William Tooke

A new and general biographical dictionary : containing an

historical and critical account of the lives and writings of the most

eminent persons in every nation : particularly the British and Irish

: from the earliest accounts of time to the present p

William Tooke

A new and general biographical dictionary : containing an historical and critical account of the lives and writings of the most eminent persons in every nation : particularly the British and Irish : from the earliest accounts of time to the present p

ISBN/EAN: 9783741183195

Manufactured in Europe, USA, Canada, Australia, Japa

Cover: Foto ©Andreas Hilbeck / pixelio.de

Manufactured and distributed by brebook publishing software (www.brebook.com)

William Tooke

A new and general biographical dictionary : containing an

historical and critical account of the lives and writings of the most

eminent persons in every nation : particularly the British and Irish

: from the earliest accounts of time to the present p

A NEW AND GENERAL

BIOGRAPHICAL

DICTIONARY.

1798.

VOL. VIII.

A

NEW and GENERAL

BIOGRAPHICAL

DICTIONARY;

CONTAINING

AN HISTORICAL AND CRITICAL ACCOUNT

OF THE

LIVES and WRITINGS

OF THE

Moſt Eminent Perſons

IN EVERY NATION;

PARTICULARLY THE BRITISH AND IRISH;

From the Earlieſt Accounts of Time to the preſent Period.

WHEREIN

Their remarkable Actions and Sufferings,
Their Virtues, Parts, and Learning,
ARE ACCURATELY DISPLAYED.

With a CATALOGUE of their LITERARY PRODUCTIONS.

A NEW EDITION, IN FIFTEEN VOLUMES.

GREATLY ENLARGED AND IMPROVED.

VOL. VIII.

LONDON:

Printed for G. G. and J. Robinson, J. Johnson, J. Nichols, J. Sewell,
H. L. Gardner, F. and C. Rivington, W. Otridge and Son,
G. Nicol, E. Newbery, Hookham and Carpenter,
R. Faulder, W. Chapman and Son, J. Deighton,
D. Walker, J. Anderson, T. Payne, J. Lowndes,
P. Macqueen, J. Walker, T. Egerton, T.
Cadell, jun. and W. Davies, R. Edwards,
Vernor and Hood, J. Nunn, Murray
and Highley, T. N. Longman, Lay
and Hurst, and J. White.

1798.

HEATH (BENJAMIN), a lawyer of eminence, and town-clerk of Exeter, was a celebrated scholar and an author. He wrote, 1. " An Essay towards a demonstrative Proof of the Divine Existence, Unity, and Attributes (to which is premised, a short Defence of the Argument commonly called, à priori, 1740." This pamphlet was dedicated to Dr. Oliver of Bath, and is to be ranked amongst the ablest defences of Dr. Clarke's, or rather Mr. Howe's, hypothesis; for it appears to be taken from Howe's " Living Temple." 2. " The Case of the County of Devon with respect to the Consequences of the new Excise Duty on Cyder and Perry. Published by the direction of the Committee appointed at a General Meeting of that County to superintend the Application for the Repeal of that Duty, 1763," 4to. To this representation of the Circum-stances peculiar to Devonshire, the repeal of the act is greatly to be ascribed. The piece indeed was considered as so well-timed a service to the public, that Mr. Heath received some honourable notice on account of it at a general meeting of the county. 3. " Notæ sive Lectiones ad Tragicorum Græcorum veterum, Æschyli, &c. 1752," 4to; a work which places the author's learning and critical skill in a very conspicuous light : a principal object of which was to restore the metre of the Grecian tragic poets. It is highly valued by all sound critics of our own and foreign countries. The same solidity of judge-ment apparent in the preceding, distinguished the author's last production ; 4. " A Revisal of Shakspeare's Text, wherein the alterations introduced into it by the more modern editors and critics are particularly considered, 1765," 8vo. It appears from the list of Oxford graduates, that Mr. Benjamin Heath was created D. C. L. by diploma, March 31, 1762. The brother of

this author, Mr. Thomas Heath, an alderman of Exeter, published "An Essay towards a new Version of Job," &c. in 1755.

HEBENSTREIT (JOHN ERNEST), a celebrated physician
and philologer of Leipsic, was born at Neuenhoff in the diocese
of Neustadt, in the year 1702. In 1719, he went to the university of Jena, but, not finding a subsistence there, removed
to Leipsic. He passed the greater part of his life in the latter
university, and finally died there in 1756. Besides his academical and physiological tracts, he published, in 1739, 1. "Carmen de usu partium," or Physiologia metrica, in 8vo. 2. "De
homine sano et ægroto Carmen, sistens Physiologiam, Patholo-
giam, Hygienen, Therapiam, materiam medicam, cum præfa-
tione de antiqua medicina." Leipsic, 1753, 8vo. 3. "Oratio de Antiquitatibus Romanis per Africam repertis," 1733, 4to.
4. "Museum Richterianum," &c. Leipf. 1743. And, 5. A
posthumous work, entitled, "Palæologia therapiæ," Halæ, 8vo,
1779. This author had also an elder brother, John Christian
Hebenstreit, who was a celebrated divine, and profoundly versed
in the Hebrew language. Ernesti has published an eulogium of
each, in his Opuscula Oratoria.

HECHT (CHRISTIAN), a native of Hall, and minister of
Essen in East Friezeland, died in 1748, at the age of 52. His
principal works are, 1. "Commentatio philogico-critico-exe-
getica," &c. 2. "Antiquitas Hebræorum inter Judæos in Polonia," &c. Besides these, he wrote several smaller works in
German. He had a brother, Godfrey Hecht, who was the author of several very learned dissertations.

HECQUET (PHILIP), a French physician of singular merit
and skill, but a strong partizan of the use of warm water and
of bleeding; for which reason he was ridiculed by Le Sage in his
Gil Blas, under the name of Dr. Sangrado. He was born at
Abbeville, in 1661, and practised first in that city, then at Port-
royal, and lastly, at Paris. He was not properly san grado, for
he took the degree of doctor in 1697; and in 1698 had more
business than he could attend. Though attached to the most
simple mode of life, he was obliged to keep his carriage, in
which he studied with as much attention as in his closet. In
1712, he was appointed dean of the faculty of medicine, and
superintended the publication of a sort of dispensary, called,
"The New Code of Pharmacy," which was published some
time afterwards. Hecquet was no less zealous in religious matters than studious in his own profession, and is said never to have
prescribed in doubtful cases, without having a previous recourse
to prayer. He lived in the most abstemious manner, and in
1727 retired to a convent of Carmelites in Paris, where he
continued accessible only to the poor, to whom he was a friend,
a comforter, and a father. He died in 1737, at the age of 76.

This

This able phyfician publifhed feveral works, none of them devoid of merit. They are thus enumerated. 1. " On the indecency of men-midwives, and the obligation of women to nurfe their own children," 12mo, 1728. The reafons he adduces on thefe fubjects are both moral and phyfical. 2. " A Treatife on the difpenfations allowed in Lent," 2 vols. 12mo. 1705 and 1715. His own abftemious fyftem inclined him very little to allow the neceffity of any indulgence. 3. " On Digeftion, and the Diforders of the Stomach," 2 vols. 12mo. 4. " Treatife on the Plague," 12mo. 5. " Novus Medicinæ confpectus," two vols. 12mo. 6. " Theological Medicine," two vols. 12mo, 7. " Natural Medicine," ditto. 8. " De purganda Medicinâ a curarum fordibus," 12mo. 9. " Obfervations on Bleeding in the Foot," 12mo. 10. " The Virtues of common Water," two vols. 12mo. This is the work in which he chiefly fupports the doctrines ridiculed by Le Sage. 11. " The abufe of Purgatives," 12mo. 12. " The roguery of Medicine," in three parts, 12mo. 13. " The Medicine, Surgery, and Pharmacy of the Poor," 3 vols. 12mo ; the beft edition is in 1742. 14. " The Natural Hiftory of the Convulfions," in which he very fagacioufly referred the origin of thofe diforders to roguery in fome, a depraved imagination in others, or the confequence of fome fecret malady. The life of this illuftrious phyfician has been written at large by M. le Fevre de St. Marc, and is no lefs edifying to Chriftians than inftructive to medical ftudents.

HEDELIN (FRANCIS), at firft an advocate, afterwards an ecclefiaftic, and abbé of Aubignac and Meimac; was born at Paris in 1604. Cardinal Richelieu, whofe nephew he educated, gave him his two abbeys, and the protection of that minifter gave him confequence both as a man of the world and as an author. He figured by turns as a grammarian, a claffical fcholar, a poet, an antiquary, a preacher, and a writer of romances; but he was moft known by his book entitled, " Pratique du Theatre," and by the quarrels in which his haughty and prefumptuous temper engaged him, with fome of the moft eminent authors of his time. The great Corneille was one of thefe, whofe difguft firft arofe from the entire omiffion of his name in the celebrated book above-mentioned. He was alfo embroiled, on different accounts, with madame Scuderi, Menage, and Richelet. The warmth of his temper exceeded that of his imagination, which was confiderable; and yet he lived at court a good deal in the ftyle of a philofopher, rifing early to his ftudies, folliciting no favours, and affociating chiefly with a few friends, as unambitious as himfelf. He defcribes himfelf as of a flender conftitution, not capable of taking much exercife, or even of applying very intenfely to ftudy, without fuffering from it in his health; yet not attached to any kind of play. " It is,"

fays

fays he, "too fatiguing for the feeblenefs of my body, or too indolent for the activity of my mind." The abbé d'Aubignac lived to the age of 72, and died at Nemours in 1676. His works are, 1. "Pratique du Theatre," Amflerdam, 1717, two vols. 8vo; alfo in a 4to edition publifhed at Paris; a book of confiderable learning, but little calculated to infpire or form a genius. 2. "Zenobie," a tragedy, in profe, compofed according to the rules laid down in his "Pratique," and a complete proof of the total inefficacy of rules to produce an interefting drama, being the moft dull and fatiguing performance that was ever reprefented. The prince of Condé faid, on the fubject of this tragedy, "We give great credit to the abbé d'Aubignac for having fo exactly followed the rules of Ariftotle, but owe no thanks to the rules of Ariftotle for having made the abbé produce fo vile a tragedy." He wrote a few other tragedies alfo, which are worfe, if poffible, than Zenobia. 3. "Macaride; or the Queen of the Fortunate Iflands," a novel. Paris, 1666, 2 vols. 8vo. 4. "Confeils d'Arifte à Celimene," 12mo. 5. "Hiftoire du tems, ou Relation du Royaume de Coqueterie," 12mo. 6. "Terence juftifié," inferted in fome editions of his "Pratique." 7. "Apologie de Spectacles," a work of no value. A curious book on fatyrs, brutes, and monfters, has been attributed to him; but though the author's name was Hedelin, he does not appear to have been the fame.

HEDERICUS, or HEDERICH (BENJAMIN), of Hain, or Groffen-hayn, in Mifnia, was born in 1675. His firft publication was an edition of Empedocles de Sphæra, with his own notes, and the Latin verfion of Septimius Florens, in 1711, Drefden, 4to. He then publifhed, a "Notitia Auctorum," in 8vo, 1714. His celebrated manual lexicon was publifhed, firft at Leipfic, in 8vo, 1722, and has been republifhed here with many additions, by Young and Patrick; but it has fince been much more improved by Ernefti, and republifhed at Leipfic, in 1767. Hederich publifhed other lexicons on different fubjects, and died in 1748. Ernefti fays of him, that he was a good man, and very laborious, but not a profound fcholar in Greek, nor well qualified for compiling a lexicon for the illuftration of Greek authors.

HEEMSKIRK. See HEMSKIRK.

HEIDEGGER (JOHN HENRY), a proteflant divine of Switzerland, born at Urfevellon, a village near Zurich, in 1633. He was firft a teacher of Hebrew and philofophy at Heidelberg, then of divinity and ecclefiaftical hiftory at Steinfurt; and laftly, of morality and divinity at Zurich, where he died in 1698. He publifhed, 1. "Exercitationes felectæ de Hiftoriâ facrâ Patriarcharum," in two volumes, 4to, the firft of which appeared at Amflerdam, in 1667, the latter in 1671. 2. "De ratione

ftudiorum

sudiorum opufcula aurea," &c. 12mo, Zurich, 1670. 3. " Tumulus Tridentini Concilii," Zurich, 1690, 4to. 4. " Historia Papatûs," Amſt. 1698, 4to. There is alſo aſcribed to him, 5. A tract, " De peregrinationibus religiofis," in 8vo, 1670. And, 6. " A Syſtem of Divinity," folio, 1700.

HEIDEGGER (John James), was the ſon of a clergyman, and a native of Zurich in Switzerland, where he married, but left his country in confequence of an intrigue. Having had an opportunity of vifiting the principal cities of Europe, he acquired a taſte for elegant and refined pleaſures, which, united to a ſtrong inclination for voluptuoufnefs, by degrees qualified him for the management of public amufements. In 1708, when he was near 50 years old, he came to England on a negotiation from the Swifs at Zurich ; but, failing in his embaffy, he entered as a private foldier in the guards for protection. By his fprightly, engaging converfation, and infinuating addrefs, he foon worked himfelf into the good graces of our young people of fafhion ; from whom he obtained the appellation of " the Swifs count [A]." He had the addrefs to procure a fubfcription, with which in 1709 he was enabled to furnish out the opera of Thomyris [B]," which was written in Englifh, and performed at the queen's theatre in the Haymarket. The mufic, however, was Italian ; that is to fay, airs felected from feveral operas by Bononcini, Scarlatti, Steffani, Gafparini, and Albinoni. Moft of the fongs in " Thomyris" were excellent, thofe by Bononcini efpecially : Valentini, Margarita, and Mrs. Tofis fung in it ; and Heidegger by this performance alone was a gainer of 500 guineas [c]. The judicious remarks he made on feveral defects in the conduct of our operas in general, and the hints he threw out for improving the entertainments of the royal theatre, foon eſtablifhed his character as a good critic. Appeals were made to his judgement ; and fome very magnificent and elegant decorations, introduced upon the ftage in confequence of his advice, gave fuch fatisfaction to George II. who was fond of operas, that, upon being informed to whofe genius he was indebted for thefe improvements, his majefty was pleafed from that time to countenance him, and he foon obtained the chief management of the Opera-houfe in the Haymarket. He then undertook to improve another fpecies of diverfion, not lefs agreeable to the king, which was the mafquerades, and over thefe he always prefided at the king's theatre. He was like-

[A] He is twice noticed under this title in the " Tatler," Nos. 12, and 18 ; and in Mr. Duncombe's " Collection of Letters of feveral eminent Perfons deceafed," is a humorous dedication of Mr. Hughs's " Vifion of Chaucer," to " the Swifs Count."

[B] There was another opera of the fame name, by Peter Motteux, in 1719.
[c] " Thomyris" and " Camilla," were both revived in 1726 ; but neither then fucceeded.

wife appointed mafter of the revels. The nobility now careffed him fo much, and had fuch an opinion of his tafte, that all fplendid and elegant entertainments given by them upon particular occafions, and all private affemblies by fubfcription, were fubmitted to his direction [D].

From the emoluments of thefe feveral employments, he gained a regular and confiderable income; amounting, it is faid, in fome years, to 5000l. which he fpent with much liberality; particularly in the maintenance of perhaps fomewhat too luxurious a table; fo that it may be faid, he raifed an income, but never a fortune. His foibles, however, if they deferve fo harfh a name, were completely covered by his charity, which was boundlefs. After a fuccefsful mafquerade, he has been known to give away feveral hundred pounds at a time. "You know poor objects of diftrefs better than I do," he would frequently fay to the father of the gentleman who furnifhed this anecdote, "Be fo kind as to give away this money for me." This well-known liberality, perhaps, contributed much to his carrying on that diverfion with fo little oppofition as he met with.

That he was a good judge of mufic, appears from his opera: but this is all that is known of his mental abilities [E]; unlefs we add, what we have good authority for faying in honour to his *memory*, that he walked from Charing-crofs to Temple-bar, and back again; and when he came home, wrote down every fign on each fide the Strand.

As to his perfon, though he was tall and well made, it was not very pleafing, from an unufual hardnefs of features [F]. But he was the firft to joke upon his own uglinefs; and he once laid a wager with the earl of Chefterfield, that, within a certain given time, his lordfhip would not be able to produce fo hideous a face in all London. After ftrict fearch, a woman was found, whofe features were at firft fight thought ftronger than Heidegger's; but, upon clapping her head-drefs upon himfelf, he was univerfally allowed to have won the wager. Jolly, a well-known taylor, carrying his bill to a noble duke; his grace, for evafion,

[D] The writer of this note has been favoured with the fight of an amethyft fnuff box fet in gold, prefented to Heidegger in 1731, by the duke of Lorrain, afterwards emperor of Germany, which Heidegger very highly valued, and bequeathed to his executor Lewis Way, efq; of Richmond, and which is now (July 1784) in the poffeffion of his fon Benjamin Way, efq;

[E] Pope (Dunciad, I. 289.) calls the bird which attended on the goddefs,

"——— a monfter of a fowl,
Something betwixt a Heidegger and owl."

And explains Heidegger to mean "a ftrange bird from Switzerland, and not (as fome have fuppofed) the name of an eminent perfon, who was a man of parts, and, as was faid of Petronius, Arbiter Elegantiarum."

[F] There is a mezzotinto of Heidegger by J. Faber, 1742, (other copies dated 1749) from a painting by Vanloo, a ftriking likenefs, now (1784) in the poffeffion of Peter Crawford, efq. His face is alfo introduced in more than one of Hogarth's prints.

said,

said, " Damn your ugly face, I never will pay you till you bring me an uglier fellow than yourself!" Jolly bowed and retired, wrote a letter, and sent it by a servant to Heidegger; saying, " his grace wished to see him the next morning on particular business." Heidegger attended, and Jolly was there to meet him; and in consequence, as soon as Heidegger's visit was over, Jolly received the cash.

The late facetious duke of Montagu (the memorable contriver of the bottle conjurer at the theatre in the Haymarket) gave an entertainment at the Devil-tavern, Temple-bar, to several of the nobility and gentry, selecting the most convivial, and a few hard drinkers, who were all in the plot. Heidegger was invited, and a few hours after dinner, was made so dead drunk that he was carried out of the room, and laid insensible upon a bed. A profound sleep ensued; when the late Mrs. Salmon's daughter was introduced, who took a mould from his face in plaster of Paris. From this a mask was made, and a few days before the next masquerade (at which the king promised to be present, with the countess of Yarmouth) the duke made application to Heidegger's valet de chambre, to know what suit of clothes he was likely to wear; and then procuring a similar dress, and a person of the same stature, he gave him his instructions. On the evening of the masquerade, as soon as his majesty was seated (who was always known by the conductor of the entertainment and the officers of the court, though concealed by his dress from the company) Heidegger, as usual, ordered the music to play " God save the King;" but his back was no sooner turned, than the false Heidegger ordered them to strike up " Charly over the Water." The whole company were instantly thunderstruck, and all the courtiers, not in the plot, were thrown into a stupid consternation. Heidegger flew to the music-gallery, swore, stamped, and raved, accused the musicians of drunkenness, or of being set on by some secret en. my to ruin him. The king and the countess laughed so immoderately, that they hazarded a discovery. While Heidegger stayed in the gallery, " God save the King" was the tune; but when, after setting matters to rights, he retired to one of the dancing-rooms, to observe if decorum was kept by the company, the counterfeit stepping forward, and placing himself upon the floor of the theatre, just in front of the music gallery, called out in a most audible voice, imitating Heidegger, damned them for blockheads, had he not just told them to play " Charly over the Water?" A pause ensued; the musicia s, who knew his character, in their turn thought him either drunk or mad; but, as he continued his vociferation, " Charly" was played again. At this repetition of the supposed affront, some of the officers of the guards, who always attended upon these occasions, were for

ascending

aſcending the gallery, and kicking the muſicians out; but the late duke of Cumberland, who could hardly contain himſelf, interpoſed. The company were thrown into great confuſion. "Shame! Shame!" reſounded from all parts, and Heidegger once more flew in a violent rage to that part of the theatre facing the gallery. Here the duke of Montagu, artfully addreſſing himſelf to him, told him, "the king was in a violent paſſion; that his beſt way was to go inſtantly and make an apology, for certainly the muſicians were mad, and afterwards to diſcharge them." Almoſt at the ſame inſtant, he ordered the falſe Heidegger to do the ſame. The ſcene now became truly comic in the circle before the king. Heidegger had no ſooner made a genteel apology for the inſolence of his muſicians, but the falſe Heidegger advanced, and, in a plaintive tone, cried out, "Indeed, Sire, it was not my fault, but that devil's in my likeneſs." Poor Heidegger turned round, ſtared, ſtaggered, grew pale, and could not utter a word. The duke then humanely whiſpered in his ear the ſum of his plot, and the counterfeit was ordered to take off his maſk. Here ended the frolic; but Heidegger ſwore he would never attend any public amuſement, if that witch the wax-work woman did not break the mould, and melt down the maſk before his face [G].

Being once at ſupper with a large company, when a queſtion was debated, which nation of Europe had the greateſt ingenuity; to the ſurpriſe of all preſent, he claimed that character for the Swiſs, and appealed to himſelf for the truth of it. "I was born a Swiſs," ſaid he, "and came to England without a farthing, where I have found means to gain 5000l. a year, and to ſpend it. Now I defy the moſt able Engliſhman to go to Switzerland, and either to gain that income, or to ſpend it there." He died Sept. 4, 1749, at the advanced age of 90 years, at his houſe at Richmond in Surrey, where he was buried. He left behind him one natural daughter, miſs Pappet, who was married Sept. 2, 1750, to captain (afterwards ſir Peter) Denis [H].

[G] To this occurrence the following imperfect ſtanzas, tranſcribed from the hand-writing of Pope, are ſuppoſed to relate. They were found on the back of a page containing ſome part of his tranſlation, either of the "Iliad," or "Odyſſey," in the Britiſh Muſeum.

XIII.

Then he went to the ſide-board, and call'd
  for much liquor,
And glaſs after glaſs he drank quicker and
  quicker;
    So that Heidegger quoth,
    May, ſaith on his oath,

Of two hogſheads of Burgundy, Satan
  drank both.
Then all like a —— the Devil appear'd,
And ſtrait the whole tables of diſhes he
  clear'd;
    Then a friar, then a nun,
    And then he put on
A face all the company took for his own.
Even thine, O falſe Heidegger! who wert
  ſo wicked
To let in the Devil——

[H] Who died June 12, 1778, being then vice-admiral of the red. See memoirs of him in Gent. Mag. 1780, p. 268.

Part

Part of this lady's fortune was a houfe at the north-weft corner of Queen-fqaare, Ormond-ftreet, which fir Peter afterwards fold to the late Dr. Campbell, and purchafed a feat in Kent, pleafantly fituated near Weftram, then called Valence, but now (by its prefent proprietor, the earl of Hillfborough) Hill Park.

HEINECCIUS (JOHN-GOTLIEB), a German lawyer, was born at Eifemborg in 1681, and trained in the ftudy of philofophy and law. He became profeffor of philofophy at Hall, in 1710, and of law in 1721, with the title of counfellor. In 1724, he was invited to Franeker; and, three years after, the king of Pruffia influenced him to accept the law-profefforfhip at Francfort upon the Oder. Here he continued till 1733, when the fame prince almoft forced him to refume the chair at Hall, where he remained till his death in 1741, although he had ftrong invitations from Denmark, Holland, &c. His principal works (for they are numerous) are, 1. "Antiquitatum Romanorum Jurifprudentiam illuftrantium fyntagma." The beft edition of which is the fifth, publifhed at Leward in 1777. 2. "Elementa Juris Civilis fecundum ordinem Inftitutionum & Pandectarum," 2 vols. 8vo. 3. "Elementa Philofophiæ Rationalis & Moralis, quibus præmiffa hiftoria Philofophica." This is reckoned a good abridgment of logic and moralitv. 4. "Hiftoria Juris Civilis, Romani ac Germanici." 5. "Elementa Juris Naturæ & Gentium." 6. "Fundamenta ftyli Cultioris;" a work of his youth, but much approved, and often reprinted, with notes by Gefner and others. Alfo feveral academic differtations upon various fubjects. His works were publifhed collectively at Geneva in 1744, and form eight volumes in quarto.

HEINECKEN (CHRISTIAN HENRY), a child, greatly celebrated for the wonderfully premature developement of his talents, was born at Lubeck, Feb. 6, 1721, and died there, June 27, 1725, after having difplayed the moft amazing proofs of intellectual powers. He could talk at ten months old, and fcarcely had completed his firft year of life, when he already knew and recited the principal facts contained in the five books of Mofes, with a number of verfes on the creation; at 13 months he knew the hiftory of the Old Teftament, and the New at 14; in his 30th month, the hiftory of the nations of antiquity, geography, anatomy, the ufe of maps, and nearly 8000 Latin words. Before the end of his third year, he was well acquainted with the hiftory of Denmark, and the genealogy of the crowned heads of Europe; in his fourth year, he had learned the doctrines of divinity, with their proofs from the Bible; ecclefiaftical hiftory; the inftitutes; 200 hymns, with their tunes; 80 pfalms; entire chapters of the Old and New Teftament; 1500 verfes and fentences from ancient Latin claffics; almoft the whole Orbis Pictus of Comenius, whence he had derived all his knowledge of the Latin language; arithmetic; the hiftory of the European empires and

kingdoms;

kingdoms; could point out in the maps whatever place he was
afked for, or paffed by in his journies, and recite all the ancient
and modern hiftorical anecdotes relating to it. His ftupendous
memory caught and retained every word he was told: his ever
active imagination ufed, whatever he faw or heard, inftantly
to apply fume examples or fentences from the Bible, geography,
profane or ecclefiaftical hiftory, the Orbis Pictus, or from ancient
claffics. At the court of Denmark, he delivered twelve fpeeches
without once faultering; and underwent public examinations
on a variety of fubjects, efpecially the hiftory of Denmark.
He fpoke German, Latin, French, and Low Dutch, and was
exceedingly good-natured and well-behaved, but of a moft tender and delicate bodily conftitution; never ate any folid food,
but chiefly fubfifted on nurfes milk, not being weaned till
within a very few months of his death, at which time he was
not quite four years old. There is a differtation on this child,
publifhed by M. Martini at Lubeck, in 1730, where the author
attempts to affign the natural caufes for the aftonifhing capacity
of this great man in embryo, who was juft fhewn to the world,
and fnatched away.

HEINSIUS (DANIEL), a celebrated fcholar and critic, profeffor of politics and hiftory at Leyden, and alfo librarian of the
univerfity there, was born at Ghent in Flanders, May 1580, of
an illuftrious family, who had poffeffed the firft places in the ma-
giftracy of that town. He was frequently removed in the
younger part of his life. He began his ftudies at the Hague,
and afterwards went with his parents into Zeland, where he was
inftructed in polite literature and philofophy. He comprehended very well the principles of morality and politics, but
did not relifh logic, and had an unconquerable averfion to
grammar. He difcovered early a ftrong propenfity to poetry,
and began to make verfes, before he knew any thing of profody
or the rules of art. He compofed a regular elegy, at ten years
of age, upon the death of a play-fellow; and there are feveral
epigrams and little poems of his, which were written when he
was not above twelve, and fhew a great deal of genius and facility.

He is reprefented, however, as having been a very idle boy,
and not likely to make any progrefs in Greek and Latin learning; on which account his father fent him, at fourteen years of
age, to ftudy the law in the univerfity of Franeker. But from
that time, as if he had been influenced by a fpirit of contradiction, nothing would pleafe him but claffics; and he applied himfelf there to Greek and Latin authors, as obftinately as he had
rejected them in Zeland. He afterwards removed to Leyden,
where he became a pupil of Jofeph Scaliger; and was obliged
to the encouragement and care of that great man for the perfection

tion to which he afterwards arrived in literature, and which at the beginning of his life there was so little reason to expect. He published an edition of "Silius Italicus," in 1600; and he added to it notes of his own, which he called "Crepundia Siliana," to shew that they were written when he was extremely young. He was made Greek professor at eighteen, and afterwards succeeded Scaliger in the professorship of politics and history. When he was made librarian to the university, he pronounced a Latin oration, afterwards published, in which he described the duties of a librarian, and the good order and condition in which a library should be kept. He died Feb. 25, 1655, after having done great honour to himself and country by various works of ability and learning. He distinguished himself as a critic by his labours upon Silius Italicus, Theocritus, Hesiod, Seneca, Homer, Hesychius, Theophrastus, Clemens Alexandrinus, Ovid, Livy, Terence, Horace, Prudentius, Maximus Tyrius, &c. He published two treatises "De Satira Horatiana," which Balzac affirms to be master-pieces in their way. He wrote poems in various languages, which have been often printed, and always admired. He was the author of several prose works, some of which were written in an humorous and satirical manner; as "Laus Asini," "Laus Pediculi," &c.

The learned have all joined in their praises of Heinsius. Gerard Vossius says, that he was a very great man; and calls him the ornament of the Muses and the Graces. Causabon admires him equally for his parts and learning. Pareus calls him the Varro of his age. Barthius ranks him with the first writers. Bochart pronounces him a truly great and learned man; and Selden speaks of him, as "tam severiorum quam amœniorum literarum sol;" a light to guide us in our gay as well as severe pursuits in letters. Some however have thought, that he was not so well formed for criticism; and Le Clerc, in his account of the Amsterdam edition of Bentley's "Horace," has the following passage: "Daniel Heinsius," says he, "was doubtless a learned man, and had spent his life in the study of criticism. Yet, if we may judge by his Horace, he was by no means happy in his conjectures, of which our author Bentley has admitted only one, if my memory does not deceive me; for I cannot recollect the place where he passes this judgement of Daniel Heinsius. But he speaks much more advantageously of his son Nicolas Heinsius; who, though not so learned a man as his father, had yet a better taste for criticism [1]."

We must not forget to observe, that Daniel Heinsius was highly honoured abroad as well as at home; and received uncommon marks of respect from foreign potentates. Gustavus Adolphus, king of Sweden, gave him a place among his coun-

[1] Bibl. Chois. XXVI. p. 262.

fellows of state; the republic of Venice made him a knight of their order of St. Mark; and pope Urban VIII. was such an admirer of his fine talents and consummate learning, that he made him great offers, if he would come to Rome; "to rescue that city from barbarism," as the pontiff is said to have expressed himself.

HEINSIUS (NICOLAS), the son of Daniel, was born at Leyden in 1620, and became as great a Latin poet, and a greater critic than his father. His poems have been several times printed: but the best edition is that of Amsterdam, 1666. Some have admired them so much, as to think him worthy to be called "The Swan of Holland." He wrote notes upon, and gave editions of, Virgil, Ovid, Valerius Flaccus, Claudian, Prudentius, &c. Bentley, in a note upon Horace, 2 Sat. vi. 108, calls his edition of Virgil, "editio castigatissima." His Claudian is dedicated, in a Latin poem, to Christina queen of Sweden; and his Ovid to Thuanus. At his death, which happened at the Hague in 1681, he disowned all his works; and expressed the utmost regret at having left behind him so many "Monuments of his vanity," as he called them. Nicolas Heinsius was as much distinguished by his great employments in the state, as he was by his parts and learning. All the learned of his time speak well of him; and he is represented as having been possessed of good qualities as well as great ones.

HELE (THOMAS), by birth an Englishman, arrived at the singular distinction of being admired in France as a writer in the French language. He was born in Gloucestershire about the year 1740. He began his career in the army, and served in Jamaica till the peace of 1763. A desire of seeing the most remarkable parts of Europe, now carried him into Italy, where he was so captivated with the beauty of the climate, and the innumerable objects of liberal curiosity which presented themselves, that he continued there several years. About the year 1770, having satisfied his curiosity in Italy, he turned his thoughts to France, and went to Paris. There also he studied the state of the arts, and was particularly attentive to the theatre. At length he began to write for the Italian comedy, which had principally attracted his notice, and wrote with considerable success. The pieces for that theatre are written chiefly in French, with French titles, and only one or two characters in Italian. He wrote, 1. "Le Jugement de Midas," on the contest between French and Italian music, which was much applauded. But his 2. "Amant jaloux," had still more success. 3. His third piece, "Les Evenemens imprevus," met with some exceptions, on which he modestly withdrew it, and after making the corrections suggested, brought it forward again, and had the pleasure to find it much approved. The comedies of this writer are

are full of plot, the action lively and interesting: his verfification is not esteemed by the French to be of consummate perfection, nor his profe always pure; yet his dialogue constantly pleafed, and was allowed to have the merit of nature and found compofition. Mr. Hele died at Paris, of a confumptive disorder, in December, 1780; and it may possibly be long before another Englishman will be fo distinguished as a writer in the French language. We take this account from French authors, who write his name d'Héle, perhaps it was properly Hale or Dale.

HELENA, the emprefs, mother of Constantine, and one of the faints of the Romish communion, owed her elevation to the charms of her perfon. She was of obfcure origin, born at the little village of Drepanum in Bithynia, where the first fituation in which we hear of her was that of hoftefs of an inn. Constantius Chlorus became enamoured of her, probably there, and married her; but, on being affociated with Dioclefian in the empire, divorced her to marry Theodora, daughter of Maximilian Hercules. The accession of her fon to the empire drew her again from obfcurity; fhe obtained the title of Augufta, and was received at court with all the honours due to the mother of an emperor. Her many virtues rivetted the affection of her fon to her, and, when he became a christian, fhe alfo was converted; yet fhe did not fcruple to admonifh him when fhe difapproved his conduct. When fhe was near eighty years old, fhe planned and executed a journey to the Holy Land, where fhe is faid to have affifted at the difcovery of the true crofs of Chrift, reported by the Romanifts to have been accompanied by many miracles. In the year 328, foon after this difcovery, fhe died at the age of 80. Helena, wherever fhe went, left proofs of a truly Chriftian liberality; fhe relieved the poor, orphans, and widows; built churches, and in all refpects fhewed herfelf worthy of the confidence of her fon, who fupported her in thefe pious efforts by an unlimited permiffion to draw upon his treafures. At her death, he paid her the highest honours, had her body fent to Rome to be depofited in the tomb of the emperors, and raifed her native village to the rank of a city, with the new name of Helenopolis. She proved her prudence and political wifdom by the influence fhe always retained over her fon, and, by the care fhe took to prevent all interference of the half-brothers of Conftantine, fons of Conftantius Chlorus and Theodora; who, being brought into notice after her death, by the injudicious liberality of the emperor, were maffacred by their nephews as foon as they fucceeded their father in the empire.

HELIODORUS, a native of Emefa in Phoenicia, and bifhop of Tricca in Theffaly, flourifhed in the reigns of Theodofius and Arcadius towards the end of the fourth century. In his youth he wrote a romance, by which he is now better known, than

than by his subfequent bifhopric of Tricca. It is entitled,
" Ethiopics," and relates the amours of Theagenes and Chari-
clea, in ten books. The learned Huetius is of opinion, that
Heliodorus was among the romance-writers, what Homer was
among the poets [K]; that is, the fource and model of an infinite
number of imitations, all inferior to their original. The firft
edition of the Ethiopics was printed at Bafil, 1533, with a dedication
to the fenate of Nuremberg, prefixed by Vincentius Opfopæus;
who informs us, that a foldier preferved the MS. when the library of Buda was plundered. Bourdelot's notes upon this romance are very learned; and were printed at Paris, in 1619, with
Heliodorus's Greek original, and a Latin tranflation, which had
been publifhed by Stanillaus Warfzewicki, a Polifh knight, (with
the Greek) at Bafil, in 1551. A notion has prevailed, that a
provincial fynod, being fenfible how dangerous the reading of
Heliodorus's Ethiopics was, to which the author's rank was
fuppofed to add great authority, required of the bifhop, that he
fhould either burn the book, or refign his dignity; and that the
bifhop chofe the latter. But this ftory is thought to be entirely
fabulous; as depending only upon the fingle teftimony of Nicephorus, an ecclefiaftical hiftorian of great credulity and little
judgement: not to mention, how difficult it is to fuppofe, that
Socrates fhould omit fo memorable a circumftance in the paffage;
where he obferves, that Heliodorus " wrote a love-tale in his
youth, which he entitled, Ethiopics." Valefius, in his notes
upon this paffage, not only rejects the account of Nicephorus as
a mere fable, but feems inclined to think, that the romance
itfelf was not written by Heliodorus bifhop of Tricca; of
which, however, Huetius entertained no doubt. Some have fancied, as Opfopæus and Melancthon, that this romance was in
reality a true hiftory; but Fabricius thinks this as incredible, as
that Heliodorus, according to others, wrote it originally in the
Ethiopic tongue. Some again have afferted, that Heliodorus
was not a Chriftian, from his faying at the end of his book,
that he was a Phœnician, born in the city of Emefa, and of the
race of the fun; fince, they fay, it would be madnefs in a Chriftian, and much more in a bifhop, to declare, that he was defcended from that luminary. This objection Bayle, who
quotes it, anfwers in the following manner: " It is certain,"
fays he, " that feveral Chriftians in the fourth century mentioned the ancientnefs of their nobility; why then fhould not we
believe, that Heliodorus mentioned his? He did not believe that
his family was really defcended from the fun; but he might
imagine, that he fhould diftinguifh it by that mark. This was a
title, by which his family had been known a long time, and

which was honourable to him: and though the principle was
falfe, yet one might infer from it fome confequences favourable
to his family with regard to its antiquity. Such a motive might
engage a Chriftian thus to diftinguifh the nobility of his extraction. Add to this, that Heliodorus was not yet a bifhop, when
he wrote his romance; he was ftill in all the fire of his youth;
and as he did not put his name to his work, he might with more
liberty make his defcent known by the ancient tradition of his
family." Bayle refers us, in the courfe of this folution, to a
differtation of Balzac at the end of his "Socrate Chretien:"
where it is obferved among other things, that St. Jerom makes
St. Paul to be defcended from Agamemnon, and that Synefius
boafted his defcent from Hercules.

Befides the Ethiopics, Cedrenus tells us of another book of
Heliodorus, concerning the Philofopher's Stone, or the art of
tranfmuting metals into gold, which he prefented to Theodofius
the Great; and Fabricius has inferted in his "Bibliotheca
Græca," a chemical Greek poem written in Iambic verfe,
which he had from a MS. in the king of France's library, and
which carries the name of Heliodorus, bifhop of Tricca; but
leaves it very juftly queftionable, whether it be not a fpurious
performance. Socrates relates, in the book and chapter above
cited, that this bifhop introduced the cuftom of depofing thofe
minifters who lay with their wives after ordination; which
Bayle thinks a profitable argument in favour of the prelate's
chaftity; and adds, that he appears from his romance to have
been a lover of this virtue.

HELLANICUS of Mitylene, an ancient Greek hiftorian,
born in the year A. C. 496, twelve years before the birth of
Herodotus. He wrote a hiftory "of the earlieft Kings of various Nations, and the Founders of Cities;" which is mentioned
by feveral ancient authors, but is not extant. He lived to the
age of 85. There was another Hellanicus of much later times,
who was a Milefian.

HELMONT (John Baptist van), commonly called Van
Helmont, from a borough and caftle of that name in Brabant,
was a perfon of quality, and a man of great learning, efpecially
in phyfic and natural philofophy; and born at Bruffels in 1577.
But, inftead of relating the particulars of his life, we will make
him relate them himfelf, as he does in the two introductory chapters to his works: for nothing can give a jufter notion of the
man, or, indeed, be more entertaining to the curious reader.

"In the year 1580 [t]," fays he, "a moft miferable one to
the Low Countries,. my father died. I, the youngeft and leaft
efteemed of all my brothers and fifters, was bred a fcholar; and

[t] Ortus Medicinæ, p. 14. Amft. 1652.

in the year 1594, which was to me the 17th, had finished the course of philosophy. Upon seeing none admitted to examinations at Louvain, but in a gown, and masked with a hood, as though the garment did promise learning, I began to perceive, that the taking degrees in arts was a piece of mere mockery; and wondered at the simplicity of young men, in fancying that they had learned any thing from their doting professors. I entered, therefore, into a serious and honest examination of myself, that I might know by my own judgement, how much I was a philosopher, and whether I had really acquired truth and knowledge: but found myself altogether destitute, save that I had learned to wrangle artificially. Then came I first to perceive, that I knew nothing, or at least that which was not worth knowing. Natural philosophy seemed to promise something of knowledge, to which therefore I joined the study of astronomy. I applied myself also to logic and the mathematics, by way of recreation, when I was wearied with other studies; and made myself a master of Euclid's Elements, as I did also of Copernicus's Theory De revolutionibus orbium cœlestium: but all these things were of no account with me, because they contained little truth and certainty; little but a parade of science falsely so called. Finding after all, therefore, that nothing was found, nothing true, I refused the title of master of arts, though I had finished my course; unwilling, that professors should play the fool with me, in declaring me a master of the seven arts, when I was conscious to myself that I knew nothing.

" A wealthy canonry was promised me then, so that I might, if I pleased, turn myself to divinity; but saint Bernard affrighted me from it, saying, that ' I should eat the sins of the people.' I begged therefore of the Lord Jesus, that he would vouchsafe to call me to that profession, in which I might please him most. The Jesuits began at that time to teach philosophy at Louvain, and one of the professors expounded the disquisitions and secrets of magic. Both these lectures I greedily received; but instead of grain, I reaped only stubble, and fantastic conceits void of sense. In the mean time, left an hour should pass without some benefit, I run through some writings of the stoics, those of Seneca, and especially of Epictetus, who pleased me exceedingly. I seemed, in moral philosophy, to have found the quintessence of truth, and did verily believe, that through stoicism I advanced in Christian perfection; but I discovered afterwards in a dream, that stoicism was an empty and swollen bubble, and that by this study, under the appearance of moderation, I became, indeed, most self-sufficient and haughty. Lastly, I turned over Mathiolus and Dioscorides; thinking with myself nothing equally necessary for mortal man to know and admire, as the wisdom and goodness of God in vegetables; to the end that he might not
only

only crop the fruit for food, but also minister of the fame to his other neceffities. My curiofity being now raifed upon this branch of ftudy, I enquired, whether there were any book, which delivered the maxims and rule of medicine? for I then fuppofed, that medicine was not altogether a mere gift, but might be taught, and delivered by difcipline, like other arts and fciences: at leaft I thought, if medicine was a good gift coming down from the Father of lights, that it might have, as an human fcience, its theorems and authors, into whom, as into Bazaleel and Aholiab, the fpirit of the Lord had infufed the knowledge of all difeafes and their caufes, and alfo the knowledge of the properties of things. I enquired, I fay, whether no writer had defcribed the qualities, properties, applications, and proportions of vegetables, from the hyffop even, to the cedar of Libanus? A certain profeffor of medicine anfwered me, that none of thefe things were to be looked for either in Galen or Avicen. I was very ready to believe this, from the many fruitlefs fearches I had made in books for truth and knowledge before; however, following my natural bent, which lay to the ftudy of nature, I read the inftitutions of Fuchfius and Fernelius; in whom I knew I had furveyed the whole fcience of medicine, as it were in an epitome. Is this, faid I, fmiling to myfelf, the knowledge of healing? Is the whole hiftory of natural properties thus fhut up in elementary qualities? Therefore I read the works of Galen twice; of Hippocrates once, whofe aphorifms I almoft got by heart; all Avicen; as well as the Greeks, Arabians, and moderns, to the tune of 600 authors. I read them ferioufly and attentively through; and took down, as I went along, whatever feemed curious, and worthy of attention; when at length, reading over my common-place book, I was grieved at the pains I had beftowed, and the years I had fpent, in throwing together fuch a mafs of ftuff. Therefore I ftraightway left off all books whatever, all formal difcourfes, and empty promifes of the fchools; firmly believing every good and perfect gift to come down from the Father of lights, more particularly that of medicine.

"I have attentively furveyed fome foreign nations; but I found the fame fluggifhnefs, in implicitly following the fteps of their forefathers, and ignorance among them all. I then became perfuaded, that the art of healing was a mere impofture, originally fet on foot by the Greeks for filthy lucre's fake; till afterwards the Holy Scriptures informed me better. I confidered, that the plague, which then raged at Louvain, was a moft miferable difeafe, in which every one forfook the fick; and faithlefs helpers, diftruftful of their own art, fled more fwiftly than the unlearned common people, and homely pretenders to cure it. I propofed to myfelf to dedicate one falutation to the miserable infected ; and although then no medicine was made known to me but trivial ones, yet God preserved my innocency from so cruel an enemy. I was not indeed sent for, but went of my own accord ; and that not so much to help them, which I despaired of doing, as for the sake of learning. All that saw me, seemed to be refreshed with hope and joy ; and I myself, being fraught with hope, was persuaded, that, by the mere free gift of God, I should sometimes obtain a mastery in the science. After ten years travel and studies from my degree in the art of medicine taken at Louvain, being then married, I withdrew myself, in 1609, to Vilvord ; that being the less troubled by applications, I might proceed diligently in viewing the king-doms of vegetables, animals, and minerals. I employed myself some years in chemical operations. I searched into the works of Paracelsus ; and at first admired and honoured the man, but at last was convinced, that nothing but difficulty, obscurity, and error, was to be found in him. Thus tired out with search after search, and concluding the art of medicine to be all deceit and uncertainty, I said with a sorrowful heart, ' Good God ! how long wilt thou be angry with mortal man, who hitherto has not disclosed one truth, in healing, to thy schools ? How long wilt thou deny truth to a people confessing thee, needful in these days, more than in times past ? Is the sacrifice of Molech pleasing to thee ? wilt thou have the lives of the poor, widows, and fa-therless children, consecrated to thyself, under the most miser-:able torture of incurable diseases ? How is it, therefore, that thou ceasest not to destroy so many families through the uncer-tainty and ignorance of physicians ?' Then I fell on my face, and said, Oh, Lord, pardon me, if favour towards my neigh-bour hath snatched me away beyond my bounds. Pardon, par-don, O Lord, my indiscreet charity ; for thou art the radical good of goodness itself. Thou hast known my sighs ; and that I confess myself to be, to know, to be worth, to be able to do, to have, nothing ; and that I am poor, naked, empty, vain. Give, O Lord, give knowledge to thy creature, that he may affectionately know thy creatures ; himself first, other things besides himself, all things, and more than all things, to be ul-timately in thee.'

" After I had thus earnestly prayed, I fell into a dream ; in which, in the sight or view of truth, I saw the whole universe, as it were, some chaos or confused thing without form, which was almost a mere nothing. And from thence I drew the con-ceiving of one word, which did signify to me this following : ' Behold thou, and what things thou seest, are nothing. What-ever thou dost urge, is less than nothing itself in the sight of the Most High. He knoweth all the bounds of things to be done : thou at least may apply thyself to thy own safety.' In this conception

ception there was an inward precept, that I fhould be made a phyfician ; and that, fome time or other, Raphael himfelf fhould be given unto me. Forthwith therefore, and for thirty whole years after, and their nights following in order, I laboured always to my coft, and often in danger of my life, that I might obtain the knowledge of vegetables and minerals, and of their natures and properties alfo. Meanwhile, I exercifed myfelf in prayer, in reading, in a narrow fearch of things, in fifting my errors, and in writing down what I daily experienced. At length I knew with Solomon, that I had for the moft part hitherto perplexed my fpirit in vain ; and I faid, Vain is the knowledge of all things under the fun, vain are the fearchings of the curious. Whom the Lord Jefus fhall call unto wifdom, he, and no other, fhall come ; yea, he that hath come to the top, fhall as yet be able to do very little, unlefs the bountiful favour of the Lord fhall fhine upon him. Lo, thus have I waxed ripe of age, being become a man ; and now alfo an old man, unprofitable, and unacceptable to God, to whom be all honour."

From the account here given by himfelf, it is eafy to conceive, that Van Helmont, at his firft appearance in the world, would pafs for no better than an enthufiaft and a madman. He certainly had in him a ftrong mixture of both enthufiafm and madnefs : neverthelefs he was very acute and very profound, and difcovered in many cafes a wonderful penetration and infight into nature. By his fkill in phyfic, he performed fuch unexpected cures, that he was put into the inquifition, as a man that did things beyond the reach of nature. He cleared himfelf before the inquifitors ; but, to be more at liberty, retired afterwards into Holland. He died Dec. 30, 1644, and the day before wrote a letter to a friend at Paris, in which were thefe words : " Praife and glory be to God for evermore, who is pleafed to call me out of the world ; and, as I conjecture, my life will not laft above 24 hours. For this day I find myfelf firft affaulted by a fever, which, fuch is the weaknefs of my body, muft, I know, finifh me within that fpace." A few days before that, he faid to his fon Francis Mercurius Van Helmont, " Take all my writings, as well thofe that are crude and uncorrected, as thofe that are thoroughly purged, and join them together. I now commit them to thy care ; finifh and digeft them according thy own judgment. It hath fo pleafed the Lord Almighty, who attempts all things powerfully, and directs all things fweetly."

John Caramuel Lobkowiz has given a good account of this phyfician and philofopher in a very few words. " Helmont," fays he, " for I knew the man, was pious, learned, famous : a fworn enemy of Galen and Ariftotle. The fick never languifhed long under his hands ; being always killed or cured in two or three days. He was sent for chiefly to those who were given up by other physicians; and, to the great grief and indignation of such physicians, often restored the patient unexpectedly to health. His works were published in folio. They are one continued satire against the Peripatetics and Galenists; very voluminous, but not very profitable for instruction in physic." His son, Francis Mercure, who had some fame, was said in his epitaph to be, " Nil patre inferior," but falsely. He died in 1699 at 81.

HELOISE, the concubine, and afterwards the wife, of Peter Abelard (a nun, and afterwards prioress of Argenteuil; and lastly, abbess of the Paraclete, was born about the beginning of the 12th century. The history of her amour with Abelard having been already related in our account of him, we refer the reader to it; and shall content ourselves here, with giving some particulars of Heloise, which we have either not mentioned at all, or but very slightly, under that article.

This lady has usually been celebrated for her great beauty and, her great learning. In the age she lived, a young girl with a very small share of erudition, might easily pass for a miracle. This however is not said to derogate from Heloise's merit, who certainly deserves an honourable place among the very learned women: as she was skilled, not only in the Latin language, but also in the Greek and Hebrew. This Abelard expressly declares in a letter, which he wrote to the nuns of the Paraclete. As to those who ascribe to her a ravishing beauty, we may upon very good grounds presume them to be mistaken. Abelard must have been as good a judge of it as any one; he must have had more reason to exaggerate, than to diminish in his account of it, yet he contents himself with saying, that " as she was not the last of her sex in beauty, so in letters she was the first;" " Cum per faciem non esset infima, per abundantium literarum erat suprema:" a very flat elogium, supposing her to have been an accomplished beauty, and by no means consistent with the passion which Abelard entertained for her. But Abelard's poetry may account for this supposed beauty in Heloise: his verses were filled with nothing but love for her, which, making the name of this mistress to fly all over the world, would naturally occasion persons to ascribe charms to her, which nature had not given. Her passion, on the other hand, was as extravagant for Abelard; and her encomiums upon him have set him perhaps as much too high in the opinion of the women, as she herself has stood in the opinion of the men. Take a little of her language by way of specimen: " What wife, what maid, did not languish for you when absent, and was not all in a flame with love, when you was near? What queen or great lady did

not

not envy my joys and my bed? Two qualities you had, seldom to be found among the learned, by which you could not fail to gain all women's hearts: poetry, I mean, and music. With thefe you unbended your mind after its philofophic labours, and wrote many love verfes, which by their fweetnefs and harmony have caufed them to be fung in every corner of the world, fo that even the illiterate found your praife. And as the greateft part of your fongs celebrated our loves, they have fpread my name to many nations, and kindled there the envy of the women againft me." In the mean time Abelard was very handfome and very accomplifhed; though probably neither fo handfome nor accomplifhed as, according to Heloife, to make every woman frantic, who fhould caft her eyes upon him.

When Abelard confented to marry Heloife, fhe ufed a thoufand arguments to put him out of conceit with the conjugal tie. "I know my uncle's temper," faid fhe to him; "nothing will appeafe his rage againft you: and then what glory will it be to me to be your wife, fince I fhould ruin your reputation by it? What curfes have I not reafon to fear, if I rob the world of fo bright a luminary as you are? What injury fhall I not do the church? What forrow fhall I not give the philofophers? What a fhame and injury will it be to y u, whom nature has formed for the public good, to give yourfelf up entirely to a woman? Confider thefe words of St. Paul, 'Art thou loofed from a wife, feek not a wife.' And if the counfel of this great apoftle, and the exhortations of the holy fathers, cannot diffuade you from that heavy burden, confider at leaft what the philofophers have faid of it. Hear Theophraftus, who has proved by fo many reafons, that a wife man ought not to marry. Hear what Cicero, when he had divorced his wife Terentia, anfwered to Hirtius, who propofed a match to him with his fifter: that ' he could not divide his thoughts between philofophy and a wife.' Befides, what conformity is there between maid fervants and fcholars, inkhorns and cradles, books and diftaffs, pens and fpindles? How will you be able to bear, in the midft of philofophical and theological meditations, the cries of children, the fongs of nurfes, and the difturbance of houfe-keeping?" Afterwards, in the correfpondence which fhe kept up with him, when fhe had renounced the world many years, and engaged in a monaftic life, fhe reprefented to him the difinterreftednefs of her affection; and how fhe had neither fought the honour of marriage, nor the advantages of a dowry, nor her own pleafure, but the fingle fatisfaction of poffeffing her dear Abelard. She tells him, that although the name of wife feems more holy and of greater dignity, yet fhe was always better pleafed with that of his miftrefs, his concubine, or even ftrum-

pet;

pet; and declares in the moſt ſolemn manner, that ſhe had rather be the whore of Peter Abelard, than the lawful wife of the
emperor of the world [N]. "Deum teſtem invoco," ſays ſhe,
" ſi me Auguſtus univerſo præſidens mundo matrimonii honore
dignaretur, totumque mihi orbem confirmaret in perpetuo præ-
ſidendum, charius mihi & dignius videretur TUA DICI MERE-
TRIX, quam illius imperatrix [O]." I know not, ſays Bayle,
how this lady meant; but we have here one of the moſt myſte-
rious refinements in love. It has been, continues he, for ſeveral ages believed, that marriage deſtroys the principal poignancy
of this ſort of ſalt, and that when a man does a thing by engage-
ment, duty, and neceſſity, as a taſk and drudgery, he no longer
finds the natural charms of it; ſo that, according to theſe nice
judges, a man takes a wife " ad honores," and not " ad deli-
cias." "Marriage," as Montaigne obſerves, " has on its ſide,
profit, juſtice, honour, and conſtancy; a flat but more univerſal
pleaſure. Love is founded only upon pleaſure, which is more
touching, ſprightly, and exquiſite; a pleaſure inflamed by difficulty. There muſt be in it ſting and ardour: 'tis no more
love if without darts and fire. The bounty of the ladies is too
profuſe in marriage: it blunts the edge of affection and deſire [P]." And this perhaps made a Roman emperor ſay to his
wife, "Patere me per alias exercere cupiditates meas, nam uxor
nomen eſt dignitatis, non voluptatis [Q]:" that is, " ſuffer me
to ſatisfy my deſires with other women, for ſpouſe is the name of
dignity, not of pleaſure."

Heloiſe died May 17, 1163, about 20 years after her beloved
Abelard, and was buried in his grave. A moſt ſurpriſing miracle happened, if we may believe a MS. chronicle of Tours,
when the ſepulchre was opened, in order to lay Heloiſe's body
there, viz. "That Abelard ſtretched out his arms to receive her,
and cloſely embraced her:" but ſome have ventured to ſuppoſe,
that this may be a fiction. The letters of Heloiſe, together
with their anſwers, may be found in Abelard's works, where
more may be ſeen of this celebrated amour. Love certainly
begets much folly and madneſs among the ſons of men: yet,
upon comparing the loves of Abelard and Heloiſe with the loves
of the reſt of mankind, one ſhall be apt to apply to the former,
what the ſervant in the play ſaid of his maſter's younger ſon,
when he compared him with his elder: "Hic vero eſt, qui ſi
occeperit amare, ludum jocumque dices fuiſſe illum alterum,
præut hujus rabies quæ dabit:" that is, "If this frantic ſpark
ſhall once take it into his head to be a lover, you will ſay that

all that the other has done is but mere fport and jeft, compared with the pranks which he will play [R]."

HELSHAM (RICHARD), doctor of phyfic, profeffor of that fcience and of natural philofophy, in the univerfity of Dublin, was author of a celebrated courfe of twenty-three lectures on natural philofophy, publifhed after his death by Dr. Bryan Robinfon. Thefe lectures were long in high eftimation, paffed through feveral editions, and are only fuperfeded now from the neceffity of keeping pace in fuch works with the progrefs of difcoveries. They are clear and plain, though fcientific.

HELVETIUS (ADRIAN), a phyfician of Holland, was born in 1656. He journeyed to Paris, without any defign of fixing there, and only to fee that new world and fell fome medicines, but accident detained him very unexpectedly. The dyfentery then prevailed in that city; and all who applied to him are faid to have been infallibly cured. His fuccefs was celebrated; and Louis XIV. ordered him to publifh the remedy, which produced fuch certain and furprifing effects. He declared it to be *fpecacuanha*, and received 1000 louis-d'-ors for the difcovery. He fettled in Paris, became phyfician to the duke of Orleans, and was alfo made infpector general of the military hofpitals. He died in 1721, leaving fome works behind him; the principal of which is, "Traité des Maladies de plus frequentes, & des Remedies fpecifiques pour les guerir," 2 vols. 8vo.

HELVETIUS (JOHN-CLAUDE), fon of the above, was born in 1685, and died in 1755. He was firft phyfician to the queen, counfellor of ftate, and greatly efteemed by the town as well as court. He was, like his father, infpector-general of the military hofpitals. He was a member of the Academy of Sciences at Paris, of the Royal Society in London, and of the Academies of Pruffia, Florence, and Bologna. He cured Louis XV. of a dangerous diforder, which attacked him at the age of feven years, and obtained afterwards the entire confidence of the queen alfo. Whenever he attended as a phyfician, he was regarded as a friend, fuch was the goodnefs and benevolence of his character. He was particularly attentive to the poor. He was the author of, 1. "Idée Générale de l'économie animale, 1722," 8vo. 2. "Principia Phyfico-Medica, in tyronum Medicinæ gratiam confcripta," 2 vols. 8vo. This latter work, though drawn up for pupils, may yet be ferviceable to mafters.

HELVETIUS (CLAUDE ADRIAN), born at Paris in 1515, was fon of the preceding Helvetius. He ftudied under the famous father Porée in the college of Louis the Great, and his tutor, difcovering in his compofitions remarkable proofs of genius, was particularly attentive to his education. An early af-

[a] Terent. Eunuch, Act. II. Sc. iv.

C 4

fociation

fociation with the wits of his time, gave him the defire to become an author, but his principles unfortunately became tainted with falfe philofophy. He did not publifh any thing till the year 1758, when he produced his celebrated book "de l'Efprit," which appeared firft in one volume 4to., and afterwards in three volumes, 12mo. This work was very juftly condemned by the parliament of Paris, as confining the faculties of man to animal fenfibility, and removing at once the reftraints of vice and the encouragements to virtue. Attacked in various ways at home, on account of thefe principles, he vifited England in 1764, and the next year went into Pruffia, where he was received with honourable attention by the king. When he returned into France, he led a retired and domeftic life on his eftate at Voré. Attached to his wife and family, and ftrongly inclined to benevolence, he lived there more happily than at Paris, where, as he faid, he "was obliged to encounter the mortifying fpectacle of mifery that he could not relieve." To Marivaux, and M. Saurin, of the French Academy, he allowed penfions; that, for a private benefactor, were confiderable [s], merely on the fcore of merit; which he was anxious to fearch out and to affift. Yet, with all this benevolence of difpofition, he was ftrict in the care of his game, and in the exaction of his feudal rights. He was maltred'hotel to the queen, and, for a time, a farmer-general, but quitted that lucrative poft to enjoy his ftudies. When he found that he had beftowed his bounty upon unworthy perfons, or was reproached with it, he faid, "If I was king, I would correct them; but I am only rich, and they are poor, my bufinefs therefore is to aid them." Nature had been kind to Helvetius, fhe had given him a fine perfon, genius, and a conftitution which promifed long life. This laft, however, he did not attain, for he was attacked by the gout in his head and ftomach, under which complaint he languifhed fome little time, and died in December 1771. His works were, 1. The Treatife "De l'Efprit," "on the Mind," already mentioned: of which various opinions have been entertained. It certainly is one of thofe which endeavour to degrade the nature of man, too nearly to that of mere animals; and even Voltaire, who called the author at one time, a true philofopher, has faid that it is filled with common place truths, delivered with great parade, but without method, and difgraced by ftories very unworthy of a philofophical production. The ideas of virtue and vice, according to this book, depend chiefly upon climate. 2. "Le Bonheur," or "happinefs," a poem in fix cantos; publifhed after his death, in 1772, with fome fragments of epiftles. His poetical ftyle is ftill more affected than his profe, and though he produces fome fine verfes, he is more frequently

[s] To the former 2000, to the latter 3000 livres; near 100 and 150l. fterling.

fliff

ftiff and forced. His poem on happinefs is a declamation, wherein he makes that great objeë depend, not on virtue, but on the cultivation of letters and the arts. 3. " De l'Homme," 2 vols 8vo. another philofophical work, not lefs bold than the firft. A favourite paradox, produced in this book, under a variety of different forms, is, " that all men are born with equal talents, and owe their genius folely to education." This book is even more dangerous than that on the mind, becaufe the ftyle is clearer, and the author writes with lefs referve. He fpeaks fometimes of the enemies of what he called philofophy, with an afperity that ill accords with the general mildnefs of his charaëter.

HELVICUS (CHRISTOPHER), profeffor of the Greek and Eaftern languages, and of divinity, in the univerfity of Gieffen, was born in 1581, at Sprendlingen, a little town near Frankfort, where his father was minifter. He went through his ftudies in Marpurg, where he took his degree of M. A. in 1599, having taken his bachelor's in 1595. He was a moft early genius; compofed a prodigious number of Greek verfes at 15; and was capable of teaching Greek, Hebrew, and even philofophy, before he was 20. The Hebrew he poffeffed fo entirely, that he fpoke it as fluently as if it had been his native language. He thoroughly read the Greek authors; and even ftudied phyfic for fome time, though he had devoted himfelf to the miniftry. In 1605, he was chofen to teach Greek and Hebrew, in the college which the landgrave had lately eftablifhed at Gieffen; and which the year after was converted into an univerfity by the emperor, who endowed it with privileges. Having difcharged for five years the feveral duties of his employment with great reputation, he was appointed divinity profeffor in 1610. He married this year; yet continued as affiduous as ever in the offices of his profeffion. A church was offered him in Moravia in 1611, and a profefforfhip at Hamburg with a confiderable ftipend: but he refufed both thofe offers. In 1613, he took the degree of D. D. at the command of the landgrave; who fent him to Frankfort, that he might view the library of the Jews, who had been lately driven away by popular tumults. Helvicus, fond of reading the rabbins, bought feveral of their books on that occafion. He died in the flower of his age, in 1617; and his lofs was bewailed after a very peculiar manner. All the German poets of the Augfburg confeffion compofed elegies, to deplore his immature death. A collection was made of his poems, which were printed with his funeral fermon and fome other pieces, under the title of " Cippus Memorialis," by the care of Winckleman colleague to Helvicus.

. He was reputed to have had a moft fkilful and methodical way of teaching languages. He was a good grammarian; and publifhed feveral grammars, as Latin, Greek, Hebrew, Chaldee, Syriac:

Syriac: but they were only abridgements. His Hebrew and Latin Lexicons were only, by way of essay, calculated for youth. He was not only a good grammarian, but also an able chronologer. His chronological tables have gone through several editions, and been greatly esteemed, though they are not, as it is difficult to conceive they should be, quite free from errors. He published them in 1609, under the title of " Theatrum Historicum, five Chronologiæ Syftema Novum, &c." and brought them down from the beginning of the world to 1612; but they were afterwards revised and continued by John Balthasar Schuppius, son-in-law to the author, and professor of eloquence and history in the university of Marpurg. Helvicus had projected writing a great number of books; and it is plain by the books he actually published, that, had he lived threescore years, his works might have made several volumes in folio. They are not interesting enough to make a particular and minute account of them necessary: his chronology being the only one, whose use has not been superseded.

HELYOT (Pierre), perhaps Elliot, properly, as he was of British extraction. He was a religious of the order of Piepus near Paris, which is a branch of that of St. Francis. His fame is founded on a large work, the toil of twenty-three years, in eight volumes quarto, which is, " A History of Monastic Orders, religious and military, and of secular congregations of both sexes," &c. &c. He was born in 1660, and died in 1716. His work is full of learned research, and more correct than any thing on that subject which had then appeared. He was a man of exemplary piety, and a neat, though not elegant, or natural writer.

HEMELAR (John), a very learned man, born at the Hague, was a fine poet and orator; and to be compared, says Gronovius [τ], with the Roman Atticus for his probity, tranquillity of life, and absolute disregard of honours and public employments. He went to Rome, and spent six years in the palace of cardinal Cesi. He wrote there a panegyric on pope Clement VIII. which was so graciously received, that he was offered the post of librarian to the Vatican, or a very good benefice. He accepted the latter, and was made a canon in the cathedral at Antwerp. Lipsius had a great esteem for him, as appears from letters he wrote to him. He was Grotius's friend, and published verses to congratulate him on his deliverance from confinement. He was uncle by the mother's side to James Golius, the learned professor at Leyden, who gained so vast a reputation by his profound knowledge in the Oriental languages: but Golius, who was a zealous protestant, was greatly disaffected to him, for

[τ] Joann. Fred. Gronov. in Orat. Funeb. Jacobi Golii, p. 7.

having

having converted his brother Peter to popery. He applied himfelf much more to the ftudy of polite literature and to the fcience of medals, than to theology. " He publifhed, fays Gronovius, extremely ufeful commentaries upon the medals of the
Roman emperors, from the time of Julius Cæfar down to Juftinian, taken from the cabinets of Charles Arfchot and Nicholas
Rocoxius: wherein he concifely and accurately explains by
marks, figures, &c. whatever is exquifite, elegant, and fuitable
or agreeable to the hiftory of thofe times, and the genius of the
monarchs, whether the medals in queftion be of gold, filver, or
brafs, whether caft or ftruck in that immortal city. It is a kind
of ftorehoufe of medals; and neverthelefs in this work, from
which any other perfon would have expected prodigious reputation, our author has been fo modeft as to conceal his name."
This work of Hemelar's, which is in Latin, is not eafily to be
met with, yet it has been thrice printed: firft at Antwerp, in
1614, at the end of a work of James Biæus; fecondly, in 1627,
4to; and thirdly, in 1654, folio. The other works of this
canon are fome Latin poems and orations. He died in 1640.
He is fometimes called Hamelar.

HEMMINGFORD (WALTER DE), a regular canon of Gif-
borough-abbey, near Cleveland in Yorkfhire, flourifhed in the
XIVth century in the reign of Edward III. He had a ftrong
genius for learning, which by his induftry was improved to a
great degree. Hiftory was his particular inclination; and upon
this fubject it was that he became an author. He begins from
the Norman conqueft, and continues to the reign of king Edward the IId. from the year of our Lord 1066 to 1308. The
work is written with great care and exactnefs, and in a ftyle
good enough confidering the time. Gale enumerates five copies
of his hiftory, two at Trinity-college, Cambridge, one at the
Herald's-office, one in the Cotton library, and one which he had
himfelf. This author died at Gifborough in 1347.

HEMSKIRK, or HEEMSKIRK (MARTIN), an eminent
painter, was a peafant's fon, and born at a village of that name
in Holland, in 1498. In his youth he was extremely dull, and
nothing was expected from him; but afterwards he became a
correct painter, eafy and fruitful in his inventions. He went to
Rome, and intended to ftay there a long time; but at the end of
three years, returned to his own country. He fettled at Haerlem, and lived there the remainder of his days. Moft of his
works were engraved. Vafari gives a particular account of
them, commends them, and fays, Michael Angelo was fo
pleafed with one of the prints, that he had a mind to colour it.
Neverthelefs it is vifible from the prints of Hemfkirk's works,
that he did not underftand the *chiaro ofcuro*, and that his manner
of

of defigning was dry. He died in 1574, at 76 years of age having lived much longer than has been thought ufual for painters.

HEMMERLIN or MALLEOLUS (FELIX), a canon of Zurich in 1428. He was put in prifon for fome political offence. Two works of his in folio, and in black letter, are much fought by fome collectors of curiofities, one is 1. " Opufcula varia ; fcilicet. de Nobilitate et rufticitate dialogus," &c. 2. " Variæ oblectationis opufcula ; nempe contra validos mendicantes contra Eeghardos et Beghinos," &c. They are written with a coarfe kind of humour.

HEMSTERHUIS (TIBERIUS), or Hemfterhufius, one of the moft famous critics of his country, the fon of Francis Hemfterhuis, a phyfician, was born at Groningen, Feb. 1, 1685. After obtaining the rudiments of literature from proper mafters, and from his father, he became a member of his native univerfity in his fourteenth year, 1598. He there ftudied for fome years, and then removed to Leyden, for the fake of attending the lectures of the famous James Perizonius. He was here fo much noticed by the governors of the univerfity, that it was expected he would fucceed James Gronovius as profeffor of Greek. Havercamp, however, on the vacancy was appointed, through the intrigues, as Ruhnkenius afferts, of fome who feared they might be eclipfed by young Hemfterhuis ; who in 1705, at the age of 19, was called to Amfterdam, and appointed profeffor of mathematics and philofophy. In the former of thefe branches he had been a favourite fcholar of the famous John Bernouilli. In 1717, he removed to Franeker, on being chofen to fucceed Lambert Bos as profeffor of Greek ; to which place, in 1738, was added the profefforfhip of hiftory. In 1740 he removed to Leyden to accept the fame two profefforfhips in that univerfity. It appears that he was married, becaufe his father-in-law, J. Wild, is mentioned. He died in 1766, having enjoyed to the laft the ufe of all his faculties. He publifhed, 1. " The three laft books of Julius Pollux's Onomafticon," to complete the edition of which, feven books had been finifhed by Lederlin. This appeared at Amfterdam in 1706. On the appearance of this work, he received a letter from Bentley, highly praifing him for the fervice he had there rendered to his author. But this very letter was nearly the caufe of driving him entirely from the ftudy of Greek criticifm : for in it Bentley tranfmitted his own conjectures on the true readings of the paffages cited by Pollux from comic writers, with particular view to the reftoration of the metre. Hemfterhuis had himfelf attempted the fame, but when he read the criticifms of Bentley, and faw their aftonifhing juftnefs, and acutenefs, he was fo hurt at the inferiority of his own, that he refolved, for the time, never again to open a Greek book. In a month or two this timidity went off, and he

returned

returned to thefe ftudies with redoubled vigour, determined to
take Bentley for his model, and to qualify himfelf, if poffible,
to rival one whom he fo greatly admired. 2. "Select Colloquies
of Lucian, and his Timon." Amft. 1708. 3. "The Plutus
of Ariftophanes, with the Scholia," various readings and notes,
Harlingen, 8vo. 1744. 4. "Part of an edition of Lucian," as
far as the 521ft page of the firft volume ; it appeared in 1743 in
three volumes quarto. The extreme flowness of his proceeding
is much complained of by Gefner and others, and was the reafon why he made no further progrefs. 5. "Notes and emendations on Xenophon Ephefius," inferted in the 3—6 volumes
of the Mifcellanea Critica of Amfterdam, with the fignature
T. S. H. S. 6. "Some obfervations upon Chryfoftom's Ho-
mily on the Epiftle to Philemon," fubjoined to Raphelius's Annotations on the New Teftament. 7. "Inaugural Speeches on
Various Occafions." 8. "There are alfo letters from him to
J. Matth. Gefner and others," and he gave confiderable aid to
J. St. Bernard, in publifhing the "Ec1ogæ Thomæ Magiftri,"
at Leyden, in 1757 [u]. Ruhnkenius holds up Hemfterhufius
as a model of a perfect critic [x], and indeed, according to his
account, the extent and variety of his knowledge, and the acutenefs of his judgment were very extraordinary.

HENAULT (JOHN D'), a French poet, was the fon of a
baker at Paris, and at firft a receiver of the taxes at Fores.
Then he travelled into Holland and England, and was employed
by the fuperintendant Fouquet, who was his patron. After his
return to France, he foon became diftinguifhed as one of the
fineft geniufes of his age ; and gained a prodigious reputation by
his poetry. His fonnet on the mifcarriage of Mad. de Guerchi
is looked upon as a mafter-piece, though it is not written according to the rules of art, and though there happened to be a
barbarifm in it. He alfo wrote a fatirical poem againft the minifter Colbert, which is reckoned by Boileau among his beft
pieces. This was written, by way of revenging the difgrace
and ruin of his patron Fouquet, which Henault afcribed to Colbert : yet the minifter did not act upon this occafion as Richelieu would have done, but with more good fenfe and generofity [y]. Being told of this fonnet, which made a great noife,
he afked, "Whether there were any fatirical ftrokes in it againft
the king?" and being informed there was not, "Then," faid
he, "I fhall not mind it, nor fhew the leaft refentment againft
the author." Henault was a man who loved to refine on pleafures, and to debauch with art and delicacy : and fo far, confidering him as a poet, fome allowances might be made. But

[u] Vriemot Athenæ Frifiacæ. [x] Ruhnkenii Elogium. Tib. Hemfterhufii.
[y] See Art. Graudier.

he was strangely wrongheaded in one respect; for he professed atheism, and gloried in it with uncommon affectation. He went to Holland, on purpose to visit Spinoza, who nevertheless did not much esteem him. Spinoza considered him probably as one of those fashionable gentry, with which every country abounds, who are ready to take up singularities in religion, not from rational conviction, but from a profligate spirit of vain-glory: and on this account might be led to despise the man, whatever he might determine of his opinions. Spinoza did not mistake him, if he considered him in this light; for when sickness and death came to stare him in the face, things took a very different turn. Henault then became a convert, and was for carrying matters to the other extreme; for his confessor was forced to prevent his receiving the Viaticum or Sacrament, with a halter about his neck, in the middle of his bed-chamber. This is not unfrequently the case: men believe or disbelieve, have religion or none, without ever consulting reason, but just as constitution and humour direct; and so it is, that they usually behave ridiculously in whichever state we view them. He died in 1682.

He had printed at Paris, 1670, in 12mo. a small collection of his works, under the title of " Oeuvres Diverses," or " Miscellanies:" containing sonnets, and letters in verse and prose to Sappho, who was probably the celebrated madam des Houlieres, to whom he had the honour to be preceptor. Among these is the following imitation from this passage in the second act of Seneca's Thyestes:

> " Illi mors gravis incubat,
> Qui notus nimis omnibus,
> Ignotus moritur sibi."

" Heureux est l'inconnu, qui s'est bien su connoître:
Il ne voit pas de mal à mourir plus qu'à naître:
Il s'en va comme il est venu.
Mais helas! que la mort fait une horreur extrême:
A qui meurt de tous trop connu,
Et trop peu connu de soy-même!"

That is, " Happy is the obscure man, who is well known to himself: he sees no more harm in dying, than in being born: he leaves the world as he came into it. But alas! how extremely horrible must death be to that man, who dies too much known to others, and too little to himself!" This shews the philosopher as well as the poet, and is equally distant from atheism and superstition: " O, si sic omnia."—Henault had translated three books of Lucretius: but his confessor having raised in him scruples and fears, he burnt this work, so that there remains nothing of it, but the first 100 lines, which had been copied by his friends. Voltaire says, that " he would have

have gained great reputation, had thefe books that were loft been preferved, and been equal to what we have of this work."

HENAULT (CHARLES JOHN FRANCIS), was born at Paris, Feb. 8, 1685. His great grandfather, Remi Henault, ufed to be of Lewis XIII's party at tennis, and that prince called him " The Baron," becaufe of a fief which he poffeffed near Triel. He had three fons, officers of horfe, who were all killed at the fiege of Cafal. John Remi, his father, an efquire, and lord of Mouffy, counfellor to the king, and fecretary to the council, kept up the honour of the family, and becoming farmer-general, made his fortune. He was honoured with the confidence of the count de Pontchartrain; and, being of a poetical turn, had fome fhare in the criticifms which appeared againft Racine's tragedies. He married the daughter of a rich merchant at Calais, and one of her brothers being prefident of that town, entertained the queen of England, on her landing there in 1689. Another brother, counfellor in the parliament of Metz, and fecretary to the duke of Berry, was affociated with Mr. Crozat in the armaments, and, dying unmarried, left a great fortune to his fifter.

Young Henault early difcovered a fprightly, benevolent difpofition, and his penetration and aptnefs foon diftinguifhed itfelf by the fuccefs of his ftudies. Claude de Lifle, father of the celebrated geographer, gave him the fame leffons in geography and hiftory which he had before given to the duke of Orleans, afterwards regent. Thefe inftructions have been printed in feven volumes, under the title of " Abridgment of Univerfal Hiftory."

On quitting college, Henault entered the congregation of the oratory, where he foon attached himfelf to the ftudy of eloquence: and, on the death of the Abbé Rene, reformer of La Trappe, he undertook to pronounce his panegyric, which not meeting the approbation of father Maffilon, he quitted the oratory after two years, and his father bought for him, of marfhal Villeroi, the *lieutenance des chaffes*, and the government of Corbeil. At the marfhal's he formed connections and even intimate friendfhips with many of the nobility, and paffed the early part of his life in agreeable amufements, and in the livelieft company, without having his religious fentiments tainted. He affociated with the wits till the difpute between Rouffeau and De la Motte foon gave him a difguft for thefe trifling focieties. In 1707, he gained the prize of eloquence at the French Academy, and another next year, at the Academy des jeux Floraux. About this time, M. Reaumur, who was his relation, came to Paris, and took leffons in geometry under the fame mafter, Guinée. Henault introduced him to the Abbé Bignon, and this was the firft ftep of his illuftrious courfe. In 1713, he brought a tragedy on the ftage,

under

under the difguifed name of Fufelier. As he was known to the
public only by fome flighter pieces, " Cornelia the Veftal" met
with no better fuccefs. He therefore locked it up, without printing. In his old age his paffion for thefe fubjects revived, and
Mr. Horace Walpole being at Paris in 1768, and having formed
a friendfhip with him as one of the amiable men of his nation,
obtained this piece, and had it printed at his prefs at Strawberry-
hill, from whence a beautiful edition of Lucan had before iffued. In 1751, Mr. Henault, under a borrowed name, brought
out a fecond tragedy, entitled " Marius," which was well
received and printed. The French biographers, however,
doubt whether this was not really by M. Caux, whofe name
it bore.

He had been admitted counfellor in parliament in 1706, with
a difpenfation on account of age, and in 1710, prefident of the
firft chamber of inquefts. Thefe important places, which he
determined to fill in a becoming manner, engaged him in the
moft folid ftudies. The excellent work of Mr. Domat charmed
him, and made him eager to go back to the fountain head. He
fpent feveral years in making himfelf mafter of the Roman
law, the ordonances of the French king, their cuftoms, and public law. M. de Morville, procureur-general of the great council,
being appointed ambaffador to the Hague in 1718, engaged Henault to accompany him. His perfonal merit foon introduced
him to the acquaintance of the moft eminent perfonages at that
time there. The grand penfionary, Heinfius, who, under the
exterior of Lacedemonian fimplicity, kept up all the haughtinefs of that people, loft with him all that hauteur which France
itfelf had experienced from him in the negociations for the treaty
of Utrecht.

The agitation which all France felt by Law's fyftem, and the
confequent fending of the parliament into exile, was a trial to
the wife policy of the prefident Henault. His friendfhip for the
firft prefident, De Mefmes, led him to fecond all the views of
that great magiftrate: he took part in all the negociations, and
was animated purely by the public good, without any private
advantage. On the death of the cardinal du Bois, in 1723, he
fucceeded in his place at the French Academy. Cardinal Fleury
recommended him to fucceed himfelf as director, and he pronounced the eloge of M. de Malezieux.

Hiftory was his favourite ftudy ; not a bare collection of dates,
but a knowledge of the laws and manners of nations ; to obtain
which he drew inftruction from private converfations, a method
he fo ftrongly recommends in his preface. After having thus
difcuffed the moft important points of public law, he undertook
to collect and publifh the refult of his inquiries, and he is defervedly

fervedly accounted the firft framer of chronological abridgements; in which, without ftopping at detached facts, he attends
only to thofe which form a chain of events that perfect or alter
the government and character of a nation, and traces only the
fprings which exalt or humble a nation, extending or contracting the fpace it occupies in the world. His work has had the
fortune of thofe literary phænomena, where novelty and merit
united excite minds eager after glory, and fire the ardour of
young writers to prefs after a guide whom few can overtake.
The firft edition of the work, the refult of 40 years reading,
appeared in 1744, under the aufpices of the chancellor Daguef-
feau, with the modeft title of " An Effay." The fuccefs it
met with furprifed the author. He made continual improvements
in it, and it has gone through nine editions, and been tranflated
into Italian, Englifh, and German, and even into Chinefe. As
the beft writers are not fecure from criticifm, and are indeed the
only ones that deferve it, the author read to the Academy of
Belles Lettres a defence of his abridgement.

All the ages and events of the French monarchy being prefent to his mind, and his imagination and memory being a vaft
theatre whereon he beheld the different movements and parts of
the actors in the feveral revolutions, he determined to give a
fpecimen of what paft in his own mind, and to reduce into the
form of a regular drama, one of the periods of French hiftory,
the reign of Francis II. which, though happy only by being
fhort, appeared to him one of the moft important by its confequences, and moft eafy to be confined within a dramatic compafs. His friend the chancellor highly approved the plan, and
wifhed it to be printed. It accordingly went through five editions; the harmony of dates and facts is exactly obferved in it,
and the paffions interefted without offence to hiftoric truth.

In 1755, Henault was chofen an honorary member of the Academy of Belles Lettres, having been before elected into the academies of Nanci, Berlin, and Stockholm. The queen alfoappointed
him fuperintendant of her houfe. His natural fprightlinefs relieved
her from the ferious attendance on his private morning lectures.
The company of perfons moft diftinguifhed by their wit and
birth, a table more celebrated for the choice of the guefts than
its delicacies, the little comedies fuggefted by wit, and executed
by reflection, united at his houfe all the pleafures of an agreeable and innocent life. All the members of this ingenious fociety contributed to render it pleafing, and the prefident was
not inferior to any. He compofed three delightful comedies:
" La Petite Maifon," " Le Jaloux de Soi-meme," and " Le
Reveil d'Epimenide." The fubject of the laft was the Cretan
philofopher, who is pretended to have flept 27 years. He is introduced fancying that he had flept but one night, and aftonifhed

at the change in the age of all around him : he miftakes his miftrefs for his mother ; but, difcovering his miftake, offers to
marry her, which fhe refufes, though he ftill continues to love
her. The queen was particularly pleafed with this piece. She
ordered the prefident to reftore the philofopher's miftrefs to her
former youth : he introduced Hebe, and this epifode produced
an agreeable entertainment.

He was now in fuch favour with her majefty, that, on the
place of fuperintendant becoming vacant by the death of M. Bernard de Conbert, mafter of requefts, and the fum he had paid
for it being loft to his family, Henault folicited it in favour of
feveral perfons, till at laft the queen beftowed it on himfelf, and
confented that he fhould divide the profits with his predeceffor's
widow.—On the queen's death he held the fame place under the
dauphinefs.

A delicate conftitution made him liable to much illnefs, which,
however, did not interrupt the ferenity of his mind. He made
feveral journies to the waters of Plombieres : in one of thefe
he vifited the depofed king Staniflaus at Luneville ; and in another accompanied his friend the marquis de Pauliny, ambaffador
to Switzerland.

In 1763 Henault drew near his end. One morning, after a quiet
night, he felt an oppreffion, which the faculty pronounced a
fuffocating cough. His confeffor being fent to him, he formed his
refolution without alarm. He mentioned afterwards, that he re-
collected having then faid to himfelf, " What do I regret ?" and
called to mind that faying of madame de Sevigne, " I leave
here only dying creatures." He received the facraments. It was
believed the next night would be his laft ; but by noon the next
day he was out of danger. " Now," faid he, " I know what
death is. It will not be new to me any more " He never forgot it during the following feven years of his life, which, like
all the reft, were gentle and calm. Full of gratitude for the
favours of Providence, refigned to its decrees, offering to the
author of his being a pure and fincere devotion ; he felt his infirmities without complaining, and perceived a gradual decay with
unabated firmnefs. He died Dec. 24, 1771, in his 86th year.
He married, in 1714, a daughter of M. le Bas de Montargis,
keeper of the royal treafure, &c. who died in 1728, without
leaving any iffue. He treated as his own children, thofe of his
fifter, who had married, in 1713, the count de Jonfac, and by him
had three fons and two daughters. The two younger fons were
killed, one at Bruffels, the other at Lafelt, both at the head of the
regiments of which they were colonels ; the eldeft long furvived,
and was lieutenant-general and governor of Collioure and Port
Vendre in Rouffillon. The elder daughter married M. le Veneur,
count

count de Tillieres, and died in 1757; the fecond married the marquis d'Aubeterre, ambaffador to Vienna, Madrid, and Rome.

HENLEY (ANTHONY), [A], was the fon of fir Robert Henley, of the Grange in Hampfhire, defcended from the Henleys of Henley in Somerfetfhire; of whom fir Andrew Henley was created a baronet in 1660. This fir Andrew had a fon of the fame name, famous for his frolics and profufion. His feat, called Bramefley, near Hartley-row, in the county of Southampton, was very large and magnificent. He had a great eflate in that and the other weflern counties, which was reduced by him to a very fmall one, or to nothing. Sir Robert Henley of the Grange, his uncle, was a man of good fenfe and œconomy. He held the mafter's place of the King's-bench court, on the pleas fide, many years; and by the profits of it, and good management, left his fon, Anthony Henley, of the Grange, of whom we now treat, poffeffed of a very fine fortune, above 3000l. a year, part of which arofe from the ground-rents of Lincoln's-inn-fields.

Anthony Henley was bred at Oxford, where he diftinguifhed himfelf by an early relifh for polite learning. He made a great proficiency in the ftudy of the claffics, and particularly the ancient poets, by which he formed a good tafte for poetry, and practifed it with fuccefs. Upon his coming to London, he was prefently received into the friendfhip and familiarity of perfons of the firft rank, for quality and wit, particularly the earls of Dorfet and Sunderland. The latter had efpecially a great efteem and affection for him; and as every one knew what a fecret influence he had on affairs in king William's court, it was thought ftrange that Mr. Henley, who had a genius for any thing great, as well as any thing gay, did not rife in the ftate, where he would have fhone as a politician, no lefs than he did at Will's and Tom's as a Wit. But the Mufes and pleafure had engaged him. He had fomething of the character of Tibullus, and, except his extravagance, was poffeffed of all his other qualities; his indolence, his gallantry, his wit, his humanity, his generofity, his learning, his tafte for letters. There was hardly a contemporary author, who did not experience his bounty. They foon found him out, and attacked him with their dedications; which, though he knew how to value as they deferved, were always received as well as the addreffers could wifh; and his returns were made fo handfomely, that the manner was as grateful as the prefent.

There was, for a long time, a ftrict friendfhip between Mr. Henley and Richard Norton of Southwick in Hampfhire, efq. who was often chofen to reprefent that county. This gentleman had the fame paffion for the Mufes; 'and the fimilarity there was in their pleafures and ftudies, made that friendſhip the more firm and affectionate. They both lived to a good age before they married, and perhaps the breach that happened between them was one reafon of their entering both into the ftate of matrimony much about the fame time. Mr. Healey married Mary youngeſt daughter and co-heirefs of the him. Peregrine Bertie, fifter to the countefs Pawlet, with whom he had 30,000l. fortune, and by her he left feveral children. Of thefe Anthony, the eldeſt, died in 1745; and Robert, the fecond fon, was created baron Henley and lord keeper of the great feal in 1760; became lord chancellor in 1761; and earl of Northington in 1764.

On becoming a hufband and a father, Mr. Henley relinquifhed his gay mode of life, and confented to be chofen a member of parliament for Andover in 1698; after which he was conſtantly the reprefentative for either Weymouth, or Melcombe Regis, in the county of Dorfet. He was always a zealous affertor of liberty in the houfe of commons, and on all other occafions conftant to that courfe which has furnifhed Britain with fo many patriots; the greateſt inftance of which was, his moving in the houfe for an addrefs to her majeſty, that fhe would be gracioufly pleafed to give Mr. Benjamin Hoadly fome dignity in the church, for ftrenuoufly afferting and vindicating the principles of that revolution which is the foundation of our prefent eſtablifhment in church and ftate. This made him odious to all the Jacobites, Nonjurors, and fome others; and fome impotent endeavours were ufed to have him laid afide in the queen's laſt parliament; but he carried his election both at his corporation, and afterwards in the houfe of commons.

Mr. Henley wrote feveral compofitions, though he did not put his name to them; and very frequently affifted the writers of the " Tatler" and " Medley [в]." No man wrote with more wit and more gaiety. He affected a low fimplicity in his writings, and in particular was extremely happy in touching the manners and paffions of parents and children, mafters and fervants, peafants and tradefmen, ufing their expreffions fo naturally and aptly, that he has very frequently difguifed by it both his merit and character.

His moſt darling diverfion was mufic, of which he was entirely mafter; his opinion was the ftandard of tafte; and after the Italian mufic was introduced, no opera could be fure of applaufe, till it had received his approbation. He was fuch an admirer of Purcell's mufic, and the Englifh manner, that he did

[в] No. XXXI, of " The Medley," in particular was his; and feveral " Tatlers," both in the firſt volumes of Steele, and in Harrifon's fifth volume.

not

not immediately relifh the Italian ; but his good judgment foon
threw off that partiality, and he was at laft much attached to it,
Whether he compofed himfelf, we know not ; but he fung with
art, and played on feveral inflruments with judgment. He
wrote feveral poems for mufic, and almoft finifhed the opera of
" Alexander" fet by Purcell. As Mr. Henley's tafte inclined him
to mufic, that of his friend Mr. Norton was led to the drama. He
had a theatre at Southwick, where Betterton, Booth, Mills, Wilks,
Mrs. Barry, Mrs. Bracegirdle, Mrs. Oldfield, and all the firft
players, were entertained for two or three months in the vaca-
tion, and acted comedies and tragedies, in which the owner of
the houfe had frequently a part. Thefe reprefentations were
given with complete decorations, mufic, &c. and were eagerly
attended by company, from the diftance of many miles. Garth
in his preface to the Difpenfary, has highly praifed Henley,
who was his friend ; and his death, which happened in 1711,
was very generally lamented.

HENLEY (JOHN), better known by the appellation of " Orator Henley," has furnifhed the world [c] with memorials of himfelf, which are in fome refpects worth preferving. He was
born at Melton Mowbray, Leicefterfhire, Aug. 3, 1792. His
father, the rev. Simon Henley, and his grand-father, by his mother's fide (John Dowel, M. A.) were both vicars of that parifh. His grand-father by his father's fide, John Henley, M. A.
was likewife a clergyman, rector of Salmonby and Thetford in
Lincolnfhire. He was educated among the Diffenters, and con-
formed at the reftoration. Henley was bred up firft in the
free-fchool of Melton, under Mr. Daffy, a diligent and expert grammarian. From this fchool he was removed to that of
Okeham in Rutland, under Mr. Wright, eminent for his knowledge of the Latin, Greek and Hebrew languages.

He was hence removed, about the age of 17, to St. John's-college in Cambridge ; where, on his examination by Dr Gower then
mafter, Dr. Lambert, Dr. Edmundfon, and others, he was, he tells
us, particularly approved, While an undergraduate at St. John's,
he wrote a letter to the " Spectator," dated from that college,
Feb. 3, 1712, figned Peter de Quir, abounding with quaintnefs
and local wit. He began here to be uneafy ; he was more inclined to difpute than to affent to any points of doctrine, and
fancied himfelf able to reform the whole fyftem of academical
education.

After he had commenced bachelor of arts, he was firft defired
by the truftees of the fchool in Melton to affift in, and then to
take the direction of, that fchool ; which he increafed and raifed
from a declining to a flourifhing condition. He eftablifhed here,

[c] In the " Oratory Tranfactions," No. 1. under the fictitious name of Welftede.

he

he tells us, a practice of improving elocution, by the public
speaking of passages in the classics, morning and afternoon, as
well as orations, &c. Here he was invited by a letter from the
rev. Mr. Newcome, to be a candidate for a fellowship in St.
John's; but as he had long been absent, and therefore lessened
his personal interest, he declined appearing for it. Here likewise he began his " Universal Grammar," and finished ten languages, with dissertations prefixed, as the most ready introduction to any tongue whatever. In the beginning of this interval
he wrote a poem on " Esther," which was approved by the
town, and well received. On the occasion of his " Grammars," Dr. Hutchinson wrote him a complimentary letter.

He was ordained a deacon by Dr. Wake, then bishop of
Lincoln; and after having taken his degree of M. A. was admitted to priest's orders by Dr. Gibson, his successor in that see.
He did not long consent to rest in the country, but, impatient
to obtain wealth and fame in London, resigned his offices of
master and curate, and entered upon his new career.

In town, he produced several publications; as, a translation of
Pliny's " Epistles," of several works of abbé Vertot, of Montfau-
con's " Italian Travels" in folio, and many other books. His most
efficient patron was the earl of Macclesfield, who gave him a
benefice in the country, the value of which to a resident would
have been above 80l. a year; he had likewise a lecture in the
city; and, according to his own account, preached more charity-
sermons about town, was more numerously followed, and raised
more for the poor children, than any other preacher, however
dignified or distinguished. This popularity, with his enterprising
spirit, and *introducing regular action into the pulpit*, were " the
true causes," he says, " why some obstructed his rising in town,
from envy, jealousy, and a dislish of those who are not qualified to be complete spaniels. For there was no objection to
his being tossed into a country benefice by the way of the sea,
as far as Galilee of the Gentiles (like a pendulum swinging one
way as far as the other.)" Not being able to obtain preferment
in London, and not choosing to return into the country, he
struck out the plan of his Lectures, or Orations, which he puffed
in the most barefaced manner, as may be seen in the following
specimen.

" That he should have the assurance to frame a plan, which
no mortal eyer thought of; that he should singly execute what
would sprain a dozen of modern doctors of the tribe of Issa-
char; that he should have success against all opposition; challenge his adversaries to fair disputations, without any offering to
dispute with him; write, read, and study 12 hours a day, and
yet appear as untouched by the yoke, as if he never wore it;
compose three dissertations each week, on all subjects, however
uncom-

uncommon, treated in all lights and manners by himfelf, without affiftance, as fome would detract from him ; teach in one
year, what fchools and univerfities teach in five ; offer to learn
—to fpeak and—to read ; not be terrified by cabals, or menaces, or infults, or the grave nonfenfe of one, or the frothy
fatire of another ; that he fhould ftill proceed and mature this
bold fcheme, and put the church, and all that, in danger ;—
This man muft be a— a— a— &c. [D]"

Henley preached on Sundays upon theological matters, and
on Wednefdays upon all other fciences. He declaimed fome
years againft the greateft perfons, and occafionally, fays Warburton, did Pope that honour. The poet in return thus blazons
him to infamy :

    " But, where each fcience lifts its modern type,
Hiftory her pot, Divinity his pipe,
While proud Philofophy repines to fhow,
Difhoneft fight! his breeches rent below ;
Imbrown'd with native bronze, lo Henley ftands,
Tuning his voice, and balancing his hands.
How fluent nonfenfe trickles from his tongue !
How fweet the periods, neither faid, nor fung!
Still break the benches, Henley! with thy ftrain,
While Kennet, Hare, and Gibfon preach in vain.
O great reftorer of the good old ftage,
Preacher at once, and Zany of thy age !
O worthy thou of Ægypt's wife abodes,
A decent prieft, where monkies were the gods !
But Fate with butchers plac'd thy prieftly ftall,
Meek modern faith to murder, hack, and maul :
And bade thee live to crown Britannia's praife,
In Toland's, Tindal's, and in Woolfton's days."

This ftrange man ftruck medals, which he difperfed as tickets
to his fubfcribers : a ftar rifing to the meridian, with this motto,
" ad fumma ;" and below, " Inveniam viam, aut faciam."
Each auditor paid 1s. His audience was generally compofed of
the loweft ranks ; and it is well known, that he once collected
a vaft number of fhoe-makers, by announcing that he could
teach them a fpeedy mode of operation in their bufinefs, which
proved only to be, the making of fhoes by cutting off the tops
of ready-made boots. He was author of a weekly paper of un-
intelligible nonfenfe, called " The Hyp Doctor," for which
fecret fervice he had 100l. a year given him. Henley ufed, every
Saturday, to print an advertifement in " The Daily Advertifer,"
containing an account of the fubjects on which he intended to

[D] Oratory Tranfactions, p. 15.

difcourfe in the enfuing evening, at his Oratory near Lincoln's-Inn-fields. The advertifement had a fort of motto before it, which was generally a fneer at fome public tranfaction of the preceding week [D]. Henley died Oct. 14, 1756. In his account of himfelf he affumes the credit of confiderable learning, and a ftrong zeal for knowledge; but, if we may judge from the fpecimens we have feen of his compofitions, thefe were only the boafts of empiricifm. Both his ftyle and his thoughts are low; vanity and cenforioufnefs are the moft confpicuous qualities.

Orator Henley is a principal figure in two very humorous plates of Hogarth; in one of which he is " chriftening a child;" in the other, called " The Oratory," he is reprefented on a fcaffold, a monkey (over whom is written *Amen*) by his fide; a box of pills, and " The Hyp Doctor," lying befide him. Over his head " The Oratory: Inveniam viam, aut faciam." Over the door, " Ingredere ut proficias." A parfon receiving the money for admiffion. Under him, " The Treafury." A butcher ftands as porter. On the left hand, Modefty in a cloud; Folly in a coach; and a gibbet prepared for Merit; people laughing. One marked " The Scout," introducing a puritan divine [E].

HENNUYER (JOHN), the bifhop of Lifieux, fo juftly celebrated for his humanity at the time of the dreadful maffacre of St. Bartholomew, had been confeffor to Henry II. of France, and bifhop of Lodéve. In the reign of Charles IX. when the royal lieutenant of his province communicated to him the order to maffacre all the proteftants in the diocefe of Lifieux, he did the act for which he is fo juftly immortalized. He figned a formal and official oppofition to the order; for which ftriking act of clemency, it is wonderful to fay, he was not cenfured or perfecuted by the bigotry of the court. The beauty of virtue exacted refpect. He died in 1577, univerfally refpected, having gained over more by his mildnefs than any bigot by his fury.

HENRY II. (PLANTAGENET), king of England, fon of Geoffrey Plantagenet, count of Anjou, and of Matilda, daughter of Henry I. was born in 1132. He was educated chiefly under the care of his uncle, the accomplifhed Robert earl of Gloucefter, at Briftol; and during that period, is faid to have formed his

[D] Dr. Cobden, one of George II's chaplains, having in 174°, preached a fermon at St. James's, from thefe words: " Take away the wicked from before the king, and his throne fhall be eftablished in righteoufnefs;" it gave fo much difpleafure, that the doctor was ftruck out of the lift of chaplains; and the next Saturday, the following parody of his text appeared as a motto to Henley's advertifements:

" Away with the wicked before the king,
And away with the wicked behind him;
His throne it will blefs
With righteoufnefs,
And we fhall know where to find him."

[E] This defcription is taken from the " Biographical anecdotes of Hogarth," by Mr. Nichols, who doubts, however, whether " The Oratory" be a genuine production of Hogarth.

attachment to the beautiful Rofamond, daughter of lord Clifford. In the long civil contelt between his mother and king Stephen, he was too young to take a confpicuous part; but in 1147 he departed for Normandy, which his father had fecured. In 1149 he returned to England, to affert his claim to the crown, and went publicly in great fplendor to Scotland, where he received knighthood from David king of Scotland. In 1150, he was invefted with the dukedom of Normandy, and in 1151 married Eleanor heirefs of Poitou and Guienne. In 1153, on the death of Euftace, fon of Stephen, he was folemnly acknowledged as fucceffor to that monarch, whom he actually fucceeded in 1154. He commenced his reign by the redrefs of feveral grievances, renewing the charter of Henry I. and the laws of Edward the Confeffor. He difmiffed the foreign mercenaries, reftored the coinage, enforced the laws againft offenders, and deftroyed the caftles of the haughty nobles which Stephen had imprudently permitted to be built. In 1159, he carried war into France, to enforce his claim to the earldom of Touloufe; but Louis VII. king of France, throwing himfelf into that capital, he raifed the fiege, and the war was foon terminated by an accommodation very honourable to Henry. Among the abufes which he was anxious to reform, were the exorbitant power of the clergy, and the great relaxation of morals then prevalent in that order; and the contelt that enfued, proved fatal in 1170 to Becket archbifhop of Canterbury, who had been his chancellor and principal favourite. He was engaged in feveral wars, and was generally fuccefsful. Ireland he invaded, and finally accomplifhed the conqueft of it in 1168. He alfo compelled William, king of Scotland, to do homage to him for his dominions, in 1175. The latter part of his life and reign were rendered turbulent and unhappy by the frequent rebellions of his fons aided by the kings of France. He refifted them with various fuccefs, but not without much anguifh at their ingratitude; till at length, the junction of his youngeft and favourite fon John, in the confederacy againft him, overpowered his patience, and is faid to have brought on the fever which proved fatal to him in his 57th year, at Chinon in Touraine, A. D. 1189. Henry was diftinguifhed above moft princes by valour, prudence, generofity, genius, extent of knowledge, for the time in which he lived, fkill in the arts of government, conftantly exerted in the formation of the moft falutary laws. To counterbalance thefe great qualities, he had exceffive pride, immoderate ambition, and a total want of command over his paffions. The life of this prince, written by lord Lyttelton, is well known as an important and valuable piece of Englifh hiftory; and fully fhews how well the fubject of it deferves to be commemorated as one of

the

the ableſt, and, in political qualities, moſt diſtinguiſhed of our Engliſh monarchs.

HENRY IV. (of Bourbon), king of France. The moſt illuſtrious of the French monarchs alſo was a Henry. He was born in 1553, in the caſtle of Pau, the capital of Beárn, being the ſon of Antony of Bourbon, king of Navarre, and Joan d'Albret. By his deſcent from Robert of Clermont, fifth ſon of Louis IX. (called St. Louis) he became heir to the crown of France. He was educated in a hardy manner ; and from his earlieſt years gave the ſtrongeſt proofs of an intrepid and noble charaĉter. His mother being a proteſtant, he was educated in that perſuaſion, and was for many years the chief of that party. Henry was early initiated in war, being preſent at the battle of Jarnac, in 1569, when he was only ſixteen years of age ; and he there ſhewed great marks of military talent. After the peace of St. Germain, in 1570, he was taken to court, and two years afterwards married the princeſs Margaret of Valois, ſiſter to Charles IX. It was during the rejoicings for this marriage, that the horrible maſſacre of St. Bartholomew's eve was perpetrated by that perfidious and cruel court. The young prince of Navarre was kept for three years afterwards a kind of ſtate priſoner. He eſcaped in 1576, and put himſelf at the head of the Hugonot, or proteſtant party, where he expoſed himſelf to all the hazards of a civil war, as much as the meaneſt ſoldier ; harraſſed without intermiſſion, undergoing the greateſt hardſhips, and frequently in want of neceſſaries. In 1587, he gained the victory of Courtras, where he performed the moſt ſignal acts of valour. By the death of his mother he became king of Navarre in 1572, and king of France by that of Henry III. in 1589. He did not here ſucceed to a quiet throne ; the famous league was ſtrong in force againſt him, while he had few friends, few ſtrong places, no money, and a ſmall army. His reſources were his courage and activity. In the year of his acceſſion he gained the battle of Arques, and that of Ivry, in 1590. Here it was that he made his famous addreſs to his ſoldiers: " If you loſe your ſtandards, rally round my white plume ; you will always find it in the path of honour and glory." Henry now laid ſiege to Paris, which he puſhed to great extremities ; but, during the ſiege, ſome conferences were held between the chiefs of the two parties, which ended in a kind of accommodation: the king agreed to abjure proteſtantiſm, which he did at St. Denys, in 1593 ; after which he was crowned at Chartres, and the year following Paris opened her gates to him. In the year 1595, was publiſhed the celebrated edict of Nantes, giving a degree of toleration to the proteſtants, and much tranquillity to the kingdom, till it was revoked with ſo much impolicy by Louis XIV. In the ſame year he was involved in a war with Spain, which

which continued to 1598. The duke of Mayenne, chief of the leaguers, had submitted in 1596, and the duke of Mercœur in 1598, after which period his kingdom enjoyed peace, with hardly any interruption, till his death. Beloved as Henry was in general for his many virtues, and his very conciliating manners, the fanatics never could pardon his former attachment to the protestant cause, and almost every year produced some attempt upon his life. One, at length, named Ravaillac, to the great misfortune of France, succeeded in his enterprise, and gave him, on May 14, 1610, a wound which proved fatal. He died in the 57th year of his age, and the 22d of his reign. His first marriage with Margaret of Valois, had been annulled, and he married afterwards Mary of Medicis, by whom he left three sons and three daughters. There is, perhaps, no prince recorded in history, of whom so many anecdotes are extant, as of Henry IV. Most of them tend to display a singular liveliness and generosity of character, with a goodness of heart, which endeared his memory to his countrymen in the strongest manner, till they imbibed an indiscriminating antipathy against all monarchs. " My wish is," said he, " that every peasant in my kingdom should have a fowl in the pot on Sundays;" an expression which well illustrates the benevolence of his disposition. It is still more proved by what he said to his excellent and justly-favoured minister, Sully, when he was dangerously ill in 1598. " My friend, I have no fear of death; you have seen me brave it in a thousand instances; but I regret losing my life before I have been able, by governing my subjects well, and alleviating all their burthens, to demonstrate to them that I love them as my own children." His actions were conformable to these expressions, and he was continually employed in plans to make his people flourishing and happy. A violent turn for gallantry, and some particular amours, to which he devoted himself too much, are the chief faults imputed to this prince, whose virtues, actions, and character, have given occasion to the only able attempt towards an epic poem that his country has produced, the Henriade of Voltaire. It is impossible even for foreigners to read the history of Henry IV. without much interest; no wonder, therefore, that his countrymen have loved so much to dwell upon it.

HENRY (PHILIP), one of the fathers of Nonconformity [F], or, as he was called by some of his admirers, " the good, the heavenly Mr. Henry," was born at Whitehall, in 1631 : his father, John Henry, was page of the back-stairs to the king's second son, James duke of York. About twelve years old he was admitted into Westminster-school, under Mr. Thomas Vincent, then usher ; very diligent in his business, but who grieved

[F] The life of Mr. Philip Henry, by Matthew Henry, 1765.

fo much at the dulnefs of many of his fcholars, that he fell into
a confumption, and was faid to be " killed with falfe Latin." In
the regular time, he was taken into the upper fchool under Dr.
Bufby, with whom he was a great favourite; and was employed by
him, with fome others, in collecting materials for that excellent
Greek grammar which he afterwards publifhed. Soon after the
civil wars broke out, there was a daily morning lecture, fet up
at the abbey church, by the affembly of divines. His pious
mother requefted Dr. Bufby to give her fon leave to attend this,
and likewife took him with her every Thurfday to Mr. Cafe's
lecture, at St. Martin's: fhe took him alfo to the monthly fafts
at St. Margaret's, where the houfe of commons attended; and
where the fervice was carried on with great ftrictnefs and folemnity, from eight in the morning till four in the evening: in
thefe, as he himfelf has curioufly expreffed it, he had often
" fweet meltings of foul."

He was elected from Weftminfter to Chrift-church Oxford,
where he was admitted a ftudent in 1648, and vigoroufly applied
himfelf to the proper ftudies of the place. When he had completed his mafter's degree, he was entertained in the family of
judge Pulefton, at Emeral in Flintfhire, to take the care of
his fons, and to preach at Worthenbury. He was ordained to
the work of the miniftry in this place in 1657, according to the
known directory of the affembly of divines, and the common
ufage of the prefbyterians. He foon after married the only
daughter and heirefs of Mr. Daniel Mathews, of Broad-oak,
near Whitchurch, by whom he became poffeffed of a competent
eftate. When the king and epifcopacy were reftored, he refufed
to conform; was ejected, and retired with his family to Broad-
oak. Here, and in this neighbourhood, he fpent the remainder
of his life, about twenty-eight years; relieving the poor, em-
ploying the induftrious, inftructing the ignorant, and exercifing
every opportunity of doing good. His moderation in his nonconformity was eminent and exemplary; and upon all occafions
he bore teftimony againft uncharitable and fchifmatical feparation. In church-government, he defired and wifhed for apb.
Ufher's reduction of epifcopacy. He thought it lawful to join
in the common-prayer in the public affemblies; which, during
the time of his filence and reftraint, he conftantly attended with
his family, with reverence and devotion.

Upon the whole, his character feems to have been highly exemplary and praife-worthy: and it may be afked, as Dr. Bufby
afked him, " What made him a nonconformift?" The reafon
which he principally infifted on was, that he could not fubmit to
be re-ordained. He was fo well fatisfied with his call to the
miniftry, and folemn ordination to it, by the laying on the
hands of the prefbytery, that he durft not do that which looked
like

like a renunciation of it as null and finful, and would at leaft
be a tacit invalidating and condemning of all his adminiftra-
tions. Defpairing to fee an accommodation, he kept a meeting
at Broad-oak, and preached to a congregation in a barn.

HENRY (MATTHEW), an eminent diffenting teacher [o],
and a voluminous writer, was the fon of the foregoing, and born
in 1662. He continued under his father's eye and care till about
eighteen; and had the greateft advantages of his education from
him, both in divine and human literature. He was very expert
in the learned languages, efpecially in the Hebrew, which had
been made familiar to him from his childhood; and from firft to
laft, the ftudy of the fcriptures was his moft delightful employment. For further improvement, he was placed in 1680 at an
academy at Iflington. He was afterwards entered in Gray's-
inn, for the ftudy of the law; where he went on with his ufual
diligence, and became acquainted with the civil law, and the mu-
nicipal law of his own country. His proficiency was foon obferved; and it was the opinion of thofe who knew him, that his
great induftry, quick apprehenfion, tenacious memory, and
ready utterance, would render him very eminent in that profeffion. But he adhered to his firft refolution of making divinity his ftudy and bufinefs, and attended the moft celebrated
preachers in town; and, as an inftance of his judgement,
was beft pleafed with Dr. Stillingfleet for his ferious practical
preaching; and with Dr. Tillotfon, for his admirable fermons
againft popery, at his lectures at St. Lawrence Jewry. In
1686, he returned into the country, and preached feveral times
as a candidate for the miniftry with fuch fuccefs and approbation,
that the congregation at Chefter invited him to be their paftor.
To this place he was ordained in 1687, where he lived about
twenty-five years. He had feveral calls from London, which
he conftantly declined; but was at laft prevailed on to accept a
very important and unanimous one from Hackney. He died in
1714, at Nantwich, of an apoplectic fit, upon a journey, and
was interred at Trinity-church in Chefter.

He was univerfally lamented; every pulpit of the Diffenters
gave notice of the great breach that was made in their church;
every fermon was a funeral fermon for Mr. Henry. The writings he publifhed, befides feveral fingle fermons, are, 1. "A
Difcourfe concerning the Nature of Schifm, 1689." 2. "The
Life of Mr. Philip Henry, 1696." 3. "A Scripture Catechifm, 1702." 4. "Family Hymns, 1702." 5. "The Com-
municant's Companion, 1704." 6. "Four Difcourfes againft
Vice and Immorality, 1705." 7. "A Method for Prayer,
1710." 8. "Directions for daily Communion with God, 1712."
9. "Expofitions of the Bible," 5 vols. folio.

[o] Life of Matt. Henry, by W. Tong, 1716.

HENRY (ROBERT), author of a history of England on a new plan, which has been generally and highly approved, was the son of James Henry, a farmer, at Muirtown in the parish of St. Ninian's, Scotland, and of Jean Galloway his wife, of Stirling-shire [H]. He was born on Feb. 18, 1718; and, having early resolved to devote himself to a literary profession, was educated first under a Mr. John Nicholson, at the parish school of St. Ninian's, and for some time at the grammar school at Stirling. He completed his academical studies at the university of Edinburgh, and afterwards became master of the grammar school of Annan. He was licensed to preach on the 27th of March, 1746, and was the first licentiate of the presbytery of Annan, after its erection into a separate presbytery. Soon after he received a call from a congregation of presbyterian dissenters at Carlisle, where he was ordained in November, 1748. In this station he remained twelve years, and, on the 13th of August, 1760, became pastor of a dissenting congregation in Berwick upon Tweed. Here, in 1763, he married the daughter of Mr. Balderston, a surgeon, and though he had no children, enjoyed to the end of his life a large share of domestic happiness. In 1768, he was removed from Berwick, to be one of the ministers of Edinburgh, and was minister of the church of the New Grey Friars, from that time till November, 1776. He then became colleague-minister in the old church, and in that station remained till his death, which happened in November, 1790. The degree of Doctor in Divinity was conferred on him by the university of Edinburgh, in 1770; and in 1774, he was unanimously chosen moderator of the general assembly of the church of Scotland, and is the only person on record who obtained that distinction the first time he was a member of the assembly.

It is thought to have been about 1763, that Dr. Henry first conceived the idea of his history of Great Britain; the plan of which is indisputably his own. In every period it arranges, under seven distinct heads, or chapters, 1. The civil and military history of Great Britain; 2. The history of religion; 3. The history of our constitution, government, laws, and courts of justice; 4. The history of learning, of learned men, and of the chief seminaries of learning; 5. The history of arts; 6. The history of commerce, shipping, money, &c.; and 7. The history of manners, customs, &c. Under these heads, which extend the province of an historian greatly beyond its usual limits, and compel him to attend to all these points uniformly and regularly, every thing curious or interesting in the history of any country may be comprehended. The first volume of his history, in quarto, was published in 1771, the second in 1774, the third in 1777, the fourth in 1781,

[a] Life of Dr. Henry, prefixed to Vol. VI. 4to, of his history.

and

and the fifth, (which brings down the hiſtory to the acceſſion of Henry VII.) in 1785. The ſixth volume, a poſthumous work, the greater part of which he had prepared for publication before his death, appeared in 1793. Dr. Henry publiſhed his volumes originally at his own riſk, and ſuffered for ſome time from the malignity of unfair attacks from his own country. The Engliſh critics were more liberal, and very early allowed to his work that merit which has ſince been univerſally acknowledged. In 1786, when an octavo edition was intended, Dr. Henry conveyed the property to meſſrs. Cadell and Strahan, for the ſum of 1000l. reſerving to himſelf what remained unſold of the quarto edition. His profits on the whole, including this ſum, he found to amount to 3,300l. a ſtrong proof of the intrinſic merit of the work. The proſecution of this hiſtory had been his favourite object for almoſt thirty years of his life. He had naturally a ſound conſtitution, with a more equal and a larger portion of animal ſpirits than is commonly poſſeſſed by literary men. From the year 1789, his bodily ſtrength was ſenſibly impaired, yet he perſiſted ſteadily in preparing his ſixth volume.

Henry was naturally fond of ſociety, and few men enjoyed it more perfectly, or were capable of contributing ſo much to the pleaſures of ſociety. Though his literary purſuits might have ſuppoſed to have given him ſufficient employment, he always found time for ſocial converſation, for the offices of friendſhip, and for objects of public utility. Of the public ſocieties in Edinburgh he was always one of the moſt uſeful and indefatigable members; and he converſed with the ardour, and even the gaiety of youth, long after his bodily ſtrength had yielded to the infirmities of age. His library he left to the magiſtrates of Linlithgow, &c. under ſuch regulations as he conceived would tend to form a library calculated to diffuſe knowledge and literature in the country. Both as a man, and as an author, he has left a character which will, and ought to be eſteemed.

HENRY (DAVID), a writer in the Gentleman's Magazine, and an active manager in the conduct of that publication for more than half a century, was born in December, 1710, and educated as a printer. He found an early friend in Mr. Cave of St. John's Gate, whoſe ſiſter he married in 1736. Mr. Henry publiſhed, 1. in 1772, "The complete Engliſh Farmer, or a practical Syſtem of Huſbandry," but without a name. This was the reſult of his attention to a conſiderable farm which he occupied at Beckenham. 2. "An hiſtorical Account of all the Voyages round the World," 4 vols. 8vo, 1774. 3. Several ſmaller works, containing deſcriptions of the curioſities of London,

don, as the Tower, St. Paul's, &c. improved by him through several succeffive editions. He died on the 5th of June, 1792.

HERACLITUS, a famous philosopher of antiquity, and founder of a sect, was born at Ephesus, and flourished about the 69th Olympiad, in the time of Darius Hystaspes [1]. He gave early figns of profound wisdom, and was of an exceedingly high spirit. Being defired to take upon him the supreme power, he flighted it, becaufe the city in his opinion was prepoffeffed with an ill way of governing. He retired to the temple of Diana, and played at dice there with the boys; faying to the Ephefians that flood about him, "Worft of men, what do ye wonder at? is it not better to do thus, than to govern you?" Darius wrote to this philofopher to come and live with him; but he refufed the monarch's offer, and returned the following rude and infolent anfwer to his letter: "All men living refrain from truth and juftice, and purfue unfatiablenefs and vain-glory, by reafon of their folly: but I, having forgot all evil, and fhunning the fociety of inbred pride and envy, will never come to the kingdom of Perfia, being contented with a little according to my own mind." He is faid to have continually bewailed the wicked lives of men, and as often as he came among them to have fallen into tears; in which, by the way, he was not near fo wife as Democritus, who made the follies of men the conftant object of his laughter. At laft, growing into a great hatred of mankind, he retired into the mountains, and lived there, feeding upon grafs and herbs. But this diet bringing him into a dropfy, he was conftrained to return to the city; where he afked the phyficians, "Whether they could of a fhower make a drought?" They not underftanding his enigmatical manner, which he conftantly ufed, he fhut himfelf up in an ox-ftall, hoping that the hydropical humours would be extracted by the warmth of the dung: but this doing him no good, he died at 60 years of age. His writings gained fo great a reputation, that his followers were called Heraclitians. Laertius fpeaks of a treatife upon nature, divided into three books; one concerning the univerfe, the fecond politic, the third theologic. This work he depofited in the temple of Diana; and, as fome affirm, he affected to write obfcurely, that he might only be read by the more learned. It is related, that Euripides brought this book of Heraclitus to Socrates to be read; and afterwards afking his opinion of it, "The things," faid Socrates, "which I underftand in it, are excellent, and fo I fuppofe are thofe which I underftand not; but they require a Delian diver."

HERALDUS (DESIDERIUS), in French Herault, a counfellor of the parliament of Paris, has given good proofs of un-

[1] Diogenes Laertius.

X   common

common learning by very different works. His "Adverfaria," appeared in 1599; which little book, if the "Scaligerana" may be credited, he repented having publifhed. His notes on Tertullian's "Apology," on "Minutius Fœlix," and on "Arnobius," have been efteemed. He alfo wrote notes on Martial's "Epigrams." He difguifed himfelf under the name of David Leidhreſſerus, to write a political differtation on the independence of kings, fome time after the death of Henry IV. He had a controverfy with Salmafius "de jure Attico ac Romano:" but did not live to finifh what he had written on that fubject. What he had done, however, was printed in 1650. He died in June 1649. Guy Patin fays [K], that "he was looked upon as a very learned man, both in the civil law and in polite literature; and wrote with great facility on any fubject he pitched on." Daille, fpeaking of fuch proteftant writers as condemned the executing of Charles I. king of England, quotes the "Pacifique Royal en deuil," by Herault. This author, fon to our Defiderius Heraldus, was a minifter in Normandy, when he was called to the fervice of the Walloon-church of London under Charles I. and he was fo zealous a royalift, that he was forced to fly to France, to efcape the fury of the commonwealths-men. He returned to England after the Reftoration, and refumed his ancient employment in the Walloun-church at London: fome time after which he obtained a canonry in the cathedral of Canterbury, and enjoyed it till his death.

HERBELOT (BARTHOLOMEW D'), an eminent orientalift of France, was born at Paris Dec. 14, 1625 [L]. When he had gone through claffical literature and philofophy, be applied himfelf to the oriental languages; and efpecially to the Hebrew, for the fake of underftanding the original text of the Old Teftament. After a continual application for feveral years, he took a journey to Rome, upon a perfuafion that converfing with Armenians, and other Eaftern people who frequented that city, would make him perfect in the knowledge of their languages. Here he was particularly efteemed by the cardinals Barberini and Grimaldi, and contracted a firm friendfhip with Lucas Holftenius and Leo Allatius. Upon his return from this journey, in which he did not fpend above a year and a half, Fouquet invited him to his houfe, and fettled on him a penfion of 1500 livres. The difgrace of this minifter, which happened foon after, did not hinder Herbelot from being preferred to the place of Interpreter for the Eaftern languages; becaufe, in reality, there was nobody elfe fo fit for it: for Voltaire fays, "he was the firft among the French who underftood them [M]."

Some years after, he took a second journey into Italy, where he acquired so great a reputation, that persons of the highest distinction for their rank and learning solicited his acquaintance. The grand duke of Tuscany Ferdinand II. whom he had the honour to see first at Leghorn, gave him extraordinary marks of his esteem; had frequent conversations with him; and made him promise to visit him at Florence. Herbelot arrived there July 2, 1666, and was received by a secretary of state, who conducted him to a house prepared for him, where he was entertained with great magnificence, and had a chariot kept for his use, at the expence of the grand duke. These were very uncommon honours. But this was not all; for a library being at that time exposed to sale at Florence, the duke desired Herbelot to see it, to examine the MSS. in the oriental languages, and to select and value the best: and when this was done, the generous prince made him a present of them; and it was undoubtedly the most acceptable present he could have made him.

The distinction with which he was received by the duke of Tuscany, taught France to know his merit, which had hitherto been but little regarded; and he was afterwards recalled and encouraged by Colbert, who encouraged every thing that might do honour to his country. The grand duke was very unwilling to let him go, and even refused to consent, till he had seen the express order of the minister for his return. When he came to France, the king often did him the honour to converse with him, and gave him a pension of 1500 livres. During his stay in Italy, he began his "Bibliotheque Orientale, or Universal Dictionary, containing whatever related to the Knowledge of the Eastern World;" and he finished it in France. This work, equally curious and profound, comprises the substance of a great number of Arabic, Persian, and Turkish books, which he had read; and informs us of an infinite number of particulars unknown before in Europe. He wrote it at first in Arabic, and Colbert had a design to print it at the Louvre, with a set of types cast on purpose. But after the death of that minister, this resolution was waved; and Herbelot translated his work into French, in order to render it more universally useful. He committed it to the press, but had not the satisfaction to see the impression finished; for he died Dec. 8, 1695, and it was not published till 1697. It is a large folio. What could not be inserted in this work, was digested by him under the title of "Anthologie:" but this was never published, any more than a Turkish, Persian, Arabian, and Latin dictionary, to which, as well to other works, he had given the last hand.

He was no less conversant in the Greek and Latin learning, than in the oriental languages and history. He was indeed an universal scholar; and, what was very valuable in him, his modesty

modefty was equal to his erudition, and his uncommen abilities
were accompanied with the utmoſt probity, piety, charity, and
other Chriſtian virtues, which he pracliſed uniformly through
the courſe of a long life.

HERBERT (MARY), counteſs of Pembroke [N], and a very
illuſtrious female, became wife of Henry earl of Pembroke in
1576, and lived in the reigns of Elizabeth and James I. She
was alſo the fiſter of ſir Philip Sidney; whoſe "Arcadia," from
being dedicated to her, was denominated by the author himſelf,
"the Counteſs of Pembroke's Arcadia." She was a great encourager of letters; and not only an encourager in others, but a careful
cultivator of them herſelf. She tranſlated from the French a tragedy, called, "Annius, 1595," in 12mo. She is ſuppoſed alſo
to have made an exact tranſlation of "David's Pſalms" into Engliſh metre; and ſome pſalms by her are printed in Harrington's
"Nugæ Antiquæ, 1779," in 3 vols. 12mo. She died at her
houſe in Alderſgate-ſtreet, London, Sept. 25, 1621. Oſborn,
in his memoirs of the reign of king James, gives her this character. "She was," ſays he, "that fiſter of ſir Philip Sidney,
to whom he addreſſed his Arcadia; and of whom he had no
other advantage, than what he received from the partial benevolence of fortune in making him a man; (which yet ſhe did,
in ſome judgements, recompenſe in beauty) her pen being nothing ſhort of his, as I am ready to atteſt,—having ſeen incom-
parable letters of her's. But, leſt I ſhould ſeem to treſpaſs upon
truth, which few do unſuborned, (as I proteſt I am, unleſs by
her rhetoric) I ſhall leave the world her epitaph, in which the
author doth manifeſt himſelf a poet in all things but untruth:

> "Underneath this ſable hearſe
> Lies the ſubject of all verſe:
> Sidney's ſiſter, Pembroke's mother.
> Death! ere thou kill'ſt ſuch another,
> Fair, and good, and learn'd, as ſhe,
> Time ſhall throw a dart at thee."

HERBERT (EDWARD), lord Herbert, of Cherbury in Shropſhire [O], and eminent Engliſh writer, was deſcended from a very
ancient family, and born, 1581, at Montgomery-caſtle in Wales.
At the age of fourteen, he was entered as a gentleman-commoner
at Univerſity-college in Oxford, where he laid, ſays Wood,
the foundation of that admirable learning, of which he was afterwards a complete maſter [P]. From thence he travelled
abroad, and applied himſelf to military exerciſes in foreign
countries, by which he became a moſt accompliſhed gentleman.
After his return he was made Knight Banneret, when prince

[N] Biographia Dramatica.   [O] Walton's Life of Mr. George Herbert.
[P] Athen. Oxon.

E 2   Henry

Henry was installed Knight of the Garter, July 2, 1603. He was afterwards one of the counsellors to king James for military affairs. Next he was sent ambassador to Louis XIII. of France, to mediate for the relief of the protestants of that realm, then besieged in several parts; but was recalled in July, 1621, on account of a dispute between him and the constable de Luines [q]. Camden informs us, that he had treated the constable irreverently, "irreverenter tractasset:" but Walton tells us that "he could not subject himself to a compliance with the humours of the duke de Luines, who was then the great and powerful favourite at court: so that, upon a complaint to our king, he was called back into England in some displeasure; but at his return gave such an honourable account of his employment, and so justified his comportment to the duke and all the court, that he was suddenly sent back upon the same embassy."

Another writer relates this more particularly. Sir Edward, while he was in France, had private instructions from England to mediate a peace for the protestants in France; and, in case of a refusal, to use certain menaces. Accordingly, being referred to de Luines, he delivered to him the message, reserving his threatenings till he saw how the matter was relished. De Luines had concealed a gentleman behind the curtain of the reformed religion; who, being an ear-witness of what passed, might relate to his friends what little expectations they ought to entertain of the king of England's intercession. De Luines was very haughty, and would needs know what our king had to do in this affair. Sir Edward replied, " It is not to you, to whom the king my master oweth an account of his actions; and for me it is enough that I obey him. In the mean time I must maintain, that my master hath more reason to do what he doth, than you to ask why he doth it. Nevertheless, if you desire me in a gentle fashion, I shall acquaint you farther." Upon this, de Luines bowing a little, said, " Very well." The ambassador then gave him some reasons; to which de Luines said, " We will have none of your advices." The ambassador replied, " that he took that for an answer, and was sorry only, that the affection and good-will of the king his master was not sufficiently understood; and that, since it was rejected in that manner, he could do no less than say, that the king his master knew well enough what to do." De Luines answered, " We are not afraid of you." The ambassador smiling a little, replied, " If you had said you had not loved us, I should have believed you, and given you another answer. In the mean time all that I will tell you more is, that we know very well what we have to do." De Luines upon this, rising from his chair with a fashion and countenance a little discom-

pofed, faid, " By God, if you were not monfieur the ambaffador, I know very well how I would ufe you." Sir Edward
Herbert rifing alfo from his chair, faid, that as he was the king
of Great Britain's ambaffador, fo he was alfo a gentleman ; and
that his fword, whereon he laid his hand, fhould give him fatisfaction, if he had taken any offence." After which, de Luines
making no reply, the ambaffador went on towards the door, and
de Luines feeming to accompany him, fir Edward told him, that
" there was no occafion to ufe fuch ceremony after fuch language,"
and fo departed, expecting to hear farther from him. But no
meffage being brought from de Luines, he had, in purfuance of
his inftructions, a more civil audience from the king at Coignac ;
where the marfhal of St. Geran told him, that " he had offended
the conftable, and was not in a place of fecurity there :" to
which he anfwered, that " he thought himfelf to be in a place
of fecurity, wherefoever he had his fword by him." De Luines
refenting the affront, procured Cadinet his brother, duke of
Chaun, with a train of officers, of whom there was not one,
as he told king James, but had killed his man, to go as an ambaffador extraordinary: who mifreprefented the affair fo much
to the difadvantage of fir Edward, that the earl of Carlifle, who
was fent to accommodate the mifunderftanding which might
arife between the two crowns, got him recalled; until the gentleman who ftood behind the curtain, out of a regard to truth
and honour, related all the circumftances fo, as to make it appear, that though de Luines gave the firft affront, yet fir Edward
had kept himfelf within the bounds of his inftructions and
honour. He afterwards fell on his knees to king James, before
the duke of Buckingham, requefting, that a trumpeter, if not
an herald, might be fent to de Luines, to tell him, that he had
made a falfe relation of the whole affair; and that fir Edward
Herbert would demand fatisfaction of him fword in hand.
The king anfwered, that he would take it into confideration ;
but de Luines died foon after, and fir Edward was fent again
ambaffador to France [R].

In 1625, fir Edward was advanced to the dignity of a baron
of the kingdom of Ireland, by the title of lord Herbert of
Caftle-Ifland; and, in 1631, to that of lord Herbert of Cherbury in Shropfhire. After the breaking out of the civil wars,
he adhered to the parliament; and, Feb. 25, 1644, " had an
allowance granted him for his livelihood, having been fpoiled
by the king's forces[s]," as Whitelocke fays; or as Wood relates it, " received fatisfaction from the members of that houfe,
for their caufing Montgomery caftle to be demolifhed[T]." He
died at his houfe in Queen-ftreet, London, Aug. 20, 1648; and

[s] Lloyd, &c. p. 101L.   [t] Memorials of the Englifh Affairs, p. 104.
[t] Ath. Oxon.

was

was buried in the chancel of St. Giles's in the Fields, with this
infcription upon a flat marble ftone over his grave: " Heic in-
humatur corpus Edvardi Herbert equitis Balnei, baronis de Cherbury & Caftle-Ifland, auctoris libri, cui titulus eft, De Veritate. Reddor ut herbæ, vicefimo die Augufti anno Domini
1648."

This noble lord was the author of fome very fingular and memorable works: the firft of which was his book, " De Veritate,"
which we have feen juft mentioned in his epitaph. It was printed
at Paris in 1624, and r printed there in 1633; after which it was
printed in London, in 1645, under this title; " De Verirate,
prout diftinguitur à revelatione, à verifimili, à poffibili, à falfo.
Cui operi additi funt duo alii tractatus: primus de caufis errorum; alter de Religione Laici." The defign of it to affert the
fufficiency, univerfality, and abfolute perfection of natural religion, with a view to difcard all extraordinary revelation as
needlefs; and on this account it is, that he has very juftly been
ranked among the deifts. A learned and candid author, however, has lately publifhed a moft extraordinary anecdote relating
to him, which, if true, fhews him to have been a moft confcientious deift: and this writer feems to confider it as a fact.
He tells us, that it is taken " from a MS. life of lord Herbert
drawn up from memorials penned by himfelf, and which is now
in the poffeffion of a gentleman of diftinction [u]." His book
" De Veritate," was, we are informed, his favourite work;
yet as it was written in a manner fo very different from what
had been heretofore written on that fubject, his lordfhip had
great doubts within himfelf, whether he fhould publifh or rather fupprefs it. This the MS. life above-mentioned, fets forth
in his lordfhip's own words; after which it reprefents him
relating the following furprifing incident, as he calls it. " Being
thus doubtful in my chamber," fays lord Herbert, " one fair
day in the fummer, my cafement being open towards the fouth,
the fun fhining clear, and no wind ftirring, I took my book,
' De Veritate,' in my hands, and kneeling on my knees, de-
voutly faid thefe words: O thou eternal God, author of this
light, which now fhines upon me, and giver of all inward
illuminations, I do befeech thee, of thine infinite goodnefs,
to pardon a greater requeft than a finner ought to make. I am
not fatisfied enough, whether I fhall publifh this book: if it
be for thy glory, I befeech thee give me fome fign from
heaven; if not, I fhall fupprefs it.' I had no fooner fpoken
thefe words, but a loud, though yet gentle noife, came forth
from the heavens, for it was like nothing on earth, which
did fo chear and comfort me, that I took my petition as

[u] Leland's View of Deiftical Writers, Vol. I. p. 469.

granted,

granted, and that I had the sign I demanded; whereupon also I resolved to print my book. This, how strange soever it may seem, I protest before the eternal God, is true: neither am I any way superstitiously deceived herein, since I did not only clearly hear the noise, but in the serenest sky that ever I saw, being without all cloud, did, to my thinking, see the place from whence it came." The celebrated Gassendi wrote a confutation of this book, "De Veritate," at the desire of Peirescius and Elias Diodati, and finished it at Aix, without publishing it: and when lord Herbert paid him a visit in Sept. 1647, Gassendi was surprised to find, that this piece had not been delivered to him, for he had sent him a copy: upon which he ordered another copy to be taken of it, which that nobleman carried with him to England. It was afterwards published in Gassendi's works, under the title of "Ad librum D. Edvardi Herberti Angli de Veritate epistola;" but is imperfect, some sheets of the original being lost.

His "History of the Life and Reign of Henry VIII." was published in 1649, a year after his death, and is a work which has always been much admired. Nicolson, in his English "Historical Library [x]," says, that lord Herbert "acquitted himself in this history with the like reputation, as the lord chancellor Bacon gained by that of Henry VIIth. For in the public and martial part this honourable author has been admirably particular and exact from the best records that were extant; though as to the ecclesiastical, he seems to have looked upon it as a thing out of his province, and an undertaking more proper for men of another profession." In 1663, appeared his book "De Religione Gentilium, errorumque apud eos causis [y]." The first part was printed at London, in 1645; and that year he sent the MS. of it to Gerard Vossius, as appears from a letter of his lordship's, and Vossius's answer. An English translation of this work was published in 1705, under this title: "The ancient Religion of the Gentiles, and Causes of their Errors considered. The Mistakes and Failures of the Heathen Priests and wise Men, in their Notions of the Deity and Matters of Divine Worship, are examined with regard to their being destitute of Divine Revelation." Lord Herbert wrote also in 1630, "Expeditio Buckinghami ducis in Ream insulam," which was published in 1656; and "Occasional Verses," published in 1665, by his son Henry Herbert, and dedicated to Edward lord Herbert, his grandson. He was, upon the whole, as Wood tells us [z], "a person well studied in the arts and languages, a good philosopher and historian, and understood men as well as books,"

[x] Part I. p. 226, 1696, 8vo. [y] Clarorum Virorum ad Voss. Epist. & Vossi Epistola. [z] Athen. Oxon.

but

but Chriſtian Kortholt, on account of his book "De Veritate," has ranked him with Hobbes and Spinoſa, in his diſſertation, entitled, "De tribus impoſtoribus magnis, Edvardo Herbert, Thoma Hobbes, & Benedicto Spinoſa Liber," printed at Kiloni in 1680.

HERBERT (George), an Engliſh poet and divine [A], was brother of the preceding, and born at Montgomery-caſtle in Wales, Apr. 3, 1593. He was educated at Weſtminſter-ſchool; and being a king's ſcholar, was elected to Trinity-college in Cambridge, about 1608. He took both the degrees in arts, and became fellow of his college: and in 1619, was choſen orator of the univerſity, which office he held eight years. During that time he had learned the Italian, Spaniſh, and French languages very perfectly: hoping, ſays his biographer, that he might in time, as his predeceſſors ſir Robert Naunton and ſir Francis Netherſole had done, obtain the place of ſecretary of ſtate; for he was at that time highly eſteemed by the king and the moſt eminent of the nobility. This and the love of a court-converſation, "mixed," ſays the ſame author, "with a laudable ambition to be ſomewhat more than he then was," drew him often from Cambridge to attend his majeſty, wherever the court was: and the king gave him a ſinecure, which queen Elizabeth had formerly conferred on ſir Philip Sidney, worth about 120l. per ann. His ambition, however, was diſappointed: for upon the death of the duke of Richmond and the marquis of Hamilton, his hopes of court preferment were at an end, and he entered into orders. July 1626, he was collated to a prebend in the church of Lincoln; and about 1630, he married a lady, who was nearly related to the earl of Danby. The ſame year, he was inducted into the rectory of Bemerton near Saliſbury; where he diſcharged the duties of his function in a moſt exemplary manner. We have no exact account of the time of his death; but it is ſuppoſed to have happened about 1635. His poems, entitled, "The Temple," were printed at London in 1635, 12mo: and his "Prieſt to the Temple, or, The Country Parſon's Character and Rules of holy Life," was publiſhed in 1652. His works have ſince been publiſhed together in a volume, 12mo, but are now little read. Nevertheleſs, he was highly valued by the moſt eminent perſons of his age. Dr. Donne inſcribed to him a copy of Latin verſes; and lord Bacon dedicated to him his "Tranſlation of ſome Pſalms into Engliſh Metre."

HERBERT (William), earl of Pembroke, was born at Wilton in Wiltſhire, April 8, 1580, and admitted of New-college in Oxford in 1592, where he continued about two years [B]. In 1601, he ſucceeded to his father's honours and eſtate; was

[A] Walton's Life of Herbert, Lond. 1675.　　[B] Ath. Oxon.

made

made knight of the garter in 1604; and governor of Portfmouth
fix years after. In 1626, he was elected chancellor of the univerfity of Oxford; and about the fame time made lord fteward
of the king's houfhold. He died fuddenly at his houfe called
Baynard's-caftle, in London, April 10, 1630; according to the
calculation of his nativity, fays Wood, made feveral years before by Mr. Thomas Allen, of Gloucefter-hall. Clarendon
relates, concerning this calculation, that fome confiderable perfons connected with lord Pembroke being met at Maidenhead,
one of them at fupper drank a health to the lord fteward: upon
which another faid, that he believed his lordfhip was at that time
very merry; for he had now outlived the day, which it had been
prognofticated upon his nativity he would not outlive; but he
had done it now, for that was his birth-day, which had completed his age to 50 years. The next morning, however, they
received the news of his death [c]. Whether the noble hiftorian really believed this and other accounts relating to aftrology,
apparitions, providential interpofitions, &c. which he has inferted in his hiftory, we do not prefume to fay: he delivers
them, however, as if he did not actually difbelieve them. Lord
Pembroke was not only a great favourer of learned and ingenious
men, but was himfelf learned, and endued with a confiderable
fhare of poetic genius. All that are extant of his productions
in this way, were publifhed with this title: " Poems written by
William earl of Pembroke, &c. many of which are anfwered
by way of repartee by fir Benjamin Rudyard, with other poems
written by them occafionally and apart, 1660," 8vo.
  The character of this noble perfon is not only one of the moft
amiable in lord Clarendon's hiftory, but is one of the beft drawn.
" He was," fays the great hiftorian, " the moft univerfally beloved and efteemed of any man of that age; and having a great
office in the court, he made the court itfelf better efteemed, and
more reverenced in the country: and as he had a great number of friends of the beft men, fo no man had ever the confidence to avow himfelf to be his enemy. He was a man very
well bred, and of excellent parts, and a graceful fpeaker upon
any fubject, having a good proportion of learning, and a ready
wit to apply it, and enlarge upon it: of a pleafant and facetious humour, and a difpofition affable, generous, and magnificent.—He lived many years about the court before in it, and
never by it; being rather regarded and efteemed by king James,
than loved and favoured.—As he fpent and lived upon his own
fortune, fo he ftood upon his own feet, without any other fupport than of his proper virtue and merit.—He was exceedingly
beloved in the court, becaufe he never defired to get that for

[c] Hift. of Rebellion, b. 1.

himfelf

himself which others laboured for, but was still ready to promote the pretences of worthy men: and he was equally celebrated in the country, for having received no obligations from the court, which might corrupt or sway his affections and judgment.—He was a great lover of his country, and of the religion and justice which he believed could only support it: and his friendships were only with men of those principles.—Sure never man was planted in a court who was fitter for that soil, or brought better qualities with him to purify that air. Yet his memory must not be flattered, that his virtues and good inclinations may be believed: he was not without some alloy of vice, and without being clouded by great infirmities, which he had in too exorbitant a proportion. He indulged to himself the pleasures of all kinds, almost in all excesses. He died exceedingly lamented by men of all qualities, &c."

HERBERT (Thomas), an eminent person of the same family, was born at York, where his grand-father was an alderman, and admitted of Jesus-college, Oxford, in 1621 [D]: but before he took a degree, removed to Trinity-college in Cambridge. He made a short stay there, and then went to wait upon William earl of Pembroke, recorded in the preceding article; who owning him for his kinsman, and intending his advancement, sent him in 1626 to travel, with an allowance to bear his charge. He spent four years in visiting Asia and Africa; and then returning, waited on his patron at Baynard's-castle in London. The earl dying suddenly, his expectations of preferment were at an end; upon which he left England a second time, and visited several parts of Europe. After his return he married, and now being settled, gave himself up to reading and writing. In 1634, he published in folio, "A Relation of some Years Travels into Africa and the great Asia, especially the Territories of the Persian Monarchy, and some Parts of the Oriental Indies, and Isles adjacent." The edition of 1677 is the fourth, and has several additions. This work was translated by Wiquefort into French, with "An Account of the Revolutions of Siam in 1647, Paris, 1663," in 4to. All the impressions of Herbert's book are in folio, and adorned with cuts.

Upon the breaking out of the civil wars, he adhered to the parliament; and, by the endeavours of Philip earl of Pembroke, became not only one of the commissioners of parliament to reside in the army of sir Thomas Fairfax, but a commissioner also to treat with those of the king's party for the surrender of the garrison at Oxford. He afterwards attended that earl, especially in Jan. 1646, when he, with other commissioners, was sent from the parliament to the king at Newcastle about peace, and to bring his majesty nearer London. While the king was at

Oldenby,

Oldenby, the parliament commiffioners, purfuant to inftructions, addreffed themfelves to his majefty, and defired him to
difmifs fuch of his fervants as were there and had waited on
him at Oxford: which his majefty with great reluctance confented to do. He had taken notice in the mean time of Mr.
James Harrington, the author of the "Oceana," and Mr. Thomas Herbert, who had followed the court from Newcaftle; and
being certified of their fobriety and education, was willing to receive them as grooms of his bedchamber with the others that
were left him ; which the commiffioners approving, they were
that night admitted. Being thus fettled in that honourable office, and in good efteem with his majefty, Herbert continued
with him when all the reft of the chamber were removed ; even
till his majefty was brought to the block. The king, though
he found him, fays Wood, to be prefbyterianly affected ; yet
withal found him very obfervant and loving, and therefore en-
trufted him with many matters of moment. At the reftoration
he was made a baronet by Charles II. " for faithfully ferving
his royal father during the two laft years of his life ;" as the letters patent for that purpofe expreffed. He died at his houfe in
York, March 1, 1681-2.

Befides the travels already mentioned, he was the author of
other things. He wrote in 1678, " Threnodia Carolina, containing an hiftorical Account of the two laft Years of the Life
of King Charles I." and the occafion of it was this. The parliament having a little before taken into confideration the appointing of 70,000l. for the funeral of that king, and for a
monument to be erected over his grave, fir William Dugdale,
then garter king of arms, fent to our author, living at York, to
know of him, whether the king had ever fpoke in his hearing,
where his body fhould be interred. To this fir Thomas Herbert returned a large anfwer, with many obfervations concerning his majefty; which fir William Dugdale being pleafed with,
defired him by another letter, to write a treatife of the actions
and fayings of the king, from his firft confinement to his death:
and accordingly he did fo. He wrote alfo an account of the
laft days of that king, which was publifhed by Wood in the 2d
volume of his " Athenæ Oxonienfes." At the defire of his
friend John de Laet of Leyden, he tranflated fome books of his
" India Occidentalis:" he affifted alfo fir William Dugdale, in
compiling the third volume of his " Monafticon Anglicanum."
A little before his death, he gave feveral MSS. to the public library at Oxford, and others to that belonging to the cathedral
at York ; and in the Afhmolean Mufeum at Oxford, there are
feveral collections of his, which he made from the regifters
of the archbifhops of York, given to that repofitory by fir William Dugdale.

HERBINIUS (John), a native of Bitfchen in Silefia, deputed by the Polifh proteflant churches to thofe of Germany, Holland, &c. in 1664. This employment leading him to travel, he took the opportunity of examining fuch matters as interefled his curiofity, particularly cataracts and water-falls, wherever they were to be found. Several of his publications were on thefe fubjeects; as, 1. " De Admirandis Mundi Cataractis," &c. 4to, Amflerdam, 1678. 2. " Kiovia fubterranea." 3. " Terræ motus et quietis examen." He wrote alfo, 4. " De flatu Ecclefiarium Auguflanæ confeffionis in Polonia," 4to, 1670. 5. " Tragicocomœdia, et Ludi innocui de Juliano Imperatore Apoflata," &c. He died in 1676, at the age of 44 years only.

HERITIER (Nicolas l'), a French poet of the laft century. He was nephew to du Vair, a celebrated keeper of the feals. His original profeffion was military, but being difabled by a wound from actual fervice, he bought the place of treafurer to the French guards. He was afterwards appointed hiftoriographer of France, and died in 1680. He wrote only two tragedies, of no great merit, " Hercule furieux," and " Clavis," and a few fugitive poems, fome of which have a degree of elevation, particularly the " Portrait d'Amaranthe."

HERITIER (Marie Jeanne l'), de Villandon, was a daughter of the preceding, and born at Paris, in 1664. She inherited a tafte and talent for poetry, and was efteemed alfo for the fweetnefs of her manners, and the dignity of her fentiments. The academy of the " Jeux Floraux," received her as a member in 1696, and that of the " Ricovrati," at Padua in 1697. She died at Paris in 1734. Her works are various, in profe and verfe, 1. " A Tranflation of Ovid's Epiftles," fixteen of them in verfe. 2. " La Tour ténébreufe," an Englifh tale. 3. " Les Caprices du Deftin," another novel. 4. " L'ware puni," a novel in verfe; with a few poems of an elegiac or complimentary nature.

HERMAN (Paul), a celebrated botanift of the 17th century, and a native of Halle in Saxony. He practifed as a phyfician in the Dutch fettlements at Ceylon, and afterwards became profeffor of botany at Leyden. He died in 1695. His principal works are, 1. " A Catalogue of the Plants in the public garden at Leyden," 8vo, 1687. 2. " Cynofura Materiæ Medicæ," 2 vols. 4to. 3. " Lugduno-Batavæ Flores," 1690. 4. " Paradifus Païavus," 1705. 5. " Mufeum Zeylanicum," 1717.

HERMANN (James), a mathematician of Bâle, a friend of Leibnitz, and much known throughout Europe, moft parts of which he vifited. He was firft mathematical profeffor at Padua; from 1724 to 1727, he was with the czar Peter I. affifting him in forming an academy; afterwards profeffor of morality at Bâle,

Bâle, where he died in 1733, at the age of 55. His works are various, on fubjects of pure and mixed mathematics.

HERMANT (GODEFROI), a learned and pious doctor of the Sorbonne, and a voluminous author, was born at Beauvais, in 1617, and difplayed early propenfities for learning. Potier bifhop and earl of Beauvais fent him to the various colleges of Paris for education. He obtained a canonry of Beauvais, was rector of the univerfity of Paris in 1646, and died in 1690, after being excluded from his canonry and the Sorbonne for fome eccleliaftical difpute. Hermant had the virtues and defects of a reclufe ftudent, and was much efteemed for his talents and piety, by Tillemont and others of the folitaries at Port Royal. His ftyle was noble and majeftic, but fometimes rather inflated. His works are numerous: 1. " The Life of St. Athanafius," 2 vols. 4to. 2. Thofe of " St. Bafil and Gregory Nazianzen," of the fame extent. 3. " The Life of St. Chryfoftom," written under the name of Menart. And 4. That of " St. Ambrofe," both in 4to. 5. A tranflation of fome tracts from St. Chryfoftom. 6. Another from St. Bafil. 7. Several polemical writings againft the Jefuits, who therefore became his mortal enemies, and contrived to interfere with his monumental honours after death, by preventing the infcription of a very commendatory epitaph. 8. " A Defence of the Church againft Labadie." 9. " Index Univerfalis totius juris Ecclefiaftici," folio. 10. " Difcours Chrétien fur l'etabliffement du Bureau des pauvres de Beauvais," 1653. A life of him has been publifhed by Baillet.

HERMAS Paftor, or Hermas commonly called the Shepherd, was an ancient father of the church, and is generally fuppofed to have been the fame whom St. Paul mentions in Rom. xvi. 14. He is ranked amongft thofe who are called Apoftolical Fathers, from his having lived in the times of the Apoftles: but who he was, what he did, and what he fuffered, for the fake of Chriftianity, are all in a great meafure, if not altogether, unknown to us. He feems to have belonged to the church at Rome, when Clement was bifhop of it; that is, according to Dodwell, from the year 64 or 65 to the year 81 [1]. This circumftance we are able to collect from his " Second Vifion," of which, he tells us, he was commanded to communicate a copy to Clement. What his condition was before his converfion, we know not; but that he was a man of fome confideration, we may conclude from what we read in his " Third Vifion;" where he owns himfelf to have been formerly unprofitable to the Lord, upon the account of thofe riches, which afterwards he feems to have difpenfed in works of charity and beneficence. What he did after his converfion we

[1] Cave's Hift. Liter. Vol. I. p. 30.

may

have no account; but that he lived a very strict life we may reasonably conjecture, since he is said to have had several extraordinary revelations vouchsafed to him, and to have been employed in several messages to the church, both to correct their manners, and to warn them of the trials that were about to come upon them. His death, if we may believe the "Roman Martyrology," was conformable to his life; where we read, that being "illustrious for his miracles, he at last offered himself a worthy sacrifice unto God." But upon what grounds this account is established, Baronius himself could not tell us; insomuch that in his "Annals" he durst not once mention the manner of his death, but is content to say, that "having undergone many labours and troubles in the time of the persecution under Aurelius, (and that too without any authority) he at last rested in the Lord July the 26th, which is therefore observed in commemoration of him [F]." And here we may observe a very pleasant mistake, and altogether worthy of the "Roman Martyrology." For Hermas, from a book of which we shall speak immediately, being sometimes called by the title of "Pastor, or Shepherd [G]," the martyrologist has very gravely divided the good man into two saints: and they observe the memorial of Hermas May the 9th, and of Pastor July the 26th.

The book just mentioned, and for which chiefly we have given Hermas a place in this work, is, as we have observed, entitled, "The Shepherd;" and is the only remains of this father. Ancients and moderns are not a little divided in their judgements of this book [H]. Some there are, and those nearest to the time when it was written, who put it almost upon a level with the canonical Scriptures. Irenæus quotes it under the very name of Scripture. Origen, though he sometimes moderates his opinion of it, upon the account of those who did not think it canonical, yet in his "Comments on the Epistle to the Romans," gives this character of it, that "he thought it to be a most useful writing, and was, as he believed, divinely inspired [I]." Eusebius tells us, that "though being doubted by some, it was not esteemed canonical, yet it was by others judged a most necessary book, and as such read publicly in the churches:" and St. Jerome, having in like manner observed that it was read in some churches,"* makes this remarks upon it, that it "was indeed a very profitable book [K]." And yet after all we find this same book, not only doubted of by others among the ancient fathers, but slighted even by some of those who had elsewhere spoken well of it. Thus Jerome in his "Comments [L]," exposes the absurdity of

[F] Baron. Annal. Eccl. ad ann. 164.
[G] Martyrolog. Rom. ad Maij 1s. & Jul. 26vi.
[H] Lib. iv. Adverf. Hæref.
[I] Hist. Ecclef. l. lil. c. 3.
[K] Catalog. Script. Ecclef.
[L] In Habac. l. 14.

that apocryphal book, as he calls it, which in his "Catalogue of Writers," he had fo highly applauded. Tertullian, who fpake of it decently, if not honourably, while a catholic, rejected it with fcorn, after he was turned montanift [M]: and moft of the other fathers, who have fpoken of it well themfelves, yet plainly enough infinuate, that there were others who did not put the fame value upon it. The moderns in general have not efteemed it fo highly; and, indeed, as Dupin obferves [N], " whether we confider the manner it is written in, or the matter it contains, it does not appear to merit much regard." The firft part, for it is divided into three, is called " Vifions," and contains many vifions, which are explained to Hermas by a woman, who reprefents the church. Thefe vifions regard the ftate of the church, and the manners of the Chriftians. The fecond, which is the moft ufeful, is called " Commands," and comprehends many moral and pious inftructions, delivered to Hermas by an angel: and the third is called " Similitudes." Many ufeful leffons are taught in thefe books, but the vifions, allegories, and fimilitudes, are apt to tire; and Hermas had probably been more agreeable as well as more profitable, if he had enforced his precepts with that fimplicity with which the apoftles themfelves were content.

The original Greek of this piece is loft, and we have nothing but a Latin verfion of it, except fome fragments preferved in the quotations of other authors; which, it is obfervable, are fufficient to evince the fidelity of this verfion. The belt edition of it is that of 1698; where it is to be found among the other apoftolical fathers, illuftrated with the notes and corrections of Cotelerius and Le Clerc. With them alfo it was tranflated into Englifh by archbifhop Wake, and publifhed with a large preliminary difcourfe relating to each father; the beft edition of which tranflation is that of 1710.

HERMES, an Egyptian legiflator, prieft, and philofopher, lived, as fome think, in the year of the world 2076, in the reign of Ninus, after Mofes: and was fo fkilled in all profound arts and fciences, that he acquired the furname of Trifmegiftus, or " thrice great." Clemens Alexandrinus has given us an account of his writings, and a catalogue of fome of them [O]; fuch as, the book containing the Hymns of the Gods; another " De rationibus vitæ regiæ;" four more " De aftrologia," that is, " De ordine fixarum ftellarum, & de conjunctione & illuminatione Solis & Lunæ; ten more, entitled, " Ἱερατικα," or which treat of laws, of the gods, and of the whole doctrine and difcipline of the priefts. Upon the whole, Clemens makes Hermes the author of thirty-fix books of divinity and philo-

[M] De Orat. r. alt. De Pufic. c. a. [N] Bibloth. des Ant. Ecclef. Tom. 1.
p. 82. [O] Strom. lib. vi.

fophy,

fophy, and fix of phyfic; but they are all loft. There goes indeed one under his name, whofe title is "Poemander;" but this is agreed by all to be fuppofititious, and Cafaubon imagines it to be written about the beginning of the fecond century, by fome Platonizing Chriftian; who, to enforce Chriftianity with a better grace upon Pagans[p], introduces Hermes Trifmegiftus delivering, as it were long before, the greateft part of thofe doctrines which are comprifed in the Chriftian's creed.

This philofopher has ftood exceedingly high in the opinion of mankind, ancients as well as moderns; higher perhaps than he would have done if his works had been extant; for there is an advantage in being not known too much. Very great things, however, have been faid of him in all ages. Thus Plato tells us[q], that he was the inventor of letters, of ordinary writing, and hieroglyphics. Cicero fays, that he was governor of Egypt, and invented letters, as well as delivered the firft laws to the people of that country[a]. Suidas fays, that he flourifhed before Pharaoh, and acquired the furname of Trifmegiftus, becaufe he gave out fomething oracular concerning the Trinity. Though the ancients are by no means precife in their encomiums, yet they feem to have conceived a wonderful opinion of him; and the moderns have done the fame. Hermes, fays Gyraldus, was called Thrice Great, becaufe he was the greateft philofopher, the greateft prieft, and the greateft king[s]. Polydore Vergil obferves, that he divided the day into twelve hours, from his obfervation of a certain animal confecrated to Serapis by the Egyptians, which made water twelve times a day at a certain interval[T]: fuch was his marvellous fagacity and infight into things. Laftly, when the great lord chancellor Bacon, endeavoured to do juftice to the merits of our James I. he could think of no better means for this purpofe, than by comparing him to Hermes Trifmegiftus. Thefe are his words addreffed to that king, in the entrance of his immortal work "De Augmentis Scientiarum;" "Tuæ vero majeftati etiam illud accedit, quod in eodem pectoris tui fcrinio facræ literæ cum profanis recondantur; adeo ut cum Hermete illo Trifmegifto triplici gloria infigniaris, poteftate regis, illuminatione facerdotis, eruditione philofophi:" that is, "but this is peculiar to your majefty, that the treafures of facred as well as profane learning are all repofited in your royal breaft; fo that you may juftly be compared to that famous Hermes Trifmegiftus of old, who was at once diftinguifhed by the glory of a king, the illuminations of a prieft, and the learning of a philofopher."

[p] Exercitat. 1. in Baron. Num. 10, P. 75.

[q] In Phædro & Philebo.

[a] De Natur. Deor. L. III.

[s] In Dial. II. de Poet.

[T] De Invent. Rat. L ii. c. 5.

HERMO.

HERMOGENES, of Tarfus, a Greek rhetorician of the fecond century, a remarkable inftance of early maturity and early deficiency of talents. At fifteen he taught rhetoric publicly; at feventeen he wrote his art of rhetoric; and at twenty, two books περὶ ἰδεῶν, or on oratorical forms: but in his twenty-fifth year he loft his memory, and the faculty of fpeech, which he never recovered, though he lived to be old. Antiochus the fophift, therefore faid of him, " that he was an old man in his Infancy, and an infant in his age." Of his book on oratory, which confilled of five parts, the firft part only is loft. There are extant alfo, 2. " De inventione Oratoriâ," four books. 3. " De furmis," above-mentioned. 4. " Methodus apti et ponderofi generis dicendi." Thefe were publifhed by Aldus in 1509, with the other Greek rhetoricians, and in two or three fubfequent editions. The beft is that of Gafpar Laurentius, publifhed at Geneva, in 1614, in 8vo. He flourifhed after A. D. 161.

HERMOGENES, an heretic of the fecond century, was a native of Africa, a painter, and ftoic philofopher. He was ftill alive in the days of Tertullian, according to Fleury. Tillemont makes him flourifh in the year 200; but according to Du Frefnoy, he did not preach his erroneous opinions concerning the origin of the world, and the nature of the foul, till the year 208. He eftablifhed matter as the firft principle, and made *Idea* the mother of all the elements; for which reafon his followers were commonly called *Materiarians*. By his affertion of the felf-exiftence and improduction of matter, he endeavoured to give an account (as ftoic philofophers had done before him) of the original of evils, and to free God from the imputation of them. He argued thus: God made all things either out of himfelf, or out of nothing, or out of pre-exiftent matter. He could not make all things out of himfelf, becaufe, himfelf being always unmade, he fhould then really have been the maker of nothing: and he did not make all out of nothing, becaufe, being effentially good, he would have made every thing in the beft manner, and fo there could have been no evil in the world: but fince there are evils, and thefe could not proceed from the will of God, they muft needs rife from the fault of fomething, and therefore of the matter out of which things were made. Some modern fects do alfo, at this day, affert the uncreatednefs of matter; but thefe fuppofe, as the ftoics did, body to be the only fubftance. Seleucus and Hermias embraced the fame opinion. His followers denied the refurrection, rejected water-baptifm, afferted that angels were compofed of fire and fpirit, and were the creators of the foul of man; and that Chrift, as he afcended, divefted himfelf of human nature, and left his body in the fun. Tertullian has written againft him.

HEROD the Great, so called rather from his power and talents, than his goodness, was a native of Ascalon in Judea, and thence sometimes called the Ascalonite. He was born seventy years before the Christian æra, the son of Antipater an Idumean, who appointed him to the government of Galilee. He at first embraced the party of Brutus and Cassius, but, after their death, that of Antony. By him he was named tetrarch, and afterwards, by his interest, king of Judea in the year 40, A. C. After the battle of Actium, he so successfully paid his court to Augustus, that he was by him confirmed in his kingdom. On all occasions he proved himself an able politician, and a good soldier. But he was far from being master of his passions, and his rage very frequently was directed against his own family. Aristobulus, brother to his beloved wife Mariamne, her venerable grandfather Hyrcanus, and finally she herself, fell victims to his jealousy and fury. His keen remorse for her death rendered him afterwards yet more cruel. He put to death her mother Alexandra, and many others of his family. His own sons Alexander and Aristobulus, having excited his suspicions, he destroyed them also, which made Augustus say, that it was better to be Herod's hog than his son. Among his good actions was the rebuilding of the temple at Jerusalem, which he performed in nine years, with great magnificence ; and in the time of a famine he sold many valuable and curious articles he had collected, to relieve the sufferers. To Augustus he paid the utmost adulation, and even divine honours. At the birth of our Saviour, his jealousy was so much excited by the prophetic intimations of his greatness, that he slaughtered all the infants in Bethlehem, in hopes of destroying him among the number. But his tyranny was now nearly at an end, and two or three years after the birth of Christ he died of a miserable disease at the age of more than 70. He had nine or ten wives, of which number Mariamne was the second. A little before his death, soured yet more by his acute sufferings, he attempted a greater act of cruelty than any he had performed in his former life. He sent for all the most considerable persons in Judea, and ordered that as soon as he was dead they should all be massacred, that every great family in the country might weep for him. But this savage order was not executed. Some have supposed that he affirmed the character of the Messiah, and that the persons who admitted that claim were those called in the gospel Herodians. But this is by no means certain. Herod was the first who shook the foundations of the Jewish government. He appointed the high-priests, and removed them at his pleasure, without regard to the laws of succession, and he destroyed the authority of the national council. But by his credit with Augustus, by his power, and the very magnificent buildings he erected, he gave a temporary splendor to that nation. His son, Herod

Antipas

Antipas (by his fifth wife Cleopatra) was tetrarch of Galilee after his death.

HERODIAN, a Greek historian, who flourished under the reigns of Severus, Caracalla, Heliogabalus, Alexander, and Maximin. His history contains eight books; at the beginning of the first of which he declares, that he will only write of the affairs of his own time, such as he had either known himself, or received information of from creditable persons: and for this he was indeed very well qualified, on account of the public employments in which he was engaged, for he might boast of having passed through the greatest offices of the state. About the end of his second book he acquaints us, that his history shall comprehend a period of 72 years, and relate the government of all the emperors that succeeded one another, from the reign of Marcus Aurelius Antonius the philosopher, to that of the younger Gordianus: and accordingly his eighth book ends with the unworthy slaughter of the two old men Balbinus and Maximin, which was committed on them by the Prætorian soldiers, for the sake of advancing Gordian to the throne.

Herodian may be ranked with the best historians, and is remarkable for good faith and freedom of sentiment. His faith, however, has been thought by the critics to be less strict when he comes to Alexander and Maximin, and he has been blamed for want of due exactness in chronological notices. His style is neat, perspicuous, and pleasing, occasionally eloquent, particularly in the speeches he inserts, which are concise but full of acuteness, and importance. Herodian was translated into Latin by Angelus Politianus, and may therefore be read, as the Camdenian professor observed [u], either in Greek or Latin; " for," says he, " I don't know which of the two deserves the greater praise; Herodian, for writing so well in his own language, or Politian, for translating him so happily, as to make him appear like an original in a foreign one." This, however, is paying no small compliment to Politian; for Photius [x] tells us, that Herodian's style is very elegant and perspicuous; and adds, to complete his character, that, considering all the virtues of an historian, there are few to whom Herodian ought to give place. Julius Capitolinus mentions Herodian, in his " Life of Clodius Albinus," as a good historian; but accuses him, in his " two Maximins," of bearing too hard upon the memory of Alexander Severus, and his mother Mammæa. This charge however does not seem to be well supported, and Causabon and Bœcler [y] incline to acquit him of it. It is remarkable, that he speaks

[u] Wheat de legend. Hist. &c. p. 74. Cant. 1684.
[x] Bibliothec. c. 99.
[y] Causf. in notis ad Capit. in Maxim. Bœcl. præfat. in Herod.

very

very refpe&fully of the clemency of Severus, who reigned
fourteen years, without taking away the life of any one, otherwife than by the ordinary courfe of juftice; which he notes as
an inftance very rare, and without example fince the reign of
Antoninus the philofopher. As to Mammea, though he juftly
blames her ill conduct in the government of the ftate, yet he
very much commends her care in the education of her fon; efpecially for excluding from him all thofe pefts of courts, which
flatter the corrupt inclinations of princes, aand cherifh in them
the feeds of vice, and for admitting only perfons that were virtuous in their lives and of approved behaviour. We are obliged
to this hiftorian, as well as to Dion Caffius, for acquainting us
with the ceremonies which the Pagans ufed at the confecration
of their emperors. In the beginning of his fourth book he has
given us fo particular a defcription of all the funeral honours
done to the afhes of Severus, which his children tranfported in
an alabafter cheft from England, that it would be difficult to find
a relation more exact and inftructive.

Though we have confidered Herodian hitherto as an hiftorian
only, yet Suidas informs us, that he wrote many other books,
which have not been preferved from the ruins of time. Herodian
was publifhed by Henry Stephens, in 1581, 4to; by Bœcler
at Strafbourg in 1662, 8vo; and by Hudfon at Oxford, in 1669,
8vo. The lateft edition, with a prodigious quantity of notes
variorum, is that Irmifch, in two large volumes, 8vo, publifhed
at Leipfic in 1789.

HERODOTUS, an ancient Greek hiftorian of Halicarnaffus
in Caria, was born in the firft year of the 74th Olympiad; that
is, about 484 years before Chrift [z]. This time of his birth
is fixed by a paffage in Aulus Gellius, Book xv. chap. 23. which
makes Hellanicus 65, Herodus 53, and Thucydides 40 years
old, at the commencement of the Peloponnefian war. The
name of his father was Lyxes, of his mother, Dryo. The city
of Halicarnaffus being at that time under the tyranny of Lyg-
damis, grandfon of Artemifia queen of Caria, Herodotus quitted
his country, and retired to Samos; whence he travelled over
Egypt, Greece, Italy, &c. and in his travels acquired the knowledge of the hiftory and origin of many nations. He then
began to digeft the materials he had collected into order, and
compofed that hiftory, which has preferved his name amongft
men ever fince. He wrote it in the ifle of Samos, according
to the general opinion [A]; but the elder Pliny is of another
mind, and affirms it to have been written at Thurium, a town
in that part of Italy then called Magna Græcia, whither Herodotus had retired with an Athenian colony, and where he is

[z] Suidas in voce Ἡροδότος.   [A] Hift. Nat. L. xii. c. 4.

fuppofed

fuppofed to have died, not however before he had returned into
his own country, and by his influence expelled the tyrant Lyg-
damis. At Samos he ftudied the Ionic dialect, in which he
wrote, his native dialect being Doric. Lucian informs us [a],
that when Herodotus left Caria to go into Greece, he began to
confider with himfelf, what he fhould do to obtain celebrity and
lafting fame, in the moft expeditious way, and with as little
trouble as poffible. His hiftory, he prefumed, would eafily
procure him fame, and raife his name among the Grecians, in
whofe favour it was written: but then he forefaw, that it would
be very tedious, if not endlefs, to go through the feveral cities
of Greece, and recite it to each refpective city; to the Athenians, Corinthians, Argives, Lacedæmonians, &c. He thought
it moft proper therefore to take the opportunity of their affem-
bling all together; and accordingly recited his work at the
Olympic games, which rendered him more famous than even
thofe who had obtained the prizes. None were ignorant of
his name, nor was there a fingle perfon in Greece, who had
not either feen him at the Olympic games, or heard thofe fpeak
of him who had feen him there; fo that wherever he came,
the people pointed to him with their fingers, faying, " This
is that Herodotus, who has written the Perfian wars in the
Ionic dialect; this is he who has celebrated our victories."

His work is divided into nine books, which, according to the
computation of Dionyfius Halicarnaffenfis, contain the moft remarkable occurrences within a period of 240 years; from the
reign of Cyrus the firft king of Perfia, to that of Xerxes, when
the hiftorian was living. Thefe nine books are called after the
nine Mufes, each of which is diftinguifhed by the name of a
Mufe: and this has given birth to two difquifitions among the
learned, firft, whether they were fo called by Herodotus himfelf;
and fecondly, for what reafon they were fo called. As to the
firft, it is generally agreed that Herodotus did not impofe thefe
names himfelf; but it is not agreed why they were impofed by
others. Lucian, in the place referred to above, tells us, that
thofe names were given them by the Grecians at the Olympic
games, when they were firft recited, as the beft compliment that
could be paid the man who had taken pains to do them fo much
honour. Others have thought, that the name of Mufes have
been fixed upon them by way of reproach, and were defigned to
intimate, that Herodotus, inftead of true hiftory, had written a
great deal of fable. But be this as it will: with regard to the
truth of his hiftory, it is well known that he has been accufed by
feveral authors. Thucydides is fuppofed to have had him in

his eye, though he only speaks of authors in general, when he blames those histories which were written for no other end but to divert the reader [c]. Strabo accuses Herodotus particularly of this fault, and says, that he trifles very agreeably, interweaving extraordinary events with his narration, by way of ornament [D]. Juvenal likewise aims at him in that memorable passage:

"———— creditur olim
Velificatus Athos, & quicquid Græcia mendax
Audet In historia."————

But none have ventured to attack him with so much freedom as Plutarch, who conceived a warm resentment against him, for casting an odium upon his countrymen the Thebans. This he owns to have been the motive to his writing that little treatise, to be found in his works, " Of the Malignity of Herodotus [e];" in which he accuses the historian, says La Mothe le Vayer, of having maliciously taxed the honour, not only of the Thebans and Corinthians, but almost all the Greeks, out of partiality to the Medes, and in order to raise the glory of his country higher in the person of Artemisia queen of Halicarnassus; whose heroic actions in the battle of Salamis he so exaggerates, that this princess alone takes up the greatest part of the narration. Plutarch indeed confesses, that it is one of the best written and most agreeable pieces that can be read; but adds, that amidst the charms of his narrative, he makes his readers swallow the poison of detraction; and he compares the malignity he imputes to him, to cantharides covered with roses. Some think Plutarch's criticism is written with all the ill-nature which he ascribes to Herodotus: but, says the author just cited, " I have too much veneration for that worthy master of Trajan, to be fully satisfied with such an answer; and, to say the truth, it is hard to consider, how Herodotus speaks of Themistocles, especially in his Urania, where he accuses him of rapines and secret correspondence with the Persians, without believing that Plutarch had reasons for what he said." Herodotus, however, has not wanted persons to defend him: Aldus Manutius, Joachim Camerarius, and Henry Stephens, have written apologies for him ; and among other things, have very justly observed, Camerarius in particular, that he seldom relates any thing of doubtful credit, but produces the authority on which his narration is grounded; and if he has no certain authority to fix it upon, uses always the terms, " ut ferunt, ut ego audivi, &c." And for fear he should be mistaken when he relates any thing wonderful, he declares expressly of a particular in his " Polyhymnia," what he desires may be applied to

[c] Thucyd. Hist. l. l.   [D] Geograph. l. xvii.
[e] Jugemens des Historiens Grecs & Latins.

his

his hiftory in general, that " though he thinks it right to relate
what he has heard, yet he is far from believing, or delivering as
true and well-grounded facts, all which he relates [F]." As for
thofe relations, fuch as feeing the fun on the northern fide of the
heavens, and other things which were fuppofed to be natural
wonders among the ancients, and made him pafs for a fabulous
writer, it is well known, that modern voyages and difcoveries
have abundantly confirmed the truth of many of them.

Befides this hiftory, he promifed, in two places of his firft
book, to write another of Affyria: but this, fays Voffius, was
never finifhed, at leaft not publifhed; otherwife it would have
been mentioned probably by fome of the ancient writers. Not
but Ariftotle, fays he, has blamed Herodotus for faying, that
" an eagle drank during the fiege of Nineveh, " becaufe that
bird was known never to drink [O];" which paffage, not being
found in the nine books extant, has made fome imagine, that
Ariftotle took it from the hiftory of Affyria. But this is hardly
a fufficient proof; not to mention, that where Ariftotle mentions
this miftake, fome read Hefiod inftead of Herodotus. There is
afcribed alfo to Herodotus a " Life of Homer," which is ufually
printed at the end of his works; but, as Voffius obferves, there
is no probability that this was written by the hiftorian, becaufe
the author of that life does not agree with him about the time
when the poet lived; for he fays, that Homer flourifhed about
168 years after the Trojan war, and 622 years before Xerxes's
expedition into Greece; but Herodotus in his " Euterpe" affirms,
that Homer and Hefiod preceded him 400 years, and confequently flourifhed a much longer time after the taking of Troy
[H]. Befides, the ftyle of this piece is very different from that
of Herodotus; and the author mentions feveral things of Homer,
which do not at all agree with what the ancients have faid of
that poet.

Herodotus wrote in the Ionic dialect, and his ftyle and manner
have ever been admired by all readers of tafte. Cicero, in his
fecond book, " De Oratore," fays, that " he is fo very eloquent
and flowing, that he pleafed him exceedingly;" and in his
" Brutus," that " his ftyle is free from all harfhnefs, and glides
along like the waters of a ftill river." He calls him alfo the
Father of Hiftory; becaufe he was, if not the firft hiftorian,
the firft who brought hiftory to that degree of perfection. Quin-
tilian has given the fame judgement of Herodotus. " Befides
the flowing fweetnefs of his ftyle, even the dialect he ufes has
a peculiar grace, and feems to exprefs the harmony of num-

[F] Polyb. c. 152, and Camerarii Proœm.
in Herodotum.
[O] Hift. Animal. l. viii. c. 18.

[2] Vide Xylandri Annotadones in
Plutarchum de vita Homeri.

bers.

bers. Many," fays he, " have written hiftory well; but every body owns, that there are two hiftorians preferable to the reft, though extremely different from each other. Thucydides is clofe, concife, and fometimes even crowded in his fentences: Herodotus is fweet, copious, and exuberant. Thucydides is more proper for men of warm paffions; Herodotus for thofe of a fedater turn. Thucydides excels in orations: Herodotus in narrations. The one is more forcible; the other more agreeable [1]." Dionyfius of Halicarnaffus fays, that Herodotus is the model of the Ionic dialect, as Thucydides is of the Attic: and in his comparifon of thefe two hiftorians, gives almoft throughout, the preference to Herodotus. But this determination, we think, will depend a good deal upon the tempers and views of thofe who read thefe hiftorians: they, who feek chiefly pleafure and entertainment, will probably like Herodotus the beft; but they who would reap the fruits which juft hiftory always affords, will find their ends more completely anfwered by reading Thucydides. There have been feveral editions of Herodotus; two by Henry Stephens, in 1570 and 1592; one by Gale at London in 1679; and one by Gronovius at Leyden in 1715. But the beft is that of Weffelingius, publifhed at Amfterdam in 1763. There is alfo an elegant edition in duodecimo, publifhed at Glafgow. The hiftory of Herodotus has been twice tranflated into Englifh, once by Littlebury, in two vols. 8vo, without notes: the fecond time by Mr. Beloe, in four vols. with many ufeful and entertaining remarks. There is alfo an excellent French tranflation, by M. Larcher, with very learned notes.

HEROPHILUS of Chalcedon, an ancient phyfician, flourifhed almoft five hundred years before Chrift. Cicero, Pliny, and Plutarch mention him. Fallopius fays, that he was the greater anatomift, and underftood the ftructure of the human body better, and made more difcoveries therein than Erafiftratus his cotemporary. He is alfo faid to have difcovered the lacteal veffels; and gave names to the various parts of the body, which they retain to this day. He was a great lover of botany, as well as phyfic and furgery; and is faid to have made fome confiderable improvement in each of them. Galen calls him a confummate phyfician, and a very great anatomift; and fays, that thefe two great anatomifts diffected many human bodies at Alexandria in Egypt; Tertullian fays 600, and calls him " Herophilus ille Medicus aut Lanius;" as they are faid to have diffected condemned criminals alive. He is faid alfo to have difcovered the nerves, and their ufe. He makes three forts of them; the firft to convey fenfation, the fecond to move the bones, and the

[1] Inftit. Orat. l. ix. & x.

third

third the mufcles. He alfo mentions the optic nerves, the re-
tina, and the tunica arachnoides, and choroides; the lacteals,
mefenteric glands, and the glandulæ proftatæ; and is the firft
that wrote any thing diftinctly with exactnefs on the pulfe.

HERRERA TORDESILLAS (ANTONIO DE), a Spanifh
hiftorian of great fame; firft fecretary to Vefpafian Gonzaga,
viceroy of Naples, and afterwards grand hiftoriographer of India,
with a confiderable penfion under Philip II. He did not receive
his money unearned, but publifhed a general hiftory of India
from 1492 to 1554, in four volumes, folio. A very fhort time
before his death he received from Philip IV. the appointment of
fecretary of ftate. He died in 1625, at the age of 60. His
hiftory of India is a very curious work, carried to a great detail,
and chargeable with no defects, except too great a love for the
marvellous, a degree of national vanity, and too great inflation
in the ftyle. He publifhed alfo a general hiftory of Spain, from
1554 to 1598, which has been lefs efteemed than the other
work. It is in three volumes, folio.

HERRERAS (FERDINAND DE), a poet of Seville, remarkable for elegance of ftyle, and facility of verfification. He publifhed lyric and heroic poetry in 1582; and fome works in profe,
as, 1. " A Life of Sir Thomas More." 2. " An Account of
the War in Cyprus, and the Battle of Lepanto." 3. " Notes
on Garcilaffo de la Vega."

HERRING (Dr. THOMAS), was the fon of the Rev. John
Herring, rector of Walfoken, in Norfolk; at which place he
was born, 1693. He was educated at Wifbech fchool, in the
Ifle of Ely; and at Jefus-college in Cambridge, where he was
entered 1710. He was chofen fellow of Corpus Chrifti college in 1716; and continued a tutor there upwards of feven years.
He entered into prieft's orders in 1719, and was fucceffively
minifter of Great Shelford, Stow cum Qui, and Trinity in
Cambridge. In 1722, Fleetwood bifhop of Ely made him
his chaplain, and foon after prefented him to Rettindon in
Effex, and to the rectory of Barly in Hertfordfhire. In 1726,
the hon. fociety of Lincoln's-Inn chofe him their preacher;
and, about the fame time, he took his doctor's degree, and was
appointed chaplain in ordinary to his majefty. In 1731, he was
prefented to the rectory of Blechingley in Surrey; and towards
the clofe of the year, promoted to the deanery of Rochefter.
In 1737, he was confecrated bifhop of Bangor; and in 1743,
tranflated to the archiepifcopal fee of York, on the demife of
Dr. Blackburn.

When the rebellion broke out in Scotland, and the Highlanders defeated the king's troops at Prefton-pans, the archbifhop
contributed much to remove the general panic, and awaken the
nation from its lethargy. He convened the nobility, gentry,

and

and clergy of his diocese, and addressed them in a noble and
animated speech; which had such an effect upon his auditory,
that a subscription ensued to the amount of 40,000l. and the
example was successfully followed by the nation in general. On
the death of Dr. Potter, in 1747, he was translated to the see of
Canterbury. In 1753, he was seized with a violent fever,
which brought him to the brink of the grave; and though he did
in some measure recover, yet from that time he might be rather
said to languish, than to live. He retired to Croydon, declined
all public business, and saw little other company than his relations and particular friends.

After languishing about four years, he expired March 13,
1757; and, agreeably to the express direction of his will, was
interred in a private manner, in the vault of Croydon church.
He expended upwards of 6000l. in repairing and adorning the
palaces and gardens of Lambeth and Croydon. He possessed
the virtues of public and private life in a most eminent degree,
and was a true friend to civil and religious liberty.

In 1763, a volume of his "Sermons on public Occasions"
was printed, which bear the strongest marks of unaffected piety
and benevolence; and the profits of the edition were given to
the treasurer of the London Infirmary, for the use of that charity. There is inserted in the preface an elegy, sacred to his
memory, by the Rev. Mr. Fawkes. A volume of his "Letters" has also been published by the Rev. Mr. Duncombe.

HERSENT (CHARLES), or Hersan, a French divine, known
chiefly for a violent satire which he wrote against cardinal Richelieu, under the feigned name of Optatus Gallus, which, having
been condemned and burnt by the parliament of Paris, is become very scarce, and therefore sells at from 60 to 100 livres,
among French collectors. It is entitled, "Optati Galli de
cavendo Schismate, Liber Parœneticus," and was published at
Paris in 1640, in 8vo. There is, however a counterfeit edition,
bearing the same date, which is distinguished from the true by a
very few differences, as *superiorum* for *superiore*, in p. 7, &c.
In this book the author maintained that the Gallican church was
in danger of separating from Rome, like the English, and strenuously maintained the supremacy of the pope. The cardinal
employed three or four writers to answer this anonymous assail-
ant, but the author in the mean time retired to Rome, where
after a time his violence and indiscretion involved him with the
inquisition, on some points respecting the doctrine of grace,
which he handled in a "Panegyric on St. Louis." He was cited,
refused to appear, and was excommunicated. He therefore returned to France, where he died in 1660. There are extant also
by him, a paraphrase on Solomon's Song, in prose, published in
1635; some funeral orations, sermons, and attacks against the
congregation

congregation of the Oratory, which he had quitted; with a few other pieces. His chief promotion was that of chancellor to the church of Metz.

HERVEY (JAMES), an English divine of exemplary virtue and piety, was born at Hardingstone, in Northamptonshire, in 1714; had his education at the grammar-school at Northampton, and at Lincoln-college in Oxford. After a residence of seven years, he left the university; and became, in 1736, curate to his father, then possessed of the living of Weston-Favell. He was afterwards curate at Biddeford, and several other places in the West. In 1750, at his father's death, he succeeded to the livings of Weston and Collingtree; which being within five miles of each other, he attended alternately with his curate, till his ill health confined him to Weston. Here he afterwards constantly resided, and diligently pursued his labours both in his ministerial office and in his study, as long as possible, under the disadvantage of a weak constitution. He died on Christmas-day, 1758, in his forty-fifth year. His charity was remarkable. It was always his desire to die just even with the world, and to be, as he called it, his own executor. His fund almost expired with his life; what little remained he desired might be given in warm clothing to the poor, in that severe season. In point of learning, though not in the first class of scholars, he was far from being deficient. He was master of the three learned languages, and well read in the classics. But for a more minute account of every part of his character, we must refer the reader to his life, prefixed to his "Letters," published in two volumes, 8vo.

His other writings are, 1. "Meditations and Contemplations: containing Meditations among the Tombs; Reflections on a Flower Garden; and a Descant on Creation, 1746," 8vo. He sold the copy, after it had passed through several editions; which sale, and the profits of the former impressions, amounted to about 700l. The whole of this he gave in charity; saying, that as Providence had blessed his attempt, he thought himself bound to relieve his fellow-creatures with it. 2. "Contemplations on the Night and Starry Heavens; and a Winter Piece, 1747," 8vo. Both these have been turned into blank verse, in imitation of Dr. Young's "Night Thoughts," by Mr. Newcomb. 3. "Remarks on Lord Bolingbroke's Letters on the Study and Use of History, so far as they relate to the History of the Old Testament, &c. in a Letter to a Lady of Quality, 1753," 8vo. 4. "Theron and Aspasio; or, a Series of Dialogues and Letters on the most important Subjects, 1755," 3 vols. 8vo. Some of the principal points which he endeavours to illustrate in this work, are the following: the beauty and excellence of the Scriptures; the ruin and depravity of human nature; its happy recovery founded on the atonement, and effected by the

Spirit

Spirit of Chrift. But the grand article is, the imputed righteoufnefs of Chrift; his notion of which has been cenfured, and attacked by feveral writers. He introduces moft of his dialogues
with defcriptions of fome of the moft delightful fcenes of the
creation. To diverfify the work, fhort fketches of philofophy
are alfo occafionally introduced, eafy to be underftood, and calculated to entertain the imagination, as well as improve the
heart. 5. Some "Sermons," the third edition publifhed after
his death, 1759. 6. An edition of "Jenks's Meditations, 1757,"
with a ftrong recommendatory preface. 7. A recommendatory
preface to "Burnham's pious Memorials," publifhed in 1753,
8vo. 8. "Eleven Letters to Wefley." 9. "Letters to Lady
Frances Shirley, 1782," 8vo. In the younger part of his life
he wrote fome copies of verfes, which fhewed no contemptible
genius for poetry; but thefe were fuppreffed by his own defire.

HERVEY (Augustus John), third earl of Briftol, fecond
fon of John lord Hervey, by Mary daughter of brigadier-ge-
neral Lapell, was born May 19, 1724. Choofing a maritime
life, he paffed through the fubordinate ftations, and was a lieutenant in the year 1744. In the fame year he firft faw mifs
Chudleigh at the houfe of Mrs. Hanmer, her aunt, in Hampfhire; where they were privately married, Aug. 4, in that year.
A few days after, Mr. Hervey was obliged to embark for Jamaica in vice-admiral Davers's fleet. At his return his lady and
he lived together, and were confidered by their relations as man
and wife. In January, 1747, he was advanced to the rank of
poft-captain; and in the fame year his lady brought him a fon,
though fhe continued a maid of honour to the year 1764. This
circumftance gave occafion to the following ænigmatical epigram
by the late lord Chefterfield.

> "A wife, whom yet no hufband dares to name,
> A mother, whom no children dare to claim;
> All this is true, but it may yet be faid,
> This wife, this mother, ftill remains a *maid*."

Soon after this event, a coolnefs arofe between captain Hervey
and his wife, which increafed till they both became defirous of
a feparation. In Jan. 1747, he was appointed to command the
Princeffa, and ferved in the Mediterranean under admirals Medley and Byng: and after the peace, in Jan. 1752, he obtained
the Phœnix of 22 guns. In the courfe of two wars, the courage, zeal, and activity, of captain Hervey were diftinguifhed in
the Mediterranean, off Breft, at the Havannah, and in other
places. During the fame period, he was gradually advanced to
the command of a 74 gun fhip; and, at the peace in 1763, he
was appointed one of the grooms of the bed-chamber to the
king. In 1771 he was created one of the lords of the admiralty; and in 1775, on the death of his brother, without iffue,
he

he became earl of Briftol, after having reprefented the borough
of St. Edmund's Bury in four parliaments. He now refigned
his places, and was created an admiral. In the beginning of the
American war, captain Hervey was a ftrenuous advocate for the
meafures of the miniftry; but changing his politics in the year
1778, continued to the end of it as violent an opponent; · not
without very ftriking appearances of inconfiftency, on feveral
occafions. He died in 1779, when his titles, and as much of
his eftate as he could not leave away, devolved to his brother the
bifhop of Derry, as he left no legitimate heir. The affair of
his marriage, which attracted much public notice at the time,
was briefly thus:—After nine years of preparation, his wife,
who had long lived with the duke of Kingfton, obtained her
fuit in the commons, in 1768, by which it was decided,that
their marriage never had been legal, and was void. She then
was married to the duke of Kingfton, in 1769. But, it appearing afterwards that the decifion had been fraudulently obtained,
fhe was indicted in 1775 for bigamy, tried in the houfe of peers,
and found guilty, but as a peerefs, was difcharged from corporal
punifhment. The following well drawn character of lord
Briftol, written by a contemporary peer in the fea-fervice,
feems to juftify the infertion of his name in this place; though
there can be no doubt that it is in fome degree heightened by perfonal partiality; and the character of a good officer is too common in our navy to demand particular notice.

" The active zeal and diligent affiduity with which the earl
of Briftol ferved, had for fome years impaired a conftitution
naturally ftrong, by expofing it to the unwholefomenefs of variety of climates, and the infirmities incident to conftant fatigue of body and anxiety of mind. His family, his friends,
his profeffion, and his country, loft him in the 56th year of his
age.

" The detail of the merits of fuch a man cannot be uninterefting, either to the profeffion he adorned, or the country
which he ferved, and the remembrance of his virtues muft be
pleafing to thofe who were honoured with his efteem; as every
hour and every fituation of his life afforded frefh opportunities for
the exercife of fuch virtues, they were beft known to thofe who
faw him moft. But however ftrong and perfect their impreffion,
they can be but inadequately defcribed, by one who long enjoyed the happinefs of his friendfhip, and advantage of his
example, and muft ever lament the privation of his fociety.

" He engaged in the fea-fervice when he was ten years old:
the quicknefs of his parts, the decifion of his temper, the ex
cellency of his underftanding, the activity of his mind, the eagernefs of his ambition, his indefatigable induftry, his unremitting diligence, his correct and extenfive memory, his ready and

accurate judgement, the promptitude, clearness, and arrangement with which his ideas were formed, and the happy perspicuity with which they were expressed, were advantages peculiar to himself; his early education under captain William Hervey, and admiral Byng, (two of the best officers of their time) with his constant employment in active service from his first going to sea, till the close of the last war [K], had furnished ample matter for experience, from which his penetrating genius, and just observation, had deduced that extensive and systematic knowledge of minute circumstances and important principles, which is necessary to form an expert seaman and a shining officer: with the most consummate professional skill, he possessed the most perfect courage that ever fortified an heart, or brightened a character; he loved enterprise, he was cool in danger, collected in distress, decided in difficulties, ready and judicious in his expedients, and persevering in his determinations; his orders in the most critical situations, and for the most various objects, were delivered with a firmness and precision, which spake a confidence in their propriety, and facility in their execution, that ensured a prompt and successful obedience in those to whom they were addressed.

" Such was his character as an officer, which made him deservedly conspicuous in a profession, as honourable to the individual, as important to the public : nor was he without those qualifications and abilities, which could give full weight to the situation in which his rank and connexions had placed him in civil life ; his early entrance into his profession had indeed deprived him of the advantages of a classical education ; this defect was however more than balanced by the less ornamental, but more solid instruction of the school he studied in: as a member of parliament, he was an eloquent, though not a correct speaker: those who differed from him in politics, confessed the extent of his knowledge, the variety of his information, and the force of his reasoning, at the same time that they admired the ingenuity with which he applied them to the support of his opinions.

" He was not more eminent for those talents by which a country is served, than distinguished by those qualities which render a man useful, respected, esteemed, and beloved in society. In the general intercourse of the world, he was an accomplished gentleman, and agreeable companion; his manners were noble as his birth, and engaging as his disposition ; he was humane, benevolent, compassionate, and generous; his humanity was conspicuous in his profession ; when exercised towards the seamen, the sensibility and attention of a commander they adored, was the most flattering relief that could be afforded to the suf-

[K] This was written in 1780.

ferings

ferings or diſtreſſes of thoſe who ſerved with him ; when exerted towards her enemies, it did honour to his country, by exemplifying in the moſt ſtriking manner, that generoſity which is the peculiar characteriſtic, and moſt diſtinguiſhed virtue of a brave, free, and enlightened people. In other ſituations his liberality was extenſive without oſtentation, and generally beſtowed where it would be moſt felt and leaſt ſeen, upon modeſt merit, and ſilent diſtreſs; his friendſhips were warm, and permanent beyond the grave, extending their influence to thoſe who ſhared the affections, or enjoyed the patronage of their objects. His reſentment was open, and his forgiveneſs ſincere; it was the effect, perhaps the weakneſs, of an excellent mind, that with him, an injury which he had forgiven, was as ſtrong a claim to his protection, as a favour received could be to his gratitude.

" This bright picture is not without its ſhades ; he had faults; the impetuoſity of his nature, and the eagerneſs with which he purſued his objects, carried him ſometimes to lengths not juſtifiable; and the high opinion he juſtly entertained of his own parts, made him too eaſily the dupe and prey of intereſted and deſigning perſons, whom his cooler judgment would have deteſted and deſpiſed, had they not had cunning enough to diſcover and flatter his vanity, and ſufficient art to avail themſelves of abilities which they did not poſſeſs.—But let it be remembered, that his failings were thoſe of a warm temper, and unguarded diſpoſition ; his virtues thoſe of an heart formed for every thing amiable in private, every thing great in public life."

HERWART, or HERVART (JOHN FÆDERIC), chancellor of Bavaria at the beginning of the ſeventeenth century, and of a noble family in Augſburg, publiſhed ſome works in which his learning was more diſplayed than his genius, in ſupporting the moſt extravagant ſyſtems. Theſe are, 1. " Chronologia nova et vera," two parts, 4to, 1622 and 1626. 2. " Admiranda Ethicæ Theologicæ Myſteria propalata, de antiquiſſima veterum nationum ſuperſtitione, qua lapis Magnes pro Deo habitus colebatur." Monach. 1626, in 4to. It was here ſupported, as the title intimates, that the ancient Egyptians worſhipped the magnet, &c. 3. " An Apology for the Emperor Louis of Bavaria, againſt the falſhoods of Bzovius."

HESHUSIUS (TILLEMANNUS), a German proteſtant theologian, born at Weſel in the dutchy of Cleves, in 1526. He taught theology in ſeveral cities of Germany, but was of ſo turbulent a ſpirit as to be exiled almoſt from every one. He died at the age of 62, in 1588. His works are, 1. " Commentaries on the Pſalms." 2. " On Iſaiah." 3. " On all the Epiſtles of St. Paul." 4. " A Treatiſe on Juſtification and the Lord's Supper." 5. " Sexcenti errores, pleni Blaſphemiis in Deum, quos Romana pontificiaque Eccleſia contra Deum
ſurenter

furenter defendit." This is scarce. 6. Other miscellaneous productions.

HESIOD, a very ancient Greek poet, but whether contemporary with, or older or younger than Homer, is not yet agreed among the learned; nor is there light enough in antiquity to settle the point exactly. His father, as he tells us [1], was an inhabitant of Cuma, in one of the Æolian isles, now called Taio Nova; and removed from thence to Ascra, a village of Bœotia at the foot of mount Helicon, where Hesiod was probably born, and called, as he often is, Ascræus from it. Of what quality his father was, is no where said; but that he was driven by misfortunes from Cuma to Ascra, Hesiod himself informs us. His father seems to have prospered better at Ascra, than he did in his own country; yet Hesiod could arrive at no higher fortune, than keeping of sheep at the top of Helicon. Here the Muses met with him, and received him into their service. To this account, which is to be found in the beginning of his "Generatio Deorum," Ovid alludes in these two lines:

" Nec mihi sunt visæ Clio, Cliusque sorores,
Servanti pecudes vallibus, Ascra, tuis."

Nor Clio nor her sisters have I seen,
As Hesiod saw them in the Ascræan green.

Upon the death of the father, an estate was left, which ought to have been equally divided between the two brothers Hesiod and Perses; but Perses defrauded him in the division, by corrupting the judges. Hesiod was so far from resenting this injustice, that he expresses a concern for those poor mistaken mortals who place their happiness in riches only, even at the expence of their virtue. He lets us know, that he was not only above want, but capable of assisting his brother in time of need; which he often did, though he had been so ill used by him. The last circumstance he mentions relating to himself, is his conquest in a poetical contention. Archidamas king of Eubœa, had instituted funeral games in honour of his own memory, which his sons afterwards took care to have performed. Here Hesiod was a competitor for the prize in poetry, and won a tripod, which he consecrated to the Muses. Plutarch, in his " Banquet of the Seven Wise Men," makes Periander give an account of the poetical contention at Chalcis, in which Hesiod and Homer are made antagonists. Hesiod was the conqueror, and dedicated the tripod, which he received for his victory, to the Muses, with this inscription:

" This Hesiod vows to th' Heliconian nine,
In Chalcis won from Homer the divine."

[1] Opera et dies.

We

We are told, that Philip of Macedon and his son Alexander had a dispute on this subject. The prince declared in favour of Homer; his father told him, "that the prize had been given to Hesiod;" and asked him, whether "he had never seen the verses Hesiod had inscribed upon the tripos, and dedicated to the Muses on mount Helicon?" Alexander allowed it; but said, that Hesiod "might well get the better, when kings were not the judges, but ignorant ploughmen and rustics." The authority of these relations is however questioned by learned men; especially by such as will not allow these two poets to have been contemporaries, but make Hesiod between thirty and forty years the older of the two.

Hesiod, having entered himself into the service of the Muses, discontinued the pastoral life, and applied himself to the study of arts and learning. When he was grown old, for it is agreed by all that he lived to a very great age, he removed to Locris, a town about the same distance from Parnassus, as Ascra was from Helicon. The story of his death, as told by Solon in Plutarch's "Banquet," is very remarkable. The man with whom Hesiod lived at Locris, a Milesian born, ravished a maid in the same house: and though Hesiod was entirely ignorant of the fact, yet being maliciously accused to her brothers as an accomplice, he was injuriously slain with the ravisher, and thrown with him into the sea. It is added, that when the inhabitants of the place heard of the crime, they drowned the perpetrators, and burned their houses. We have the knowledge of some few monuments, which were framed in honour of this poet. Pausanias, in his Bœotics, informs us, that his countrymen the Bœotians, erected to him an image with a harp in his hand; and relates in another place, that there was likewise a statue of Hesiod in the temple of Jupiter Olympicus. Ursinus and Bolssard have exhibited a breast with a head, a trunk without a head, and a gem of him; and Ursinus says, that there is a statue of brass of him in the public college at Constantinople. The "Theogony" and "Works and Days," are the only undoubted pieces of this poet now extant: though it is supposed, that these poems have not descended perfect and finished to the present times. The "Theogony, or Generation of the Gods," Fabricius [L] makes indisputably the work of Hesiod; "nor is it to be doubted," adds he, "that Pythagoras took it for his, who feigned that he saw in hell the soul of Hesiod tied in chains to a brass pillar, for what he had written concerning the nature of the Gods." This doubtless was the poem, which gave Herodotus occasion to say, that Hesiod and Homer were the first who introduced a Theogony among the Grecians; the first who gave names to the

Gods, aſcribed to them honours and arts, and gave particular
deſcriptions of their perſons. The " Works and Days" of
Heſiod, Plutarch aſſures us, were uſed to be ſung to the harp.
Virgil has ſhewn great reſpect to this poet, and taken occaſion
to pay a very high compliment to him :

" Hos tibi dant calamos, en accipe, Muſæ,
Aſcræo quos ante ſeni ; quibus ille ſolebat
Cantando rigidas deducere montibus ornus. "

He was indeed much obliged to him, and propoſed him as his
pattern in his Georgics, though in truth he has greatly excelled
him.   There is alſo in the works of Heſiod a large fragment
of another poem, called the " Shield of Hercules," which ſome
have aſcribed to him, and ſome have rejected.   Manilius [M]
has given a high character of this poet and his works.   Hein-
ſius in the preface to his edition of Heſiod remarks, that among
all the poets, he ſcarce knew any but Homer and Heſiod, who
could repreſent nature in her true native dreſs ; and tells us, that
nature had begun and perfected at the ſame time her work in
theſe two poets, whom for that very reaſon he makes no ſcruple
to call Divine.   In general, the merit of Heſiod has not been
eſtimated ſo highly ; and it is certain that, when compared with
Homer, he muſt paſs for a very moderate poet : though in defining
their different degrees of merit, it may perhaps be but reaſonable
to conſider the different ſubjects, on which the genius of each was
employed.   A good edition of Heſiod's works was publiſhed by
Le Clerc at Amſterdam, in 1701.   Robinſon's in 4to, publiſhed
at Oxford in 1737, is alſo eſteemed ; but the beſt at preſent is
Loeſner's in 8vo, Leipſic, 1778.

HESSELS (JOHN), or Heſſelius, a celebrated profeſſor of
theology at Louvain, where he was born in the year 1522.
Being ſent as a legate to the council of Trent, he greatly diſtinguiſhed himſelf by his profound erudition.   He was particularly converſant in the works of St. Auſtin and St. Jerom, and
was more remarkable for judgement than for eloquence.   After
having been afflicted by the ſtone, he died of an apoplexy at the
early age of 44, in the year 1566, and was buried in the church
of St. Peter at Louvain, of which he was a canon.   He wrote
a great number of controverſial works againſt the proteſtants,
which in his time were much eſteemed.   Alſo, 1. " Commentaries on St. Matthew, and ſeveral of the Epiſtles."   2. " A
famous Catechiſm," containing a vaſt maſs of moral and theological learning.   His epitaph ſays, " Hæreſes ſuo tempore graſ-
ſantes tum vivâ voce, tum editis libris ſtrenuè profligavit."   " The
hereſies which were ſpreading in his time he ſtoutly defeated

[M] In Aſtronom.

both

both by fpeeches and books." Which means no more than that he wrote ably againſt the reformers.

HESYCHIUS, a celebrated grammarian of Alexandria; whom Iſaac Caſaubon has declared to be, in his opinion, of all the ancient critics, whoſe remains are extant, the moſt learned and inſtructive, for thoſe who would apply themſelves in earneſt to the ſtudy of the Greek language. Who or what Hefychius was, and indeed at what time precifely he lived, are circumſtances which there is not light enough in antiquity to determine; as Fabricius himſelf owns [N], who has laboured abundantly about them. He has left us a learned lexicon or vocabulary of Greek words, from which we may perceive, that he was a Chriſtian, or, at leaſt, that he had a thorough and intimate knowledge of Chriſtianity; for he has inſerted in his work the names of the apoſtles, evangeliſts, and prophets, as well as of thoſe ancient writers who have commented upon them. Some ſay, that he was a diſciple of Gregory of Nazianzen, and that he was extremely well verſed in the Sacred Scriptures: and Sixtus Sinenſis is of opinion that he ought to be placed about the end of the fourth century. The firſt edition of Hefychius's lexicon was puliſhed in folio by Aldus at Venice in 1513; then appeared one by Schrevelius, at Leyden in 4to, in 1668, in Greek only. The beſt edition is in two volumes, folio; the firſt publiſhed by Alberti at Leyden in 1746; the ſecond, completed by Ruhnkenius, after the death of Alberti, and publiſhed in 1766. This is a complete and excellent edition, abounding in learned and uſeful notes. It is reckoned one of the beſt editions exiſting of any ancient author. But, after all the labours of the acuteſt men, much yet remains to be corrected and diſcovered in this work.

Julius Scaliger has ſpoken with great contempt of Hefychius, and calls him a frivolous author, who has nothing that is good in him: " but," ſays Baillet, " I believe this critic is very ſingular in his opinion. His ſon Joſeph on the contrary declares, that Hefychius is a very good author, though we have nothing left of him but an epitome, and though his citations are loſt beyond recovery. Meric Caſaubon alſo eſteems him a moſt excellent grammarian; and Menage calls him the moſt learned of all the makers of dictionaries. Well therefore might Barthius pronounce it as he does, a moſt unpardonable crime [O], in him who took upon him to epitomize Hefychius, and to ſeparate from the vocabulary the teſtimonies of ancient authors."

HEVELIUS (JOHN), or Hevelke, a celebrated aſtronomer and mathematician, was born at Dantzick, Jan. 28, 1611. His parents, who were of rank and fortune, gave him a liberal education; in which he diſcovered early a propenſity to natural

[N] Biblioth. Græc. IV. p. 540, &c. [O] Jugemens des Sçavans, Tom. II.
p. 585. Paris, 1718.

philoſophy

philofophy and aftronomy. He ftudied mathematics under Peter Crugerus, in which he made a wonderful progrefs; and learned alfo to draw, to engrave, and to work both in wood and iron in fuch a manner, as to be able to frame mechanical inftruments. In 1630, he fet out upon his travels, in which he fpent four years, paffing through Holland, England, France, and Germany; and upon his return was fo taken up with civil affairs, that he was obliged to intermit his ftudies for fome years. Mean while, his mafter Crugerus, knowing well the force of his genius, and entertaining no fmall expectations from him, ufed all the means he could devife to bring him back to aftronomy; and fucceeded fo well, that, in 1639, Hevelius began to apply himfelf entirely to it. He confidered very wifely, that hypothefes, however they may fhew the ingenuity of their inventors, are of but little ufe in the promotion of real knowledge; and that facts are the only foundation, on which any folid fcience can be raifed. He therefore began his application by building an obfervatory upon the top of his houfe, which he furnifhed with inftruments for making the moft accurate obfervations. He conftructed excellent telefcopes himfelf, and began his obfervations with the moon, whofe various phafes and fpots he noted very accurately; " with a view," as he fays, " of taking lunar eclipfes with greater ex-actnefs [r], and removing thofe difficulties, which frequently arife for want of being able to fettle more precifely the quantity of an eclipfe." When he had finifhed his courfe of obfervations, and prepared a great number of fine engravings upon copper with his own hands, he publifhed his work at Dantzick, 1647, under the title of, " Selenographia, five, Lunæ defcriptio; atque accurata tam macularum ejus quam motuum diverforum, aliarumque omnium viciffitudinum phafiumque, telefcopii ope deprehenfarum, delineatio:" to which he added, by way of ap-pendix, the phafes of the other planets, as they are feen through the telefcope, with obfervations upon them, upon the fpots of the Sun and Jupiter in particular; all engraved by himfelf upon copper, and diftinctly placed before the eyes of the reader. At the entrance of this work there is a handfome mezzotinto of himfelf by Falck, as he then was in his 36th year, with an en-comium in Latin verfe engraved under it; which, as we take it to contain no more than is ftrictly due to his merit, is here given for the entertainment of the reader: the verfes are bad enough, but the compliment was well deferved:

" Contemplare virum, qui cœli fydera primus,
  Quæ vidit, fculpfit; mente manuque valens.
Hactenus ut nemo: quod teftareris, Alhafen;
  Si in vivis effes, tu, Galilæe, quoque.
Expreffit cœlo Faleki celeberrima dextra
  Hevelium, patriæ nobile fidus humi."

[r] Præfat. ad Selenograp.

After

After this, Helvetius continued to make his observations upon the heavens, and to publish, from time to time, whatever he thought might tend to the advancement of astronomy. In 1654, he published two epistles: one to the famous astronomer Ricciolus, " De motu Lunæ libratorio;" another to the no less famous Bulialdus, " De utriusque luminaris defectu " In 1656, a dissertation " De natura Saturni faciei, ejusque phasibus certa periodo redeuntibus." In 1661, " Mercurius in sole visus." In 1662, " Historiola de nova stella in collo Ceti." In 1665, " Prodromus Cometicus, or the History of a Comet, which appeared in 1664." In 1666, " The History of another Comet, which appeared in 1665;" and, in 1668, " Cometographia, cometarum naturam, & omnium à mundo condito historiam exhibens." He sent copies of this work to several members of the Royal Society at London, and among the rest to Hooke; whom we mention particularly, because of a very warm dispute which this present accidentally occasioned soon after between these philosophers. In return for the " Cometographia," Hooke sent Hevelius a description of the dioptric telescope, with an account of the manner of using it; and at the same time recommended it to him, as greatly preferable to telescopes with plain sights. This gave rise to the dispute between them; the point of which was, " whether distances and altitudes could be taken with plain sights any nearer than to a minute." Hooke asserted that they could not; but that, with an instrument of a span radius, by the help of a telescope, they might be determined to the exactness of a second. Hevelius, on the other hand, insisted, that, by the advantage of a good eye and long use, he was able with his instruments to come up even to that exactness; and appealing to experience and facts, sent by way of challenge eight distances, each between two different stars, to be examined by Hooke. Thus the affair rested for some time with outward decency, but not without some inward enmity between the parties. In 1673, Hevelius published the first part of his " Machina Cœlestis," as a specimen of the exactness both of his instruments and observations; and sent several copies as presents to his friends in England, but omitted Hooke. This, it is supposed, occasioned Hooke to print, in 1674, " Animadversions on the first part of the Machina Cœlestis;" in which he treated Hevelius with a very magisterial air, and threw out several unhandsome reflections, which were greatly resented; and the dispute grew afterwards so public, and rose to such a height, that, in 1679, Halley went, at the request of the Royal Society, to examine both the instruments and the observations made with them. Halley gave a favourable judgement of both, in a letter to Hevelius; and Hooke managed the controversy so ill, that he was universally condemned, though the preference has since been given to tele-

scopic

fcopic fights. Hevelius, however, could not be prevailed with to make ufe of them: whether he thought himfelf too experienced to be informed by a young aftronomer, as he confidered Hooke; or whether, having made fo many obfervations with plain fights, he was unwilling to alter his method, left he might bring their exactnefs into queftion; or whether, being by long practice accuftomed to the ufe of them, and not thoroughly apprehending the ufe of the other, nor well underftanding the difference, is uncertain. Befides Halley's letter, Hevelius received many others in his favour, which he took the opportunity of inferting among the aftronomical obfervations in his " Annus Climacterricus," printed in 1685. In a long preface prefixed to this work, he fpoke with more confidence and greater indignation than he had done before; and particularly exclaimed againft Hooke's dogmatical and magifterial manner of affuming a kind of dictatorfhip over him. This revived the difpute; and caufed feveral learned men to engage in it. The book itfelf being fent to the Royal Society, an account was given of it at their requeft by Dr. Wallis; who, among other things took notice, that " Hevelius's obfervations had been mifreprefented, fince it appeared from this book, that he could diftinguifh by plain fights to a fmall part of a minute." About the fame time, Molyneux alfo wrote a letter to the fociety, in vindication of Hevelius againft Hooke's " Animadverfions." Hooke drew up an anfwer to this letter, which was read likewife before the fociety; wherein he obferved, " that he was not the aggreffor, and denied that he had intended to depreciate Hevelius."

In 1679, Hevelius had publifhed the fecond part of his " Machina Coeleftis;" but the fame year, while he was at a feat in the country, he had the misfortune to have his houfe at Dantzick burnt down. By this calamity he is faid to have fuftained feveral thoufand pounds damage; having not only his obfervatory and all his valuable inftruments and aftronomical apparatus deftroyed, but alfo a great number of copies of his " Machina Coeleftis;" which accident has made this fecond part very fcarce, and confequently very dear. In 1690, were publifhed a defcription of the heavens, called, " Firmamentum Sobiefcianum," in honour of John III. king of Poland; and " Prodromus aftronomiae, & novae tabulae folares, una cum catalogo fixarum," In which he lays down the neceffary preliminaries for taking an exact catalogue of the ftars. Both thefe works however were pofthumous; for Hevelius died January 28, 1687, which was the day of his birth, on which he entered upon his 77th year. He was a man greatly efteemed by his countrymen, not only on account of his fkill in aftronomy, but as an excellent and worthy magiftrate. He was made a burgomafter of Dantzick; which office he is faid to have executed with the utmoft integrity and applaufe.

applaufe. He was alfo very highly efteemed by foreigners; and not only by foreigners fkilled in aftronomy and the fciences, but by foreign princes and potentates: as appears abundantly evident from a collection of their letters, which were printed at Dantzick in 1687.

HEURNIUS (John), a celebrated phyfician, born at Utrecht in 1543. After having made himfelf mafter of every thing belonging to his art at Louvain, Paris, Padua, Turin, he was invited to Leyden to be profeffor there. He is faid to have been the firft in this place who taught anatomy by lectures upon human bodies. He died of the ftone in 1601. There are feveral of his productions extant, but the moft capital is, " A Treatife upon Diforders of the Head." It is, fays Julius Scaliger, " as much fuperior to his other works, as the head is fuperior to other parts of the body;" but Scaliger's praifes as well as his cenfures were for the moft part extravagant. Heurnius publifhed Hippocrates in Greek and Latin, with explanatory commentaries, which have undergone many editions: the fourth was at Amflerdam, 1688, in 12mo. Gerrard Voffius calls him *fummum Medicum*; and fays, that he was his mafter *in fcientiâ naturali*. His works were publifhed in folio at Leyden in 1658. He had a fon named Otto, who alfo obtained fome celebrity.

HEUSINGER, (John Michael), a celebrated Saxon divine and fcholar, was born in September, 1690, at Sunderhaufen in Thuringia [Q]. He ftudied at home and at Gotha, when having determined for the clerical profeffion, he removed in 1708 to Halle. Hence, after a fhort ftay, he went to Jena, where he purfued his theological ftudies under the celebrated Buddeus, and his philological under Danzius. In 1711, he returned to Halle; but, being obliged by ill health to change the air, he took a literary tour to Eifenach, Caffel, Marpurg, and Gieffen. At the latter of thefe places he fettled, and took pupils, in 1715; but in 1722, undertook the care of a fchool at Laubach. In 1730 he was appointed a profeffor at Gotha, where he remained till 1738, when by particular invitation he gave up that fituation for a fimilar one of more profit at Eifenach. Heufinger was married, and had a fon and two daughters. He died in March, 1751. This philologer is highly praifed by his biographer for learning, piety, good temper, and found judgement. He publifhed feveral editions of claffical books; as, " Julian's Cæfars," with notes, Gotha, 1736. " Æfop's Fables," in Greek. " Phædrus." " Three Orations of Cicero." " Cornelius Nepos," Eifenach, 1747, and others; befides feveral valuable editions of modern philological works. His original productions confift

[Q] Hiftes de Vitis Philol. noftra æt. clariff. Tom. I.

G 4   chiefly

chiefly of academical profusions and difputations, of which his biographer gives a long lift.

HEUSINGER (JAMES FREDERICK), was a nephew of the former, under whom he made his principal ftudies at Gotha [R]. He was born in 1719, at Ufingen in Wetteravia, near Eifenach; and, when prepared by his uncle for academical lectures, completed his education at Jena. There, after fome time, he began to teach philology, and continued his lectures for fix years; but in 1750 removed to Wolfenbuttel, where he was at firft fecond mafter of the principal fchool; but in 1759 became head mafter. Thefe fituations he filled with the greateft credit; being a good grammarian, a found critic, and an admirable interpreter of Greek and Latin authors. He died in 1778, having made himfelf famous by feveral very learned publications; the chief of which are, 1. " A Specimen of Obfervations on the Ajax and Electra of Sophocles," 1746, at Jena. 2. " An edition of Plutarch on Education, with the Verfion of Xylander corrected, and his own Annotations," Leipfic, 1749. This tract, however, Wyttenbach pronounces to be one of thofe that are falfely afcribed to Plutarch. 3. " Flavii Mallii Theodori, de metris liber;" from old manufcripts. This was printed in 4to, at Wolfenbuttel, in 1759.]. F. Heufinger was twice married and left a fon, who is alfo a man of learning.

HEYLIN (Dr. PETER), an Englifh divine, defcended from an ancient family at Pentric-Heylin in Montgomeryfhire, was born at Burford in Oxfordfhire, Nov. 29, 1600 [S]. In 1613, he was entered of Hart-hall in Oxford, and two years after chofen a demy of Magdalen college. He had, while at fchool, given a fpecimen of his genius for dramatie poetry, in a tragicomedy on the wars and fate of Troy; and now compofed a tragedy, entitled, " Spurius," which was fo approved by his fociety, that the prefident, Dr. Langton, ordered it to be acted in his apartments. After this, he read cofmographical lectures in the college, which being a very unufual thing, and he very converfant in that branch of fcience, fo much recommended him to the fociety, that he was chofen fellow in 1619. In 1621, he publifhed his " Microcofmus, or Defcription of the World;" the chief materials of which were the lectures juft mentioned. It was univerfally approved, and fo fpeedily fold, that, in 1624, it was reprinted in the fame fize, but with confiderable additions, and again prefented to prince Charles, to whom it had been dedicated. It was foon after put into the hands of the king, who feemed at firft greatly pleafed with it; till meeting with a paffage in it, where Heylin gave precedency to the French king,

[R] Harles de Vitis Philol. noftra æt. clariff. Tom. III.
[S] Ath. Oxon. Barnard's Life of Heylin, p. 7.

and

and ſtyled France the more famous kingdom, he took ſo much offence, that he ordered the lord-keeper to ſuppreſs the book; Heylin, to make his peace with the king, declared that the error, in one of the exceptionable paſſages, was entirely the printer's, who had put *is* inſtead of *was*; and that when he himſelf mentioned the precedency of France before England, he did not ſpeak of England, as it then ſtood augmented by Scotland, and beſides he took what he did ſay from Camden's Remains. James was hereby ſatisfied, and Heylin took care, on the other hand, that the whole clauſe, which gave ſo much diſguſt, ſhould be left out in all future impreſſions. The work was afterwards ſucceſſively enlarged, till it became a great folio, and has ſince been often reprinted in that ſize.

In 1625, he went over to France, where he continued about ſix weeks, and took down in writing an account of his journey; the original manuſcript of which he gave to his friend lord Danvers, but kept a copy for himſelf, which was publiſhed about 30 years after. In April, 1627, he anſwered, *pro forma*, upon theſe two queſtions: 1. "An eccleſia unquam fuerit inviſibilis?" "Whether the church was ever inviſible?" 2. "An eccleſia poſſit errare?" "Whether the church can err?" both which determining in the affirmative, a great clamour was raiſed againſt him as a papiſt, or at leaſt a favourer of popery. Wood ſays, that Prideaux, the divinity-profeſſor, "fell foul upon him for it, calling him Bellarminian, Pontifician, and I know not what." Heylin was not eaſy under the charge of being popiſhly affected; for which reaſon, to clear himſelf from that imputation, he took an opportunity, in preaching before the king on John iv. 20. of declaring vehemently againſt ſome of the errors and corruptions of the Romiſh church. In 1628, lord Danvers, then earl of Danby, recommended him to Laud, then biſhop of Bath and Wells; by whoſe intereſt alſo, in 1629, he was made one of the chaplains in ordinary to his majeſty. On Act-Sunday 1630, he preached before the univerſity of Oxford at St. Mary's on Matth. xiii. 25. whence he took occaſion to deliver his ſentiments very freely in regard to an affair which at firſt ſight had a ſpecious appearance of promoting the honour and emolument of the eccleſiaſtical ſtate, but was in reality a moſt iniquitous ſcheme, injurious to the laity, and of no ſervice where it was pretended to avail. This was a feoffment, that ſome deſigning perſons had obtained, for the buying in of impropriations; but Heylin, ſeeing through the diſguiſe, expoſed very clearly the knavery of the deſigners. About this time he reſigned his fellowſhip, having been married near two years; in concealing which marriage he acted very unſtatutably, not to ſay diſhoneſtly, nor did his friends attempt to juſtify him for it.

In

In 1631, he publifhed his "Hiftory of that moft famous Saint and Soldier of Jefus Chrift, St. George of Cappadocia, &c. to which he fubjoined, the Inftitution of the moft Noble Order of St. George, named the Garter;" &c. which work he prefented to his majefty, to whom he was introduced by Laud, then raifed to the fee of London. It was gracioufly received by the king, and Heylin foon after reaped the fruits of it : for in Oct. 1631 he was prefented to the rectory of Hemmingford in Huntingdonfhire, to a prebend of Weftminfter in November following, and fhortly after to the rectory of Houghton in the bifhopric of Durham, worth near 400l. per annum. In April 1633, he was created D. D. and gave frefh offence to the divinity-profeffor Prideaux by the queftions he put up; which were, 1. "Whether the church hath authority in determining controverfies of faith?" 2. "Whether the church hath authority of interpreting the Sacred Scriptures?" 3. "Whether the church hath authority of appointing rites and ceremonies?" Of all which he maintained the affirmative. Prideaux, however, in the courfe of this difpute, is faid to have laid down fome tenets, which gave as much offence to Laud, who was chancellor of Oxford, and to the king, whom Laud informed of them, as Heylin's had given to him; as, "That the church was a mere chimera"—"That it did not teach nor determine any thing."—"That controverfies had better be referred to univerfities than to the church, and might be decided by the literati there, even though bifhops were laid afide." Heylin afterwards found an opportunity of revenging himfelf on Prideaux, for the rough treatment he had received from him. This divine, we are told, had delivered a lecture on the fabbath, fomewhat freer than fuited the rigid orthodoxy of the times; of which, however, not much notice was taken. But fhortly after, when the king, by publifhing the book of fports on Sundays, had raifed a violent outcry throughout the nation againft himfelf and Laud, Heylin tranflated this lecture into Englifh, and publifhed it with a preface in 1633-4, to the great vexation of Prideaux, who hereby fuffered much in the efteem and affection of the puritans.

Williams, bifhop of Lincoln and dean of Weftminfter, having incurred the king's and Laud's difpleafure, was now fufpended and imprifoned, whereupon Heylin was made treafurer of the church of Weftminfter in 1637; and was alfo prefented by the prebendaries, his brethren, to the rectory of Iflip near Oxford. This he exchanged in 1638, for that of South-Warnborough in Hampfhire; and the fame year was made one of the juftices of the peace for that county. In 1639, he was employed by Laud to tranflate the Scotch liturgy into Latin; and was chofen by the college of Weftminfter their clerk, to reprefent them in convocation. But the feafon was coming on, when

men

men of his principles had reason to be afraid. A cloud was gathered, which threatened to overwhelm all who, like him, had distinguished themselves as champions for royal or ecclesiastical prerogative. To shelter himself therefore from the impending storm, he withdrew from the metropolis, where he had long basked in the sun-shine of a court, to his parsonage; but not thinking himself secure there, retreated soon after to Oxford, then garrisoned by the king, and the seat of his residence. On this the parliament voted him a delinquent, and dispatched an order to their committee at Portsmouth, to sequester his whole estate, and seize upon his goods. In consequence of this severe decree, he was deprived of his most curious and valuable library, it being carried with his houshold furniture to that town. He was employed by the king at Oxford to write a periodical paper, which was published weekly in that city, entitled " Mercurius Aulicus;" but in 1645, when the king's affairs became desperate, and the " Mercurius Aulicus" no longer supported, he quitted Oxford, and wandered from place to place, himself and his family reduced to the utmost straits. At Winchester he stayed for a while with his wife, &c. but that city being at length delivered up to the parliament, he was forced to remove again. In 1648, he went to Minster-Lovel in Oxfordshire, the seat of his elder brother, which he farmed for the six or seven years following of his nephew colonel Heylin, and spent much of his time in writing. On quitting this farm, he went to Abingdon in Berkshire, where he also employed himself much in composing treatises, which he published from time to time. Upon the Restoration of Charles II. he was restored to all his spiritualities, and undoubtedly expected from that prince some very eminent dignity in the church, as he had heroically exerted himself in behalf of it, as well as of the crown; and endured so much on that account, during their suffering condition. Here, however, he was utterly disappointed, being never raised above the subdeanery of Westminster. This was matter of great vexation to him, and of wonder to many others, who did not sufficiently consider the qualities of the man ; which though well suited to the tool of a party, were not the fittest recommendations to preferment, or most proper for an eminent ecclesiastical station. He died May 8, 1662, and was interred before his own stall, within the choir of the abbey.

Wood has given the character of him, and tells us, that he was " a person endowed with singular gifts, of a sharp and pregnant wit, solid and clear judgement. In his younger years he was accounted an excellent poet, but very conceited and pragmatical ; in his elder, a better historian, a noted preacher, and a ready extemporaneous speaker. He had a tenacious memory to a miracle. He was a bold and undaunted man among his friends and foes, though of a very mean port and presence; and therefore by some of them he was accounted too high and proud for his function. A constant assertor of the church's right and the king's prerogative; a severe and vigorous opposer of rebels and schismatics. In some things too much a party-man to be an historian, and equally an enemy to popery and puritanism." His writings are numerous, but not very valuable; and almost the only work by which he is at present known, is his "Cosmography;" which, however, is in no very high esteem, being superseded by publications abundantly superior in the kind.

HEYWOOD (John), an admired English poet and jester of his time, was born in London, and educated at Oxford: but the severity of an academical life not suiting his gay and airy temper, he retired to his native place, and became known to all the men of wit, and especially to sir Thomas More, with whom he was very familiar. He was one of the first who wrote English plays; and is said to have been very well skilled in vocal and instrumental music. He found means to become a favourite with Henry VIII. and was well rewarded by that monarch, for the mirth and quickness of his conceits. He was afterwards equally valued by queen Mary, and had often the honour to display his wit and humour before her; which he did, it seems, even when she lay languishing on her death-bed. After the decease of that princess, being a bigoted papist, and finding the protestant religion likely to prevail under queen Elizabeth, he entered into a voluntary exile, and went and settled at Mechlin in Brabant, where he died in 1565. He wrote several plays; " A Dialogue in verse concerning English Proverbs;" " 500 Epigrams;" " The Spider and Fly, a Parable, 1556," in a pretty thick 4to. Before the title of this last work is his figure given, from head to foot, printed from a wooden cut, with a fur gown, on his head a round cap, his chin and lips close shaved, and a dagger hanging at his girdle. There are 77 chapters in this work, at the beginning of each of which is the portrait of the author, either standing or sitting before a table, with a book on it, and a window near it hung round with cobwebs, flies, and spiders. What would the present age say of an author, whose book should be so full of himself? He left two sons, both eminent men: the eldest of whom, Ellis Heywood, was born in London, and educated at All-souls-college in Oxford, of which he was elected fellow in 1547. Afterwards he travelled into France and Italy; continued some time at Florence, under the patronage of cardinal Pole; and became such an exact master of the Italian tongue, that he wrote a book in that language, entitled, " Il Moro," 8vo, Firenz. 1556. He then went to Antwerp, and thence to Louvain, where he died in the 12th year after his entrance into the society of the Jesuits; which was about 1572.

HEYWOOD (Jasper), the younger fon of John abovementioned, was born in London about 1535, and educated at Merton-college in Oxford; of which he was chosen fellow, but obliged to resign, for fear of expulsion, on account of his immoralities, in 1558. He was then elected fellow of All-fouls, but left the university, and soon after England. In 1561, he became a popish priest; and the year after, being at Rome, was entered among the Jesuits. After he had passed two years in the study of divinity, he was sent to Diling in Switzerland; whence being called away by pope Gregory XIII. in 1581, he was sent into England, where he was appointed provincial of the Jesuits. After many peregrinations, he died at Naples in 1597. Before he left England the first time, he translated three tragedies of Seneca; and wrote "Various Poems and Devices;" some of which are printed in a book, entitled, " The Paradife of Dainty Devices, 1573," 4to.

HEYWOOD (Thomas), an actor, and a writer of plays, in the reigns of queen Elizabeth, James I. and Charles I. has not had the time of his birth and death recorded. Winstanley fays, he was one of the most voluminous writers of his age: and, in a preface to one of his plays, he tells us, that it was one preferved out of 220; of which number only 24 now remain. He displayed much learning in his " Actor's Vindication;" but what rank he held on the stage none of his biographers have informed us. Langbaine obferves of him, that he was a general scholar and tolerable linguist, as his tranflations from Lucian, Erafmus, and from other Latin as well as Italian authors, sufficiently shew: the wits and poets, however, have always held him cheap.

HEYWOOD (Eliza), a most voluminous female writer, was the daughter of a tradefman in London, and died in 1756, aged about 63. Her genius leading her to novel-writing, she took Mrs. Manley's " Atalantis" for her model, and produced " The Court of Arimania," " The New Utopia," with other pieces of a like kind. The loofenefs of thefe works were the oftenfible reafon of Pope for putting her into his " Dunciad;" but it is most probable, that some provocation of a private and perfonal nature was the real motive to it. She feemed, however, to be convinced of her error; fince, in the numerous volumes fhe publifhed afterwards, fhe generally appeared a votary of virtue, and preferved more purity and delicacy of fentiment. Her latter writings are, 1. " The Female Spectator," 4 vols. 2. " Epiftles for the Ladies," 2 vols. 3. " Fortunate Foundling," 1 vol. 4. " Adventures of Nature," 1 vol. 5. " Hiflory of Betfey Thoughtlefs," 4 vols. 6. " Jenny and Jemmy Jeffamy," 3 vols. 7. " Invifible Spy," 2 vols. 8. " Hufband and Wife," 2 vols. all in 12mo; and a pamphlet, entitled, " A Prefent for a Servant-Maid."

When

When young, she attempted dramatic poetry, but with no great success; none of her plays being either much approved at first, or revived afterwards. She had also an inclination for the theatre as a performer, and was on the stage at Dublin in 1715. It would be natural to impute gallantry to such a woman, yet nothing criminal was ever laid to her charge. On the contrary, she is represented as not only good-natured, affable, lively, and entertaining, but as a woman also of strict decorum, delicacy, and prudence; whatever errors, from a gaiety and vivacity of spirit, she might have committed in her younger years.

HICKES (GEORGE), an English divine, of uncommon abilities and learning, was born June 20, 1642, at Newsham in Yorkshire, where his parents were settled on a very large farm. He was sent to the grammar-school at North Allerton, and thence in 1659, to St. John's-college in Oxford. Soon after the Restoration, he removed to Magdalen-college, from thence to Magdalen-hall; and at length, in 1664, was chosen fellow of Lincoln-college, taking the degree of M. A. the year after. June 1666, he was admitted into orders, became a public tutor, and discharged that office with great reputation, for seven years. Being then in a bad state of health, he was advised to ramble about the country: upon which sir George Wheeler, who had been his pupil, and had conceived a filial affection for him, invited him to accompany him in his travels. They set out in Oct. 1673, and made the tour of France; after which they parted, Hickes being obliged to return to take his degree of B. D. At Paris, where he staid a considerable time, he became acquainted with Mr. Henry Justell, who in confidence told him many secret affairs; particularly that of the intended revocation of the edict of Nantes, and of a design in Holland and England to set aside the family of the Stuarts. He committed to him also his father's MS. of the "Codex canonum ecclesiæ universalis," to be presented in his name to the university of Oxford.

After his return home, in May, 1675, he took the degree just mentioned, being about that time rector of St. Ebbe's church in Oxford; and, in Sept. 1676, was made chaplain to the duke of Lauderdale. In May 1677, his grace being to be made high-commissioner of Scotland, took his chaplain with him into that kingdom; and, in April 1678, sent him up to court, with Dr. Burnet, archbishop of Glasgow, to lay before the king the proceedings in Scotland. He returned the month following, and was desired by Sharp, archbp. of St. Andrew's, to accept the degree of D. D. in that university, as a testimony of his and his country's great esteem for him, which request the duke of Lauderdale approving, Hickes was dignified in a full convocation: and afterwards, when he returned with his patron into England, the archbishop, in his own name, and that of all his

brethren,

brethren, prefented him with 18 volumes of Labbe's "Councils," as an acknowledgement of his fervices to that church.

In Sept. 1679, he married; and, Dec. following, was created D. D. at Oxford. In March, 1679-80, the king promoted him to a prebend of Worcefter: and, in Auguft, he was prefented by Sancroft, archbifhop of Canterbury, to the vicarage of Allhallows Barking, near the Tower of London. In Dec. 1681, he was made chaplain in ordinary to the king; and, in Aug. 1683, dean of Worcefter. The bifhopric of Briftol was vacant the next year, and Hickes, it is faid, might have had it if he would: but, miffing his opportunity, the king died, and he loft his profpect of advancement; for though his church principles were very high, yet he had diftinguifhed himfelf too much by his zeal againft popery, to be any favourite with James II. In May, 1686, he left the vicarage of Barking, and went to fettle on his deanery; the bifhop of Worcefter having offered him the rectory of All-church, not far from that city, which he accepted.

Upon the Revolution in 1688, Dr. Hickes with many others, refufing to take the oaths of allegiance, fell under fufpenfion in Auguft, 1689, and was deprived the February following. He continued, however, in poffeffion till the beginning of May; when reading in the Gazette, that the deanery of Worcefter was granted to Talbot, afterwards bifhop of Oxford, Salifbury, and Durham fucceffively, he immediately drew up in his own hand-writing a claim of right to it, directed to all the members of that church; and, in 1691, affixed it over the great entrance into the choir, that none of them might plead ignorance in that particular. The earl of Nottingham, then fecretary of ftate, called it "Dr. Hickes's Manifefto againft Government;" and it has fince been publifhed by Dr. Francis Lee, in the appendix to his "Life of Mr. Kettlewell," with this title, "The Proteftation of Dr. George Hickes, and Claim of Right, fixed up in the Cathedral Church of Worcefter." Expecting hereupon the refentment of the government, he privately withdrew to London, where he abfconded for many years; till, May 1699, when lord Somers, then chancellor, out of regard to his uncommon abilities, procured an act of council, by which the attorney-general was ordered to caufe a Noli Profequi to be entered to all proceedings againft him.

Soon after their deprivation, archbp. Sancroft and his colleagues began to confider about maintaining and continuing the epifcopal fucceffion among thofe who adhered to them; and, having refolved upon it, they fent Dr. Hickes over, with a lift of the deprived clergy, to confer with king James about that matter. The doctor fet out in May, 1693, and going by the way of Holland, made it fix weeks before he arrived at St. Germains. He had feveral audiences of the king, who complied

with

with all he afked; and would have foon returned to England, but was detained fome months by an ague and fever. He arrived in February, and on the eve of St. Matthias, the confecrations were performed by Dr. Lloyd bifhop of Norwich, Dr. Turner bifhop of Ely, and Dr. White bifhop of Peterborough, at the bifhop of Peterborough's lodgings in the Rev. Mr. Giffard's houfe, Southgate. Hickes was confecrated fuffragan bifhop of Thetford, and Wagftaffe fuffragan of Ipfwich: at which folemnity Henry earl of Clarendon is faid to have been prefent. It has indeed been averred, that Hickes was once difpofed to take the oaths, in order to fave his preferments; but this is not probable. He was a man very ftrict in his principles of morality; and what he was convinced was his duty, he clofely adhered to, choofing to fuffer any thing rather than violate his confcience. Some years before he died, he was grievoufly tormented with the ftone; and at length his conftitution, though naturally ftrong, gave way to that diftemper, Dec. 15, 1715, in his 74th year.

Dr. Hickes was a man of univerfal learning; but his temper, fituation, and connections were fuch, as to fuffer him to leave us but few monuments of it, that are worth remembering: for though he wrote a great deal, the greateft part confifts of controverfial pieces on politics and religion, which are generally thrown afide after they have been once read, and are very unworthy to employ almoft the whole time of a man of real parts and learning, as he certainly was. He was particularly fkilful in the old Northern languages, and in antiquities, and has given us fome works on thefe fubjects, which will be valued when all his other writings are forgotten. He was deeply read in the primitive fathers of the church, whom he confidered as the beft expofitors of Scripture; and as no one better underftood the doctrine, worfhip, conftitution, and difcipline of the Catholic church in the firft ages of Chriftianity, fo it was his utmoft ambition and endeavour to prove the church of England perfectly conformable to them.

The principal works of Dr. Hickes are the three following: 1. " Inftitutiones Grammaticæ Anglo-Saxonicæ & Mæfo-Gothicæ. Grammatica Iflandica Runolphi Jonæ. Catalogus librorum Septentrionalium. Accedit Edwardi Bernardi Etymologicum Britannicum, Oxon. 1689," 4to, infcribed to archbifhop Sancroft. While the dean was writing the preface to this book, there were great difputes in the houfe of commons, and throughout the kingdom, about the original contract; which occafioned him to infert therein the ancient coronation oath of our Saxon kings, to fhew, what was not very neceffary, that there is not the leaft footftep of any fuch contract. 2. " Antiquæ literaturæ Septentrionalis libri duo: quorum primus G. Hickefii S.T.P.

Linguarum

Linguarum Veterum Septentrionalium thesaurum grammatico-criticum & Archæologicum, ejusdem de antiquæ literaturæ Septentrionalis utilitate differtationem epistolarum, & Andreæ Fountaine equitis auratl numifmata Saxonica & Dano-Saxonica, complectitur: alter continet Humfredi Wanleii librorum Veterum Septentrionalium, qui In Angliæ Bibliothecis extant, catalogum historico-criticum, nec non multorum veterum codicum Septentrionalium alibi extantium notitiam, cum totius operis fex indicibus, Oxon, 1705," folio. Foreigners as well as Englishmen, who had any relifh for antiquities, have justly admired this fplendid and laborious work. The great duke of Tufcany's envoy fent a copy of it to his mafter, which his highnefs looking into, and finding full of ftrange characters, called a council of the Dotti, and commanded them to perufe and give him an account of. They did fo, and reported it to be an excellent work, and that they believed the author to be a man of a particular head; for this was the envoy's compliment to Hickes, when he went to him with a prefent from his mafter. 3. Two volumes of Sermons [T], most of which were never before printed,

[T] He publifhed alfo many fmaller works, moft of them controverfial. The firft was 4. "A Letter fent from beyond the Seas to one of the chief Minifters of the Nonconforming Party, &c. 1674;" which was afterwards reprinted in 1684, under the title of, "The Judgement of an anonymous Writer concerning thefe following Particulars; firft, a Law for difabling a Papist to inherit the Crown; fecondly, the Execution of penal Laws againft Proteftant Diffenters; thirdly, a Bill of Comprehenfion: all briefly difcuffed in a Letter, fent from beyond the Seas to a Diffenter ten Years ago." This letter was In reality an anfwer to his elder brother Mr. John Hickes, a Diffenting minifter, bred up in Cromwell's time at the college of Dublin; whom the doctor always endeavoured to convince of his errors, but without fuccefs. John perfifted in them to his death, and at laft fuffered from his rebellion under the duke of Monmouth; though, upon the doctor's unwaried application, the king would have granted him his life, but that he had been falfely informed, that this Mr. Hickes was the perfon who advifed the duke of Monmouth to take upon him the title of king. 5. "Ravillac Redivivus, being a Narrative of the ate Tiial of Mr James Mitchel, a Conventicle Preacher, who was executed Jan. 11, 1677, for an Attempt on the Perfon of the Archbifhop of St. Andrew's,

&c." 6. "The Spirit of Popery fpeaking out of the Mouths of fanatical Proteftants: or, the laft Speeches of Mr. John Kid and Mr. John King, two Prefbyterian Minifters, who were executed for high Treafon at Edinburgh, on Aug. 14, 1679." Thefe pieces were publifhed in 1680, and they were occafioned by his attendance on the duke of Lauderdale in quality of chaplain. The fpirit of faction, however, made them much read, and did the author confiderable fervice with feveral great perfonages, and even with the king. 7. "Jovian; or, an Anfwer to Julian the Apoftate;" printed twice in 1683, 8vo. This is an ingenious and learned tract in defence of paffive obedience and non-refiftance, againft the celebrated Samuel Johnfon, the author of "Julian." 8. "The Cafe of Infant Baptifm, 1683;" printed in the fecond vol. of the "London Cafes, 1685," in 4to. 9. "Speculum beatæ Virginis, a Difcourfe on Luke i. 28, of the due Praife and Honour of the Virgin Mary, by a true Catholic of the Church of England, 1686." 10. "An Apologetical Vindication of the Church of England, in Anfwer to her Adverfaries, who reproach her with the Englifh Herefies and Schifms, 1686," 4to; reprinted, with many additions, a large preface, and an appendix of "Papers relating to the Schifms of the Church of Rome, 1706," 8vo. 11. "The celebrated

printed, with a preface by Mr. Spinckes, 1713, 8vo. After his death was published another volume of his Sermons, with some pieces relating to schism, separation, &c. Besides the works enumerated here and in the note, there are many prefaces and recommendations written by him, at the earnest request of others, either authors or editors. But an account of these would be neither important in itself, nor materially illustrative of his character.

HIERO I. king of Syracuse, whose victories at the Olympic and Pythian games were celebrated by Pindar, succeeded his brother Gelon, but by no means emulated his virtues. Though, towards the end of his reign, his intimacy with Simonides, Pindar, Epicharmus, and other learned men, whom he invited to his court, had considerably softened his manners. At first he

brated Story of the Theban Legion no Fable: in Answer to the Objections of Dr. Gilbert Burnet's Preface to his Translation of Lactantius de moribus persecutorum, with some Remarks on his Discourse of Persecution;" written in 1687, but not published till 1714, for reasons given in the preface. 11. "Reflections upon a Letter out of the Country to a Member of this present Parliament, occasioned by a Letter to a Member of the House of Commons, concerning the Bishops lately in the Tower, and now under Suspension, 1689." The author of the letter, to which these reflections are an answer, was generally presumed to be Dr. Burnet; though that action was afterwards contradicted. 13. "A Letter to the Author of a late Paper, entitled, A Vindication of the Divines of the Church of England, &c. in Defence of the History of passive Obedience, 1689." The author of the "Vindication" was Dr. Fowler, bishop of Gloucester, though his name was not to it. 14. "A Word to the Wavering, in Answer to Dr. Gilbert Burnet's Enquiry into the present State of Affairs, 1689." 15. "An Apology for the new Separation, in a Letter to Dr. Sharp, Archbishop of York, &c. 1691." 16. "A Vindication of some among ourselves against the false Principles of Dr. Sherlock, &c. 1692." 17. Some Discourses on Dr. Burnet and Dr. Tillotson, occasioned by the late Funeral Sermon of the former upon the latter, 1695." It is remarkable, that in this piece Hickes has not scrupled to call Tillotson an Atheist; which may serve to convince the reader, that no talents, natural or acquired, can secure a man from fanaticism, whose zeal is under no restraint from reason.

18. "The Pretences of the Prince of Wales examined and rejected, &c. 1701." 19. A letter in the "Philosophical Transactions," entitled, "Epistola viri Rev. D. G. Hickesii S. T. P. ad D. HanaSloane, M.D. & S. R. Secr. de variis lectionibus inscriptionis, quæ in statua Tagis exaratur per quatuor alphabeta Hetrusca." 20. "Several Letters which passed between Dr. G. Hickes and a Popish Priest, &c. 1705." The person, on whose account this book was published, was the lady Theophila Nelson, wife of Robert Nelson, esq; 21. "A second Collection of controversial Letters, relating to the Church of England and the Church of Rome, as they passed between Dr. G. Hickes and an honourable Lady, 1710." This lady was the lady Gratiana Carew of Hadcomb in Devonshire. 22. "Two Treatises; one of the Christian Priesthood, the other of the Dignity of the Episcopal Order, against a book entitled, The Rights of the Christian Church." The third edition in 1711, enlarged into two volumes, 8vo. 23. "A seasonable and modest Apology in behalf of the Rev. Dr. Hickes and other Nonjurors, in a Letter to Thomas Wise, D.D. 1710." 24. "A Vindication of Dr. Hickes, and the Author of the seasonable and modest Apology; from the Reflections of Dr. Wise, &c. 1712." 25. "Two Letters to Robert Nelson, Esq; relating to Bishop Bull;" published in Bull's life. 26. "Some Queries proposed to civil, canon, and common Lawyers, 1712;" printed after several editions, in 1714, with another title, "Seasonable Queries relating to the Birth and Birth-right of a certain Person."

was hated for his violence and avarice; as much as Gelon had
been beloved for mildnefs and equity. His brother Thrafydæus
he endeavoured to remove by giving him a dangerous command,
againſt the Crotoniatæ. Thrafydæus, fufpecting the defign,
refufed to go. Hence arofe a difagreement, and the brother
took refuge in the court of Theron, king of Agrigentum. Hoſ-
tilities were commenced on both fides, but by the mediation of
Theron, the brothers were reconciled, and peace eſtabliſhed.
After the death of Theron, his fon and fucceſſor Thrafydæus
made war againſt Hiero, which ended in the defeat and depofal
of the former. Hiero died in 461, A. C. and was fucceeded
by his brother Thrafybulus.

HIERO II. a prince of eminent virtues, and defcended from
the Gelon mentioned in the preceding article. But his mother
was of flaviſh extraction, for which reaſon his father Hierocles
had once determined to expofe the child. Hiero, as he grew
up, was diſtinguiſhed for a fine countenance, a graceful and robuſt
perfon, and noble ſtature, with great excellence in all military
exercifes; he was affable and polite in converfation, of ſtrict
integrity in bufinefs, and of great moderation in command.
For thefe merits, he was greatly favoured and admired by Pyrrhus. He was about thirty years of age when the Syracufan
foldiers, without the confent of the citizens, raifed him to the
chief command civil and military, which appointment the citizens, though difpleafed at the right of nomination affumed by
the army, unanimoufly confirmed. Seven years after this event,
and in the year 268 A. C. he was declared king by all the citizens of Syracufe, and afterwards by all the cities of Sicily, then
in alliance againſt Carthage. But foon after the Syracufans
and Carthaginians united againſt the Romans, on the breaking out of the firſt Punic war. The Roman conful Appius
Claudius, coming into Sicily to aid the Mamertines, befieged
by the Carthaginians in Meſſina, Hiero gave him battle before
that city, and performed prodigies of valour, but could not refiſt
the fortune and courage of Rome. The Carthaginians alfo were
defeated foon after; and their power in Sicily was fo broken,
that Hiero thought it prudent to make peace with the Romans.
This happened in 263 A. C. and from that time to his death,
which was near 50 years, he continued the faithful friend and
ally of Rome. He thus preferved his country in peace, of
which advantage he made the wifeſt and moſt benevolent ufe, by
encouraging the arts, and endeavouring to render his people
happy. Archimedes, the celebrated mathematician, was related
to him, and he felt the greateſt fatisfaction in examining the
proofs of his genius, and giving him occafion to difplay them.
Hiero was magnificent in every thing, in building palaces, arfe-
nals, temples, and ſhips. Of the latter, he caufed one to be

built,

built, which for magnitude and workmanship surpassed every thing that was ever attempted in ancient times. It proved, however, too large for any port in Sicily, and he presented it to Ptolemy king of Egypt, probably Philadelphus. Hiero died in the year 215, A. C. at the age of more than ninety; his subjects regretted him as a father. He was succeeded by an unworthy grandson, named Hieronymus.

HIEROCLES; a great persecutor of the Christians in the beginning of the fourth century, was at first president of Bithynia, and afterwards governor of Alexandria: in both which situations he acted very furiously against the Christians. Lactantius relates, that at the time he was teaching rhetoric in Bithynia, and the Christian church under persecution, two authors set themselves to insult and trample upon the truth that was oppressed. One of these writers was a philosopher, who managed so very ill, that although he had the magistrate to support his arguments, his work was despised and soon neglected. " There was another," says Lactantius, meaning Hierocles, " who wrote more sharply upon the subject. He was then one of the judges, and had been the chief promoter of the bloody persecution, which the Christians suffered under the emperor Dioclesian: but not contented with crushing them by his power, he endeavoured also to destroy them with his pen. For he composed two small books, not indeed professedly against the Christians, lest he should seem to inveigh against them as an enemy; but addressed to the Christians, that he might be thought to advise them kindly as a friend [u]." Though Lactantius has not mentioned the name of Hierocles in this passage, yet it may be put past all doubt, that he meant him: for speaking of this author a little further, he says, " Ausus est libros suos nefarios, ac Dei hostes φιλαληθεις annotare;" that is, he had the assurance to intitle his abominable and impious books, LOVERS OF TRUTH. Now Eusebius wrote a book, which is still extant, against these two books of Hierocles, and, together with his name, has produced their title at full length; Λογοι φιλαληθεις προς Χριςιανας [x], i. e. " Sermones veri amantes ad Christianos;" which circumstance, joined to the account given by both Eusebius and Lactantius of these Λογοι φιλαληθεις, proves beyond all reply, that the writer Lactantius spoke of, was no other than Hierocles.

In these books Hierocles, as we learn from the writings of these fathers, and from the fragments preserved of him by Eusebius, endeavoured to prove, that the Holy Scripture is false, by shewing it to be inconsistent with itself. He insisted upon

[u] Instit. Divin. l. v. c. 2.
[x] Euseb. Dem. Evang. p. 111, 112.

some points, which seemed to him to contradict each other; and he collected so many peculiarities relating to Christianity, that, as Lactantius says, he may well appear to have been a Christian himself. He abused Peter and Paul, and the other disciples, as though they had been the contrivers of the cheat; and yet he confessed at the same time, that they wanted skill and learning, for that some of them gained their livelihood by fishing. He asserted also, that Christ himself being banished by the Jews, assembled 900 men, at the head of whom he robbed and plundered the country: and to evade the consequence of Christ's miracles, which he did not deny, but imputed to magic, he pretended to prove, that Apollonius had performed such or even greater wonders. Eusebius undertook, in his book against Hierocles, to confute the latter part of this work; but, as Cave says [y], "he has done it very indifferently, his confutation being little more than a bare running over of Philostratus's Life of Apollonius." Lactantius did not design to make a particular answer to Hierocles; for he is so far from following him closely, that he never answers directly any objection transcribed from his books. His design was, to establish the foundations of the gospel, and to ruin those of Paganism; and he thought, as he tells us, that this would be answering at once all that the adversaries of Christianity had published, or would publish for the future.

It is reported by Eusebius, that the martyr Ædesius, transported with an holy zeal, ventured to approach Hierocles, while he was presiding at the trial of some Christians of Alexandria, and to give him a box on the ear; upbraiding him at the same time with his infamous cruelty. The remains of Hierocles were collected into one vol. 8vo, by bishop Pearson, and published at London in 1654, with a learned dissertation upon him and his writings prefixed.

HIEROCLES, a Platonic philosopher of the fifth century, taught at Alexandria with great reputation, and was admired for the strength of his mind, and the beauty and nobleness of his expressions. He wrote seven books upon Providence and Fate, and dedicated them to the philosopher Olympiodorus, who by his embassies did the Romans great services, under the emperors Honorius and Theodosius the younger. These books however are lost; and all we know of them is by the extracts, which are to be met with in Photius. This philosopher married only with a design to have children, as did also his disciple Theosebius; which shews us, that the most celebrated Platonic philosophers were persuaded, that these were the true rules and real bounds of matrimony; and that all beyond these limits was a disorder, or at least a licentiousness, in which wise men ought not to in-

[y] Hist. Litter. Tom. I. p. 344. Edit. 1740.

H 3 dulge

dulge themfelves. Thus Theofebius, finding that his wife was barren, made a ring of chaftity, and gave it her. "Formerly," faid he to her, "I made you a prefent of a ring of generation; but now I give you a ring which will help you to lead a conti- nent life. You may continue with me if you pleafe, and if you can contain yourfelf; but if you do not like this condition, you may marry another man. I confent to it; and the only favour I beg of you is, that we may part friends." This Pho- tius relates, who tells us alfo, that fhe accepted the offer; but whether the former or latter offer, we know not. Hierocles wrote alfo "A Commentary upon the Golden Verfes of Py- thagoras," which is ftill extant, and has feveral times been pub- lifhed with thofe verfes.

HIERONYMUS, or as he is commonly called, Jerom [z], a very celebrated father of the church, was born of Chriftian parents at Strido, a town fituated upon the confines of Pannonia and Dalmatia, about 329. His father Eufebius, who was a man of rank and fubftance, took the greateft care of his edu- cation; and, after grounding him well in the language of his own country, fent him to Rome, where he was placed under the beft mafters in every branch of literature. Donatus, well known for his "Commentaries upon Virgil and Terence," was his mafter in grammar, as Jerom himfelf tells us [A]: and under this mafter he made a prodigious progrefs in every thing relating to the belles lettres. He had alfo mafters in rhetoric, Hebrew, and in divinity, who conducted him through all parts of learn- ing, facred and profane; through hiftory, antiquity, the know- ledge of languages, and of the difcipline and doctrines of the various fects in philofophy; fo that he might fay of himfelf, as he afterwards did, with fome reafon, "Ego philofophus, rhetor, grammaticus, dialecticus, Hebræus, Græcus, Latinus, &c." He was particularly careful to accomplifh himfelf in rhetoric, or the art of fpeaking, becaufe, as Erafmus fays [B], he had obferved, that the generality of Chriftians were defpifed as a rude illiterate fet of people; on which account he thought, that the unconverted part of the world would fooner be drawn over to Chriftianity, if it were but fet off and enforced in a manner fuitable to the dignity and majefty of it: "Sperans futurum," fays Erafmus, "ut plures facris literis delectarentur, fi quis theologiæ majeftatem dignitate fermonis æquaffet." But though he was fo converfant with profane learning in his youth, he renounced it entirely afterwards, and did all he could to make others renounce it alfo; for he relates a vifion, which

[z] Cave's Hift. Liter. Vol. L. p. 267. Oxon. 1740.
[A] Apolog. 1. adv. Ruff.
[B] Hieronymi Vita ab Erafmo præfix. operib. Bafil. 1526.

he

he pretended was given to him, " in which he was dragged to the tribunal of Chrift, and terribly threatened, and even fcourged, for the grievous fin of reading fecular and profane writers, Cicero, Virgil, and Horace, whom for that reafon he refolved never to take into his hands any more." If Jerom, as an Italian Ciceronian facetioufly obferved upon this paffage, was whipped for being a Ciceronian, that is, for writing altogether in the ftyle and manner of Cicero, he fuffered what he did not deferve, and might have pleaded Not guilty: in the mean time, as a certain author remarks [c]. Jerom " was a very good writer for the time in which he lived;" and we may add, would not in any time have been reckoned a bad one.

When he had finifhed his education at Rome, and reaped all the fruits which books and good mafters could afford, he refolved, for his further improvement, to travel. He had a mind, fays Erafmus, to imitate Pythagoras, Plato, Apollonius, and other great men, who vifited foreign countries for the fake of enlarging and perfecting that knowledge abroad, which they had acquired by ftudy and application at home. After being baptized therefore at Rome, when an adult, he made the tour of Gaul ; and ftayed a long time in every city through which he paffed, that he might have opportunity and leifure to examine the public libraries, and to vifit the men of letters, with which that country then abounded. He ftaid fo long at Treveris, that he tranfcribed with his own hand a large volume of Hilary's concerning Synods, which fome time after he ordered to be fent to him in the deferts of Syria. From hence he went to Aquileia, where he became firft acquainted with Ruffinus, who was a prefbyter in that town, and with whom he contracted an intimate friendfhip. When he had travelled as long as he thought expedient, and feen every thing that was curious and worth his notice, he returned to Rome ; where he began to deliberate with himfelf, what courfe of life he fhould take. Study and retirement were what he moft defired, and he had collected an excellent library of books; but Rome, he thought, would not be a proper place to refide in: it was not only too noify and tumultuous for him, but as yet had too much of the old leaven of Paganifm in it. He had objections likewife againft his own country, Dalmatia, whofe inhabitants he reprefents, in one of his epiftles, as entirely funk in fenfuality and luxury, regardlefs of every thing that was good and praife-worthy, and gradually approaching to a ftate of barbarifm : " in mea patria rufticitatis vernacula," fays he, " deus venter eft, & in diem vivitur; & fanctior eft ille, qui ditior eft." After a confultation therefore with his friends, he determined to retire into fome very remote region ; and therefore leaving his country, parents, substance, and taking nothing with him but his books, and as much money as would be sufficient for his journey, he set off from Italy for the Eastern parts of the world. Having passed through Dalmatia, Thrace, and some provinces of Asia Minor, his first care was to pay a visit to Jerusalem; for in those days such a journey was considered as a necessary act of religion, and incumbent upon all who were in a condition to take it; and a man would have had but a low reputation for piety, who had not visited the holy ground, and adored the blessed footsteps of his Saviour. From Jerusalem he went to Antioch, where he fell into a danger-ous fit of illness; but having the good fortune to recover from it, he left Antioch, and set forward in quest of some more retired habitation; and after rambling over several cities and countries, with all which he was dissatisfied on account of the customs and manners of the people, he settled at last in a most frightful desert of Syria, which was scarcely inhabited by any thing but wild beasts. This however was no objection to Jerom: it was rather a recommendation of the place to him; for, says Erasmus, " he thought it better to cohabit with wild beasts and wild men, than with such sort of Christians as were usually found in great cities; men half Pagan, half Christian; Christians in nothing more than in name."

He was in his 31st year, when he entered upon this monastic course of life; and he carried it, by his own practice, to that height of perfection, which he ever after enforced upon others so zealously by precept. He divided all his time between devo-tion and study: he exercised himself much in watchings and fastings; slept little, eat less, and hardly allowed himself any recreation. He applied himself very severely to the study of the Holy Scriptures, which he is said to have gotten by heart; as well as to the study of the Oriental languages, which he consi-dered as the only keys that could let him into their true sense and meaning. After he had spent four years in this dreadful situ-ation, and laborious way of life, his health grew so impaired, that he was obliged to return to Antioch: where the church at that time was divided by factions, Meletius, Paulinus, and Vi-talis all claiming a right to the bishopric of that place. Jerom being a son of the church of Rome, where he was baptized, would not espouse any party, till he knew the sense of his own church upon this contested right. Accordingly, he wrote to Damasus, then bishop of Rome, to know whom he must con-sider as the lawful bishop of Antioch; and upon Damasus's naming Paulinus, Jerom acknowledged him as such, and was ordained a priest by him in 378.

From this time his reputation for piety and learning began to spread abroad, and be known in the world. He went soon after
to

to Conftantinople, where he fpent a good deal of time with Gregory Nazianzen; whom he did not difdain to call his mafter, and owned, that of him he learned the right method of expounding the Holy Scriptures. Afterwards, in 382, he went to Rome with Paulinus, bifhop of Antioch, and Epiphanius, bifhop of Salamis in the ifle of Cyprus; where he foon became known to Damafus, and was made his fecretary. He acquitted himfelf in this poft very well, and yet found time to compofe feveral works. Upon the death of Damafus, which happened in 385, he began to entertain thoughts of travelling again to the Eaft; to which he was moved chiefly by the difturbances and vexations he met with from the Origenifts, or followers of Origen, at Rome. For thefe, when they had in vain endeavoured, fays Cave, to draw him over to their party, raifed infamous reports and calumnies againft him. They charged him, among other things, with a criminal paffion for one Paula, an eminent matron, in whofe houfe he had lodged during his refidence at Rome, and who was as illuftrious for her piety as for the fplendor of her birth, and the dignity of her rank. For thefe and other reafons he was determined to quit Rome, and accordingly embarked for the Eaft in Auguft 385, attended by a great number of monks and ladies, whom he had perfuaded to embrace the afcetic way of life. He failed to Cyprus, where he paid a vifit to Epiphanius; and arrived afterwards at Antioch, where he was kindly received by his friend Paulinus. From Antioch he went to Jerufalem; and the year following from Jerufalem into Egypt. Here he vifited feveral monafteries: but finding to his great grief the monks every where infatuated with the errors of Origen, he returned to Bethlehem, a town near Jerufalem, that he might be at liberty to cherifh and propagate his own opinions, without any difturbance or interruption from abroad [D].

[D] This whole peregrination is particularly related by himfelf, in one of his pieces againft Ruffinus; and, as it is very charaƈterifƈic, and fhews much of his fpirit and manner of writing, we think it may not be difagreeable to the reader to fee it in his own language. " Vis noffe profeƈtidais meæ de urbe ordinem? Narrabo breviter. Menfe Augufto, flantibus Erefiis, cum fanƈto Vincentio prefbytero, et adolefcente fratre, & aliis monachis, qui nunc Hierofolymæ continuantur, navim in Romano portu fecurus afcendi, maxima me fanƈtorum frequentia profequente. Veni Rhegium: in Scyllæo latore paululum fteti; ubi veteres didici fabulas, & præcipitem fallacis Ulixis curfum, & Syrenarum cantica, & infatiabilem Charybdis voraginem. Camque mihi accolæ illius loci multa narrarent, darentque confilium, ut non ad Protei columnas, fed ad Ionæ portum navigarem; hunc enim fugientium & perbantorum, illum fecuri hominis effe curfum, malui per Malæas & Cycladas Cyprum pergere, ubi fufceptus à venerabili Epifcopo Epiphanio, cujus tu teftimonio gloriaris. veni Antiochium, ubi fruitus fum communione pontificis confeffurifque Paulini; & deduƈtus ab eo, med'a hieme & frigore gravidium, intravi Hierofolymam. Vidi multa miracula; & quæ prius ad me fama pertulerat, oculorum indicio comprobavi. Inde contendi Ægyptum: luftravi monafteria Nitriæ; & inter fanƈtorum choros afrides latere perfpexi. Protinus concito gradu Bethlehem meam reverfus fum, ubi adoravi præfepe & incunabula Salvatoris, &c." Apud. 3. Adv. Ruffinum.

He

He had now fixed upon Bethlehem, as the propereſt place of abode for him, and beſt accommodated to that courſe of life which he intended to purſue; and was no ſooner arrived here, than he met with Paula, and other ladies of quality, who had followed him from Rome, with the ſame view of devoting themſelves to a monaſtic life. His fame for learning and piety was indeed ſo very extenſive, that numbers of both ſexes flocked from all parts and diſtances, to be trained up under him, and to form their manner of living according to his inſtructions. This moved the pious Paula to found four monaſteries; three for the uſe of females, over which ſhe herſelf preſided, and one for males, which was committed to Jerom. Here he enjoyed all that repoſe which he had long deſired; and he laboured abundantly, as well for the ſouls committed to his care, as in compoſing great and uſeful works. He had enjoyed this repoſe probably to the end of his life, if Origeniſm had not prevailed ſo mightily in thoſe parts: but, as Jerom had an abhorrence for every thing that looked like hereſy, it was impoſſible for him to continue paſſive, while theſe aſps, as he calls them above, were inſinuating their deadly poiſon into all who had the misfortune to fall in their way. This engaged him in terrible wars with John, biſhop of Jeruſalem, and Ruffinus of Aquileia, which laſted many years. Ruffinus and Jerom had of old been intimate friends; but Ruffinus having of late years ſettled in the neighbourhood of Jeruſalem, and eſpouſed the part of the Origeniſts, the enmity between them was on that account the more bitter. Jerom had alſo ſeveral other quarrels upon his hands; for as hereſy was to receive no quarter from this ſaint, ſo his righteous ſoul was perpetually vexed from one quarter or another. In 410, when Rome was beſieged by the Goths, many fled from thence to Jeruſalem and the Holy Land, and were kindly received by Jerom into his monaſtery. He died in 420, which was the 91ſt year of his age; and is ſaid to have preſerved his vivacity and vigour to the laſt.

Eraſmus, who wrote his life, and gave the firſt edition of his works in 1526, ſays, that he was "undoubtedly the greateſt ſcholar, the greateſt orator, and the greateſt divine, that Chriſtianity had then produced [ε]." Suppoſing this true, as perhaps it is, may we not wonder at Eraſmus for his partiality to Jerom, and his prejudices againſt Origen? Origen, ſays Jortin [ɤ], "was very learned and ingenious, and indefatigably induſtrious: his whole life from his early years was ſpent in examining, teaching, and explaining the Scriptures, to which he joined the ſtudy of philoſophy and polite literature." So much, would Eraſmus reply, may be fairly ſaid of Jerom. But Origen "was humble, modeſt,

[ε] Eraſm. Epiſt. L u. 19. [ɤ] Remarks on Eccleſ. Hiſt. Vol. II. p. 334.

and

and patient under great injuries and cruel treatment," which
cannot be so fairly said of Jerom; who, it is well known,
was of a temper just the reverse of this. Jerom, says a late
noble author [G], was " an impudent and scurrilous Hunga-
rian, and wrote against his adversaries with all the ferocity
of a modern huslar ;" which, though the language of an
enemy, is not advanced altogether without reason ; for let us
only hear what a friend would say. Cave, in particular, never
yet was charged with want of justice to the fathers, and therefore may reasonably be supposed to speak the truth, when the
account is disadvantageous to the party concerned. Jerom,
says this historian of the ecclesiastical writers [H], " was, with
Erasmus's leave, a hot and furious man, who had no command
at all over his passions. When he was once provoked, he
treated his adversaries in the roughest manner, and did not even
abstain from invective and satire: witness what he has written
against Ruffinus, who was formerly his friend; against John,
bishop of Jerusalem, Jovinian, Vigilantius, and others. Upon
the slightest provocation, he grew excessively abusive, and threw
out all the ill language he could rake together, *tota convitiorum
plustra evomit*, without the least regard to the situation, rank,
learning, and other circumstances, of the persons he had to
do with. And what wonder," says Cave, " when it is common
with him to treat even St. Paul himself in very harsh and insolent terms? charging him, as he does, with solecisms in language, false expressions, and a vulgar use of words?" We do
not quote this with any view of detracting from the real merit
of Jerom, but only to note the partiality of Erasmus, in defending, as he does very strenuously, this most exceptionable
part of his character, his want of candour and spirit of
persecution; to which Erasmus himself was so averse, that he
has ever been highly praised by protestants, and as highly dis-
praised by papists, for placing all his glory in moderation.

Jerom was as exceptionable in many parts of his literary character, as he was in his moral, whatever Erasmus or his pane-
gyrists may have said to the contrary: instead of an orator, he
was rather a declaimer; and, though he undertook to translate
so many things out of Greek and Hebrew, he was not accurately skilled in either of those languages ; and did not reason
clearly, consistently, and precisely, upon any subject. This
has been shewn in part already by Le Clerc, in a book entitled,
" Quæstiones Hieronymianæ," printed at Amsterdam in 1700,
by way of critique upon the Benedictine edition of his works.
In the mean time we are ready to acknowledge, that the writ-

[G] Bolingbroke's Philosophical Works, Essay iv. Sect. 41.
[H] Hist. Liter. Tom. I. p. 268.

ings of Jerom are useful, and deserve to be read by all who have
any regard for sacred antiquity. They have many uses in common with other writings of ecclesiastical authors, and many peculiar to themselves. The writings of Jerom teach us the doctrines,
the rites, the manners, and the learning of the age in which he
lived; and these also we learn from the writings of other fathers.
But the peculiar use of Jerom's works is, 1. Their exhibiting to
us more fragments of the ancient Greek translators of the Bible,
than the works of any other father; 2. Their informing us of
the opinions which the Jews of that age had of the signification
of many Hebrew words, and of the sense and meaning they
put upon many passages in the Old Testament; and, 3. Their
conveying to us the opinion of Jerom himself; who, though he
must always be read with caution, on account of his declamatory
and hyperbolical style, and the liberties he allowed himself of
feigning and prevaricating upon certain occasions, will perhaps,
upon the whole, be found to have had more judgement as well
as more learning than any father who went before him.

There have been several editions of his works; the first, as
we have observed above, by Erasmus at Basil in 1526, which,
we may add, was dedicated to Warham, archbishop of Canterbury; the last at Paris in 1693, by a Benedictine monk, whom
Le Clerc, in the book above-mentioned, has shewn not to have
been perfectly qualified for the work he undertook, though his
edition is reckoned the best that has been given.

HIFFERMAN (PAUL), a minor author of the present century, much patronized and befriended by Garrick, was born in
the county of Dublin in 1719, and educated for a popish priest,
first in Ireland, and afterwards, for many years, in France. Yet
after all, he took his degree of batchelor in physic, and returned
to Dublin that he might practise in that line. Indolence, however, prevented his application to that or any profession, and he
came to London about 1753, where he subsisted very scantily and
idly, as an author, for the remainder of his life; producing several works, but none of any great merit, and living in a mean
manner, chiefly by the contributions of his friends, and by various
not very honourable expedients. He was a tolerable scholar,
but his character was singular and eccentric, and though several
were entertained by his oddities, none could give him their
esteem. He lived, however, with some of the most celebrated
men of his time, Foote, Garrick, Murphy, Goldsmith, Kelly,
Bickerstaff, who tolerated his faults, and occasionally supplied
his necessities. One of his peculiar fancies was to keep the
place of his lodging a secret, which he did so completely, that he
refused to disclose it even when dying, to a friend who supported
him, and actually received his last contributions through the
channel of the Bedford coffee-house. When he died, which

was

was in June, 1777, it was difcovered that he had lodged in one of the obfcure courts near St. Martin's-lane. Dr. Hifferman, as he was ufually called, was author of the following works. 1. "The Ticklers," a fet of periodical and political papers, publifhed in Dublin about 1750. 2. "The Tuner," a fet of periodical papers, publifhed in London in 1753. 3. "Mifcellanies in profe and verfe," 1754. 4. "The Ladies Choice," a dramatic *petite piece*, acted at Covent-garden in 1759. 5. "The Wifhes of a free People," a dramatic poem, 1761. 6. "The New Hippocrates," a farce, acted at Drury-lane in 1761, but not publifhed. 7. "The Earl of Warwick," a tragedy, from the French of La Harpe, 1764. 8. "Dramatic Genius," an effay, in five books, 1770. 9. "The Philofophic Whim," a farce, 1774. 10. "The Heroine of the Cave," a tragedy, left unfinifhed by Henry Jones, author of the "Earl of Effex," completed by Hifferman, and acted at Drury-lane in 1774.

HIGDEN (RALPH), one of our early chroniclers, who died in 1363, was the author of a work, often confulted by Englifh hiftorians, called the "Polychronicon." The exact title of it is, "Radulphi Higdeni polychronici libri VII. ex Anglico in Latinum converfi, a Johanne Trevifa, et editi cura Gulielmi Caxtoni." The beft edition is a folio, printed in 1642. It is chiefly a compilation, and extends from Adam to the year 1357. The part that is entirely original, is only in the laft book; but the whole is formed with fuch judgment, that it is refpected, and often cited as an original work.

HIGGINS, or HIGINS (JOHN), one of the principal writers in the fourth edition of that early collection of poetical narratives, "The Mirror for Magiftrates:" and a man, as it appears from his fhare in that work, of confiderable talents in poetry, for his time. Higgins lived at Winfham in Somerfetfhire [1], was a clergyman, educated at Oxford, and was engaged in the inftruction of youth. He compiled, 1. The "Flofculi of Terence," on the plan of a former collection by Udal, mafter of Eton. 2. He publifhed alfo, "Holcot's Dictionaire, newly corrected, amended, fet in order, and enlarged, with many names of men, townes, beaftes, fowles, &c. by which you may find the Latine or French name of any Englifhe worde you will. By John Higgins, late Student in Oxforde." Printed for Marfhe, in folio, 1572. 3. "The Nomenclator of Adrian Junius," tranflated into Englifh, in conjunction with Abraham Fleming, and publifhed at London for Newberie and Durham, in 1585, in 8vo. From the dedication to this book he feems to have been connected with the fchool of Ilminfter, a neighbouring town in Somerfetfhire. He appears to have been living fo late

[1] Warton's Hiftory of Poetry, Vol. III. chap. 32.

as the year 1602; for in that year he publiſhed, 4. An anſwer to a work of controverſy by one William Perkins, concerning Chriſt's deſcent to Hell, which was dated at Winſham. The former editions of the "Mirror for Magiſtrates," were publiſhed in 1563, 1571, and 1574. His edition appeared in 1587. The dedication is dated a year earlier. In this he wrote a new induction in the octave ſtanza, and without aſſiſtance from friends began a new ſeries of hiſtories, from Albanact the youngeſt ſon of Brutus, and the firſt king of Albanie, or Scotland, to the emperor Caracalla. There were alſo a few additions by other writers, in the poems relating to Britiſh perſonages after the Conqueſt.

HIGGONS (Sir THOMAS), ſon of Dr. Thomas Higgons, ſome time rector of Weſtburgh in Shropſhire [κ], was born in that county; became a commoner of St. Alban's-hall in the beginning of 1638, at the age of 14; when he was put under the tuition of Mr. Edward Corbet, fellow of Merton-college, and lodged in the chamber under him in that houſe. Leaving the univerſity without a degree, he retired to his native country. He married the widow of Robert earl of Eſſex; and delivered an oration at her funeral, Sept. 16, 1656. "Oratione funebri, à marito ipſo, more priſco laudata ſuit," is part of this lady's epitaph. He married, ſecondly, Bridget daughter of Sir Bevil Greenvill of Stow, and ſiſter to John earl of Bath; and removed to Grewell in Hampſhire; was elected a burgeſs for Malmſbury in 1658, and for New Windſor in 1661. His ſervices to the crown were rewarded with a penſion of 500l. a year, and gifts to the amount of 4000l. [L]. He was afterwards knighted; and in 1669, was ſent envoy extraordinary to inveſt John George

[κ] Nichol's Select Collection of Poems, Vol. V. p. 42.
[L] "King Charles II. ſold Dunkirk to Louis XIV. and gave him Engliſh oak enough to build the very fleet that afterwards attacked and defeated one of ours, in Bantry Bay on the couſt of Ireland. This puts me in mind of the foreſight of a gentleman, who had been ſome time envoy from the king to the princes and ſtates of Italy, and who, in his return home, made the coaſt of France his road; in order to be as uſeful to his country as poſſible, and to his ſovereign too, as he thought. In his audience of the king, he told his majeſty, that the French were hard at work, building men of war in ſeveral of their ports, and that ſuch a haſty increaſe of the naval power of France could not but threaten England's ſovereignty of the ſeas, and conſequently portend deſtruction to her trade. The gentleman

was in the right, for our trade and ſovereignty of the ſeas are dependent on each other; they muſt live or die together. But what a compliance do you think he met with for his fidelity! really ſuch a one as I would hardly have believed, had I been told of it by any perſon but his own ſon, the late Mr. Bevil Higgons, whoſe works, both in proſe and verſe, have made him known to all the men of letters in Britain, and whoſe attachment to the family of Stuart, even to his dying day, puts his veracity in this point out of diſpute. The recompenſe was a ſevere reprimand from the king, as the forerunner to the laying him aſide, for talking of things which his majeſty told him it was not his buſineſs to meddle with." I forget (ſays Mr. Nichols) from which of the political writers between 1730 and 1740 this anecdote was tranſcribed; moſt probably "The Craftſman."

duke of Saxony with the order of the Garter. About four years after, he was fent envoy to Vienna, where he continued three years. In 1685 he was elected burgefs for St. Germain's, " being then," fays Wood, " accounted a loyal and accomplished perfon, and a great lover of the regular clergy." He died fuddenly, of an apoplexy, in the King's-bench court, having been fummoned there as a witnefs, Nov. 24, 1691; and was buried in Winchefter cathedral near the relics of his firft wife. His literary productions are, 1. " A Panegyric to the King, 1660," folio. 2. " The Funeral Oration on his firft Lady, 1656." 3. " The Hiftory of Ifoof Bafla, 1684." He alfo tranflated into Englifh, " The Venetian Triumph;" for which he was complimented by Waller, in his Poems; who has alfo addreffed a poem to Mrs. Higgons. Mr. Granger, who ftiles Sir Thomas " a gentleman of great merit," was favoured by the dutchefs dowager of Portland with a MS. copy of his Oration; and concludes, from the great fcarcity of that pamphlet, that " the copies of it were, for certain reafons, induftriously collected and deftroyed, though few pieces of this kind have lefs deferved to perifh. The countefs of Effex had a greatnefs of mind which enabled her to bear the whole weight of infamy which was thrown upon her; but it was, neverthelefs, attended with a delicacy and fenfibility of honour which poifoned all her enjoyments. Mr. Higgons had faid much, and I think much to the purpofe, in her vindication; and was himfelf fully convinced from the tenor of her life, and the words which fhe fpoke at the awful clofe of it, that fhe was perfectly innocent.—In reading this interefting oration, I fancied myfelf ftanding by the grave of injured innocence and beauty; was fenfibly touched with the pious affection of the tendereft and beft of hufbands doing public and folemn juftice to an amiable and worthy woman, who had been grofsly and publicly defamed. Nor could I withhold the tribute of a tear; a tribute which, I am confident, was paid at her interment by every one who loved virtue, and was not deftitute of the feelings of humanity. This is what I immediately wrote upon reading the oration. If I am wrong in my opinion, the benevolent reader, I am fure, will forgive me. It is not the firft time that my heart has got the better of my judgement." " I am not afraid," Mr. Nichols adds, " of being cenfured for having tranfcribed this beautiful paffage."

HIGGONS (BEVIL), younger fon of Sir Thomas [M], (and firft coufin to the late earl of Granville) by Bridget his fecond wife; at the age of fixteen, became a commoner of St. John's-college, Oxford, in Lent term 1686; and went afterwards to Cambridge, and then to the Middle Temple. Wood enume-

[M] Nichols's Select Collection of Poems, Vol. I. p. 128.

rates five of his poems. He wrote some others; and was the author of a tragedy, entitled, "The Generous Conqueror, or the Timely Discovery," acted at Drury-lane, and printed in 4to, 1702 [N]. He was a steady adherent to the cause of the exiled family; and accompanied king James into France, where he maintained his wit and good-humour undepressed by his misfortunes. He published a poem " on the Peace of Utrecht." On the publication of bishop Burnet's " History of his own Times," he wrote some strictures on it, in a volume entitled, " Historical and Critical Remarks;" the second edition of which was printed in 8vo, 1727; and, in the same year, published " A short View of the English History with Reflections, political, historical, civil, physical, and moral; on the Reigns of the Kings; their Characters, and Manners; their Successions to the Throne, and other remarkable Incidents to the Revolution 1688. Drawn from authentic Memoirs and MSS." " These papers," he tells us in his preface, " lay covered with dust 36 years, till every person concerned in the transactions mentioned were removed from the stage."

HIGHMORE (JOSEPH), an eminent painter [O], was born in the parish of St. James, Garlickhithe, London, June 13, 1692, being the third son of Mr. Edward Highmore [R], a coal-merchant in Thames-street. Having such an early and strong inclination to painting, that he could think of nothing else with pleasure, his father endeavoured to gratify him in a proposal to his uncle, who was serjeant-painter to king William, and with whom Mr. (afterward Sir James) Thornhill [Q] had served his apprenticeship. But this was afterwards for good reasons declined, and he was articled as clerk to an attorney, July 18, 1707; but so much against his own declared inclination, that in about three years he began to form resolutions of indulging his natural disposition to his favourite art, having continually employed his leisure hours in designing, and in the study of geometry, perspective, architecture, and anatomy, but without any instructors except books. He had afterwards an opportunity of improving himself in anatomy, by attending the lectures of Mr. Cheselden, besides entering himself at the Painter's Academy in Great Queen-street, where he drew ten years, and had the honour to be particularly noticed by sir Godfrey Kneller, who distinguished him by the name of " the Young Lawyer." On June 13, 1714,

[N] See the prologue to this tragedy in lord Lansdowne's Poems, p. 220.

[O] Gen. Mag. 1-80, p. 176.

[P] His grandfather, Abraham, who was first cousin to Nathaniel, the celebrated physician, being a lieutenant-colonel in the royal service, had, in return for his losses, an honourable augmentation to his arms, as mentioned in the Gentleman's Magazine for 1772," p. 449.

[Q] The Highmores and Thornhills were connected by marriage; Edward, the uncle of sir James, marrying Susanna, the daughter of Nathaniel Highmore, rector of Purse Candell, Dorsetshire, sister to the physician.

2

his

his clerkſhip expired; and on March 26, 1715, he began painting as a profeſſion, and ſettled in the city. In the ſame year
Dr. Brook Taylor publiſhed his " Linear Perſpective: or, a
new Method of repreſenting juſtly all Manner of Objects as
they appear to the Eye, in all Situations." On this complete
and univerſal theory our artiſt grounded his ſubſequent practice;
and it has been generally allowed, that few, if any, of the profeſſion at that time, were ſo thoroughly maſters of that excellent,
but intricate ſyſtem. In 1716, he married Miſs Suſanna Hiller,
daughter and heireſs of Mr. Anthony Hiller, of Effingham in
Surrev; a young lady in every reſpect worthy of his choice.
For Mr. Cheſelden's Anatomy of the Human Body, publiſhed
in 1722, he made drawings from the real ſubjects at the time of
diſſection, two of which were engraved for that work, and appear, but without his name, in tables xii. and xiii. In the
ſame year, on the exhibition of " The Conſcious Lovers,"
written by Sir Richard Steele, Mr. Highmore addreſſed a letter
to the author, on the limits of filial obedience, pointing out a
material defect in the character of Bevil, with that clearneſs and
preciſion for which, in converſation and writing, he was always
remarkable, as the pencil by no means engroſſed his whole attention [r]. His reputation and buſineſs increaſing, he took
a more conſpicuous ſtation, by removing to a houſe in Lincoln's-
Inn-fields, in March 1723-4; and an opportunity ſoon offered
of introducing him advantageouſly to the nobility, &c. from his
being deſired, by Mr. Pine the engraver, to make the drawings
for his prints of the Knights of the Bath, on the revival of that
order, in 1725. In conſequence of this, ſeveral of the Knights
had their portraits alſo by the ſame hand, ſome of them whole
lengths; and the duke of Richmond, in particular, was attended
by his three eſquires, with a perſpective view of king Henry
the VIIth's chapel. This capital picture is now at Godwood.
The artiſt was alſo ſent for to St. James's, by George I. to paint
the portrait of the late duke of Cumberland, from which Smith
ſcraped a mezzotinto.

In 1728, Mr. Hawkins Browne, then of Lincoln's-Inn, who had
always a juſt ſenſe of Highmore's talents and abilities, addreſſed to
him a poetical epiſtle " On Deſign and Beauty;" and, ſome years
after, an elegant Latin Ode, both now collected in his poems
[s]. In the ſummer of 1732, Mr. Highmore viſited the continent, in company with Dr. Pemberton, Mr. Benj. Robins,
and two other friends, chiefly with a view of ſeeing the gallery
of pictures belonging to the elector Palatine at Duſſeldorp, col-

[a] This he allowed to be publiſhed,   [s] See the Letter, with a tranſlation, in
for the firſt time, in the " Gentleman's   the " Gentleman's Magazine for 1768,"
Magazine for 1768," p. 404.   p. 392.

lected by Rubens, and supposed to be the best in Europe. At Antwerp also he had peculiar pleasure in contemplating the works of his favourite master. In their return they visited the principal towns in Holland. In 1734, he made a like excursion, but alone, to Paris, where he received great civilities from some of his countrymen, particularly the duke of Kingston, Dr. Hickman (his tutor), Robert Knight, esq; (the late cashier), &c. Here he had the satisfaction of being shewn, by cardinal de Polignac, his famous group of antique statues, the court of Lycomedes, then just brought from Rome, and since purchased by the king of Prussia, and destroyed at Charlottenbourg, in 1760, by the Russians. In 1742. he had the honour to paint the late prince and princess of Wales, for the duke of Saxe Gotha; as he did some years after, the late queen of Denmark, for that court. The publication of Pamela, in 1744, gave rise to a set of paintings by Mr. Highmore, which were engraved by two French engravers, and published by subscription, in 1745. In the same year he painted the only original of the late General Wolfe, then about 18. His Pamela introduced him to the acquaintance and friendship of the excellent author, whose picture he drew, and for whom he painted the only original of Dr. Young. In 1750 he had the great misfortune to lose his excellent wife. On the first institution of the Academy of Painting, Sculpture, &c. in 1753, he was elected one of the professors; an honour, which, on account of his many avocations, he desired to decline. In 1754 he published, " A critical Examination of those two Paintings [by Rubens] on the cieling of the Banqueting-house at Whitehall, in which Architecture is introduced, so far as relates to Perspective; together with the Discussion of a Question which has been the Subject of Debate among Painters:" printed in 4to, for Nourse. In the solution of this question, he proved that Rubens, and several other great painters, were mistaken in the practice, and Mr. Kirby, and several other authors, in the theory and practice: and in the eighteenth volume of the " Monthly Review," he animadverted (anonymously) on Mr. Kirby's unwarrantable treatment of Mr. Ware, and detected and exposed his errors, even where he exults in his own superior science. Of the many portraits which Mr. Highmore painted, in an extensive practice of 46 years, (of which several have been engraved) it is impossible and useless to discuss particulars. Some of the most capital in the historical branch, which was then much less cultivated than it is at present, shall only be mentioned, viz. " Hagar and Ishmael," a present to the Foundling-hospital: " The Good Samaritan," painted for Mr. Shepherd of Campsey Ash: " The finding of Moses," purchased at his sale by colonel (now general) Lister: " The Harlowe Family," as described in " Clarissa," now in the possession

feſſion of Thomas Watkinſon Payler, eſq; at Heden in Kent:
" Clariſſa," the portrait mentioned in that work: " The Graces
unveiling Nature," drawn by memory from Rubens: " The
Clementina of Grandiſon," and " the Queen-mother of Edward
IV. with her younger Son, &c. in Weſtminſter-abbey :" the
three laſt in the poſſeſſion of his ſon.

In 1761, on the marriage of his daughter to the Rev. Mr.
Duncombe, ſon to one of his oldeſt friends, he took a reſolution
of retiring from buſineſs, and diſpoſing of his collection of pictures, which he did by auction, in March, 1762; and ſoon after
removed to the houſe of his ſon-in-law at Canterbury, where he
paſſed the remainder of his life, without ever reviſiting the metropolis. But though he had laid down the pencil, he never wanted
employment: ſo active and vigorous was his mind, that, with a
conſtitutional flow of ſpirits, and a reliſh for inſtructive ſociety,
he was " never leſs alone than when alone ;" and, beſides his
profeſſional purſuits (abovementioned), to philoſophy, both natural and moral, and alſo divinity, he laudably dedicated his
time and attention. No man had more clearneſs and preciſion
of ideas, or a more ardent deſire to know the truth ; and, when
known, conſcientiouſly to purſue it. With ſtrong paſſions,
ever guided by the ſtricteſt virtue, he had a tender, ſuſceptible
heart, always open to the diſtreſſes of his fellow-creatures, and
always ready to relieve them. His capital work of the literary
kind was his " Practice of Perſpective, on the Principles of
Dr. Brook Taylor, &c." written many years before, but not
publiſhed till 1763, when it was printed for Nourſe, in one
vol. 4to. This not only evinced his ſcientific knowledge of the
ſubject, but removed, by its perſpicuity, the only objection that
can be made to the ſyſtem of Dr. Taylor. It accordingly received, from his friends and the intelligent public, the applauſes
it deſerved. In 1765, he publiſhed (without his name) " Obſervations on a Pamphlet intituled, ' Chriſtianity not founded on
Argument,' [by Dodwell];" in which, after ſhewing that it is
a continued irony, and lamenting that ſo ample a field ſhould be
offered the author of it for the diſplay of his ſophiſtry, he gives
up creeds, articles, and catechiſms, as out-works raiſed by fallible men, and, confining himſelf to the defence of the Goſpel,
or citadel, ſhews, that pure primitive Chriſtianity, though aſ-
ſaulted by infidels, will ever remain impregnable. His opinion
of Rubens may be ſeen in the Gent. Mag. for 1766, p. 353,
under the title of " Remarks on ſome Paſſages in Mr. Webb's
' Enquiry into the Beauties of Painting, &c." In the ſame
year he publiſhed, with only his initials, " J. H." two ſmall
volumes of " Eſſays, moral, religious, and miſcellaneous; with
a tranſlation in Proſe of Mr. Browne's Latin Poem on the Immortality of the Soul," ſelected from a large number written at

his leisure, at different periods of his life. " As such," says Dr. Hawkesworth [т], " they do the author great credit. They are not excursions of fancy, but efforts of thought, and indubitable indications of a vigorous and active mind." In the Gent. Mag. for 1769, p. 287, he communicated " A natural and obvious Manner of constructing Sun-dials, deduced from the Situation and Motion of the Earth with respect to the Sun," explained by a scheme; and in that for 1778, p. 526, his remarks on colouring, suggested by way of a note on the " Epistle to an eminent Painter," will shew that his talents were by no means impaired at the age of 86. He retained them, indeed, to the last, and had even strength and spirit sufficient to enable him to ride out daily on horseback, the summer before he died. A strong constitution, habitual temperance, and constant attention to his health in youth as well as in age, prolonged his life, and preserved his faculties to his 88th year, when he gradually ceased to breathe; and, as it were, fell asleep, on March 3, 1780. He was interred in the south aisle of Canterbury cathedral [v], leaving one son, Anthony, educated in his own profession ; and a daughter, Susanna, mentioned above.

His abilities as a painter appear in his works, which will not only be admired by his contemporaries, but by their posterity ; as his time, like those of Rubens and Vandyck, instead of being impaired, are improved by time, which some of them have now withstood above 60 years. His idea of beauty, when he indulged his fancy, was of the highest kind; and his knowledge of perspective gave him great advantages in family-pieces, of which he painted more than any one of his time. He could take a likeness by memory as well as by a sitting, as appears by his picture of the duke of Lorrain (the late emperor), which Faber engraved ; and those of king George II. (in York assembly-room) ; Queen Caroline, the two Miss Gunnings, &c. Like many other great painters, he had " a poet for his friend," in the late Mr. Browne; to which may be added, a poem addressed to him in 1726, by the Rev. Mr. Bunce, at that time of Trinity-hall, Cambridge, who succeeded Mr. Highmore, and in 1780, was vicar of St. Stephen's near Canterbury.

HIGHMORE (NATHANIEL), a native of Fordingbridge, in Hampshire, a celebrated anatomist, and the first in this country who wrote " a Systematical Treatise on the Structure of the Human Body." He made many discoveries in Natural History and Anatomy; the *maxillary sinus*, in particular, is called from his name, *Antrum Highmorianum*. He has left the following

[т] In his Review of them, Gent. Mag. Vol. XXXV. p. 238.
[v] " A Thought at his Grave," 195.

was printed in Gent. Mag. 1780, p. 144; and verses to him by Mr. Bunce, in p.

works, 1. " Corporis Humani difquifitio Anatomica," folio, 1651. 2. " The Hiftory of Generation." 3. " De Paffione Hyfterica," 8vo, 1660. Highmore died March 21, 1684, at the age of 71.

HILARIUS, or HILARY, an ancient father of the Chriftian church, who flourifhed in the fourth century, was born, as St. Jerom tells us, at Poicliers in France; but in what year, is not any where mentioned. His parents were of rank and fubftance, and had him liberally educated in the Pagan religion, which they themfelves profeffed, and which Hilary did not forfake till many years after he was grown up; when reflecting, as Dupin fays, upon the grofs errors of Paganifm, he was by little and little conducted to the truth, and at laft confirmed in it by reading the Holy Scriptures. After he was perfectly inftructed in the Chriftian religion, he was baptized, together with his wife and daughter, who were alfo converted with him. He was advanced to the bifhopric of Poicliers in 355, as Baronius fixes it; though Cave [x] fees no reafon why he might not be made bifhop of that place fome years before. As foon as he was raifed to this dignity, he became a moft zealous champion of the orthodox faith, and diftinguifhed himfelf particularly againft the Arians, whofe doctrines were at that time gaining ground in France. In 356, he was fent by Conftantius to fupport the party of Athanafius at the fynod of Beterra, or Beziers, againft Saturninus bifhop of Arles, who had juft before been excommunicated by the bifhops of France; but Saturninus intrigued with fo much art againft him, that he prevailed with the emperor, who was then at Milan, to order him to be banifhed. Accordingly, Hilary was banifhed to Phrygia, where he continued four years, and applied himfelf during that time to the compofing of feveral works. He wrote his twelve books upon the Trinity, which Cave calls " a noble work," and which have been fo much admired by the orthodox believers. He wrote alfo " A Treatife concerning Synods," which he addreffed to the bifhops of France; wherein he explains to them the fenfe of the Eaftern churches upon the doctrine of the Trinity, and alfo their manner of holding councils. This treatife was drawn up by Hilary, after the council of Ancyra in 358, whofe canons he fets forth in it; and before the councils of Rimini and Seleucia, which were called in the beginning of 359. Some time after he was fent to the council of Seleucia, where he defended the Gallican bifhops from the imputation of Sabellianifm, which the Arians had fixed upon them; and boldly afferted the found and orthodox faith of the Weftern bifhops. He was fo favourably received, and fo much refpected

[x] Hiftor. Liter. Tom. I. p. 243. Oxon. 1740.

I 3

by this council, that they admitted him as one who should give
in his opinion, and assist in a determination among their bishops;
but finding the greater part of them to be Arian, he would not
act. Nevertheless he continued at Seleucia, till the council was
over; when, seeing the orthodox faith in the utmost peril, he
followed the deputies of the council to Constantinople, and petitioned the emperor for leave to dispute publicly with the Arians,
The Arians, perceiving what a powerful adversary they were
likely to find in Hilary, contrived to have him sent to France,
whither passing through Italy he arrived in 360, without being
absolved in the mean time from the sentence of banishment.
However, after the catholic bishops had recovered their usual
liberty and authority under Julian the Apostate, Hilary assembled
several councils in France, to re-establish the ancient orthodox
faith, and to condemn the determinations of the synods of Rimini and Seleucia. He condemned Saturninus bishop of Arles,
but pardoned those who acknowledged their error; and, in
short, he exerted himself so heartily in this great affair, that, as
Sulpicius Severus says, it was agreed on all hands, that France
was in a great measure freed from Arianism by the single influence and endeavours of Hilary. He extended his care likewise
on this account to Italy and foreign churches, and was particu-
cularly qualified, as Ruffinus observes, to recover men from the
error of their ways, because he was "vir natura lenis, placidus,
simulque eruditus, & ad persuadendum commodissimus:" "an
excellent observation," says the candid Dupin, "and very proper lesson of instruction to all who are employed in the conversion of Heretics."
    About 367, Hilary had another opportunity of distinguishing
his zeal against Arianism. The emperor Valentinian coming
to Milan, issued an edict, by which he obliged all to acknowledge Auxentius for their bishop. Hilary, persuaded that Auxentius was in his heart an Arian, presented a petition to the
emperor, in which he declared Auxentius to be a blasphemer,
whose opinions were opposite to those of the church. Upon this
the emperor ordered Hilary and Auxentius to dispute publicly;
where Auxentius, after many subtleties and evasive shifts to
prevent being deposed from his bishopric, was forced to own,
that Jesus Christ "was indeed God, of the same substance
and divinity with the Father." The emperor believed this profession sincere, and embraced his communion; but Hilary continued still to call him an heretic, and most wicked prevaricator
with God and man; on which account he was ordered to depart
from Milan, as one who disturbed the peace of the church.
Hilary died the latter end of this year, after many struggles and
endeavours to support the catholic faith. His works have been
published several times: but the last and best edition of them
                                                        was

was given by the Benedictines in 1693 at Paris. Of his twelve books upon the Trinity, Jerom has spoken thus: "Hilarius, meorum confeſſor temporum & epiſcopus, duodecim Quintiliani libros & ſtylo imitatus eſt & numero [v]." And Eraſmus, in the preface to that edition which he gave of Hilary's works, ſays, that in theſe books he ſeems to have taken pains to ſhew, "quicquid ingenio, quicquid eloquentia, quicquid ſacrarum literarum cognitione poſſet." He was likewiſe a man of great piety as well as abilities and learning, of which the ancient author of his life, attributed to Fortunatus, has given us this inſtance. He tells us, that when Hilary went to Phrygia into baniſhment, leaving his wife and daughter behind him at Poictiers, he had a viſion, which informed him, that a young man of great wealth and power wanted to marry his daughter; but that Hilary prevented the match by his prayers, in which he earneſtly begged, that ſhe might only be married to Jeſus Chriſt. The author adds, that after his return from exile, upon her expreſſing an inclination to be married, Hilary prayed the Lord again, to take her from this vain world to himſelf: the reſult of which was, it is ſaid, that the young lady, as well as her mother, whom we muſt ſuppoſe to have been upon this occaſion too much in her intereſt, died in a very ſhort time after. A ſtory of this kind proves at leaſt the opinion held of the perſon of whom it is told.

HILARIUS, another Romiſh ſaint of that name, who was of Arles. He was born in 401, of rich and noble parents, and educated urder St. Honoratus abbot of Lérins. When Honoratus was promoted to the ſee of Arles, Hilarius, afterwards his ſucceſſor, attended him. When he was himſelf promoted to that dignity, he held ſeveral councils, and preſided in that at Rome in 441. In conſequence of ſome falſe accuſations, he was partly degraded by pope Leo, but his merit was afterwards fully perceived by that prelate. He died at the age of 48, yet worn out by his eccleſiaſtical labours. He has the higheſt character for piety, and all virtues. His works are, 1. "Homilies," under the name of Euſebius of Emeſa. 2. "The Life of St. Honoratus," his predeceſſor. 3. Various ſmaller works. The former Hilary is the perſon moſt known by the name of St. Hilary.

HILDEBERT, biſhop of Mans, and afterwards archbiſhop of Tours, in the 12th century, was born at Lavardin, a town in France. He is ſaid by Bayle to have led a very diſſolute life, before he was raiſed to the epiſcopal character. Ivo biſhop of Chartres, reproached him in the following terms: "Some of the moſt ancient perſons of the church of Mans, who ſay they

[v] Epiſt. ad Mag. Tom. II. p. 318.

are very well acquainted with your former way of living, affert, that you indulged yourself in fenfual pleafures to that degree, that after you was made an archdeacon, you ufed to lie with a whole tribe of concubines, by whom you have had many boys and girls [z]." Hildebert, however, was a man of great learning, as well as merit in many refpects. Maimbourg commends him highly, calls him the bleffed Hildebert, and afferts him to have been one of the moft holy and moft learned prelates, the Gallican church ever had. "We have fome letters," fays he, "and other beautiful works of his in the collection of the fathers. St. Bernard ftyles him the excellent pontiff and chief fupport of the church; whom the moft celebrated writers mention with great elogium, and whofe holinefs God himfelf was pleafed to fhew, and to honour by the miracles which were performed at his tomb. And on this occafion, to do his memory the juftice it deferves, I think myfelf obliged to obferve, that they who, on the credit of a letter of Ivo of Chartres, have afferted the diffolutenefs of his life, when he was made bifhop of Mans, have entirely miftaken him for another; being mifled by the infcription of that letter [A], in which they found Ildeberto inftead of Aldeberto, as the ancient manufcripts read it." But Maimbourg's criticifm, which is taken from Jurer's "Notes on Ivo of Chartres's Life," has not availed at all in Hildebert's favour; fince it is well known, that no other perfon who was raifed from an archdeacon to a bifhop, was elected bifhop of Mans in Ivo's time, but Hildebert.

Maimbourg relates afterwards, that Hildebert was tranflated from the bifhopric of Mans to the archbifhopric of Tours by pope Honorius II. in 1125; and obferves, that this prelate, finding king Lewis the Big to have given two canonfhips in his diocefe during the vacancy of that fee, went himfelf to court to make his humble reprefentations to the king. His majefty heard him; but, as he would not be fatisfied with the fentence that was given, and demanded a canonical judgement, all the income of his archbifhopric was feized upon, on account of his obftinacy. This made him have recourfe to the moft humble petitions; and he recommended his cafe to a bifhop, for whom the king had a great efteem. "I do not write to you," fays he, "with a defign to complain of the king's proceedings againft me; nor to roufe you by my expoftulation; nor to raife clamours, troubles, feditions, and ftorms againft the Lord's Anointed; nor to demand, that the feverities and cenfures of the church be made ufe of againft him. Far from it; I only beg of you, that by your kind and charitable offices, you would prevail upon his majefty, not to exert the weapons of his anger and indignation

[z] Ivo's Letter the 37th.   [A] Hift. du Lutheranifme, Liv. ii. p. 191.

againft

againſt a poor biſhop, full of years, and who deſires nothing but
reſt [a]."

Hildebert wrote a very pointed letter againſt the court of Rome.
The deſcription he gives of the vices of that court, is very
lively and elegant; and we find as lively and elegant a tranſlation of it, in French, by M. du Pleſſis Mornay, in his " Myſ-
tére d'Iniquité." He was only biſhop of Mans when he wrote
that letter; but when he wrote another to pope Honorius II.
complaining that all the cauſes were carried to Rome by way of.
appeal, he was archbiſhop of Tours. He wrote alſo a deſcription
of Rome in Latin verſe, which ends with theſe two lines:

" Urbs felix, ſi vel Dominis urbs illa careret,
    Vel Dominis eſſet turpe carere fide."

That is,

" Happy city, if it had no maſters; or if it were ſcandalous
for thoſe maſters to be unfaithful."

HILDESLEY (MARK), a truly primitive prieſt and biſhop,
was ſon of Mark Hildeſley, rector of Houghton and Witton in
the county of Huntingdon, who died about 1724 or 1725, when
the living was offered to his ſon by ſir John Barnard, to hold on
terms for a minor, which he declined. He was born at Marſton,
in the county of Kent, 1698, educated at the Charter-houſe, at
nineteen removed to Trinity-college, Cambridge, whereof he
was elected fellow in 1723. In 1724 he was appointed Whitehall preacher by biſhop Gibſon; in 1731 preſented by his college to the vicarage of Hitchin, and in 1535 to the neighbouring rectory of Holwell in the county of Bedford, by R. Radcliffe, Eſq; who had a ſingular reſpect for his many amiable
and engaging qualities, and always called him father Hildeſley.
This rectory he retained with the maſterſhip of an hoſpital in
Durham, given him by the biſhop of that ſee, after his promotion to the ſee of Sodor and Man. He diſtinguiſhed himſelf
by a diligent attendance on the duties of his extenſive pariſh,
which had been much neglected by his predeceſſor, took his
conſtant rounds in viſiting his pariſhioners both in town and
country, and preaching alternately with his curate at both livings; and every Friday evening in the year at ſeven, inſtructed
and catechiſed the younger part in the church, and on Good
Fridays diſtributed books to them. He generally preached from
memory or ſhort notes, and at a viſitation at Baldock, delivered
the whole diſcourſe to the clergy from memory, with a very
agreeable addreſs. His conſtant attention to the duties of his
function, and his inability to keep a curate before he had Holwell, impaired his weakly conſtitution. He beſtowed great

[a] Hild. Epiſt. vi. apud Lucam Dacherium, Tom. XIII.

expence,

expence, foon after his inflitution, on his vicarage-houfe, which was before a poor mean dwelling; and he took four or fix felect boarders into his houfe for inftruction. His exemplary conduct in this humble ftation recommended him to the duke of Athol as a fit fucceffor to the worthy bifhop Wilfon, whofe noble defign of printing a tranflation of the whole Bible in the Manks language he brought to the moft happy conclufion, immediately after his confecration in 1755, and died within ten days of its completion, of a paralytic ftroke, Dec. 7, 1772. He was buried, according to his defire, as near to his predeceffor as poffible. His farewel fermon at Hitchin drew tears from all who heard it; and when he vifited the parifh two years after, on his return to England from his fee, he recognized affectionately the meaneft of his friends and catechumens. He preached another affectionate difcourfe to them, and when he left the town, the ftreets were crouded with multitudes to pay him every mark of reverence, which he returned with equal kindnefs.

HILL (JOSEPH), an Englifh divine, famous chiefly for having publifhed, in 1676, an edition of Schrevelius's Greek lexicon, augmented with 8000 words, and purged of as many faults. He was born at Leeds in 1624, educated at St. John's-college, Cambridge, where he took his degrees, and was afterwards chofen fellow of Magdalen-college in that univerfity. He imbibed the puritanical doctrines, and was proctor during the prevalence of that party in 1659. After the Reftoration, he refufed to conform, and was therefore ejected in 1662. He then travelled through France and Germany, and paffed two years at Leyden. In 1667, he was chofen paftor of the Englifh congregation at Middleburg.; but, after a time, refigned that fituation and returned to England. He finally fettled at Rotterdam, where he continued till his death, which happened in 1707.

HILL (WILLIAM), author of fome learned notes, grammatical, critical, and geographical, on Dionyfius Periegetes; which were publifhed in London in 1688, after his death. He had been a fellow of Merton-college, Oxford, and was afterwards mafter of a fchool in Dublin. He died in 1667. To his notes are fubjoined maps, with an explanation of them, and geographical inftitutes for young ftudents. The edition is common, and has the text of Dionyfius from H. Stephens, and the commentary of Euftathius.

HILL (AARON), a poet; was the eldeft fon of George Hill, of Malmefbury-Abbey in Wiltfhire, and was born in Beaufortbuildings, London, Feb. 10, 1685. He was fent to Weftminfter-fchool, which, however, he left, on account of family diftrefs, occafioned by his father's mifmanagement, at fourteen years of age. Shortly after he formed a refolution of paying a vifit to his relation lord Paget, then ambaffador at Conftantinople;

and

and accordingly embarked for that place, March 2, 1700.
When he arrived, lord Paget received him with much surprise,
as well as pleasure; wondering, that a person so young should
run the hazard of such a voyage, to visit a relation whom he
only knew by character. The ambassador immediately provided for him a very learned ecclesiastic in his own house; and,
under his tuition, sent him to travel, so that he had an opportunity of seeing Egypt, Palestine, and a great part of the
East. With lord Paget he returned home about 1703, and in
his journey saw most of the courts in Europe. A few years after,
he was defired to accompany Sir William Wentworth, who was
then going to make the tour of Europe; and with him he travelled two or three years. About 1709, he published his first
poem, entitled, " Camillus," in honour of the earl of Peterborough, who had been general in Spain: and being the same
year made master of the theatre in Drury-lane, he wrote his first
tragedy, " Elfrid, or the Fair Inconstant," at the desire of the
famous actor Booth, which he began, and completed in a little
more than a week. In 1710, he was master of the opera-house
in the Hay-market; and then wrote an opera called " Rinaldo,"
which met with great success, and was the first that Handel composed after he came to England. His genius seems to have
been best adapted to the business of the stage; and while he held
the management, he conducted both the theatres to the satisfaction of the public; but, having some misunderstanding with the
lord-chamberlain, he relinquished it in a few months.

But Hill was not only a poet, he was also a great projector.
Among the Harleian MSS. 7524, is a letter from him to the lord-
treasurer, dated April 12, 1714, on a subject by which " the
nation might gain a million annually." In 1715, he undertook
to make an oil, as sweet as that from olives, of the beech-nuts,
and obtained a patent for the purpose: but, from some cause or
other, the undertaking came to nothing. In 1716, he wrote
another tragedy, called " The Fatal Vision, or the Fall of Siam:"
to which he prefixed this motto out of Horace,

" I not for vulgar admiration write:
To be well read, not much, is my delight."

About 1718, he wrote a poem, called " The Northern Star,"
upon the actions of the czar Peter the Great; and several years
after was complimented with a gold medal from the empress
Catherine, according to the czar's desire before his death. He
was also to have written his life from papers of the czar's, which
were to have been sent to him: but the death of the czarina,
quickly after, prevented it. In 1728, he made a journey to
the North of Scotland, where he had been about two years before; having contracted with the York-buildings company, concerning

cerning many woods of great extent in that kingdom, for timber for the uses of the navy. He found some difficulties in this affair: for when the trees were by his orders chained together into floats, the Highlanders refused to venture themselves on them down the river Spey, till he first went himself to convince them there was no danger. In this passage he found a great obstacle in the rocks, on which he ordered fires to be made when the river was low, and great quantities of water to be thrown; by which means they were broken to pieces, and thrown down, so that the passage became easy for the floats. This project, however, like the former, came to nothing; upon which, after a stay of several months in the Highlands, he quitted Scotland, and went to York. In that retirement in the North, he wrote a poem, called "The Progress of Wit, being a Caveat for the use of an eminent Writer." This was intended for Pope, who had been the aggressor in the "Dunciad," and, as Hill's friends say, was made very uneasy by it. The first eight lines are as follows:

> " Tuneful Alexis, on the Thame's fair side,
> The ladies' play-thing, and the Muses pride,
> With merit popular, with wit polite,
> Easy though vain, and elegant though light:
> Desiring and deserving others praise,
> Poorly accepts a fame he ne'er repays:
> Unborn to cherish, sneakingly approves,
> And wants the soul to spread the worth he loves."

In 1731, he met the greatest shock affliction ever gave him, though it is said he was born to combat it in all its shapes: and that was in the loss of a wife, to whom he had been married twenty years. She was the only daughter of Edmund Morris, esq; of Stratford in Essex, by whom he had nine children, and also a handsome fortune. He wrote the following epitaph for a monument he designed to erect over grave:

> " Enough, cold stone! suffice her long-lov'd name;
> Words are too weak to pay her virtue's claim.
> Temples, and tombs, and tongues shall waste away,
> And power's vain pomp in mould'ring dust decay.
> But ere mankind a wife more perfect see,
> Eternity, O Time! shall bury thee."

It would not be a small task to enumerate all his productions in poetry and prose. Four volumes have been published, in 8vo, since his death; but they have never been in much favour with the public, and we cannot undertake to make them so. Affectation both in the thoughts, and in the manner of expressing them, rather than want of genius, may account for their imperfect success. His last production was a tragedy called "Merope," taken from

Voltaire,

Voltaire, which was brought upon the stage in Drury-lane by
Garrick. There are some lines in the beginning of it, which
may be considered as a prophecy of his own approaching dis-
solution:

> " Cover'd in fortune's shade, I rest reclin'd:
> My griefs all silent; and my joys resign'd.
> With patient eye life's evening gloom survey:
> Nor shake th' out-hastening sands, nor bid them stay.
> Yet while from life my setting prospects fly,
> Fain would my mind's weak offspring shun to die, &c."

He died Feb. 8, 1750, as it is said, in the very minute of the
earthquake, after enduring a twelvemonth's torment of body with
great calmness and resignation. He was interred in the same
grave with his wife, in the great cloister of Westminster-abbey.
The following judgement of A. Hill, is found enough for us
to adopt [c]. " His character," it is said, " seems to have been
almost as singular as his adventures. Born of a good family, and
endowed with some natural talents, he might perhaps have arrived at that eminence to which he aspired, could he have confined himself to any single pursuit. But he was one of those
enterprising spirits, that attempt every thing; and, for want of
discerning their proper province, bring nothing to perfection.
He travelled much, read much, and wrote much; and all, as it
should seem, to very little purpose. His intimate acquaintance
with the most eminent persons of an age so fruitful in *Beaux
Esprits* inflamed his natural ardour to distinguish himself in the
Belles Lettres. He fancied that he was destined to be a great
poet; and the high compliments he received from one that was
really such (namely, Mr. Pope) confirmed him in that error.——
From poetry to music the passage was natural and easy: but from
composing dramas, to be set to the extracting oil from beech-
nuts, was a transition quite peculiar to such a versatile genius
as Hill."

HILL (Sir JOHN), an English writer, and most extraordinary
character [D], was the son of a Mr. Theophilus Hill, a clergyman of Peterborough or Spalding, and born about the year
1716. He was bred an apothecary, and set up in St. Martin's-
lane, Westminster; but marrying early, and without a fortune
on either side, he was obliged to look round for other resources
than his profession. Having, therefore, in his apprenticeship,
attended the botanical lectures, which are periodically given
under the patronage of the apothecary's company, and being
possessed of quick natural parts, he soon made himself acquainted
with the theoretical, as well as practical parts of botany; after

[c] Memoirs of the Life of Handel, p. 80.
[D] Annual Register, for the year 1775.—Biographia Dramatica.

which,

which, being recommended to the late duke of Richmond and
lord Petre, he was by them employed in the infpection and arrangement of their botanic gardens. Affifted by the liberality
of thefe noblemen, he executed a fcheme of travelling over
feveral parts of this kingdom, to gather fome of the moft rare
and uncommon plants, accounts of which he afterwards publifhed by fubfcription. But, after great refearches, and the exertion of uncommon induftry, which he poffeffed in a peculiar
degree, this undertaking turned out by no means adequate either
to his merits or expectations.

The ftage next prefented itfelf, as a foil in which genius
might ftand a chance of flourifhing: but this plan proved likewife abortive; and, after two or three unfuccefsful attempts at
the Hay-market and Covent-garden, he was obliged to relinquifh
all pretenfions to the fock and bufkin, and apply again to his
botanical enquiries, and his bufinefs as an apothecary. In the
courfe of thefe purfuits, he was introduced to the acquaintance
of Martin Folkes and Henry Baker, efqrs. both of the Royal
Society, and through them to the literary world; where he was
received and entertained on every occafion with much candour
and friendly warmth: in fhort, he was confidered by them as a
young man of great natural and acquired knowledge, ftruggling
againft the tide of misfortune, and in this view pitied and encouraged.

At length, about 1746, (at which time he had the trifling appointment of apothecary to one or two regiments in the Savoy)
he tranflated from the Greek a fmall tract of Theophraftus,
" On Gems," which he publifhed by fubfcription; and this,
being well executed, procured him friends, reputation, and
money. Encouraged by this fuccefs, he engaged in works of
greater extent and importance. The firft he undertook, was
" A General Natural Hiftory," 3 vols. folio. He next engaged
in conjunction with George Lewis Scott, efq. for a " Supplement to Chambers's Dictionary." At the fame time he undertook the " Britifh Magazine;" and, when engaged in thefe and
a number of other works, fome of which feemed to require a
man's whole attention, he carried on a daily effay under the title
of " Infpector." Notwithftanding all this employment, he was
a conftant attendant upon every place of public amufement;
where he collected, by wholefale, a great variety of private intrigue, and perfonal fcandal, which he as freely retailed again to
the public, in his " Infpectors" and " Magazines." It would
make a folio, inftead of an article in this work, were we to trace
Dr. Hill (for he had now obtained a diploma from the college
of St. Andrew's, in Scotland) through all his various purfuits in
life. Let it fuffice to fay, that from this fuccefsful period, he
commenced a man of fafhion, kept his equipage, dreffed, went

into

into all polite companies, laughed at the drier studies, and in every respect claimed the character of a man of *bon ton*. His writings supported him in all this for a time ; and, notwithstanding the graver part of them were only compilations, and the lighter part such as could produce no great copy-money, yet there is no doubt that he made, for several years, a considerable income.

But the disposition of Dr. Hill was greatly changed with his circumstances: from being humble and diffident, he had become vain and self-sufficient: there appeared in him a pride, which was perpetually claiming a more than ordinary homage ; and a vindictive spirit, which could never forgive the refusal of it. Hence his writings abounded with attacks on the understandings, morals, or peculiarities of others, descending even to personal abuse and scurrility. This licence of his pen engaged him frequently in disputes and quarrels; and an Irish gentleman, supposed to be ridiculed in an " Inspector," proceeded so far as even to cane him, in the public gardens at Ranelagh. He had a paper war with Woodward the comedian ; was engaged with Henry Fielding in the affair of Elizabeth Canning; and concerned in a contest with the Royal Society. He attacked this body, first in a pamphlet, entitled, " A Dissertation on Royal Societies;" and afterwards in a 4to volume, called " A Review of the Works of the Royal Society." The latter work was ushered into the world with an abusive dedication to Martin Folkes ; against whom, and Mr. Baker above-mentioned, his early patrons, the weight of his malignity was aimed. The cause of both these productions was the discouragement he met with, when he was desirous to offer himself as a candidate for admittance into that Society.

By personal abuse, malignant altercation, proud and insolent behaviour, together with the slovenliness and inaccuracy of careless and hasty productions, he wrote himself out of repute both with booksellers and the town; and, after some time, sunk in the estimation of the public, nearly as fast as he had risen. He found, however, as usual, resources in his own invention. He applied himself to the preparation of certain simple medicines : namely, " the Essence of Water-dock ; Tincture of Valerian ; Pectoral Balsam of Honey ; and Tincture of Bardana." The well-known simplicity of these preparations, led the public to judge favourably of their effects; they had a rapid sale, and once more enabled the doctor to live in splendor.

Soon after the publication of the first of these medicines, he obtained the patronage of the earl of Bute ; under which, he published a very pompous and voluminous botanical work, entitled, " A System of Botany." To wind up the whole of so extraordinary a life, having, a year or two before his death, presented an elegant set of his botanical works to the king of Sweden,

Sweden, that monarch invested him with one of the orders of his court, in consequence of which he assumed the title of Sir John. He died Nov. 1775, of the gout, though he professed to cure it in others. As to his literary character, and the rank of merit in which his writings ought to stand, Hill's greatest enemies could not deny that he was master of considerable abilities, and an amazing quickness of parts. The rapidity of his pen was ever astonishing, and we have been credibly informed, that he has been known to receive, within one year, no less than 15col. for the works of his own single hand; which, as he was never in such estimation as to be entitled to any extraordinary price for his copies, is, we believe, at least three times as much as ever was made by any one writer in the same period of time. But, had he written much less, his works would probably have been much more read. The vast variety of subjects he handled, certainly required such a fund of universal knowledge, and such a boundless genius, as were never, perhaps, known to centre in any one man; and it is not therefore to be wondered, if, in regard to some, he appears very inaccurate, in some very superficial, and, in others, altogether inadequate to the task he had undertaken. His works on philosophical subjects, seemed most likely to have procured him fame, had he allowed himself time to digest the knowledge he possessed, or preserved that regard to veracity which the relation of scientific facts so rigidly demands. His novels, of which he has written many, such as "The History of Mr. Lovell," (in which he had endeavoured to persuade the world he had given the detail of his own life) "The Adventures of a Creole," "The Life of Lady Frail," &c. have, in some parts of them, incidents not disagreeably related, but the most of them are no more than narratives of private intrigues; containing throughout, the grossest calumnies, and endeavouring to blacken and undermine the private characters of many respectable and amiable personages. In his "Essays," which are by much the best of his writings, there is, in general, a liveliness of imagination, and adroitness in the manner of extending, perhaps some very trivial thought: which, at first, is pleasing enough, and may by many be mistaken for wit; but, on a nearer examination, will be found to lose much of its value. A continual use of smart short periods, bold assertions, and bolder egotisms, produces a transient effect, but seldom tempts the spectator to take a second glance. The utmost that can be said of Hill is, that he had talents, but that, in general, he either greatly misapplied them, or most miserably hackneyed them for profit. As a dramatic writer he stands in no estimation, nor has he been known in that view by any thing but three very insignificant pieces: namely, 1. "Orpheus," an opera, 1740. 2. "The Critical Minute," a farce, published in 1754, but not acted. 3. "The Rout,"

Rout," a farce, 1754. Some smart epigrams by Garrick and others, on his joint occupations of poet and physician, will be remembered longer than his own dramas. Some of them run thus:

" For physic and farces, his equal there scarce is,
His farces are physic, his physic a farce is."

Another.

" Thou essence of dock, of valerian, and sage,
At once the disgrace and the pest of this age,
The worst that we wish thee, for all thy vile crimes,
Is to take thy own physic, and read thy own rhymes."

Answer.

The wish must be in form revers'd
To suit the doctor's crimes;
For if he takes his physic first,
He'll never read his rhymes!"

HILL (ROBERT), a man remarkable for his perseverance and talent in learning many languages by the aid of books alone, and that under every disadvantage of laborious occupation and extreme poverty. His extraordinary character was made known to the world by Mr. Spence in 1757, who, in order to promote a subscription for him, published a comparison between him and the famous Magliabecchi, with a short life of each [z]. From this account it appears that he was born January 11, 1699, at Miswell near Tring, in Hertfordshire; that he was bred a taylor, which trade and that of a stay-maker, he practised throughout life, sometimes adding to them that of a schoolmaster. He was three times married, and the increase of his family, with the extravagance of his second wife, kept him always in great penury. He worked in general, or taught by day, and studied by night; in which way he acquired the Latin, Greek, and Hebrew languages, with a good knowledge of arithmetic. As he could proceed only as he accidentally picked up books in a very cheap way, his progress was slow, but by his unremitting diligence, very steady. According to his own account, he was seven years acquiring Latin, twice as much in learning Greek, but Hebrew he found so easy, that it cost him little time. He wrote, 1. Remarks on Berkeley's "Essay on Spirit." 2. "The Character of a Jew." 3. "Criticisms on Job," He was a modest sensible man, fond of studying the Scriptures, and a zealous member of the Church of England. He died at Buckingham, in July, 1777, after having been confined to his bed about a year and a half. During this time, he employed the hours in which he was able to sit up, in his favourite study of the Old Testament in Hebrew, which he frequently said, now

[z] This tract was reprinted in Dodsley's two volumes of "Fugitive Pieces," in 1761. The amount of the subscriptions there stated is only 89l. 19s.

more than repaid him for the trouble he had taken to acquire the language. It is probable, that the notice into which he was brought by Mr. Spence fecured him afterwards from the extremities of poverty.

HILLEL the Elder, one of the Jewifh doctors of the Mifchna, flourifhed about 30 years before the Chriftian æra, and lived to an advanced age. He was born of an illuftrious Jewifh family in Babylon, but was made prefident of the Sanhedrim at Jerufalem, which dignity remained in his family for fix generations. He defended the oral traditions of the Jews, which he firft reduced into order in fix *Sedarim* or treatifes. He took great pains to procure an accurate text of the Bible.

HILLEL, the Prince, great grandfon of Judas Hakkadofh, and one of the principal writers of the Gemara, or comment on the Mifchna. He flourifhed in the middle of the fourth century.

HILLIARD (NICHOLAS), a celebrated Englifh painter, who drew Mary queen of Scots in water-colours, when fhe was but 18 years of age; wherein he fucceeded to admiration, and gained a general applaufe. He was goldfmith, carver, and portrait-painter to queen Elizabeth, whofe picture he drew feveral times; particularly once, when he made a whole length of her, fitting on her throne. Donne has celebrated this painter in a poem, called " The Storm ;" where he fays,

> " An hand, an eye,
> By Hilliard drawn, is worth an hiftory."

HIMERIUS, a Greek fophift and grammarian, who flourifhed under the emperors Conftantius and Julian, and was living after the death of the latter, in the year 363. He was a native of Prufias in Bithynia, and a rival of Anatolius and Prœnefius, after whofe death he eftablifhed himfelf in the fchool of rhetoric at Athens. Eunapius, who writes fome account of him, commends his ftyle, which was formed on that of Ariftides. He delighted in making clandefline attacks upon the Chriftians. Photius defcribes his declamations, and gives fome extracts; but a copy of them has been found, and an edition was promifed by Weinfdorf.

HINCKLEY (JOHN), fon of Robert Hinckley of Coton in Warwickfhire [F], was born in that county in 1617. His parents being puritanically inclined, he was bred in that perfuafion under Mr. Vynes, a celebrated fchoolmafter of Hinckley. In Midfummer or April term, 1634, he was admitted a ftudent in St. Alban's-hall, under the tuition of Mr. Robert Sayer; but before he became B. A. was converted, by the preaching of Dr. Wentworth, from the opinions he had imbibed in infancy.

[F] Nichals's Hiftory of Afton-Flamvile and Burbach.

About

About the time he had completed the degree of M. A. he entered into orders, was patronized by the family of Purefoy of Wadley near Faringdon, Berks; vicar of Colefhill in that county, afterwards of Drayton in Leiceflerfhire, on the prefentation of George Purefoy, efq; in 1662, rector of Northfield in Worceflerfhire; and in 1679, B. and D. D. He died April 13, 1691, and was buried in the chancel of Northfield church, where feveral epitaphs record part of the hiftory of his family. The publications of Dr. Hinckley are, 1. " Four Sermons; viz. 1. at the Affizes at Reading; 2. at Abingdon; 3. and 4. at Oxford, 1657," 8vo. 2. " Matrimonial Inftruction to Perfons of Honour," printed with the " Four Sermons." 3. " Epiftola veridica ad homines φιλοπραλτωνΐας, 1659," 4to, (reprinted in his " Fafciculus Literarum"). 4. " Oratio pro ftatu Eccleſiæ fluctuantis," printed with art. 3. 5. " Sermon at the Funeral of George Purefoy the Elder, of Wadley in Berks, efq; who was buried by his Anceftors at Drayton in Leiceflerfhire, 21 April, 1661; 1661," 4to. 6. " A Perfuafive to Conformity, by Way of Letter to the Diffenting Brethren, 1670," 8vo. 8. " Fafciculus Literarum; or, Letters on feveral Occafions [ᴏ], 1680," 8vo.

HINCMAR, or HINCMARUS, a celebrated archbifhop of Rheims, to which fee he was advanced in 845. He was bred in the monaftery of St. Denys, which, with the abbé Hilduin, he laboured to reform. When he became a bifhop, he proved a zealous defender of the rights of the Gallican church; but is thought to have proceeded rather too warmly againft a monk named Gotefcalcus, whofe opinions were condemned as unorthodox. The latter days of Hincmar were difturbed by the incurfions of the Normans, which drove him from his metropolitan city; and he died at Epernei in 882. The beft edition of his work is that publifhed by P. Sirmond, in 1645, which amounts to two volumes. He wrote on various fubjects of hiftory and divinity; and difplayed abundant learning in theology and jurifprudence; but his ftyle was harfh and barbarous, difgraced by all the faults of his time.

HIPPARCHIA, a celebrated lady of antiquity [ʜ], was born at Maronea, a city of Thrace, and flourifhed in the time of

[ᴏ] The firft half part of this book contains Letters between Mr. Baxter and Dr. Hinckley, wherein many things are difcuffed which are repeated in Baxter's " Plea for the Nonconformift." There are four in number, written by each, and our author's third Letter was written foon after Baxter's book " Of Church Divifions" came forth; he having not only obliquely reflected on, but let fall direct and downright expreffions againft Dr. Hinckley's

fecond Letter, particularly fignifying his difcontent both of Hinckley and his book. The reafon of the publication of thefe Letters five years after their firft penning, was occafioned by that mean and fcornful account which Baxter had given in many of his writings of Hinckley's Letters: the laft of which Letters was anfwered by Baxter in his third, " Of the Caufe of Peace, &c."

[ʜ] Diogen. Laert. de vit. Ph. lib. vi.

Alexander;

Alexander. She addicted herself to philosophy, and was so charmed with the discourses of the cynic Crates, that she was determined at all events to marry him. She was courted by a great many lovers, who were handsome men, and distinguished by their rank and riches; and her relations pressed her to choose an husband from these. But she answered, that she had sufficiently considered the affair, and was persuaded no one could be richer and handsomer than Crates; and that, if they would not marry her to him, she would slab herself. Upon this her friends had recourse to Crates himself, and desired him to exert all his eloquence, and to use all his authority with this maid to cure her of her passion. He did so; but she still continued obstinate and resolved. At last, finding arguments ineffectual, he displayed his poverty before her: he shewed her his crooked back, his cloak, his bag; and told her, that she could not be his wife, without leading such a life as his sect prescribed. She declared herself infinitely pleased with the proposal, and took the habit of the order. She loved Crates to such a degree, that she rambled every where, and went to entertainments with him; though this was what the other Grecian ladies never did. Nay, she did not even scruple to pay him conjugal duty in the open streets: for, as Apuleius relates, he led her for that purpose to the portico, which was one of the most stately public buildings in Athens, and where the greatest number of people continually resorted. It was one of the tenets of the Stoics, not to be ashamed of any thing that was natural, under which pretence they allowed themselves thus to insult the public morals. Hipparchia, wrote some things, which have not been transmitted down to us: among which were "Tragedies: Philosophical Hypotheses, or Suppositions; some Reasonings and Questions proposed to Theodorus, surnamed the Atheist." She once dined with Theodorus at Lysimachus's house, and proposed a subtle objection to him, which she only refuted by action: she said, "If I should commit the same action, which you had lawfully committed, I could not be charged with committing an unlawful action. Now if you should beat yourself, you would act lawfully; if therefore I should beat you, I could not be charged with committing an unlawful action." Theodorus did not lose time in answering like a logician, but, to shew her that different objects, circumstances, and connections, make different actions, went immediately up to her, and pulled open her clothes. But Hipparchia was too well trained a Stoic to be disconcerted by a little indecency, and continued the dispute without alarm.

HIPPARCHUS, one of the sons of Pisistratus monarch of Athens, who, after the death of his father, in the year 528, A. C. reigned jointly with his brother Hippias. These young men inherited the love of letters from their father, protected

and

and rewarded ingenious and learned men, such as Simonides,
and others; and might long have retained their power, had not
Hipparchus given an affront to the sister of a spirited young man.
This youth was Harmodius, for whom Hipparchus, according
to the manners of those times, had conceived a passion. Being
slighted by Harmodius, he took occasion to revenge himself by
turning his sister out of a public ceremony of religion, where
she was walking in procession. Exasperated at this insult, Harmodius, with his friend Aristogiton, conspired against Hipparchus, whom they slew in the year 514, A. C. As this action led
to the destruction of the usurped monarchical power of the Pisis-
tratidæ, the Athenians, with true Republican spirit, always
highly honoured the memory of Harmodius and Aristogiton.
His brother Hippias reigned tyrannically after his death, and
was expelled in about three years.

HIPPARCHUS, a celebrated ancient astronomer, was born,
as Strabo and Suidas inform us, at Nice in Bithynia, and flourished between the 154th and the 163d Olympiads; that is, between 160 and 125 before the birth of Christ. That he flourished within this period, we have as strong a proof as can be
desired; since it is taken from the astronomical observations he
made in that space of time. Hipparchus is supposed to have
been the first, who from vague and scattered observations reduced astronomy into a science, and prosecuted the study of it
systematically [1]. Pliny mentions him very often, and always in
terms of high commendation. He was the first, as that author tells
us, who attempted to take the number of the fixed stars, " rem,"
says he, " Deo improbam [k];" and his catalogue is preserved
in Ptolemy's " Almagest," where they are all noted according
to their longitudes and apparent magnitudes. Pliny places him
amongst those men of a sublime genius, who, by foretelling the
eclipses, taught mankind, that they ought not to be frightened
at these phænomena. Thales was the first among the Greeks,
who could discover when there was to be an eclipse. Sulpitius
Gallus among the Romans began to succeed in this kind of pre-
diction; and gave an essay of his skill very seasonably, the day
before a battle was fought. " After them [L]," says Pliny,
" came Hipparchus, who foretold the course of the sun and
moon for 600 years, calculated according to the different manner
of reckoning the months, days, and hours used by several nations, and for the different situations of places." He admires
him for taking an account of all the stars, and for acquainting
us with their situations and magnitudes: for by these means, says
he, posterity will be able to discover, not only whether they are
born and die, but also whether they change their places, and

[1] Hist. Natur. lib. ii. c. 26.   [k] Lib. vii. 5.   [L] Lib. ii. c. 12.

whether they increase or decrease. Hipparchus is also memorable for being the first who discovered the precession of the equinoxes, or a very slow apparent motion of the fixed stars from west to east, by which in a great number of years they will perform a complete revolution.

The first observations he made were in the isle of Rhodes, which gained him the name Rhodius, and has made some moderns imagine, that there were two ancient astronomers of that name: afterwards he cultivated this science in Bithynia and Alexandria only. One of his works is still extant, namely, his "Commentary upon Aratus's Phænomena." It is properly a criticism upon Aratus ; for Hipparchus charges him with having plundered Eudoxus's books, and transcribed even those observations in which Eudoxus was mistaken. He makes the same remarks against Aratus the grammarian, who wrote "A Commentary on Aratus's Phænomena." Peter Victorius is the first who published this "Commentary" of Hipparchus. Petavius gave afterwards a more correct edition of it : to which he added a Latin translation made by himself. Hipparchus composed several other works [M], of which honourable mention is made by many writers of antiquity ; and upon the whole, it is universally agreed, that astronomy is greatly obliged to him for laying originally that rational and solid foundation, on which all succeeding professors of this science have built their improvements.

HIPPIAS. See HIPPARCHUS.

HIPPOCRATES, the father of physic and prince of physicians, was born in the island of Cos, in the first year of the 80th Olympiad, or A. C. 460, and flourished at the time of the Peloponnesian war. He was the first man we know of, who laid down precepts concerning physic ; and was supposed to descend from Hercules and Æsculapius. He was first a pupil of his own father Heraclides, then of Herodicus, then of Gorgias of Leontinum the orator, and according to some, of Democritus of Abdera [N]. After being instructed in physic and all the liberal arts, and losing his parents, he left his own country : but what were his motives, authors are not agreed. Some say, that he was obliged to fly for burning the library in Cnidus, of which he had been appointed the keeper [o]. This Pliny relates from Varro, and assigns also the motive which induced him to commit so atrocious an act ; namely, that, "having transcribed from ancient books every thing relating to his own art, he might, by destroying them afterwards, pass the better for an original himself [P]." Soranus, junior, a writer of uncertain age, whose life of Hippocrates was published by Fabricius, tells us, that he was divinely ad-

[M] Vossius de Scient. Mathem. p. 160. [o] Tzetzes Chiliad. p. 139.
[N] Fabricii Bibl. Græc. tom. I. p. 142. [P] Plin. Nat. Hist. lib. xxxix. 4.

monished

monished in a dream, to go and settle in Thessaly; as Galen, we know, pretended since to be led to the study of physic by a dream which happened to his father. Be this as it will, it is certain that he left Cos, and practised physic all over Greece; where he was so much admired for his skill, as to be sent for publicly with Euryphon, a man superior to him in years, to Perdiccas king of Macedonia, who was then thought to be consumptive. But Hippocrates, as soon as he arrived, pronounced the disorder to be entirely mental, as it really was found to be. For upon the death of his father Alexander, Perdiccas fell in love with Philas, his father's mistress; and this Hippocrates discerning by the great change her presence always wrought upon him, soon effected a cure, which one would think might easily have been effected without the help of such a physician, or even of any physician. He was also entreated by the people of Abdera, to come and cure Democritus of a supposed madness. Their epistle to him on this occasion is to be found in most of the editions of his works; and, as it is curious, and gives a just and full idea of his very extensive fame, we will here present it to the reader in a translation.

"Our city, Hippocrates, is in very great danger, together with that person, who, we hoped, would ever have been a great ornament and support to it. But now, O ye gods! it is much to be feared, that we shall only be capable of envying others, since he through extraordinary study and learning, by which he gained it, is fallen into sickness; so that it is much to be feared, that if Democritus become mad, our city will become desolate. For he is got to such a pitch, that he entirely forgets himself, watches day and night, laughs at all things little and great, esteeming them as nothing, and spends his whole life in this frantic manner. One marries a wife; another trades; another pleads; another performs the office of a magistrate, goeth on an embassy, is chosen officer by the people, is put down, falls sick, is wounded, dies. He laughs at all these, observing some to look discontented, others pleased: moreover, he enquires what is done in the infernal places, and writes of them: he affirms the air to be full of images, and says, he understands the language of birds. Rising in the night, he often sings to himself; and says, that he sometimes travels to the infinity of things, and that there are innumerable Democrituses like him: thus, together with his mind, he destroyeth his body. These are the things which we fear, Hippocrates: these are the things which trouble us. Come therefore quickly, and preserve us by your advice, and despise us not, for we are not inconsiderable; and if you restore him, you shall not fail either of money or fame. Though you prefer learning before wealth, yet accept of the latter, which shall be offered to you in great abundance. If our city were all

K 4   gold,

gold, we would give it to reflore Democritus to health: we think our laws are fick, Hippocrates: come, then, beft of men, and cure a moft excellent perfon. Thou wilt not come as a phyfician, but as a guardian of all Ionia, to encompafs us with a facred wall. Thou wilt not cure a man, but a city, a languifhing fenate, and prevent its diffolution: thus becoming our lawgiver, judge, magiftrate, and preferver. To this purpofe we expect thee, Hippocrates: all thefe, if you come, you will be to us. It is not a fingle obfcure city, but all Greece, which befeecheth thee to preferve the body of wifdom. Imagine, that Learning herfelf comes on this embaffy to thee, begging, that thou wilt free her from this danger. Wifdom is certainly nearly allied to every one, but efpecially to us, who dwell fo near her. Know for certain, that the next age will own itfelf much obliged to thee, if thou defert not Democritus, for the truth which he is capable of communicating to all. Thou art allied to Æfculapius by thy family, and by thy art: he is defcended from the brother of Hercules, from whom came Abdera, whofe name, as you have heard, our city bears: wherefore even to him will the cure of Democritus be acceptable. Since therefore, Hippocrates, you fee a moft excellent perfon falling into madnefs, and a whole people into diftrefs, haften, we befeech you, to us. It is ftrange, that the exuberance of good fhould become a difeafe: that Democritus, by how much he excelled others in acutenefs of wifdom, fhould fo much the fooner fall into madnefs, while the ordinary unlearned people of Abdera enjoy their wits as formerly: and that even they, who before were efteemed foolifh, fhould now be moft capable of difcerning the indifpofition of the wifeft perfon. Come therefore, and bring along with you Æfculapius, and Epione the daughter of Hercules, and her children, who went in the expedition againft Troy: bring with you receipts and remedies againft ficknefs: as the earth plentifully affords fruits, roots, herbs, and flowers, to cure madnefs, fhe can never do it more happily than now, for the recovery of Democritus. Farewell."

Hippocrates, after writing an anfwer to this letter from the fenate of Abdera, in which he commended their love of wifdom and wife men, went; but upon his arrival, inftead of finding Democritus mad, declared that he found all his fellow-citizens fo, and him the only man in his fenfes. He heard many lectures, and learned much philofophy from him; which has made Celfus and others imagine, that Hippocrates was the difciple of Democritus, though it is probable they never faw each other till this interview, which was occafioned by the Abderites. Hippocrates had alfo public invitations to other countries. Thus when a plague attacked the Illyrians and the Pæonians, the kings of thofe countries begged of him to come to their relief: he

did

did not go, but learning from the meffengers the courfe of the winds there, he concluded, that the diftemper would come to Athens; and, foretelling what would happen, applied himfelf to take care of the city and the ftudents. He was indeed fuch a lover of Greece, that when his fame had reached as far as Perfia, and upon that account Artaxerxes had intreated him by his governor of the Hellefpont, to come to him, upon an offer of great rewards, he refufed to leave it. He alfo delivered his own country from a war with the Athenians, that was juft ready to break out, by prevailing with the Theffalians to come to their affiftance: for which he received very great honours from the Coans. The Athenians alfo conferred great honours upon him; they admitted him next to Hercules in the Eleufinian ceremonies; gave him the freedom of the city; and voted a public maintenance for him and his family in the Prytanæum, or council-houfe at Athens, where none were maintained at the public charge, but fuch as had done fignal fervice to the ftate He died among the Lariffæans about the time that Democritus is faid to have died; fome fay, in his 90th year, others in his 85th, others in his 104th, and others in his 109th. He was buried between Gyrton and Lariffa, where his monument is fhewn even to this day. It would be endlefs to tranfcribe the fine things that have been faid of him, or to relate the honours that have been done to his memory. His countrymen the Coans kept his birth-day as a feftival; and indeed no wonder that he fhould have divine honours paid him, fince, on account of his wonderful fkill and forefight in this art, he paffed with the Grecians for a God. He taught his art, as he practifed it, with great candour and liberality; fo that Macrobius had reafon to fay, that he knew not how to deceive any more than to be deceived [q]. We have already had occafion to mention one fpecimen of his open and ingenuous temper under the article of Celfus; but to give a larger view of it, we will here fubjoin his oath, which is a curiofity with which the Englifh reader will not be difpleafed.

The OATH of HIPPOCRATES.

"I fwear by Apollo the phyfician, by Æfculapius, by his daughters Hygeia and Panacea, and by all the Gods and Goddeffes, that, to the beft of my power and judgement, I will faithfully obferve this oath and obligation. The mafter that has inftructed me in the art, I will efteem as my parents; and fupply, as occafion may require, with the comforts and neceffaries of life. His children I will regard as my own brothers; and if they defire to learn, I will inftruct them in the fame art, without

[q] Somnium Scip. L. L.

any reward or obligation. The precepts, the explanations, and whatever else belongs to the art, I will communicate to my own children, to the children of my master, to such other pupils as have subscribed the Physician's Oath, and to no other persons. My patients shall be treated by me, to the best of my power and judgement, in the most salutary manner, without any injury or violence: neither will I be prevailed upon by another to administer pernicious physic, or be the author of such advice myself; nor will I recommend to women a pessary to procure abortion: but will live and practise chastely and religiously. Cutting for the stone I will not meddle with, but will leave it to the operators in that way. Whatever house I am sent for to attend, I will always make the patient's good my principal aim, avoiding as much as possible all voluntary injury and corruption, especially all venereal matters, whether among men or women, bond or free. And whatever I see or hear in the course of a cure, or otherwise, relating to the affairs of life, nobody shall ever know it, if it ought to remain a secret. May I be prosperous in life and business, and for ever honoured and esteemed by all men, as I observe this solemn oath : and may the reverse of all this be my portion, if I violate it, and forswear myself."

His works have often been printed in separate pieces, as well as together; and amongst them this Oath, which has been much admired, and commented on by several persons; by Meibomius in particular, who published it by itself in 4to, at Leyden, 1643.

HIPPONAX, an Ephesian satiric poet, who flourished in the 60th Olympiad, that is, about 540 years before the Christian æra. He was so remarkably ugly and deformed, that certain painters and sculptors amused themselves by displaying representations of him to public ridicule. Caricatures were probably not common in those days; for Hipponax was so offended at the insult, that he exercised against the offenders all the force of his satyric vein; and, as it is said, with such effect, that two of them, sculptors of Chios, Bupalus and Anthermus, hanged themselves. But Pliny contradicts the story; Hist. Nat. xxxvi. 5. Hipponax is said to be the inventor of the scazontic verse, which is an iambic, terminating with a spondee, instead of an iambic foot.

HIRE (PHILIP DE LA), an eminent French mathematician and astronomer, was born at Paris, March 18, 1640 [a]. His father Laurence, who was painter in ordinary to the king, professor in the academy of painting and sculpture, and much celebrated in his line, intended him also for the same occupation ; and with that view taught him the principles of design, and such branches of mathematics as related to those arts; but died, when

[a] Nicero, Hommes Illustres, Tom. V.

Philip

Philip was no more than 17. Falling afterwards into an ill
habit of body, he projected a journey into Italy; which he conceived might contribute not less to the recovery of his health,
than to bring him to perfection in his art. He set out in 1660,
and was not deceived in his expectations; for he soon found himself well enough to contemplate the remains of antiquity, with
which Italy abounds. He applied himself also to geometry, to
which he had indeed more propensity than to painting, and which
soon afterwards engrossed him entirely. The retired manner in
which he spent his time in Italy, very much suited his disposition; and he would willingly have continued longer in that
country, but for the importunity of his mother, who prevailed
upon him to return, after an absence of about four years.

Being again settled in Paris, he continued his mathematical
studies, applying himself to them with the utmost intense-
ness: and he afterwards published works, which gained him so
much reputation, that he was made a member of the academy
of Sciences in 1678. The minister Colbert having formed a
design of a better chart or map of the kingdom than any which
had hitherto been taken, de la Hire was nominated, with Picard,
to make the necessary observations. He went to Bretagne in
1679, to Guyenne in 1680, to Calais and Dunkirk in 1681,
and into Provence in 1682. In these peregrinations he did
not confine his attention to their main object, but philoso-
phized upon every thing that occurred, and particularly upon the
variations of the magnetic needle, upon refractions, and upon
the height of mountains, as determined by the barometer. In
1683, he was employed in continuing the meridian line, which
Picard had begun in 1669. De la Hire continued it to the
north of Paris, while Cassini pushed it on to the south: but
Colbert dying the same year, the work was left unfinished. He
was next employed, with other geometricians of the academy,
in taking the necessary levels for those grand aqueducts, which
Louis XIV. was about to make.

Geometry, however, did not take up all his time and labour;
he employed himself upon other branches of mathematics and
philosophy. Even painting itself, which he may seem to have
discarded so long ago, had a place in those hours which he set
apart for amusement. The great number of works which he
published, together with his continual employments as professor
of the Royal College and of the Academy of Architecture, to
which places his great merit had raised him, give us a vast idea
of the labours he underwent. His days were always spent in
study, his nights very often in astronomical observations; and he
seldom sought any other relief from his labours, but a change
of one for another. He was twice married, and had eight children. He had the exterior politeness, circumspection, and prudence

dence of Italy, for which country he had a fingular regard; and on this account appeared in the eyes of the French, too referved, and retired into himfelf. Neverthelefs, he was a very honeft difintereſted man, and a good Chriſtian. He died April 21, 1718, aged 78.

He was the author, as we have faid, of a vaſt number of works: the principal of which are thefe: "Nouvelle Methode en Geometrie pour les fections des fuperficies coniques & cylindriques, 1673," 4to. 2. "De la Cycloide, 1677," 12mo. 3. "Nouveaux Elemens des fections coniques: les lieux Geometriques: la conſtruction ou effection des equations, 1679," 12mo. 4. "La Gnomonique, &c. 1682," 12mo. 5. "Sectiones Conicæ in novem libros diſtributæ, 1655," folio. This was confidered as an original work, and gained the author a great reputation all over Europe. 6. "Tabulæ Aſtronomicæ, 1687, and 1702," 4to. 7. "Veterum Mathematicorum Opera, Græcè & Latinè pleraque nunc primum edita, 1693," folio. This edition had been begun by M. Thevenot; who dying, the care of finiſhing it was committed to de la Hire. It ſhews that the author's ſtrong application to mathematical and aſtronomical ſtudies, had not hindered him from acquiring a very competent knowledge of the Greek tongue. Befides thefe and other ſmaller works, there are a vaſt number of his pieces fcattered up and down in journals, and particularly in the "Memoirs of the Academy of Sciences." M. de Fontenelle wrote an eulogium upon him.

HISCAM, or HISJAM, the fifteenth caliph of the race of Ommiades, and the fourth fon of Abdalmelech, fucceeded his brother J. zid II. in the year 723. His moſt confpicuous actions were thofe of vanquiſhing Khacam of Turkeſtan, and making war againſt the emperor Leo the Ifaurian, and Conſtantine Copronymus. He died in 743, after a reign of 19 years. He was fludiouſly ſplendid in his apparel, and always was attended by a train of 600 camels, employed to carry his wardrobe. The Greek hiſtorians call him Ifam.

HOADLY (BENJAMIN), a prelate of uncommon talents, was the fon of the Rev. Samuel Hoadley, who kept a private fchool many years, and was afterwards maſter of the public grammar-fchool at Norwich. He was born at Weſterham in Kent, Nov. 14, 1676. His academical education he had at Catharine-hall in Cambridge, where he was entered in 1692, and afterwards became a fellow of that fociety. In 1706, he publiſhed "Some Remarks on Dr. Atterbury's Sermon at the Funeral of Mr. Bennet;" and two years afterwards "Exceptions" againſt another Sermon by the fame author, on the power of "Charity to cover Sin." In 1709, a difpute arofe between thefe combatants, concerning the doctrine of non-refiſtance,

occa-

occafioned by a work of Hoadly's, entitled, "The Meafures of Obedience;" fome pofitions in which Atterbury endeavoured to confute in a Latin Sermon, preached that year before the London clergy. Hoadly fignalized himfelf fo eminently in this debate, that the houfe of Commons gave him a particular mark of their regard, by reprefenting in an addrefs to the queen, the fignal fervices he had done to the caufe of civil and religious liberty. At this time, when his principles were unpopular, and the fury of party virulence let loofe upon him, Mrs. Howland fpontaneoufly prefented him to the rectory of Streatham in Surry. Soon after the acceffion of George I. his abilities and attachment were properly regarded; and he was made bifhop of Bangor in 1715, which fee, however, from an apprehenfion of party fury, as was faid, he never vifited, but ftill remained in town, preaching againft what he confidered as the inveterate errors of the clergy. Among other difcourfes he made at this crifis, one was upon thefe words, "My kingdom is not of this world:" which, producing the famous Bangorian controverfy, as it was called, employed the prefs for many years. The manner in which he explained the text was, that the clergy had no pretenfions to any temporal jurifdictions; but this was an-fwered with great vehemence by Dr. Snape; and, in the courfe of the debate, the argument infenfibly changed, from the rights of the clergy to that of princes, in the government of the church. Bifhop Hoadly ftrenuoufly maintained, that temporal princes had a right to govern in ecclefiaftical polities. His moft able opponent was the celebrated William Law, who, in fome material points, may be faid to have gained a complete victory. He was afterwards involved in another difpute with Dr. Hare, upon the nature of prayer: he maintained, that a calm, rational, and difpaffionate manner of offering up our prayers to heaven, was the moft acceptable method of addrefs. Hare, on the con-trary, infifted, that the fervour of zeal was what added merit to the facrifice; and that prayer, without warmth, and without coming from the heart, was of no avail. This difpute, like the former, for a time excited many opponents, but has long fub-fided. From the bifhopric of Bangor, he was tranflated fuccef-fively to thofe of Hereford, Salifbury, and Winchefter, of which laft fee he continued bifhop more than 26 years.

A monument is erected to his memory in the weft ifle of the cathedral at Winchefter. The infcription is in Latin, drawn up by himfelf. The principal contents and dates as follows: "He was the fon of Samuel Hoadly, a prefbyter of the church of England, and for many years inftructor of a private fchool, and afterwards of the public fchool at Norwich; and of Martha Pickering, daughter of the Rev. Benjamin Pickering, born at Wefterham in Kent, Nov. 14, 1676. Admitted into Catharine-hall,

hall, Cambridge, 1692; of which hall he was afterwards chofen a fellow. Afternoon lecturer for ten years at St. Mildred in the Poultry, London, from 1701. Rector of St. Peter's Poor, London, for 16 years, from 1704. Alfo rector of Streatham in Surrey, for 13 years, from 1710. Confecrated bifhop of Bangor, March 18, 1715. Confirmed bifhop of Hereford, Nov. 23, 1721. Confirmed bifhop of Salifbury, Oct. 19, 1723. Confirmed bifhop of Winchefter, Sept. 26, 1734. His firft wife was Sarah Curtis, by whom he had two fons, Benjamin, M. D. and John, LL. D. chancellor of the diocefe of Winchefter. His fecond wife was Mary Newey, daughter of the Rev. Dr. John Newey, dean of Chichefter. He died April 17, 1761, aged 85. On a fmall tablet underneath, are thefe words: " Patri amantiffimo, veræ religionis ac libertatis publicæ vindici, de fe, de patriâ, de genere humano optimè merito, hoc marmor pofuit J. Hoadly, filius fuperftes."

His conftant motto was, " Veritas & Patria."

As a writer, he poffeffed uncommon talents; his greateft defect was in his ftyle, extending his periods to a difagreeable length, for which Pope has thus recorded him:

" ———— Swift for clofer ftyle,
But Hoadly for a period of a mile."

In his character, he was naturally facetious, eafy, and complying, fond of company, from which however he would frequently retire, for the purpofes of ftudy or devotion; happy in every place, but peculiarly fo in his own family, where he took all opportunities of inftructing by his influence and by example. In his tenets he was far from adhering ftrictly to the doctrines of the church; fo far, indeed, that it is a little to be wondered on what principles he continued throughout life to profefs conformity. But as he took great latitude himfelf, fo he was ready alfo to allow it to others. His doctrine, that fincerity is fufficient for acceptance, whatever be the nature of opinions, is favourable to fuch indulgence, but far from defenfible on the genuine principles of Chriftianity [a]. He was of courfe in high favour with all who wifhed to mould religion according to their own imaginations.

It would far exceed the limits of our page to name all the pamphlets and tracts which bifhop Hoadly wrote; but a complete catalogue of them may be found at the end of the life written by his fon the chancellor, which is copied alfo in the " Biographia Britannica." The admirable Ode of Akenfide, there alfo in-

[a] Archbifhop Secker one day, at his table, when the Monthly Reviewers were laid, by one of the company, to be Chrif- tians, replied, " If they were, it was certainly ' fecundum ufum Winton."

ferted, reflects equal honour on the poet and the bifhop. The following humbler tribute, written foon after his death, is lefs generally known:

"While Fortune fmiles, let Pride's vain minions claim
From Wilton's hand their fcanty fhare of fame:
From Parian ftatues let their names be fought,
How well the Patriot liv'd, or Hero fought. ·
No proud infcriptions Hoadley's worth demands,
On firmer grounds its furer bafis ftands.
When fails the fculptur'd urn, the breathing buft
Sinks down to ruin, mouldering in the duft,
Thy works, illuftrious Hoadly, fhall furvive,
And there embalm'd thy honour'd name fhall live:
The lateft ages there fhall wondering find
How great thy learning, and how pure thy mind."

HOADLY (BENJAMIN), M D. eldeft fon of the bifhop of Winchefter, was born Feb. 10, 1705-6, in Broad-ftreet, educated, as was his younger brother, at Dr. Newcome's at Hackney, and Benet-college, Cambridge; being admitted penfioner April 8, 1722, under archbifhop Herring, then tutor there. Here he took a degree in phyfic in 1727; and, particularly applying to mathematical and philofophical ftudies, was well known (along with the learned and ingenious doctors David Hartley and Davies, both late of Bath, who with him compofed the whole clafs) to make a greater progrefs under the blind profeffor Saunderfon than any ftudent then in the univerfity. When his late majefty was at Cambridge in April 1728, he was upon the lift of perfons to be created doctors of phyfic: but either by chance or management, his name was not found in the laft lift; and he had not his degree of M. D. till about a month after, by a particular mandamus. Through this tranfaction it appeared, that Dr. Snape had not forgotten or forgiven the name of Hoadley; for he not only behaved to him with great ill-manners, but obftructed him in it as much as lay in his power. He was F. R. S. very young, and had the honour of being made known to the learned world as a philofopher, by "A Letter from the Rev. Dr. Samuel Clarke to Mr. Benjamin Hoadly, F. R. S. occafioned by the prefent Controverfy among the Mathematicians concerning the Proportion of Velocity and Force in Bodies in Motion." He was made regiftrar of Hereford while his father filled that fee; and was appointed phyfician to his majefty's houfhold fo early as June 9, 1742. It is remarkable, that he was for fome years phyfician to both the royal houfholds; having been appointed to that of the prince of Wales, Jan. 4, 1745-6, in the place of Dr. Lamotte, a Scotch phyfician, whom the prince had himfelf ordered to be ftruck out of the lift, on

fome

some imprudent behaviour at the Smyrna-coffee-house at the time of the rebellion in 1745. The appointment was attended with some circumstances of particular honour to Dr. Hoadley. This, happening at a time when the two branches of the royal family were not on good terms, is a strong testimony in favour of Dr. Hoadley. He is said to have filled these posts with singular honour. He married, 1. Elizabeth daughter of Henry Betts, esq; of Suffolk, counsellor at law, by whom he had one son, Benjamin, that died an infant. 2. Anne, daughter and co-heiress of the honourable general Armstrong, by whom he left no issue. He died in the life-time of his father, Aug. 10, 1757, at his house at Chelsea, since sir Richard Glyn's, which he had built ten years before. He published, 1. " Three Letters on the Organs of Respiration, read at the Royal College of Physicians, London, A. D. 1737, being the Gulstonian lectures for that Year. To which is added, an Appendix, containing Remarks on some Experiments of Dr. Houlton, published in the Transactions of the Royal Society for the Year 1736, by Benjamin Hoadly, M. D. Fellow of the College of Physicians, and of the Royal Society, London, 1740," 4to. 2. " Oratio Anniversaria in Theatro Coll. Medicor. Londinensium, ex Harveii instituto habita die 18° Oct. A. D. 1742, à Benj. Hoadly, M. D. Coll. Med. & S. R. S. 1742," esteemed a very elegant piece of Latin. 3. " The Suspicious Husband, a Comedy." 4. " Observations on a Series of Electrical Experiments, by Dr. Hoadley and Mr. Wilson, F. R. S. 1756," 4to. The doctor was, in his private character, an amiable humane man, and an agreeable sprightly companion. In his profession, he was learned and judicious; and, as a writer, there needs no further testimony to be borne to his merit, than the very pleasing comedy he has left behind him, which, whenever represented, continually affords fresh pleasure to the audience. It is hardly necessary to mention to any one, the least conversant with theatrical affairs, that we mean " The Suspicious Husband, a Comedy, 1747," 8vo.

HOADLY (JOHN), LL.D. This gentleman was the youngest son of Dr. Benjamin Hoadly, bishop of Winchester. He was born in Broad-street, Oct. 8, 1711, and educated at Mr. Newcome's school in Hackney, where he gained great applause by performing the part of Phocyas in " The Siege of Damascus." In June 1730, he was admitted at Corpus-Christi college in Cambridge, and about the same time at the Temple, intending to study the law. This design, however, he soon abandoned; for in the next year we find he had relinquished all thoughts of the law as a profession. He took the degree of LL. B. in 1735; and, on the 29th of November following, was appointed chancellor of Winchester, ordained deacon by his father, Dec. 7, and priest the 21st of the same month. He was immediately

received

received into the prince of Wales's houshold as his chaplain, as he afterwards was in that of the princess dowager, May 6, 1751.

His several preferments he received in the following order of time: the rectory of Michelmersh, March 8, 1737; that of Wroughton in Wiltshire, Sept. 8, 1737; and that of Alresford, and a prebend of Winchester, 29th of November in the same year. On June 9, 1743, he was instituted to the rectory of St. Mary near Southampton, and on Dec. 16, 1746, collated to that of Overton. He had the honour to be the first person on whom archbishop Herring conferred the degree of a doctor. In May, 1760, he was appointed to the mastership of St. Cross; and all these preferments he enjoyed until his death, except the living of Wroughton, and the prebend of Winchester. He wrote some Poems in "Dodsley's Collection," and is supposed very materially to have assisted his brother in "The Suspicious Husband." He likewise published an edition of his father's works in 3 vols. folio. After living to the age of 64, the delight of his friends, he died March 16, 1776, and with him the name of Hoadly became extinct. He was the author of five dramas: 1. "The Contrast," a comedy, acted at Lincoln's-inn-fields, 1731, but not printed. 2. "Love's Revenge," a pastoral, 1737. 3. "Phœbe," another pastoral, 1748. 4. "Jeptha," an oratorio, 1737. 5. And another, entitled, "The Force of Truth," 1764. He also revised Lillo's "Arden of Feversham;" and wrote the fifth act of Miller's "Mahomet." He left several dramatic works in MS. behind him; and, among the rest, "The House-keeper, a Farce," on the plan of "High Life below Stairs," in favour of which piece it was rejected by Mr. Garrick, together with a tragedy on a religious subject. So great, however, was the doctor's fondness for theatrical exhibitions, that no visitors were ever long in his house before they were solicited to accept a part in some interlude or other. He himself, with Garrick and Hogarth, once performed a laughable parody on the scene in "Julius Cæsar," where the ghost appears to Brutus. Hogarth personated the spectre; but so unretentive was his memory, that, although his speech consisted only of a few lines, he was unable to get them by heart. At last they hit on the following expedient in his favour. The verses he was to deliver were written in such large letters on the outside of an illuminated paper lanthorn, that he could read them when he entered with it in his hand on the stage. Hogarth prepared the play-bill on this occasion, with characteristic ornaments. The original drawing is still preserved, and we could with it were engraved: as the slightest sketch from the design of so grotesque a painter, would be welcome to the collectors of his works.

Dr. Hoadly's tragedy was on the story of lord Cromwell, and he once intended to give it to the stage. In a letter dated June 27, 1765, he says, " My affair with Mr. Garrick is coming upon the carpet again ;" Aug. 1, 1765, he thus apologizes to Mr. Bowyer, to whom he intended to present the copy-right: " Your kind concern, &c. demanded an earlier acknowledgement, had I not delayed till an absolute answer came from my friend David Garrick with his fixed resolution never more ' to strut and fret his hour upon the stage again.' This decree has unhinged my schemes with regard to lord Cromwell, for nothing but the concurrence of so many circumstances in my favour (his entire disinterested friendship for me and the good doctor's memory; Mrs. Hoadly's bringing on a piece of the doctor's at the same time ; the story of mine being on a religious subject, &c. and the peculiar advantage of David's unparalleled performance in it), could have persuaded me to break through the prudery of my profession, and (in my station in the church) produce a play upon the stage."

HOBBES, or HOBBS (Thomas), was born at Malmsbury in Wiltshire, April 5, 1588, his father being minister of that town. The Spanish Armada was then upon the coast of England; and his mother is said to have been so frighted at the alarm which it occasioned, that she was brought to bed of him before her time [т]. After having made a considerable progress in the learned languages at school, he was sent, in 1603, to Magdalen-hall in Oxford; and, in 1608, by the recommendation of the principal, taken into the family of the right honourable William Cavendish lord Hardwicke, soon after created earl of Devonshire, as tutor to his son William lord Cavendish. Hobbes ingratiated himself so effectually with this young nobleman, and with the peer his father, that he was sent abroad with him on his travels in 1610, and made the tour of France and Italy. Upon his return with lord Cavendish, he became known to persons of the highest rank, and eminently distinguished for their abilities and learning. The chancellor Bacon admitted him to a great degree of familiarity, and is said to have made use of his pen, for translating some of his works into Latin. He was likewise much in favour with lord Herbert of Cherbury; and the celebrated Ben Jonson had such an esteem for him, that he revised the first work which he published, viz. his " English Translation of the History of Thucydides." This Hobbes undertook, as he tells us himself, " with an honest view of preventing, if possible, those disturbances, in which he was apprehensive his country would be involved, by shewing in the history

[т] Thomas Hobbes Malmsburiensis vita, à seipso conscripta, &c. Vitæ Hobbianæ Auctarium, &c. Historia & Antiquitates Oxonienses, &c.

of the Peloponnefian war, the fatal confequences of inteftine troubles." This has always been efteemed one of the beft tranflations that we have of any Greek writer; and the author himfelf fuperintended the maps and indexes. But while he meditated this defign, his patron the earl of Devonfhire died in 1626; and in 1628, the year his work was publifhed, his fon died alfo. This lofs affected him to fuch a degree, that he very willingly accepted an offer of going abroad a fecond time with the fon of Sir Gervafe Clifton, whom he accordingly accompanied into France, and ftaid there fome time. But while he continued there, he was folicited to return to England, and to refume his concern for the hopes of that family, to which he had attached himfelf fo early, and owed fo many and fo great obligations.

In 1631, the countefs dowager of Devonfhire was defirous of placing the young earl under his care, who was then about the age of 13. This was very fuitable to his inclinations, and he difcharged that truft with great fidelity and diligence. In 1634, he republifhed his tranflation of Thucydides, and prefixed to it a dedication 'to that young nobleman, in which he gives a high character of his father, and reprefents in the ftrongeft terms his obligations to that illuftrious family. The fame year he accompanied his noble pupil to Paris, where he applied his vacant hours to natural philofophy, and more efpecially to mechanifm, and the caufes of animal motion. He had frequent converfations upon thefe fubjects with father Merfenne, a man defervedly famous, who kept up a correfpondence with almoft all the learned in Europe. From Paris he attended his pupil into Italy, and at Pifa became known to Galileo, who communicated to him his notions very freely. After having feen all that was remarkable in that country, he returned in 1637 with the earl of Devonfhire into England. The troubles in Scotland now grew high; and, as popular difcontent is always contagious, began to fpread themfelves fouthward, and to threaten difturbance throughout the kingdom. Hobbes, feeing this, thought he might do good fervice, by turning himfelf to politics, and compofing fomething by way of antidote to the peftilential opinions which then prevailed. This engaged him to commit to paper certain principles, obfervations, and remarks, out of which he compofed his book " De Cive," and which grew up afterwards into that fyftem which he called his " Leviathan."

Not long after the meeting of the long parliament Nov. 3, 1640, when all things fell into confufion, he withdrew, for the fake of living in quiet, to Paris; where he affociated himfelf with thofe learned men, who, under the protection of cardinal Richelieu, fought, by conferring their notions together, to promote every kind of ufeful knowledge. He had not been long there, when by the good offices of his friend Merfenne, he became

came

came known to Des Cartes, and afterwards held a correspondence with him upon mathematical subjects, as appears from the
letters of Hobbes published in the works of Des Cartes. But
when that philosopher printed afterwards his " Meditations,"
wherein he attempted to establish points of the highest confequence from innate ideas, Hobbes took the liberty of dissenting
from him; as did also Gassendi, with whom Hobbes contracted
a very close friendship, which was not interrupted till the death
of the former. In 1642, he printed a few copies of his book
" De Cive," which raised him many adversaries, by whom he
was charged with instilling principles of a dangerous tendency.
Immediately after the appearance of this book, Des Cartes gave
this judgement upon it to a friend: " I am of opinion," says he,
[v], " that the author of the book ' De Cive,' is the same person
who wrote the third objection against my ' Meditations.' I
think him a much greater master of morality, than of meta-
physics or natural philosophy; though I can by no means approve of his principles or maxims, which are very bad and extremely dangerous, because they suppose all men to be wicked,
or give them occasion to be so. His whole design is to write in
favour of monarchy, which might be done to more advantage
than he has done, upon maxims more virtuous and solid. He
has wrote likewise greatly to the disadvantage of the church and
the Roman Catholic religion, so that if he is not particularly
supported by some powerful interest, I do not see how he can
escape having his book censured." The learned Conringius
[x] censures him very roughly for boasting in regard to this performance, " that though physics were a new science, yet civil
philosophy was still newer, since it could not be styled older than
his book ' De Cive:' whereas," says Conringius, " there is nothing good in that work of his, that was not always known."

Among many illustrious persons, who upon the shipwreck of
the royal cause retired to France for safety, was sir Charles Cavendish, brother to the duke of Newcastle ; and this gentleman,
being skilled in every branch of mathematics, proved a constant
friend and patron to Hobbes, who, by embarking in 1645 in a
controversy about the quadrature of the circle, was grown so
famous, that in 1647 he was recommended to instruct Charles
prince of Wales, afterwards Charles II. in that kind of learning. His care in the discharge of this office, gained him the
esteem of that prince in a very great degree: and though he afterwards withdrew his public favour from Hobbes, on account
of his writings, yet he always retained a sense of the services
he had done him; shewed him various marks of his favour,
after he was restored to his dominions ; and, as some say, had

[v] Epist. Ren. des Cart. Tom. III. p. 504.   [x] De Civil. Prudent. cap. viv.

his

his picture hanging in his closet. This year also was printed in Holland, by the care of M. Sorbiere, a second and more complete edition of his book " De Cive," to which are prefixed, two Latin letters to the editor, one by Gassendi, the other by Merfenne, in commendation of it. While Hobbes was thus employed at Paris, he was attacked by a violent fit of illness, which brought him so low, that his friends began to despair of his recovery. Among those who visited him in this weak condition, was his friend Merfenne; who, taking this for a favourable opportunity, began, after a few general compliments of condolence, to mention the power of the church of Rome to forgive sins: but Hobbes immediately replied, " Father, all these matters I have debated with myself long ago. Such kind of business would be troublesome to me now; and you can entertain me on subjects more agreeable: when did you see Mr. Gassendi?" Merfenne easily understood his meaning, and, without troubling him any farther, suffered the conversation to turn upon general topics. Yet some days afterwards, when Dr. Cosins, afterwards bishop of Durham, came to pray with him, he very readily accepted the proposal, and received the sacrament at his hands, according to the forms appointed by the church of England.

In 1650, was published at London a small treatise by Hobbes, entitled, " Human Nature," and another, " De corpore politico, or, of the Elements of the Law." The latter was presented to Gassendi, and read by him a few months before his death; who is said first to have killed it, and then to have delivered his opinion of it in these words: " This treatise is indeed small in bulk, but in my judgement the very marrow of science." All this time Hobbes had been digesting with great pains his religious, political, and moral principles into a complete system, which he called the " Leviathan," and which was printed in English at London in that and the year following. He caused a copy of it, very fairly written on vellum, to be presented to Charles II but after that monarch was informed, that the English divines considered it as a very bad book, and tending to subvert both religion and civil government, he is said to have withdrawn his countenance from the author, and by the marquis of Ormond to have forbidden him to come into his presence. After the publication of his " Leviathan," Hobbes returned to England, and passed the summer commonly at his patron the earl of Devonshire's seat in Derbyshire, and his winters in town; where he had for his intimate friends some of the greatest men of the age; such as Dr. Harvey, Selden, Cowley, &c. In 1654, he published his " Letter upon Liberty and Necessity," which occasioned a long controversy between him and Bramhall, bishop of Londonderry. About this time he began the controversy

with

with Wallis, the mathematical profeſſor at Oxford, which laſted as long as Hobbes lived, and in which he had the misfortune to have all the mathematicians againſt him. It is indeed ſaid, that he came too late to this ſtudy, to excel in it; and that, though for a time he maintained his credit, while he was content to proceed in the ſame track with others, and to reaſon in the accuſtomed manner from the eſtabliſhed principles of the ſcience, yet when he began to digreſs into new paths, and ſet up for a reformer, inventor, and improver of geometry, he loſt himſelf extremely. But notwithſtanding theſe debates took up much of his time, yet he publiſhed ſeveral philoſophical treatiſes in Latin.

Such were his occupations till 1660, when upon the king's reſtoration he quitted the country, and came up to London. He was at Saliſbury-houſe with his patron, when the king paſſing by one day accidentally ſaw him. He ſent for him, gave him his hand to kiſs, enquired kindly after his health and circumſtances; and ſome time after directed Cooper, the celebrated miniature-painter, to take his portrait. His majeſty likewiſe afforded him another private audience, ſpoke to him very kindly, aſſured him of his protection, and ſettled a penſion upon him of 100l. per annum out of his privy purſe. Yet this did not render him entirely ſafe; for, in 1666, his "Leviathan," and treatiſe "De Cive," were cenſured by parliament, which alarmed him much; as did alſo the bringing of a bill into the houſe of commons to puniſh atheiſm and profaneneſs. When this ſtorm was a little blown over, he began to think of procuring a beautiful edition of his pieces that were in Latin; but finding this impracticable in England, he cauſed it to be undertaken abroad, where they were publiſhed in 1668, 4to, from the preſs of John Bleau. In 1669, he was viſited by Coſmo de Medicis, then prince, afterwards duke of Tuſcany, who gave him ample marks of his eſteem; and having received his picture, and a complete collection of his writings, cauſed them to be depoſited, the former among his curioſities, the latter in his library at Florence. Similar viſits he received from ſeveral foreign ambaſſadors, and other ſtrangers of diſtinction; who were curious to ſee a perſon, whoſe ſingular opinions and numerous writings had made ſo much noiſe all over Europe. In 1672, he wrote his own life in Latin verſe, when, as he obſerves, he had completed his 84th year: and, in 1674, he publiſhed in Engliſh verſe four books of Homer's "Odyſſey," which were ſo well received, that it encouraged him to undertake the whole "Iliad" and "Odyſſey," which he likewiſe performed, and publiſhed in 1675. Theſe were not the firſt ſpecimens of his poetic genius, which he had given to the public: he had publiſhed many years before, about 1637, a Latin poem entitled, "De Mirabilibus

Pecci,

Pecci, or, Of the Wonders of the Peak." But his poetry is
below criticism, and has been long exploded. In 1674, he took
his leave of London, and went to spend the remainder of his
days in Derbyshire; where however he did not remain in-
active, notwithstanding his advanced age, but published from
time to time several pieces to be found in the collection of his
works, namely, in 1676, his "Dispute with Laney bishop of Ely,
concerning Liberty and Necessity;" in 1678, his "Decameron
Physiologicum, or, Ten Dialogues of Natural Philosophy;" to
which he added a book, entitled, "A Dialogue between a Philosopher and a Student of the Common Law of England."
June 1679, he sent another book, entitled, "Behemoth, or,
A History of the Civil Wars from 1640 to 1660," to an eminent bookseller, with a letter setting forth the reasons for his
communication of it, as well as for the request he then made,
that he would not publish it till a proper occasion offered. The
book however was published as soon as he was dead, and
the letter along with it; of which we shall give an extract, because it is curious.—"I would fain have published my Dialogue
of the Civil Wars of England long ago, and to that end I presented it to his majesty; and some days after, when I thought
he had read it, I humbly besought him to let me print it. But
his majesty, though he heard me graciously, yet he flatly refused
to have it published: therefore I brought away the book, and
gave you leave to take a copy of it; which when you had done,
I gave the original to an honourable and learned friend, who
about a year after died. The king knows better, and is more
concerned in publishing of books than I am; and therefore I
dare not venture to appear in the business, lest I should offend
him. Therefore I pray you not to meddle in the business.
Rather than to be thought any way to further or countenance the
printing, I would be content to lose twenty times the value of
what you can expect to gain by it. I pray do not take it ill; it
may be I may live to send you somewhat else as vendible as that,
and without offence. I am, &c." However he did not live to
send his bookseller any thing more, this being the last piece that
went from himself: for, October following, he was afflicted
with a suppression of urine; and his physician plainly told him,
that he had little hopes of curing him. Nov. 20, the earl of
Devonshire removing from Chatsworth to another seat called
Hardwick, Hobbes obstinately persisted in desiring that he might
be carried too, though this could no way be done, but by laying
him upon a feather-bed. He was not much discomposed with
his journey, yet within a week after lost, by a stroke of the
palsy, the use of his speech, and of his right side entirely; in
which condition he remained for some days, taking little nourishment, and sleeping much, sometimes endeavouring to speak,

but

but not being able. He died Dec. 4, 1679, in his 92d year. Wood tells us, that after his phyfician gave him no hop s of a cure, he faid, " Then I fhall be glad to find a hole to creep out of the world at." He obferves alfo, that his not defiring a mi- nifter, to receive the facrament before he died, ought in charity to be imputed to his being fo fuddenly feized, and afterwards deprived of his fenfes; the rather, becaufe the earl of Devon- fhire's chaplain declared, that within the two laft years of his life he had often received the facrament from his hands with feeming devotion.

He was a man of prodigious capacity, and went to the bottom of whatever he undertook to examine: his genius was lively and penetrating, but, at the fame time, he was ftudious and indefatigable in his enquiries. Confidering his great age, he was a man of no very extenfive reading. Homer, Virgil, Thucydides, and Euclid, were authors with whom he was moft delighted. He ufed to fay upon this fubject, that " if he had read as much as others, he fhould have been as ignorant as they." As to his character and manners, they are thus defcribed by Dr. White Kennet, in his " Memoirs of the Cavendifh Family [Y]." " The earl of Devonfhire," fays he, " for his whole life entertained Mr. Hobbes in his family, as his old tutor rather than as his friend or confident. He let him live under his roof in eafe and plenty, and in his own way, without making ufe of him in any public, or fo much as domeftic affairs. He would often exprefs an ab- horrence of fome of his principles in policy and religion; and both he and his lady would frequently put off the mention of his name, and fay, ' He was a humourift, and nobody could ac- count for him.' There is a tradition in the family of the man- ners and cuftoms of Mr. Hobbes fomewhat obfervable. His profeffed rule of health was to dedicate the morning to his exer- cife, and the afternoon to his ftudies. At his firft rifing, there- fore, he walked out, and climbed any hill within his reach; or, if the weather was not dry, he fatigued himfelf within doors by fome exercife or other, to be in a fweat: recommending that practice upon this opinion, that an old man had more moifture than heat, and therefore by fuch motion heat was to be acquired, and moifture expelled. After this he took a comfortable break- faft; and then went round the lodgings to wait upon the earl, the countefs, and the children, and any confiderable ftrangers, paying fome fhort addreffes to all of them. He kept thefe rounds till about twelve o'clock, when he had a little dinner pro- vided for him, which he eat always by himfelf without cere- mony. Soon after dinner he retired to his ftudy, and had his candle with ten or twelve pipes of tobacco laid by him; then

[Y] Page 107, &c.

fhutting

fantting his door, he fell to fmoaking, thinking, and writing for feveral hours. He retained a friend or two at court, and efpecially the lord Arlington, to protect him if occafion fhould require. He ufed to fay, that it was lawful to make ufe of ill inftruments to do ourfelves good: ' If I were call," fays he, ' into a deep pit, and the devil fhould put down his cloven foot, I would take hold of it to be drawn out by it.' Towards the end of his life he had very few books, and thofe he read but very little; thinking he was now able only to digeft what he had for-'merly fed upon. If company came to vifit him, he would be free in difcourfe till he was preffed or contradicted; and then he had the infirmities of being fhort and peevifh, and referring to his writings for better fatisfaction. His friends, who had the liberty of introducing ftrangers to him, made thefe terms with them before their admiffion, that they fhould not difpute with the old man, nor contradict him."

After mentioning the apprehenfions Hobbes was under, when the parliament cenfured his book, and the methods he took to efcape perfecution, Dr. Kennet proceeds in the following terms: " It is not much to be doubted, that upon this occafion he began to make a more open fhew of religion and church communion. He now frequented the chapel, joined in the fervice, and was generally a partaker of the holy facrament: and whenever any ftrangers in converfation with him feemed to queftion his belief, he would always appeal to his conformity in divine fervices, and referred them to the chaplain for a teftimony of i. Others thought it a mere compliance to the orders of the family, and obferved, that in city and country he never went to any parifh church; and even in the chapel upon Sundays, he went out after prayers, and turned his back upon the fermon; and when any friend afked the reafon of it, he gave no other but this, ' they could teach him nothing, but what he knew.' He did not conceal his hatred to the clergy; but it was vifible that the hatred was owing to his fear of their civil intereft and power. He had often a jealoufy, that the bifhops would burn him: and of all the bench he was moft afraid of the bifhop of Sarum, becaufe he had moft offended him; thinking every man's fpirit to be remembrance and revenge. After the Reftoration, he watched all opportunities to ingratiate himfelf with the king and his prime minifters; and looked upon his penfion to be more valuable, as an earneft of favour and protection, than upon any other account. His following courfe of life was to be free from danger. He could not endure to be left in an empty houfe. Whenever the earl removed he would go along with him, even to his laft ftage, from Chatfworth to Hardwick. When he was in a very weak condition, he dared not to be left behind, but made his way upon a feather-bed in a coach, though he furvived the
journey

journey but a few days. He could not bear any difcourfe of death, and feemed to caft off all thoughts of it: he delighted to reckon upon longer life. The winter before he died, he made a warm coat, which he faid muft laft him three years, and then he would have fuch another. In his laft ficknefs his frequent queftions were, Whether his difeafe was curable? and when intimations were given that he might have eafe, but no remedy, he ufed this expreffion, ' I fhall be glad to find a hole to creep out of the world at ;' which are reported to have been his laft fenfible words; and his lying fome days following in a filent ftupefaction, did feem owing to his mind more than to his body. The only thought of death, that he appeared to entertain in time of health, was to take care of fome infcription on his grave. He would fuffer fome friends to dictate an epitaph, among which he was beft pleafed with this humour, ' This is the true philofopher's ftone, &c."

After this account of Hobbes, which, though undoubtedly true in the main, feems rather too ftrongly coloured, it will be but juftice to fubjoin what lord Clarendon has faid of him. This noble perfon, during his banifhment, wrote a book in 1670, which was printed fix years after at Oxford with this title, " A brief View of the dangerous and pernicious Errors to Church and State in Mr. Hobbes's Book, intituled, Leviathan." In the introduction the earl obferves, that Mr. Hobbes's " Leviathan" " contains in it good learning of all kinds, politely extracted, and very wittily and cunningly digefted in a very commendable, and in a vigorous and pleafant ftyle: and that Mr. Hobbes himfelf was a man of excellent parts, of great wit, fome reading, and fomewhat more thinking; one who has fpent many years in foreign parts and obfervations; underftands the learned as well as the modern languages; hath long had the reputation of a great philofopher and mathematician; and in his age hath had converfation with very many worthy and extraordinary men: to which it may be, if he had been more indulgent in the more vigorous part of his life, it might have had greater influence upon the temper of his mind; whereas age feldom fubmits to thefe queftions, enquiries, and contradictions, which the laws and liberty of converfation require. And it hath been always a lamentation among Mr. Hobbes's friends, that he fpent too much time in thinking, and too little in exercifing thofe thoughts in the company of other men of the fame, or of as good faculties; for want whereof his natural conftitution, with age, contracted fuch a morofity, that doubting and contradicting men were never grateful to him. In a word, Mr. Hobbes is one of the moft ancient acquaintance I have in the world; and of whom I have always had a great efteem, as a man, who, befides his eminent parts, learning, and knowledge,

hath

? ath been always looked upon as a man of probity, and of a life free from fcandal."

There have been few perfons, whofe writings have had a more pernicious influence in fpreuding irreligion and infidelity than thofe of Hobbes; and yet none of his treatifes are directly levelled againft revealed religion. He fometimes affects to fpeak with veneration of the facred writings, and exprefsly declares, that though the laws of nature are not laws, as they proceed from nature, yet " as they are given by God in Holy Scripture, they are properly called laws; for the Holy Scripture is the voice of God, ruling all things by the greateft right [z]." But though he feems here to make the laws of Scripture the laws of God, and to derive their force from his fupreme authority, yet elfewhere he fuppofes them to have no authority, but what they derive from the prince or civil power. He fometimes feems to acknowledge infpiration to be a fupernatural gift, and the immediate hand of God: at other times he treats the pretence to it as a fign of madnefs, and reprefents God's fpeaking to the prophets in a dream, to be no more than the prophets dreaming that God fpake unto them. He afferts, that we have no affurance of the certainty of Scripture, but the authority of the church [a], and this he refolves into the authority of the commonwealth; and declares, that til' the fovereign ruler had prefcribed them, " the precepts of Scripture were not obligatory laws, but only counfel or advice, which he that was counfelled might without injuftice refufe to obferve, and being contrary to the laws could not without injuftice obferve;" that the word of the interpreter of Scripture is the word of God, and that the fovereign magiftrate is the interpreter of Scripture, and of all doctrines, to whofe authority we muft ftand. Nay, he carries it fo far as to pronounce [b], that Chriftians are bound in confcience to obey the laws of an infidel king in matters of religion; that " thought is free, but when it comes to confeffion of faith, the private reafon muft fubmit to the public, that is to fay, to God's lieutenant." Accordingly he allows the fubject, being commanded by the fovereign, to deny Chrift in words, holding the faith of him firmly in his heart; it being in this " not he, that denieth Chrift before men, but his governor and the laws of his country." In the mean time he acknowledges the exiftence of God [c], and that we muft of neceffity afcribe the effects we behold to the eternal power of all powers, and caufe of all caufes; and he reproaches thofe as abfurd, who call the world, or the foul of the world, God. But then he denies that we know any thing more of him than that he exifts, and feems plainly to make him corporeal;

[z] De Cive, c. III. C. 33.
[a] Leviathan, p. 196.

[z] De Cive, c. 17. Leviathan, p. 269, 283, 284.
[c] Leviathan, p. 238. 271.

fo**r**

for he affirms, that whatever is not body is nothing at all.
And though he sometimes seems to acknowledge religion and its
obligations, and that there is an honour and worship due to
God ; prayer, thankfgivings, oblations, &c. yet he advances
principles, which evidently tend to fubvert all religion. The
account he gives of it is this, that " from the fear of power
invifible, feigned by the mind, or imagined from tales, publicly
allowed, arifeth religion ; not allowed, fuperftition:" and he
refolves religion into things which he himfelf derides, namely,
" opinions of ghofts, ignorance of fecond caufes, devotion to
what men fear, and taking of things cafual for prognoftics." He
takes pains in many places to prove man a neceffary agent, and
openly derides the doctrine of a future ftate: for he fays, that the
belief of a future ftate after death, " is a belief grounded upon
other men's faying, that they knew it fupernaturally ; or, that they
knew thofe, that knew them, that knew others that knew it fupernaturally." But it is not revealed religion only, of which Hobbes
makes light ; he goes farther, as will appear by running over a
few more of his maxims. He afferts, " that, by the law of
nature, every man hath a right to all things, and over all perfons;
and that the natural condition of man is a ftate of war, a war
of all men againft all men: that there is no way fo reafonable
for any man, as by force or wiles to gain a maftery over all
other perfons that he can, till he fees no other power ftrong
enough to endanger him: that the civil laws are the only rules
of good and evil, juft and unjuft, honeft and difhoneft ; and
that, antecedently to fuch laws, every action is in its own nature indifferent ; that there is nothing good or evil in itfelf, nor
any common laws conftituting what is naturally juft and unjuft ;
that all things are meafured by what every man judgeth fit, where
there is no civil government, and by the laws of fociety, where
there is: that the power of the fovereign is abfolute, and that
he is not bound by any compacts with his fubjects : that nothing
the fovereign can do to the fubject, can properly be called injurious or wrong ; and that the king's word is fufficient to take
any thing from the fubject if need be, and that the king is judge
of that need." This fcheme evidently ftrikes at the foundation
of all religion, natural and revealed. It tends not only to fubvert the authority of Scripture, but to deftroy God's moral government of the world. It confounds the natural differences of
good and evil, virtue and vice. It deftroys the beft principles
of the human nature; and inftead of that innate benevolence,
and focial difpofition which fhould unite men together, fuppofes
all men to be naturally in a ftate of war with one another. It
erects an abfolute tyranny in the ftate and church which it confounds, and makes the will of the prince or governing power
the fole ftandard of right and wrong.

Such

Such principles in religion and politics would, as it may be imagined, raise a man adversaries. Hobbes accordingly was attacked by many considerable persons, and, what may seem more strange, by such as wrote against each other. For instance, Harrington in his " Oceana," falls very often on Hobbes; and so does sir Robert Filmer in his " Observations concerning the Original of Government." We have already mentioned Bramhall and Clarendon; the former argued with great acuteness against that part of his system, which relates to liberty and necessity, and afterwards attacked the whole in a piece, called " The Catching of the Leviathan," published in 1685; in which he undertakes to demonstrate out of Hobbes's own works, that no man, who is thoroughly an Hobbist, can be " a good Christian, or a good commonwealth's man, or reconcile himself to himself." Tenison, afterwards archbishop of Canterbury, gave a summary view of Hobbes's principles, in a book, called " The Creed of Mr. Hobbes examined, 1670;" to which we may add the two dialogues of Dr. Eachard between Timothy and Philautus, and Dr. Parker's book, entitled, " Disputationes de Deo & Divina Providentia." Dr. Henry More has also in different parts, of his works canvassed and refuted several positions of Hobbes; and the philosopher of Malmesbury is said to have been so ingenuous as to own, that " whenever he discovered his own philosophy to be unsustainable, he would embrace the opinions of Dr. More." But the two greatest works against him were, Cumberland's book " De legibus Naturæ," and Cudworth's " Intellectual System:" for these authors do not employ themselves about his peculiar whimsies, or in vindicating revealed religion from his exceptions and cavils, but endeavour to establish the great principles of all religion and morality, which his scheme tended to subvert, and to shew, that they have a real foundation in reason and nature.

There is one peculiarity related of Hobbes, which we have not yet mentioned in the course of our account of him, but with which it shall be closed: it is, that he was afraid of apparitions and spirits. His friends indeed have called this a fable [D]. " He was falsely accused," say they, " by some, of being afraid to be alone, because he was afraid of spectres and apparitions: vain bugbears of fools, which he had chased away by the light of his philosophy." They do not however deny, that he was afraid of being alone; they only insinuate, that it was for fear of being assassinated. In the mean time, Bayle observes, that Hobbes's principles of philosophy were not proper to rid him from the fear of apparitions or spirits [E]: " a man," says he, " would not only be very rash, but also very extrava-

[D] Vita Hobbes, p. 106.   [E] Art. HOBBES, note x.

gant,

gant, who should pretend to prove, that there never was any person that imagined he saw a spectre; and I do not think that the most obstinate unbelievers have maintained this. All that they say amounts to no more, than that the persons, who have thought themselves eye-witnesses of the apparitions of spirits, had disturbed imaginations. They confess then, that there are certain places in our brain, that being affected in a certain manner excite the image of an object, which has no real existence out of ourselves; and make the man, whose brain is thus modified, believe he sees at two paces distance a frightful spectre, a hobgoblin, a threatening phantom. The like happens in the heads of the most incredulous, either in their sleep, or in the paroxysms of a violent fever. Will they maintain after this, that it is impossible for a man awake, and not in a delirium, to receive in certain places of his brain, an impression almost like that, which by the laws of nature is connected with the appearance of a phantom? If they are forced to acknowledge that this is possible, they cannot promise that a spectre will never appear to them; that is, that they shall never, when awake, believe they see either a man or a beast, when they are alone in a chamber. Hobbes then might believe, that a certain combination of atoms, agitated in his brain, might expose him to such a vision; though he was persuaded, that neither an angel nor the soul of a dead man was to be concerned in it. He was timorous to the last degree, and consequently had reason to distrust his imagination, when he was alone in a chamber in the night; for, in spite of him, the remembrance of what he had read and heard concerning apparitions would revive, though he was not persuaded of the reality of any such things. These images, joined with the timorousness of his temper, might play him an unlucky trick: and it is certain, that a man as incredulous as he was, but of greater courage, would be astonished to think he saw one, whom he knew to be dead, enter into his chamber. These apparitions in dreams are very frequent, whether a man believes the immortality of the soul or not. Supposing they should once happen to an incredulous man awake, as they do frequently in his sleep, we allow that he would be afraid, though he had never so much courage: and therefore for a stronger reason we ought to believe, that Hobbes would have been terribly affrighted at it."

HOCHSTETTER (ANDREW, ADAM), a protestant divine, born at Tubingen, in 1688, and successively professor of eloquence, of moral philosophy, and of divinity in that university; of which finally he became rector. He died at the same place in April, 1717. His principal works are, 1. "Collegium Pufsendorfianum." 2. "De Festo Expiationis, et Hirco Azazel."

3. "De

3. " De Conradino, ultimo ex Suevis duce." 4. " De rebus
Elbigenfibus." His hiftorical works are in moſt eſteem.

HODGES (Nathaniel), an Engliſh phyſician [r], was
the ſon of Dr. Thomas Hodges, dean of Hereford, of
whom there are three printed ſermons. He was educated
in Weſtminſter-ſchool, and became a ſtudent of Chriſt-church,
Oxford, in 1648. In 1651 and 1654, he took the degrees
of B. and M. A. and, in 1659, accumulated the degrees of
B. and M. D. He ſettled in London, and continued there during the plague in 1665: by which, fays Wood, he obtained a
great name and practice among the citizens, and was in 1672
made fellow of the College of Phyſicians. Neverthelefs, he
afterwards fell into unfortunate circumſtances, and was confined
for debt in Ludgate priſon, where he died in 1684. His body
was interred in the church of St. Stephen's, Walbrook, London,
where a monument- is erected to him. He is author of two
works: 1. " Vindiciæ Medicinæ & Medicorum :" " An Apology for the Profeſſion and Profeſſors of Phyſic, &c. 1660," 8vo.
2. " ΛΟΙΜΟΛΟΓΙΑ : five, peſtis nuperæ apud populum
Londinenſem graſſantis narratio hiſtorica," 1672, 8vo. A tranſlation of it into Engliſh was printed at London in 1720, 8vo,
under the following title : " Loimologia, or, an Hiſtorical Account of the Plague of London in 1665, with precautionary Directions againſt the like Contagion. By Nath. Hodges, M. D.
and Fellow of the College of Phyſicians, who reſided in the
City all that Time. To which is added, an Eſſay on the different
Cauſes of Peſtilential Diſeaſes, and how they become contagious.
With Remarks on the Infection now in France, and the moſt
probable Means to prevent its ſpreading here. By John Quincy,
M. D." In 1721, there was printed at London, in 8vo, " A
Collection of very valuable and ſcarce Pieces relating to the laſt
Plague in 1665;" among which is " An Account of the firſt
Rife, Progrefs, Symptoms, and Cure of the Plague, being the
Subſtance of a Letter from Dr. Hodges to a Perſon of Quality, dated from his Houfe in Watling Street, May the 8th,
1666." The author of the preface to this collection calls our
author " a faithful hiſtorian and diligent phyſician;" and tells
us, that " he may be reckoned among the beſt obſervers in any
age of phyſic, and has given us a true picture of the plague in
his own time."

HODY (Humphrey), an eminent Engliſh divine [o], was
born Jan. 1, 1659, at Odcombe in the county of Somerſet, of
which place his father was rector. He difcovered while a boy,

[r] Athen. Oxon. Vol. II.   de Græcis Illuftribus Linguæ Græcæ la-
[o] De vita & ſcriptis Hum. Hodii ſtauratoribus, &c.
diſſertatio, p. 5, 6. Prefixed to his book,

a vaſt propenſity to learning; and, in 1676, was admitted into Wadham-college, Oxford, of which he was choſen fellow in 1684. When he was but 21, he publiſhed his " Diſſertation againſt Ariſteas's Hiſtory of the Seventy-two Interpreters." The ſubſtance of that hiſtory of Ariſteas, concerning the 72 Greek interpreters of the Bible, is this: Ptolemy Philadelphus, king of Egypt, and founder of the noble library at Alexandria, being deſirous of enriching that library with all ſorts of books, committed the care of it to Demetrius Phalareus, a noble Athenian then living in his court. Demetrius being informed, in the courſe of his enquiries, of the Law of Moſes among the Jews, a quainted the king with it; who thereupon ſignified his pleaſure, that a copy of that book, which was then only in Hebrew, ſhould be ſent for from Jeruſalem, with interpreters from the ſame place to tranſlate it into Greek. A deputation was accordingly ſent to Eleazar the high-prieſt of the Jews at Jeruſalem; who ſent a copy of the Hebrew original, and 72 interpreters, ſix out of each of the twelve tribes, to tranſlate it into Greek. When they were come to Egypt, the king cauſed them to be conducted into the iſland of Pharos near Alexandria, in apartments prepared for them, where they completed their tranſlation in 72 days. Such is the ſtory told by Ariſteas, who is ſaid to be one of king Ptolemy's court. Hody ſhews that it is the invention of ſome Helleniſt Jew; that it is full of anachroniſms and groſs blunders; and, in ſhort, was written on purpoſe to recommend and give greater authority to the Greek verſion of the Old Teſtament, which from this ſtory hath received the name of the Septuagint. This diſſertation was received with the higheſt applauſe by all the learned, except Iſaac Voſſius. Charles du Freſne ſpoke highly of it in his obſervations on the " Chronicon Paſchale," publiſhed in 1688; and Menage, in his notes upon the ſecond edition of " Diogenes Laertius," gave Hody the titles of " eruditiſſimus, doctiſſimus, elegantiſſimus, &c." but Voſſius alone was greatly diſſatisfied with it. He had eſpouſed the contrary opinion, and could not bear that ſuch a boy as Hody ſhould preſume to contend with one of his age and reputation for letters. He publiſhed therefore an Appendix to his " Obſervations on Pomponius Mela," and ſubjoined an anſwer to this diſſertation of Hody's; in which, however, he did not enter much into the argument, but contents himſelf with treating Hody very contemptuouſly, vouchſafing him no better title than Juvenis Oxonienſis, and ſometimes uſing a great deal worſe language. When Voſſius was aſked afterwards, what induced him to treat a young man of promiſing hopes, and who had certainly deſerved well of the republic of letters, ſo very harſhly, he anſwered, that he had received ſome time before a rude Latin epiſtle from Oxford, of which he ſuſpected Hody to be the

I   author;

author; and that this had made him deal more feverely with him, than he fhould otherwife have done. Voffius had indeed received fuch a letter; but it was written, according to the affertion of Creech, the tranflator of Lucretius, without Hody's knowledge or approbation. When Hody publifhed his " Differtation, &c." he told the reader in his preface, that he had three other books prepared upon the Hebrew Text, and Greek Verfion; but he was now fo entirely drawn away from thefe ftudies by other engagements, that he could not find time to complete his work, and to anfwer the objections of Voffius, till more than twenty years after. In 1704, he publifhed it altogether, with this title, " De Bibliorum textibus originalibus, verfionibus Græcis, & Latina Vulgata, libri IV. &c." The firft book contains his differtation againft Arifteas's hiftory, which is here reprinted with improvements, and an anfwer to Voffius's objections. In the fecond he treats of the true authors of the Greek verfion, called the Septuagint; of the time when, and the reafons why, it was undertaken, and of the manner in which it was performed. The third is a hiftory of the Hebrew text, the Septuagint verfion, and of the Latin Vulgate; fhewing the authority of each in different ages, and that the Hebrew text hath been always moft efteemed and valued. In the fourth he gives an account of the reft of the Greek verfions, namely, thofe of Symmachus, Aquila, and Theodotion; of Origen's " Hexapla," and other ancient editions; and fubjoins lifts of the books of the Bible at different times, which exhibit a concife, but full and clear view, of the canon of Holy Scripture.—Upon the whole, he thinks it probable, that the Greek verfion, called the Septuagint, was done in the time of the two Ptolemies, Lagus and Philadelphus; and that it was not done by order of king Ptolemy, or under the direction of Demetrius Phalereus, in order to be depofited in the Alexandrine library, but by Hellenift Jews for the ufe of their own countrymen.

In 1689, he wrote the "Prolegomena" to John Malela's " Chronicle" printed at Oxford; and the year after was made chaplain to Stillingfleet bifhop of Worcefter, being tutor to his fon at Wadham-college. The deprivation of the bifhops, who had refufed the oaths to king William and queen Mary, engaged him in a controverfy with Dodwell, who had till now been his friend, and had fpoken handfomely and affectionately of him, in his " Differtations upon Irenæus," printed in 1689. The pieces Hody publifhed on this occafion were, in 1691, " The Unreafonablenefs of a Separation from the new Bifhops: or, a Treatife out of Ecclefiaftical Hiftory, fhewing, that although a bifhop was unjuftly deprived, neither he nor the church ever made a feparation, if the fucceffor was not an heretic. Tranflated out of an ancient manuscript in the public library at Oxford [u]." He translated it afterwards into Latin, and prefixed to it some pieces out of ecclesiastical antiquity, relating to the same subject. Dodwell publishing an answer to it, entitled, "A Vindication of the deprived Bishops," &c. in 1692; Hody replied, in a treatise which he styled, "The Case of Sees vacant by an unjust or uncanonical Deprivation stated; in Answer to a Piece intituled, A Vindication of the deprived Bishops, &c. Together with the several Pamphlets published as Answers to the Baroccian Treatise, 1693." The part he acted in this controversy recommended him so powerfully to Tillotson, who had succeeded Sancroft in the see of Canterbury, that he made him his domestic chaplain in May, 1694. Here he drew up his dissertation "concerning the Resurrection of the same Body," which he dedicated to Stillingfleet, whose chaplain he had been from 1690. Tillotson dying November following, he was continued chaplain by Tenison his successor; who soon after gave him the rectory of Chart near Canterbury, vacant by the death of Wharton. This, before he was collated, he exchanged for the united parishes of St. Michael's Royal and St. Martin's Vintry, in London, being instituted to these in Aug. 1695. In 1696, at the command of Tenison, he wrote "Animadversions on Two Pamphlets lately published by Mr. Collier, &c." When sir William Perkins and sir John Friend were executed that year for the assassination-plot, Collier, Cook, and Snatt, three nonjuring clergymen, formally pronounced upon them the absolution of the church, as it stands in the office for the visitation of the sick, and accompanied this ceremony with a solemn imposition of hands. For this imprudent action they were not only indicted, but also the archbishops and bishops published "A Declaration of their Sense concerning those irregular and scandalous Proceedings." Snatt and Cook were cast into prison. Collier absconded, and from his privacy published two pamphlets to vindicate his own, and his brethren's conduct; the one called, "A Defence of the Absolution given by Sir William Perkins at the Place of Execution;" the other, "A Vindication thereof, occasioned by a Paper, intituled, A Declaration of the Sense of the Archbishops and Bishops, &c." in answer to which Hody published the "Animadversions" abovementioned.

March, 1698, he was appointed regius professor of Greek in the university of Oxford; and instituted to the archdeaconry of Oxford in 1704. In 1701, he bore a part in the controversy about the convocation, and published upon that occasion, "A History of English Councils and Convocations, and

[u] One of the Baroccian MSS.

of

of the Clergy's fitting in Parliament, in which is also comprehended the History of Parliaments, with an Account of our ancient Laws." He died Jan. 20, 1706, and was buried in the chapel belonging to Wadham-college, where he had received his education, and to which he had been a benefactor: for, in order to encourage the study of the Greek and Hebrew languages, of which he was so great a master himself, he founded in that college ten scholarships of 10l. each; and appointed, that five of the scholars should apply themselves to the study of the Hebrew, and five to the study of the Greek language. He left behind him in MS. " An Account of those learned Grecians, who retired to Italy, before and after the taking of Constantinople by the Turks, and restored the Greek Tongue and Learning in these Western Parts of the World." It was published in 1742, by Dr. S. Jebb, under this title, " De Græcis illustribus linguæ Græcæ literarumque humaniorum instauratoribus, eorum vitis, scriptis, & elogiis libri duo. E. Codd. potissimum MSS. aliisque authenticis ejusdem ævi monimentis deprompsit Humfredus Hodius, S. T. P. haud ita pridem Regius Professor & Archidiaconus Oxon."

HOË (MATTHIAS DE HORNEGG), of a noble family at Vienna, was born Feb. 24, 1580. After being eight years superintendant of Plaven in Saxony, he took holy orders at Prague in 1611. In 1613 he left Prague, and was appointed principal preacher to the elector of Saxony at Dresden; and there he died March 4, 1645. He was a strenuous Lutheran, and wrote with zeal against Calvinists as well as Papists. His works, which are very numerous both in Latin and German, are not at this day much esteemed, or indeed known. Their titles, however, are given by the writer of his life, and among them we find, " Solida detestatio Papæ et Calvinistarum," 4to. " Apologia pro B. Luthero contra Lampadium," 4to, Leipsic, 1611. " Philosophiæ Aristotelicæ, partes tres." " Septem verborum Christi explicatio." The greater part of his tracts appear evidently, from their titles, to be controversial.

HOELTZLINUS (JEREMIAS), a philologer born at Nuremberg, but settled at Leyden, and best known by his edition of Apollonius Rhodius, which was published there in 1641. This edition is generally esteemed; but Ruhnkenius, in his second Epistola Critica, calls the editor " tetricum et ineptum Apollonii Commentatorem;" and his commentary has been censured also by other learned men. He published in 1628, a German translation of the Psalms, which has the credit of being accurate. He died in 1641.

HOESCHELIUS (DAVID), a learned German, was born at Augsburg in 1556; and spent his life in teaching the youth in the college of St. Anne, of which he was made principal, by the magiftrates of Augfburg, in 1593. They made him their library-keeper alfo, and he acquitted himfelf incomparably well in this poft : for he collected a great number of MSS. and printed books, efpecially Greek, and alfo of the beft authors and the beft editions, with which he enriched their library. Neither did he let the MSS. lie there, as a treafure buried under ground ; but publifhed the moft fcarce and curious of them, to which he added his own notes. His publications were very numerous, among which were editions of the following authors, or at leaft of fome part of their works ; Origen, Philo Judæus, Bafil, Gregory of Nyffen, Gregory of Nazianzen, Chryfoftom, Hori Apollinis Hieroglyphica, Appian, Photius, Procopius, Anna Comnena, &c. To fome of thefe he made Latin tranflations, while he publifhed others in Greek only, with the addition of his own notes. Huetius has commended him [1], not only for the pains he took to difcover old manufcripts, but alfo for his fkill and abi-lity in tranflating them. He compofed, and publifhed in 1595, " A Catalogue of the Greek MSS. in the Augfburg library," which, for the judgement and order with which it is drawn up, is reckoned a mafterpiece in its kind. He may juftly be ranked among thofe who contributed to the revival of good learning in Europe: for, befides thefe labours for the public, he attended his college clofely ; and not only produced very good fcholars, but fuch a number of them, that he is faid to have furnifhed the bar with one thoufand, and the church with two thoufand young men. He died at Augfburg in 1617, much lamented ; for he was a man of good as well as great qualities, and therefore not lefs be-loved than admired.

HOFFMAN (MAURICE), a phyfician, was born of a good family, at Furftenwalde, in the electorate of Brandenbburg, Sept. 20, 1621 [x] ; and was driven early from his native coun-try by the plague, and alfo by the war that followed it. His pa-rents, having little idea of letters or fciences, contented them-felves with having him taught writing and arithmetic ; but Hoff-man's tafte for books and ftudy made him very impatient under this confined inftruction, and he was refolved, at all events, to be a fcholar. He firft gained over his mother to his fcheme ; but fhe died when he was only 15. This, however, fortunately proved no impediment to his purpofe ; for the fchoolmafter of Furftenwalde, to which place after many removals he had now re-turned, was fo touched with his good natural abilities and ftrong difpofition for learning, that he was at the pains of inftructing him in fecret. His father, convinced at length of his very uncommon talents, permitted him to follow his inclinations ; and,

[1] De claris interpretibus, p. 229.
[2] Nicron, Homines Illuftres, Tom. XVI.

in 1637, fent him to ſtudy in the college of Cologne. Famine
and the plague drove him from hence to Kopnik, where he buried his father; and, in 1638, he went to Altdorf, to an uncle
by his mother's ſide, who was a profeſſor of phyſic. Here he
finiſhed his ſtudies in claſſical learning and philoſophy, and then
applied himſelf, with the utmoſt ardour, to phyſic. In 1641,
when he had made ſome progreſs, he went to the univerſity of
Padua, which then abounded with men very learned in all ſciences.
Anatomy and botany were the great objects of his purſuit; and
he became very deeply ſkilled in both. Bartholin tells us, that
Hoffman, having diſſected a turkey-cock [1], diſcovered the
panacretic duct, and ſhewed it to Verſungus, a celebrated ana-
tomiſt of Padua, with whom he lodged; who, taking the hint
from thence, demonſtrated afterwards the ſame veſſel in the
human body. When he had been at Padua about three years, he
returned to Altdorf, to aſſiſt his uncle, now growing infirm, in
his buſineſs; and taking the degree of doctor, he applied himſelf
very diligently to practice, in which he had abundant ſucceſs, and
acquired great fame. In 1648, he was made profeſſor extraordinary in anatomy and ſurgery; in 1649, profeſſor of phyſic,
and ſoon after member of the college of phyſicians; in 1653,
profeſſor of botany, and director of the phyſic-garden. He
acquitted himſelf very ably in theſe various employments, not
neglecting in the mean time the buſineſs of his profeſſion; in
which his reputation was ſo high and extenſive, that many
princes of Germany appointed him their phyſician. He died of
an apoplexy in 1698, aged 76, after having publiſhed ſeveral
botanical works, and married three wives, by whom he had
eighteen children. His works are, 1. " Altdorfi deliciæ hor-
tenſes," 4to, 1677. 2. " Appendix ad Catalogum, Plantarum
hortenſium," 4to, 1691. 3. " Deliciæ ſilveſtres," 4to, 1677.
4. " Florilegium Altdorfinum," 4to, 1676, &c.

HOFFMAN (JOHN MAURICE), ſon of the former by his
firſt wife, was born at Altdorf in 1653; and ſent to ſchool at
Herſzpruck, where having acquired a competent knowledge of
the Greek and Latin tongues, he returned to his father at Altdorf
at 16, and ſtudied firſt philoſophy, and then phyſic. He went
afterwards to Frankfort upon the Oder, and propoſed to viſit the
United Provinces and England; but being prevented by the wars,
he went to Padua, where he ſtudied two years. Then making a
tour of part of Italy, he returned to Altdorf, in 1674, and was
admitted to the degree of M. D. He ſpent two years in perfecting the knowledge he had acquired; and then, in 1677, was
made profeſſor extraordinary in phyſic, which title, in 1681,
was changed to that of profeſſor in ordinary. He now applied

[1] Anatomia Renovata, L. III. c. xliii.

M 3   himſelf

himself earneftly to the practice of phyfic; and in procefs of
time his fame was fpread fo far, that he was fought by perfons of the firft rank. George Frederic, marquis of Anfpach,
of the houfe of Brandenbourg, chofe him in 1695 for his phyfician; and about the latter end of the year, Hoffman attended
this prince into Italy, and renewed his acquaintance with the
learned there. Upon the death of his father in 1698, he was
chofen to fucceed him in his places of botanic profeffor and director of the phyfic garden. He was elected alfo the fame year
rector of the univerfity of Altdorf; a poft, which he had occupied in 1686. He loft his great friend and patron, the marquis
of Anfpach, in 1703; but found the fame kindnefs from his
fucceffor William Frederic, who preffed him fo earneftly to come
nearer him, and made him withal fuch advantageous offers, that
Hoffman in 1713 removed from Altdorf to Anfpach, where he
died in 1727. He had married a wife in 1681, by whom he had
five children. He publifhed alfo fome botanical books, which
are highly efteemed, and " De differentiis alimentorum," 4to,
1677, &c.

HOFFMAN (FREDERICK), an eminent phyfician, was born
at Hall near Magdeburg, in 1660; took a doctor of phyfic's
degree in 1681; was made profeffor of phyfic at Hall in 1693;
and filled the chair till his death, which happened in 1742.
His works were collected at Geneva in fix large folios,
1748—1754: and there are doubtlefs things good and curious in this collection: but there are many frivolous, and
many very frequently repeated. Notwithftanding the imperfections of fo enormous a mafs, Hoffman has defervedly been
reckoned among the beft writers in phyfic. The moft remarkable circumftances of his life are, his journey into Holland and
England, where he became intimately acquainted with Paul
Herman and Robert Boyle; his never taking any fees, as he
was fupported by an annual ftipend; and his curing thofe great
perfonages the emprefs, the emperor Charles VI. and Frederic I.
king of Pruffia, of inveterate difeafes. To thefe may be
added, that he firft taught that acid and mineral waters might
be taken with milk, with fafety and advantage, which phyficians
before had generally reckoned pernicious; that he firft difcovered
the virtues of the Seltzer and Lauchftad waters, in preventing and
curing ftubborn difeafes; and that he prepared and recommended
an acid cathartic falt from the waters of Sedlic, which was commonly ufed in Germany. He furvived his 80th year.

HOFFMAN (DANIEL), a Lutheran minifter, fuperintendant
and profeffor at Helmftad, was the author of fome controverfy
towards the end of the 16th century. He ftarted fome difficulties
about fubfcribing the Concord, and refufed to concur with Dr.
Andreas in defence of this confeffion. He would not acknowledge

ledge the ubiquity, but only that the body of Jefus Chrift was
prefent in a great many places; this difpute though laid afleep
foon after, left a fpirit of curiofity and contradiction upon
peoples minds, fo that in a little time they began to difagree
and argue very warmly upon feveral other points, Hoffman
being always at the head of the party. Among other things it
was argued, whether philofophy was to be allowed in theological
controverfies, and how far. Hoffman and Beza wrote againft
each other upon the fubject of the Holy Eucharift. Hoffman
accufed Hunnius, an eminent Lutheran minifter, for having
mifreprefented the book of the Concord; for here, fays Hoffman,
the caufe of election is not made to depend upon the qualifications of the perfon elected; but Hunnius, fays he, and Mylius
affert, that the decree of election is founded upon the forefight
of faith. Hunnius and Mylius caufed Hoffman to be condemned
at a meeting of their divines in 1593, and threatened him with
excommunication, if he did not comply. The year following,
Hoffman publifhed an apology againft their cenfure. Hofpinian
gives the detail of this controverfy: he obferves, that fome divines of Leipfic, Jena, and Wittemburg, would have had Hoffman publickly cenfured as a Calvinift, and fuch a heretic as was
not fit to be converfed with; others, who were more moderate,
were for admonifhing him by way of letter before they came to
extremities: this latter expedient was approved, and Hunnius
wrote to him in the name of all his brethren. Hoffman's apology was an anfwer to this letter, in which he gives the reafons
for refufing to comply with the divines of Wittemburg, and pretends to fhew that they were grofsly miftaken in feveral articles of
faith. He muft not be confounded with *Melchior Hoffman*, a fa-
natic of the 16th century, who died in prifon at Strafburgh.
There was alfo a *Gafper Hoffman* (the name being common),
a celebrated profeffor of medicine at Altdorf; who was born at
Gotha in 1572, and died in 1649; and who left behind him
many medical works [M].

HOFFMAN (JOHN JAMES). Of this laborious compiler very
little is related; the periods of his birth and death are both unknown. He was a native of Bâle; but his great work, the
" Lexicon Univerfale Hiftorico-Geographico-Poetico-Philofo-
phico-Politico-Philologicum," was firft publifhed at Geneva, in
1677, in two volumes, folio. This being received by the learned
with great avidity, he publifhed, a few years after, a fupplement;
which was alfo rapidly fold off. In 1698, fome of the principal
bookfellers at Leyden, encouraged by this fuccefs of the work,
and having received from the author all his fubfequent collections,
and many other additions from various learned men, digefted the

whole, with the supplement, into one alphabet, and published it in four volumes, folio. In this form it is now known as a most useful book of reference, and finds a place in every learned library. For this edition the author also wrote a new preface.

HOGARTH (WILLIAM), a truly great and original genius [N], is said by Dr. Burn, to have been the descendant of a family originally from Kirkby Thore in Westmoreland. His grandfather, a plain yeoman, possessed a small tenement in the vale of Bampton, a village about fifteen miles north of Kendal in that county, and had three sons. The eldest assisted his father in farming, and succeeded to his little freehold. The second settled in Troutbeck, a village eight miles north-west of Kendal, and was remarkable for his talent at provincial poetry. The third, Richard, educated at St. Bee's, who had been a schoolmaster in the same county, went early to London, where he was employed as a corrector of the press, and appears to have been a man of some learning; a dictionary in Latin and English, which he composed for the use of schools, being still extant in manuscript. He married in London; and kept a school [o] in Ship court, in the Old Bailey. The subject of the present article, and his sisters Mary and Anne, are believed to have been the only product of the marriage.

William Hogarth was born in 1697, or 1698, in the parish of St. Martin, Ludgate. The outset of his life, however, was unpromising. "He was bound," says Mr. Walpole, "to a mean engraver of arms on plate." Hogarth probably chose this occupation, as it required some skill in drawing, to which his genius was particularly turned, and which he contrived assiduously to cultivate. His master, it since appears, was Mr. Ellis Gamble, a silversmith of eminence, who resided in Cranbourn-street, Leicester-fields. In this profession it is not unusual to bind apprentices to the single branch of engraving arms and cyphers on every species of metal; and in that particular department of the business young Hogarth was placed; "but, before his time was expired, he felt the impulse of genius, and that it directed him to painting."

During his apprenticeship, he set out one Sunday, with two or three companions, on an excursion to Highgate. The weather being hot, they went into a public-house, where they had not been long, before a quarrel arose between some persons in the same room. One of the disputants struck the other on the head with a quart pot, and cut him very much. The blood running down the man's face, together with the agony of the

[N] Nichol's Biographical Anecdotes of Hogarth, 1782.
[o] He published, in 1712, a volume of Latin exercises, for the use of his own school, under the title of "Dissertationes Grammaticales; five Examen Octo Pierium Orationis, interrogatorium & responsorium, Anglo-Latinum," 8vo.

wound,

wound, which had diftorted his features into a moft hideous grin, prefented Hogarth, who fhewed himfelf thus early " apprifed of the mode Nature had intended he fhould purfue," with too laughable a fubject to be overlooked. He drew out his pencil, and produced on the fpot one of the moft ludicrous figures that ever was feen. What rendered this piece the more valuable was, that it exhibited an exact likenefs of the man, with the portrait of his antagonift, and the figures in caricature of the principal perfons gathered round him.

How long he continued in obfcurity we cannot exactly learn; but the firft piece in which he diftinguifhed himfelf as a painter, is fuppofed to have been a reprefentation of Wanftead Affembly. The figures in it, we are told, were drawn from the life, and without any circumftances of burlefque. The faces are faid to have been extremely like, and the colouring rather better than in fome of his late and more highly finifhed performances. 'From the date of the earlieft plate that can be afcertained to be the work of Hogarth, it may be prefumed that he began bufinefs, on his own account, at leaft as early as 1720.

His firft employment feems to have been the engraving of arms and fhop-bills. The next ftep was to defign and furnifh plates for bookfellers; and here we are fortunately fupplied with dates. Thirteen folio prints, with his name to each, appeared in Aubry de la Motraye's Travels, in 1723; feven fmaller prints for Apuleius' Golden Afs, in 1724; fifteen head-pieces to Beaver's Military Punifhments of the Ancients, five frontif-pieces for the tranflation of Caffandra, in five volumes, 12mo, 1725; feventeen cuts for a duodecimo edition of Hudibras, (with Butler's head) in 1726; two for Perfeus and Andromeda, in 1730; two for Milton [the date uncertain]; and a variety of others between 1726 and 1733. Mr. Bowles, at the Black Horfe in Cornhill, was one of his earlieft patrons, who paid him very low prices His next friend in that line was Mr. Philip Overton, who rewarded him fomewhat better for his labour and ingenuity.

There are ftill many family pictures by Hogarth exifting, in the ftyle of ferious converfation-pieces. What the prices of his portraits were, Mr. Nichols ftrove in vain to difcover; but he fufpected that they were originally very low, as the perfons who were beft acquainted with them chofe to be filent on the fubject. At Rivenhall, in Effex, the feat of Mr. Weftern, is a family-picture, by Hogarth, of Mr. Weftern and his mother, chancellor Hoadly, archdeacon Charles Plumptre, the Rev. Mr. Cole of Milton near Cambridge, and Mr. Henry Taylor the curate there, 1736. In the gallery of Mr. Cole of Milton, was alfo a whole length picture of Mr. Weftern by Hogarth, a ftriking refemblance, He is drawn fitting in his fellow-commoner's habit,

habit, and square cap with a gold taffel, in his chamber at Clare-hall, over the arch towards the river; and the artift, as the chimney could not be expreffed, has drawn a cat fitting near it, agreeable to his humour, to fhew the fituation: Mr. Weftern's mother, whofe portrait is in the converfation-piece at Rivenhall, was a daughter of fir Anthony Shirley.

It was Hogarth's cuftom to fketch out on the fpot any remarkable face which particularly ftruck him, and of which he wifhed to preferve the remembrance. A gentleman ftill living afferts, that being once with him at the Bedford coffee-houfe, he obferved him drawing fomething with a pencil on his nail. Enquiring what had been his employment, he was fhewn a whimfical countenance of a perfon who was then at a fmall diftance.

It happened in the early part of Hogarth's life, that a nobleman who was uncommonly ugly and deformed, came to fit to him for his picture. It was executed with a fkill that did honour to the artift's abilities; but the likenefs was rigidly obferved, without even the neceffary attention to compliment or flattery. The peer, difgufted at this counterpart of his dear felf, never once thought of paying for a reflector that would only infult him with his deformities. Some time was fuffered to elapfe before the artift applied for his money; but afterwards many applications were made by him (who had then no need of a banker) for payment, but without fuccefs. The painter, however, at laft hit upon an expedient, which he knew muft alarm the nobleman's pride, and by that means anfwer his purpofe. It was couched in the following card: " Mr. Hogarth's dutiful refpects to lord ——; finding that he does not mean to have the picture which was drawn for him, is informed again of Mr. H.'s neceffity for the money; if, therefore, his lordfhip does not fend for it in three days, it will be difpofed of, with the addition of a tail, and fome other little appendages, to Mr. Hare, the famous wild-beaft man; Mr. H. having given that gentleman a conditional promife of it for an exhibition-picture, on his lordfhip's refufal." This intimation had the defired effect. The picture was fent home, and committed to the flames.

Mr. Walpole has remarked, that if our artift " indulged his fpirit of ridicule in perfonalities, it never proceeded beyond fketches and drawings," and wonders " that he never, without intention, delivered the very features of any identical perfon." But this elegant writer, who may be faid to have received his education in a court, had perhaps few opportunities of acquaintance among the low popular characters with which Hogarth occafionally peopled his fcenes. The friend who contributed this remark, was affured by an ancient gentleman of unqueftionable veracity and acuteuefs of remark, that almoft all the perfonages

fonages who attended the levee of the Rake were undoubted portraits; and that in " Southwark Fair," and the " Modern Midnight Converfation," as many more were difcoverable. In the
former plate he pointed out Effex the dancing-mafter; and in
the latter, as well as in the fecond plate to the " Rake's Progrefs,"
Figg the prize-fighter. He mentioned feveral others by name,
from his immediate knowledge both of the painter's defign and
the characters reprefented; but the reft of the particulars by
which he fupported his affertions, have efcaped the memory of
our informant. While Hogarth was painting the " Rake's Progrefs," he had a fummer refidence at Ifleworth; and never failed
to queftion the company who came to fee thefe pictures, if they
knew for whom one or another figure was defigned. When they
gueffed wrongly, he fet them right.

The duke of Leeds has an original fcene in the Beggar's
Opera, painted by Hogarth. It is that in which Lucy and Polly
are on their knees, before their refpective fathers, to intercede
for the life of the hero of the piece. All the figures are either
known or fuppofed to be portraits. If we are not mifinformed,
the late fir Thomas Robinfon (better known perhaps by the name
of long fir Thomas) is ftanding in one of the fide-boxes. Macheath, unlike his fpruce reprefentative on our prefent ftage, is
a flouching bully; and Polly appears happily difencumbered of
fuch a hoop as the daughter of Peachum within the reach of
younger memories has worn. The duke gave 35l. for this picture
at Mr. Rich's auction. Another copy of the fame fcene was bought
by the late fir William Saunderfon; and is now in the poffeffion
of fir Harry Gough. Mr. Walpole has a picture of a fcene
in the fame piece, where Macheath is going to execution.
In this alfo the likeneffes of Walker and mifs Fenton, afterwards dutchefs of Bolton, (the original Macheath and Polly) are
preferved.

In the year 1726, when the affair of Mary Tofts, the rabbit-
breeder of Godalming, engaged the public attention, a few of
the principal furgeons fubfcribed their guinea-a-piece to Hogarth,
for an engraving from a ludicrous fketch he had made on that
very popular fubject. This plate, amongft other portraits, contains that of St. André, then anatomift to the royal houfhold,
and in high credit as a furgeon.

In 1727, Hogarth agreed with Morris, an upholfterer, to
furnifh him with a defign on canvas, reprefenting the element
of earth, as a pattern for tapeftry. The work not being performed to the fatisfaction of Morris, he refufed to pay for it;
and the artift, by a fuit at law, recovered the money.

In 1730, Hogarth married the only daughter of fir James
Thornhill, by whom he had no child. This union, indeed, was
a ftolen one, and confequently without the approbation of fir
James,

James, who, confidering the youth of his daughter, then barely
18, and the flender finances of her hufband, as yet an obfcure
artift, was not eafily reconciled to the match. Soon after this
period, however, he began his "Harlot's Progrefs [p];" and
was advifed by lady Thornhill to have fome of the fcenes in it
placed in the way of his father-in-law. Accordingly, one
morning early, Mrs. Hogarth undertook to convey feveral of
them into his dining-room. When he arofe, he enquired
whence they came; and being told by whom they were introduced, he cried out, "Very well; the man who can furnifh
reprefentations like thefe, can alfo maintain a wife without a
portion." He defigned this remark as an excufe for keeping his
purfe-ftrings clofe; but, foon after, became both reconciled and
generous to the young people. An allegorical cieling by fir
James Thornhill is at the houfe of the late Mr. Huggins, at
Headly Park, Hants. The fubject of it is the ftory of Zephyrus
and Flora; and the figure of a fatyr and fome others were
painted by Hogarth.

In 1732, he ventured to attack Mr. Pope, in a plate called
"The Man of Tafte;" containing a view of the gate of Bur-
lington-houfe; with Pope white-wafhing it, and befpattering
the duke of Chandos's coach. This plate was intended as a
fatire on the tranflator of Homer, Mr. Kent the architect, and
the earl of Burlington. It was fortunate for Hogarth that he
efcaped the lafh of the firft. Either Hogarth's obfcurity at
that time was his protection, or the bard was too prudent to
exafperate a painter who had already given fuch proof of his
abilities for fatire. What muft he have felt who could complain
of the "pictured fhape" prefixed to "Gulliveriana," "Pope
Alexander's Supremacy and Infallibility examined," &c. by
Ducket, and other pieces, had fuch an artift as Hogarth undertaken to exprefs a certain tranfaction recorded by Cibber?

Soon after his marriage, Hogarth had fummer lodgings at
South-Lambeth; and, being intimate with Mr. Tyers, contributed to the improvement of The Spring Gardens at Vauxhall,
by the hint of embellifhing them with paintings, fome of which
were the fuggeftions of his own truly comic pencil. For his
affiftance, Mr. Tyers gratefully prefented him with a gold ticket
of admiffion for himfelf and his friends, infcribed

IN PERPETUAM BENEFICII-MEMORIAM.

This ticket remained in the poffeffion of his widow, and was
by her occafionally employed.

In 1733, his genius became confpicuoufly known. The third
fcene of his "Harlot's Progrefs," introduced him to the notice

[p] The coffin in the laft plate is infcribed Sept. 2, 1731.

of

of the great. At a board of treafury which was held a day or two after the appearance of that print, a copy of it was fhewn by one of the lords, as containing, among other excellencies, a ftriking likenefs of fir John Gonfon. It gave univerfal fatisfaction; from the treafury each lord repaired to the print-fhop for a copy of it, and Hogarth rofe completely into fame.

The ingenious abbé du Bos has often complained, that no hiftory-painter of his time went through a feries of actions, and thus, like an hiftorian, painted the fucceffive fortune of an hero, from the cradle to the grave. What Du Bos wifhed to fee done, Hogarth performed. He launches out his young adventurer a fimple girl upon the town, and conducts her through all the viciffitudes of wretchednefs to a premature death. This was painting to the underftanding and to the heart; none had ever before made the pencil fubfervient to the purpofes of morality and inftruction; a book like this is fitted to every foil and every obferver, and he that runs may read. Nor was the fuccefs of Hogarth confined to his figures. One of his excellencies confifted in what may be termed the furniture of his pieces; for as in fublime and hiftorical reprefentations the fewer trivial circumftances are permitted to divide the fpectator's attention from the principal figures, the greater is their force; fo in fcenes copied from familiar life, a proper variety of little domeftic images contributes to throw a degree of verifimilitude on the whole. " The Rake's levee-room," fays Mr. Walpole, " the nobleman's dining-room, the apartments of the hufband and wife in Marriage à la Mode, the alderman's parlour, the bed-chamber, and many others, are the hiftory of the manners of the age." The novelty and excellence of Hogarth's performances foon tempted the needy artift and print-dealer to avail themfelves of his defigns, and rob him of the advantages which he was entitled to derive from them. This was particularly the cafe with the " Midnight Converfation," the " Harlot's" and " Rake's Progreffes," and others of his early works. To put a ftop to depredations like thefe on the property of himfelf and others, and to fecure the emoluments refulting from his own labours, as Mr. Walpole obferves, he applied to the legiflature, and obtained an act of parliament, 8 George II. chap. 38, to veft an exclufive right in defigners and engravers, and to reftrain the multiplying of copies of their works without the confent of the artift. This ftatute was drawn by his friend Mr. Huggins, who took for his model the eighth of Queen Anne, in favour of literary property; but it was not fo accurately executed as entirely to remedy the evil; for, in a caufe founded on it, which came before lord Hardwicke in chancery, that excellent lawyer determined, that no affignee, claiming under an affignment from the original inventor, could take any benefit by it. Hogarth, immediately after the paffing of

the

the act, published a small print, with emblematical devices, and an inscription expressing his gratitude to the three branches of the legislature. Small copies of the "Rake's Progress," were published by his permission.

In 1745, Hogarth sold about twenty of his capital pictures by auction; and in the same year acquired additional reputation by the six prints of "Marriage à la Mode," which may be regarded as the ground-work of a novel called "The Marriage Act," by Dr. Shebbeare, and of "The Clandestine Marriage."

Hogarth had projected a "Happy Marriage," by way of counterpart to his "Marriage à la Mode." A design for the first of his intended six plates he had sketched out in colours; and the following is as accurate an account of it as could be furnished by a gentleman who, long ago, enjoyed only a few minutes sight of so great a curiosity. The time supposed was immediately after the return of the parties from church. The scene lay in the hall of an antiquated country mansion. On one side, the married couple were represented sitting. Behind them was a group of their young friends of both sexes, in the act of breaking bride-cake over their heads. In front appeared the father of the young lady, grasping a bumper, and drinking, with a seeming roar of exultation, to the future happiness of her and her husband. By his side was a table covered with refreshments. Jollity rather than politeness was the designation of his character. Under the screen of the hall, several rustic musicians in grotesque attitudes, together with servants, tenants, &c. were arranged. Through the arch by which the room was entered, the eye was led along a passage into the kitchen, which afforded a glimpse of sacerdotal luxury. Before the dripping-pan stood a well-fed divine, in his gown and cassock, with his watch in his hand, giving directions to a cook, dressed all in white, who was employed in basting a haunch of venison. Among the faces of the principal figures, none but that of the young lady was completely finished. Hogarth had been often reproached for his inability to impart grace and dignity to his heroines. The bride was therefore meant to vindicate his pencil from so degrading an imputation. The effort, however, was unsuccessful. The girl was certainly pretty; but her features, if we may use the term, were uneducated. She might have attracted notice as a chambermaid, but would have failed to extort applause as a woman of fashion. The clergyman and his culinary associate were more laboured than any other parts of the picture. It is natural for us to dwell longest on that division of a subject which is most congenial to our private feelings. The painter sat down with a resolution to delineate beauty improved by art; but seems, as usual, to have deviated into meanness; or could not help neglecting his original purpose, to luxuriate in such ideas as his situation

fituation in early life had fitted him to exprefs. He found himfelf, in fhort, out of his element in the parlour, and therefore
haftened, in queft of eafe and amufement, to the kitchen fire.
Churchill, with more force than delicacy, once obferved of him,
that he only painted the *backfide* of nature. It muft be allowed,
that fuch an artift, however excellent in his walk, was better
qualified to reprefent the low-born parent, than the royal preferver of a foundling.

Soon after the peace of Aix la Chapelle, he went over to
France, and was taken into cuftody at Calais, while he was
drawing the gate of that town, a circumftance which he has recorded in his picture, entitled, " O the Roaft Beef of Old
England !" publifhed March 26, 1749. He was actually carried before the governor as a fpy; and, after a very ftrict examination, committed a prifoner to Granfire, his landlord, on his
promife that Hogarth fhould not go out of his houfe till he
was to embark for England. Soon after this period he purchafed a fmall houfe at Chifwick; where he ufually paffed the
greateft part of the fummer feafon, yet not without occafional
vifits to his houfe in Leicefter-fields.

In 1753, he appeared to the world in the character of an author, and publifhed a 4to volume, entitled, " The Analyfis
of Beauty, written with a View of fixing the fluctuating Ideas
of Tafte." In this performance he fhews, by a variety of examples, that a curve is the line of beauty, and that round fwelling
figures are moft pleafing to the eye; and the truth of his opinion
has been countenanced by fubfequent writers on the fubject. In
this work, the leading idea of which was hieroglyphically thrown
out in a frontifpiece to his works in 1745, he acknowledges
himfelf indebted to his friends for affiftance, and particularly to
one gentleman for his corrections and amendments of at leaft
a third part of the *wording.* This friend was Dr. Benjamin
Hoadly the phyfician, who carried on the work to about the
third part, (chap. ix.) and then, through indifpofition, declined the
friendly office with regret. Mr. Hogarth applied to his neigh-
bour, Mr. Ralph; but it is impoffible for two fuch perfons to
agree, both alike vain and pofitive. He proceeded no further
than about a fheet, and they then parted friends, and feem to
have continued fuch. The kind office of finifhing the work,
and fuperintending the publication, was laftly taken up by Dr.
Morell, who went through the remainder of the book. The
preface was in like manner corrected by the Rev. Mr. Townley.
The family of Hogarth rejoiced when the laft fheet of the
" Analyfis" was printed off; as the frequent difputes he had with
his coadjutors, in the progrefs of the work, did not much har-
monize his difpofition. This work was tranflated into German
by Mr. Mylins, when in England, under the author's infpection;

and

and the tranflation was printed in London, price five dollars. A new and correct edition was in 1754, propofed for publication at Berlin, by Ch. Fr. Vok, with an explanation of Mr. Hogarth's fatirical prints, tranflated from the French; and an Italian tranflation was publifhed at Leghorn in 1761.

Hogarth had one failing in common with moft people who attain wealth and eminence without the aid of liberal education. He affected to defpife every kind of knowledge which he did not poffefs. Having eftablifhed his fame with little or no obligation to literature, he either conceived it to be needlefs, or decried it becaufe it lay out of his reach. His fentiments, in fhort, refembled thofe of Jack Cade, who pronounced fentence on the clerk of Chatham, becaufe he could write and read. Till, in evil hour, this celebrated artift commenced author, and was obliged to employ the friends already mentioned to correct his " Analyfis of Beauty," he did not feem to have difcovered that even fpelling was a neceffary qualification; and yet he had ventured to ridicule the late Mr. Rich's deficiency as to this particular, in a note which lies before the Rake whofe play is refufed while he remains in confinement for debt. Before the time of which we are now fpeaking, one of our artift's common topics of declamation, was the ufeleffnefs of books to a man of his profeffion. In " Beer-ftreet, among other volumes configned by him to the paftry-cook, we find " Turnbull on Ancient Painting," a treatife which Hogarth fhould have been able to underftand, before he ventured to condemn. Garrick himfelf, however, was not more ductile to flattery. A word in favour of " Sigifmunda," might have commanded a proof print, or forced an original fketch out of our artift's hands. The perfon who fupplied this remark owed one of Hogarth's fcarceft performances to the fuccefs of a compliment, which might have feemed extravagant even to fir Godfrey Kneller.

The following well-authenticated ftory will alfo ferve to fhew how much more eafy it is to detect ill-placed or hyperbolical adulation refpecting others, than when applied to ourfelves. Hogarth being at dinner with the celebrated Chefelden, and fome other company, was told that Mr. John Freke, furgeon of St. Bartholomew's hofpital, a few evenings before at Dick's coffee-houfe, had afferted that Greene was as eminent in compofition as Handel. " That fellow Freke," replied Hogarth, " is always fhooting his bolt abfurdly one way or another! Handel is a giant in mufic; Greene only a light Florimel kind of a compofer."—" Ay," faid the informant, " but at the fame time Mr. Freke declared you were as good a portrait-painter as Vandyck." —" There he was in the right," adds Hogarth: " and fo by G— I am, give me my time, and let me choofe my fubject!"

Hogarth

Hogarth was the moſt abſent of men. At table he would ſometimes turn round his chair as if he had finiſhed eating, and as ſuddenly would return it, and commence his meal again. I may add, that he once directed a letter to Dr. Hoadly, thus,— "To the Doctor at Chelſea." This epiſtle, however, by good luck, did not miſcarry; and was preſerved by the late chancellor of Wincheſter, as a pleaſant memorial of his friend's extraordinary inattention. Another remarkable inſtance of Hogarth's abſence was related by one of his intimate friends. Soon after he ſet up his carriage, he had occaſion to pay a viſit to the lord-mayor (Mr. Beckford). When he went, the weather was fine; but buſineſs detained him till a violent ſhower of rain came on. He was let out of the manſion-houſe by a different door from that at which he entered; and, ſeeing the rain, began immediately to call for a hackney-coach. Not one was to be met with on any of the neighbouring ſtands; and the artiſt ſallied forth to brave the ſtorm, and actually reached Leiceſter-fields without beſtowing a thought on his own carriage, till Mrs. Hogarth (ſurpriſed to ſee him ſo wet and ſplaſhed) aſked him where he had left it.

A ſpecimen of Hogarth's propenſity to merriment, on the moſt trivial occaſions, is obſervable in one of his cards requeſting the company of Dr. Arnold King to dine with him at the Mitre. Within a circle, to which a knife and fork are the ſupporters, the written part is contained. In the centre is drawn a pye, with a mitre on the top of it; and the invitation concludes with the following ſport on three of the Greek letters— to *Eta Beta Pi*. The reſt of the inſcription is not very accurately ſpelt. A quibble by Hogarth is ſurely as reſpectable as a conundrum by Swift.

In one of the early exhibitions at Spring-Gardens, a very pleaſing ſmall picture by Hogarth made its firſt appearance. It was painted for the earl of Charlemont, in whoſe collection it remains; and was entitled, "Picquet, or Virtue in Danger," and ſhews us a young lady, who, during a *tête-à-tête*, had juſt loſt all her money to a handſome officer of her own age. He is repreſented in the act of returning her a handful of bank-bills, with the hope of exchanging them for a ſofter acquiſition, and more delicate plunder. On the chimney-piece a watch-caſe and a figure of Time over it, with this motto—NUNC. Hogarth has caught his heroine during this moment of heſitation, this ſtruggle with herſelf, and has marked her feelings with uncommon ſucceſs.

In the "Miſer's Feaſt," Mr. Hogarth thought proper to pillory ſir Iſaac Shard, a gentleman proverbially avaricious. Hearing this, the ſon of ſir Iſaac, the late Iſaac Pacatus Shard, eſq; a young man of ſpirit, juſt returned from his travels, called at the painter's to fee the picture; and among the reft, afking the Cicerone " whether that odd figure was intended for any particular perfon;" on his replying, " that it was thought to be very like one fir Ifaac Shard;" he immediately drew his fword, and flafhed the canvas. Hogarth appeared inftantly in great wrath; to whom Mr. Shard calmly juftified what he had done, faying, " that this was a very unwarrantable licence; that he was the injured party's fon, and that he was ready to defend any fuit at law;" which, however, was never inftituted.

About 1757, his brother-in-law, Mr. Thornhill, refigned the place of king's ferjeant painter in favour of Mr. Hogarth. " The laft memorable event in our artift's life," as Mr. Walpole obferves, " was his quarrel with Mr. Wilkes, in which, if Mr. Hogarth did not commence direct hoftilities on the latter, he at leaft obliquely gave the firft offence, by an attack on the friends and party of that gentleman. This conduct was the more furprifing, as he had all his life avoided dipping his pencil in political contefts, and had early refufed a very lucrative offer that was made, to engage him in a fet of prints againft the head of a court-party. Without entering into the merits of the caufe, I fhall only ftate the fact. In September, 1762, Mr. Hogarth publifhed his print of ' The Times.' It was anfwered by Mr. Wilkes in a fevere ' North Briton.' On this the painter exhibited the caricatura of the writer. Mr. Churchill, the poet, then engaged in the war, and wrote his ' Epiftle to Hogarth,' not the brighteft of his works, and in which the fevereft ftrokes fell on a defect that the painter had neither caufed nor could amend—his age; and which, however, was neither remarkable nor decrepit; much lefs had it impaired his talents, as appeared by his having compofed but fix months before, one of his moft capital works, the fatire on the Methodifts. In revenge for this epiftle, Hogarth caricatured Churchill, under the form of a canonical bear, with a club and a pot of porter—*& vitulâ tu dignus & hic*—never did two angry men of their abilities throw mud with lefs dexterity.

" When Mr. Wilkes was the fecond time brought from the Tower to Weftminfter-hall, Mr. Hogarth fkulked behind in a corner of the gallery of the court of Common Pleas; and while the chief juftice Pratt, with the eloquence and courage of old Rome, was enforcing the great principles of Magna Charta, and the Englifh conftitution, while every breaft from him caught the holy flame of liberty, the painter was wholly employed in caricaturing the perfon of the man, while all the reft of his fellow-citizens were animated in his caufe, for they knew it to be their own caufe, that of their country, and of its laws. It was declared to be fo a few hours after by the unanimous fentence of the judges of that court, and they were all prefent.

                                                    " The

" The print of Mr. Wilkes was foon after publifhed, *drawn from the life by William Hogarth.* It muft be allowed to be an excellent compound caricatura, or a caricatura of what nature had already caricatured. I know but one fhort apology that can be made for this gentleman, or, to fpeak more properly, for the perfon of Mr. Wilkes. It is, that he did not make himfelf, and and that he never was folicitous about the cafe of his foul, as Shakefpeare calls it, only fo far as to keep it clean and in health. I never heard that he once hung over the glaffy ftream, like another Narciffus, admiring the image in it, nor that he ever ftole an amorous look at his counterfeit in a fide mirrour. His form, fuch as it is, ought to give him no pain, becaufe it is capable of giving pleafure to others. I fancy he finds himfelf tolerably happy in the clay-cottage, to which he is tenant for life, becaufe he has learnt to keep it in good order. While the fhare of health and animal fpirits, which heaven has given him, fhall hold out, I can fcarcely imagine he will be one moment peevifh about the outfide of fo precarious, fo temporary a habitation, or will even be brought to own, *ingenium Galbæ male habitat. Monfieur oft mal logé.*

" Mr. Churchill was exafperated at this perfonal attack on his friend. He foon after publifhed the ' Epiftle to William Hogarth,' and took for the motto, *ut pictura poefis.* Mr. Hogarth's revenge againft the poet terminated in vamping up an old print of a pug-dog and a bear, which he publifhed under the title of ' The Bruifer C. Churchill (once the Revd. !)' in the character of a Ruffian Hercules, &c."

At the time when thefe hoftilities were carrying on in a manner fo virulent and difgraceful to all the parties, Hogarth was vifibly declining in his health. In 1762, he complained of an inward pain, which, continuing, brought on a general decay that proved incurable [q]. This laft year of his life he employed in retouching his plates, with the affiftance of feveral engravers whom he took with him to Chifwick. Oct. 25, 1764, he was

[q] It may be worth obferving, that in " Independence," a poem which was not publifhed by Churchill till the laft week of September, 1764, he confiders his antagonift as a departed Genius:

" Hogarth would draw him (Envy muft allow)
E'en to the life, was HOGARTH LIVING NOW."

How little did the fportive fatirift imagine, that the power of pleafing was fo foon to ceafe in both! Hogarth died in four weeks after the publication of this poem; and Churchill furvived him but nine days. In fome lines which were printed in November, 1764, the compiler of this article took occafion to lament that

" —— Scarce had the friendly tear,
For Hogarth fhed, efcap'd the generous eye
Of feeling Pity, when again it flow'd
For Churchill's fate. Ill can we bear the lofs
Of Fancy's twin-born offspring, clofe ally'd
In energy of thought, though different paths
They fought for fame! Though jarring paffions fway'd
The living artifts, let the funeral wreath
Unite their memory!"

conveyed

conveyed from thence to Leicester-fields, in a very weak condition, yet remarkably chearful; and, receiving an agreeable letter from the American Dr. Franklin, drew up a rough draught of an anfwer to it; but going to bed, he was feized with a vomiting, upon which he rung his bell with fuch violence that he broke it, and expired about two hours afterwards. His diforder was an aneurifm; and his corpfe was interred in the churchyard at Chifwick, where a monument is erected to his memory, with an infcription by his friend Mr. Garrick.

It may be truly obferved of Hogarth, that all his powers of delighting were reftrained to his pencil. Having rarely been admitted into polite circles, none of his fharp corners had been rubbed off, fo that he continued to the laft a grofs uncultivated man. The flighteft contradiction tranfported him into rage. To fome confidence in himfelf he was certainly entitled; for, as a comic painter, he could have claimed no honour that would not moft readily have been allowed him; but he was at once unprincipled and variable in his political conduct and attachments. He is alfo faid to have beheld the rifing eminence and popularity of fir Jofhua Reynolds with a degree of envy; and, if we are not mifinformed, frequently fpoke with afperity both of him and his performances. Juftice, however, obliges us to add, that our artift was liberal, hofpitable, and the moft punctual of paymafters; fo that, in fpite of the emoluments his works had procured to him, he left but an inconfiderable fortune to his widow. His plates indeed were fuch refources to her as could not fpeedily be exhaufted. Some of his domeftics had lived many years in his fervice, a circumftance that always reflects credit on a mafter. Of moft of thefe he painted ftrong likeneffes, on a canvas which was left in Mrs. Hogarth's poffeffion.

His widow had alfo a portrait of her hufband, and an excellent buft of him by Roubilliac, a ftrong refemblance; and one of his brother-in-law Mr. Thornhill, much refembling the countenance of Mrs. Hogarth. Several of his portraits alfo remained in her poffeffion, but at her death were difperfed.

Of Hogarth's fmaller plates many were deftroyed. When he wanted a piece of copper on a fudden, he would take any plate from which he had already worked off fuch a number of impreffions as he fuppofed he fhould fell. He then fent it to be effaced, beat out, or otherwife altered to his prefent purpofe.

The plates which remained in his poffeffion were fecured to Mrs. Hogarth by his will, dated Aug. 12, 1764, chargeable with an annuity of 80l. to his fifter Anne, who furvived him. When, on the death of his other fifter, fhe left off the bufinefs in which fhe was engaged, he kindly took her home, and generoufly fupported her, making her, at the fame time, ufeful in

the

the difpofal of his prints. Want of tendernefs and liberality to his relations was not among the failings of Hogarth.

In the year 1745, one Launcelot Burton was appointed naval officer at Deal. Hogarth had feen him by accident; and on a piece of paper, previoufly impreffed by a plain copper-plate, drew his figure with a pen in imitation of a coarfe etching. He was reprefented on a lean Canterbury hack, with a bottle flicking out of his pocket; and underneath was an infcription, intimating that he was going down to take poffeffion of his place. This was inclofed to him in a letter; and fome of his friends, who were in the fecret, protefted the drawing to be a print which they had feen expofed to fale at the fhops in London; a circumftance that put him in a violent paffion, during which he wrote an abufive letter to Hogarth, whofe name was fubfcribed to the work. But, after poor Burton's tormentors had kept him in fufpenfe throughout an uneafy three weeks, they proved to him that it was no engraving, but a fketch with a pen and ink. He then became fo perfectly reconciled to his refemblance, that he fhewed it with exultation to admiral Vernon, and all the reft of his friends. In 1753, Hogarth returning with a friend from a vifit to Mr. Rich at Cowley, flopped his chariot, and got out, being ftruck by a large drawing (with a coal) on the wall of an alehoufe. He immediately made a fketch of it with triumph; it was a St. George and the Dragon, all in ftraight lines.

Hogarth made one effay in fculpture.' He wanted a fign to diftinguifh his houfe in Leicefter-fields; and thinking none more proper than the Golden Head, he out of a mafs of cork made up of feveral thickneffes compacted together, carved a buft of Vandyck, which he gilt and placed over his door. It decayed, and was fucceeded by a head in plaifter, which in its turn was fupplied by a head of fir Ifaac Newton. Hogarth alfo modelled another refemblance of Vandyck in clay; which has alfo perifhed. His works, as his elegant biographer has well obferved, are his hiftory; and the curious are highly indebted to Mr. Walpole for a catalogue of his prints, drawn up from his own valuable collection, in 1771. But as neither that catalogue, nor his appendix to it in 1780, have given the whole of Mr. Hogarth's labours, Mr. Nichols, including Mr. Walpole's catalogue, has endeavoured, from later difcoveries of our artift's prints in other collections, to arrange them in chronological order. There are three large pictures by Hogarth, over the altar in the church of St. Mary Redcliff at Briftol. Mr. Forreft, of York-buildings, is in poffeffion of a fketch in oil of our Saviour (defigned as a pattern for painted glafs); and feveral drawings, defcriptive of the incidents that happened during a five days tour by land and water. The parties were Meffrs. Hogarth, Thornhill (fon of the late fir James), Scott (an ingenious landfcape-painter of that

name), Tothall, and Forreſt. They ſet out at midnight, at a
moment's warning, from the Bedford-Arms tavern, with each a
ſhirt in his pocket. They had all their particular departments.
Hogarth and Scott made the drawings; Thornhill the map;
Tothall faithfully diſcharged the joint officers of treaſurer and ca-
terer; and Forreſt wrote the journal. They were out five days
only; and on the ſecond night after their return, the book was
produced, bound, gilt, and lettered, and read at the ſame tavern
to the members of the club then preſent. Mr. Forreſt has alſo
drawings of two of the members, remarkable. fat men, in ludicrous ſituations. Etchings from all theſe have been made, and
the journal has been printed. A very entertaining work, by Mr.
John Ireland, entitled, " Hogarth illuſtrated," was published by
Meſſrs. Boydell, in 1792, and has ſince been reprinted. It contains the ſmall plates originally engraved for a paltry work called,
" Hogarth moralized," and an exact account of all his prints.
Since that, have appeared, " Graphic illuſtrations of Hogarth,
from Pictures, Drawings, and ſcarce Prints, in the poſſeſſion of
Samuel Ireland." Some curious articles were contained in this
volume. A ſupplementary volume to " Hogarth illuſtrated," is
now promiſed, which is to contain, the original manuſcript of
the Analyſis, with the firſt ſketches of the figures. 2. A Supplement to the Analyſis, never publiſhed. 3. Original Memo-
randa. 4. Materials for his own Life, &c.

HOLBEIN (JOHN), better known by his German name
Hans Holbein, a moſt excellent painter, was born at Baſil in
Switzerland in 1498, as many ſay; though Charles Patin places
his birth three years earlier [a], ſuppoſing it very improbable
that he could have arrived at ſuch maturity of judgement and
perfection in painting, as he ſhewed in the years 1514 and 1516,
if he had been born ſo late as 1498. He learned the rudiments
of his art from his father John Holbein, who was a painter, and
had removed from Augſburg to Baſil; but the ſuperiority of his
genius ſoon raiſed him above his maſter. He painted our Saviour's Paſſion in the town-houſe of Baſil; and alſo in the fiſh-
market of the ſame town, a Dance of Peaſants, and Death's
Dance. Theſe pieces were exceedingly ſtriking to the curious;
and the great Eraſmus was ſo affected with them, that he re-
queſted of him to draw his picture, and was ever after his friend.
Holbein, in the mean time, though a great genius and fine artiſt,
had no elegance or delicacy of manners, but was given to wine
and revelling company; for which he met with the following
gentle rebuke from Eraſmus. When Eraſmus wrote his " Moriæ Encomium," or " Panegyric upon Folly," he ſent a copy of
it to Hans Holbein, who was ſo pleaſed with the ſeveral deſcrip-

[a] Vita Joh. Holbenii à Car. Patino præfix, Eraſmi Moriæ Encomio. Baſil.
1676.

tions

tions of folly there given, that he defigned them all in the margin;
and where he had not room to draw the whole figures, paffed a
piece of paper to the leaves. He then returned the book to
Erafmus, who feeing that he had reprefented an amorous fool
by the figure of a fat Dutch lover, hugging his bottle and his
lafs, wrote under it, " Hans Holbein," and fo fent it back to
the painter. Holbein, however, to be revenged of him, drew
the picture of Erafmus for a mufty groper, who bufied himfelf
in fcraping together old MSS. and antiquities, and wrote under
it " Adagia."

It is faid, that an Englifh nobleman, who accidentally faw
fome of Holbein's performances at Bafil, invited him to come
to England, where his art was in high efteem; and promifed
him great things from the encouragement he would be fure to
meet with from Henry VIII.; but Holbein was too much engaged in his pleafures to liften to fo advantageous a propofal.
A few years after, however, moved by the neceffities to which
an increafed family and his own mifmanagement had reduced
him, as well as by the perfuafions of his friend Erafmus, who
told him how improper a country his own was to do juftice to
his merit, he confented to go to England; and he confented the
more readily, having a termagant for his wife. In his journey
thither he ftayed fome days at Strafburg, and applying, as it is
faid, to a very great mafter in that city for work, was taken in,
and ordered to give a fpecimen of his fkill. Holbein finifhed a
piece with great care, and painted a fly upon the moft eminent
part of it; after which he withdrew privily in the abfence of his
mafter, and purfued his journey, without faying any thing to
any body. When the painter returned home, he was aftonifhed
at the beauty and elegance of the drawing; and efpecially at the
fly, which, upon his firft cafting his eye upon it, he fo far took
for a real fly, that he endeavoured to remove it with his hand.
He fent all over the city for his journeyman, who was now
miffing; but after many enquiries, found that he had been thus
deceived by the famous Holbein.

After almoft begging his way to England, as Patin tells us,
he found an eafy admittance to the lord-chancellor, fir Thomas
More: for he had brought with him Erafmus's picture, and
letters recommendatory from him to that great man. Sir Thomas received him with all the joy imaginable, and kept him in
his houfe between two and three years; during which time he
drew fir Thomas's picture, and thofe of many of his friends
and relations. One day Holbein happening to mention the
nobleman who had fome years ago invited him to England, fir
Thomas was very folicitous to know who he was. Holbein
replied, that he had indeed forgot his title, but remembered his
face fo well, that he thought he could draw his likenefs; and this

he

he did fo very ftrongly, that the nobleman, it is faid, was immediately known by it. The chancellor, having now fufficiently
furnifhed and enriched his apartments with Holbein's productions, was determined to introduce him to Henry VIII. which
he did in this manner. He invited the king to an entertainment,
and hung up all Holbein's pieces, difpofed in the beft order, and
in the beft light, in the great hall of his houfe. The king, upon
his firft entrance, was fo charmed with the light of them, that
he afked, " Whether fuch an artift were now alive, and to be
had for money ?" Upon which fir Thomas prefented Holbein
to the king, who immediately took him into his fervice, and
brought him into great efteem with the nobility of the kingdom. The king from time to time manifefted the great
value he had for him, and upon the death of queen Jane,
his third wife, fent him into Flanders, to draw the picture of
the dutchefs dowager of Milan, widow to Francis Sforza, whom
the emperor Charles V. had recommended to him for a fourth
wife ; but the king's defection from the fee of Rome happening
about that time, he rather chofe to match with a Proteftant
princefs. Cromwell, then his prime minifter (for fir Thomas
More had been removed, and beheaded), propofed Anne of Cleves
to him ; but the king was not inclined to the match, till her
picture, which Holbein had alfo drawn, was prefented to him.
There, as lord Herbert of Cherbury fays, fhe was reprefented
fo very fine and charming, that the king immediately refolved
to marry her.

In England Holbein drew a vaft number of admirable portraits; among others, thofe of Henry VII. and Henry VIII.
on the wall of the palace at Whitehall, which perifhed with it
when it was burnt, though fome endeavours were made to remove that part of the wall on which the pictures were drawn.
There happened, however, an affair in England, which might have
been fatal to Holbein, if the king had not protected him. On the
report of his character, a nobleman of the firft quality came one
day to fee him, when he was drawing a figure after the life.
Holbein begged his lordfhip to defer the honour of his vifit to
another day; which the nobleman taking for an affront, broke
open the door, and very rudely went up ftairs. Holbein, hearing
a noife, came out of his chamber ; and meeting the lord at his
door, fell into a violent paffion, and pufhed him backwards from
the top of the ftairs to the bottom. Confidering, however, immediately what he had done, he efcaped from the tumult he had
raifed, and made the beft of his way to the king. The nobleman, much hurt, though not fo much as he pretended, was
there foon after him; and upon opening his grievance, the king
ordered Holbein to afk pardon for his offence. But this only
irritated the nobleman the more, who would not be fatisfied

with

with lefs than his life; upon which the king fternly replied,
"My lord, you have not now to do with Holbein, but with me;
whatever punifhment 'you may contrive by way of revenge
againft him, fhall affuredly be inflicted upon yourfell's remember, pray my lord, that I can, whenever I pleafe, make feven
lords of feven ploughmen, but I cannot make one Holbein even
of feven lords."

We cannot undertake to give a lift of Holbein's works, but
fuch a one may be found prefixed to the edition of the "Moriæ
Encomium," quoted above. There is alfo the life of Holbein
at large, with two prints of him, very unlike each other; the
one drawn when he was very young, the other when he was 45
years of age. The judgement which du Frefnoy has paffed on
this painter is, that "he was wonderfully knowing, and had
certainly been of the firft form of painters, had he travelled into
Italy; fince nothing can be laid to his charge, but only that he
had a Gothic gufto." He declares, that Holbein performed
better than Raphael [s]; and that he had feen a portrait of his
painting, with which one of Titian's could not come into com-
petition." "It is amazing to think," fays de Piles[т], "that
a man born in Switzerland, and who had never been in Italy,
fhould have fo good a tafte, and fo fine a genius for painting."
Frederic Zucchero, who travelled over England in 1574, was
greatly furprifed at the fight of Holbein's works, and faid, that
"they were not inferior to either Raphael's or Titian's." He
painted alike in every.manner; in frefco, in water-colours, in
oil, and in miniature. He was eminent alfo for a rich vein of
invention, very confpicuous in a multitude of defigns, which he
made for gravers, fculptors, jewellers, &c. He had the fame
fingularity, which Pliny mentions of Turpilius a Roman,
namely, that of painting with his left hand. He died of the
plague at London in 1554; and at his lodgings in Whitehall,
where he had lived from the time that the king became his
patron.

HOLBERG (Louis DE), a Danifh hiftorian, lawyer, and
poet; was born at Bergen in Norway, in the year 1685. His
family is faid by fome to have been low, by others noble; but it
is agreed that he commenced life in very poor circumftances,
and picked up his education in his travels through various parts
of Europe, where he fubfifted either by charity, or by his perfonal efforts of various kinds. On his return to Copenhagen,
he found means to be appointed affeffor ol the confiftory court,
which place afforded him a competent fubfiftence. He then was
able to indulge his genius, and produced feveral works, which

[s] Art of Painting, by Dryden, p. 235, 236. Lond. 1716.
[т] Lives of the Painters, &c.

gave

gave him great celebrity. Among thefe are fome comedies, a volume of which has been tranflated into French. He wrote alfo a hiftory of Denmark, in 3 vols. 4to, which has been confidered as the beft that hitherto has been produced, though rather minute and uninterefting. Two volumes of " Moral Thoughts;" and a work entitled, " The Danifh Spectator," were produced by him: and he is generally confidered as the author of the " Iter fubterraneum of Klimius," a fatirical romance, fomething in the ftyle of Gulliver's Travels. Moft of thefe have been tranflated alfo into German, and are much efteemed in that country. By his publications, and his place of affeffor, he had œconomy enough to amafs a confiderable fortune, and even in his life gave 70,000 crowns to the univerfity of Zealand, for the education of young nobleffe; thinking it right that as his wealth had been acquired by literature, it fhould be employed in its fupport. This munificence obtained him the title of baron. At his death, which happened in 1754, he left alfo a fund of 16,000 crowns to portion out a certain number of young women, felected from the families of citizens in Copenhagen.

HOLDEN (HENRY), an Englifh divine, who took the degree of doctor at Paris, and lived there till his death in 1662. He died equally regretted for his ftrict probity, and his profound erudition. We have not an exact hiftory of him; but it is probable that being a Roman catholic, he had received his education altogether in France. There are three works by him, one of which, 1. " Analyfis Fidei," was reprinted by Barbou in 1766, and contains a brief fummary of the whole œconomy of faith, its principles and motives, with their application to controverfial queftions. It is confidered as argumentative and found. 2. " Marginal Notes on the New Teftament," in 2 vols. 12mo, publifhed at Paris in 1660. 3. ",A Letter concerning Mr. White's Treatife, De Medio Animarum ftatu," in 4to, Paris, 1661. He argued from his own fources more than he compiled.

HOLDER (WILLIAM), a learned and philofophical Englifhman [v], was born in Nottinghamfhire, educated in Pembroke-hall, Cambridge, and, in 1642, became rector of Blechingdon of Oxford. In 1660, he proceeded D. D. was afterwards canon of Ely, fellow of the Royal Society, canon of St. Paul's, fub-dean of the royal chapel, and fub-almoner to his majefty. He was very accomplifhed, and a great virtuofo. He gained particular celebrity by teaching a young gentleman of diftinction, who was born deaf and dumb, to fpeak, an attempt at that time unprecedented. This gentleman's name was Alexander Popham, fon of colonel Edward Popham, who was fome time an admiral in the fervice of the long parliament. The cure was performed by him in his houfe at Blechingdon, in 1659; but Popham lofing what he had been taught by Holder, after he was called home to his friends, was fent to Dr. Wallis, who brought him to his fpeech again. On this fubject Holder publifhed a book, enti-tled, " The Elements of Speech; an Effay of Inquiry into the natural Production of Letters: with an Appendix concerning Perfons that are deaf and dumb, 1669," 8vo. In the appendix he relates, how foon, and by what methods, he brought Popham to fpeak. In 1678, he publifhed, in 4to, " A Supplement to the Philofophical Tranfactions of July, 1670, with fome Re-flections on Dr. Wallis's Letter there inferted." This was written to claim the glory of having taught Popham to fpeak, which Wallis in the letter there mentioned had claimed to him-felf: upon which the doctor foon after publifhed, " A Defence of the Royal Society and the Philofophical Tranfactions, parti-cularly thofe of July, 1670, in Anfwer to the Cavils of Dr. William Holder, 1678," 4to. Holder was fkilled in the theory and practice of mufic, and wrote, " A Treatife of the natural Grounds and Principles of Harmony, 1694," 8vo. He wrote alfo " A Difcourfe concerning Time, with Application of the natural Day, lunar Month, and folar Year, &c. 1694." 8vo. He died at Amen Corner in London, Jan. 24, 1696-7, and was buried in St. Paul's.

HOLDSWORTH (EDWARD), a very polite and elegant fcholar [x], was born about 1688, and trained at Winchefter-fchool. He was thence elected demy of Magdalen-college, Oxford, in July, 1705; took the degree of M. A. in April, 1711; became a college-tutor, and had many pupils. In 1715, when he was to be chofen into a fellowfhip, he refigned his demyfhip, and left the college, becaufe unwilling to fwear al-legiance to the new government. The remainder of his life was fpent in travelling with young noblemen and gentlemen as a tutor: in 1741, and 1745, he was at Rome in this capacity. He died of a fever at lord Digby's houfe at Colefhill in Warwick-fhire, Dec. 30, 1747. He was the author of the " Mufcipula," a poem, efteemed a mafter-piece in its kind, and of which there is a good Englifh tranflation by Dr. John Hoadly, in Vol. V. of " Dodfley's Mifcellanies." He was the author alfo of a differtation, entitled, " Pharfalia and Philippi; or the two Phi-lippi in Virgil's Georgics attempted to be explained and recon-ciled to Hiftory, 1741," 4to: and of " Remarks and Differtations on Virgil; with fome other claffical Obfervations, publifhed with feveral Notes and additional Remarks by Mr. Spence, 1768," 4to. Mr. Spence fpeaks of him in his Polymetis, as one who

[x] Anecdotes of Bowyer, by Nichols, p. 408.

underftood

underſtood Virgil in a more maſterly manner, than any perſon he ever knew.

HOLINSHED (RAPHAEL), an Engliſh hiſtorian, and famous for the Chronicles that go under his name, was deſcended from a family, which lived at Boſely in Cheſhire: but neither the place nor time of his birth, nor ſcarcely any other circumſtances of his life, are known. Some ſay, he had an univerſity education, and was a clergyman; while others, denying this, affirm, that he was ſteward to Thomas Burdett, of Bromcote in the county of Warwick, eſq. Be this as it will, he appears to have been a man of conſiderable learning, and to have a head particularly turned for hiſtory. His "Chronicles" were firſt publiſhed in 1577, in 2 vols. folio; and then in 1587 in three, the two firſt of which are commonly bound together. In this ſecond ediſion, ſeveral ſheets were caſtrated in the ſecond and third volumes, becauſe there were paſſages in them diſagreeable to queen Elizabeth and her miniſtry: but the caſtrations have ſince been reprinted apart. Holinſhed was not the ſole author or compiler of this work, but was aſſiſted in it by ſeveral other writers. The firſt volume opens with "An Hiſtorical Deſcription of the Iſland of Britaine, in three Books," by William Harriſon: and then, "The Hiſtorie of England, from the Time that it was firſt inhabited, until the Time that it was laſt conquered," by R. Holinſhed. The ſecond volume contains, "The Deſcription, Conqueſt, Inhabitation, and troubleſome Eſtate of Ireland; particularly the Deſcription of that Kingdom:" by Richard Stanihurſt. "The Conqueſt of Ireland, tranſlated from the Latin of Giraldus Cambrenſis," by John Hooker, alias Vowell, of Exeter, gent. "The Chronicles of Ireland, beginning where Giraldus did end, continued untill the Year 1509, from Philip Flatſburie, Henrie of Marleborow, Edmund Campian," &c. by R. Holinſhed; and from thence to 1586, by R. Stanihurſt and J. Hooker. "The Deſcription of Scotland, tranſlated from the Latin of Hector Boethius," by R. H. or W. H. "The Hiſtorie of Scotland, conteining the Beginning, Increaſe, Proceedings, Continuance, Acts and Government of the Scottiſh Nation, from the Original thereof unto the Yeere 1571," gathered by Raphael Holinſhed; and continued from 1571 to 1586, by Francis Boteville, alias Thin, and others. The third volume begins at "Duke William the Norman, commonly called the Conqueror; and deſcends by Degrees of Yeeres to all the Kings and Queenes of England." Firſt compiled by R. Holinſhed, and by him extended to 1577; augmented and continued to 1586, by John Stow, Fr. Thin, Abraham Fleming, and others. The time of this hiſtorian's death is unknown; but it appears from his will, which Hearne prefixed to his edition of Camden's "Annals," that it happened between 1578 and 1582.

As

As for his coadjutors; Harrison was bred at Westminster-school, sent from thence to Oxford, became chaplain to sir William Brooke, who preferred him, and died in 1593. Hooker was uncle to the famous Richard Hooker, and born at Exeter about 1524: was educated at Oxford, and afterwards travelled into Germany, where at Cologne he took a degree in law. Next he went to Strasburg, and sojourned with Peter Martyr, who instructed him in divinity. Then returning home, he married and settled in his native place; where he became a principal citizen, and was sent up as a representative, to the parliament holden at Westminster in 1571. He died in 1601 [A], after having published several works of various kinds. We know nothing of Botevile; only that Hearne [B] styles him "a man of great learning and judgement, and a wonderful lover of antiquities."

HOLLAR, or HOLLARD (WENTZEL, or WENCESLAUS), a most admired engraver, was born at Prague in Bohemia, in 1607. He was at first instructed in school-learning, and afterwards put to the profession of the law; but not relishing that pursuit, and his family being ruined when Prague was taken and plundered in 1619 [c], so that they could not provide for him as had been proposed, he removed from thence in 1627. During his abode in several towns in Germany, he applied himself to drawing and designing, to copying the pictures of several great artists, taking geometrical and perspective views and draughts of cities, towns, and countries, by land and water; wherein at length he grew so excellent, especially for his landscapes in miniature, as not to be outdone in beauty and delicacy by any artist of his time. He was but eighteen, when the first specimens of his art appeared; and the connoisseurs in his works have observed, that he inscribed the earliest of them with only a cypher of four letters, which, as they explain it, was intended for the initials of, "Wenceslaus Hollar Pragensis excudit." He employed himself chiefly in copying heads and portraits, sometimes from Rembrandt, Henzelman, Fælix Biler, and other eminent artists; but his little delicate views of Strasburgh, Cologne, Mentz, Bonn, Frankfort, and other towns along the Rhine, Danube, Necker, &c. got him much reputation; and when Howard, earl of Arundel, was sent ambassador to the emperor Ferdinand II. in 1636, he was so highly pleased with his performances, that he admitted him into his retinue. Hollar attended his lordship from Cologne to the emperor's court, and in this progress made several draughts and prints of the places through which they travelled. He took that view of Wurtz-

[A] Athen. Oxon. Vol. I. [B] Præfat. ad Camd. Ann.al. [c] Life of Hollar by Vertue, Lond. 1745.

3

burg, under which is written, " Hollar delineavit, in legatione
Arundeliana ad Imperatorem." He then made also a curious
large drawing, with the pen and pencil, of the city of Prague, which
gave great satisfaction to his patron, then upon the spot.

After lord Arundel had finished his negotiations in Germany,
he returned to England, and brought Hollar with him: where,
however, he was not so entirely confined to his lordship's service,
but that he had the liberty to accept of employment from others.
Accordingly, we soon find him to have been engaged by the
printsellers; and Peter Stent, one of the most eminent among
them, prevailed upon him to make an ample view or prospect
of and from the town of Greenwich, which he finished in two
plates, 1637; the earliest date of his works in this kingdom. In
1638, appeared his elegant prospect about Richmond; at which
time he finished also several curious plates from the fine paintings
in the Arundelian collection. In the midst of this employment,
arrived Mary de Medicis the queen-mother of France, to visit
her daughter Henrietta Maria queen of England; and with her
an historian, who recorded the particulars of her journey and
entry into this kingdom. His work, written in French, was
printed at London in 1639; and adorned with several portraits
of the royal family, etched for the purpose by the hand of Hollar. The same year was published the portrait of his patron the
earl of Arundel on horseback; and afterwards he etched another
of him in armour, and several views of his country seat at Ald-
brough in Surrey. In 1640, he seems to have been introduced
into the service of the royal family, to give the prince of Wales
some taste in the art of designing; and it is intimated, that either
before the eruption of the civil wars, or at least before he was
driven by them abroad, he was in the service of the duke of
York. This year appeared his beautiful set of figures in 28
plates, entitled, " Ornatus Muliebris Anglicanus," and containing the several habits of English women of all ranks or degrees: they are represented at full length, and have rendered him
famous among the lovers of engraving. In 1641, were published his prints of king Charles and his queen: but now the
civil wars being broke out, and his patron the earl of Arundel
leaving the kingdom to attend upon the queen and the princess Mary, Hollar was left to support himself. He applied
himself closely to his business, and published other parts of his
works, after Holbein, Vandyck, &c. especially the portraits of
several persons of quality of both sexes, ministers of state,
commanders of the army, learned and eminent authors; more
especially another set of two of female habits in divers nations
in Europe. Whether he grew obnoxious, as an adherent to the
earl of Arundel, or as a malignant for drawing so many portraits
of the royal party, is not expressly said: but now it seems he

was

was molefted, and driven to take fhelter under the protection of
one or more of them, till they were defeated, and he taken prifoner of war with them, upon the furrender of their garrifon at
Bafing-houfe in Hampfhire. This happened on Oct. 14, 1645;
but Hollar, either making his efcape, or otherwife obtaining
his liberty, went over to the continent after the earl of Arundel,
who refided at Antwerp with his family, and had tranfported
thither his moft valuable collection of pictures.

He remained at Antwerp feveral years, copying from his patron's collection, and working for printfellers, bookfellers, and
publifhers; but feems to have cultivated no intereft among men
of fortune and curiofity in the art, to difpofe of them by fubfcription, or otherwife moft to his advantage. In 1647 and
1648, he etched eight or ten of the painters' heads with his own,
with various other curious pieces, as the picture of Charles I.
foon after his death, and of feveral of the Royalifts; and in the
three following years, many portraits and landfcapes after Breug-
hill, Elfheimer, and Teniers, with the triumphs of death.
He etched alfo Charles II. ftanding, with emblems; and alfo
publifhed a print of James duke of York, ætat. 18, ann. 1651,
from a picture drawn of him when he was in Flanders, by
Teniers. He was more punctual in his dates than moft other
engravers, which have afforded very agreeable lights and directions, both as to his own perfonal hiftory and performances, and
to thofe of many others. At laft, either not meeting with encouragement enough to keep him longer abroad, or invited by
feveral magnificent and coftly works propofed or preparing in
England, wherein his ornamental hand might be employed more
to his advantage, he returned hither in 1652. Here he afterwards executed fome of the moft confiderable of his publications: but what is very ftrange, though he was an artift fuperior
to almoft moft others in genius as well as affiduity, yet he had the
peculiar fate to work here, as he had done abroad, ftill in a ftate
of fubordination, and more to the profit of other people than
himfelf. Notwithftanding his penurious pay, he is faid to have
contracted a voluntary affection to his extraordinary labour;
fo far, that he fpent almoft two-thirds of his time at it, and
would not fuffer himfelf to be drawn or difengaged from it, till
his hour-glafs had run to the laft moment propofed. Thus he
went on in full bufinefs, till the reftoration of Charles II.
brought home many of his friends, and him into frefh views of
employment. It was but two years after that memorable epocha,
that Evelyn publifhed his "Sculptura, or the Hiftory and Art
of Chalcography and engraving in Copper;" in which he gave
the following very honourable account of Hollar. "Wincef-
laus Hollar," fays he, "a gentleman of Bohemia, comes in the
next place: not that he is not before moft of the reft for his

choice and great induſtry, for we rank them very promiſcuouſly both as to time and pre-eminence, but to bring up the rear of the Germans with a deſerving perſon, whoſe indefatigable works in aqua fortis do infinitely recommend themſelves by the excellent choice which he hath made of the rare things furniſhed out of the Arundelian collection, and from moſt of the beſt hands and deſigns: for ſuch were thoſe of L. da Vinci, Fr. Parmenſis, Titian, Julio Romano, A. Mantegna, Corregio, Perino del Vaga, Raphael Urbin, Seb. del Piombo, Palma, Albert Durer, Hans Holbein, Vandyck, Rubens, Dreughel, Baſſan, Eltheimer, Brower, Artois, and divers other maſters of prime note, whoſe drawings and paintings he hath faithfully copied; beſides ſeveral books of landſcapes, towns, ſolemnities, hiſtorics, heads, beaſts, fowls, inſects, veſſels, and other ſignal pieces, not omitting what he hath etched after De Cleyn, Mr. Strcter, and Dankerty, for ſir Robert Stapleton's ' Juvenal,' Mr. Rofs's ' Silius Italicus,' ' Polyglotta Biblia,' ' The Monaſticon,' firſt and ſecond part, Mr. Dugdale's ' St. Paul's,' and ' Survey of Warwickſhire,' with other innumerable frontiſpieces, and things by him publiſhed and done after the life; and to be on that account more valued and eſteemed, than where there has been more curioſity about chimeras, and things which are not in nature: ſo that of Mr. Hollar's works we may juſtly pronounce, there is not a more uſeful and inſtructive collection to be made."

Some of the firſt things Hollar performed after the Reſtoration, were, "A Map of Jeruſalem;" " The Jewiſh Sacrifice in Solomon's Temple;" " Maps of England, Middleſex, &c." " View of St. George's Hoſpital at Windſor;" " The Gate of John of Jeruſalem near London;" and many animals, fruits, flowers, and inſects, after Barlow and others: many heads of nobles, biſhops, judges, and great men; ſeveral proſpects about London, and London iſſelf, as well before the great fire, as after its ruin and rebuilding: though the calamities of the fire and plague in 1665 are thought to have reduced him to ſuch difficulties, as he could never entirely vanquiſh. He was afterwards ſent to Tangier in Africa, in quality of his majeſty's deſigner, to take the various proſpects there of the garriſon, town, fortifications, and the circumjacent views of the country: and many of his drawings upon the ſpot, dated 1669, ſtill preſerved in the library of the late ſir Hans Sloane, were within three or four years after made public, upon ſome of which Hollar ſtyles himſelf " Stenographus Regis." After his return to England, he was variouſly employed, in finiſhing his views of Tangier for publication, and taking ſeveral draughts at and about Windſor in 1671, with many repreſentations in honour of the knights of the garter. About 1672, he travelled northward, and drew views of Lincoln, Southwell, Newark, and York Minſter; and afterwards

terwards was engaged in etching of towns, castles, churches, and
their seneftral figures, arms, &c. besides tombs, monumental effigies
with their inscriptions, &c. in such numbers as it would almost
be endless to enumerate. Few artists have been able to imitate his
works; for which reason many lovers of the art, and all the
curious, both at home and abroad, have, from his time to ours, been
fond and even zealous to collect them. But how liberal soever they
might be in the purchase of his performances, the performer himself, it seems, was so incompetently rewarded for them, that he
could not, now in his old age, keep himself free from the incum-
brances of debt; though it is visible, that he was variously and
closely employed to a short time before his death. But as many
of his plates are dated that year, in the very beginning of which
he died, it is probable they were somewhat antedated by him,
that the sculptures might appear of the same date with the book
in which they were printed: that is, in " Thoroton's Antiquities of Nottinghamshire." Some of them appear unfinished;
and the 501st page, which is entirely blank, was probably left so
for a plate to be supplied. When he was upon the verge of his
70th year, he had the misfortune to have an execution at his house
in Gardiner's-lane, Westminster: he desired only the liberty of
dying in his bed, and that he might not be removed to any other
prison but his grave. Whether this was granted him or not, we
cannot say; but he died March 28, 1677, and, as appears from
the parish register of St. Margaret's, was buried in the New
Chapel Yard, near the place of his death. Noble and valuable
as the monuments were which Hollar had raised for others, none
was erected for him: nor has any person proposed an epitaph
worthy of the fame and merits of the artist.

HOLLIS (THOMAS), esq; of Corscombe in Dorsetshire; a
gentleman whose " Memoirs" were printed in two splendid volumes, 4to, 1780, with a considerable number of plates by Bar-
tolozzi, Basire, and other engravers of eminence, and an admirable profile of himself in the frontispiece [D]. He was born
in London, April 14, 1720; and sent to school, first at Newport in Shropshire, and afterwards at St. Alban's. At 14, he
was sent to Amsterdam, to learn the Dutch and French languages, writing, and accompts; stayed there about fifteen months,
and then returned to his father, with whom he continued till his
death in 1735. To give him a liberal education, suitable to the
ample fortune he was to inherit, his guardian put him under
the tuition of professor Ward, whose picture Mr. Hollis presented to the British Museum; and, in honour of his father and
guardian, he caused to be inscribed round a valuable diamond
ring, *Mnemosynon patris tutorisque.* He professed himself a dis-

[D] Anecdotes of Bowyer, by Nichols, p. 402, 596.

fenter; and from Dr. Foster and others of that perfuafion, imbibed that ardent love of liberty, and freedom of fentiment, which ftrongly marked his character. In Feb. 1739-40, he took chambers in Lincoln's-Inn, and was admitted a law-ftudent; but does not appear ever to have applied to the law, as a profeffion. He refided there till July, 1748, when he fet out on his travels for the firft time; and paffed through Holland, Auftrian and French Flanders, part of France, Switzerland, Savoy, and part of Italy, returning through Provence, Britanny, &c. to Paris. His fellow-traveller was Thomas Brand, efq; of the Hyde in Effex, who was his particular friend. His fecond tour commenced in July 16, 1750; and extended through Holland to Embden, Bremen, Hamburg, the principal cities on the north and eaft fide of Germany, the reft of Italy, Sicily, and Malta, Lorrain, &c. The journals of both his tours are faid to be in being.

On his return home, he attempted to get into parliament; but, not being able to effect this without fome fmall appearance of bribery, he turned his thoughts entirely to other objects. He began a collection of books and medals; " for the purpofe," it is faid, " of illuftrating and upholding liberty, preferving the memory of its champions, rendering tyranny and its abettors odious, extending art and fcience, and keeping alive the honour due to their patrons and protectors." Among his benefactions to foreign libraries, none is more remarkable than that of two large collections of valuable books to the public library of Berne; which were prefented anonymoufly as by " an Englifhman, a lover of liberty, his country, and its excellent conftitution, as reftored at the happy Revolution." Switzerland, Geneva, Venice, Leyden, Sweden, Ruffia, &c. fhared his favours. His benefactions to Harvard-college commenced in 1758, and were continued to the amount of 1400l. His liberality to individuals, as well as to public focieties, cannot be fpecified here; but muft be fought in the " Memoirs" above-mentioned. Aug. 1770, he carried into execution a plan, which he had formed five years before, of retiring into Dorfetfhire; and there, in a field near his refidence at Corfcombe, dropped down and died of an apoplexy, on New-year's-day, 1774. The character of this fingular perfon was given, fome time before, in one of the public prints, as follows: " Thomas Hollis is a man poffeffed of a large fortune: above half of which he devotes to charities, to the encouragement of genius, and to the fupport and defence of liberty. His ftudious hours are devoted to the fearch of noble authors, hidden by the ruft of time; and to do their virtues juftice, by brightening their actions for the review of the public. Wherever he meets the man of letters, he is fure to affift him : and, were I to defcribe in paint this illuftrious citizen of the

world,

world, I would depict him leading by the hands Genius and
diftreffed Virtue to the temple of Reward."

If Mr. Hollis had any relations, his private affections were
not as eminent as his public fpirit, for he left the whole of his
fortune to his friend T. Brand, efq; who, on that account, took
the name of Hollis, and was as violent a zealot for liberty as
his patron. In 1764, Mr. Hollis fent to Sidney-college, Cambridge, where Cromwell was educated, an original portrait of
him by Cooper; and, a fire' happening at his lodgings in Bed-
ford-ftreet, in 1761, he calmly walked out, taking an original
picture of Milton only in his hand. A new edition of " Toland's Life of Milton" was publifhed under his direction, in 1761;
and, in 1763, he gave an accurate edition of " Algernon Syd-
ney's Difcourfes on Government," on which the pains and expence he beflowed are almoft incredible. He meditated alfo an
edition of Andrew Marvell; but did not complete it. In order
to preferve the memory of thofe patriotic heroes whom he moft
admired, he called many of the farms and fields in his eftate at
Corfcombe by their names: and, in the middle of one of thefe
fields, not far from his houfe, he ordered his corpfe to be depofited in a grave ten feet deep, and the field to be immediately
ploughed over, that no trace of his burial-place might remain.
Another of his fingularities was, to obferve his nominal birth-
day always, without any regard to the change of ftyle. He
would not be offended with being charged with fingularities;
he owned, that he affected them : " the idea of fingularity," fays
he, " by way of fhield, I try by all means to hold out." By
way of fhield: that is, againft thofe who would otherwife break
in upon his time, cuftoms, and way of living.

HOLMES (GEORGE), born at Skipton in Craven, Yorkfhire
[s]; became about 1695 clerk to William Petyt, efq; keeper of
the records at the Tower; and continued near fixty years deputy
to Mr. Petyt, Mr. Topham, and Mr. Polhill. On the death
of Mr. Petyt, which happened Oct. 9, 1707, Mr. Holmes was,
on account of his fingular abilities and induftry, appointed by
lord Halifax (then prefident of a committee of the houfe of
lords) to methodize and digeft the Records depofited in the
Tower, at a yearly falary of 200l. which was continued to his
death, Feb. 16, 1748-9, in the 87th year of his age. He was
alfo barrack-mafter of the Tower. He married a daughter of
Mr. Marfhall, an eminent fword-cutler in Fleet-ftreet, by whom
he had an only fon George, who was bred at Eton, and was
clerk under his father, but died, aged 25, many years before
him. Holmes re-publifhed the firft 17 volumes [v] of Rymer's

[r] Anecdotes of Bowyer, by Nichols,   the feventeen volumes was fold for 100
p. 97.   given. § the preface to the " Acta
[s] Before this fecond edition, a fet of Regia, 1726," 8vo.

" Fœdera,"

" Fœdera," in 1727. His curious collections of books, prints, and coins, &c. were fold by auction in 1749. His portrait was engraved by the Society of Antiquaries, with this inscription: " Vera effigies GEORGII HOLMES generofi, R. S. S. & tabularii publici in Turre Londinenfi Vicecuftodis; quo munere annos circiter LX fumma fide & diligentia perfunctus, XIV kalend. Mart. A. D. MDCCXLVIII, ætatis fuæ LXXXVII, fato demum conceffit. In fratris fui erga fe meritorum teftimonium hanc tabulam SOCIETAS ANTIQUARIORUM Londini, cujus commoda femper promovit, fumptu fuo æri incidendum curavit, MDCCXLIX. R. Van Bleeck, p. 1743. G. Vertue del. & fculp."—In Strype's London, 1754, Vol. I. p. 746, is a fac fimile of an antique infcription over the little door next to the cloifter in the Temple church. It was in old Saxon capital letters, engraved within an half circle; denoting the year when the church was dedicated, and by whom, namely, Heraclius the patriarch of the church of the Holy Refurrection in Jerufalem; and to whom, namely, the Bleffed Virgin; and the indulgence of 40 days pardon to fuch who, according to the penance enjoined them, reforted thither yearly. This infcription, which was fcarcely legible, and in 1695 was entirely broken by the workmen, having been exactly tranfcribed by Mr. Holmes, was by him communicated to Strype. Mrs. Holmes out-lived her hufband, and received of government 200l. for his MSS. about the records, which were depofited and remain in his office to this day.

HOLSTENIUS, or HOLSTEIN (LUCAS), an ingenious and learned German, was born at Hamburg in 1596; and after a liberal education in his own country, went to France, and flayed fome time at Paris, where he diftinguifhed himfelf by uncommon parts and learning. From thence he went to Rome, and attached himfelf to cardinal Francis Barberini; who took him under his protection, and recommended him to favour. He was honoured by three popes; Urban VIII. Innocent X. and Alexander VII. The firft gave him a canonry of St. Peter's; the fecond made him librarian of the Vatican; and the third fent him, in 1665, to Chriftina of Sweden, whofe formal profeffion of the Catholic faith he received at Infpruck. He fpent his life in ftudy, and died at Rome in 1661, aged 65 years. Cardinal Barberini, whom he made his heir, caufed a monument of marble to be erected over his grave, with a Latin infcription much to his honour. He was very learned both in facred and profane antiquity, had a very exact and critical difcernment, and wrote with the utmoft purity and elegance. He was not the author of any great works: what he did chiefly confifted of notes and differtations, which have been highly efteemed for the judgement and precifion with which they are drawn up. Some of thefe were publifhed by himfelf; but the greater part

were

were communicated after his death, and inserted by his friends in their editions of authors, or other works that would admit them. Though Holstenius *seems* to have been a grave man, yet there is a bon-mot in the Menagiana [o], which shews some mirth and a great deal of ready wit. Disputing one day with some vehemence against two learned men at his patron cardinal Barberini's table, he had the misfortune to break wind backwards. The cardinal smiled ; and the company could not forbear laughing out. Holstenius, however, not t e least disconcerted, turned himself to the cardinal, and said, " I may very well upon this occasion apply to your eminence this of Virgil,—Tu das epulis accumbere divum—but not the following—Ventorumque facis tempestatumque potentem :" nobody suspecting in the mean time, that it was not Ventorum, but Nimborum, in Virgil. His notes and emendations upon Eusebius's book against Hierocles, upon Porphyry's " Life of Pythagoras," upon Apollonius's " Argonautics," upon the fragments of Demophilus, Democrates, Secundus, and Sallustius the philosopher, upon Stephanus Byzantinus de Urbibus, &c. are known to all the learned, and to be found in the best editions of those authors. He wrote a " Dissertation upon the Life and Writings of Porphyry," which is printed with his notes on Porphyry's " Life of Pythagoras;" and other dissertations of his are inserted in Grævius's " Collection of Roman Antiquities," and elsewhere.

We must not forget to observe, that Holstenius was born in the Lutheran religion ; but afterwards embraced the Roman Catholic, at the intercession of Sirmond the Jesuit, who had the honour to make a convert of him.

HOLT (Sir JOHN), knight, lord chief justice of the court of King's-bench, in the reign of king William [H], was son of sir Thomas Holt, knight, serjeant at law; and born at Thame in Oxfordshire, 1642. He was educated at Abingdon-school, while his father was recorder of that town; and afterwards became a gentleman-commoner of Oriel-college, Oxford. In 1658, he entered himself of Gray's-Inn, before he took a degree; some time after which he was called to the bar, where he attended constantly, and soon became a very eminent barrister. In the reign of James II. he was made recorder of London, which office he discharged with much applause for about a year and a half; but refusing to give his hand towards abolishing the test, and to expound the law according to the king's design, he was removed from his place. In 1686, he was called to the degree of a serjeant at law, with many others. On the arrival of the prince of Orange, he was chosen a member of the convention parliament ; and appointed one of the managers for the com-

[o] Tom. I. p. 222.   [a] Life of lord chief justice Holt, 8vo.

mons at the conferences held with the lords, about the abdication and the vacancy of the throne. He had here an opportunity of displaying his abilities; and as soon as the government was settled, he was made lord chief justice of the court of King's-bench, and admitted into the king's privy-council.

In 1700, when lord Somers parted with the great seal, king William pressed chief justice Holt to accept of it: but he replied, that he never had but one chancery cause in his life, which he lost; and consequently could not think himself fitly qualified for so great a trust. He continued in his post 22 years, and maintained it with great reputation for steadiness, integrity, and complete knowledge in his profession. He applied himself with great assiduity to the functions of his important office. He was perfect master of the common law [1]; and, as his judgement was most solid, his capacity vast, and understanding most clear, so he had a firmness of mind, and such a degree of resolution, as never could be brought to swerve in the least from what he thought to be law and justice. Upon great occasions he shewed an intrepid zeal in asserting the authority of the law; for he ventured to incur the indignation of both houses of parliament, by turns, when he thought the law was with him. Several cases of the utmost importance, and highly affecting the lives, rights, liberties, and property of the people, came in judgement before him. There was a remarkable clearness and perspicuity of ideas in his definitions; a distinct arrangement of them in the analysis of his arguments; and the real and natural difference of things was made most perceptible and obvious, when he distinguished between matters which bore a false resemblance to each other. Having thus rightly formed his premises, he scarce ever erred in his conclusions; his arguments were instructive and convincing, and his integrity would not suffer him to deviate from judgement and truth, in compliance to his prince, or, as observed before, to either house of parliament. They are most of them faithfully and judiciously reported by that eminent lawyer, chief justice Raymond. His integrity and uprightness as a judge, are celebrated by the author of the "Tatler," No. 14, under the noble character of Verus the magistrate.

There happened in the time of this chief justice, a riot in Holborn, occasioned by a wicked practice then prevailing, of decoying young persons of both sexes to the plantations. The persons so decoyed they kept prisoners in a house in Holborn, till they could find an opportunity of shipping them off; which being discovered, the enraged populace were going to pull down the house. Notice of this being sent to Whitehall, a party of the guards were commanded to march to the place; but they

[1] Burnet's History, vol. II. p. 543.

first

firſt ſent an officer to the chief juſtice to acquaint him with the deſign, and to deſire him to ſend ſome of his people to attend the ſoldiers, in order to give it the better countenance. The officer having delivered his meſſage, Holt ſaid to him, " Suppoſe the populace ſhould not diſperſe at your appearance, what are you to do then?" " Sir," anſwered the officer, " we have orders to fire upon them." " Have you, Sir? (replied Holt) then take notice of what I ſay ; if there be one man killed, and you are tried before me, I will take care that you, and every ſoldier of your party, ſhall be hanged. Sir, (added he) go back to thoſe who ſent you, and acquaint them, that no officer of mine ſhall attend ſoldiers ; and let them know at the ſame time, that the laws of this kingdom are not to be executed by the ſword: theſe matters belong to the civil power, and you have nothing to do with them." Upon this, the chief juſtice ordering his tipſtaves, with a few conſtables to attend him, went himſelf in perſon to the place where the tumult was ; expoſtulated with the mob.; aſſured them that juſtice ſhould be done upon the perſons who were the objects of their indignation : and thus they all diſperſed quietly.

He married Anne, daughter of ſir John Cropley, bart. whom he left without iſſue ; and died in March, 1709, after a long lingering illneſs, in his 68th year. The following Reports were publiſhed by himſelf, in 1708, with ſome notes of his own upon them : " A Report of divers Caſes in Pleas of the Crown, adjudged and determined, in the Reign of the late King Charles the Second, with Directions for Juſtices of the Peace, and others, collected by Sir John Keyling, Knight, late Lord Chief Juſtice of his Majeſty's Court of King's-bench, from the original Manuſcript under his own Hand. To which is added, The Report of three modern Caſes, viz. Armſtrong and Liſle; the King and Plummer ; the Queen and Mawgridge."

HOLYDAY (BARTEN), an ingenious and learned Engliſh divine, was the ſon of a taylor in Oxford, and born there about 1593 [K]. He was entered early into Chriſt-church, in the time of Dr. Ravis, his relation and patron, by whom he was choſen ſtudent; and, in 1615, he took orders. He was before noticed for his ſkill in poetry and oratory, and now diſtinguiſhed himſelf ſo much by his eloquence and popularity as a preacher, that he had two benefices conferred on him in the dioceſe of Oxford. In 1618, he went as chaplain to ſir Francis Stewart, when he accompanied the count Gundamore to Spain, in which journey Holyday behaved in ſo facetious and pleaſant a manner, that the count was greatly pleaſed with him. Afterwards he became chaplain to the king, and was promoted to the archdeaconry of Oxford before 1626. In 1642, he was made a doctor of divinity by mandamus at Oxford; near which place he sheltered himself during the time of the rebellion. When the Royal party declined, he so far sided with the prevailing powers, as to undergo the examination of the Triers, in order to be inducted into the rectory of Chilton in Berkshire; for he had lost his livings, and the profits of his archdeaconry, and could not well bear poverty and distress. This drew upon him much censure from his own party; some of whom, however, says Wood, commended him, since he had thus made provision for a second wife he had lately married. After the Restoration he quitted this living, and returned to Ilsley near Oxford, to live on his archdeaconry; and had he not acted a temporizing part, it was said he might have been raised to a see, or some rich deanery. His poetry, however, got him a name in those days, and he stood fair for preferment: his philosophy also, discovered in his book " De Anima," and his well-languaged sermons, says Wood, speak him eminent in his generation, and shew him to have traced the rough parts of learning, as well as the pleasant paths of poetry. He died at Ilsley, Oct. 2, 1661.

His works consist of twenty sermons, published at different times: " Technogamia, or the Marriage of Arts, a Comedy, 1630:" this was acted by some Oxford scholars at Woodstock in 1621, before king James, who is said not to have relished it at all: " Philosophiæ polito-barbaræ specimen, in quo de Anima & ejus habitibus intellectualibus quæstiones aliquot libris duobus illustrantur, 1633," 4to.—" Survey of the World, in ten Books, a Poem, 1661," 8vo. But the work he is known and esteemed for now, is his " Translation of the Satires of Juvenal and Persius;" for though his poetry is but indifferent, yet his translation is allowed to be faithful, and his notes good. The second edition of his " Persius," was published in 1616; and the fourth at the end of the " Satires of Juvenal illustrated with Notes and Sculptures, 1673," folio. Dryden, in the dedication of his " Translation of Juvenal and Persius," makes the following critique upon our author's performance. " If," says he, " rendering the exact sense of these authors, almost line for line, had been our business, Barten Holyday had done it already to our hands; and by the help of his learned notes and illustrations, not only Juvenal and Persius, but {what is yet more obscure} his own verses might be understood." Speaking a little further on, of close and literal translation, he says, that " Holyday, who made this way his choice, seized the meaning of Juvenal, but the poetry has always escaped him."

HOLYOAKE (FRANCIS), a learned Englishman, memorable for having made an " Etymological Dictionary of Latin Words," was born at Nether Whitacre, in Warwickshire, about 1567,

1567, and studied in the university of Oxford about 1582; but it does not appear that ever he took a degree. He taught school at Oxford, and in his own country [L]; and became rector of Southam in Warwickshire, 1604. He was elected a member of the convocation of the clergy in the first year of Charles the First's reign; and afterwards in the civil wars, suffered extremely for his attachment to that king. He died in 1653, and was buried at Warwick. His "Dictionary" was first printed in 1606, 4to; and the fourth edition in 1633, augmented, was dedicated to Laud, then bishop of London. He subscribed himself In Latin, " Francifcus de facra quercu."

He had a son, Thomas, born at Southam in 1616, and afterwards a student in Queen's-college, Oxford, where he took the degrees in arts. Then he became a captain in behalf of the king, and did such service, that, strange as it may seem, he was made doctor of divinity. After the surrender of Oxford, he retired into his own country; and obtaining a licence, practiced physic till the Restoration with good success. Then taking orders, he was presented by lord Leigh to the rectory of Whitnath, near Warwick, and afterwards obtained other good preferments. He died in 1675, and left a "Dictionary, English and Latin, and Latin and English," which was published in 1677, in a large thick folio. Before it are prefixed two epistles; one by the author's son, Charles Holyoake of the Inner-temple, dedicating the work to Foulke lord Brook, who in 1674, had conferred the donative of Breamour in Hampshire; another by Dr. Barlow bishop of Lincoln, containing many things of the work and its author. " This Dictionary, however," as Wood observes, " is made upon the foundation laid by his father."

HOMBERG (WILLIAM), a celebrated chemist, was born at Batavia in the island of Java, Jan. 3, 1652, the son of John Homberg, a Saxon gentleman, governor of the arsenal of that place [M]. His father at first put him into the army, but soon after quitting the service of the Dutch, and a military life, brought him to Amsterdam, where he settled. He was now educated, by paternal indulgence, at Jena and Leipsic for the law, and was received as an advocate in 1674, at Magdebourg. But the sciences seduced him from the law; in his walks he became a botanist, and in his nocturnal rambles an astronomer. An intimacy with Otto de Guericke, who lived at Magdebourg, completed his conversion, and he resolved to abandon his first profession. Otto, though fond of mystery, consented to communicate his knowledge to so promising a pupil; but as his friends continued to press him to be constant to the law, he ere long quitted Magdebourg, and went into Italy. At Padua, and

[L] Athen. Oxon. Vol. II.   [M] Eloge par Fontenelle, &c.

Bologna,

Bologna, he pursued his favourite studies, particularly medicine, anatomy, botany, and chemistry. One of his first efforts in the latter science, was the complete discovery of the properties of the Bologna stone, and its phosphoric appearance after calcination, which Casciarolo had first observed. The efforts of Homberg, in several scientific enquiries, were pursued at Rome, in France, in England with the great Boyle, and afterward in Holland and Germany. With Baldwin and Kunckel he here pursued the subject of Phosphorus. Not yet satisfied with travelling in search of knowledge, he visited the mines of Saxony, Hungary, Bohemia, and Sweden. Having materially improved himself, and at the same time assisted the progress of chemistry at Stockholm, he returned to Holland, and thence revisited France, where he was quickly noticed by Colbert. By this interposition, he was prevailed upon to quit his intention of returning to Holland to marry, according to the desire of his father, and fixed himself in France. This step also alienated him from his religion. He renounced the Protestant communion in 1682, and thus losing all connection with his family, became dependent on Louis XIV. and his minister. This, however, after the death of Colbert, in 1683, became a very miserable and starving dependence; men of learning and science were neglected as much as before they had been patronized; and Homberg, in 1687, left Paris for Rome, and took up the profession of physic. He now pursued and perfected his discoveries on Phosphorus, and prosecuted his discoveries in pneumatics, and other branches of natural philosophy. Finding, after some time, that the learned were again patronized at Paris, he returned there in 1690, and entered into the academy of sciences under the protection of M. de Bignon. He now resumed the study of chemistry, but found his finances too limited to carry on his experiments as he wished, till he had the good fortune to be appointed chemist to the duke of Orleans, afterwards regent. In this situation he was supplied with the most perfect apparatus, and all materials for scientific investigation. Among other instruments, the large burning mirror of *Tschirnaus* was given to his care, and he made with it the most interesting experiments, on the combustibility of gold, and other substances. In examining the nature of borax, he discovered the sedative salt, and traced several remarkable properties of that production. Pleased with the researches of his chemist, the duke of Orleans in 1704, appointed him his first physician. About the same time he was strongly solicited by the elector Palatine to settle in his dominions, but he was too much attached to his present patron to quit Paris, and was besides not without an inclination of a more tender kind for mademoiselle Dodart, daughter to the celebrated physician of that name. He married her in 1708, though hitherto much averse to matrimony;
but

but enjoyed the benefit of his change of sentiments only seven years, being attacked in 1715 with a dysentery, of which he died in September of that year.

Homberg was indefatigable in application, and his manners were mild and social. Though his constitution was not robust he was rather addicted to pleasure, and was glad to forget his fatigues in the charms of good company. He did not publish any complete work, the productions he has left being only memoirs in the volumes of the academy.

HOME (DAVID), a protestant minister of a distinguished family in Scotland, but educated in France, where he passed the chief part of his life. James I. employed him to reconcile the differences between Tilenus and du Moulin, on the subject of justification; and, if possible, to reconcile the Protestants throughout Europe to one single form of doctrine; but this was found impracticable. The chief work of this Home is, his 1. " Apologia Basilica; seu Machiavelli ingenium examinatum," 4to, 1626. There are attributed to him also, 2. " Le contr' Assassin, ou reponse a l'Apologie des Jesuites," Geneve, 1612, 8vo. 3. " L'Assassinat du Roi, ou maximes du Viel de la Montagne, pratiquées en la personne de defunt Henri le Grand," 8vo, 1617. He is also the author of several compositions in the " Deliciæ Poetarum Scotorum." The times of his birth and death are not known.

HOME (HENRY), lord Kaimes, was one of the very few who, to great legal knowledge, added a considerable share of polite literature [N]. He arrived at the highest rank to which a lawyer could attain in his country, and he has left to the world such literary productions as will authorize his friends to place him, if not in the highest, yet much above the lowest class of elegant and accomplished writers.

Scotland has the honour to claim his birth, and in the same country we are informed he received his education. Adopting the law for his profession, he soon became eminent in it. His first work was in the line of his profession, and was composed in the year 1745. It was entitled, " Essays upon several Subjects concerning British Antiquities, viz. 1. Introduction of the Feudal Law into Scotland; 2. Constitution of Parliament; 3. Honour, Dignity; 4. Succession or Descent, with an Appendix upon Hereditary and Indefeasible Right;" and was printed in the Year 1746. In the preface to this performance, he says, " To our late troubles the public is indebted for the following papers, if they be of value to create a debt. After many disconsolate hours, the author took courage to think of some study that might in some measure relieve his distressed mind. A connection with

[N] Europ. Magazine, November, 1790.

the caufe of our violent and unhappy diffenfions, led him naturally to the following fpeculations, which he now gives to the
public ; anxioufly wifhing to raife a fpirit in his countrymen of
fearching into their antiquities, thofe efpecially which regard
the law and conftitution, being ferioufly convinced that nothing
will more contribute than this ftudy to eradicate a fet of political opinions, which, tending to break the peace of fociety,
have been pernicious to this ifland. If thefe papers have the
effect intended, it is well ; if not, they may at leaft ferve to bear
teftimony of fome degree of firmnefs in the author, who, amidft
the calamities of a civil war, gave not his country for loft ; but
trufting to a good caufe, and to the prevalence of good fenfe
among his countrymen, was able to compofe his mind to ftudy,
and to deal in fpeculations which are not commonly relifhed
but in times of the greateft tranquillity."

His next work was on a very different fubject, and was publifhed in the year 1751. It was called, " Effays on the Principles of Morality and Natural Religion," 8vo, and was received by the public with confiderable approbation. On the 2d
of February, 1752, he was advanced to the Bench, and took
his feat as one of the Lords of Seffion, under the title of lord
Kaimes.

The duty of an advocate being now over, lord Kaimes found
leifure to communicate to the world the refult of his ftudies. In
1759 he publifhed his " Hiftorical Law," 8vo; and in 1760,
" The Principles of Equity," in folio. In both thefe works he
aimed to unite the principles of policy and philofophy with thofe
of jurifprudence, and to treat the law rather as a rational fyftem,
fit for the attention of the ftudious in general, than an intricate
and myfterious purfuit, folely confined to the profeffors of the
fcience, and it may be afferted that in thefe defigns he was not
unfuccefsful.

Two years afterwards, in 1762, he produced " Elements of
Criticifm," in 3 vols. 8vo, a work which has paffed through
feveral editions with the higheft approbation. In 1767, he
was one of the Lords of Seffion who, in the famous Douglas
caufe, gave judgement in favour of the fon of lady Jane.
After a confiderable interval, lord Kaimes refumed his pen
and publifhed " The Gentleman Farmer, being an Attempt
to improve Agriculture, by fubjecting it to the Teft of rational Principles," 8vo, 1777 ; and this was fucceeded by
" Loofe Hints upon Education, chiefly concerning the Culture
of the Heart," 8vo, 1781. His laft publication was the refult
of great refearch and unwearied application, and muft be allowed, if not a complete work itfelf, to furnifh the moft valuable materials for The Hiftory of Man, which it profeffes it
to trace. He modeftly ftyles it only " Sketches," and indeed it
will

will hardly be confidered in any other light than a common-place book. Confidered in that point of view, it is entitled to the warmeft praife. It is ufeful and entertaining, and contains facts and reafonings which will both amufe and inftruct, and which deferve the attention equally of the legiflator and the politician, the moralift and the divine.

At length, after a life ufefully fpent in the fervice of the world, having been feveral years the fenior Lord of Seffion, lord Kaimes died, Dec. 26, 1782, leaving to the world a proof that an attention to the abftrufeft branches of learning is not incompatible with the more pleafing purfuits of tafte and polite literature.

HOMER, the moft ancient of the Greek poets extant, has been called the father of poetry. As much as he has celebrated the praifes of others, he has been fo very modeft about himfelf, that we do not find the leaft mention of him throughout his poems: fo that where he was born, who were his parents, at what exact period he lived, and almoft every circumftance of his life, remain at this day in a great meafure, if not altogether, unknown. The moft copious account we have of the life of Homer is that which goes under the name of Herodotus, and is ufually printed with his hiftory: and though it is generally fup-pofed to be fpurious, yet as it is ancient, was made ufe of by Strabo, and exhibits that idea which the later Greeks, and the Romans in the age of Auguftus, entertained of Homer, we muft content ourfelves with giving an abftract of it.

A man of Magnefia, whofe name was Menalippus, went to fettle at Cumæ, where he married the daughter of a citizen called Homyres, and had by her a daughter called Critheis. The father and mother dying, the young woman was left under the tuition of Cleonax her father's friend; and, fuffering herfelf to be deluded, was got with child. The guardian, though his care had not prevented the misfortune, was however willing to conceal it; and therefore fent Critheis to Smyrna. Critheis being near her time, went one day to a feftival, which the town of Smyrna was celebrating on the banks of the river Meles; where her pains coming upon her, fhe was delivered of Homer, whom fhe called Melefigenes, becaufe he was born on the banks of that river. Having nothing to maintain her, fhe was forced to fpin: and a man of Smyrna called Phemius, who taught literature and mufic, having often feen Critheis, who lodged near him, and being pleafed with her houfewifery, took her into his houfe to fpin the wool he received from his fcholars for their fchooling. Here fhe behaved herfelf fo modeftly and difcreetly, that Phemius married her, and adopted her fon, in whom he difcovered a wonderful genius, and the beft natural difpofition in the world. After the death of Phemius and Critheis,

Homer fucceeded to his father-in-law's fortune and fchool ; and was admired not only by the inhabitants of Smyrna, but by ftrangers, who reforted from all parts to that place of trade. A fhip-mafter called Mentes, who was a man of wit, very learned, and a lover of poetry, was fo pleafed with Homer, that he followed him clofely, and perfuaded him to leave his fchool, and to travel with him. Homer, whofe mind was then employed upon his poem of the " Iliad," and who thought it of great confequence to fee the places of which he fhould have occafion to treat, embraced the opportunity. He embarked with Mentes, and during their feveral voyages, never failed carefully to note down all that he thought worth obferving. He travelled into Egypt, whence he brought into Greece the names of their gods, and the chief ceremonies of their worfhip. He vifited Africa and Spain, in his return from which places he touched at Ithaca, and was there much troubled with a rheum falling upon his eyes. Mentes being in hafte to vifit Leucadia his native country, left Homer well recommended to Mentor, one of the chief men of the ifland of Ithaca, who took all poffible care of him. There Homer was informed of many things relating to Ulyffes, which he afterwards made ufe of in compofing his " Odyffey." Mentes returning to Ithaca, found Homer cured. They embarked together; and after much time fpent in vifiting the coafts of Peloponnefus and the iflunds, they arrived at Colophon, where Homer was again troubled with the defluxion upon his eyes, which proved fo violent, that he is faid to have loft his fight [o]. This misfortune made him refolve to return to Smyrna, where he finifhed his " Iliad." Some time after, the ill pofture of his affairs obliged him to go to Cumæ, where he hoped to have found fome relief. He ftayed by the way at a place called the New Wall, which was the refidence of a colony from Cumæ. There he lodged in the houfe of an armourer called Tichius, and recited fome hymns he had made in honour of the Gods, and his poem of Amphiarus's expedition againft Thebes. After ftaying here fome time and being greatly admired, he went to Cumæ ; and pailing through Larilfa, he wrote the epitaph of Midas, king of Phrygia, then newly dead. At Cumæ he was received with extraordinary joy, and his poems highly applauded; but when he propofed to immortalize their town, if they would allow him a falary, he was anfwered, that " there would be no end of maintaining all the Ὅμηροι or Blind Men," and hence got the name of Homer. From Cumæ he went to Phocæa, where he recited his verfes in public affem-

[o] The blindnefs of Homer has been contefted by feveral authors, and particularly by a fcholar named *Andreas Wilkius*, In a book bearing the quaint title of *Cæretis taci Homeri*. If he was blind at all, it was probably only in extreme old age.

5

blies.

blies. Here one Theftorides a fchoolmafter offered to maintain
him, if he would fuffer him to tranfcribe his verfes: which
Homer complying with through mere neceffity, the fchoolmafter
privily withdrew to Chios, and there grew rich with Homer's
poems, while Homer at Phocæa hardly earned his bread by repeating them.

Obtaining however at laft fome intimation of the fchoolmafter,
he refolved to find him out ; and landing near that place, he was
received by one Glaucus a fhepherd, at whofe door he was
near being worried by dogs; and carried by him to his mafter
at Boliffus, who, admiring his knowledge, intrufted him with
the education of his children. Here his praife began to get
abroad, and the fchoolmafter hearing of him fled before him.
He removed fome time after to Chios, where he fet up a fchool
of poetry, gained a competent fortune, married a wife, and had
two daughters; one of which died young, and the other was
married to his patron at Boliffus. Here he compofed his
" Odyffey," and inferted the names of thofe to whom he had
been moft obliged, as Mentes, Phemius, Mentor, and refolving
to vifit Athens, he made honourable mention of that city, to
difpofe the Athenians for a kind reception of him. But as he
went, the fhip put in at Samos, where he continued the whole
winter, finging at the houfes of great men, with a train of boys
after him. In the fpring he went on board again, in order to
profecute his journey to Athens; but landing by the way at
Chios, he fell fick, died, and was buried on the fea-fhore.

This is the moft regular life we have of Homer; and though
probably but little of it is exactly true, yet it has this advantage
over all other accounts which remain of him, that it is within
the compafs of probability. The only inconteftable works,
which Homer has left behind him, are the " Iliad," and the
" Odyffey." The " Batrachomyomachia," or, " Battle of the
Frogs and Mice," has been difputed, but yet is allowed to be his
by many authors. The Hymns have been doubted alfo, and
attributed by the fcholiafts to Cynæthus the rhapfodift : but
neither Thucydides, Lucian, nor Paufanias, have fcrupled to ·
cite them as genuine. We have the authority of the two former, for that to Apollo ; and of the laft for a " Hymn to Ceres,"
of which he has given us a fragment. The whole hymn has been
lately found by Matthæi at Mofcow, and was publifhed by Ruhnkenius in 1782, at Leyden. A good tranflation has fince been given
by Mr. Hole. The Hymn to Mars is objected againft; and likewife the firft to Minerva. The " Hymn to Venus" has many of
its lines copied by Virgil, in the interview between Æneas and
that goddefs in the firft " Æneid." But whether thefe Hymns are
Homer's or not, they were always judged to be nearly as ancient,
if not of the fame age with him. Many other pieces were afcribed

to

to him: " Epigrams," the " Margites," the " Cecropes," the " Destruction of Oechalia," and several more. Time may here have prevailed over Homer, by leaving only the names of these works, as memorials that such were once in being; but while the " Iliad" and " Odyssey" remain, he seems like a leader, who, though he may have failed in a skirmish or two, has carried a victory, for which he will pass in triumph through all future ages.

Homer had the sublimest, and most universal genius, that the world has ever seen; and though it is an extravagance of enthusiasm to say as some of the Greeks did, that all knowledge may be found in his writings, his knowledge was certainly very extensive, and no man could have a deeper insight into the feelings and passions of human nature. He represents great things with such sublimity, and inferior objects with such propriety, that he always makes the one admirable, and the other pleasing. Strabo, whose authority in geography is indisputable, assures us, that Homer has described the places and countries, of which he gives an account, with such accuracy, that no man can imagine who has not seen them, and no man can observe without admiration and astonishment. His poems may justly be compared with that shield of divine workmanship, so inimitably represented in the 18th book of the " Iliad;" where we have exact images of all the actions of war and employments of peace, and are entertained with a delightful view of the universe. " Homer," says sir William Temple, " was without doubt the most universal genius that has been known in the world, and Virgil the most accomplished. To the first must be allowed the most fertile invention, the richest vein, the most general knowledge, and the most lively expressions: to the last the most noble ideas, the justest institution, the wisest conduct, and the choicest elocution. To speak in the painters' terms, we find in the works of Homer the most spirit, force, and life; in those of Virgil, the best design, the truest proportions, and the greatest grace. The colouring of both seems equal, and indeed in both is admirable. Homer had more fire and rapture, Virgil more light and sweetness; or at least the poetical fire was more raging in the one, but clearer in the other; which makes the first more amazing, and the latter more agreeable. The ore was richer in the one, but in the other more refined, and better allayed to make up excellent work. Upon the whole," says he, " I think it must be confessed, that Homer was of the two, and perhaps of all others, the vastest, the sublimest, and the most wonderful genius; and that he has been generally so esteemed, there cannot be a greater testimony given, than what has been by some observed, that not only the greatest masters have found the best and truest principles of all their sciences and arts in him; but that the noblest nations have
. derived

derived from him the original of their several races, though it be
hardly yet agreed, whether his story be true or a fiction. In
short, these two immortal poets must be allowed to have so much
excelled in their kinds, as to have exceeded all comparison, to
have even extinguished emulation, and in a manner confined
true poetry, not only to their two languages, but to their very
persons."

In the mean time Homer has had his enemies; and it is certain, that Plato banished his writings from his commonwealth,
which some would fix as a blemish upon the memory of the
poet. But the true reason, why Plato would not suffer the
poems of Homer to be in the hands of the subjects of that government, was, because he did not esteem the common people
to be capable readers of them. They would be apt to pervert
his meaning, and have wrong notions of God and religion, by
taking his bold and beautiful allegories in a literal sense. Plato
frequently declares, that he loves and admires him as the best,
the most pleasant, and the divinest of all poets, and studiously
imitates his figurative and mystical way of writing: and though
he forbad his works to be read in public, yet he would never be
without them in his closet. But the most memorable enemy to
the merits of Homer was Zoilus, a snarling critic, who frequented the court of Ptolemy Philadelphus, king of Egypt.
This fellow wrote ill-natured notes upon his poems, but received no encouragement from that prince; on the contrary, he
became universally hated for his pains, and was at length put,
as some say, to a most miserable death.

It must not be forgotten, that though Homer's poems were
at first published all in one piece, and not divided into books,
yet every one not being able to purchase them entire, they were
circulated in separate pieces; and each of those pieces took its name
from the contents, as, " The Battle of the Ships;" " The
Death of Dolon;" " The Valour of Agamemnon;" " The
Grot of Calypso;" " The Slaughter of the Wooers," and the
like; nor were these entitled books, but rhapsodies, as they
were afterwards called, when they were divided into books.
Homer's poems were not known entire in Greece before the
time of Lycurgus; whither that law-giver being in Ionia carried them, after he had taken the pains to transcribe them from
perfect copies with his own hands. This may be called the
first edition of Homer that appeared in Greece, and the time of
its appearing there was about 120 years before Rome was built,
that is, about 200 years after the time of Homer. It has been
said, that the " Iliad" and " Odyssey" were not composed by
Homer in their present form, but only in separate little poems,
which being put together and connected afterwards by some other
person, make the entire works they now appear; but this is so

extravagant a conceit, that it scarcely deserved to be mentioned.

HOMMEL (CHARLES FREDERICK), a lawyer, philologer, and historian of Leipsic, was born in the year 1722. He published his first work in 1743, which was a tract in 4to. 1. "De Legum civilium et naturalium Natura." 2. "Oblectamenta Juris Feudalis, five Grammaticæ Obfervationes jus rei clientelaris, et antiquitates Germanicas, variè illuftrantes," 1755. This was also in quarto, and tends, as well as his other works, to prove the pleasing qualities and the acuteness of his mind. 3. "Literatura Juris," 8vo, 1761. 4. "Jurisprudentia numismatibus illuftrata, nec non figillis, gemmis, aliifque picturis vetuftis varie exornata," 8vo, 1763. 5. "Corpus juris civilis, cum notis variorum," 8vo, 1768. 6. "Palingenefia librorum juris veterum," &c. 3 tom. 8vo, 1768, He publifhed fome fmaller tracts, but thefe are the moft important. Hommel died in 1781.

HONDERKOETER (MELCHIOR), a Dutch painter, born at Utrecht in 1636. His particular excellence confifted in reprefenting animals, and above all birds, whofe plumage he imitated in the moft perfect manner. His touch is firm and bold, his colouring rich and mellow. His pictures are particularly efteemed in Holland, where they bear a high price, and having been diligently collected there, are lefs known in other countries. He died in 1695.

HONDIUS (JESSE), born at Wackerne, a fmall town in Flanders, in 1563, died in 1611. He was a felf-taught engraver both on copper and ivory, and a letter-founder; in all which branches he attained great excellence. He ftudied geography alfo, and in 1607 publifhed a work entitled, "Defcriptio Geographica orbis terrarum," in folio.

HONE (GEORGE PAUL), a lawyer of Nuremberg, where he was born in 1662. He became counfellor to the duke of Meinungen, and bailli of Cobourg, at which place he died in 1747. His works are chiefly thefe: 1. "Iter Juridicum, per Belgium, Angliam, Galliam, Italiam." 2. "Lexicon Topographicum Franconiæ." 3. "Hiftory of the Dutchy of Saxe-Cobourg," in German. 4. "Thoughts on the Suppreffion of Mendicity," in the fame language.

HONESTIS (PETRUS DE), or Petrus DAMIANI, fo called from his brother Damian, whom he always confidered as a father, was an Italian, born at Ravenna in 1006. He took up the monaftic life at the monaftery of St. Andrew, near Abella, and was foon diftinguifhed for his exemplary piety. About the year 1057, he was created cardinal and bifhop of Oftia by pope Stephen, though averfe to affuming thofe dignities. In the year 1059 he was employed by pope Nicolas II.

9

to reduce the church of Milan to the rule of celibacy, a matter
of no fmall difficulty; and the conteft ran fo high, that Peter was
once in danger of lofing his life. He had, however, the addrefs
to gain over the archbifhop Guido, and thus at length fucceeded
in the object of his miffion, and returned in triumph to Rome.
Difgufted with the lives of the Roman clergy, and unwilling therefore to live among them, he abdicated his bith pric in 1061, and
retired to a folitary life. In the following year, however, he was
called by the pope from his folitude, and employed on a miffion
in France. In 1069 he perfuaded the emperor Henry to relinquifh the project he had formed of divorcing his wife, and in 1072
he was employed to reconcile Ravenna to the fee of Rome.
He fucceeded in the undertaking, but died the fame year, on
his return, at the age of 66. His works were numerous, but
are not at this day much known or valued, but they are enumerated at large by Cave [o]. Among them are eight books of
epiftles, addreffed to the different orders of clergy, to princes,
and to laymen; feveral lives of faints, and a number of treatifes
on various fubjects. His works were publifhed altogether at
Rome, in three volumes, by Cajetan.

HONORATUS, bifhop of Marfeilles, flourifhed about the
year 490. He was, according to Gennadius, who celebrates
him, a man of ready and abundant eloquence. He publifhed
many homilies, fome delivered in an extemporary manner, others
regularly compofed; in which his object was to confute the
dreams of heretics, and exhort his hearers to piety. He wrote
alfo lives of many eminent leaders of the church, of which no
one is extant, except his life of St. Hilary of Arles.

HONORIUS I. a pope and a poet. He fucceeded Boniface
V. in the year 626, and died in 638. He was undoubtedly addicted to the herefy of the Monothelites, though fome writers
have laboured earneftly to acquit him of the charge. There is
ftill extant by him, an epigram on the apoftles looking up into
heaven [p], and eight epiftles.

HONTAN (THE BARON DE), was a native of Gafcony, in
the feventeenth century, and is principally known by his travels
in North America, which, however, are written in an embar-
raffed and barbarous ftyle, confounding truth and falfehood, dif-
figuring names, and difguifing facts. They contain fome
epifodes of pure fiction, particularly the narrative of the voyage
up the long river, which is fuppofed to be of equal authority
with the voyage to Lilliput. He defcribes, neverthelefs, with
fome fuccefs, the general face of the country, and the difpofition, cuftoms, government, and other particulars of the i habi-
tants. There is an edition of his travels publifhed at Amfterdam

[o] Hiftoria Literaria, &c. xi. p. 610.   [p] Biblioth. Patrum, xii. 214.
in

in 1705, in 2 vols. 12mo. He began his career in Canada as common foldier, was raifed to the rank of an officer, went to Newfoundland in the quality of royal lieutenant, there quarrelled with the governor, was broken, and retired firft in Portugal, and finally to Denmark.

HOOFT (PETRUS CORNELIUS VAN), a Dutch poet and hiftorian, but principally eminent in the latter capacity, was born at Amflerdam in 1581. He was honoured by Louis XIII. with a ribband of the order of St. Michael, probably in confequence of his hiftory of Henry IV. Frederic Henry prince of Orange being dead, Hooft was preparing to attend his funeral, when he was himfelf taken violently ill and died in 1647. His works confift of, 1. " Epigrams, Comedies, and other Poems." 2. " The Hiftory of the Low Countries, from the Abdication of Charles V. to the year 1598." A good edition of it appeared in the year 1703, in two vols. folio. 3. " A Hiftory of Henry IV. of France," in Latin. 4. " A Tranflation of Tacitus into Dutch," very highly efteemed in that country. To familiarize the ftyle of his author completely to his mind, he is faid to have read all the extant works of Tacitus fifty two times.

HOOGEVEEN (HENRY), a very celebrated Dutch philologer, was born at Leyden in the latter end of January, 1712 [Q]. His parents were poor, but of great probity ; and, had it not been for a very laudable ambition in his father to make his fon a fcholar, the obfcurity of a mechanical trade would probably have concealed his powers through life. At ten years of age he was fent to fchool, but, for a confiderable time, gave not the flighteft proof of talents for literature, fo completely depreffed was he by the wanton tyranny of a fevere mafter. When at length he was removed into another clafs, and was under a milder teacher, his powers began to expand, and took the lead among thofe of his ftanding, inftead of holding an inferior place. So early as at fifteen, he began the tafk of teaching others, to alleviate the expences of his parents, being now highly qualified for fuch an undertaking. He was employed in teaching the inferior claffes of the fchool to which he ftill belonged. While he was yet employed in his ftudies, he loft his father ; but this misfortune rather redoubled his efforts than fubdued his fpirit. In 1732, before he had exceeded his twentieth year, he obtained the appointment of co-rector (or under mafter) at Gorcum. Within nine months the magiftrates of the city of Woerden gave him an appointment there which induced him to think of matrimony. He married in March, 1733, and began the care of this fchool in May the fame year. By this wife, who died in 1738, he had three fons and two daughters. In the fame year,

[Q] Harles de vitis philologorum noftra ætate clariffimorum, t. iv. p. 114.

he

he was folicited by the magistrates of Culembourg to undertake
the care of their school, to which, with much reluctance in leaving
his former situation, he at length confented. Here he took a
fecond wife, who produced him eight children: and here, notwithstanding follicitations from other places, he continued for
feveral years. At length, much fatigued by inceffant attention
to a great number of fcholars, he went in 1745 to Breda, on a
more liberal appointment. The very next year, Breda being harraffed by a French invafion, Hoogeveen was obliged to fend his
collection of books to Leyden, and literary purfuits were at a
stand. He remained, however, fixteen years at Breda, and had
determined there to end his days, but Providence decided otherwife. The malice and turbulence of a perfon who had taken
up fome unreafonable caufe of offence againft him, inclined
him to leave Breda. His intention being known, he was liberally invited to Dort, whither he transferred his refidence in
1761. From this place, after living there three years, he
was in a manner forced away by the importunity and liberality
of the city of Delft. On his firft arrival there, he encountered
fome difficulties from calumny and malice, but he weathered the
ftorm, and remained there the remainder of his life in peace and
honour. He died about Nov. 1, 1794, leaving fome furviving
children by both his marriages.

His works are, 1. An edition of " Vigerus de Idiotifmis
Linguæ Græcæ," publifhed at Leyden in 1743, and feveral
times republifhed. His improvements to this work are of the
higheft value. 2. " An Inaugural Speech at Culembourg," in
1738. 3. An Alcaic Ode to the people of Culembourg, " De
Inundatione feliciter averruncata." 4. " An Elegiac Poem," in
defence of poets, againft Plato ; and feveral other occafional
pieces, few of which are publifhed. 5. " Doctrina particu-
larum Linguæ Græcæ," 2 vols. 4to, 1769. This great work, the
foundation of his well-earned fame, is executed with a prodigious
abundance of learning, and has been approved and received
throughout Europe. He followed Devarius profeffedly to a
certain point, but went far beyond him in copioufnefs and fagacity. A very ufeful abridgement of this work, the only fault
of which is too great prolixity, was publifhed at Delfau in the
year 1782, by Schütz. This edition will be found more ufeful
to the young ftudent than the vaft work on which it is founded,
as more eafily purchafed, and more eafily read. A pofthumous
work of this author, entitled, " Dictionarium Analogicum
Græcum," is now printing at the univerfity-prefs in Cambridge,
and will be accompanied with the life of the author, by one of
his fons, who has fucceeded him as rector of the fchool at Delft.
Unfortunately, we could not wait for the information which
this life may be expected to contain.

HOOG-

HOOGSTRATEN (DAVID VAN), a professor of the belles lettres, was born at Rotterdam in 1658, and died at Amsterdam in 1724. In the evening of Nov. 13, there suddenly arose so thick a mist, that he lost his way, and fell into a canal. He was soon taken out; but the coldness of the water, and the fright from the fall, brought on so strong an oppression upon the breast, that he died in eight days after. There are of his, 1. "Latin Poems." 2. "Flemish Poems." 3. "A Flemish and Latin Dictionary." 4. "Notes upon C. Nepos and Terence." 5. "An Edition of Phædrus," for the prince of Naſſau, 4to, in imitation of the Delphin editions. 6. A fine edition of "Janus Broukhuſius's Poems."

HOOGUE (ROMAIN DE), a Dutch deſigner and engraver, who flouriſhed towards the cloſe of the laſt century. He had a lively imagination, by which he was ſometimes led aſtray; and his works muſt be viewed with ſome allowance for incorrectneſs of deſign, and injudicious choice of ſubjects; which were in general of an allegorical caſt, or diſtinguiſhed by a kind of low caricature. His works are chiefly extant in certain editions of books, for which he was employed; as, 1. Plates for the Old and New Teſtament, in folio, publiſhed by Baſnage in 1704. 2. Plates to "the Academy of the Art of Wreſtling," in Dutch, 1674, and in French, in 1712. 3. Plates to the Bible, with Dutch explanations. 4. Plates for the Egyptian Hieroglyphics, Amſterdam, 1735, ſmall folio. 5. Plates to Fontaine's Fables, in 2 vols. 8vo, 1685. 6. To Boccace, 1695, 2 vols. 8vo. 7. To the Tales of the Queen of Navarre. 8. To the "Cent Nouvelles nouvelles," 1701, 2 vols. 8vo. Such of his plates as are to be met with, ſeparate from the works to which they belong, bear a higher price.

HOOKE (ROBERT), an eminent Engliſh mathematician and philoſopher, was ſon of Mr. John Hooke, miniſter of Freſhwater in the Iſle of Wight, and born there July 18, 1635 [a]. He was deſigned for the church; but being of a weakly conſtitution, and very ſubject to the head-ach, all thoughts of that nature were laid aſide. Thus left to himſelf, the boy followed the bent of his genius, which led him to mechanics; and employed his time in making little toys, which he did with wonderful art and dexterity. For inſtance, ſeeing an old braſs clock taken to pieces, he made a wooden one that would go: he made likewiſe a ſmall ſhip about a yard long, fitly ſhaped, maſted, and rigged, with a contrivance to make it fire ſmall guns, as it was ſailing acroſs a haven of ſome breadth. Theſe indications led his friends to think of ſome ingenious trade for him; and after his father's death, which happened in 1648, as he had alſo a turn for

[a] Life of Hooke, prefixed to his Poſthumous Works, Lond. 1705, folio.

drawing,

drawing, he was placed with fir Peter Lely; but the fmell of the oil-colours increafed his head-achs, and he quitted painting in a very fhort time. Afterwards he was kindly taken by Dr. Bufby into his houfe, and fupported there, while he attended Weftminfter-fchool. Here he not only acquired the Greek and Latin, together with an infight into Hebrew and other Oriental languages, but alfo made himfelf mafter of a good part of " Euclid's Elements [s]." Wood tells us, that while he lived with Dr. Bufby, he " learned of his own accord to play twenty leffons on the organ; and invented thirty feveral ways of flying; as himfelf and Dr. Wilkins of Wadham-college have reported."

About 1653, he went to Chrift-church, Oxford, and in 1655 was introduced to the Philofophical Society there; where, dif-covering his mechanic genius, he was firft employed to affift Dr. Willis in his operations of chemiftry, and afterwards recom-mended to Mr. Boyle, whom he ferved many years in the fame capacity. He was alfo inftructed about this time by Dr. Seth Ward, Savilian profeffor of aftronomy, in that fcience; and from henceforward diftinguifhed himfelf by many noble inven-tions and improvements of the mechanic kind. He invented feveral aftronomical inftruments for making obfervations both at fea and land; and was particularly ferviceable to Boyle, in completing the air-pump. Wood tells us, that he alfo explained " Euclid's Elements," and " Des Cartes's Philofophy," to Boyle. Nov. 1662, fir Robert Moray, then prefident, propofed him for curator of experiments to the Royal Society. He was unani-moufly accepted, and it was ordered, that Boyle fhould have the thanks of the fociety, for difpenfing with him for their ufe; and that he fhould come and fit among them, and both bring in every day three or four of his own experiments, and take care of fuch others, as fhould be mentioned to him by the fociety. He executed this office fo much to their fatisfaction, that when that body was eftablifhed by the royal charter, his name was in the lift of thofe, who were firft nominated by the council, May 20, 1663; and he was admitted accordingly, June 3, with a peculiar exemption from all payments. Sept. 28, of the fame year, he was nominated by Clarendon, chancellor of Oxford, for the degree of M. A. and Oct. 19, it was ordered, that the repofitory of the Royal Society fhould be committed to his care [T], the white gallery in Grefham-college being appointed for that ufe. May, 1664, he begun to read the aftronomical lecture at Grefham for the profeffor Dr. Pope, then in Italy; and the fame year was made profeffor of mechanics to the Royal Society by fir John Cutler, with a falary of 50l. per annum, which that

[s] Athen. Oxon.
[T] Ward's Life of Hooke in the Lives of the profeffors of Grefham-college, p. 112, 174.

gentleman,

gentleman, the founder, settled upon him for life. Jan. 11, 1664-5, he was elected by that society curator of experiments for life, with an additional salary of 30l. per annum to sir John Cutler's annuity, settled on him "pro tempore:" and, March following, was elected professor of geometry in Gresham-college.

In 1665, he published in folio, his "Micrographia, or some Philosophical Descriptions of minute Bodies, made by magnifying Glasses, with Observations and Enquiries thereupon:" and the same year, during the recess of the Royal Society on account of the plague, attended Dr. Wilkins and other ingenious gentlemen into Surrey, where they made several experiments. Sept. 19, 1666, he produced a plan of his own for rebuilding the city of London, then destroyed by the great fire; which was so approved by the lord-mayor and court of aldermen, some of whom were present at the society when it was produced, that he was appointed city-surveyor, although his design was not carried into execution. It is said, that by one part of this plan, all the chief streets, as from Leaden-hall corner to Newgate, and the like, were to have been built in regular lines, all the other cross streets to have turned out of them at right angles; and all the churches, public buildings, market-places, &c. to have been fixed in proper and convenient places. The re-building of the city, according to the act of parliament, requiring an able person to set out the ground to the several proprietors, Hooke was pitched upon, as we have said, for one of the city surveyors, and Oliver a glass painter for the other. In this employment he acquired the greatest part of that estate of which he died possessed; as appeared sufficiently evident from a large iron chest of money found after his death, locked down with a key in it, and a date of the time, which shewed it to have been so shut up for above thirty years.

In 1668, Hevelius, the famous astronomer at Dantzick, presented a copy of his "Cometographia" to Hooke, in acknowledgement for an handsome compliment, which Hooke had made him on account of his "Selenographia," printed in 1647; and Hooke in return sent Hevelius a description of the dioptric telescope, with an account of his manner of using it, and recommended it to him as preferable to those with plain sights. This circumstance gave rise to a great dispute between them, in which many learned men afterwards engaged, and which Hooke so managed, as to be universally condemned, though it has since been agreed, that he had the best side of the question. In 1671, he attacked sir Isaac Newton's "New Theory of Light and Colours;" where, though he was forced to submit in respect to the argument, he is said to have come off with a better reputation than in the former instance. The Royal Society having

having begun their meetings at Gresham-college, in Nov. 1674,
the committee in December allowed him 40l to erect a turret
over part of his lodgings, for trying his instruments, and making
astronomical observations: and the year following, he published
" A Description of Telescopes, and some other Instruments,
made by R. H. with a Postscript," complaining of some injustice done him by Oldenburg, the publisher of the " Philosophical Transactions," in regard to his invention of pendulum
watches. This charge drew him into a dispute with that gentleman, which ended in a declaration of the Royal Society in
their secretary's favour. Oldenburg dying in Aug. 1677, Hooke
was appointed to supply his place, and began to take minutes at
the meeting in October; but did not publish the " Transactions."
Soon after this, he grew more reserved than formerly; and
though he read his Cutlerian lectures, and often made experiments, and shewed new inventions before the Royal Society,
yet he seldom left any account of them to be entered in their
registers; designing, as he said, to fit them for himself, and
make them public, which however he never performed. In
1686, when sir Isaac Newton's Principia were published, he
laid claim to his discovery concerning the force and action of
gravity, which was warmly resented by that great philosopher.
Hooke was in truth a great inventor and discoverer, but so
very ambitious, that he would fain have been thought the only
man who could invent and discover. This made him frequently
lay claim to other people's inventions and discoveries; in which,
however, as well as in the present case, the point was generally
carried against him.

In 1687, his brother's daughter, Mrs. Grace Hooke, who
had lived with him several years, died; and he was so affected
with grief at her death, that he hardly ever recovered it, but
was observed from that time to grow less active, more melancholy, and, if that could be, more cynical than ever. At the
same time a chancery-suit, in which he was concerned with sir
John Cutler, on account of his salary for reading the Cutlerian
lectures, made him very uneasy, and increased his disorder.
In 1691, he was employed in forming the plan of the hospital
near Hoxton, founded by Ask alderman of London [u], who
appointed archbishop Tillotson one of his executors; and in December, the same year, Hooke was created M. D. by a warrant
from that prelate. July 18, 1696, his chancery-suit for sir John
Cutler's salary was determined in his favour, to his inexpressible
satisfaction. His joy on that occasion was found in his diary thus
expressed: " DOMSHLGISSA; that is, Deo Optimo Maximo sit
honor, laus, gloria, in sæcula sæculorum. Amen. I was born on this

[u] Birch's Life of Tillotson.

day of July, 1635, and God has given me a new birth: may I
never forget his mercies to me! whilst he gives me breath, may
I praise him!" The same year, an order was granted to him
for repeating most of his experiments, at the expence of the
Royal Society, upon a promise of his finishing the accounts,
observations, and deductions from them, and of perfecting the
description of all the instruments contrived by him; but his increasing illness and general decay rendered him unable to perform it. He continued some years in this wasting condition;
and thus languishing, till he was quite emaciated, he died March
3. 1702, at his lodgings in Gresham-college, and was buried in
St. Helen's church, Bishopsgate-street, his corpse being attended
by all the members of the Royal Society then in London.

The writer of his life, to which we have all along referred,
has given the following character of him, which, though not an
amiable one, seems to be drawn with candour and impartiality.
He was in person but a despicable figure; short of stature, very
crooked, pale, lean, and of a meagre aspect, with dark brown hair,
very long, and hanging over his face, uncut, and lank. Suitable
to this person, his temper was penurious, melancholy, mistrustful,
and jealous; which qualities increased upon him with his years.
He set out in his youth with a collegiate or rather a monastic
reclusenefs, and afterwards led the life of a cynical hermit;
scarcely allowing himself necessaries, notwithstanding the great
increase of his fortunes after the fire in London. He declared
sometimes, that he had a great project in his head, as to the
disposal of his estate, for the advancement of natural knowledge, and to promote the ends and designs for which the Royal
Society was instituted; to build a handsome fabric for the society's
use, with a library, repository, laboratory, and other conveniences
for making experiments; and to found and endow a physico-
mechanic lecture like that of sir John Cutler. But though he
was often solicited by his friends to put his designs down in
writing, and make his will as to the disposal of his estate, yet
he could never be prevailed on to do it, but died without any
will that could be found. In like manner, with respect to his
philosophical treasures, when he first became known to the
learned world, he was very communicative of his inventions and
discoveries, but afterwards grew close and reserved to a fault;
alledging for an excuse, that some persons challenged his discoveries for their own, and took occasion from his hints to perfect
what he had not finished. For this reason he would suggest nothing,
till he had time to perfect it himself; so that many things are
lost which he affirmed he knew, though he was not supposed to
know every thing which he affirmed. For instance, not many
weeks before his death, he told Mr. Waller and others, that
he knew a certain and infallible method of discovering the
longitude

longitude at fea; yet it is evident, that his friends diftrufted his affeveration of this difcovery; and how little credit was then given to it in general, appears from Waller's own account. "Hooke," fays he, "fuffering this invention to be undifcovered to the laft, gave fome perfons caufe to queftion, whether he was ever the poffeffor of it; and to doubt, whether what in theory feemed very promifing, would anfwer when put in practice. Others indeed more feverely judged, th t it was only a kind of boafling in him to affert that, which had not been performed, though attempted by many." Thus ftood the opinion of the world at his death; and nothing has fince appeared to alter it. In the religious part of his character he was fo far exemplary, that he always expreffed a great veneration for the Deity; and feldom received any remarkable benefit in life, or made any confiderable difcovery in nature, or invented any ufeful contrivance, or found out any difficult problem, without fetting down his acknowledgement to God, as many places in his diary plainly fhew. He frequently ftudied the facred writings in the originals; for he was acquainted with the ancient languages, as well as with all the parts of mathematics. "To conclude," fays Waller, "all his errors and blemifhes were more than made amends for by the greatnefs and extent of his natural and acquired parts, and more than common if not wonderful fagacity, in diving into the moft hidden fecrets of nature, and in contriving proper methods of forcing her to confefs the truth, by driving and purfuing the Proteus through all her changes to her laft and utmoft receffes.—There needs no other proof of this, than the great number of experiments he made, with the contrivances for them, amounting to fome hundreds; his new and ufeful inftruments and inventions, which were numerous; his admirable facility and clearnefs in explaining the phænomena of nature, and demonftrating his affertions; his happy talent in adapting theories to the phænomena obferved, and contriving eafy and plain, not pompous and amufing, experiments to back and prove thofe theories; proceeding from obfervations to theories, and from theories to farther trials, which he afferted to be the moft proper method to fucceed in the interpretation of nature. For thefe his happy qualifications he was much refpected by the moft learned philofophers at home and abroad; and as with all his failures he may be reckoned among the great men of the laft age, fo had he been free from them, poffibly he might have ftood in the front."

His papers being put by his friends into the hands of Richard Waller, efq; fecretary to the Royal Society, that gentleman collected fuch as he thought worthy of the prefs, and publifhed them under the title of his "Pofthumous Works," in 1705, to which he prefixed an account of his life, in folio.

HOOKE

HOOKE (NATHANIEL), celebrated for a "Roman Hiſtory," died in 1764, but we know not at what age; as indeed few particulars of him are recorded, though he is ſaid, "from 1723 till his death, to have enjoyed the confidence and patronage of men, not leſs diſtinguiſhed by virtue than by titles [x]." The firſt particular that occurs of him is from a letter to lord Oxford, dated Oct. 17, 1722; by which it appears, that, having been "ſeized with the late epidemical diſtemper of endeavouring to be rich," meaning the South-ſea infatuation, "he was in ſome meaſure happy to find himſelf at that inſtant juſt worth nothing." Some time after, however, he was recommended to Sarah, dutcheſs of Marlborough, who preſented him with 5000l. the condition of which donation was expreſsly, that he the ſaid Hooke ſhould aid and aſſiſt her the ſaid dutcheſs in drawing up and digeſting "An Account of the Conduct of the Dowager Dutcheſs of Marlborough, from her firſt coming to Court, to the Year 1710." This was done, and the work was publiſhed in 1742, 8vo; but, ſoon after, ſhe took occaſion, as was uſual with her, to quarrel with him; "becauſe," finding her without religion, "he attempted," as ſhe affirmed, "to convert her to popery." Hooke was a Myſtic and Quietiſt, and a warm diſciple of Fenelon. It was he who brought a Catholic prieſt to take Pope's confeſſion upon his death-bed; the prieſt had ſcarcely departed, when Bolingbroke coming in, flew into a great paſſion upon the occaſion.

The "Roman Hiſtory" of Hooke was firſt publiſhed in 4 vols. 4to; the firſt in 1733, the ſecond in 1745, the third in 1764, and the fourth in 1771; from the building of Rome to the ruin of the commonwealth. In 1758, he publiſhed "Obſervations on four pieces upon the Roman Senate," among which were thoſe of Middleton and Chapman; and was anſwered in an anonymous pamphlet, entitled, "A Short Review of Mr. Hooke's Obſervations, &c. concerning the Roman Senate, and the Character of Dionyſius of Halicarnaſſus, 1758," 8vo. But the author of this was Edward Spelman, eſq; who was then publiſhing an Engliſh tranſlation of Dionyſius. Hooke publiſhed alſo a tranſlation of "Ramſay's Travels of Cyrus."

HOOKER (RICHARD), an eminent Engliſh divine, and author of an excellent work, entitled, "The Laws of Eccleſiaſtical Polity, in eight Books," was born at Heavy-tree near Exeter, in 1553 [y], or, as Wood ſays, about the time of Eaſter, 1554. His parents, not being rich, intended him for a trade; but his ſchoolmaſter at Exeter prevailed with them to continue him at ſchool [z], aſſuring them, that his natural en-

[x] Anecdotes of Bowyer by Nichols, p. 594, 594.   [y] Ath. Oxon.
[z] Life of Hooker by Walton, prefixed to his Works.

dowments

dowments and learning were both fo remarkable, that he muft of neceffity be taken notice of, and that God would provide him fome patron who would free them from any future care or charge about him. Accordingly his uncle John Hooker, who was then chamberlain of the town, began to regard him; and being known to Jewell, made a vifit to that prelate at Salifbury foon after, and "befought him for charity's fake to look favourably upon a poor nephew of his, whom nature had fitted for a fcholar; but the eftate of his parents was fo narrow, that they were unable to give him the advantage of learning; and that the bifhop therefore would become his patron, and prevent him from being a tradefman, for he was a boy of remarkable hopes." The bifhop examined into his merits, found him to be what the uncle had reprefented him, and took him henceforward under his protection. He got him admitted, in 1567, one of the clerks of Corpus-chrifti college in Oxford, and fettled a penfion on him; which, with the contributions of his uncle, afforded him a very comfortable fubfiftence. In 1571, Hooker had the misfortune to lofe his patron, together with his penfion. Providence, however, raifed him up two other patrons, in Dr. Cole, then prefident of the college, and Dr. Edwyn Sandys, bifhop of London, and afterwards archbifhop of York. To the latter of thefe Jewell had recommended him fo effectually before his death, that though of Cambridge himfelf, he immediately refolved to fend his fon Edwyn to Oxford, to be pupil to Hooker, who yet was not much older; for, faid he, "I will have a tutor for my fon, that fhall teach him learning by inftruction, and virtue by example." Hooker had alfo another confiderable pupil, namely, George Cranmer, grand nephew to Cranmer the archbifhop and martyr; with whom, as well as with Sandys, he cultivated a ftrict and lafting friendfhip.

In 1577, he was elected fellow of his college; and about two years after, being well fkilled in the Oriental languages, was appointed deputy-profeffor of Hebrew, in the room of a gentleman who was difordered in his fenfes. In 1581, he entered into orders; and foon after, being appointed to preach at St. Paul's-crofs in London, was fo unhappy as to be drawn into a moft unfortunate marriage; of which, as it is one of the moft memorable circumftances of his life, we fhall here give the particulars as they are related by Walton. There was then belonging to the church of St. Paul's, a houfe called the Shunamites houfe, fet apart for the reception and entertainment of the preachers at St. Paul's-crofs, two days before, and one day after, the fermon. That houfe was then kept by Mr. John Churchman, formerly a fubftantial draper in Watling-ftreet, but now reduced to poverty. Walton fays, that Churchman was a perfon of virtue, but that he cannot fay quite fo much of his wife. To this houfe Hooker came from Oxford fo wet and weary, that he was afraid he fhould not be able to perform his duty the Sunday following: Mrs. Churchman, however, nurfed him fo well, that he prefently recovered from the ill effects of his journey. For this he was very thankful; fo much indeed that, as Walton expreffes it, he thought himfelf bound in confcience to believe all fhe faid; fo the good man came to be perfuaded by her, "that he had a very tender conftitution; and that it was beft for him to have a wife, that might prove a nurfe to him; fuch a one as might both prolong his life, and make it more comfortable; and fuch a one fhe could and would provide for him, if he thought fit to marry." Hooker, not confidering, "that the children of this world are wifer in their generation than the children of light," and fearing no guile, becaufe he meant none, gave her a power to choofe a wife for him; promifing, upon a fair fummons, to return to London, and accept of her choice, which he did in that or the year following. Now, fays Walton, the wife provided for him was her daughter Joan, who brought him neither beauty nor portion; and for her conditions, they were too like that wife's which Solomon compares to a dripping-houfe; that is, fays Wood, fhe was "a clownifh filly woman, and withal a mere Xantippe."

Hooker, now driven from his college, remained without preferment, and fupported himfelf as well as he could, till the latter end of 1584, when he was prefented by John Cheny, efq; to the rectory of Drayton Beauchamp in Buckinghamfhire, where he led an uncomfortable life with his wife Joan for about a year. In this fituation he received a vifit from his friends and pupils Sandys and Cranmer, who found him with a Horace in his hand, tending his fmall allotment of fheep in a common field; which he told them he was forced to do, becaufe his fervant was gone home to dine, and affift his wife in the houfhold bufinefs. When the fervant returned and releafed him, his pupils attended him to his houfe, where their beft entertainment was his quiet company, which was prefently denied them, for Richard was called to rock the cradle, and the reft of their welcome was fo like this, that they ftayed but till the next morning, which was long enough to difcover and pity their tutor's condition. At their return to London, Sandys acquainted his father with Hooker's deplorable ftate; who thereupon entered fo heartily into his concerns, that he got him to be made mafter of the Temple in 1585. This, though a fine piece of preferment, was not fo fuitable to Hooker's temper, as the retirement of a living in the country, where he might be free from noife; nor did he accept of it without reluctance. At the time when Hooker was chofen mafter of the Temple, one Walter Travers was afternoon-lecturer there; a man of learning and good

manners,

manners, it is said, but ordained by the presbytery of Antwerp, and warmly attached to the Geneva government. Travers had some hopes of setting up this government in the Temple, and for that purpose endeavoured to be master of it; but not succeeding, gave Hooker all the opposition he could in his sermons, many of which were about the doctrine, discipline, and ceremonies of the church; insomuch that they constantly withstood each other to the face: for, as somebody said pleasantly, " The forenoon sermon spake Canterbury, and the afternoon Geneva." The opposition became so visible, and the consequences so dangerous, especially in that place, that archbp. Whitgift caused Travers to be silenced by the high commission court. Upon that, Travers presented his supplication to the privy council, which being without effect, he made it public. This obliged Hooker to publish an answer, which was inscribed to the archbishop, and procured him as much reverence and respect from some, as it did neglect and hatred from others. In order therefore to undeceive and win these, he entered upon his famous work " Of the Laws of Ecclesiastical Polity;" and laid the foundation and plan of it, while he was at the Temple. But he found the Temple no fit place to finish what he had there designed; and therefore intreated the archbishop to remove him to some quieter situation in the following letter.

" My lord, When I lost the freedom of my cell, which was my college, yet I found some degree of it in my quiet country parsonage. But I am weary of the noise and oppositions of this place; and indeed God and nature did not intend me for contentions, but for study and quietness. And, my lord, my particular contests here with Mr. Travers have proved the more unpleasant to me, because I believe him to be a good man; and that belief hath occasioned me to examine mine own conscience concerning his opinions. And to satisfy that, I have consulted the Holy Scripture, and other laws both human and divine, whether the conscience of him, and others of his judgement, ought to be so far complied with by us, as to alter our frame of church government, our manner of God's worship, our praising and praying to him, and our established ceremonies, as often as their tender consciences shall require us. And in this examination I have not only satisfied myself, but have began a treatise, in which I intend the satisfaction of others, by a demonstration of the reasonableness of our Laws of Ecclesiastical Polity.—But, my lord, I shall never be able to finish what I have begun, unless I be removed into some quiet parsonage, where I may see God's blessings spring out of my mother earth, and eat my own bread in peace and privacy; a place, where I may without disturbance meditate my approaching mortality, and that great

account

account, which all flesh must give at the last day to the God of all spirits."

Upon this application he was presented, in 1591, to the rectory of Boscomb in Wiltshire; and, July the same year, to the prebend of Nether-Haven in the church of Sarum, of which he was also made sub-dean. At Boscomb he finished four books, which were entered into the register-book at Stationers-hall, March, 1592, but not printed till 1594. In 1595, he quitted Boscomb, and was presented by queen Elizabeth to the rectory of Bishop's-Bourne in Kent, where he spent the remainder of his life. In this place he composed the fifth book of his " Ecclesiastical Polity," which was dedicated to the archbishop, and published by itself in 1597. He finished there the 6th, 7th, and 8th books of that learned work; but whether we have them genuine, and as left by himself hath been a matter of much dispute. Some time after he caught cold, in a passage by water between London and Gravesend, which drew up n him an illness, that put an end to his life, when he was only in his 47th year. He died Nov. 2, 1600. His illness was severe and lingering; he continued, notwithstanding, his studies to the last. He strove particularly to finish his " Ecclesiastical Polity;" and said often to a friend, who visited him daily, that " he did not beg a long life of God for any other reason, but to live to finish the three remaining books of Polity; and then, Lord, let thy servant depart in peace," which was his usual expression. A few days before his death, his house was robbed; of which having notice, he asked, " are my books and written papers safe?" And being answered, that they were, " then," said he, " it matters not, for no other loss can trouble me."

But whatever value Hooker himself might put upon his books of " Ecclesiastical Polity," he could not give them more esteem than has been paid by the general judgement of mankind. They have been admired for the soundness of reasoning, which runs through them, and the prodigious extent of learning they every where discover; and the author has universally acquired from them the honourable titles of " the Judicious," and " the Learned." When James I. ascended the throne of England, he is said to have asked Whitgift for his friend Mr. Hooker, from whose books of " Ecclesiastical Polity" he had so much profited; and being informed by the archbishop that he died a year before the queen, he expressed the greatest disappointment, and the deepest concern. Charles I. it is well known, earnestly recommended the reading of Hooker's books to his son; and they have ever since been held in the highest veneration and esteem by all. An anecdote is preserved by the writer of his life, which, if true, shews that his fame was by no means confined to his own country, but travelled abroad; and so

far

far and fo loudly, that it reached even the ears of the pope himfelf. Cardinal Alen and Dr. Stapleton, though both in Italy
when his books were publifhed, were yet fo affected with the
fame of them, that they contrived to have them fent for; and
after reading them, are faid to have told the pope, then Clement
VIII. that " though his holinefs had not yet met with an Englifh book, as he was pleafed to fay, whofe writer deferved the
name of an author, yet there now appeared a wonder to them,
and fo they did not doubt it would appear to his holinefs, if it
was in Latin; which was, that ' a pure obfcure Englifh prieft
had written four fuch books of Law and Church Polity, in fo
majeftic a ftyle, and with fuch clear demonftrations of reafon,'
that in all their readings they had not met with any thing that
exceeded him." This begetting in the pope a defire to know
the contents, Stapleton read to him the firft book in Latin; upon
which the pope faid, " there is no learning that this man hath
not fearched into; nothing too hard for his underftanding.
This man indeed deferves the name of an author. His books
will get reverence by age; for there is in them fuch feeds of
eternity, that if the reft be like this, they fhall continue till the
laft fire fhall devour all learning:" all which, whether the pope
faid it or no, we take to be ftrictly true.

Befides the eight books of " Ecclefiaftical Polity," and his
anfwer to Travers's " Supplication," there are fome fermons of
his in being, which have been collected and printed with his
works in folio. An octavo edition has lately appeared at Oxford.

HOOPER (Dr. George), an eminent Englifh divine, was
born at Grimley in Worcefterfhire, about 1640, and educated
in grammar and claffical learning at Weftminfter-fchool, where
he was a king's fcholar. From thence he became a ftudent of
Chrift-church in Oxford, in 1656[A], where he took his degrees at the regular times; and diftinguifhed himfelf above his
contemporaries by his fuperior knowledge in philofophy, mathematics, Greek and Roman antiquities, and the Oriental languages. In 1672, he became chaplain to Morley bifhop of
Winchefter; and not long after to archbifhop Sheldon, who
begged that favour of the bifhop of Winchefter, and who in
1675 gave him the rectory of Lambeth, and afterwards the pre-
centorfhip of Exeter. In 1677, he commenced D. D. and the
fame year, being made almoner to the princefs of Orange, he
went over to Holland, where, at the requeft of her royal highnefs, he regulated her chapel according to the ufage of the
church of England. After one year's attendance, he repaffed
the fea, in order to complete his marriage, the treaty for which
had been fet on foot before his departure. This done, he went

[A] Wood's Faft, Vol. II.

back to her highness, who had obtained a promise from him to
that purpose; but, after a stay of about eight months, she consented to let him return home. In 1680, he was offered the divi-
nity-professorship at Oxford, which he declined; but was made
king's chaplain about the same time. In 1685, by the king's
command, he attended the duke of Monmouth, and had much
free conversation with him in the Tower, both the evening before, and the day of his execution. The following year he
took a share in the popish controversy, and wrote a treatise,
which will be mentioned presently with his works. In 1691,
he succeeded Dr. Sharp in the deanery of Canterbury. As he
never made the least application for preferment, queen Mary
surprised him with this offer, when the king her husband was
absent in Holland. He was made chaplain to their majesties
the same year. In 1698, when a preceptor was chosen for the
duke of Gloucester, though both the royal parents of that prince
pressed earnestly to have Hooper [B], and no pretence of any
objection was ever made against him, yet the king named bishop
Burnet for that service. In 1701, he was chosen prolocutor to
the lower house of convocation: and the same year was offered
the primacy of Ireland by the earl of Rochester, then lord lieutenant. The year after the accession of Anne to the throne, he
was nominated to the bishopric of St. Asaph. This he accepted,
though against his inclination; and in half a year after, receiving
a like command to remove to that of Bath and Wells, he earnestly requested her majesty to dispense with the order, not only
on account of the sudden charge of such a translation, as well as
a reluctance to remove, but also in regard to his friend Dr.
Kenn, the deprived bishop of that place, for whom he begged
the bishopric. The queen readily complied with Hooper's request; but the offer being declined by Kenn, Hooper at his
importunity yielded to become his successor. He sat in the see
of Bath and Wells twenty-four years and six months; and, in
1727, died at Berkley in Somersetshire, whither he sometimes
retired; and was interred, in pursuance of his own request, in
the cathedral of Wells, under a marble monument with a Latin
inscription.

Besides eight sermons, he published several books in his life-
time, and left several MSS. behind him, some of which he permitted to be printed. The following is a catalogue of both. 1.
"The Church of England free from the Imputation of Popery,
1682." 2. "A fair and methodical Discussion of the first and
great Controversy between the Church of England and the
Church of Rome, concerning the Infallible Guide: in three
Discourses." The two first of these were licensed by Dr.

[B] Boyer's Hist. of Queen Anne, under that year.

2

Morrice,

Morrice, in 1687, but the laſt was never printed. 3. "The Parſon's Caſe under the preſent Land-Tax, recommended in a Letter to a Member of the Houſe of Commons, 1689." 4. "A Diſcourſe concerning Lent, in two Parts. The firſt, an hiſtorical Account of its Obſervation: the ſecond, an Eſſay concerning its Original. This ſubdivided into two Repartitions, whereof the firſt is preparatory, and ſhews that moſt of our Chriſtian Ordinances are derived from the Jews; and the ſecond conjectures, that Lent is of the ſame Original, 1694." 5. A Paper in the "Philoſophical Tranſactions for Oct. 1699, entitled, "A Calculation of the Credibility of Human Teſtimony." 6. "New Danger of Preſbytery, 1737." 7. "Marks of a defenceleſs Cauſe." 8. "A Narrative of the Proceedings of the lower Houſe of Convocation from Feb. 10, 1700, to June 25, 1701, vindicated." 9. "De Valentinianorum Hæreſi conjecturæ, quibus illius origo ex Ægyptiaca Theologia deducitur, 1711." 10. "An Inquiry into the State of the ancient Meaſures, the Attic, the Roman, and eſpecially the Jewiſh. With an Appendix concerning our old Engliſh Money and Meaſures of Content, 1721." 11. "De Patriarchæ Jacobi Benedictione Gen. 49, conjecturæ," publiſhed by the Rev. Mr. Hunt of Hart-hall in Oxford, with a preface and notes, according to the biſhop's directions to the editor, a little before his death. The MSS. before mentioned are the two following: 1. "A Latin Sermon, preached in 1672, when he took the degree of B. D. and, 2. "A Latin Tract on Divorce." A beautiful edition of his whole works was printed at Oxford, 1757, folio.

HOPER, or HOOPER (John), memorable for being a martyr in the Proteſtant cauſe, was born in Somerſetſhire, and bred at Oxford [c]. He took a batchelor's degree in 1518; and, as is reported, was of the fraternity of Ciſtercians, commonly called White Monks: but, being weary of the order, he returned to Oxford, where, as the Catholics ſay, he was poiſoned with Lutheran principles, and became, in their language, a heretic. At the time when the ſtatute of the Six Articles came out, he left what he had; and by ſome means got to be chaplain and ſteward to ſir John Arundel, who was afterwards put to death with the protector in king Edward's days: but, being diſcovered to be a Proteſtant, he was obliged to quit his employment, and fly into France. After ſtaying there for ſome time in a diſagreeable ſituation, he returned to England, and lived with a gentleman of the name of Saintlow. But at length being ſought for, and dreading to be apprehended, he diſguiſed himſelf in a mariner's habit, made himſelf maſter of a boat, and ſailed to Ireland. Thence he went to Switzerland, where he became acquainted with Bullin-

ger, fcholar and fucceffor of Zuinglius, and where, fays Fox,
by his counfel and doctrine, he married a wife who was a Bur-
gundian, and applied very ftudioufly to the Hebrew tongue [D].

On the acceffion of Edward VI. he returned to his native
country, fettled in London, and became a frequent and popular
preacher. When Bonner was to be deprived of his bifhopric,
he was one of his accufers; which, no doubt, would recommend him as an acceptable facrifice in the following bloody reign.
By the intereft of the earl of Warwick, he was nominated and
elected bifhop of Gloucefter; but when he came to be confecrated or invefted by archbifhop Cranmer and bifhop Ridley, he
refufed to wear a canonical habit, and was thereupon put under
confinement. But, thefe ceremonies being difpenfed with by
the king's authority, he was confecrated bifhop of the aforefaid
fee, in 1550; and about two years after, he had the bifhopric
of Worcefter given to him, to keep in commendam with the
former. He now preached often, vifited his diocefes, kept great
hofpitality for the poor, and was beloved by many. But in the
perfecution under Mary, being then near fixty years of age, and
refufing to recant his opinions, he was burned in the city of
Gloucefter, and fuffered death with admirable conftancy.

He was a man of good abilities, and great learning, and publifhed many writings, fome of which are to be found in John
Fox's book of the " Acts and Monuments of the Church."

HOORNBEECK (JOHN), an illuftrious profeffor of divinity
in the univerfities of Utrecht and Leyden, was born at Haerlem
in 1617, and ftudied there till he was fixteen [E]. Then he
was fent to Leyden, and afterwards in 1635 went to ftudy at
Utrecht. In 1632, he was admitted a minifter, went to perform the functions of his office fecretly at Cologne; and was
never difcouraged by the dangers to which he was expofed, in a
city where moft of the inhabitants were zealous papifts. He
returned to Holland in 1643, and that year was made D. D.
The proofs he gave of his great learning were fuch, that he was
chofen in 1644 to fill the chair of divinity profeffor at Utrecht;
and the next year was made minifter in ordinary of the church
in that city. However difficult the functions of thefe two employments were, yet he acquitted himfelf in them with great
diligence almoft ten years. As a paftor, he often vifited the
members of his church: he encouraged the pious, inftructed the
ignorant, reproved the wicked, refuted the heretics, comforted
the afflicted, refrefhed the fick, ftrengthened the weak, cheared
the drooping, affifted the poor. As a profeffor, he took as
much care of the ftudents in divinity, as if they had been his
own children: he ufed to read not only public lectures, but

[D] Act. & Mon. Ecclef. fub. ann. 1559.   [E] Boyle's Dict.

even

even private ones, for them; and to hold ordinary and extraordinary diſputations. He was choſen to exerciſe the ſame employments at Leyden, which he had at Utrecht, and accepted them in 1654. He died in 1666; and though he was but forty-nine years of age, yet conſidering his labours it is rather a matter of wonder that he lived ſo long, than that he died ſo ſoon. He publiſhed a great number of works; didactical, polemical, practical, hiſtorical, and oratorical. He underſtood many languages, both ancient and modern; the Latin, Greek, Hebrew, Chaldaic, Syriac, Rabbinical, Dutch, German, Engliſh, French, Italian, and ſome little of Arabic and Spaniſh. He never departed one inch from the moſt ſtrict orthodoxy; and was not leſs commendable for his integrity, than for his parts and learning. Bayle ſeems to have exhibited him in his Dictionary, as the complete model of a good paſtor and divinity-profeſſor. He married at Utrecht in 1650; and left two ſons.

HOPKINS (EZEKIEL), a learned and worthy prelate, experienced a fate extremely ſingular [P]. He was born at Sandford in Devonſhire, where his father was curate; became choiriſter of Magdalen-college, Oxford, in 1649; at the age of about ſixteen, he was uſher of the ſchool adjoining, being already B.A.; he was chaplain of the college when M.A.; and would have been fellow, had his county qualified him. All this time he lived and was educated under Preſbyterian and Independent diſcipline; and about the time of the Reſtoration became aſſiſtant to Dr. Spurſtow of Hackney. He was afterwards elected preacher at one of the city churches; but the biſhop of London refuſed to admit him, as he was a popular preacher among the Fanatics. He then obtained St. Mary's church at Exeter, was countenanced by biſhop Ward, and much admired for the comelineſs of his perſon and elegance of preaching. The lord Robartes in particular (afterwards earl of Truro) was ſo pleaſed with him, that he gave him his daughter Araminta in marriage, took him as his chaplain to Ireland in 1669, gave him the deanery of Raphoe, and recommended him ſo effectually to his ſucceſſor lord Berkeley, that he was conſecrated biſhop of Raphoe, Oct. 27, 1671, and tranſlated to Londonderry in 1681. Driven thence by the forces under the earl of Tyrconnel, in 1688, he retired into England, and was elected miniſter of Aldermanbury in Sept. 1689, where he died. June 19, 1690, he publiſhed five ſingle ſermons, afterwards incorporated in two volumes; "An Expoſition of the Ten Commandments, 1692," 4to, with his portrait; and an "Expoſition of the Lord's Prayer, 1691."

HOPKINS (CHARLES), ſon of the biſhop of Londonderry, was born at Exeter; but, his father being taken chaplain to

Ireland, he received the early part of his education at Trinity-college, Dublin; and afterwards was a student at Cambridge [G]. On the rebellion in Ireland in 1688, he returned thither, and exerted his early valour in the cause of his country, religion, and liberty. When public tranquillity was restored, he came again into England, and formed an acquaintance with gentlemen of the best wit, whose age and genius were most agreeable to his own. In 1694 he published some "Epistolary Poems and Translations," which may be seen in Nichols's "Select Collection;" and in 1695 he shewed his genius as a dramatic writer, by "Pyrrhus king of Egypt," a tragedy, to which Congreve wrote the epilogue. He published also in that year, "The History of Love," a connection of select fables from "Ovid's Metamorphoses, 1695;" which, by the sweetness of his numbers and easiness of his thoughts, procured him considerable reputation. With Dryden in particular he became a great favourite. He afterwards published the "Art of Love," which, Jacob says, added to his fame, and happily brought him acquainted with the earl of Dorset, and other persons of distinction, who were fond of his company, through the agreeableness of his temper, and the pleasantry of his conversation. It was in his power to have made his fortune in any scene of life; but he was always more ready to serve others than mindful of his own affairs; and by the excesses of hard drinking, and too passionate an addiction to women, he died a martyr to the cause in the 36th year of his age." Mr. Nichols has preserved in his collection an admirable hymn, "written about an hour before his death, when in great pain." His "Court-Prospect," in which many of the principal nobility are very handsomely complimented, is called by Jacob "an excellent piece;" and of his other poems he adds, "that they are all remarkable for the purity of their diction, and the harmony of their numbers." Mr. Hopkins was also the author of two other tragedies; "Boadicea Queen of Britain, 1697;" and "Friendship improved, or the Female Warrior," with a humourous prologue, comparing a poet to a merchant, a comparison which will hold in most particulars except that of accumulating wealth. The author, who was at Londonderry when this tragedy came out, inscribed it to Edward Coke of Norfolk, esq; in a dedication remarkably modest and pathetic. It is dated Nov. 1, 1699, and concludes, "I now begin to experience how much the mind may be influenced by the body. My Muse is confined, at present, to a weak and sickly tenement; and the winter season will go near to overbear her, together with her houshold. There are storms and tempests to beat her down, or frosts to bind her up

and

and kill her; and she has no friend on her side but youth to bear her through; If that can sustain the attack, and hold out till spring comes to relieve me, one use I shall make of farther life shall be to shew how much I am, Sir, your most devoted humble servant, C. HOPKINS."

His feelings were but too accurate; he died in the course of that winter.

HOPKINS (JOHN), another son of the bishop of London-derry, was born Jan. 1, 1675 [a]. Like his elder brother, his poetry turned principally on subjects of Love; like him too, his prospects in life appear to have terminated unfortunately. He published, in 1698, " The Triumphs of Peace, or the Glories of Nassau; a Pindaric poem occasioned by the conclusion of the peace between the Confederacy and France; written at the time of his grace the duke of Ormond's entrance into Dublin." " The design of this poem," the author says in his preface, " begins, after the method of Pindar, to one great man, and rises to another; first touches the duke, then celebrates the actions of the king, and so returns to the praises of the duke again." In the same year he published " The Victory of Death; or the Fall of Beauty; a Visionary Pindaric Poem, occasioned by the ever-to-be-deplored Death of the Right Honourable the Lady Cutts," 8vo. But the principal performance of J. Hopkins was " Amasia, or the Works of the Muses, a collection of Poems in 3 vols. 1700." Each of these little volumes is divided into three books, and each book is inscribed to some beautiful patroness, amongst whom the dutchess of Grafton stands foremost. The last book is inscribed " To the memory of Amasia," whom he addresses throughout these volumes, in the character of Sylvius. There is a vein of seriousness, if not of poetry, runs through the whole performance. Many of Ovid's stories are very decently imitated; " most of them," he says, " have been very well performed by my brother, and published some years since; mine were written in another kingdom before I knew of his." In one of his dedications he tells the lady Olympia Robartes, " Your ladyship's father, the late earl of Radnor, when governor of Ireland, was the kind patron to mine: he raised him to the first steps by which he afterwards ascended to the dignities he bore; to those, which rendered his labours more conspicuous, and set in a more advantageous light those living merits, which now make his memory beloved. These, and yet greater temporal honours, your family heaped on him, by making even me in some sort related and allied to you, by his inter-marriage with your sister the lady Araminta. How imprudent a vanity is it in me to boast a

[a] Nichols's Select Collection of Poems, Vol. II. p. 322.

father

father fo meritorious! how may I be afhamed to prove myfelf
his fon, by poetry, that only qualification he fo much excelled
in, but yet efteemed no excellence. I bring but a bad proof of
birth, laying my claim in that only thing he would not own.
Thefe are, however, Madam, but the products of immaturer
years: and riper age, may, I hope, bring forth more folid
works." We have never feen any other of his writings; nor
have been able to collect any farther particulars of his life: but
there is a portrait of him, under his poetical name of Sylvius.

HORAPOLLO, or HORUS APOLLO, a grammarian,
according to Suidas, of Panoplus in Egypt, who taught firft at
Alexandria, and then at Cunftantinople, under the reign of
Theodofius. There are extant under his name two books
" concerning the Hieroglyphics of the Egyptians," which
Aldus firft publifhed in Greek in 1505, folio. They have often
been republifhed fince, with a Latin verfion and notes; but the
beft edition is that by Cornelius de Pauw at Utrecht, in 4to.
Mean while there are many Horapollos of antiquity; and it is
not certain, that the grammarian of Alexandria was the author
of thefe books. Suidas does not afcribe them to him; and Fabricius is of opinion, that they belong rather to another Horus
Apollo of more ancient ftanding, who wrote upon Hieroglyphics in the Egyptian language, and from whofe work an extract
rather than a verfion has been made of thefe two books in Greek.
The reafons of Fabricius for fo thinking, may be feen in the firft
volume of his " Bibliotheca Graeca."

HORATIUS (QUINTUS FLACCUS), an ancient Roman poet,
who flourifhed in the age of Auguftus, was born at Venufium,
a town of Apulia, or of Lucania [I]; for he himfelf does not
determine which. His birth day fell on Dec. 8, U. C. 689,
when L. Cotta and L. Manlius Torquatus were confuls [K];
and about 65 years before Chrift. He ftayed in the place of
his birth till he was ten years old, and was then removed to
Rome: for though his father was no more than the fon of a freedman, and a tax-gatherer, nor himfelf very learned, yet being a
man of good fenfe, he knew the neceffity of inftructing his fon
by fomething more than bare advice. He removed him to
Rome, therefore, for the opportunity of fetting before him the
examples of all forts of perfons, and fhewing him what behaviour he fhould imitate, and what he fhould avoid; fpurring
him on all the while to this imitation, by pointing out the good
effects of virtue, and the ill effects of vice. 'This Horace himfelf tells us [L]; in a paffage where he alludes to the old man in
Terence, who expreffes fimilar notions. " I ufe him," fays he,
fpeaking of his fon, " to look upon the lives of others, as upon

[I] Sat. 2 Lib. II.   [K] Od. 21. Lib. I.   [L] Sat. 4. Lib. I.

a mirror;

a mirror; and from their conduct to take a pattern for his own. Do this, shun that; this is praise-worthy, that to be blamed." "Confuefacio: infpicere, tanquam in fpeculum, in vitas omnium jubeo, atque ex aliis, fumere exemplum fibi. Hoc facito, hoc fugito: hoc laudi eft, hoc vitio datur [M]." Mean time, Horace did not want the beft mafters that Rome could afford; and when he was about eighteen, was fent to Athens, where he completed what his father had fo well begun, and acquired all the accomplifhments that polite learning, and a liberal education could beftow.

Brutus about this time going to Macedonia, as he paffed through Athens, took feveral young gentlemen to the army with him; and Horace, now grown up, and qualified to fet out into the world, among the reft. Brutus made him a tribune: but it is probable, that this general was pretty much ftraightened for officers and foldiers at that time, otherwife we fhall not eafily account for his advancing Horace. He would hardly make him an officer for his wit; and for courage he certainly was not diftinguifhed, as the event fhewed at the battle of Philippi, where he left the field and fled, after he had fhamefully flung away his fhield. This memorable circumftance of his life he mentioned himfelf, in an Ode to his friend Pompeius Varus, who was with him in the fame battle of Philippi, and accompanied him in his flight:

> " Tecum Philippos, & celerem fugam
> Senfi, relicta non bene parmula:"

If indeed we are to underftand this ferioufly, and not rather as a compliment to the prowefs of Auguftus and his arms. However, though running away might poffibly fave his life, it could not fecure his fortune, which he forfeited; for, being on the weaker fide, it became with thofe of others a prey to the conqueror. Thus reduced to want he applied himfelf to poetry, in which he fucceeded fo well, that he foon made himfelf known to fome of the greateft men in Rome [N]. Virgil, as he has told us, was the firft that recommended him to Mæcenas; and this celebrated patron of learning and learned men grew fo fond of him, that he became a fuitor for him to Auguftus, and fucceeded in having his eftate reftored. Auguftus was highly pleafed with his merit and addrefs, admitted him to a clofe familiarity with him in his private hours, and afterwards made him no fmall offers of preferment. The poet had the greatnefs of mind to refufe them all; and the prince was generous enough not to be offended at his freedom in fo doing. He muft have been, what his writings every where fpeak him to have been, very indifferent as to vain and oftentatious living, and the pride of a

[M] Adelph. Act. iii. Sc 3.   [N] Sat. 6. Lib. L.

court,

court, to refuse a place so honourable and advantageous as that of secretary to Augustus. But the life he loved best, and lived as much as he could, was the very reverse of a court life; a life of retirement and study, free from the noise of hurry and ambition; for he seems not serious, when he represents himself as fond of change:

   "Romæ Tibur amo ventosus, Tibure Romam,"

as it was his peculiar talent to make his satire agreeable, by seeming to rally himself when he meant to censure others.

Some time after, when Horace was about twenty-six years of age, Augustus found it necessary to make peace with Antony, that they might the better destroy young Pompey their common enemy; and for this end persons were sent to Brundusium as deputies, to conclude the treaty between them. Mæcenas going on Cæsar's part, Horace, Virgil, and some others, accompanied him thither: and Horace has described the journey in a most entertaining and humorous manner, in the fifth Satire of his first book. This happened in Pollio's consulship, who was about that time writing a history of the civil wars for the last twenty years; which occasioned Horace to address the first Ode of the second book to him, and to represent the many inconveniences to which such a work must necessarily expose him,

   "Periculosæ plenum opus aleæ
      Tractas, & incedis per ignes
      Suppositos cineri doloso:"

justly imagining, it might ruin him with Augustus, if he mentioned the true causes of the civil war between Cæsar and Pompey, and their motives for beginning it. Dacier, in his life of Horace, seems to have fixed happily enough the time of his writing some Odes and Epistles, and Bentley has gone yet further in the same design. From them it appears, that before he was thirty years of age, he had introduced himself to the acquaintance of the most considerable persons in Rome; of which this Ode to Pollio may furnish a proof: for his merit must have been well known, and his reputation well-established, before he could take the liberty he has there done with one of Pollio's high character: and he was so great a master in the science of men and manners, that he would not have taken it, if it had been in any degree improper.

His love for retirement increasing with his age, he at last resolved upon it altogether. For some years he was only at Rome in the spring, passing the summer in the country, and the winter at Tarentum. In his retirement he gave himself so entirely up to ease, that he could not be prevailed on to undertake any great work, though he was strongly solicited to it: nevertheless, his gratitude to Augustus called upon him sometimes to
                                                                sing

fing his triumphs over Pompey and Antony, or the victorious exploits of Tiberius and Drufus. His " Carmen fæculare" he compofed at the exprefs command of Auguftus; and to oblige him, wrote alfo the firft epiftle of the fecond book. That prince had kindly reproached him with having faid fo little of him in his writings; and afked him in a letter written on this occafion, " whether he thought it would difgrace him with pofterity, if he fhould f em to have been intimate with him?" upon which he addreffed the epiftle juft mentioned to him [o].

Horace embraced the Epicurean philofophy for the greateft part of his life; but at the latter end of it, feems to have leaned a little towards the Stoic. He was of a cheerful temper, fond of eafe and liberty, and went pretty far into the gallantries of his times, till age ftole in upon his amours [p]. He feems now to have maftered his paffions, and to have lived in an undifturbed and philofophical tranquillity: fo that his life in general was, as he defcribes it—" Secretum iter, & fallentis femita vitæ." While he was thus enjoying the fweets of retirement, his beloved friend and patron Mæcenas died; and this incident is fuppofed to have touched him fo fenfibly, that he did not furvive it long enough to lament him in an elegy. He had before declared, upon a dangerous fit of illnefs, which had attacked Mæcenas, that if he went, he would not ftay behind him [q].

" Ille dies utramque
Ducet ruinam: non ego perfidum
Dixi facramentum: ibimus, ibimus,
Utcunque præcedes, fupremum
Carpere iter comites parati."

Whether the lofs of his friend and patron contributed to fhorten his life, or whether he was attacked by fome diftemper immediately afterwards, is uncertain: but he died Nov. 17, as Mæcenas did, according to Dio, in the beginning of that month. This happened in the year of Rome 746, in that of Horace 57, and about eight years before Chrift. He was buried near Mæcenas's tomb, and declared in his laft words Auguftus his heir; the violence of his diftemper being fuch, that he was not able to fign his will. In his perfon he was very fhort and corpulent, as we learn from a fragment of a letter of Auguftus's to him, preferved in his life by Suetonius: where the emperor compares him to the book he fent him, which was a little fhort thick volume. He was gray-haired about forty; fubject to fore eyes, which made him ufe but little exercife; and of a conftitution probably not the beft, by its being unable to fupport him to a more advanced age, though he feems to have managed it with very great care.

[o] Horatii Vita à Suetonio. [p] Od. 2. Lib. iv. [q] Od. 17. Lib. ii.

Confident

Confident of immortal fame from his works, as all allow he
very juſtly might be, he has thus expreſſed his indifference
to any magnificent funeral rites, or fruitleſs ſorrows for his
death, (Od. xx. b. ii.)

> " Abſint inani funere næniæ
> Luctuſque turpes, & querimoniæ :
> Compeſce clamorem, ac ſepulchri
> Mitte ſupervacuos honores."

> " Mourn not, no friendly drops muſt fall,
> No ſighs attend my funeral,
>   Thoſe common deaths may crave:
> Let no diſgraceful grief appear,
> Nor damp my glory with a tear,
> And ſpare the uſeleſs honours of a grave."

CREECH.

HORNE (GEORGE), biſhop of Norwich, was born Nov. 1,
1730, at Otham near Maidſtone in Kent, where his father, the
Rev. Samuel Horne, was rector [R]. Of four ſons and three
daughters he was the ſecond ſon, and his education was commenced at home, under the inſtruction of his father. At thirteen, having made a good proficiency, he was ſent to ſchool at
Maidſtone, under the Rev. Deodatus Bye, a man of good principles, and at little more than fifteen, being elected to a Maidſtone ſcholarſhip at Univerſity-college, Oxford, he went there
to reſide. He was ſo much approved at his college, that about
the time when he took his batchelor's degree, in conſequence of
a ſtrong recommendation from that place, he was elected to a
Kentiſh fellowſhip at Magdalen. His ſtudies early were directed
to Hebrew, and to ſacred literature, and by ſome intimates of
whom he had a high opinion, he was led to conſider, and in part
to adopt, the doctrines of Hutchinſon. Mr. Jones, who has
written his life, with the zeal of a long-tried and ſteady friend,
contends that he never approved the verbal and etymological criticiſms of that author, but only that philoſophy of nature which
he thought deducible from the ſcriptures, and which Mr. Jones
himſelf prefers to the principles of Newton. It will be beſt to
give the account of this author in his own words.

" It has been hinted to me, that Dr. Horne had embraced a
ſort of philoſophy in the early part of his life, which he found
reaſon to give up towards the latter end of it. Before it can be
judged how far this may be true, a neceſſary diſtinction is to be
made. I do not recollect that his writings any where diſcover a
profeſſed attachment to the Hebrew criticiſms of Mr. Hutchinſon ; and I could prove abundantly from his private letters to

[R] Jones's Life of Horne, 8vo, 1795.

myſelf

myfelf, that he was no friend to the ufe of fuch evidence, either
in philofophy or divinity; but that he ever renounced or difbe-
lieved *that* philofophy, which afferts the true *agency* of nature,
and the refpective ufes of the *elements*, or that he did not always
admire, and fo far as he thought it prudent, infift upon it, and
recommend it, is not true[s]." The biographer then proceeds
to explain what Dr. Horne did believe; and fo far as his opinions
tended only to affert in natural philofophy the agency of an æthe-
rial fluid, or fome material caufe in producing gravity and other
attractions, we conceive that they were juft, and coincident with
what has been conjectured at leaft, if not proved, by the New-
tonians of the prefent day. But if he proceeded to a fuppofed
analogy between material and immaterial things, and compared
the agency of the Son and Holy Ghoft to that of light and air
in the natural world, it will furely be thought that he went (with
his moft refpectable and pious encomiaft) upon very uncertain
and fanciful, not to fay, prefumptuous grounds; which, with the
utmoft efteem both for him and the able writer in queftion, we
think it neceffary to fuggeft.

Whatever, in thefe fpeculative points, the opinions of Mr.
Horne might be, there is no doubt that he was, both now and
throughout his life, a good and valuable man, a fincere chriftian
in thought and in action, and finally, in all refpects worthy of
the preferment he obtained. Some of his earlieft publications
confifted, however, of attacks upon the Newtonian, and defences of the Hutchinfonian fyftem of phyfiology, as will be
feen when we enumerate his works. After a due and ftudious
preparation for orders, Mr. Horne was admitted to them at
Oxford, on Trinity Sunday, 1753, and foon after preached his
firft fermon for his friend Jones, at Finedon in Northamptonfhire. A fhort time after, he preached in London with fuch fuccefs, that a perfon, eminent himfelf for the fame talent, pronounced him, without exception, the beft preacher in England.

Mr. Horne, as he proceeded in life, was fometimes attacked
as an Hutchinfonian, and took up the pen occafionally in jufti-
fication of himfelf and others. He entered into the controverfy
about collating the Hebrew text, and took his part againft Dr.
Kennicott. About the year 1756, he had planned and begun to
execute his Commentary on the Pfalms, which he had not completed and publifhed till twenty years after. It was a work in
which he always proceeded with pleafure, but on which he do-
lighted to dwell and meditate. The character and conduct of
Mr. Horne were fo much approved in the college to which he
belonged, that on a vacancy happening in the year 1768, he was
elected prefident of that fociety. Nearly at the fame time he

[s] Life, p. 174. See alfo, p. 59, and 60.

I

married

married the daughter of Philip Burton, efq; of Eltham in Kent, by whom he had three daughters. The public fituation of Mr. Horne now made it proper for him to proceed to the degree of doctor in divinity; and he was alfo appointed one of the chaplains to the king. In 1776, Dr. Horne was elected vice-chancellor of the univerfity of Oxford, which office he held for the cuftomary period of four years. In this fituation he became known to lord North, the chancellor, and thus, it is probable, prepared the way to his fubfequent elevation. In 1781, the very year after the expiration of his office, he was made dean of Canterbury, when he would willingly have relinquifhed his cares at Oxford, to refide altogether in his native county of Kent; but yielded to the judgement of a prudent friend who advifed him to retain his fituation at Magdalen. In 1789, on the tranflation of bifhop Bagot to St. Afaph, Dr. Horne was advanced to the epifcopal dignity, and fucceeded him in the fee of Norwich. Unhappily, though he was no more than fifty-nine, he had already begun to fuffer much from infirmities. " Alas!" faid he, obfervi..g the large flight of fteps which lead into the palace of Norwich, " I am come to thefe fteps at a time of life when I can neither go up them nor down them with fafety." It happened confequently, that the church could not long be benefited by his piety and zeal. Even the charge which he compofed for his primary vifitation at Norwich, he was unable to deliver, and it was printed " as intended to have been delivered." From two vifits to Bath he had received fenfible benefit, and was mediating a third in the autumn of 1791, which he had been requefted not to delay too long. He did, however, delay it too long, and was vifited by a paralytic ftroke on the road to that place. He completed his journey, though very ill; and for a fhort time was fo far recovered as to walk daily to the pump-room; but the hopes of his friends and family were of fhort duration, for, on the 17th of January, 1792, in the 62d year of his age, his death afforded an edifying example of chriftian refignation and hope; and he was buried at Eltham in Kent, with a commendatory but very juft epitaph, which is alfo put up in the cathedral at Norwich.

It cannot often fall to the lot of the biographer to record a man fo blamelefs in character and conduct as bifhop Horne. Whatever might be his peculiar opinions on fome points, he was undoubtedly a fincere and exemplary chriftian; and as a fcholar, a writer, and a preacher, a man of no ordinary qualifications. The cheerfulnefs of his difpofition is often marked by the vivacity of his writings, and the goodnefs of his heart is every where confpicuous in them. So far was he from any tincture of covetoufnefs, that he laid up nothing from his preferments in the church. If he was no lofer at the year's end he was

perfectly

perfectly satisfied. What he gave away was bestowed with so much secresy, that it was supposed by some persons to be little; but, after his death, when the pensioners, to whom he had been a constant benefactor, rose up to look about them for some other support, it began to be known who, and how many they were.

The works of bishop Horne amount to a good many articles, which we shall notice in chronological order. 1. " The Theology and Philosophy in Cicero's Somnium Scipionis explained; or a brief attempt to demonstrate that the Newtonian System is perfectly agreeable to the notions of the wisest Ancients, and that mathematical Principles are the only sure ones," 8vo, Lond. 1751. 2. " A fair, candid, and impartial State of the Case between Sir Isaac Newton and Mr. Hutchinson," &c. 8vo, Oxford, 1753. 3. " Spicileguim Shuckfordianum; or a Nosegay for the Critics," &c. 12mo, Lond. 1754. 4. " Christ and the Holy Ghost the supporters of the spiritual Life," &c. two sermons preached before the university of Oxford, 8vo, 1755. 5. " The Almighty justified in Judgement," a sermon, 1756. 6. " An Apology for certain Gentlemen in the University of Oxford, asperfed in a late anonymous Pamphlet," 8vo, 1756. 7. " A View of Mr. Kennicott's Method of correcting the Hebrew Text," &c. 8vo. Oxford, 1760. 8. " Considerations on the Life and Death of St. John the Baptist," 8vo, Oxford, 1772. This pleasing tract contained the substance of several sermons preached annually at Magdalen-college in Oxford, the course of which had commenced in 1755. A second edition in 12mo, was published at Oxford in 1777. 9. " Considerations on the projected Reformation of the Church of England. In a Letter to the Right Hon. Lord North. By a Clergyman," 4to, London, 1772. 10. " A Commentary on the Book of Psalms," &c. &c. 4to, Oxford, 2 vols. 1776. Reprinted in 8vo, in 1778, and three times since. With what satisfaction this good man composed this pious work, may best be judged from the following passage in his preface. " Could the author flatter himself that any one would have half the pleasure in reading the following exposition, which he hath had in writing it, he would not fear the loss of his labour. The employment detached him from the bustle and hurry of life, the din of politics, and the noise of folly. Vanity and vexation flew away for a season, care and disquietude came not near his dwelling. He arose fresh as the morning to his task; the silence of the night invited him to pursue it; and he can truly say that food and rest were not preferred before it. Every psalm improved infinitely on his acquaintance with it, and no one gave him uneasiness but the last; for then he grieved that his work was done. Happier hours than those which have been spent in these meditations on the songs of Sion, he never expected to see in this world. Very

pleasantly

prefently did they pafs, and move fmoothly and fwiftly along; for when thus engaged he counted no time. They are gone, but have left a relifh and a fragrance on the mind, and the remembrance of them is fweet." 11. "A Letter to Adam Smith, LL. D. on the Life, Death, and Philofophy of David Hume, efq. By one of the People called Chriftians," 12mo, Oxford, 1777. 12. "Difcourfes on feveral Subjects and Occafions," 2 vols. 8vo, Oxford, 1779. Thefe fermons have gone through five editions. 13. "Letters on Infidelity," 12mo, Oxford, 1784. 14. "The Duty of contending for the Faith," Jude, ver. 3. preached at the primary Vifitation of the moft Reverend John Lord Archbifhop of Canterbury, July 1, 1786. To which is fubjoined, a Difcourfe on the Trinity in Unity, Matth. xxviii. 19." 4to, 1786. Thefe fermons, with fourteen others preached on particular occafions, and all publifhed feparately, were collected into one volume, 8vo, at Oxford, in 1795. The two have alfo been publifhed in 12mo, by the fociety for promoting Chriftian Knowledge, and are among the books diftributed by that fociety. 15. "A Letter to the Rev. Dr. Prieftley, by an Undergraduate," Oxford, 1787. 16. "Obfervations on the Cafe of the Proteftant Diffenters, with Reference to the Corporation and Teft Acts," 8vo, Oxford, 1790. 17. "Charge intended to have been delivered to the Clergy of Norwich, at the primary Vifitation," 4to, 1791. 18. "Difcourfes on feveral Subjects and Occafions," 8vo, vol. 3, and 4, Oxford, 1794; a pofthumous publication. The four volumes have fince been reprinted in an uniform edition. Befides thefe, might be enumerated feveral occafional papers in different periodical publications, but particularly the papers figned Z. in the "Olla Podrida," a periodical work, conducted by Mr. T. Monro, then batchelor of arts, and a demy of Magdalen-college, Oxford. But we leave thefe particulars to be fpecified by thofe who fhall write the life of the venerable bifhop on a larger fcale.

HORNECK (Dr. ANTHONY), an Englifh divine, was born at Baccharack, a town in the Lower Palatinate, in 1641 [T]. His father was recorder or fecretary of that town, a ftrict Proteftant; and the doctor was brought up in the fame manner, though fome, we find, afferted that he was originally a Papift. He was defigned for the facred miniftry from his birth, and firft fent to Heidelberg, where he ftudied divinity under Spanheim, afterwards profeffor at Leyden. When he was nineteen, he came over to England, and was entered of Queen's-college, in Oxford, Dec. 1663; of which, by the intereft of Barlow, then provoft of that college, and afterwards bifhop of Lincoln, he

[T] Life of Horneck by bifhop Kidder, p. 3.

was made chaplain soon after his admission. He was incorporated M. A. from the university of Wittemberg, Dec. 1663; and not long after made vicar of Allhallows in Oxford, a living in the gift of Lincoln-college. Here he continued two years, and was then taken into the family of the duke of Albemarle, in quality of tutor to his son lord Torrington. The duke presented him to the rectory of Doulton in Devonshire, and procured him also a prebend in the church of Exeter.' In 1669, before he married, he went over into Germany to see his friends, where he was much admired as a preacher, and was entertained with great respect at the court of the elector Palatine. At his return in 1671, he was chosen preacher in the Savoy, where he continued to officiate till he died. This however was but poor maintenance, the salary being small as well as precarious, and he continued in mean circumstances for some years after the Revolution; till, as Kidder says, it pleased God to raise up a friend, who concerned himself on his behalf, namely, the lord admiral Russel, afterwards earl of Orford. Before he went to sea, lord Russel waited on the queen to take leave; and when he was with her, begged of her, that she " would be pleased to bestow some preferment on Dr. Horneck." The queen told him, that she " could not at present think of any way of preferring the doctor;" and with this answer the admiral was dismissed. Some time after, the queen related what had passed to archbishop Tillotson; and added, that she " was anxious lest the admiral should think her too unconcerned on the doctor's behalf." Consulting with him therefore what was to be done, Tillotson advised her to promise him the next prebend of Westminster that should happen to become void. This the queen did, and lived to make good her word in 1693. In 1681, he had commenced D. D. at Cambridge, and was afterwards made chaplain to king William and queen Mary. His prebend at Exeter lying at a great distance from him, he resigned it; and Sept. 1694, was admitted to a prebend in the church of Wells, to which he was presented by Kidder, bishop of Bath and Wells. It was no very profitable thing; and if it had been, he would have enjoyed but little of it, since he died so soon after as Jan. 1696, and in his 56th year. His body being opened, it appeared at once what was the cause of his death. Both his ureters were stopped; the one by a stone that entered the top of the ureter with a sharp end; the upper part of which was thick, and much too large to enter any farther; the other by stones of much less firmness and consistence. He was interred in Westminster-abbey, where a monument, with an handsome inscription upon it, was erected to his memory.

He was, says Kidder, a man of very good learning, and had good skill in the languages. He had applied himself to the

Arabic from his youth, and retained it to his death. He had great skill in the Hebrew likewise; nor was his skill limited to the Biblical Hebrew only, but he was also a great master in the Rabbinical. He was a most diligent and indefatigable reader of the Scriptures in the original languages: "Sacras literas traclavit indefeffu ftudio," fays his tutor Spanheim of him; and adds, that he was then of an elevated wit, of which he gave a fpecimen in 1659, by publicly defending "A Differtation upon the Vow of Jephthah concerning the facrifice of his Daughter." He had great skill in ecclefiaftical hiftory, in controverfial and cafuiftical divinity; and it is faid, that few men were fo frequently confulted in cafes of confcience as Dr. Horneck. As to his paftoral care in all its branches, he is fet forth as one of the greateft examples that ever lived. "He had the zeal, the fpirit, the courage of John the Baptift," fays Kidder, "and durft reprove a great man; and perhaps that man lived not, that was more confcientious in this matter. I very well knew a great man," fays the bifhop, "and peer of the realm, from whom he had juft expectations of preferment; but this was fo far from ftopping his mouth, that he reproved him to his face, upon a very critical affair. He miffed of his preferment indeed, but faved his own foul. This freedom," continues the good bifhop, "made his acquaintance and friendfhip very defirable by every good man, that would be better. He would in him be very fure of a friend, that would not fuffer fin upon him. I may fay of him, what Pliny fays of Corellius Rufus, whofe death he laments, 'amifi meæ vitæ teftem, &c.' 'I have loft a faithful witnefs of my life;' and may add what he faid upon that occafion to his friend Calvifius, 'vereor ne negligentius vivam,' 'I am afraid left for the time to come I fhould live more carelefsly."

He was the author of fermons, and many works of the religious kind; but befides thefe, he tranflated out of German into Englifh, "A wonderful Story or Narrative of certain Swedifh Writers," printed in Glanvil's "Sadducifmus Triumphatus;" in the fecond edition of which book is a "Preface to the Wonderful Story," with an addition of a "new Relation from Sweden," tranflated by him out of German. He tranflated likewife from French into Englifh, "An Antidote againft a carelefs Indifferency in Matters of Religion; in Oppofition to thofe who believe that all Religions are alike, and that it imports not what Men profefs." This was printed at London in 1693, with an Introduction written by himfelf. He collected and publifhed "Some Difcourfes, Sermons, and Remains of Mr. Jofeph Glanvil," in 1681. He wrote likewife, in conjunction with Dr. Gilbert Burnet, "The laft Confeffion, Prayers, and Meditations of Lieutenant John Stern, delivered by him on the Cart,

Cart, immediately before his Execution, to Dr. Burnet : together with the laſt Confeſſion of George Boroſky, ſigned by him in the Priſon, and ſealed up in the Lieutenant's Pacquet. With which an Account is given of their Deportment, both in the Priſon, and at the Place of their Execution, which was in the Pall-mall, on the 10th of March, in the ſame place in which they had murdered Thomas Thynne, Eſq; on the 12th of February before, in 1681." This was publiſhed at London, in folio, 1682.

HORNIUS (GEORGE), profeſſor of hiſtory at Leyden, was born in the Palatinate, and died at Leyden in 1670. He was a little maniacal towards the end of his life; which diſorder was ſuppoſed to be occaſioned by the loſs of 6000 florins, he had entruſted with an alchemiſt at the Hague. His chief works are, 1. " Hiſtoria Eccleſiaſtica ad ann. 1666." This has been well eſteemed. 2. " De Originibus Americanis, 1652," 8vo. 3. " Geographia Vetus & Nova." 4. " Orbis Politicus." 5. Hiſtoria Philoſophiæ," in ſeven books, 4to, 1655. He was a man of vaſt reading, rather than great parts.

HORROX (JEREMIAH), an Engliſh aſtronomer, and memorable for being the firſt, from the beginning of the world, who had obſerved the paſſage of Venus over the Sun's diſk, was born at Toxteth in Lancaſhire, about 1619 [U]. From a ſchool in the country, where he acquired grammar-learning, he was ſent to Emanuel-college in Cambridge, and there ſpent ſome time in academical ſtudies. About 1633, he began with real earneſtneſs to ſtudy aſtronomy : but living at that time with his father at Toxteth, in very moderate circumſtances, and being deſtitute of books and other aſſiſtances for the proſecution of this ſtudy, he could not make any conſiderable progreſs. He ſpent ſome of his firſt years in ſtudying the writings of Lanſbergius, of which he repented and complained afterwards; neglecting in the mean time the more valuable and profitable works of Tycho Brahe, Kepler, and other excellent aſtronomers. In 1636, he contracted an acquaintance with Mr. William Crabtree of Broughton near Mancheſter, and was engaged in the ſame ſtudies; but living at a conſiderable diſtance from each other, they could have little correſpondence except by letters. Theſe, however, they frequently exchanged, communicating their obſervations to one another ; and they ſometimes conſulted Mr. Samuel Foſter, profeſſor of aſtronomy at Greſham-college in London. Horrox, having now obtained a companion in his ſtudies, aſſumed new ſpirits. Procuring aſtronomical inſtruments and books, he applied himſelf to make obſervations ; and by Crabtree's advice, laid aſide Lanſbergius, whoſe tables he found

[U] Wallis's Epiſtola Nuncupatoria, prefixed to Horrox's Opera Poſthuma.

R 2   erroneous,

erroneous, and his hypotheses inconsistent. He was pursuing his studies with great vigour and success, when he was cut off by a sudden death, Jan. 3, 1640-1.

What we have of his writings is sufficient to shew, how great a loss the world had of him. He had just finished his " Venus in Sole visa," a little before his death. He made his observations upon this new and extraordinary phænomenon at Hool near Liverpool ; but they did not appear till 1662, when Hevelius published them at Dantzick, with some works of his own, under this title, " Mercurius in Sole visus Gedani anno 1661, Maij 3, cum aliis quibusdam rerum cœlestium observationibus rarifque phænomenis. Cui annexa est Venus in Sole pariter visa anno 1639, Nov. 24, &c " Besides this work he had begun another, in which he proposed these two things: first, to refute Lansbergius's hypotheses, and to shew, how inconsistent they were with each other and the heavens; and, secondly, to draw up a new system of astronomy, agreeably to the heavens, from his own observations and those of others; retaining for the most part the Keplerian hypotheses, but changing the numbers as observations required. Wallis, from whose " Epistola Nuncupatoria" we have extracted these memoirs of Horrox, published some of his papers in 1673, under the title of " Opera Posthuma :" others were carried into Ireland by his brother Jonas Horrox, who had pursued the same studies, and died there, by which means they were lost: and others came into the hands of Mr. Jeremiah Shakerly, who, by the assistance of them, formed his " British Tables," published at London in 1653: which last papers, after Shakerly's voyage to the East-Indies, where he died, are said to have remained in the possession of a bookseller, till they were destroyed by the great fire at London in 1666.

HORSLEY (JOHN), author of a very learned and excellent work, entitled, " Britannia Romana," by which only he is known, is supposed to have been a native of Northumberland, where, at a village called Long-Horsley, near Morpeth, the family, in all probability, originated. This parent flock, if such it was, is now lost in the Witheringtons, by the marriage of the heiress of Long-Horsley, about the middle of this century, with a person of that name. We know only of two other branches; one settled in Yorkshire, the other in the West, from which latter, we understand the present learned bishop of Rochester to have sprung [u]: but the branches have been so long

[u] Dr. Priestley, with his usual accuracy of historical assertion, has said that the father and grandfather of the bishop were dissenting ministers. The truth is, that the father of the bishop was a clergyman of the church of England: his grandfather was indeed a dissenter, but not a minister; the father changed voluntarily, with Maddox, afterwards bishop of Worcester, in early youth, and the grandfather, late in life, acceded also to our communion.

separated

feparated, that they cannot trace their relationfhip to each other.
John Horfley was educated in the public grammar-fchool at Newcaftle, and afterwards in Scotland, where he took a degree; he
was finally fettled at Morpeth, and is faid, in Hutchinfon's
view of Northumberland [x], to have been paftor to a diffenting
congregation in that place. The fame author adds, from Ran-
dall's manufcripts, that he died in 1732, which was the fame
year in which his great work appeared; but the truth is, as
we learn from the journals of the time, that he died Dec. 12,
1731; a fhort time before the publication of his book. He was
a fellow of the Royal Society. A few letters from him to Roger
Gale, efq; on antiquarian fubjeéts, are inferted in Hutchinfon's
book [y]: they are all dated in 1729. His "Britannia Romana"
gives a full and learned account of the remains and vefliges of
the Romans in Britain. It is divided into three books; the firft
containing "the Hiftory of all the Roman Tranfaétions in Britain, with an account of their legionary and auxiliary forces
employed here, and a Determination of the Stations *per lineam
valli*; alfo a large Defcription of the Roman Walls, with Maps
of the fame, laid down from a geometrical Survey." The
fecond book contains, "a complete Colleétion of the Roman
Infcriptions and Sculptures, which have hitherto been difcovered in Britain, with the Letters engraved in their proper
fhape, and proportionate fize, and the reading placed under
each; as alfo an biftorical account of them, with explanatory
and critical obfervations." The third book contains, "the
Roman Geography of Britain, in which are given the originalf
of Ptolemy, Antonini Itinerarium, the Notitia, the anonymous
Ravennas, and Peutinger's Table, fo far as they relate to this
Ifland, with particular Effays on each of thofe ancient Authors,
and the feveral Places in Britain mentioned by them," with tables, indexes, &c. Such is the author's own account in his title-
page; and the learned of all countries have teftified that the
accuracy of the execution has equalled the excellence of the plan.

HORSTIUS (JAMES), an eminent phyfician, was born at
Torgau in 1537; and took the degree of M. D. in the univerfity
of Frankfort on the Oder, in 1562. He was offered the place
of public phyfician in feveral places; and he exercifed it fucceffively at Sagan and Suidnitz in Silefia, and at Iglaw in Moravia, till 1580, when he was made phyfician in ordinary to the
archduke of Auftria: and four years after, quitting that place,
he was promoted to the medical profefforfhip in the univerfity of
Helmftadt. The oration he delivered at his inftallation, "De
remoris difcentium medicinam & earum remediis," that is,
"Of the Difficulties which attend the Study of Phyfic, and the
Means to remove them," is a very good one; and printed with

his " Epiſtolæ Philoſophicæ & Medicinales, Lipſ. 1596 [z]," 8vo.
Upon enteri g on this poſt, he diſtinguiſhed himſelf by one ob-
ſervance, which was thought a great ſingularity: he joined devotion to the practice of phyſic. He always prayed to God to bleſs
his preſcriptions; and he publiſhed a form of prayer upon this
ſubject, which he preſented to the univerſity. It is eaſy to
conceive, that no book of devotion ever ſold worſe than this,
which Horſtius compoſed for the uſe of phyſicians: it muſt,
however, be obſerved to their honour, that ſeveral of them gave
him thanks for publiſhing theſe prayers, and confeſſed that their
art ſtood very much in need of God's aſſiſtance. He acquitted
himſelf worthily in his functions, and publiſhed ſome books,
which kept up the reputation he had already acquired. It muſt
not be diſſembled, that he publiſhed a " Diſſertation upon the
Golden Tooth of a Child in Sileſia;" concerning which he ſuffered himſelf to be egregiouſly impoſed upon. This golden
tooth was a thorough impoſture, contrived for the ſake of getting
money; and Van Dale has related in what manner the cheat was
diſcovered. Horſtius, in the mean time, took it for a great
prodigy, which ought to be a comfort to thoſe Chriſtians, who
were oppreſſed by the Turks; as certainly foreboding the down-
fal of the Ottoman empire. He was not, however, the only
one who made himſelf ridiculous by writing about this golden
tooth; others did the ſame: and they may ſerve as a leſſon of
caution to the curious enquirers into nature, to make themſelves
ſure of the real exiſtence of things, before they attempt to explain their cauſes. Horſtius's diſſertation was publiſhed at
Leipſic in 1595, 8vo, with another piece of his writing, " De
Noctambulis," or " Concerning thoſe who walk in their
ſleep."

He died about 1600. He married his firſt wife in 1562, by
whom he had ten children; and loſing her in 1585, he married a
ſecond two years after. If the religion of this phyſician had
been leſs tinctured with ſuperſtition, and his philoſophy leſs credulous, he would have eſcaped ſome ridicule.

HORSTIUS (GEORGE), nephew of the preceding, gained
ſuch a reputation in the practice of phyſic, that he was uſually
call'd the Æſculapius of Germany. He was born at Torgau in
1578 [A], admitted M. A. at Wittemberg in 1601, and M. D.
at Baſil in 1606. He was profeſſor of phyſic in ſeveral places,
and at laſt, in 1622, accepted the place of firſt phyſician to the
city of Ulm, which he held as long as he lived. He took
a wife in 1615, and loſt her in 1634. He married a ſecond in
June, 1635, and died of the gout in Auguſt, 1636. He publiſhed many books, ſome upon uſeful, ſome upon curious ſubjects, which have been much eſteemed. Among theſe were,

" De tuenda fanitate, 1648," 12mo. " De tuenda fanitate
ftudioforum & literatorum, 1648," 12mo. " De caufis fimi-
litudinis & diffimilitudinis in fœtu, refpectu parentum, &c.
1619," 4to. " Differtatio de natura amoris, additis refolu-
tionibus de cura furoris amatorii, de philtris, atque de pulfu
amantium, 1611," 4to, &c. Befides two daughters, he left four
fons by his firft wife; three of whom were phyficians, the other
an apothecary. Two of the phyficians, John-Daniel, and Gregory, were alfo authors.

HORTENSIUS (QUINTUS), a Roman orator, the contemporary and rival of Cicero, fo far his fenior, that he was an
eftablifhed pleader fome time before the appearance of the
latter. He pleaded his firft caufe at the age of nineteen, in the
confulfhip of L. Licinius Craffus, and Q. Mutius Scevola, 94
years before the Chriftian æra, Cicero being then in his twelfth
year. This early effort was crowned with great fuccefs, and he
continued throughout his life a very favourite orator. His enemies, however, reprefented his action as extravagant, and gave
him the name of *Hortenfia*, from a celebrated dancer of that
time. He proceeded alfo in the line of public honours, was military tribune, prætor, and, in the year 68, A. C. conful, together
with Q. Cæcilius Metellus. He was an eminent member of
the college of augurs, and was the perfon who elected Cicero
into that body, being fworn to prefent a man of proper dignity.
By him alfo Cicero was there inaugurated, for which reafon,
fays that author, it was my duty to regard him as a parent.
He died in the year 49 A. C. and Cicero, to whom the news of
that event was brought when he was at Rhodes, in his return
from Cilicia, has left a moft eloquent eulogy and lamentation
upon him, in the opening of his celebrated treatife on orators,
entitled *Brutus*. " I confidered him," fays that writer, " not,
as many fuppofed, in the light of an adverfary, or one who
robbed me of any praife, but as a companion and fharer in my
glorious labour. It was much more honourable to have fuch an
opponent, than to ftand unrivalled; more efpecially as neither
his career was impeded by me, nor mine by him; but each, on the
contrary, was always ready to affift the other by communication,
advice, and kindnefs." If, however, Cicero was fincere in his
attachment, it was furmifed that Hortenfius was not, and this
is even infinuated in one of the epiftles of Cicero. Hortenfius
amaffed great wealth, but lived at the fame time in a fplendid
and liberal manner; and it is faid that at his death his cellars
were found ftocked with 10,000 hogfheads of wine. His orations have all perifhed; but it was the opinion of Quintillian,
that they did not in perufal anfwer to the fame he obtained by
fpeaking them. Hortenfius muft have been fixty-four at the
time of his death.

HORTEN-

HORTENSIUS (LAMBERT), a philologer, a writer of verfes, and a hiftorian. His real name is unknown; he took that of Hortenfius, either becaufe his father was a gardener, or becaufe his family name fignified gardener. He was born at Montfort, in the territory of Utrecht, in the year 1501, and ftudied at Louvain. Hortenfius was for feveral years rector of the fchool at Naarden, and when that city was taken in the year 1572, he would have fallen a facrifice to the military fury, had he not been preferved by the gratitude of one who had been his pupil. His death happened at Naarden, in 1577. There are extant by him, befides fatires, epithalamia, and other Latin poems, the following works: 1. Seven books, " De bello Germanico," under Charles V. 8vo. 2. " De tumultu Anabaptiftarum," folio. 3. " De Seceffionibus Ultrajectinis," folio. 4. Commentaries on the fix firft books of the Æneid, and on Lucan. 5. Notes on four Comedies of Ariftophanes.

HOSIUS (STANISLAUS), cardinal, was born at Cracow in Poland, in 1503, of low parents, but being well educated, was, after taking his degrees, fo much diftinguifhed, as to be admitted into the Polifh fenate. He was here diftinguifhed by the acutenefs of his genius, the retentivenefs of his memory, and other accomplifhments mental and perfonal; and was advanced fucceffively to the places of fecretary to the king, canon of Cracow, bifhop of Culm, and bifhop of Warmia. He was fent by the pope Pius IV. to engage the emperor Ferdinand to continue the council of Trent, and the emperor was fo charmed with his eloquence and addrefs that he granted whatever he afked. Pius then made him a cardinal, and employed him as his legate, to open and prefide at the council. Hofius was a zealous advocate for the Romifh church, and defended it ably both in fpeeches and writings; the latter of which amounted to two folio volumes, and were often printed during his life. He died in the year 1579, at the age of 76, and was buried in the church of St. Lawrence, from which he took his title as cardinal. By his will he left his library to the univerfity of Cracow, with an annual fum to provide for its fupport and increafe. Among his works, the chief are, 1. " Confeffio Catholicæ fidei;" faid to have been reprinted, in various languages, thirty-four times. 2. " De Communione fub utraque fpecie." 3. " De facerdotum conjugio." 4. " De Miffa vulgari lingua celebranda," &c. His works were firft collectively publifhed at Cologne in 1584.

HOSPINIAN (RODOLPHUS), a learned Swifs writer, who rendered prodigious fervice to the Proteftant caufe, was born at Altdorf near Zurich, where his father was minifter, in 1547 [a]. He began his ftudies at Zurich, under the direction of

[a] Bayle's Dict.

Wolfius,

Wolfius, his uncle by his mother's fide; and made a vaft progrefs. Lofing his father in 1563, he found an affectionate
patron in his godfather Rodolphus Gualterus. He left Zurich
in 1565, in order to vifit the other univerfities; and fpent
fome time in Marpurg and Heidelberg. He was afterwards
recalled, and received into the miniftry in 1568, and the year
after took a wife, by whom he had fourteen children; neverthelefs, when fhe died in 1612, he married a fecond. They were
both good women, and made him very happy. The fame year
alfo, 1569, he obtained the freedom of the city; and was made
provifor of the abbey fchool in 1571. Though his fchool and
his cure engroffed fo much of his time, he had yet the courage
to undertake a noble work of vaft extent: and that was, " An
Hiftory of the Errors of Popery." He confidered, that the
Papifts, when defeated by the holy Scriptures, had recourfe to
tradition; were for ever boafting of their antiquity, and defpifed
the proteftants for being modern. To deprive them of this plea,
he was determined to fearch into the rife and progrefs of the
Popifh rites and ceremonies; and to examine by what gradations
the truth, which had been taught by Chrift and his apoftles, had
given way to innovations. The circumftance, which firft fuggefted this thought was, his falling accidentally into converfation
in a country alehoufe with a landlord, who was fo filly as to imagine, that the monaftic life came immediately from Paradife.
He could not complete his work, agreeably to the plan he had
drawn out; but he publifhed fome confiderable parts of it, as,
1. " De Templis: hoc eft, de origine, progreffu, ufu, & abufu
Templorum, ac omnino rerum omnium ad Templa pertinentium.
1587," folio. 2. " De Monachis: feu de origine & progreffu
monachatus & ordinum monafticorum, 1588," folio. 3. " De
Feftis Judæorum & Ethnicorum: hoc eft, de origine, progreffu,
ceremoniis, & ritibus feftorum dierum Judæorum, Græcorum,
Romanorum, Turcarum, & Indianorum, 1592," folio. 4.
" Fefta Chriftianorum," &c. 1593, folio. 5. " Hiftoria Sacra-
mentaria: hoc eft, libri quinque de Cœnæ Dominicæ prima in-
ftitutione, ejufque vero ufu & abufu, in primæva ecclefia; necnon
de origine, progreffu, ceremoniis, & ritibus Miffæ, Tranfub-
ftantiationis, & aliorum pene infinitorum errorum, quibus Cœnæ
prima inftitutio horribiliter in papatu polluta & profanata eft,"
1598, folio. 6. " Pars altera: de origine progreffu contro-
verfiæ facramentariæ de Cœna Domini inter Lutheranos, Ubi-
quiftas, & Orthodoxos, quos Zuinglianos feu Calviniftas vocant,
exortæ ab anno 1517 ufque ad 1602 dedučta, 1602," folio.
Thefe are all of them parts of his great work, which he enlarged in fucceeding editions, and added confutations of the arguments of Bellarmin, Baronius, and Gretfer. What he publifhed on the Eucharift, and another work, entitled, " Concor-

dia Difcors, &c. printed into 1607, exafperated the Lutherans in a high degree; and they wrote againſt him very abuſively. He did not publiſh any anſwer, though he had almoſt finiſhed one, but turned his arms againſt the Jeſuits; and publiſhed " Hiſtoria Jeſuitica: hoc eſt, de origine, regulis, conſtitution- ibus, privilegiis, incrementis, progreſſu, & propagatione ordinis Jeſuitarum. Item, de eorum dolis, fraudibus, impoſturis, ne- fariis facinoribus, cruentis conſiliis, falfa quoque, feditioſa, & ſanguinolenta doctrina, 1619," folio.

Theſe are his works; and they juſtly gained him high repu- tation, as they did alſo good preferment. He was appointed archdeacon of Caroline church in 1588; and, in 1594, miniſter of the abbey-church. He was deprived of his ſight for near a year by a cataract, yet continued to preach as uſual, and was happily couched in 1613. In 1623, being 76 years of age, he grew childiſh; and ſo continued till his death, which happened in 1626. The public entertained ſo high an opinion of his learning from his writings, that he was exhorted from all quar- ters to refute Baronius's " Annals;" and no one was thought to have greater abilities for the taſk. A new edition of his works was publiſhed at Geneva, 1681, in ſeven thin volumes, folio.

HOSPITAL (MICHEL DE L'), chancellor of France, was the ſon of a phyſician, and born at Aigueperſe in Auvergne, in the year 1505. His father ſent him to ſtudy in the moſt cele- brated univerſities of France and Italy, where he diſtinguiſhed himſelf at once by his genius for literature, and for buſineſs. Having diligently ſtudied juriſprudence, he was quickly advanced to very honourable poſts; being ſucceſſively auditor of the Rota at Rome, counſellor in the parliament of Paris, ambaſſador at the council of Trent when transferred to Bologna, and finally ſuperintendant of the royal finances in France. His merits in this poſt were of the moſt ſingular and exalted kind. By a ſe- vere œconomy, he laboured to reſtore the royal treaſure, exhauſted by the prodigality of the king, Henry II. and the diſhoneſt avarice of his favourites; he defied the enmity of thoſe whoſe profits he deſtroyed, and was himſelf ſo rigidly diſintereſted, that after five or ſix years continuance in this place, he was unable to give a portion to his daughter, and the deficiency was ſupplied by the liberality of the ſovereign. On the death of Henry, in 1559, the cardinal of Lorraine, then at the head of affairs, introduced l'Hoſpital into the council of ſtate. Hence he was removed by Margaret of Valois, who took him into Savoy, as her chancellor. But the confuſions of France ſoon made it ne- ceſſary to recal a man of ſuch firmneſs and undaunted integrity. In the midſt of faction and fury, he was advanced to the high office of chancellor of that kingdom, where he maintained his poſt, like a philoſopher who was ſuperior to fear, or any ſpecies

of

of weakneſs. At the breaking out of the conſpiracy of Amboiſe, in 1560, and on all other occaſions, he was the advocate for mercy and reconciliation; and by the edict of Romorantin, prevented the eſtabliſhment of the inquiſition in France. It was perhaps for reaſons of this kind, rather than from any ſolid proof, that the violent Romaniſts accuſed him of being a concealed Proteſtant; forgetting that by ſuch ſuſpicions they paid the higheſt compliment to the ſpirit of Proteſtantiſm. The queen, Catherine of Medicis, who had contributed to the elevation of l'Hoſpital, being too violent to approve his pacific meaſures, excluded him from the council of war; on which he retired to his country-houſe at Vignai near Eſtampes. Some days after, when the ſeals were demanded of him, he reſigned them without regret, ſaying, that " the affairs of the world were too corrupt for him to meddle with them." In lettered eaſe, amuſing himſelf with Latin poetry, and a ſelect ſociety of friends, he truly enjoyed his retreat, till his happineſs was interrupted by the atrocious day of St. Bartholomew, in 1572. Of this diſgraceful event, he thought as poſterity has thought; but, though his friends conceived it probable that he might be included in the proſcription, he diſdained to ſeek his ſafety by flight. So firm was he, that when a party of horſemen actually advanced to his houſe, though without orders, for the horrid purpoſe of maſſacreing him, he refuſed to cloſe his gates: " If the ſmall one," ſaid he, " will not admit them, throw open the large;" and he was preſerved only by the arrival of another party, with expreſs orders from the king to declare that he was not among the proſcribed. The perſons who made the liſts, it was added, pardoned him the oppoſition he had always made to their projects. " I did not know," ſaid he coldly, without any change of countenance, " that I had done any thing to deſerve either death or pardon." His motto is ſaid to have been

Si fractus illabatur orbis
Impavidum ferient ruinæ,

and certainly no perſon ever had a better right to aſſume that ſublime device. This excellent magiſtrate, and truly great man, died in 1573, at the age of 68 years. It has been thought that his portrait reſembles the antique heads of Ariſtotle. There are extant by him, 1. " Latin Poems," 8vo, 1732, publiſhed at Amſterdam. They are not without merit, but Chapelain extolled them much too highly, when he compared the author to Horace. His ſtile is manly, but ſometimes diffuſe. 2. " Speeches delivered in the Meeting of the States at Orleans." As an orator he ſhines much leſs than as a poet. 3. " Memoirs, containing Treaties of Peace," &c. &c. It is ſaid that he had alſo projected a hiſtory of his own time in Latin, but this he did not execute. He left only one child, a daughter, married to

Robert

Robert Hurault, whose children added the name of l'Hôpital to that of their father; but the male line of this family also was extinct in 1706. Nevertheless, the memory of the chancellor has received the highest honours within a few years of the present time. In 1777, the abbé Remi pronounced a panegyric upon him, which was crowned in the French academy; and, in the same year, Louis XVI. erected a statue of white marble to him. For a man so fond of justice, no one ever suffered so much injustice as that unfortunate monarch.

HOSPITAL (WILLIAM-FRANCIS-ANTONY, marquis DE L'), a great mathematician of France, was born of another branch of the same family in 1661. He was a geometrician almost from his infancy; for one day being at the duke de Rohan's, where some able mathematicians were speaking of a problem of Pascal's, which appeared to them extremely difficult, he ventured to say, that he believed he could solve it. They were amazed at what appeared such unpardonable presumption in a boy of fifteen, for he was then no more; nevertheless, in a few days he sent them the solution. He entered early into the army, yet always preserved his love for the mathematics, and studied them even in his tent; whither he used to retire, it is said, rot only to study, but also to conceal his application to study: for in those days, to be too knowing in the sciences was thought to derogate from nobility; and a soldier of quality, to preserve his dignity, was in some measure obliged to hide his attainments of this kind. De l'Hospital did this very well, and was never suspected of being a great mathematician. He was a captain of horse; but, being extremely short-sighted, and exposed on that account to perpetual inconveniences and errors, he at length quitted the army, and applied himself entirely to his favourite amusement. He contracted a friendship with Malbranche, judging by his "Recherche de la verité," that he must be an excellent guide in the sciences; and he took his opinion upon all occasions. His abilities and knowledge were no longer a secret: and at the age of 32 he gave a public solution of problems, drawn from the deepest geometry, which had been proposed to mathematicians in the Acts of Leipsic. In 1693, he was received an honorary member of the Academy of sciences at Paris; and published a work upon sir Isaac Newton's calculations, entitled, "L'Analyse des infinimens petits." He was the first in France who wrote on this subject: and on this account was regarded almost as a prodigy. He engaged afterwards in another work of the mathematical kind, in which he included "Les Sectiones coniques, les Lieux geometriques, la Construction des Equations," and "Une Theorie des Courbes mechaniques:" but a little before he had finished it, he was seized with a fever, of which he died Feb. 2, 1704, aged 49. It was

published

published after his death. He is reprefented to have been a very worthy, honeft, eftimable man.

HOTMAN (Francis), in Latin Hotomanus, a learned French civilian, was born in 1524 [c], at Paris, where his family, originally of Breflau in Silefia, had flourifhed for fome time. He made fo rapid a progrefs in the belles lettres, that at the age of fifteen, he was fent to Orleans to ftudy the civil law, and in three years was received doctor in that faculty. His father, a counfellor in parliament, had already defigned him for that employment; and therefore fent for him home, and placed him at the bar. But Hotman was foon difpleafed with the chicanery of the court, and applied himfelf vigoroufly to the ftudy of the Roman law and polite literature. At the age of twenty-three, he was chofen to read public lectures in the fchools of Paris: but, relifhing the opinions of Luther, on account of which many perfons were put to death in France, and finding that he could not profefs them at Paris, he went to Lyons the year after; that is, in 1548. Having now nothing to expect from his father, who was greatly irritated at the change of his religion, he left France, and retired to Geneva; where he lived fome time in Calvin's houfe. From hence he went to Laufanne, where the magiftrates of Bern gave him the place of profeffor of polite literature. He publifhed there fome books, which, however, young as he was, were not his firft publications; and married a French gentlewoman, who had alfo retired thither on account of religion. His merit was fo univerfally known, that the magiftrates of Strafburg offered him a profefforfhip of civil law; which he accepted, and held till 1561. Mean time, while he was difcharging the functions of this place, he received invitations from the duke of Prufia, the landgrave of Heffe, the dukes of Saxony, and even from queen Elizabeth of England; but did not accept them. He did not refufe, however, to go to the court of the king of Navarre, at the beginning of the troub'es; and he went twice into Germany, to defire affiftance of Ferdinand, in the name of the princes of the blood, and even in the name of the queen-mother. The fpeech he made at the diet of Frankfurt is publifhed. Upon his return to Strafburg, he was prevailed upon to go and teach civil law at Valence; which he did with fuch fuccefs, that he raifed the reputation of that univerfity. Three years after he went to be profeffor at Bourges, by the invitation of Margaret of France, fifter of Henry II. but left that city in about five months, and retired to Orleans to the heads of the party, who made great ufe of his advice. The peace which was made a month after, did not prevent him from apprehending the return of the ftorm: upon

[c] Bayle's Dict.—Niceron, Hommes Illuftres, Tom. XI.

which

which account he retired to Sancerre, and there wrote an excellent book, " De Confolatione," which his fon publifhed after
his death. He returned afterwards to his profefforfhip at Bourges,
where he was very near being killed in the maffacre of 1572:
but luckily efcaping, he left France, with a full refolution never
to return thither; and went to Geneva, where he read lectures
upon the civil law. Some time after he went to Bafil, and there
alfo taught civil law. He was fo pleafed with this fituation, that
he refufed great offers from the prince of Orange and the States-
General, who would have drawn him to Leyden. The plague
having obliged him to leave Bafil, he retired to Montbeliard,
where he loft his wife; and went afterwards to live with her fifters
at Geneva. He returned once more to Bafil, and there died in
1590, of a dropfy, which had kept him conftantly in a ftate of
indifpofition for fix years before. During this, he revifed and
digefted his works for a new edition; and they were publifhed
at Geneva in 1599, in 3 vols. fulio, with his life prefixed by
Neveletus Dofchius. The two firft contain treatifes upon the
civil law; the third, pieces relating to the government of France,
and the right of fucceffion; five books of Roman antiquities;
commentaries upon Tully's " Orations and Epiftles;" notes
upon Cæfar's " Commentaries," &c. His " Franco-Gallia,"
or, " Account of the free State of France," has been tranflated
into Englifh by lord Molefworth, author of " The Account of
Denmark." He publifhed alfo feveral other articles without
his name; but, being of the controverfial kind, they were probably not thought of confequence enough to be revived in the
collection of his works.

He was one of thofe who would never confent to be painted;
but we are told, that his picture was taken while he was in his
laft agony. His integrity, firmnefs, and piety, are highly extolled by the author of his life; yet, if Baudouin may be believed (whom however it is more reafonable not to believe, as
he was his antagonift in religious opinions) he was guilty of fome
very great enormities[D]. From the defire of money which he
difcovers in his dedications, and the means he ufed to extort it
from the great, fome have fuppofed him to be avaricious: but it
muft be remembered, that he loft his all when he changed his
religion, and had no fupplies but what arofe from reading lectures; for it does not appear that his wife brought him a fortune. It is very probable, however, that his lectures would have
been fufficient for his fubfiftence; but he was bewitched with
fchemes of finding out the philofopher's ftone, and we find him
lamenting to a friend in his laft illnefs, that he had fquandered
away his fubftance upon this hopeful project. It is certain,

[D] Refponf. ad Calvin & Bezam pro Francifco Baldulm.

therefore,

therefore, he had his weaknesses, though he was one of the greatest civilians France ever produced.

HOTTINGER (JOHN-HENRY), a very learned writer, and famous for his skill in the Oriental languages, was born at Zurich in Switzerland, in 1620 [E]. He had a particular talent for learning languages; and the progress he made in his first studies gave such promising hopes, that it was resolved he should be sent to study in foreign countries, at the public expence. He began his travels in 1638, and went to Geneva, where he studied two months under Fr. Spanheim. Then he went into France, and thence into Holland; and fixed at Groningen, where he studied divinity under Gomarus and Alting, and Arabic under Pasor. Here he intended to have remained; but being very desirous of improving himself in the Oriental languages, he went in 1639 to Leyden, to be tutor to the children of Golius, who was the best skilled in those languages of any man in the world. By the instructions of Golius, he improved greatly in the knowledge of Arabic, and also by the assistance of a Turk, who happened to be at Leyden. Besides these advantages, Golius had a fine collection of Arabic books and MSS. from which Hottinger was suffered to copy what he pleased, during the fourteen months he staid at Leyden. In 1641, he was offered, at the recommendation of Golius, the place of chaplain to the ambassador of the States-General to Constantinople; and he would gladly have attended him, as such a journey would have co-operated wonderfully with his grand design of perfecting himself in the Eastern languages: but the magistrates of Zurich did not consent to it: they chose rather to recall him, in order to employ him for the glory and advantage of their public schools. They permitted him first, however, to visit England; and the instant he returned from that country, they appointed him professor of ecclesiastical history; and a year after, in 1643, gave him two professorships, that of catechetical divinity, and that of the Oriental tongues.

He married at twenty-two, and began to publish books at twenty-four. New professorships were bestowed upon him in 1653, and he was admitted into the college of canons. In 1655, the elector Palatine, desirous to restore the credit of his university of Heidelberg, obtained leave of the senate of Zurich for Hottinger to go there, on condition that he should return at the end of three years: but before he set out for that city, he went to Basil, and there took the degree of D. D. He arrived at Heidelberg the same year, and was graciously received in that city. Besides the professorship of divinity of the Old Testament, and the Oriental tongues, he was appointed principal of

[E] Niceron, Hommes Illustres, Tom. VIII.—Bayle's Dict.

the

the Collegium Sapientiæ. He was rector of the university the
year following, and wrote a book concerning the re-union of
the Lutherans and Calvinists; which he did to pleafe the elector,
who was rather zealous in that affair: but party-animofities, and
that itch of difputation fo natural to mankind, rendered his performance ineffectual. Hottinger accompanied this prince to the
electoral diet of Frankfort in 1658, and there had a conference
with Job Ludolf. It is well known, that Ludolf had acquired a vaft knowledge of Ethiopia; and he, in conjunction
with Hottinger, concerted meafures for fending into Africa
fome perfons fkilled in the Oriental tongues, who might make
exact enquiries concerning the ftate of the Chriftian religion in
that part of the world. He was not recalled to Zurich till 1661,
his fuperiors at the elector's earneft requeft having prolonged the
term of years for which they lent him: and he then returned,
honoured by the elector with the title of Ecclefiaftical-coun-
fellor.

Many employments were immediately conferred on him:
among the reft, he was elected prefident of the commiffioners
who were to revife the German tranflation of the Bible. A
civil war breaking out in Switzerland in 1664, he was fent into
Holland on ftate affairs. Many univerfities would willingly have
drawn Hottinger to them, but were not able. That of Leyden
offered him a profefforfhip of divinity in 1667; but, not
obtaining leave of his fuperiors, he refufed it. The Dutch
were not difheartened at this refufal, but infifted that he fhould
be lent them: upon which the magiftrates of Zuric confented,
in complaifance to the ftates of Holland, who had interefted
themfelves in this affair. As he was preparing for this journey,
he unfortunately loft his life, June 5, 1667, in the river which
paffes through Zurich. He went into a boat, with his wife,
three children, his brother-in-law, a friend, and a maid-fervant,
in order to go and let out upon leafe an eftate which he had two
leagues from Zurich. The boat ftriking againft a pier, which
lay under water, overfet: upon which Hottinger, his brother-
in-law, and friend, efcaped by fwimming. But when they looked
upon the women and children, and faw the danger they were
in, they jumped back into the water: the event of which was,
that Hottinger, his friend, and three children loft their lives,
while his wife, his brother-in-law, and fervant-maid were faved.
His wife was the only daughter of Huldric, minifter of Zurich,
a man of very great learning, and brought him feveral children: for befides the three who were drowned with him, and
thofe who died before, he left four fons and two daughters.

He began to be author, as we have obferved, at twenty-four;
and he feems to have been fo pleafed with that character, that
he was afterwards for ever publifhing books. Bayle fays, "is
was

was not very difficult for him to do this, since he was very laborious and blessed with a very happy memory:" but in saying this he seems to imply an insinuation against his parts and judgement. It is neverthelefs surprising, that a man, who had possessed so many academical employments, was interrupted with so many visits, (for every body came to see him, and confulted him as an oracle) and was engaged, as he was, in a correspondence with all the literati of Europe, should have found time to write more than forty volumes, especially when it is considered, that he did not reach fifty years of age. We shall mention some of the most confiderable of his works; and those particularly, as being the most interesting, which relate to Oriental literature. 1. " Exercitationes Anti-Morinianæ, de Pentateucho Samaritano, &c. 1644," 4to. Morin had afferted, in the strongest manner, the authenticity of the Samaritan Pentateuch; which he preferred to the Hebrew text, upon a pretence that this had been corrupted by the Jews; and it was to combat this opinion, that Hottinger wrote these Exercitations. This work, though the first, is, in the judgement of father Simon, one of the best he wrote; and if he had never written any thing more, it is probable that he would have left higher notions of his abilities: for certainly it was no small enterprise for him, so early in life, to attack, on a very delicate and knotty subject, and with supposed success too, one of the most learned men in Europe at that time.

The next works we shall mention relate immediately to Oriental affairs; and may always be of use, although we should confider him as a mere collector. 2. " Thefaurus Philologicus, feu clavis fcripturæ, qua quicquid fere Orientalium, Hebræorum maxime & Arabum, habent monumenta de religione ejufque variis fpeciebus, Judaifmo, Samaritanifmo, Muhammedifmo, Gentilifmo, de theologia & theologis, verbo Dei, &c. breviter & aphoriftice ita referatur & aperitur, ut multiplex inde ad philologiæ & theologiæ ftudiofos fructus redundare poffit, 1649," 4to. There was a fecond edition in 1649, in 4to, " in qua Samaritica, Arabica, Syriaca fuis quæque nativis characteribus exprimuntur." 3. " Hiftoria Orientalis, quæ ex variis Orientalium monumentis collecta agit, primo, de Muhammedifmo, ejufque caufis tum procreantibus tum confervantibus: fecundo, de Saracenifmo, feu religione veterum Arabum: tertio, de Chaldaifmo, feu fuperftitione Nabatæorum, Chaldæorum, Charranæorum: quarto, de ftatu Chriftianorum & Judæorum tempore orti & nati Muhammedanifmi: quinto, de variis inter ipfos Muhammedanos circa religionis dogmata & adminiftrationem fententiis, fchifmatis, & hærefibus excitatis, &c. 1651," 4to. No man was better qualified to write on Oriental affairs than Hottinger, as he was fkilled in moft of the languages which were anciently, as well as at prefent, fpoken in the Eaft:

namely, the Hebrew, Syriac, Chaldee, Arabic, Turkish, Persian, and Coptic; 4. " Promptuarium, five Bibliotheca Orientalis, exhibens catalogum five centurias aliquot tam auctorum, quam librorum Hebraicorum, Syriacorum, Arabicorum, Ægyptiacorum: addita mantissa Bibliothecarum aliquot Europæarum, 1658," 4to. Baillet does not speak very advantageously of this work of Hottinger, whom he accuses of not being very accurate in any of his compositions: and indeed his want of accuracy is a point pretty well agreed on by both Papists and Protestants. 5. " Etymologicon Orientale, five Lexicon Harmonicum Heptaglotton, &c. 1661," 4to. The feven languages contained in this Lexicon are, the Hebrew, Chaldee, Syriac, Arabic, Samaritan, Ethiopic, and Rabbinical.

These are the principal, if not the only works of Hottinger, which are of any ufe: and they are by far more valuable for containing materials of a curious nature, and which were before only acceffible to perfons fkilled in Oriental languages, than for any ingenuity, accuracy, or judgement in the writer. If the reader is particularly defirous of feeing an exact catalogue of the works of this laborious man, he may confult the " Bibliotheca Tigurina;" or the Latin life of Hottinger, publifhed by Heidegger at Zurich, 1667: in either of which places he will find them all drawn up and digefted into regular order. We cannot help repeating, that the number of them is aftonifhing.

HOUBIGANT (CHARLES FRANCIS), a pious and learned tranflator of the Hebrew Scriptures, and commentator on them, was born at Paris in 1686. He was a prieft of the congregation named the oratory; and being, by the misfortune of deafnefs, deprived of the chief comforts of fociety, addicted himfelf tho more earneftly to books, in which he found his conftant confolation. Of a difpofition naturally benevolent, with great firmnefs of foul, goodnefs of temper, and politenefs of manners, he was held in very general eftimation, and received honours and rewards from the pope (Bened. XIV.) and from his countrymen, which he had never thought of foliciting. Though his income was but fmall, he dedicated a part of it to found a fchool near Chantilly; and the purity of his judgement, joined to the ftrength of his memory, enabled him to carry on his literary labours to a very advanced age. Even when his faculties had declined, and were further injured by the accident of a fall, the very fight of a book, that well known confoler of all his cares, reftored him to peace and rationality. He died in 1783, at the advanced age of 98. His works, for which he was no lefs efteemed in foreign countries than in his own, were chiefly thefe: 1. An edition of the Hebrew Bible, with a Latin verfion and notes, publifhed at Paris in 1753, in 4 vols. folio. This is the moft valuable and important work of the author, and contains the Hebrew text
corrected

corrected by the foundest rules of criticism, a Latin version, and useful notes: and prefixed to each book is a very learned preface. Benedict XIV. who justly appreciated the value and difficulty of the work, honoured the author with a medal, and some other marks of approbation; and the clergy of his own country, unsolicited, conferred a pension on him. 2. A Latin translation of the Pfalter, from the Hebrew, 12mo, 1746. 3. Another of the Old Testament at large, in 1753, in 8 vols, 8vo. 4. " Racines Hebraiques, 1732," 8vo. 5. " Examen du Pfautier des Capuchins," 12mo. 6. A French translation of an English work, by one Forbes, entitled, " Thoughts on Natural Religion." 7. Most of the works of Charles Leslie translated, 8vo, Paris, 1770. Father Houbigant is said also to have left several works in manuscript, which, from the excellence of those he published, may be conjectured to be well deserving of the press.

HOVEDEN (ROGER DE), an English historian who flourished in the reign of Henry II. He was born at York, of a good family, and lived beyond the year 1204, but the exact periods of his birth and death are not known. He is said to have had some situation in the family of Henry II. and to have been employed by that monarch in confidential services, such as visiting monasteries. He was by profession a lawyer, but, like other lawyers of that time, in the church, and also a professor of theology at Oxford. After the death of Henry, he applied himself diligently to the writing of history, and composed annals, which he commenced at 731, the period where Bede left off, and continued to the third year of king John. These annals were first published by Saville among the Historici Anglici, in 1595, and reprinted at Frankfort in 1601, folio. They are in two books. Leland says of him [P], " If we consider his diligence, his knowledge of antiquity, and his religious strictness of veracity, he may be considered as having surpassed, not only the rude historians of the preceding ages, but even what could have been expected of himself. If to that fidelity, which is the first quality of a historian, he had joined a little more elegance of Latin style, he might have stood the first among the authors of that class." Vossius says, that he wrote also a history of the Northumbrian kings [Q], and a life of Thomas à Becket: Edward the Third caused a diligent search to be made for the works of Hoveden, when he was endeavouring to ascertain his title to the crown of Scotland. Saville bears the same testimony to his fidelity that we have seen given by Leland.

HOUGH (JOHN), bishop of Worcester, memorable for the noble stand he made when president of Magdalen-college in Oxford, against James II. was born in Middlesex, in 1650. He

[P] De Scriptoribus Britannicis, cap. 203. p. 229.
[Q] De Historicis Latinis, l. ii. cap. 56.

was brought up at Birmingham in Warwickshire, and thence
removed to Magdalen-college, Oxford, in 1669; of which, in
1675, he was elected fellow. Upon the breaking out of the
Popish plot in 1679, his chamber was searched on a suspicion
that he corresponded with one of that religion; but nothing was
discovered against him; and, in 1681, being appointed domestic
chaplain to the duke of Ormond, chancellor of the university,
but then lord lieutenant of Ireland, he attended his patron to
Dublin. No vacancies, as we suppose, of any consequence
happening, he returned the year after, unpreferred, to England;
where, in 1685, he was collated to a prebend in the church of
Worcester [H]. In April, 1687, he was statutably elected president of his college by a majority of the fellows, after they had
rejected a mandamus from James II. in behalf of Anthony Farmer, M. A. of that house; but he was soon removed from his
presidentship by the ecclesiastical commissioners, and Parker
bishop of Oxford put into his place. But when the prince of
Orange declared his intention of coming to England, Magdalen-college was restored to its rights, and Hough to his presidentship [I]. "It is disputable," says a certain writer, "whether he shewed greater courage and constancy, or prudence and
temper, in the management of so important a contest with a
misguided crown; and whether he displayed a greater love of
the liberties of his country, in baffling the instruments of an
illegal ecclesiastical commission, or integrity and conscience in
adhering so firmly to the statutes of his college, and his own
oath, in opposition to all the artifices as well as menaces of an
arbitrary court; in his engaging by his weighty influence the
members of that learned body to act unanimously; and in confirming by his own example, their resolutions to sacrifice their
interest to their duty on that great occasion."

After the Revolution, he was nominated by king William, in
April, 1690, to the bishopric of Oxford [K]; and translated to
the see of Litchfield and Coventry in Aug. 1699. On the death
of Tenison, in 1715, the archbishopric of Canterbury was
offered to him, the acceptance of which he is said to have declined
out of modesty [L]; but, upon the decease of bishop Lloyd,
Hough succeeded him in the see of Worcester, Sept. 1717.
He was a great benefactor wherever he came. When he removed from the see of Oxford to that of Litchfield and Coventry, he did not merely repair, but almost rebuild as well as
adorn the episcopal house at Eccleshall; and, upon his translation to the see of Worcester, he rebuilt so great a part of the
episcopal palace there, and made such improvements in his other

[H] Willis's Account of the Cathe- John Hough, p. 6.
dr.ls, Vol. II, p. 437.   [K] Athen. Oxon.
[I] Some Account of the Life of Dr. [L] Same Account, &c. p. 19.

feat, the caftle of Hartlebury, that he is fuppofed to have expended upon both thefe houfes at leaft 7000l. Thefe fchemes were executed with fo nice a judgement, that he left little to be done by any of his fucceffors towards perfecting either of thofe epifcopal refidences; except the founding of a library at Hartlebury, which bifhop Hurd has with great and laudable liberality accomplifhed. He was not many years under 70, when he entered upon the fee of Worcefter; yet he lived upwards of 26 years bifhop of that place. A little before his death, he wrote a letter to his friend lord Digby, where we find the following remarkable words: " I am weak and forgetful—In other refpects I have eafe to a degree beyond what I durft have thought on, when years began to multiply upon me. I wait contentedly for a deliverance out of this life into a better, in humble confidence, that by the mercy of God, through the merits of his Son, I fhall ftand at the refurrection on his right-hand. And when you, my lord, have ended thofe days which are to come, which I pray may be many and comfortable, as innocently and as exemplary as thofe which are paffed, I doubt not of our meeting in that ftate, where the joys are unfpeakable, and will always endure." He died March 8, 1743, having extended his age to the beginning of his 93d year, and almoft to complete the 53d year of his epifcopate.

HOULIERES (ANTONIETTA DE LA GARDE DES), of all the French ladies who have ftudied poetry, has fucceeded the beft; for her verfes ftill continue to be more read than thofe of any other of her fex. She was born at Paris in 1638, had all the charms of her fex, and wit enough to fhine in the age of Louis XIV. Her tafte for poetry was cultivated by the celebrated poet Henault, who is faid to have inftructed her in all he knew, or imagined he knew. She did her mafter great honour; but the misfortune was, fhe not only imitated him in his poetry, but alfo in his irreligion; for her verfes favour ftrongly of epicureanifm. She compofed in all ways; epigrams, odes, eclogues, tragedies; but fucceeded beft in the idyllium or paftoral, which fome affirm fhe carried to perfection. She died at Paris in 1694, and left a daughter of her own name, who had fome talent for poetry, but inferior to that of her mother. The firft verfes, however, compofed by this lady, bore away the prize at the French academy; which was highly to her honour, if it be true, as is reported, that Fontenelle wrote at the fame time, and upon the fame fubject. She was a member of the academy of the Ricovrati of Padua, as was her mother, who was alfo of that of Arles. She died at Paris in 1718. The works of thefe two ladies were collectively publifhed in 1747, in 2 vols. 12mo. Several maxims of the elder of thefe ladies are much cited by French writers; as, that on gaming, " On commence par être dupe, on finit par être fripon." People begin dupes, and end rogues And that on self-love: " Nul n'eſt content de ſa fortune, ni mécontent de ſon eſprit." No one is ſatisfied with his fortune, or diſſatisfied with his talents.

HOUTEVILLE (CLAUDE FRANCIS), a native of Paris, was eighteen years a member of the congregation called the Oratory, and afterwards ſecretary to cardinal Dubois, by whom he was much eſteemed. He was appointed, in 1742, 'perpetual ſecretary to the French academy, but did not long enjoy his preferment, for he died the ſame year, being about fifty-four years old. He publiſhed a work, entitled, " La verite de la Religion Chrétienne prouvée par les faits," the latter editions of which are far ſuperior to the firſt. There are few important objections which have been brought againſt Chriſtianity, even ſince his time, to which he has not furniſhed a ſound reply; but he had written in an affected and epigrammatic ſtyle, which being juſtly expoſed by the abbé des Fontaines, he went over his work with great care, and removed moſt of the objections.

HOWARD (HENRY), earl of Surrey, was the eldeſt ſon of Thomas duke of Norfolk [M]. We cannot preciſely fix the time of his birth, but in all probability it was about 1520, as he was educated with Henry Fitzroy, a natural ſon of Henry VIII. who was born about that time. This favourite ſon of the king's was created earl of Richmond; and, as Leland informs us, had a ſpirit turned to martial affairs, was maſter of the languages, and diſplayed an excellent taſte in polite literature; all which talents were undoubtedly improved by the mutual intercourſe and emulation between him and his noble companion. The place of their ſtudies and diverſions at home, was Windforcaſtle; which is the ſcene of many of Howard's poems on his miſtreſs Geraldine, the moſt celebrated beauty of her time. They went together to Paris, and jointly purſued thoſe ſtudies and recreations in France, which they firſt cultivated in England. The duke of Richmond died ſoon after their return, about the year 1536.

After the death of his friend, which he did not ſoon forget, having loſt in him not only a congenial ſoul but a brother, (as Richmond had juſt been united to his ſiſter lady Mary Howard) this young nobleman ſeems to have turned his thoughts chiefly to the buſineſs of the field, where he diſtinguiſhed himſelf by a ſuperior courage and conduct. He was preſent in almoſt all the great actions of Henry's reign, and his name is renowned in its tournaments. It is not known at what period his travels took place, but he travelled like a hero of romance, proclaiming the charms of his miſtreſs Geraldine, and ſupporting them with the weapons

[M] Walpole's Catalogue of noble authors.

of

of knight-errantry. History has not recorded the real name of the fair Geraldine, but it has been very happily conjectured, by the prefent earl of Orford, that she was the lady Elizabeth Fitzgerald, second daughter of the earl of Kildare; so that her poetical title very closely reprefents her real name. He commanded at the famous battle of Flodden-field, in which he gave such extraordinary proofs of his gallantry, that he was foon after created earl of Surrey. In an expedition of his own, he was unfortunate. Endeavouring to cut off a convoy to Boulogne, he was defeated; a difgrace which he foon repaired, by gaining many advantages over the enemy. To this fingle inftance of ill fuccefs, fome afcribe his lofs of the king's favour. Others, with more shew of probability, affign his difgrace to the king's jealoufy of his very brilliant character, and a fufpicion of his defigning to wed the princefs Mary, and thereby afpiring to the crown. The earl of Surrey, however, upon a very frivolous pretence of having been guilty of treafon, was, after all his fervices to his prince and country, left to the trial of a common jury; who, in compliance with the king's paffions, bringing him in guilty, he was foon after beheaded on Tower-hill. The accufation was only that he had faid, " the king was ill-adv   ;" and that he had quartered certain royal arms with his own; which be proved, by the teftimony of the heralds, to belong to his family.

He was the firft of the Englifh nobility who had any familiar intercourfe with the Mufes; and far furpaffed his contemporaries in purity of language, and harmony of numbers. Puttenham, in his Art of Englifh Poetry, fays, " That fir Thomas Wyat, and Henry earl of Surrey, were the two chieftains, who, having travelled into Italy, and there tafted the fweet and ftately mrafures and ftyle of the Italian poetry, greatly polifhed our rude and homely manner of vulgar poetry, from what it had been before: and therefore may be juftly called, the reformers of our Englifh poetry and ftyle." There has hardly been a poet of note fince this nobleman's time, who hath not paid fome refpect to his memory. Sir Philip Sidney, Churchyard, Drayton, Dryden, Fenton, Pope, and many other authors, have given their teftimonies to his merits; but it will be fufficient to quote a few beautiful lines from Pope's " Windfor Foreft," where the poet artfully applies the praifes of Surrey to lord Lanfdown.

" Here noble Surrey felt the facred rage,
Surrey, the Granville of a former age.
Matchlefs his pen, victorious was his lance,
Bold in the lifts, and graceful in the dance.
In the fame fhades the Cupids tuned his lyre,
To the fame notes of love and foft defire:
Fair Geraldine, bright object of his vow,
Then fill'd the groves, as heav'nly Mira now."

His

His poems, together with some others of his famous contemporaries, were published in one vol. 8vo, London, 1717. They have been republished lately in the general collection of the *British Poets*, printed under the care of Dr. Anderson at Edinburgh; with the exception of his two books of the Æneid, the second and fourth, wherein he gave the first specimen of English blank verse. These are so very scarce, that they could not be procured for that edition; but will soon be republished, with his other poems, under the direction of a very eminent critic in English poetry. The character of Surrey, as drawn by Mr. Warton, in his history of English poetry, must not be omitted. " In the Sonnets of Surrey," says that classical and able critic, " we are surprised to find nothing of that metaphysical cast, which marks the Italian poets, his supposed masters, especially Petrarch. Surrey's sentiments are for the most part natural and unaffected; arising from his own feelings, and dictated by the present circumstances. His poetry is alike unembarrassed by learned allusions, or elaborate conceits. If he copies Petrarch, it is in Petrarch's best manner, where he descends from his Platonic abstractions, his refinements of passion, his exaggerated compliments, and his play up opposite sentiments, into a track of tenderness, simplicity, and nature. Surrey, for his justness of thought, correctness of style, and purity of expression, may justly be pronounced the first English classical poet. He unquestionably is the first polite writer of love-verses in our language." It may be added that, as the inventor of blank verse, he bestowed a present of inestimable value upon his country. He gave the enchanted spear with which Milton was enabled to unhorse the epic poets of all countries.

HOWARD (Sir ROBERT), an English writer of some abilities and learning, was a younger son of Thomas earl of Berkshire, and educated at Magdalen-college in Oxford [N]. During the civil war, he suffered with his family, who adhered to Charles I. but at the Restoration was made a knight, and chosen for Stockbridge in Hampshire, to serve in the parliament which began in May, 1661. He was afterwards made auditor of the exchequer, and was reckoned a creature of Charles II. whom the monarch advanced on account of his faithful services, in cajoling the parliament for money. In 1679, he was chosen to serve in parliament for Castle-Rising in Norfolk: and re-elected for the same place in 1688. He was a strong advocate for the Revolution, and became so fiery and passionate an abhorrer of the nonjurors, that he disclaimed all manner of conversation and intercourse with persons of that description. His obstinacy and pride procured him many enemies, and among them the duke

[F] Athen. Oxon.

of

of Buckingham; who intended to have exposed him under the name of Bilboa in the "Rehearsal," but afterwards altered his resolution, and levelled his ridicule at a much greater name, under that of Bayes. He was so extremely positive, and so sure of being in the right upon every subject, that Shadwell the poet, though a man of the same principles, could not help ridiculing him in his comedy of the Sullen Lovers, under the character of sir Positive At-all. In the same play there is a lady Vaine, a courtezan, which the wits then understood to be the mistress of sir Robert; whom he afterwards married. He published, 1. Poems and plays. 2. "The History of the Reigns of Edward and Richard II. with Reflections and Characters of their chief Ministers and Favourites; also a Comparison of these Princes with Edward I. and III. 1690," 8vo. 3. "A letter to Mr. Samuel Johnson, occasioned by a scurrilous pamphlet, entitled, Animadversions on Mr. Johnson's Answer to Jovian, 1692," 8vo. 4. "The History of Religion, 1694," 8vo. 5. "The fourth book of Virgil translated, 1660," 8vo. 6. "Statius's Achilleis translated, 1660," 8vo.

There was an Edward Howard, esq; likewise, a descendant of the same family, who exposed himself to the severity of our satirists, by writing bad plays.

HOWARD (JOHN), the indefatigable friend of the poor and unfortunate, was born at Hackney, in the year 1726. His father, who kept a carpet warehouse in Long-lane, Smithfield, dying while he was very young, left him to the care of guardians, by whom he was apprenticed to a wholesale grocer in the city of London [o]. His constitution appearing too weak for attention to trade, and his father having left him, and an only sister, in circumstances which placed them above the necessity of pursuing it, he bought out the remainder of his indentures before the time, and took a tour in France and Italy. On his return, he lodged at the house of a Mrs. Lardeau, a widow, in Stoke-Newington, where he was so carefully attended by the lady, that though she was many years older than himself, he formed an attachment to her, and in 1752 made her his wife. She was possessed of a small fortune, which he generously presented to her sister. She lived, however, only three years after their union, and he was a sincere mourner for her loss. About this time he became a fellow of the Royal Society; and, in 1756, being desirous to view the state of Lisbon after the dreadful earthquake, he embarked for that city. In this voyage, the Hanover frigate, in which he sailed, was taken by a French privateer, and the inconveniences which he suffered during his subsequent confinement in France, are supposed to have awakened his sympathies with

[o] Mr. Newnham, grandfather to alderman Newnham.

peculiar

peculiar ſtrength in favour of priſoners, and to have given riſe
to his plans for rendering priſons leſs pernicious to health. It is
ſuppoſed, that after his releaſe, he made the tour of Italy. On
his return, he fixed himſelf at Brokenhurſt, a retired and pleaſant villa near Lymington, in the New Foreſt. Mr. Howard
married a ſecond time in 1758; but this lady, a daughter of a
Mr. Leeds, of Cro ton in Cambridgeſhire, died in child-bed
of her only child, a ſon, in the year 1765. Either before, or
ſoon after the death of his ſecond wife, he left Lymington, and
purchaſed an eſtate at Cardington, near Bedford, adjoining to
that of his relation Mr. Whitbread. Here he much conciliated
the poor by giving them employment, building them cottages,
and other acts of benevolence; and regularly attended the congregations of diſſenters at Bedford, being of that perſuaſion.
His time was alſo a good deal occupied by the education of his
only ſon, a taſk for which he is ſaid to have been little qualified.
With all his benevo'ence of heart, he is aſſerted to have been diſpoſed to a rigid ſeverity of diſcipline, ariſing probably from a
very ſtrict ſenſe of rectitude, but not well calculated to form a
tender mind to advantage. In 1773, he ſerved the office of
ſheriff, which as he has ſaid himſelf, "brought the diſtreſs of
priſoners more immediately under his notice," and led to his
benevolent deſign of viſiting the gaols and other places of confinement throughout England, for the ſake of procuring alleviation
to the miſeries of the ſufferers. In 1774, truſting to his intereſt
among the ſectaries at Bedford, he offered himſelf as a candidate
for that borough, but was not returned; and endeavouring to
gain his ſeat by petition, was unſucceſsful. He was, however,
in the ſame year, examined before the houſe of commons, on
the ſubject of the priſons, and received the thanks of the houſe
for his attention to them. Thus encouraged, he completed his
inſpection of the Britiſh priſons, and extended his views even to
foreign countries. He travelled with this deſign, three times
through France, four through Germany, five through Holland,
twice through Italy, once in Spain and Portugal, and once alſo
through the northern ſtates, and Turkey. Theſe excurſions were
taken between the years 1775 and 1787. In the mean time,
his ſiſter died, and left him a conſiderable property, which he
regarded as the gift of Providence to promote his humane deſigns, and applied accordingly. He publiſhed alſo in 1777,
"The State of the Priſons in England and Wales, with preliminary Obſervations, and an Account of ſome Foreign Priſons,"
dedicated to the Houſe of Commons; in 4to. In 1780, he
publiſhed an appendix to this book, with the narrative of his
travels in Italy; and in 1784, republiſhed it, extending his account to many other countries. About this time, his benevolence had ſo much attracted the public attention, that a large
ſubſcription

fubfcription was made for the purpofe of erecting a ftatue to his
honour; but he was too modeft and fincere to accept of fuch a
tribute, and wrote himfelf to the fubfcribers to put a ftop to it.
" Have I not one friend in England," he faid, when he firft
heard of the defign, " that would put a ftop to fuch a proceeding?" In 1789, he publifhed " An Account of the principal
Lazarettos in Europe, with various Papers relative to the Plague,
together with further Obfervations on fome foreign Prifons and
Hofpitals; and additional remarks on the prefent State of thofe
in Great Britain and Ireland." He had publifhed alfo, in 1780,
a tranflation of a French account of the Baftile; and, in 1789,
the duke of Tufcany's new code of civil law, with an Englifh
tranflation.

In his book on Lazarettos, he had announced his intention of
revifiting Ruffia, Turkey, and fome other countries, and extending his tour in the Eaft. " I am not infenfible," fays he, " of
the dangers that muft attend fuch a journey. Trufting, however, in the protection of that kind Providence which has hitherto preferved me, I calmly and cheerfully commit myfelf to
the difpofal of unerring wifdom. Should it pleafe God to cut
off my life in the profecution of this defign, let not my conduct be uncandidly imputed to rafhnefs or enthufiafm, but to a
ferious, deliberate conviction, that I am purfuing the path of
duty; and to a fincere defire of being made an inftrument of
more extenfive ufefulnefs to my fellow-creatures, than could be
expected in the narrower circle of a retired life." He did actually fall a facrifice to this defign; for in vifiting a fick patient
at Cherfon, who had a malignant epidemic fever, he caught the
diftemper, and died, Jan. 20, 1790.

Mr. Howard was, in his own habits of life, rigidly temperate,
and even abftemious; fubfifting entirely, at one time, on pota-
toes; at another, chiefly on tea and bread and butter; of courfe,
not mixing in convivial fociety, nor accepting invitations to
public repafts. His labours have certainly had the admirable
effect of drawing the attention of this country to the regulation
of public prifons. In many places his improvements have been
adopted, and perhaps in all our gaols fome advantage has been
derived from them. We may hope that thefe plans will terminate in fuch general regulations, as will make judicial confinement, inftead of the means of confirming and increafing depravity, (as it has been too generally) the fuccefsful inftrument of
amendment in morality, and acquiring habits of induftry.
While the few criminals, and probably very few, who may be
too depraved for amendment, will be compelled to be beneficial
to the community by their labour; and, being advantageoufly
fituated in point of health, may fuffer nothing more than that
reftraint which is neceffary for the fake of fociety, and that exertion

ertion which they ought never to have abandoned. Confidered as the firft mover of thefe important plans, Howard will always be honoured with the gratitude of his country: and his monument, lately erected in St. Paul's cathedral, is a proof that this gratitude is not inert. The monument is at the fame time, a noble proof of the fkill and genius of the artift, Mr. Bacon, and reprefents Mr. Howard in a Roman drefs, with a look and attitude expreffive of benevolence and activity, holding in one hand a fcroll of plans for the improvement of prifons, hofpitals, &c. and in the other a key; while he is trampling on chains and fetters. The epitaph is too long to be inferted, and contains, indeed, a fketch of his life; but concludes in words which we alfo heartily adopt: " He trod an open, but unfrequented path, to immortality, in the ardent and unremitted exercife of Chriftian charity: may this tribute to his fame excite an emulation of his truly glorious atchievements!"

HOWE (JOHN, efq;) was the younger brother of fir Scroop Howe, of a good family in Nottinghamfhire [P]. In the convention-parliament, which met at Weftminfter, Jan. 22, 1688-9, he ferved for Cirencefter, and was conftantly chofen for that borough, or as a knight of the fhire for the county of Gloucefter, in the three laft parliaments of king William, and in the three firft of queen Anne. In 1696, he was a ftrenuous advocate for fir John Fenwick; and his pleading in behalf of that unfortunate gentleman, fhews his extenfive knowledge of the laws, and averfion to unconftitutional meafures. In 1699, when the army was reduced, it was principally in confideration of Mr. Howe's remonftrances, that the houfe of commons agreed to allow half-pay to the difbanded officers; and when the partition-treaty was afterwards under the confideration of that houfe, he expreffed his fentiments of it in fuch terms, that king William declared, that if it were not for the difparity of their rank, he would demand fatisfaction with the fword. At the acceffion of queen Anne, he was fworn of of her privy-council, April 21, 1702; and, on June 7 following, conftituted vice-admiral of the county of Gloucefter. Before the end of that year, Jan. 4, 1702-3, he was conftituted paymafter-general of her majefty's guards and garrifons. " He feemed to be pleafed with, and joined in the Revolution, and was made vice-chamberlain to queen Mary; but having afked a grant, which was refufed him, and given to lord Portland, he fell from the court, and was all that reign the moft violent and open antagonift king William had in the houfe. A great enemy to foreigners fettling in England; moft claufes in acts againft them being brought in by him. He is indefatigable in

[o] Nichols's Select Collection of Poems, Vol. I. p. 209. Vol. VIII. p. 285.

whatever

HOWELL.

269

whatever he undertakes; witnefs the old Eaft-India company, whofe caufe he maintained till he fixed it upon as fure a foot as the new; even when they thought themfelves paft recovery. He lives up to what his vifible eftate can afford; yet purchafes, inftead of running in debt. He is endued with good natural parts, attended with an unaccountable boldnefs; daring to fay what he pleafes, and will be heard out; fo that he paffeth with fome for the fhrew of the houfe. On the queen's acceffion to the throne, he was made a privy-counfellor, and paymafter of the guards and garrifons. He is a tall, thin, pale-faced man, with a very wild look; brave in his perfon, bold in expreffing himfelf, a violent enemy, a fure friend, and feems to be always in a hurry. Near fifty years old." Such is the character given of this gentleman by Macky, in 1703. A new privy-council being fettled, May 10, 1708, according to act of parliament, relating to the union of the two kingdoms, he was, among the other great officers, fworn into it. He continued paymafter of the guards and garrifons till after the acceffion of George I. who appointed Mr. Walpole to fucceed him, in Sept. 23, 1714; the privy-council being alfo diffolved, and a new one appointed to meet on Oct. 1 following, he was left out of the lift. Retiring to his feat at Stowell in Gloucefterfhire, he died there in 1721, and was buried in the chancel of the church of Stowell.

Mr. Howe was author of " A panegyric on King William," and of feveral fongs and little poems; and is introduced in Swift's celebrated ballad, " On the Game of Traffic." He married Mary, daughter and co-heir of Humphrey Bafkerville, of Pantryllos in Herefordfhire, efq; widow of fir Edward Morgan, of Laternam in Monmouthfhire, bart. by whom he was father to the firft lord Chedworth.

HOWELL. (JAMES), an Englifh writer [P], was the fon of Thomas Howell, minifter of Abernant in Caermarthenfhire, and born about 1596. He was fent to the free-fchool at Hereford; and entered of Jefus-college, Oxford, in 1610. His elder brother Thomas Howell was already a fellow of that fociety, afterwards king's chaplain, and was nominated in 1644 to the fee of Briftol. James Howell, having taken the degree of B. A. in 1613, left college, and removed to London; for being, fays Wood, " a pure cadet, a true Cofmopolite, not born to land, leafe, houfe, or office, he had his fortune to make; and being withal not fo much inclined to a fedentary, as an active life, this fituation pleafed him beft, as moft likely to anfwer his views." The firft employment he obtained was that of fteward to a glafs-houfe in Broad-ftreet, which was procured for him by fir Robert

[P] Athen. Oxon.

Manfel,

Manfel, who was principally concerned in it. The proprietors of this work, intent upon improving the manufactory, came to a refolution to fend an agent abroad, who fhould procure the beft materials and workmen ; and they made choice of Howell for this purpofe, who fetting off in 1619, vifited feveral of the principal places in Holland, Flanders, France, Spain, and Italy. Dec. 1621, he returned to London; having executed the purpofe of his miffion very well, and particularly having acquired a mafterly knowledge in the modern languages. "Thank God," fays he, "I have this fruit of my foreign travels, that I can pray unto him every day of the week in a feparate language, and upon Sunday in feven [q]."

Soon after his return, he quitted his ftewardfhip of the glafshoufe ; and having experienced the pleafures of travelling, laid his plan for more employments of the fame kind. In 1622, he was fent into Spain, to recover a rich Englifh fhip, feized by the viceroy of Sardinia for his mafter's ufe, on pretence of its having prohibited goods on board. In 1623, during his abfence abroad, he was chofen fellow of Jefus-college in Oxford, upon the new foundation of fir Eubule Theloal : for he had taken unremitting care to cultivate his intereft in that fociety. He tells fir Eubule, in his letter of thanks to him, that he "will referve his fellowfhip, and lay it by as a good warm garment againft rough weather, if any fall on him :" in which he was followed by Prior, who alledged the fame reafon for keeping his fellowfhip at St. John's-college in Cambridge. Howell returned to England in 1624 ; and was foon after appointed fecretary to lord Scrope, afterwards earl of Sunderland, who was made lord-prefident of the North. This office carried him to York ; and while he refided there, the corporation of Richmond, without any application from himfelf, and againft feveral competitors, chofe him one of their reprefentatives, in the parliament which began in 1627. In 1632, he went as fecretary to Robert earl of Leicefter, ambaffador extraordinary from Charles I. to the court of Denmark, on occafion of the death of the queen dowager, who was grandmother to that king: and there gave proofs of his oratorical talents, in feveral Latin fpeeches before the king of Denmark, and other princes of Germany. After his return to England, his fortune proved more unftable than ever: for, except an inconfiderable affair, on which he was difpatched to Orleans in France by fecretary Windebank in 1635, he was for fome years deftitute of any employment. At laft, in 1639, he went to Ireland, and was well received by lord Strafford, the lord-lieutenant, who had before made him very warm profeffions of kindnefs. The lieutenant employed him as an affiftant-clerk upon fome bufinefs to Edinburgh,

[q] Howell's Letters, Vol. I.

and afterwards to London; but his rising hopes were ruined by the unhappy fate which soon overtook the earl of Strafford. In 1640, he was dispatched upon some business to France; and the same year was made clerk of the council, which post was the most fixed in point of residence, and the most permanent in its nature, that he had ever enjoyed. But his royal master, having departed from his palace at Whitehall, was not able to secure his continuance long in it: for, in 1643, being come to London upon some business of his own, all his papers were seized by a committee of the parliament, his person secured, and, in a few days after, he was committed close prisoner to the Fleet. This at least he himself makes the cause of his imprisonment: but Wood insinuates, that he was thrown into prison, for debts contracted through his own extravagance; and indeed some of his own letters give room enough to suspect it. But whatever was the cause, he bore it cheerfully; among many proofs of which the following epitaph upon himself is one.

" Here lies entomb'd a walking thing,
Whom Fortune with the states did fling
Between these walls. Why? ask not that:
That blind whore doth she knows not what."

He had now no resource except his pen: and he applied himself therefore wholly to write and translate books. This work he managed so well, that it brought him a comfortable subsistence, during his long stay in that prison, where he was confined till some time after the king's death; and as he got nothing by his discharge but his liberty, he was obliged to continue the same employment afterwards. His numerous productions, written rather out of necessity than choice, shew, however, a readiness of wit, and an exuberant fancy. Though always a firm Royalist, he does not seem to have approved the measures pursued by Buckingham, Laud, and Strafford; and was far from approving the imposition of ship-money, and the policy of creating and multiplying monopolies. Yet the unbridled insolence and outrages of the Republican governors so much disgusted him, that he was not displeased when Oliver assumed the sovereign power under the title of protector; and in this light he addressed him on that occasion in a speech, which shall be mentioned presently. His behaviour under Cromwell's tyranny was no more than prudential, and was so considered; for Charles II. at his restoration, thought him worthy of his notice and favour: and his former post under the council being otherwise disposed of, a new place was created, by the grant of which he became the first historiographer royal in England. He died Nov. 1666, and was interred in the Temple-church, London, where a monument was erected to his memory, with the following

ing inscription; which was taken down when the church was repaired in 1683, and has not since been replaced. " Jacobus Howell Cambro-Britannus, Regius Historiographus in Anglia primus, qui post varios peregrinationes tandem naturæ cursum peregit, satur annorum & famæ; domi forisque huc usque erraticus, hic fixus 1666."

His works were numerous. 1. " Dodona's Grove, or, The Vocal Forest, 1640." 2. " The Vote:" a poem, presented to the king on New-year's day, 1641. 3. " Instructions for forraine Travell : shewing by what Course, and in what compass of Time, one may take an exact Survey of the Kingdomes and States of Christendome, and arrive to the practical Knowledge of the Languages to good Purpose, 1642." Dedicated to Prince Charles. Reprinted in 1650, with additions. These works were published before he was thrown into prison. 4. " Casual Discourses and Interlocutions between Patricius and Peregrin, touching the Distractions of the Times." Written soon after the Battle of Edgehill, and the first book published in Vindication of the king. 5. " Mercurius Hibernicus: or, a Discourse of the Irish Massacre, 1644." 6. " Parables reflecting on the Times, 1644." 7. " England's Tears for the present Wars, &c. 1644." 8. " Preheminence and Pedigree of Parliaments, 1644." 9. " Vindication of some Passages reflecting upon him in Mr. Prynne's Book, called The Popish Royal Favourite, 1644." 10. " Epistolæ Ho-Elianæ :" " Familiar Letters Domestic and Foreign, divided into sundry Sections, partly historical, partly political, partly philosophical, 1645." Another collection was published in 1647 ; and both these, with the addition of a third, came out in 1650. A few additional letters appeared in some subsequent editions: of which the eleventh was printed in 8vo, 1754. It is not, indeed, to be wondered, that these letters have run through so many editions; since they not only contain much of the history of his own times, but are also interspersed with many pleasant stories properly introduced and applied. It cannot be denied, that he has given way frequently to very low witticisms, the most unpardonable instance of which is, his remark upon Charles the First's death, where he says, " I will attend with patience how England will thrive, now that she is let blood in the Basilical vein, and cured as they say of the king's evil:" but it may be said, that he was led into this manner by the humour of the times. Wood relates, it does not appear on what authority, that " many of these letters were never written before the author of them was in the Fleet, as he pretends they were, but only feigned and purposely published to gain money to relieve his necessities:" be this as it will, he allows that they " give a tolerable history of those times," which if true is very sufficient to recommend them.

1

These

These letters are almost the only work of Howell that is now regarded: the rest are very obscure. But we shall proceed in the account. 11. "A Nocturnal Progress: or, a Perambulation of most Countries in Christendom, performed in one Night by strength of Imagination, 1645." 12. "Lustra Ludovici: or the Life of Lewis XIII. King of France, &c." 13. "An Account of the deplorable State of England in 1647, &c." 1647. 14. "Letter to Lord Pembroke concerning the Times, and the sad Condition both of Prince and People, 1647." 15. "Bella Scot-Anglica: A Brief of all the Battles betwixt England and Scotland, from all Times to this present, 1648." 16. "Corollary declaring the Causes, whereby the Scot is come of late Years to be so heightened in his Spirits." 17. "The Instruments of a King: or, a short Discourse of the Sword, Crown, and Sceptre, &c. 1648." 18. "Winter-Dream, 1649." 19. "A Trance, or News from Hell, brought first to Town by Mercurius Acheronticus, 1649." 20. "Inquisition after Blood, &c. 1649." 21. "Vision, or Dialogue between Soul and Body, 1651." 22. "Survey of the Signory of Venice, &c. 1651." 23. "Some sober Inspections made into the Carriage and Consults of the late long Parliament, whereby occasion is taken to speak of Parliaments in former Times, and of Magna Charta: with some Reflections upon Government in general, 1653." Dedicated to Oliver lord protector, whom he compares to Charles Martel, and compliments in language much beyond the truth, and the sentiments of his own heart. The fourth edition of this book came out in 1660, with several additions. 24. "History of the Wars of Jerusalem epitomised." 25. "Ah, Ha; Tumulus, Thalamus: two Counter-Poems: the first an Elegy on Edward late Earl of Dorset: the second an Epithalamium to the Marquis of Dorchester, 1653." 26. "The German Diet: or Balance of Europe, &c. 1653," folio. The author's portrait at whole length is set before the title. 27. "Parthenopeia: or, the History of Naples, &c. 1654." 28. "Londinopolis, 1657." A short discourse, says Wood, mostly taken from Stowe's "Survey of London." 29. "Discourse of the Empire, and of the Election of the King of the Romans, 1658." 30. "Lexicon Tetraglotton: An English-French-Italian-Spanish Dictionary, &c. 1660." 31. "A Cordial for the Cavaliers, 1661." Answered immediately by sir Roger L'Estrange, in a book entitled, "A Caveat for the Cavaliers:" replied to by Mr. Howell, in the next article. 32. "Some sober Inspections made into those Ingredients that went to the Composition of a late Cordial for the Cavaliers, 1661." 33. "A French Grammar, &c." 34. "The Parley of Beasts, &c. 1660." 35. "The second Part of casual Discourses and Interlocutions between Patricius and Peregrin, &c. 1661." 36. "Twelve Treatises

of the late Revolutions, 1661." 37. " New Englifh Grammar
for Foreigners to learn Englifh; with a Grammar for the Spanifh and Caftilian Tongue, with fpecial Remarks on the Portu-
guefe Dialect, for the fervice of her Majefty, 1662." 38.
" Difcourfe concerning the Precedency of Kings, 1663." 39.
" Poems:" collected and publifhed by ferjeant-major P. F. that
is, Payne Fifher, who had been poet-laureat to Cromwell. The
editor tells us, that his author Howell " may be called the
prodigy of the age for the variety of his volumes: for there hath
paffed the prefs above forty of his works on various fubjects,
ufeful not only to the prefent times, but to all pofterity. And
it is to be obferved," fays he, " that in all his writings there is
fomething ftill new, either in the matter, method, or fancy, and
in an untrodden tract." He publifhed next, 40. " A Treatife
concerning Ambaffadors, 1664." 41. " Concerning the furrender
of Dunkirk, that it was done upon good Grounds, 1664."
Befides thefe original works, he tranflated feveral from foreign
languages; as, 1. " St. Paul's late Progrefs upon Earth about a
Divorce betwixt Chrift and the Church of Rome, by reafon of
her Diffolutenefs and Exceffes, &c. 1644." The author of
this book publifhed it about 1642, and was forced to fly from
Rome on that account. He withdrew in the company, and
under the conduct of one, who pretended friendfhip for him;
but who betrayed him at Avignon, where he was firft hanged and
then burnt. 2. " A Venetian Looking-glafs: or, a Letter
written very lately from London to Cardinal Barberini at Rome,
by a Venetian Clariffimo, touching the prefent Diftempers in
England, 1648." 3. " An exact Hiftory of the late Revolutions in Naples, &c. 1650." 4. " A Letter of Advice from
the prime Statefmen of Florence, how England may come to
herfelf again, 1659." All thefe were tranflated from the Italian.
He tranflated alfo from the French, " The Nuptials of Peleus
and Thetis, &c. 1654;" and from the Spanifh, " The Procefs
and Pleadings in the Court of Spain, upon the Death of Anthony
Afcham, Refident for the Parliament of England, &c. 1651."
Laftly, he publifhed, in 1649, " The late King's Declaration in Latin, French, and Englifh:" and in 1751, " Cottoni
Pofthuma, or divers choice Pieces of that renowned Antiquary
Sir Robert Cotton, Knight and Baronet," in 8vo.
HOZIER (Pierre d'), a man famous in his time, and even
celebrated by Boileau, for his fkill in genealogies, was born of a
good family at Marfeilles, in 1592, and bred to military fervice;
but very early applied himfelf with great zeal to that ftudy for
which he became fo famous. By his probity as well as talents,
he obtained the confidence of Louis XIII. and XIV. and enjoyed the benefit of their favour in feveral lucrative and honourable pofts. After rifing through feveral appointments, fuch
as

as judge of arms, in 1641, and certifier of titles in 1643, he was admitted in 1654 to the council of state. He died at Paris in 1660. Hozier was author of a history of Britany, in folio, and of many genealogical tables.

HUARTE (JOHN), a native of French Navarre, though he is usually supposed to be a Spaniard, lived in the 17th century. He gained great fame by a work which he published in Spanish, upon a very curious and interesting subject. The title of it runs thus: " Examen de ingenios para las Sciencias, &c. or, an examination of such geniuses, as are fit for acquiring the sciences, and were born such : wherein, by marvellous and useful secrets, drawn from true philosophy both natural and divine, are shewn the gifts and different abilities found in men, and for what kind of study the genius of every man is adapted in such a manner, that whoever shall read this book attentively, will discover the properties of his own genius, and be able to make choice of that science in which he will make the greatest improvement." This book has been translated into several languages, and gone through several impressions. It was translated into Italian, and published at Venice in 1582; at least the dedication of that translation bears this date. It was translated into French by Gabriel Chappuis in 1580; but there is a better French version than this by Savinien d'Alquie, printed at Amsterdam in 1672. He has taken in the additions inserted by Huarte in the last edition of his book, which are considerable both in quality and quantity. It has been translated also into Latin, and lastly, into English. This very admired author has been highly extolled for acuteness and subtlety, and undoubtedly had a great share of these qualities: Bayle however thinks, that " it would not be prudent for any person to rely either on his maxims or authorities; for," says he, " he is not to be trusted on either of these heads, and his hypotheses are frequently chimerical, especially when he pretends to teach the formalities to be observed by those who would beget children of a virtuous turn of mind. There are, in this part of his book, a great many particulars repugnant to modesty: and he deserves censure for publishing, as a genuine and authentic piece, a pretended letter of Lentulus the proconsul from Jerusalem to the Roman senate, wherein a portrait is given of Jesus Christ, a description of his shape and stature, the colour of his hair, the qualities of his beard, &c."

HUBER (ULRIC), a native of Dockum in the Dutch territories, was famous as a lawyer, an historian, and a philologer. He was born in 1635; and became professor at Francker, and afterwards at Lewarde. He published, 1. in 1662, Seven Dissertations, " De genuina ætate Assyriorum, et regno Medorum." Also, 2. A treatise, " De Jure civitatis." 3. " Jurisprudentia Frisiaca." 4. " Specimen Philosophiæ civilis." 5. " Institu-

tiones

tiones Hiftoriæ civilis:" and feveral other works. From 1688, he was engaged in violent controverfy with Perizonius, on fome points of jurifprudence, and on his work laft-mentioned, the " Inftitutiones hiftoriæ civilis." He died in 1694. The dif-pute with Perizonius was carried on with fufficient fcurrility on both fides.

HUBER (ZACHARIAS), fon of the former, born at Fra-neker, in 1669; and afterwards advanced to the fame pro-feſſorſhips. He publiſhed in 1690, 1. A Differtation, " De vero fenfu atque interpretatione, legis IX. D. de lege Pompeia, de parricidis," Francker, 4to. 2. Alfo, " Differtationum libri tres, quibus explicantur &c. felecta juris publici, facri, pri-vatique capita." Francker, 1702. He died [R] in 1732.

HUBER (MARY), a voluminous female author, born at Ge-neva, in 1710, died at Lyons in 1753. Her principal works are thefe that follow. 1. " Le monde fou, préferé au monde Sage," 1731—1744, in 8vo. 2. " Le Syftême des Theologiens anciens et modernes, fur l'etat des ames féparées des corps," 12mo, 1731—1739. 3. " Suite du même ouvrage, fervant de réponfe a M. Ruchat," 12mo, 1731—1739. 4. " Réduction du Spec-tateur Anglois." This was an abridgement of the Spectator, and appeared in 1753, in fix parts, duodecimo; but did not fucceed. 5. " Lettres fur la Religion effentielle à l'homme," 1739—1754. Mary Huber was a Proteftant, and this latter work in particular, was attacked by the divines of the Romish communion. She had wit and knowledge, but was fumetimes obfcure, from wanting the talent to develope her own ideas.

HUBERT (MATTHEW), a celebrated French preacher, con-temporary with Bourdaloue, whom, indeed, he could not rival, but was fkilful enough to pleafe; being efteemed by him one of the firft preachers of the time. He was a prieft of the congre-gation of the Oratory, and no lefs remarkable for his gentle piety, and profound humility than for his eloquence. He excelled confequently rather in the touching ftyle of the facred, than the vivid manner of the temporal orator. He was ufed to fay, that his brother Maffillon was fit to preach to the mafters, and himfelf to the fervants. He died in 1717, at the age of 77; after difplay-ing his powers in the provinces, in the capital, and at court. Eight years after his death, in 1725, his fermons were publiſhed at Paris, in 6 vols. 12mo, and were much approved by all per-fons of piety and tafte. " His manner of reafoning," fays his editor, father Monteuil, " had not that drynefs which frequently deftroys the effect of a difcourfe; nor did he employ that ftudied elocution which frequently enervates the ftyle by an excefs of poliſh." The beft compofition in thefe volumes, is the funeral

oration

oration on Mary of Auſtria. As a trait of his humility, it is
related, that, on being told by a perſon in a large company, that
they had been fellow-ſtudents; he replied, " I cannot eaſily
forget it, ſince you not only lent me books, but gave me
cloches "

HUBNER (JOHN), a native of Luſatia, or, according to
ſome authorities, of Torgau in Saxony, highly celebrated for his
ſkill in hiſtory, geography, and genealogy, was born in 1668.
His works were chiefly written in the form of queſtion and
anſwer, and ſo popular in Germany, that his introduction
to geography went through a vaſt number of editions in that
country, and has been tranſlated into Engliſh, French, and other
languages. They are calculated rather for the inſtruction of the
ignorant, than the ſatisfaction of the learned; but are well executed in their way. Hubner was profeſſor of geography at Leipſic,
and rector of the ſchool at Hamburgh, in which city he died in
1731. His queſtions on modern and ancient geography, were
publiſhed at Leipſic in 1693, in 8vo, under the title of " Kurtze
Fragen aus der newen und alten Geographie." He publiſhed,
2. in 1697, and ſeveral ſubſequent years, in ten volumes, ſimilar
queſtions on political hiſtory, entitled, " Kurtze Fragen aus
der Politiſchen Hiſtorie, bis zum Aufgang des Siebenzenden
ſæculi." 3. His next work was, Genealogical Tables, with genealogical queſtions ſubjoined, 1708, &c. 4. Supplements to
the preceding works. 5. Lexicons, reſembling our Gazetteers,
for the aid of common life, entitled, " Staats, Zeitungs, und
Converſations-Lexico." 6. A Genealogical Lexicon. 7.
" Bibliotheca Hiſtorica Hamburgenſis," Leipſic, 1715. And,
8. " Muſeum Geographicum." The two laſt were more
eſteemed by the learned than any of his other works.

HUDSON (Captain HENRY), an eminent Engliſh navigator,
who flouriſhed in high fame in the beginning of the laſt century.
Where he was born and educated, we have no certain account;
nor have we of any private circumſtances of his life. The
cuſtom of diſcovering foreign countries for the benefit of
trade, not dying with queen Elizabeth, in whoſe reign it had
been zealouſly purſued, Hudſon, among others, attempted to
find out a paſſage by the north to Japan and China. His firſt
voyage was in 1607, at the charge of ſome London merchants; •
and his firſt attempt was for the north-eaſt paſſage to the Indies.
He departed therefore on the firſt of May; and after various
adventures through icy ſeas, and regions intenſely cold, returned
to England, and arrived in the Thames, Sept. 15. The year
following he undertook a ſecond voyage for diſcovering the ſame
paſſage, and accordingly ſet ſail with fifteen perſons only, April
22; but not ſucceeding, returned homewards, and arrived at
Graveſend, on Aug. 26. What we are to think of the veracity

of his accounts, may be doubted, when we find in his journal of
this voyage, the mention of a mermaid, which he says was seen
when they were about 76 degrees north latitude. These are
his words. "The 15th of June, one of our company looking overboard saw a mermaid, and calling up some of the company to see her, one more came up, and she was then come
close to the ship's side, looking earnestly on the men [s]. Soon
after a sea came and overturned her. From the navel upwards
her back and breasts were like a woman's, her body as big as
one of us, her skin very white, and long black hair hanging
down behind. In her going down they saw her tail, like the
tail of a porpous, and speckled like mackarel." In this instance
he was at least credulous, for he does not say that he saw it himself.

Not disheartened by his former unsuccessful voyages, he undertook again, in 1609, a third voyage to the same parts, for further discoveries; and was fitted out by the Dutch East-India
company. He sailed from Amsterdam, with twenty men, English and Dutch, March 25; and on April 25, doubled the north
cape of Finmark in Norway. He kept along the coasts of Lap-
land towards Nova Zembla, but found the sea so full of ice,
that he could not proceed. Then turning about, he went towards America, and arrived at the coast of New France on July
18. He sailed from place to place, without any hopes of succeeding in their grand scheme; and the ship's crew disagreeing,
and being in danger of mutinying, he pursued his way homewards, and arrived Nov. 7, at Dartmouth in Devonshire: of
which he gave advice to his directors in Holland, sending them
also a journal of his voyage. In 1610, he was again fitted out
by some gentlemen, with a commission to try, if through any of
those American inlets, which captain Davis saw, but durst not
enter, on the western side of Davis's Streights, any passage
might be found to the South Sea. They sailed from St. Catharine's, April 17, and on June 4, came within sight of Greenland.
On the 9th they were off Forbisher's Streights, and on the 15th
came in sight of Cape Desolation. Thence they proceeded north-
westward, among great quantities of ice, until they came to the
mouth of the streights that bear Hudson's name. They advanced in those streights westerly, as the land and ice would
permit, till they got into the bay, which has ever since been
called by the bold discoverer's name, "Hudson's Bay." He
gave names to places as he went along; and called the country
itself "Nova Britannia, or New Britain. He sailed above
100 leagues south into this bay, being confident that he had

[s] Purchas's Pilgrims, Part iii, Edit. 1625. p. 575.—Harris's Voyages, Vol. I.
Edit. 1705, p. 566.

found the defired paffage; but perceiving at laft that it was only
a bay, he refolved to winter in the moft fouthern point of it,
with an intention of purfuing his difcoveries the following
fpring. Upon this he was fo intent, that he did not confider
how unprovided he was with neceffaries to fupport himfelf during a fevere winter in that defolate place. On Nov. 3, however, they drew their fhip into a fmall creek, where they would
all infallibly have perifhed, if they had not been unexpected'y
and providentially fupplied with uncommon flights of wild
fowl, which ferved them for provifion. In the fpring, when
the ice began to wafte, Hudfon, in order to complete his difcovery, made feveral efforts of various kinds: but, notwithftanding all his endeavours, he found himfelf neceffitated to abandon
his enterprife, and to make the beft of his way home; and
therefore diftributed to his men, with tears in his eyes, all the
bread he had left, which was only a pound to each: though it
is faid other provifions were afterwards found in the fhip. In
his defpair and uneafinefs, he had let fall fome threatening
words, of fetting fome of his men on fhore; upon which a few
of the fturdieft, who had before been very mutinous, entered his
cabin in the night, tied his arms behind him, and expofed him
in his own fhallop at the weft end of the ftreights, with his fon,
John Hudfon, and feven of the moft fick and infirm of his men.
There they turned them adrift, and it is fuppofed that they
all perifhed, being never heard of more.. The crew proceeded
with the fhip for England; but going on fhore near the ftreight's
mouth, four of them were killed by favages. The reft, after
enduring the greateft hardfhips, and ready to die for want, arrived at Plymouth, Sept. 1611.

HUDSON (Dr. JOHN), a learned Englifh critic, was born
at Widehope near Cockermouth in Cumberland, 1662[T]; and,
after having been educated in grammar and claffical learning, was
entered in 1676 of Queen's-college, Oxford. Soon after he had
taken the degree of M. A. he removed to Univerfity-college, of
which he was chofen fellow in March, 1686, and became a moft
confiderable and efteemed tutor. He afterwards diftinguifhed
himfelf alfo by publifhing feveral valuable editions of Greek
and Latin authors. In April, 1701, on the refignation of Dr.
Thomas Hyde, he was elected principal keeper of the Bodleian
library; and, in June following, accumulated the degrees of B.
and D. D. With this librarian's place, which he held till his
death, he kept his fellowfhip till June 1711, when, according
to the ftatutes of the college, he would have been obliged
to refign it; but he had juft before difqualified himfelf for

[T] Athenæ, Vol. II. Col. 940; Edit. 1721.—Ant. Hall, Præf. ł. J. Hudfon, Jofephum.

holding

holding it any longer, by marrying Margaret, daughter of fir Robert Harrifon, knight, an alderman of Oxford, and a mercer, In 1712, he was appointed principal of St. Mary-hall by the chancellor of the univerfity, through the interoft of Dr. Radcliffe: and it is faid, that to Hudfon's intereft with this phyfician, the univerfity of Oxford is obliged for the wonderfully ample benefactions fhe afterwards received from him. Hudfon's ftudious and fedentary way of life brought him at length into an ill habit of body, which, turning to a dropfy, kept him about a year in a very languifhing condition. He died, Nov. 27, 1719, leaving a widow, and one daughter.

His publications were as follow: 1. "Introductio ad Chronographiam: five ars chronologica in Epitomen redacta, 1691," 8vo. Extracted from Beveridge's Treatife on that fubject, for the ufe of his pupils. 2. "Velleius Paterculus, cum variis lectionibus, & notis, & indice, 1693," 8vo. A fecond edition, with the notes enlarged, in 1711. 3. "Thucydides, 1696," folio. A neat and beautiful edition, but fomewhat eclipfed in its credit by that of Duker and Walfe. 4. "Geographiæ Veteris Scriptores Græci Minores. Cum Differtationibus & Annotationibus Henrici Dodwelli," 8vo. The firft publifhed in 1698, the fecond in 1703, and the third and fourth in 1712. 5. "Dionyfii Halicarnaffenfis opera omnia, 1704," 2 vols. folio. A beautiful and valuable edition, enriched with the various readings of an ancient copy in the Vatican library, and of feveral manufcripts in France. The learned editor has fubjoined to his own notes feveral of Sylburgius, Portus, Stephens, Cafauboh, and Valefius. 6. "Dionyfius Longinus, 1710," 4to. and 1718, 8vo. A very beautiful edition, and the notes, like all the reft of Hudfon's, very fhort. 7. "Moeris Atticifta, de vocibus Atticis & Hellenicis. Gregorius Martinus de Græcorum literarum pronunciatione, 1712," 8vo. 8. "Fabulæ Æfopicæ," Greek and Latin, 1718, 8vo. 9. "Flavii Jofephi Opera," he had juft finifhed, but did not live to publifh. He had proceeded as far as the third index, when, finding himfelf unable to go quite through, he recommended the work to his intimate friend Mr. Antony Hall, who publifhed it in 1720, in 2 vols. folio. It is a correct and beautiful edition, and fuperior in thofe refpects to Havercamp's, but not in the number or value of the notes. The care of Mr. Hall extended not only to the works of his deceafed friend, but to his family, for he married his widow.

Dr. Hudfon intended, if he had lived, to publifh a catalogue of the Bodleian library, which he had caufed to be fairly tranfcribed in 6 vols. folio. He was an able affiftant to feveral editors in Oxford, particularly to Dr. Gregory in his "Euclid," and to the induftrious Mr. Hearne in his "Livy," &c. He corresponded with many learned men in foreign countries:

tries: with Muratori, Salvini, and Bianchini, in Italy; with Boivin,
Kuiter, and Lequien, in France; with Olearius, Menckenius,
Chriftopher Wolfius, and, whom he chiefly efteemed, John
Albert Fabricius, in Germany; Eric Benzel, in Sweden; Fre,
deric Roftgard, in Denmark; with Pezron, Reland, Le Clerc,
in Holland, &c. He ufed to complain of the vaft exp[.] nce of
foreign letters; for he was far from being rich, never having
been pollefled of any ecclefiaftical preferment; of which he ufed
alfo to make frequent and heavy complaints.

HUET (Peter Daniel), bifhop of Avranches in France, a
very great as well as polite fcholar, was born of a good family at
Caen in Normandy, Feb. 8, 1630 [v]. His parents dying when
he was fcarcely out of his infancy, Huet fell into the hands of
guardians, who neglected him: his own invincible and feemingly
innate love of letters, however, made him amends for all difadvan-
tages; and he finifhed his ftudies in the belles lettres before he was
thirteen years of age. In the profecution of his philofophical
ftudies, he met with an excellent profeflor, father Mambrun, a
Jefuit; who, after Plato's example, directed him to begin by
learning a little geometry. Huet went further than his tutor
defired; and contracted fuch a relifh for it, that he flighted in a
manner all his other ftudies. He went through every branch of
mathematics, and maintained public thefes at Caen, a thing never
before done in that city. Having pafled through his claffes, it
was his bufinefs to ftudy the law, and to take his degrees in it;
but two books that were then publifhed, feduced him from this
purfuit. Thefe were, " The Principles of Des Cartes," and
" Bochart's Sacred Geography." He was a great admirer of
Des Cartes, and adhered to his philofophy for many years; but
afterwards faw the falfenefs and vanity of it, and, as we fhall
fee, wrote alfo againft it. " A leffon of caution this," fays his
panegyrift, " to all, to embrace no fyftem whatever, till they
have carefully examined the principles on which it is built: fince
even the wifeft and moft difcerning men are through fuch rafhnefs or inadvertency liable to be deceived." Bochart's geography
made a vaft impreffion upon him, as well on account of the
immenfe erudition with which it abounds, as by the prefence
of its author, who was minifter of the Proteftant church at
Caen. This book, being full of Greek and Hebrew learning,
infpired Huet with an ardent defire of being verfed in thofe
languages. To affift his progrefs in thefe ftudies, he contracted
a friendfhip with Bochart, and put himfelf under his directions.

At the age of twenty years and one day, he was delivered by
the cuftom of Normandy from the tuition of his guardians: and

[v] Eloge Hiftorique de Mr. Huet, par Mr. l'abbé Olivet, prefixed to his Traite
Philofophique de la Foibleffe de l'Efprit humain.—Huetii Commentarius de rebus ad
eum pertinentibus, p. 16.

foon after took a journey to Paris, not fo much from curiofity to fee the place, as for the fake of purchafing books, and making himfelf acquainted with the learned men of the times. He foon became known to Sirmond, Petavius, Vavaffor, Naudé, and, in fhort, to almoft all the fcholars in France. About two years after, he had alfo an opportunity of introducing himfelf to the learned in other parts of Europe: for Chriftina of Sweden having invited Bochart to her court, Huet accompanied him, and they fet out in April, 1652. He faw Salmafius at Leyden, and Ifaac Voffius at Amfterdam. He often vifited the queen, who would have engaged him in her fervice; but Bochart not having been very gracioufly received, through the intrigues of Bourdel another phyfician, who was jealous of him, and the queen's fickle temper being known to every body, Huet declined all offers, and after a ftay of three months returned to France. The chief fruit of his journey was a copy of a manufcript of Origen's "Commentaries upon St. Matthew," which he tranfcribed at Stockholm; and the acquaintance he contracted with the learned men in Sweden and Holland, through which he paffed. Upon his return to his own country, he refumed his ftudies with more vigour than ever, in order to publifh his manufcript of Origen. While he was employed in tranflating this work, he was led to confider the rules to be obferved in tranflations, as well as the different manners of the moft celebrated tranflators. This gave occafion to his firft performance, which came out at Paris in 1661, under this title, "De interpretatione libri duo:" and it is written in the form of a dialogue between Cafaubon, Fronto Ducæus, and Thuanus. M. de Segrais tells us [x], that "nothing can be added to this treatife, either with refpect to ftrength of critical judgement, variety of learning, or elegance of ftyle; which laft," fays abbé Olivet, "is fo very extraordinary, that it might have done honour to the age of Auguftus." This book was firft printed in a thin 4to, but afterwards in 12mo, and 8vo. In 1688, were publifhed at Rouen, in 2 vols. folio, his "Origenis Commentaria, &c. cum Latina interpretatione, notis & obfervationibus;" to which is prefixed, a large preliminary difcourfe, wherein is collected all that antiquity relates of Origen. The interval of fixteen years, between his return from Sweden and the publication of this work, was fpent entirely in ftudy, excepting a month or two every year, when he went to Paris; during which time he gave the public a fpecimen of his fkill in polite literature, in an elegant collection of poems, entitled, "Carmina Latina & Græca;" which were publifhed at Utrecht in 1664, and afterwards enlarged in feveral fucceffive editions. While he was employed upon his "Commentaries

[x] Preface de Virgile, Num. 35.

of

of Origen," he had the misfortune to quarrel with his friend
and master Bochart; who defiring one day a fight of his manuscript, for the sake of confulting some paffages about the Eucharift, which had been greatly controverted between Papifts and
Proteftants, difcovered an hiatus or defect, which feemed to determine the fenfe in favour of the Papifts, and reproached Huet
with being the contriver of it. Huet at firft thought that it was
a defect in the original MS. but upon confulting another very
ancient MS. in the king's library at Paris, he found that he had
omitted fome words in the hurry of tranfcribing, as he fays, and
that the miftake was his own. Bochart, ftill fuppofing that this
was a kind of pious fraud in Huet, to fupport the doctrine of
the church of Rome in regard to the Eucharift, alarmed the
Proteftants every where, as if Origen's " Commentaries" were
going to be very unfairly publifhed; and by that means diffolved
the friendfhip which had fo long fubfifted between Huet and himfelf.

In 1659, Huet was invited to Rome by Chriftina, who had
abdicated her crown, and retired thither; but, remembering the
cool reception which Bochart had experienced from her majefty,
after as warm an invitation, he refufed to go. Thofe, fays
Olivet, who judge of actions by events, will fuppofe him to have
acted very wifely in continuing in France; for ten years after,
when Boffuet was appointed by the king preceptor to the Dauphin, Huet was chofen for his colleague, with the title of fub-pre-
ceptor, which honour had fome time been defigned him by the duke
de Montaufier, governor to the Dauphin. He went to court in
1670, and ftayed there till 1680, when the Dauphin was married. Though his employment muft of neceffity occupy a confiderable part of his time, he found enough to complete his
" Demonftratio Evangelica," which, though fo great and laborious a work, was begun and ended amidft the embarraffments of
a court. It was publifhed at Paris in 1679, in folio; and has
been reprinted fince in folio, quarto, and octavo. Huet owns,
that this work was better received by foreigners, than by his
own countrymen; many of whom confidered it as a work full
of learning indeed, but utterly devoid of that demonftration
to which it fo formally and pompoufly pretends. Others, lefs
equitable, borrowed from it, and attacked it at the fame time,
to cover their plagiarifm; which, though Huet complains of it
very heavily, is not a fate peculiar to him or his book; there
being hardly any country, which will not afford inftances of authors who have been fo treated. Father Simon had a defign of
making an abridgement of this work; but Huet being informed
that his purpofe was only to alter it as he thought proper, to add
to it, and ftrike out of it at pleafure, defired him to excufe himfelf that trouble. We muft not forget the fervice which Huet

at

at this time performed to the republic of letters, by promoting
the editions of the classics, "in usum Delphini:" for though
the first idea of the commentaries for the use of the Dauphin was
started by the duke de Montausier, yet it was Huet who formed
the plan, and directed the execution, as far as the capacity of
the persons employed in that work would permit. He undertook, he tells us, only to promote and conduct the work, " pro-
curator esse & ιροδιακτης, non & operarius;" but at last came in
for a share of it. For when Michael Faye, who took upon him
the care of setting out Manilius, but was not equal to the task,
found himself puzzled, as he often did, with passages in that
obscure author, he had recourse to Huet ; who, having formerly
read him with great attention, and made several notes and observations upon him, was thereupon induced to digest them into
order, and to publish them, as he did at the end of the Delphin
edition of that author, in 1679. We must remember also to
observe, that he had been chosen a member of the French academy ; and that his speech pronounced on the occasion before that
illustrious body, had been published at Paris in 1674.

While he was employed in composing his " Demonstratio
Evangelica," the sentiments of piety, which he had cherished
from his earliest youth, moved him to enter into orders, which
he did at 46 years of age. In 1678, he was presented by the
king to the abbey of Aunay in Normandy, which was so agreeable to him, that he retired there every summer, after he had left
the court. In 1685, he was nominated to the bishopric of Sois-
sons ; but before the bulls for his institution were expedited, the
abbey de Sillery having been nominated to the see of Avranches,
they exchanged bishoprics with the consent of the king ; though,
by reason of the differences between the court of France and that
of Rome, they could not be consecrated till 1692. In 1689, he
published his " Censura Philosophiæ Cartesianæ," and addressed
it to the duke de Montausier: it appears, that he was greatly
piqued at the Cartesians, when he wrote this book. He was
displeased, that these philosophers preferred those who cultivate
their reason, to those who only cultivate their memory ; and required, that men should endeavour more to know themselves,
than to know what was done in former ages [v]. " What,"
says he, " because we are men of learning, shall this make us
obnoxious to the raillery of the Cartesians?" There was, indeed,
no occasion for raillery in the case ; yet the preference of reason
to mere memory is too clear to be denied. In 1690, he published in Caen, in 4to, his " Quæstiones Alnetanæ de Concordia
Rationis & Fidei:" which is written in the form of a dialogue,
after the manner of Cicero's Tusculan Questions. It is di-

[v] Cent. Phil. Cart. cap. viii. p. 7.

vided

vided into three books: in the firft of which the author lays down
the rules, whereby the agreement between faith and reafon is to
be regulated; the fecond compares the doctrines of Chriftianity
with the doctrines of Paganifm; and the third the practical precepts of each, and how they tend to improve and perfect human
life in piety and morals. This is not only a very learned, but
a very entertaining work; being written in an elegant and polite manner, and in moft excellent Latin, like all the reft of his
works.

In 1699, he refigned his bifhopric of Avranches, and was
prefented to the abbey of Fontenay, near the gates of Caen.
His love to his native place determined him to fix there, for
which purpofe he improved the houfe and gardens belonging to
the abbot. But feveral grievances and law-fuits coming upon
him, he removed to Paris; and lodged among the Jefuits in the
Maifon Profeffé, whom he had made heirs to his library, referving to himfelf the ufe of it while he lived. Here he fpent
the laft 20 years of his life, dividing his time between devotion
and ftudy. He did not, like fome pious men, confider the Bible
as the only book to be read, but thought that all other books
muft be read, before it could be rightly underftood. He employed
himfelf chiefly in writing notes on the vulgate tranflation: for which
purpofe he read over the Hebrew text 24 times; comparing it,
as he went along, with the other Oriental texts, and, as his panegyrift tells us, fpent every day two or three hours in this
work from 1681 to 1712. He was then feized with a very fevere diftemper, which confined him to his bed for near fix
months, and brought him fo very low, that he was given up by
his phyficians, and received extreme unction. Recovering, however, by degrees, he applied himfelf to the writing of his life,
which was publifhed at Amfterdam in 1718, in 12mo, under
the title of " Pet. Dan. Huetii, Epifcopi Abrincenfis, Commentarius de rebus ad eum pertinentibus:" where the critics have
wondered, that fo great a mafter of Latin as Huetius was, and
who has written it, perhaps as well as any of the moderns,
fhould be guilty of a folecifm in the very title of his book; as he
was in writing " eum," when he fhould have manifeftly written
" fe." This performance, though drawn up in a very amufing
and entertaining manner, and with great elegance of ftyle, is not
executed with that order and exactnefs, which appear in his
other works; his memory being then decayed, and afterwards
declining more and more, fo that he was no longer capable of a
continued work, but only committed detached thoughts to paper. Olivet in the mean time relates a moft remarkable fingularity of him, namely, that " for two or three hours before his
death, he recovered all the vigour of his genius and memory."
He died Jan. 26, 1721, in his 91ft year.

Befides

Befides the works which we have mentioned in the courfe of this memoir, he publifhed others of a fimilar nature, viz. " De l'Origine des Romans, 1670." " De la fituation du Paradis Terreftre, 1691." " Nouveaux Memoires pour fervir à l'Hiftoire du Cartefianifme, 1692." " Statuts Synodaux pour le diocefe d'Avranches, &c. 1693 ;" to which were added three fupplements in the years 1695, 1696, 1698. " De Navigationibus Salomonis, Amft. 1698." " Notæ in Anthologiam Epigrammatum Græcornm, Ukraj. 1700." " Origines de Caen, Roan, 1702." " Lettres la Monf. Perrault, fur le Parallele des Anciens & des Modernes du 10 Oct. 1692," printed without the author's knowledge in the third part of the " Pieces Fugitives, Paris, 1704." " Examen du fentiment de Longin fur ce paffage de la Genefe, Et Dieu dit, que la Lumiere foit faite, & la Lumiere fut faite," inferted in tome the 10th of Le Clerc's " Bibliotheque Choifée, Amft. 1706." Huet, in his " Demonftratio Evangelica," had afferted, that there was nothing fublime in this paffage, as Longinus had obferved, but that it was perfectly fimple. Meffrs. de Port Royal and Boileaux, who gave tranflations of Longinus, afferted its fublimity on that very account ; and this occafioned the " Examen" juft mentioned. " Lettre à M. Foucault confeiller d'etat fur l'origine de la poefie Françoife, du 16 Mar. 1706," inferted in the " Memoires de Trevoux, in 1711." " Lettre de M. Morin, (that is, of M. Huet) de l'academie des infcriptions à M. Huet, touchant le livre de M. Tolandus Anglois, intitulé, Adeifidæmon, & origines Judaicæ :" inferted in the " Memoirs de Trevoux" for Sept. 1709, and in the collection, which the abbé Tilladet publifhed of Huet's works, under the title of " Differtations fur diverfes matieres de la Religion & de Philologie, 1612." " Hiftoire de Commerce & de la navigation des Anciens, 1716." After his death were publifhed, " Traité Philofophique de la foiblesse de l'efprit humain, Amft. 1723." " Huetiana, ou penfées diverfes de M. Huet, 1722." Thefe contain thofe loofe thoughts he committed to paper after his laft illnefs, when, as we have already obferved, he was incapable of producing a connected work. " Diana de Caftro, ou le faux Yncas, 1728." A romance, written when he was very young. There are yet in being other MSS. of his, which, as far as we know, have not been publifhed ; viz. " A Latin tranflation of Longus's Loves of Daphnis and Chloe ;" " An Anfwer to Regis with regard to Des Cartes's Metaphyfics ;" " Notes upon the Vulgate Tranflation of the Bible ;" and a collection between 5 and 600 letters in Latin and French written to learned men.

To conclude, " when we confider," as Olivet fays, " that he lived to 90 years of age and upwards, that he had been a hard ftudent from his infancy, that he had had almoft all his time to

himfelf,

himfelf, that he had enjoyed an uninterrupted ftate of good health, that he had always fomebody to read to him even at his meals, that in one word, to borrow his own language, neither the heat of youth, nor a multiplicity of bufinefs, nor the love of company, nor the hurry of the world, had ever been able to moderate his invincible love of letters, we muft needs conclude him to have been one of the moft learned men that any age has produced."

HUGHES (JOHN), an Englifh poet [z], was fon of a citizen of London, and born at Marlborough in Wiltfhire, Jan. 29, 1677. He was brought early to London, and received the rudiments of learning there in private fchools. He had a weak or at leaft a delicate conftitution, which perhaps reftrained him from feverer ftudies, and inclined him to purfue the fofter arts of poetry, mufic, and drawing; in each of which he made a confiderable progrefs. His acquaintance with the Mufes and the Graces did not render him averfe to bufinefs; he had a place in the office of Ordnance, and was fecretary to feveral commiffions under the great feal for purchafing lands, in order to the better fecuring of the royal docks and yards at Portfmouth, Chatham, and Harwich. He continued, however, to purfue his natural inclination to letters, and added to a competent knowledge of the learned an intimate acquaintance with the modern languages. The firft teftimony he gave the public of his poetic vein, was in a poem " on the peace of Ryfwick," printed in 1697, and received with uncommon approbation. In 1699, " The Court of Neptune" was written by him on king William's return from Holland; and, the fame year, a fong on the duke of Gloucefter's birth-day. In 1702, he publifhed, on the death of king William, a Pindaric ode, entitled, " Of the Houfe of Naffau," which he dedicated to Charles duke of Somerfet; and in 1703 his " Ode in Praife of Mufic," was performed with great applaufe at Stationers-hall.

His numerous performances, for he had all along employed his leifure hours in tranflations and imitations from the ancients, had by this time introduced him, not only to the wits of the age, fuch as Addifon [A], Congreve, Pope, Southerne, Rowe, and others, but alfo to fome of the greateft men in the kingdom; and among thefe to the earl of Wharton, who offered to carry him over, and to provide for him; when appointed lord-

[z] Account of the Life of Hughes, prefixed to his poems.

[A] " His acquaintance with the great writers of his time," fays Dr. Johnfon, " appears to have been very general; but of his intimacy with Addifon there is a remarkable proof. It is told, on good authority, that ' Cato' was finifhed and played by his perfuafion. It had long wanted the laft act, which he was defired by Addifon to fupply. If the requeft was fincere, it proceeded from an opinion, whatever it was, that did not laft long; for when Hughes came in a week to fhew him his firft attempt, he found half the act written by Addifon himfelf."

lieutenant

lieutenant of Ireland : but, having other views at home, he declined the offer.

Hughes [a] had hitherto suffered the mortifications of a narrow fortune ; but in 1717 the lord chancellor Cowper set him at ease, by making him secretary to the Commissions of the peace ; in which he afterwards, by a particular request, desired his successor lord Parker to continue him. He had now affluence ; but such is human life, that he had it when his declining health could neither allow him long possession nor full enjoyment. His last work was his tragedy, "The Siege of Damascus ;" after which a *Siege* became a popular title. This play, which continues on the stage, and of which it is unnecessary to add a private voice to such continuance of approbation, is not acted or printed according to the author's original draught, or his settled intention. He had made Phocyas apostatize from his religion ; after which the abhorrence of Eudocia would have been reasonable, his misery would have been just, and the horrors of his repentance exemplary. The players, however, required that the guilt of Phocyas should terminate in desertion to the enemy ; and Hughes, unwilling that his relations should lose the benefit of his work, complied with the alteration. He was now weak with a lingering consumption, and not able to attend the rehearsal ; yet was so vigorous in his faculties, that only ten days before his death he wrote the dedication to his patron lord Cowper. On Feb. 17, 1720, the play was represented, and the author died. He lived to hear that it was well received ; but paid no regard to the intelligence, being then wholly employed in the meditations of a departing Christian.

A few weeks before he died, he sent, as a testimony of gratitude, to his noble friend earl Cowper, his own picture drawn by sir Godfrey Kneller, which he had received as a present from that painter : upon which the earl wrote him the following letter. "24 Jan. 1719-20. Sir, I thank you for the most acceptable present of your picture, and assure you, that none of this age can set an higher value on it than I do, and shall while I live : though I am sensible posterity will outdo me in that particular. I am, with the greatest esteem and sincerity, Sir, your most affectionate and obliged humble servant, COWPER."

A man of his character was undoubtedly regretted ; and Steele devoted an essay, in the paper called "The Theatre," to the memory of his virtues. In 1735, his poems were collected and published in 2 vols. 12mo, under the following title : "Poems on several Occasions, with some select Essays in Prose." Hughes was also the author of other works in prose. "The Advices from Parnassus," and "The Political Touchstone of Boccalini," trans-

[a] Dr. Johnson's Life of Hughes.

lated

lated by feveral hands, and printed in folio 1706, were revifed,
correected, and had a preface prefixed to them, by him. He
tranflated himfelf the following works: namely, "Fontenelle's
Dialogues of the Dead, and Difcourfe concerning the Ancients
and Moderns;" "the Abbé Vertot's Hiftory of the Revolutions
in Portugal;" and "Letters of Abelard and Heloifa." He wrote
the preface to the colleection of the "Hiftory of England" by
various hands, called, "The Complete Hiftory of England,"
printed in 1706, in 3 vols. folio; in which he gives a clear, fatisfactory, and impartial account of the hiftorians there collected.
Several papers in the "Tatlers," "Speectators," and "Guardians," were written by him. He is fuppofed to have written
the whole, or at leaft a confiderable part, of the Lay-Monaftery;
confifting of Effays, Difcourfes, &c. publifhed fingly under the
title of the 'Lay-Monk:' being the Sequel of the 'Speectators.'
The fecond edition of this was printed in 1714, 12mo. Laftly,
he publifhed, in 1715, an accurate edition of the works of Spenfer, in 6 vols. 12mo: to which are prefixed the "Life of Spenfer," "An Effay on Allegorical Poetry," "Remarks on the
Fairy-Queen, and other Writings of Spenfer;" and a Gloffary,
explaining old words; all by Mr. Hughes. This was a work
for which he was well qualified, as a judge of the beauties of
writing, but he wanted an antiquary's knowledge of the obfolete
words. He did not much revive the curiofity of the public; for
near thirty years elapfed before his edition was reprinted. The
character of his genius we fhall tranfcribe from the correfpondence of Swift and Pope. "A month ago," fays Swift, "was
fent me over, by a friend of mine, the works of John Hughes,
Efq. They are in profe and verfe. I never heard of the man
in my life, yet I find your name as a fubfcriber. He is too grave
a poet for me; and I think among the mediocrifts, in profe as
well as verfe." To this Pope returns: "To anfwer your queftion as to Mr. Hughes; what he wanted in genius, he made up
as an honeft man; but he was of the clafs you think him."

HUGHES (JABEZ), younger brother of Mr. John Hughes,
and, like him, a votary of the Mufes, and an excellent fcholar.
He publifhed, in 1714, in 8vo, a tranflation of "The Rape of
Proferpine," from Claudian, and "The Story of Sextus and
Erietho," from Lucan's "Pharfalia," book vi. Thefe tranf-
lations, with notes, were reprinted in 1723, 12mo. He alfo
publifhed, in 1717, a tranflation of Suetonius's "Lives of the
Twelve Cæfars," and tranflated feveral "Novels" from the Spa-
nifh of Cervantes, which are inferted in the "Select Colleection
of Novels and Hiftories," printed for Watts, 1729. He died
Jan. 17, 1731, in his 46th year. A pofthumous volume of his
"Mifcellanies in Verfe and Profe" was publifhed in 1737. The

widow accompanied the lady of governor Byng to Barbadoes, and died there in 1740.

HUGHES (Jabez), of a different family from the former, though of the same name, fellow of Jesus-college, Cambridge, and called by bishop Atterbury [c] "a learned hand," is known to the republic of letters as editor of St. Chrysostom's treatise "On the Priesthood." Two letters of his to Mr. Bonwicke are printed in "The Gentleman's Magazine [D]," in one of which he says "I have at last been prevailed on to undertake an edition of St. Chrysostom's περὶ ἱερωσύνης; and I would beg the favour of you to send me your octavo edition. I want a small volume to lay by me; and the Latin version may be of some service to me, if I cancel the interpretation of Fronto Ducæus." A second edition of this treatise was printed at Cambridge in Greek and Latin, with notes, and a preliminary dissertation against the pretended "Rights of the Church, &c." in 1712. A good English translation of St. Chrysostom "On the Priesthood," a posthumous work by the Rev. John Bunce, M. A. was published by his son (vicar of St. Stephen's near Canterbury) in 1760.

HUGO of Cluni, a saint of the Romish Calendar, (not the only one of the name, for there was a St. Hugo, bishop of Grenoble, in 1080,) was of a very distinguished family in Burgundy; and was born in 1023. When he was only 15, he rejected all worldly views, and entered into the monastic life at Cluni, under the guidance of the Abbot Odilon. After some years, he was created Prior of the Order, and Abbot in 1048, at the death of Odilon. In this situation he extended the reform of Cluni to so many monasteries, that, according to an ancient author, he had under his jurisdiction above ten thousand monks. In 1758, he attended pope Stephen when dying, at Florence; and in 1074, he made a religious pilgrimage to Rome. Some epistles written by him, are extant in Dacherius's Spicilegium. There are also some other of his works in the "Bibliotheque de Cluni." He died in 1108 or 9, at or about the age of 85. He is said to have united moderation with his exemplary piety; and was embroiled, at one time, with the bishop of Lyons, for saying the prayer for the Emperor Henry IV, when that prince was under excommunication.

HUGO (Herman), a learned Jesuit, was born at Brussels, in 1588; and died of the plague at Rhimberg in 1639. He published his first work in 1617, which was, "De prima scribendi origine, et universæ rei literariæ antiquitate," 8vo. Antwerp. This book was republished by Trotzius in 1738, with

[c] Epistolary Correspondence, Vol. II. p 295.   [D] Vol. XLVIII. p. 583, 673.

3   many

many notes. 2. "Obfidio Bredana, fub Ambrofio Spinola," folio, Antwerp, 1629. 3. "Militia equeftris, Antiqua et nova," Antw. folio, 1630. 4. His "*Pia Defideria*," the work by which he is beft known, were firft publifhed in octavo in 1632. They are alfo printed in 32mo. with all the clearnefs of Elzevir, and adorned with rather fanciful engravings. His *Pia Defideria* are in Latin verfe, of which they contain 45 copies, and are illuf-ftrated by curious cuts. The whole confifts of three books, the fubjects of which are thus arranged. B. 1. "Gemitus Animæ peni-tentis." 2. "Vota animæ fanctæ." 3. "Sufpiria animæ aman-tis." They confift of long paraphrafes in elegiac verfe, on va-rious paffages of fcripture. His verfification is ufually good, but he wants fimplicity and fublimity; yet he is fometimes poeti-cal, though his Mufe is not like that of David.

HUGO (CHARLES LOUIS), a voluminous author in Latin and French; though his works, from their fubjects, are little known here. He was a Canon of the Premonftratenfian Order, a Doctor of Divinity, Abbé of Etival, and titular bifhop of Ptolemais. He died at an advanced age, in 1735. His works are, 1. "Annales Præmonftratenfium," a Hiftory of his own order, and a very laborious work, in two volumes folio; illuftrated with plans of the monafteries, and other curious particulars; but accufed of fome remarkable errors. 2. "Vie de St. Norbert Fondateur des Præmontrés," 4to. 1704. 3. "Sacræ antiqui-tatis monumenta hiftorica, dogmatica, diplomatica," two vo-lumes in folio, 1725. 4. "Traité hiftorique et critique de la Maifon de Lorraine," 8vo. 1711. This being a work of fome boldnefs, not only the name of the author, but that of the place where it was printed, was concealed: the former being profef-fedly *Balricourt*, the latter Berlin, inftead of Nanci. Yet the au-thor was traced out, and fell under the cenfure of the parliament, in 1712. In 1713, he publifhed, 5. another work, entitled, "Reflexions fur les deux Ouvrages concernant la Maifon de Lor-raine," where he defends his former publication.

HULSEMANN (JOHN), a Lutheran divine, was born in 1602, at Efens, in Eaft Friezeland; and died in 1661. He had travelled through moft countries of Europe, but fixed him-felf at Leipfic in 1646, where he became Profeffor of Divinity, and furintendant. He was a very voluminous author; wrote commentaries on the facred books, and feveral other valuable works on fubjects of divinity.

HUME (DAVID) [1], a celebrated philofopher and hiftorian, was defcended from a good family in Scotland, and born at Edin-burgh April 26, 1711. Being a younger brother with a very flender patrimony, and of a ftudious, fober, induftrious turn, he

[1] Life, written by himfelf, prefixed to his Hiftory of England.

was deſtined by his family to the law; but, being ſeized with
an early paſſion for letters, he found an inſurmountable aver-
ſion to any thing elſe; and, as he relates, while they fancied
him to be pouring upon Voet and Vinnius, he was occupied with
Cicero and Virgil. His fortune however being very ſmall, and
his health a little broken by ardent application to books, he was
tempted, or rather forced, to make a feeble trial at buſineſs;
and, in 1734, went to Briſtol, with recommendations to ſome
eminent merchants: but, in a few months, found that ſcene totally unfit for him. He ſeems, alſo, to have conceived ſome
perſonal diſguſt againſt the men of buſineſs in that place; for,
though he was by no means addicted to ſatire, yet we can ſcarcely
interpret him otherwiſe than ironically, when, ſpeaking in his
Hiſtory (anno 1660) of James Naylor's entrance into Briſtol
upon a horſe, in imitation of Chriſt, he preſumes it to be " from
the difficulty in that place of finding an aſs!"

Immediately on leaving Briſtol, he went over to France, with
a view of proſecuting his ſtudies in privacy; and practiced a very
rigid frugality, for the ſake of maintaining his independency
unimpaired. During his retreat there, firſt at Rheims, but
chiefly at La Fleche, in Anjou, he compoſed his " Treatiſe of
of Human Nature;" and, coming over to London in 1737, he
publiſhed it the year after. It met with no manner of ſucceſs:
" it fell," ſays he, " dead-born from the preſs." In 1742, he
printed, with more ſucceſs, the firſt part of his " Eſſays." In
1745, he lived with the marquis of Annandale, the ſtate of that
nobleman's mind and health requiring ſuch an attendant: the
emoluments of the ſituation muſt have been his motive for undertaking ſuch a charge. He then received an invitation from
general St. Clair, to attend him as a ſecretary to his expedition;
which was at firſt meant againſt Canada, but ended in an incur-
ſion upon the coaſt of France. Next year, 1747, he attended
the general in the ſame ſtation, in his military embaſſy to the
courts of Vienna and Turin: he then wore the uniform of an
officer, and was introduced to theſe courts as aid-de-camp to the
general. Theſe two years were almoſt the only interruptions
which his ſtudies received during the courſe of his life; his ap-
appointments, however, had made him in his own opinion " independent; for he was now maſter of near 1000l."

Having always imagined, that his want of ſucceſs, in publiſhing the " Treatiſe of Human Nature," proceeded more from
the manner than the matter, he caſt the firſt part of that work
anew, in the " Enquiry concerning Human Underſtanding,"
which was publiſhed while he was at Turin; but with little
more ſucceſs. He perceived, however, ſome ſymptoms of a
riſing reputation: his books grew more and more the ſubject of
converſation; and " I found," ſays he, " by Dr. Warburton's
railing,

railing, that they were beginning to be efteemed in good company." In 1752, were publifhed at Edinburgh, where he then lived, his " Political Difcourfes;" and the fame year, at London, his " Enquiry concerning the Principles of Morals." Of the former he fays, " that it was the only work of his, which was fuccefsful on the firft publication, being well received abroad and at home :" and he pronounces the latter to be, " in his own opinion, of all his writings, hiftorical, philofophical, or literary, incomparably the beft ; although it came unnoticed and unobferved into the world."

In 1754, he publifhed the firft volume, in 4to, of " A Portion of Englifh Hiftory, from the Acceffion of James I. to the Revolution." He ftrongly promifed himfelf fuccefs from this work, thinking himfelf the firft Englifh hiftorian that was free from bias in his principles : but he fays, " that he was herein miferably difappointed ; and that, inftead of pleafing all parties, he had made himfelf obnoxious to all." He was, as he relates, " fo difcouraged with this, that, had not the war at that time been breaking out between France and England, he had certainly retired to fome provincial town of the former kingdom, changed his name, and never more have returned to his native country." He recovered himfelf, however, fo far, as to publifh, in 1756, his fecond volume of the fame hiftory ; and this was better received. " It not only rofe itfelf," he fays, " but helped to buoy up its unfortunate brother." Between thefe publications came out, along with fome other fmall pieces, his " Natural Hiftory of Religion :" which, though but indifferently received, was in the end the caufe of fome confolation to him ; becaufe, as he expreffes himfelf,—" Dr. Hurd wrote a pamphlet againft it, with all the illiberal petulance, arrogance, and fcurrility, which diftinguifh the Warburtonian fchool ;" fo well aware was he, that, to an author, attack of any kind is much more favourable than neglect. Dr. Hurd, however, was only the oftenfible author ; he has fince declared exprefsly, that it proceeded from Warburton himfelf [r]. In 1759, he publifhed his " Hiftory of the Houfe of Tudor ;" and, in 1761, the more early part of the Englifh Hiftory : each, in two vols. 4to. The clamour againft the former of thefe was almoft equal to that againft the hiftory of the two firft Stuarts ; and the latter was attended with but tolerable fuccefs : but he was now, he tells us, grown callous againft the impreffions of public cenfure. He had, indeed, what he would think good reafon to be fo ; for the copy-money, given by the bookfellers for his hiftory, exceptionable as it was deemed, had made him not only independent but opulent.

[r] Life of Warburton.
Being

Being now about fifty, he retired to Scotland, determined never more to set his foot out of it; and carried with him "the satisfaction of never having preferred a request to one great man, or even making advances of friendship to any of them." But, while meditating to spend the rest of his life in a philosophical manner, he received, in 1763, an invitation from the earl of Hertford, to attend him on his embassy to Paris; which at length he accepted, and was left there *chargé d'affaires*, in the summer of 1765. In the beginning of 1766, he quitted Paris; and in the summer of that year, went to Edinburgh, with the same view as before, of burying himself in a philosophical retreat: but, in 1767, he received from Mr. Conway, a new invitation to be under-secretary of state, which, like the former, he did not think it expedient to decline. He returned to Edinburgh in 1769, "very opulent," he says, "for he possessed a revenue of 1000l. a year, healthy, and, though somewhat stricken in years, with the prospect of enjoying long his ease." In the spring of 1775, he was struck with a disorder in his bowels; which, though it gave him no alarm at first, proved incurable, and at length mortal. It appears, however, that it was not painful, nor even troublesome or fatiguing: for he declares, that "notwithstanding the great decline of his person, he had never suffered a moment's abatement of his spirits; that he possessed the same ardour as ever in study, and the same gaiety in company; insomuch," says he, "that, were I to name a period of my life, which I should most choose to pass over again, I might be tempted to point to this latter period."

The life written by himself, from which these materials are extracted, is dated April 18, 1776; he died the 25th of August following. His works, as corrected by himself, are printed in 4to and 8vo; but there is a posthumous piece, not included among them; yet, in point of composition, not inferior to any of them. It is entitled, "Dialogues concerning Natural Religion," in 8vo.

HUMPHREY (LAURENCE), a learned English writer, was born at Newport Pagnell in Buckinghamshire, about 1527, and had his school education at Cambridge; after which he became first a demy, then a fellow, of Magdalen-college in Oxford [G]. He took the degree of M. A. in 1552, and about that time was made Greek reader of his college, and entered into orders. In June, 1555, he had leave from his college to travel into foreign countries; he went to Zurich, and associated himself with the English there, who had fled from their country on account of their religion. After the death of queen Mary, he returned to England; and was restored to his fellowship in Magdalen-college,

● [G] Athen. Oxon. Vol. I.

from which he had been expelled, because he did not return within the space of a year, which was one condition on which he was permitted to travel; another was, that he should refrain from all heretical company. In 1560, he was appointed the queen's profeffor of divinity at Oxford; and the year after elected prefident of his college. In 1562, he took both the degrees in divinity; and, in 1570, was made dean of Gloucefter. In 1580, he was removed to the deanery of Winchefter; and had probably been promoted to a bifhopric, if he had not been dif-affected to the church of England. For Wood tells us, that from the city of Zurich, where the preaching of Zuinglius had fafhioned people's notions, and from the correfpondence he had at Geneva, he brought back with him fo much of the Cal-. vinift both in doctrine and difcipline, that the beft which could be faid of him was, that he was a moderate and confcientious Non-conformift. This was at leaft the opinion of feveral divines, who ufed to call him and Dr. Fulke of Cambridge, ftandard-bearers among the Nonconformifts; though others thought they grew more conformable in the end. Be this as it will, " fure it is," fays Wood, " that Humphrey was a great and general fcholar, an able linguift, a deep divine; and for his excellency of ftyle, exactnefs of method, and fubftance of matter in his writings, went beyond moft of our theologifts." He died in Feb. 1590, N. S.; leaving a wife, by whom he had twelve children.

His writings are, 1. " Epiftola de Græcis literis, & Homeri lectione & imitatione;" printed before a book of Hadrian Junius, entitled, " Cornu-copiæ," at Bafil, 1558. 2. " De Religionis confervatione & reformatione, deque primatu regum, Baf. 1559." 3. " De ratione interpretandi auctores, Baf. 1559." 4. " Optimates: five de nobilitate, ejufque antiqua origine, &c. Baf. 1560." 5. " Joannis Juelli Angli, Epifcopi Sarifburienfis, vita & mors, ejufque veræ doctrinæ defenfio, &c. Lond. 1573." 6. " Two Latin Orations fpoken before queen Elizabeth: one in 1572, another in 1575." 7. " Sermons;" and 8. " Some Latin Pieces againft the Papifts, Campian in particular." Wood quotes Tobias Matthew, an eminent archbifhop, who knew him well, as declaring, that " Dr. Humphrey had read more fathers, than Campian the Jefuit ever faw; devoured more than he ever tafted; and taught more in the univerfity of Oxford, than he had either learned or heard."

HUNIADES (JOHN CORVINUS), waiwode of Tranfylvania, and general of the armies of Ladiflas king of Hungary, was one of the greateft commanders of his time. He fought againft the Turks like a hero, and, in 1442 and 1443, gained important battles againft the generals of Amurath; and obliged that prince to retire from Belgrade, after befieging it feven months. In the battle of Varnes, fo fatal to the Chriftian caufe, and in

which

which Ladiflas fell, Corvinus was not lefs diftinguifhed than in his more fortunate contefts ; and, being appointed governor of Hungary, became proverbially formidable to the Turks. In 1448, however, he fuffered a defeat from them. He was more fortunate afterwards, and in 1456, obliged Mahomet II. alfo to relinquifh the fiege of Belgrade, and died the 10th of September in the fame year. Mahomet, though an enemy, had generofity enough to lament the death of fo great a man ; and pride enough to alledge as one caufe for his regret, that the world did not now contain a man againft whom he could deign to turn his arms, or from whom he could regain the glory he had fo lately loft before Belgrade. The pope is faid to have fhed tears on the news of his death ; and Chriftians in general lamented Huniades, as their beft defender againft the Infidels.

HUNNIUS (Giles), a celebrated Lutheran divine, was born at Winende, a village in the dutchy of Wirtemburg, in the year 1550. He was educated at the fchools in that vicinity, and took his degree in arts at Tubingen, in 1567. He then applied himfelf earneftly to the ftudy of theology, and was fo remarkable for his progrefs in it, that in 1576 he was made profeffor of divinity at Marpurg. About the fame period, he married. He was particularly zealous againft the Calvinifts, and not long after this time began to write againft them, by which he gained fo much reputation, that in 1592 he was fent for into Saxony to reform that electorate, was made divinity-profeffor at Wittemburg, and a member of the ecclefiaftical confiftory. In thefe offices he proved very vigilant in difcovering thofe who had departed from the Lutheran communion ; and, from the accounts of the feverities practifed againft thofe who would not conform to that rule, it appears that nothing lefs than a ftrong perfecution was carried on by him and his colleagues. In 1595, he was appointed paftor of the church at Wittemburg, and in the fame year publifhed his moft celebrated polemical work entitled, " Calvinus Judaizans," in which he charges that reformer with all poffible herefies. At the fame time he carried on a controverfy with Huberus, about Predeftination and Election [H]. Againft Calvin he wrote with fuch acrimony that Bayle fays, not without probability, that, if he had been poffeffed of fimilar power, he would probably have done no lefs to him than he did to Servetus. Hunnius was prefent at the conference at Ratifbon in 1601, between the Lutherans and Roman Catholics. He died of an inflammation brought on by the ftone, in April 1603. His works have been collected in five volumes, and contain, funeral orations, a catechifm, prayers, colloquies, notes on fome of the evangelifts, &c. &c. His acrimony in writing went beyond his judgement.

[H] See alfo in Hoffman (Daniel).

HUNTER

HUNTER (ROBERT, efq;), author of the celebrated "Letter on Enthufiafm," and, if Coxeter be right in his MS. conjecture in his title-page of the only copy extant, of a farce called
" Androboros [1]." He was appointed lieutenant-governor of
Virginia in 1708, but taken by the French in his voyage thither.
Two excellent letters, addreffed to colonel Hunter while a prifoner at Paris, which reflect equal honour on Hunter and Swift,
are printed in the 12th vol. of the Dean's Works, by one of
which it appears, that the " Letter on Enthufiafm" had been
afcribed to Swift; as it has ftill more commonly been to the earl
of Shaftefbury. In 1710, he was appointed governor of New-
York, and fent with 2700 Palatines to fettle there. From Mr.
Gough's " Hiftory of Croyland Abbey," we learn, that Mr.
Hunter was a major-general, and that, during his government of
New-York, he was directed by her majefty to provide fubfiftence
for about 3000 Palatines (the number ftated in the alienating act)
fent from Great Britain to be employed in raifing and manu-
facturing naval ftores; and by an account ftated in 1734, it
appears that the governor had difburfed 20,000l. and upwards,
in that undertaking, no part of which was ever re-paid. He
returned to England in 1719; and on the acceffion of George II.
was continued governor of New-York and the Jerfeys. On account of his health, he obtained the government of Jamaica,
where he arrived in Feb. 1728; died March 31, 1734; and
was buried in that ifland. His epitaph, written by the Rev. Mr.
Flemming, may be feen below [K].

HUNTER (WILLIAM, M. D.), was born May 23, 1718,
at Kilbride in the county of Lanerk [L]. He was the feventh
of ten children [M], of John and Agnes Hunter, who refided on
a fmall

[1] Biographia Dramatica.
[K] Hic chara recumbont e tuvia
    ROBERTI HUNTER,
Hujus lofula nuperrime praefecti;
qui nihil à patrum gloria mutuatus
fuae nobilitatis virtute emicuit.
Mirae corporis pulchritudini
    fuavitatem ingenii,
rerum & literarum fcientiae,
    morum comitatem adjecit.
    In bello illuftris,
far in pace minus infignis,
negotiis cum fapientia & fortitudine,
otium cum dignitate & elegantia
        exercuit.
Hic ergo, lector candide,
    ad defuncti tumulum
laudis pende vectigalia
quae viventis verecundia
' accipere non fuftinuit.
Huic doloris debitum pofteri
lachrymarum fluctu folvite,

qui dum publicam falutem
    follicitus curaret
    fuam fatigatus deperdidit.
[L] This article is abridged from the
excellent Life of Dr. Hunter by S. F. Simmons, M. D. F. R. S. to which our readers are referred for a fuller account of Dr.
Hunter's writings.
[M] Thefe were John, Elizabeth, Andrew, Janet, James, Agnes, William,
Dorothea, Ifabella, and John. Of the
fons, John the eldeft, and Andrew died
young; James, born in 1715, was a writer
to the fignet at Edinburgh, who, difliking
the profeffion of the law, came to London
in 1743, with an intention to ftudy anatomy under his brother William, but was
prevented from purfuing this plan by ill
health, which induced him to return to
Long Caldarwood, where he died foon after,
aged 28 years; John, the youngeft, is the
fubject of the enfuing article.—Of the
                    daughters,

a small estate in that parish, called Long Calderwood, which had long been in the possession of his family. His great grandfather, by his father's side, was a younger son of Hunter of Hunterston, chief of the family of that name. At the age of fourteen, his father sent him to the college of Glasgow; where he passed five years, and by his prudent behaviour and diligence acquired the esteem of the professors, and the reputation of being a good scholar. His father had designed him for the church, but the necessity of subscribing to articles of faith was to him a strong objection. In this state of mind he happened to become acquainted with Dr. Cullen, who was then just established in practice at Hamilton, under the patronage of the duke of Hamilton. By the conversation of Dr. Cullen, he was soon determined to devote himself to the profession of physic. His father's consent having been previously obtained, he went, in 1737, to reside with Dr. Cullen. In the family of this excellent friend and preceptor he passed nearly three years, and these, as he has been often heard to acknowledge, were the happiest years of his life. It was then agreed, that he should prosecute his medical studies at Edinburgh and London, and afterwards return to settle at Hamilton, in partnership with Dr. Cullen.

Mr. Hunter set out for Edinburgh in Nov. 1740, and continued there till the following spring, attending the lectures of the medical professors, and amongst others those of the late Dr. Alexander Monro. He arrived in London in the summer of 1741, and took up his residence at Mr. (afterwards Dr.) Smellie's, who was at that time an apothecary in Pall-mall. He brought with him a letter of recommendation to his countryman Dr. James Douglas, from Mr. Foulis, printer at Glasgow, who had been useful to the doctor in collecting for him different editions of Horace. Dr. Douglas was then intent on a great anatomical work on the bones, which he did not live to complete, and was looking out for a young man of abilities and industry whom he might employ as a dissecter. This induced him to pay particular attention to Mr. Hunter, and finding him acute and sensible, he after a short time invited him into his family, to assist in his dissections, and to superintend the education of his son. Mr. Hunter having communicated this offer to his father and Dr. Cullen, the latter readily and heartily gave his concurrence to it; but his father, who was very old and infirm, and expected his return with impatience, consented with reluctance. His father did not long survive; dying Oct. 30, following, aged 78.

daughters, Elizabeth, Agnes, and Isabella, died young; Janet married Mr. Buchanan of Glasgow, and died in 1749; Dorothea, married the late Rev. James Baillie, D. D.

professor of divinity in the university of Glasgow, by whom she had a son Matthew Baillie, now a very eminent physician, and two daughters.

. Mr.

Mr. Hunter having accepted Dr. Douglas's invitation, was by his friendly assistance enabled to enter himself as a surgeon's pupil at St. George's hospital under Mr. James Wilkie, and as a dissecting pupil under Dr. Frank Nichols, who at that time taught anatomy with considerable reputation. He likewise attended a course of lectures on experimental philosophy by Dr. Defaguliers. Of these means of improvement he did not fail to make a proper use. He soon became expert in dissection, and Dr. Douglas was at the expence of having several of his preparations engraved. But before many months had elapsed, he had the misfortune to lose this excellent friend. Dr. Douglas died April 1, 1742, in his 67th year, leaving a widow and two children. The death of Dr. Douglas, however, made no change in his situation. He continued to reside with the doctor's family, and to pursue his studies with the same diligence as before. In 1743, he communicated to the Royal Society " An Essay on the Structure and Diseases of articulating Cartilages [N]." This ingenious paper, on a subject which till then had not been sufficiently investigated, affords a striking testimony of the rapid progress he had made in his anatomical enquiries. As he had it in contemplation to teach anatomy, his attention was directed principally to this object; and it deserves to be mentioned as an additional mark of his prudence, that he did not precipitately engage in this attempt, but passed several years in acquiring such a degree of knowledge, and such a collection of preparations, as might insure him success. After waiting some time for a favourable opening, he succeeded Mr. Samuel Sharpe as lecturer to a private society of surgeons in Covent-garden, began his lectures in their rooms, and soon extended his plan from surgery to anatomy. This undertaking commenced in the winter of 1746. He is said to have experienced much solicitude when he began to speak in public, but applause soon inspired him with courage; and by degrees he became so fond of teaching, that for many years before his death he was never happier than when employed in delivering a lecture.

The profits of his two first courses were considerable [O], but by contributing to the wants of different friends, he found him-

[N] Phil. Trans. Vol. XLII.

[O] Mr. Watson, F.R.S. who was one of Mr. Hunter's earliest pupils, accompanied him home after his introductory lecture. Mr. Hunter, who had received about 70 guineas from his pupils, and had got the money in a bag under his cloak, observed to Mr. Watson, that it was a larger sum than he had ever been master of before.—Dr. Pulteney, in his " Life of Linnæus," has not thought it superfluous to record the slender beginning from which that great naturalist rose to ease and affluence in life. " Exivi patria virginti sex nummis aureis dives," are Linnæus's own words. Anecdotes of this sort deserve to be recorded, as an encouragement to young men, who, with great merit, happen to possess but little advantages of fortune.

self at the return of the next season obliged to defer his lectures
for a fortnight, merely because he had not money to defray the
necessary expence of advertisements. This circumstance taught
him to be more reserved in this respect. In 1747 he was admitted a member of the corporation of surgeons, and in the
spring of the following year, soon after the close of his lectures,
he set out in company with his pupil, Mr. James Douglas, on
a tour through Holland to Paris. His lectures suffered no interruption by this journey, as he returned to England soon enough
to prepare for his winter course, which began about the usual
time. At first he practised both surgery and midwifery, but the
former he always disliked; and, being elected one of the sur-
geon-men-midwives first to the Middlesex, and soon afterwards
to the British lying-in hospital, and recommended by several of
the most eminent surgeons of that time, his line was thus determined. Over his countryman Dr. Smellie, notwithstanding his
great experience, and the reputation he had justly acquired, he
had a great advantage in person and address. The most lucrative
part of the practice of midwifery was at that time in the hands
of sir Richard Manningham and Dr. Sandys. The former of
these died, and the latter retired into the country a few years
after Mr. Hunter began to be known in midwifery. Although
by these incidents he was established in the practice of midwifery, it is well known that, in proportion as his reputation
increased, his opinion was eagerly sought in all cases where any
light, concerning the seat or nature of any disease, could be expected from an intimate knowledge of anatomy. In 1750, he
obtained the degree of M. D. from the university of Glasgow,
and began to practise as a physician. About this time he quitted
the family of Mrs. Douglas, and went to reside in Jermyn-
street. In the summer of 1751 he re-visited his native country,
for which he always retained a cordial affection. His mother
[r] was still living at Long Calderwood, which was now become his property by the death of his brother James. Dr,
Cullen, for whom he always entertained a sincere regard, was
then established at Glasgow. During this visit, he shewed his
attachment to his little paternal inheritance, by giving many
instructions for repairing and improving it, and for purchasing
any adjoining lands that might be offered for sale. As he and
Dr. Cullen were riding one day in a low part of the country,
the latter, pointing out to him Long Calderwood at a considerable distance, remarked how conspicuous it appeared. "Well,"
said he, with some degree of energy, "if I live, I shall make
it still more conspicuous." After this journey to Scotland, to
which he devoted only a few weeks, he was never absent from

[r] Mrs. Hunter died Nov. 3, 1751, aged 66 years.

London,

London, unless his professional engagements, as sometimes happened, required his attendance at a distance from the capital.

In 1762, we find him warmly engaged in controversy, supporting his claim to different anatomical discoveries, in a work entitled, " Medical Commentaries," the style of which is correct and spirited. As an excuse for the tardiness with which he brought forth this work, he observes in his introduction, that it required a good deal of time, and he had little to spare; that the subject was unpleasant, and therefore he was very seldom in the humour to take it up. In 1762, when our present excellent queen became pregnant, Dr. Hunter was consulted; and two years after he had the honour to be appointed physician extraordinary to her majesty. About this time his avocations were so numerous, that he became desirous of lessening his fatigue, and having noticed the ingenuity and assiduous application of the late Mr. William Hewson, F. R. S. who was then one of his pupils, he engaged him first as an assistant, and afterwards as a partner in his lectures[Q]. This connexion continued till 1770, when some disputes happened, which terminated in a separation. Mr. Hewson was succeeded in the partnership by Mr. Cruikshank, whose anatomical abilities are deservedly respected.

April 30, 1767, Dr. Hunter was elected F. R. S. and the year following communicated to that learned body, " Observations on the Bones, commonly supposed to be Elephants Bones, which have been found near the River Ohio in America [a]." This was not the only subject of natural history on which Dr. Hunter employed his pen; for in a subsequent volume of the " Philosophical Transactions," we find him offering his " Remarks on some Bones found in the Rock of Gibraltar," which he proves to have belonged to some quadruped. In the same work likewise he published an account of the Nyl-ghau, an Indian animal, not described before, and which, from its strength and swiftness, promised, he thought, to be an useful acquisition to this country.

In 1768, Dr. Hunter became F. S. A. and the same year, at the institution of a Royal Academy of Arts, he was appointed by his majesty to the office of professor of anatomy. This appointment opened a new field for his abilities, and he engaged in it, as he did in every other pursuit of his life, with unabating zeal. He now adapted his anatomical knowledge to the objects of painting and sculpture, and the novelty and justness of his observations proved at once the readiness and the extent of his genius.

[Q] Of the life of this ingenious anatomist no account had been printed, till Dr. Hahn, professor of physic in the university of Leyden, prefixed some anec-

dotes of him to a Latin translation of his works published in that city.

[a] Phil. Trans. Vol. LVIII.

In January, 1781, he was unanimously elected to succeed the late Dr. John Fothergill as president of the Society of Physicians of London. "He was one of those," says Dr. Simmons, "to whom we are indebted for its establishment, and our grateful acknowledgements are due to him for his zealous endeavours to promote the liberal views of this institution, by rendering it a source of mutual improvement, and thus making it ultimately useful to the public." As his name and talents were known and respected in every part of Europe, so the honours conferred on him were not limited to his own country. In 1780 the Royal Medical Society at Paris elected him one of their foreign associates; and in 1782 he received a similar mark of distinction from the Royal Academy of Sciences in that city. We come now to the most splendid of Dr. Hunter's medical publications, "The Anatomy of the Human Gravid Uterus." The appearance of this work, which had been begun so early as the year 1751 (at which time ten of the thirty-four plates it contains were completed), was retarded till the year 1775, only by the author's desire of sending it into the world with fewer imperfections. This great work is dedicated to the king. In his preface to it we find the author very candidly acknowledging, that in most of the dissections he had been assisted by his brother, Mr. John Hunter. This anatomical description of the Gravid Uterus, was not the only work which Dr. Hunter had in contemplation to give to the public. He had long been employed in collecting and arranging materials for a history of the various concretions that are formed in the human body. He seems to have advanced no further in the execution of this design, than to have nearly completed that part of it which relates to urinary and biliary concretions. Among Dr. Hunter's papers have likewise been found two introductory lectures, which are written out so fairly, and with such accuracy, that he probably intended no further correction of them, before they should be given to the world. In these lectures Dr. Hunter traces the history of anatomy from the earliest to the present times, along with the general progress of science and the arts. He considers the great utility of anatomy in the practice of physic and surgery; gives the ancient divisions of the different substances composing the human body, which for a long time prevailed in anatomy; points out the most advantageous mode of cultivating this branch of natural knowledge; and concludes with explaining the particular plan of his own lectures. Besides these MS. he has also left behind him a considerable number of cases of dissection [s]. The same year

[s] The work on the Gravid Uterus was published without a descriptive account. In 1795, Dr. Baillie published, from Dr. Hunter's papers, improved by his own observations, a book intended to supply this defect. It is entitled, "An Anatomical Description of the Human Gravid Uterus, and its Contents. By the late W. Hunter, M.D. &c." and forms a thin quarto.

in

in which the tables of the Gravid Uterus made their appearance, Dr. Hunter communicated to the Royal Society, "An Essay on the Origin of the Venereal Disease." After this paper had been read to the Royal Society, Dr. Hunter, in a conversation with the late Dr. Musgrave, was convinced that the testimony on which he placed his chief dependence was of less weight than he had at first imagined; he therefore very properly laid aside his intention of giving his Essay to the public.

In 1777, Dr. Hunter joined with Mr. Watson in presenting to the Royal Society " A short Account of the late Dr. Maty's Illness, and of the Appearances on Dissection [τ];" and the year following he published his " Reflections on the Section of the Symphysis Pubis."

We must now go back a little in the order of time, to describe the origin and progress of Dr. Hunter's Museum, without some account of which these memoirs would be very incomplete. When he began to practise midwifery, he was desirous of acquiring a fortune sufficient to place him in easy and independent circumstances. Before many years had elapsed, he found himself in possession of a sum adequate to his wishes in this respect, and this he set apart as a resource of which he might avail himself, whenever age or infirmities should oblige him to retire from business. He has been heard to say, that he once took a considerable sum from this fund for the purposes of his museum, but that he did not feel himself perfectly at ease till he had restored it again. After he had obtained this competency, as his wealth continued to accumulate, he formed a laudable design of engaging in some scheme of public utility, and at first had it in contemplation to found an anatomical school in this metropolis. For this purpose, about 1765, during the administration of Mr. Grenville, he presented a memorial to that minister, in which he requested the grant of a piece of ground in the Mews for the site of an anatomical theatre. Dr. Hunter undertook to expend 7000l. on the building, and to endow a professorship of anatomy in perpetuity. This scheme did not meet with the reception it deserved.—In a conversation on this subject soon afterwards with the earl of Shelburne, his lordship expressed a wish that the plan might be carried into execution by subscription, and very generously requested to have his name set down for 1000 guineas. Dr. Hunter's delicacy would not allow him to adopt this proposal. He chose rather to execute it at his own expence, and accordingly purchased a spot of ground in Great Windmill-street, where he erected a spacious house, to which he removed from Jermyn-street in 1770. In this building, besides a handsome amphi-

[τ] Philos. Transf. Vol. LXVII.

theatre and other convenient apartments for his lectures and diffections, there was one magnificent room, fitted up with great elegance and propriety as a museum.

Of the magnitude and value of his anatomical collection, some idea may be formed, when we consider the great length of years he employed in making anatomical preparations, and in the dissection of morbid bodies; added to the eagerness with which he procured additions, from the collections that were at different times offered for sale in London. His specimens of rare diseases were likewise frequently increased by presents from his medical friends and pupils, who, when any thing of this sort occurred to them, very justly thought they could not dispose of it more properly than by placing it in Dr. Hunter's museum. Before his removal to Windmill-street, he had confined his collection chiefly to specimens of human and comparative anatomy, and of diseases; but now he extended his views to fossils, and likewise to the branches of polite literature and erudition. In a short space of time he became possessed of "the most magnificent treasure of Greek and Latin books that has been accumulated by any person now living, since the days of Mead." A cabinet of ancient medals contributed likewise greatly to the richness of his museum. A description [u] of part of the coins in this collection, struck by the Greek free cities, has been published by the doctor's learned friend Mr. Combe. In a classical dedication of this elegant volume to the queen, Dr. Hunter acknowledges his obligations to her majesty. In the preface, some account is given of the progress of the collection, which had been brought together since the year 1770, with singular taste, and at the expence of upwards of 20,000l. In 1781, the museum received a valuable addition of shells, corals, and other curious subjects of natural history, which had been collected by the late Dr. Fothergill, who gave directions by his will that his collection should be appraised after his death, and that Dr. Hunter should have the refusal of it at 500l. under the valuation. This was accordingly done, and Dr. Hunter purchased it for the sum of 1200l.

Dr. Hunter, at the head of his profession, honoured with the esteem of his sovereign, and in the possession of every thing that his reputation and wealth could confer, seemed now to have attained the summit of his wishes. But these sources of gratification were embittered by a disposition to the gout, which harrassed him frequently during the latter part of his life, notwithstanding his very abstemious manner of living. About ten years before his death his health was so much impaired, that, fearing

[u] "Nummorum veterum populorum & urbium qui in museo Gulielmi Hunteri asservantur descriptio figuris illustrata. Opera & studio Caroli Combe, S. R. & S. A. Soc. Londini, 1783," 4to.

he

he might foon become unfit for the fatigues of his profeffion, he began to think of retiring to Scotland. With this view he requefted his friends Dr. Cullen and Dr. Baillie, to look out for a pleafant eftate for him. A confiderable one, and fuch as they thought would be agreeable to him, was offered for fale about that time in the neighbourhood of Alloa. A defcription of it was fent to him, and met with his approbation: the price was agreed on, and the bargain fuppofed to be concluded. But when the title-deeds of the eftate came to be examined by Dr. Hunter's counfel in London, they were found defective, and he was advifed not to complete the purchafe. After this he found the expences of his mufeum increafe fo faft, that he laid afide all thoughts of retiring from practice.

This alteration in his plan did not tend to improve his health. In the courfe of a few years the returns of his gout became by degrees more frequent, fometimes affecting his limbs, and fometimes his ftomach, but feldom remaining many hours in one part. Notwithftanding this valetudinary ftate, his ardour feemed to be unabated. In the laft year of his life he was as eager to acquire new credit, and to fecure the advantage of what he had before gained, as he could have been at the moft enterprifing part of his life. At length, on Saturday, March 15, 1783, after having for feveral days experienced a return of wandering gout, he complained of great head-ach and naufea. In this ftate he went to bed, and for feveral days felt more pain than ufual, both in his ftomach and limbs. On the Thurfday following he found himfelf fo much recovered, that he determined to give the introductory lecture to the operations of furgery. It was to no purpofe that his friends urged to him the impropriety of fuch an attempt. He was determined to make the experiment, and accordingly delivered the lecture, but towards the conclufion his ftrength was fo exhaufted that he fainted away, and was obliged to be carried to bed by two fervants. The following night and day his fymptoms were fuch as indicated danger; and on Saturday morning Mr. Combe, who made him an early vifit, was alarmed on being told by Dr. Hunter himfelf, that during the night he had certainly had a paralytic ftroke. As neither his fpeech nor his pulfe were affected, and he was able to raife himfelf in bed, Mr. Combe encouraged him to hope that he was miftaken. But the event proved the doctor's idea of his complaint to be but too well founded; for from that time till his death, which happened on Sunday, March 30, he voided no urine without the affiftance of the catheter, which was occafionally introduced by his brother; and purgative medicines were adminiftered repeatedly, without procuring a paffage by ftool. Thefe circumftances, and the abfence of pain, feemed to fhew that the inteftines and bladder had loft their fenfibility and power of contraction; and it was reasonable to presume, that a partial palsy had affected the nerves distributed to those parts. The latter moments of his life exhibited an instance of calmness and fortitude that well deserves to be recorded. Turning to his friend Mr. Combe, "If I had strength enough to hold a pen," said he, "I would write how easy and pleasant a thing it is to die."

By his will, the use of his museum, under the direction of trustees, devolved to his nephew Matthew Baillie, and in case of his death, to Mr. Cruikshank for the term of thirty years, at the end of which period the whole collection is bequeathed to the university of Glasgow. The sum of 8000l. sterling is left as a fund for the support and augmentation of the collection. The trustees are Dr. George Fordyce, Dr. David Pitcairne, and Mr. Charles (since Dr.) Combe, to each of whom Dr. Hunter bequeathed an annuity of 20l. for thirty years, that is, during the period in which they will be executing the purposes of the will. Dr. Hunter has likewise bequeathed an annuity of 100l. to his sister, Mrs. Baillie, during her life, and the sum of 2000l. to each of her two daughters. The residue of his estate and effects goes to his nephew. On Saturday, April 5, his remains were interred in the rector's vault of St. James's church, Westminster.

Of the person of Dr. Hunter, it may be observed, that he was regularly shaped, but of a slender make, and rather below a middle stature. There are several good portraits of him extant. One of these is an unfinished painting by Zoffany, who has represented him in the attitude of giving a lecture on the muscles at the Royal Academy, surrounded by a groupe of academicians. His manner of living was extremely simple and frugal, and the quantity of his food was small as well as plain. He was an early riser, and when business was over, was constantly engaged in his anatomical pursuits, or in his museum. There was something very engaging in his manner and address, and he had such an appearance of attention to his patients when he was making his enquiries, as could hardly fail to conciliate their confidence and esteem. In consultation with his medical brethren, he delivered his opinions with diffidence and candour. In familiar conversation he was chearful and unassuming. All who knew him allowed, that he possessed an excellent understanding, great readiness of perception, a good memory, and a sound judgement. To these intellectual powers he united uncommon assiduity and precision, so that he was admirably fitted for anatomical investigation. As a teacher of anatomy, he was long and deservedly celebrated. He was a good orator, and having a clear and accurate conception of what he taught, he knew how to place in distinct and intelligible points of view, the most abstruse ftrufe fubje&s of anatomy and phyfiology. How much he contributed to the improvement of medical fcience in general, may be colle&ed from the concife view we have taken of. his writings. The munificence he difplayed in the caufe of fcience has likewife a claim to our applaufe. Dr. Hunter facrificed no part of his time or his fortune to voluptuoufnefs, to idle pomp, or to any of the common obje&s of vanity that influence the purfuits of mankind in general. He feems to have been animated with a defire of diftinguifhing himfelf in thofe things which are in their nature laudable ; and being a batchelor, and without views for eftablifhing a family, he was at liberty to indulge his inclination. Let us, therefore, not withhold the praife that is due to him ; and undoubtedly his temperance, his prudence, his perfevering and eager purfuit of knowledge, conftitute an example which we may with advantage to ourfelves and to fociety, endeavour to imitate.

HUNTER (JOHN), younger brother of Dr. Hunter, one of the moft profound anatomifts, fagacious and expert furgeons, and acute obfervers of nature, that any age has produced, was born at Long Calderwood, abovementioned, July 14, 1728 [x]. At the age of ten years he loft his father, and being the youngeft of ten children, was fuffered to employ himfelf in amufement rather thau ftudy, though fent occafionally to a grammar-fchool. He had reached the age of twenty before he felt a wifh for more a&ive employment, and hearing of the reputation his brother William had acquired in London as a teacher of anatomy, made a propofal to go up to him as an affiftant. His propofal was kindly accepted, and, in September 1748, he arrived in London. It was not long before his difpofition to excel in anatomical purfuits was fully evinced, and his determination to proceed in that line confirmed and approved. In the fummer of 1749, he attended Mr. Chefelden at Chelfea-hofpital, and there acquired the rudiments of furgery. In the fubfequent winter, he was fo far advanced in the knowledge of anatomy, as to inftru& his brother's pupils in diffe&ion, and, from the conftant occupation of the doctor in bufinefs, this tafk in future devolved almoft totally upon him. In the fummer of 1750, he again attended at Chelfea, and in 1751 became a pupil at St. Bartholomew's, where he conftantly attended when any extraordinary operation was to be performed. After having paid a vifit to Scotland, he entered as a gentleman-commoner in Oxford, at St. Mary-hall, though with what particular view does not appear. His profeffional ftudies, however, were not interrupted, for in 1754, he became a pupil at St. George's hofpital, where, in 1756, he was ap-

[x] Life of John Hunter, by his brother-in-law Everard Home, prefixed to his pofthumous treatife on the blood.

pointed

pointed houfe-furgeon. In the winter of 1755, Dr. Hunter admitted him to a partnerſhip in his lectures.

The management of anatomical preparations was at this time a new art, and very little known; every preparation, therefore, that was ſkilfully made, became an object of admiration; many were wanting for the uſe of the lectures, and Dr. Hunter having himſelf an enthuſiaſm for the art, his brother had every advantage in the proſecution of that purſuit towards which his own diſpoſition pointed ſo ſtrongly; and of which he left ſo noble a monument in his Muſeum of Comparative Anatomy. Mr. Hunter purſued the ſtudy of anatomy with an ardour and perſeverance of which few examples can be found. By this cloſe application for ten years, he made himſelf maſter of all that was already known, and ſtruck out ſome additions to that knowledge. He traced the ramifications of the olfactory nerves upon the membranes of the noſe, and diſcovered the courſe of ſome of the branches of the fifth pair of nerves. In the gravid uterus, he traced the arteries of the uterus to their termination in the placenta. He alſo diſcovered the exiſtence of the lymphatic veſſels in birds. In comparative anatomy, which he cultivated with indefatigable induſtry, his grand object was, by examining various organizations formed for ſimilar functions, under different circumſtances, to trace out the general principles of animal life. With this object in view, the commoneſt animals were often of conſiderable importance to him; but he alſo took every opportunity of purchaſing thoſe that were rare, or encouraged their owners to ſell the bodies to him when they happened to die.

By exceſſive attention to theſe purſuits, his health was ſo much impaired, that he was threatened with conſumptive ſymptoms, and being adviſed to go abroad, obtained the appointment of a ſurgeon on the ſtaff, and went with the army to Belleiſle, leaving Mr. Hewſon to aſſiſt his brother. He continued in this ſervice till the cloſe of the war in 1763, and thus acquired his knowledge of the nature and treatment of gun-ſhot wounds. On his return to London, to his emoluments from private practice, and his half-pay, he added thoſe which aroſe from teaching practical anatomy, and operative ſurgery; and, that he might be more enabled to carry on his enquiries in comparative anatomy, he purchaſed ſome land at Earl's-court near Brompton, where he built a houſe. Here alſo he kept ſuch animals alive as he purchaſed, or were preſented to him; ſtudied their habits and inſtincts, and cultivated an intimacy with them, which with the fiercer kinds, was not always ſupported without perſonal riſk. It is recorded by his biographer, that, on finding two leopards looſe, and likely to eſcape or be killed, he went out, and ſeizing them with his own hands, carried them back to their

den.

den. The horror he felt afterwards, at the danger he had run, would not, probably, have prevented him from making a fimilar effort, had a like occafion arifen.

On the fifth of February, 1767, Mr. Hunter was elected a fellow of the Royal Society; and, in order to make that fituation as productive of knowledge as poffible, he prevailed on Dr. George Fordyce, and Mr. Cumming (the celebrated watchmaker) to form a kind of fubfequent meeting at a coffee-houfe, for the purpofe of philofophical difcuffion, and enquiry into difcoveries and improvements. To this meeting, fome of the firft philofophers of the age very fpeedily acceded, among whom none can be more confpicuous than fir Jofeph Banks, Dr. Solander, Dr. Mafkelyne, fir Geo. Shuckburgh, fir Harry Englefield, fir Charles Blagden, Dr. Noothe, Mr. Ramfden, and Mr. Watt of Birmingham. About the fame time, the accident of breaking his *tendo Achillis*, led him to fome very fuccefsful refearches into the mode in which tendons are re-united; fo completely does a true philofopher turn every accident to the advantage of fcience. In the year 1768, Dr. Hunter having finifhed his houfe in Windmill-ftreet, gave up to his brother that which he had occupied in Jermyn-ftreet; and in the fame year, by the intereft of the doctor, Mr. Hunter was elected one of the furgeons to St. George's-hofpital. In the year 1771, he married mifs Home, the eldeft daughter of Mr. Home, furgeon to Burgoyne's regiment of light-horfe, by whom he had two fons and two daughters [y]. In 1772, he undertook the profeffional education of his brother-in-law Mr. Everard Home, then leaving Weftminfter-fchool, who has affiduoufly purfued his fteps, ably recorded his merits, and fuccefsfully emulates his reputation.

As the family of Mr. Hunter increafed, his practice and character alfo advanced; but the expence of his collection abforbed a very confiderable part of his profits. The beft rooms in his houfe were filled with his preparations, and his mornings, from fun-rife to eight o'clock, were conftantly employed in anatomical and philofophical purfuits. The knowledge which he thus obtained, he applied moft fuccefsfully to the improvement of the art of furgery; was particularly ftudious to examine morbid bodies, and to inveftigate the caufe of failure when operations had not been productive of their due effect. It was thus that he perfected the mode of operation for the Hydrocele, and made feveral other improvements of different kinds. At the fame time the volumes of the Philofophical Tranfactions bear teftimony to his fuccefs in comparative anatomy, which was his favourite, and

[y] Only one fon and one daughter lived to grow up. The fon is now an officer in the army, and the daughter is married to captain James Campbell, eldeft fon of fir James, and nephew of the late fir Archibald Campbell.

may be called almost his principal pursuit. When he met with natural appearances which could not be preserved in actual preparations, he employed able draughtsmen to represent them on paper; and for several years, he even kept one in his family, expressly for this purpose. In Jan. 1776, Mr. Hunter was appointed surgeon-extraordinary to his majesty. In the autumn of the same year, he had an illness of so severe a nature as to turn his mind to the care of a provision for his family in case of his decease; when, considering that the chief part of his property was vested in his collection, he determined immediately to put it into such a state of arrangement as might make it capable of being disposed of to advantage at his death. In this he happily lived to succeed in a great measure, and finally left his museum so classed as to be fit for a public situation.

Mr. Hunter, in 1781, was elected into the Royal Society of Sciences and Belles Lettres at Gottenburg; and, in 1783, into the Royal Society of Medicine, and the Royal Academy of Surgery at Paris. In the same year, he removed from Jermyn-street, to a larger house in Leicester-square, and, with more spirit than consideration, expended a very great sum in buildings adapted to the objects of his pursuits. He was, in 1785, at the height of his career as a surgeon, and performed some operations with complete success, which were thought by the profession to be beyond the reach of any skill. His faculties were now in their fullest vigour, and his body sufficiently so to keep pace with the activity of his mind. He was engaged in a very extensive practice, he was surgeon to St. George's hospital, he gave a very long course of lectures in the winter, had a school of practical anatomy in his house, was continually engaged in experiments concerning the animal œconomy, and was from time to time producing very important publications. At the same time he instituted a medical society, called, " Lyceum Medicum Londinense," which met at his lecture-rooms, and soon rose to considerable reputation. On the death of Mr. Middleton, surgeon-general, in 1786, Mr. Hunter obtained the appointment of deputy surgeon-general to the army; but in the spring of the year he had a violent attack of illness, which left him, for the rest of his life, subject to peculiar and violent spasmodic affections of the heart. In July, 1787, he was chosen a member of the American Philosophical Society. In 1790, finding that his lectures occupied too much of his time, he relinquished them to his brother-in-law Mr. Home ; and in this year, on the death of Mr. Adair, he was appointed inspector-general of hospitals, and surgeon-general of the army. He was also elected a member of the Royal College of Surgeons in Ireland.

The death of Mr. Hunter was perfectly sudden, and the consequence of one of those spasmodic seizures in the heart to which he
                                                                    had

had now for feveral years been fubject. It happened on the 16th
of October, 1793. Irritation of mind had long been found
to bring on this complaint; and on that day, meeting with fome
vexatious circumftances at St. George's hofpital, he put a degree
of conftraint upon himfelf to fupprefs his fentiments, and in
that ftate went into another room; where in turning round to
a phyfician who was prefent, he fell, and inftantly expired without a groan. Of the diforder which produced this effect, Mr.
Home has given a clear and circumftantial account, of a very
interefting nature to profeffional readers. Mr. Hunter was fhort
in ftature, but uncommonly ftrong, active, and capable of great
bodily exertion. The prints of him by Sharp, from a picture
by fir Jofhua Reynolds, give a forcible and accurate idea of his
countenance. His temper was warm and impatient; but his
difpofition was candid and free from referve, even to a fault.
He was fuperior to every kind of artifice, detefted it in others,
and in order to avoid it, expreffed his exact fentiments, fometimes too openly and too abruptly. His mind was uncommonly
active; it was naturally formed for inveftigation, and fo attached
to truth and fact, that he defpifed all unfounded fpeculation, and
proceeded always with caution upon the folid ground of experiment. At the fame time his acutenefs in obferving the refult
of thofe experiments, his ingenuity in contriving, and his adroit-
nefs in conducting them, enabled him to deduce from them advantages which others would not have derived. It has been
fuppofed, very falfely, that he was fond of hypothefis; on the
contrary, if he was defective in any talent, it was in that of
imagination; he purfued truth on all occafions with mathematical precifion, but he made no fanciful excurfions. Converfation in a mixed company, where no fubject could be connectedly
purfued, fatigued inftead of amufing him; particularly towards
the latter part of his life. He flept little; feldom more than
four hours in the night, and about an hour after dinner. But his
occupations, laborious as they would have been to others, were far
from being fatiguing to him, being fo perfectly congenial to his
mind. He fpoke freely and fometimes harfhly of his cotem-
poraries; but he confidered furgery as in its infancy, and being
very anxious for its advancement thought meanly of thofe profeffors whofe exertions to promote it were unequal to his own.
Money he valued no otherwife than as it enabled him to purfue
his refearches; and in his zeal to benefit mankind, he attended too
little to the interefts of his own family. Altogether he was a
man fuch as few ages produce; and by his great contributions to
the ftores of knowledge, will ever deferve the gratitude and veneration of pofterity.

The contributions of Mr. Hunter, to the Tranfactions of the
Royal Society, cannot eafily be enumerated: his other works

appeared in the following order. 1. A treatife on " the natural Hiftory of the human Teeth," 4to, 1771 ; a fecond part to which was added in 1778. 2. " A Treatife on the Venereal Difeafe," 4to, 1786. 3. " Obfervations on certain Parts of the Animal Œconomy," 4to, 1786. 4. " A Treatife on the Blood, Inflammation, and Gun-fhot Wounds," 4to. This was a pofthumous work, not appearing till the year 1794; but it had been fent to the prefs in the preceding year, before his death. There are alfo fome papers by Mr. Hunter in the " Tranfactions of the Society for the Improvement of medical and chirurgical Knowledge," which were publifhed in 1793. The collection of comparative anatomy which Mr. Hunter left behind him, muft be confidered as a proof of talents, affiduity, and labour, which cannot be contemplated without furprife and admiration. His attempt in this collection has been to exhibit the gradations of nature from the moft fimple ftate in which life is found to exift, up to the moft perfect and complex of the animal creation, to man himfelf. By his art and care, he has been able fo to expofe and preferve in a dried ftate, or in fpirits, the correfponding parts of animal bodies, that the various links in the chain of perfectnefs may be readily followed, and clearly underftood. They are claffed in the following order : firft, the parts conftructed for motion ; fecondly, the parts effential to animals as refpecting their own internal œconomy ; thirdly, parts fuperadded for purpofes concerned with external objects ; fourthly, parts defigned for the propagation of the fpecies, and the maintenance and prefervation of the young. To go further into thefe particulars, would lead us to a detail inconfiftent with the nature of this work : but they are of the moft curious kind, and may be found defcribed in a manner at once clear and inftructive, in the life of J. Hunter, from which we have taken this account.

HUNTINGTON (ROBERT), a learned Englifh divine, was born at Deorhyrft in Glouceflerfhire where his father was minifter, in 1636. Having been educated in fchool-learning at Briftol, he was fent to Merton-college, Oxford, of which in due time he was chofen fellow[z]. He went through the ufual courfe of arts and fciences with great applaufe, and then applied himfelf moft diligently to divinity, and the Oriental languages. The latter became afterwards of infinite fervice to him ; for he was chofen chaplain to the Englifh factory at Aleppo, and failed from England in Sept. 1670. During his eleven years refidence in this place, he applied himfelf particularly to fearch out and procure manufcripts; and for this purpofe maintained a correfpondence with the learned and eminent of every profeffion and degree,

[z] D. Roberti Huntingtoni Vita, fcriptore T. Smith, Lond. 1704, 8vo.

which

which his knowledge in the Eastern languages, and especially
the Arabic, enabled him to do. He travelled also for his diver-
sion and improvement, not only into the adjacent, but even into
distant places; and after having carefully visited almost all Galilee and Samaria, he went to Jerusalem. In 1677, he went,
into Cyprus; and the year after, undertook a journey of 150
miles, for the sake of beholding the venerable ruins of the once
noble and glorious city of Palmyra: but, instead of having an
opportunity of viewing the place, he and they that were with
him were very near being destroyed by two Arabian princes,
who had taken possession of those parts. He had better success
in a journey to Egypt in 1680, where he met with several curi-
·osities and mannscripts; and had the pleasure of conversing with
John Lascaris, archbishop of mount Sinai.

In 1682, he embarked, and landed in Italy; and having visited Rome, Naples, and other places, taking Paris in his way,
where he stayed a few weeks, he arrived, after many dangers
and difficulties, safe in his own country. He retired immediately to his fellowship at Merton-college; and, in 1683, took
the degrees in divinity. About the same time, through the recommendation of bishop Fell, he was appointed master of Trinity-college in Dublin, and went over thither, though against
his will; but the troubles that happened in Ireland at the Revolution forced him back for a time into England; and though he
returned after the reduction of that kingdom, yet he resigned
his mastership in 1691, and came home, with an intention to
quit it no more. In the mean time he sold for 700l. his fine
collection of MSS. to the curators of the Bodleian library;
having before made a present of thirty-five. In 1692, he was
presented by sir Edward Turnor to the rectory of Great Hal-
lingbury in Essex, and the same year he married. He was offered about that time the bishopric of Kilmore in Ireland, but
refused it: in 1701, however, he accepted that of Raphoe, and
was consecrated in Christ-church, Dublin, Aug. 20. He survived his consecration but twelve days; for he died Sept. 2, in
his 66th year, and was buried in Trinity-college chapel.

All that he published himself was, " An Account of the Porphyry Pillars in Egypt," in the " Philosophical Transactions,
Nº 161." Some of his " Observations" are printed in " A
Collection of curious Travels and Voyages," in 2 vols. 8vo,
by Mr. J. Ray; and thirty-nine of his letters, chiefly written
while he was abroad, were published by Dr. T. Smith, at the
end of his life.

HUNTORST (GERARD), one of the best Dutch painters of
his time, was born at Utrecht in 1592. He was a disciple of
Blomeart, and afterwards went to Rome; where having studied
design, he exercised it in drawing night-pieces with the utmost
succefs.

fuccefs. When he returned to Utrecht, he applied himfelf to hiftory-painting. He had a vaft number of fcholars from Antwerp. He taught alfo the queen of Bohemia's children to defign. Charles I. invited him over to England, and for him he executed feveral noble works. He afterwards returned to Holland, where he painted for the prince of Orange. The time of his death is not mentioned.

HURE (CHARLES), a French divine of fome eminence, was born at Champigny-fur-Youne, in 1639, the fon of a labourer. He made it his object to know every thing that could throw any light upon theology; and with this view he ftudied the Oriental languages. He was a member of the learned fociety of Port-Royal, where he imbibed at once his zeal for religion and for letters. He was afterwards profeffor of the learned languages in the univerfity of Paris, and principal of the college of Bencourt. He died in 1717. There are extant by him, 1. A Dictionary of the Bible, 2 vols. folio, lefs full, and lefs complete, than that of Calmet, publifhed in 1715. 2. An edition of the Latin Teftament, with notes, which are much efteemed, 2 vols. 12mo. 3. A French tranflation of the former, with the notes from the Latin augmented, 4 vols. 12mo, 1702. 4. " A Sacred Grammar," with rules for underftanding the literal fenfe of the Scripture. He was confidered as a Janfenift; and by fome faid to be only Quefnel a little moderated.

HUSS (JOHN), a celebrated divine and martyr, was born at a town in Bohemia, called Huffenitz, about the year 1376[A]; and liberally educated in the univerfity of Prague. Here he took the degree of B. A. in 1393, and that of mafter in 1395; and we find him, in 1400, in orders, and a minifter of a church in that city. About this time the writings of our countryman Wicklif had fpread themfelves among the Bohemians, and were particularly read by the ftudents at Prague, among the chief of whom was Hufs; who, being greatly taken with Wicklif's notions, and having abundance of warmth in his compofition, began to preach and write with great zeal againft the fuperftitions and errors of the church of Rome. He fucceeded fo far, that the fale of indulgences began greatly to decreafe and grow cold among the Bohemians; and the pope's party cried aloud, that there would foon be an end of religion, if meafures were not taken to oppofe the reftlefs endeavours of the Huffites. With a view, therefore, of preventing this danger, Subinco, the archbifhop of Prague, iffued forth two mandates in 1408; one, addreffed to the members of the univerfity, by which they were ordered to bring together all Wicklif's writings, that fuch as were found to contain any thing erroneous or heretical might

[A] Cave Hift. Liter. Tom. II. Append. p. 102. Oxon. 1740.

be

be burnt; the other to all curates and ministers, commanding
them to teach the people, that, after the consecration of the
elements in the holy Sacrament, there remained nothing but the
real body and blood of Christ, under the appearance of bread
and wine. Huss, whose credit and authority in the university
were very great, as well for his piety and learning, as on account
of considerable services he had done, found no difficulty in
persuading many of its members of the unreasonableness and
absurdity of these mandates: the first being, as he said, a plain
encroachment upon the liberties and privileges of the university,
whose members had an indisputable right to possess, and to read
all sorts of books; the second, inculcating a most abominable
error. Upon this foundation they appealed to Gregory XII.
and the archbishop Subinco was summoned to Rome. But, on
acquainting the pope that the heretical notions of Wicklif were
gaining ground apace in Bohemia, through the zeal of some
preachers who had read his books, a bull was granted him for
the suppression of all such notions in his province. By virtue of
this bull, Subinco condemned the writings of Wicklif, and proceeded against four doctors, who had not complied with his mandate, in bringing in their copies. Huss and others, who were
involved in this sentence, protested against this procedure of the
archbishop, and appealed from him a second time, in June,
1410. The matter was then brought before John XXIII. who
ordered Huss, accused of many errors and heresies, to appear in
person at the court of Rome, and gave a special commission
to cardinal Colonna to cite him. Huss, however, under the
protection and countenance of Wenceslaus king of Bohemia,
did not appear, but sent three deputies to excuse his absence,
and to answer all which should be alledged against him. Colonna paid no regard to the deputies, nor to any defence they
could make; but declared Huss guilty of contumacy to the court
of Rome, and excommunicated him for it. Upon this the deputies appealed from the cardinal to the pope, who commissioned
four other cardinals to examine into the affair. These commis-
saries confirmed all that that Colonna had done [a]. Nay, they
did more; the excommunication, which was limited to Huss,
they extended to his friends and followers: they declared him an
Heresiarch, and pronounced an interdict against him.

All this time, utterly regardless of what was doing at Rome,
Huss continued to preach and write with great zeal against the
errors and superstitions of that church, and in defence of Wicklif and his doctrines. He preached directly against the pope,
the cardinals, and the clergy of that party; and at the same
time published writings, to shew the lawfulness of exposing the

[a] Dupin Nouvel. Bibl. Eccles. Tom. XII. p. 132. Paris, 1700.

vices of ecclesiastics. In 1413, the religious tumults and seditions were become so violent, that Subinco applied to Wenceslaus to appease them. Wenceslaus banished Huss from Prague; but still the disorders continued. Then the archbishop had recourse to the emperor Sigismond, who promised him to come into Bohemia, and assist in settling the affairs of the church; but before Sigismond could be prepared for the journey, Subinco died in Hungary. About this time bulls were published by John XXIII. at Prague against Ladislaus king of Naples; in which a crusade was proclaimed against that prince, and indulgences promised to all who would go to the war. This furnished Huss, who had returned to Prague upon the death of Subinco, with a fine occasion of preaching against indulgences and crusades, and of refuting these bulls: and the people were so affected and inflamed with his preaching, that they declared pope John to be antichrist. Upon this, some of the ringleaders among the Hussites were seized and imprisoned; which, however, was not consented to by the people, who were prepared to resist, till the magistrate had promised that no harm should happen to the prisoners. But he did not keep his word: they were executed in prison; which the Hussites discovering, took up arms, rescued their bodies, and interred them honourably, as martyrs, in the church of Bethlehem, which was Huss's church.

Things went on thus at Prague and in Bohemia, till the council of Constance was called; where it was agreed between the pope and the emperor, that Huss should appear, and give an account of himself and his doctrine. The emperor promised for his security against any danger, and that nothing should be attempted against his person; upon which he set out, after declaring publicly, that he was going to the council of Constance, to answer the accusations that were formed against him; and challenging all people, who had any thing to except to his life and conversation, to do it without delay. He made the same declarations in all the towns through which he passed, and arrived at Constance, Nov. 3, 1414. Here he was accused in form, and a list of his heretical tenets laid before the pope and the prelates of the council. He was summoned to appear the twenty-sixth day after his arrival; and declared himself ready to be examined, and to be corrected by them, if he should be found to have taught any doctrine worthy of censure. The cardinals soon after withdrew, to deliberate upon the most proper method of proceeding against Huss; and the result of their deliberations was, that he should be imprisoned. This accordingly was done, notwithstanding the emperor's parole for his security; nor were all his prince's endeavours afterwards sufficient to release him, though he exerted himself to the utmost. Huss was tossed about from prison to prison for six whole

months,

months, suffering great hardships and pains from those who had
the care of him; and at last was condemned of herefy by the
council, in his absence and without a hearing, for maintaining,
that the Euchariſt ought to be adminiſtered to the people in both
kinds. The emperor, in the mean time, complained heavily of
the contempt that was ſhewn to himſelf, and of the uſage that was
employed towards Huſs; inſiſting, that Huſs ought to be allowed
a fair and public hearing. Therefore, on the 5th and 7th of
June, 1415, he was brought before the council, and permitted
to ſay what he could in behalf of himſelf and his doctrines;
but every thing was carried on with noiſe and tumult, and Huſs
ſoon given to underſtand, that they were not diſpoſed to hear
any thing from him, but a recantation of his errors; which,
however, he abſolutely refuſed, and was ordered back to priſon.
July 6, he was brought again before the council; where he was
condemned of herefy, and ordered to be burnt. The ceremony
of his execution was this: he was firſt ſtripped of his ſacerdotal
veſtments by biſhops nominated for that purpoſe; next he was
formally deprived of his univerſity-degrees; then he had a paper-
crown put upon his head, painted round with devils, and the
word Hereſiarch inſcribed in great letters; then he was delivered over to the magiſtrate, who burnt him alive, after having
firſt burnt his books at the door of the church. He died with
great firmneſs and reſolution; and his aſhes were afterwards
gathered up and thrown into the Rhine. His writings, which
are very numerous and learned, were collected into a body,
when the art of printing began.

HUTCHESON (Dr. FRANCIS), a very fine writer and excellent man, was the ſon of a diſſenting miniſter in Ireland, and
was born Aug. 8, 1694 [c]. He diſcovered early a ſuperior
capacity, and ardent thirſt after knowledge; and when he had
gone through his ſchool-education, was ſent to an academy to
begin his courſe of philoſophy. In 1710, he removed from the
academy, and entered a ſtudent in the univerſity of Glaſgow in
Scotland. Here he renewed his ſtudy of the Latin and Greek
languages, and applied himſelf to all parts of literature, in which
he made a progreſs ſuitable to his uncommon abilities. Afterwards he turned his thoughts to divinity, which he propoſed to
make the peculiar ſtudy and profeſſion of his life; for the proſecution of which he continued ſeveral years longer at Glaſgow.

He then returned to Ireland; and, entering into the miniſtry,
was juſt about to be ſettled in a ſmall congregation of Diſſenters
in the north of Ireland, when ſome gentlemen about Dublin,
who knew his great abilities and virtues, invited him to ſet up

[c] Account of his Life, prefixed to his Syſtem of Moral Philoſophy. Glaſgow,
1755.

a private academy in that city. He complied with the invitation,
and met with much succefs. He had been fixed but a fhort
time in Dublin, when his fingular merits and accomplifhments
made him generally known; and his acquaintance was fought
by men of all ranks, who had any tafte for literature, or any
regard for learned men. Lord Molefworth is faid to have
taken great pleafure in his converfation, and to have affifted him
with his criticifms and obfervations upon his " Enquiry into the
Ideas of Beauty and Virtue," before it came abroad. He received the fame favour from Dr. Synge, bifhop of Elphin, with
whom he alfo lived in great friendfhip. The firft edition of
this performance came abroad without the author's name, but
the merit of it would not fuffer him to be long concealed. Such
was the reputation of the work, and the ideas it had raifed of
the author, that lord Granville, who was then lord-lieutenant of
Ireland, fent his private fecretary to enquire at the bookfeller's
for the author; and when he could not learn his name, he left
a letter to be conveyed to him: in confequence of which he
foon became acquainted with his excellency, and was treated by
him, all the time he continued in his government, with diftinguifhing marks of familiarity and efteem.

From this time his acquaintance began to be ftill more courted
by men of diftinction, either for ftation or literature, in Ireland.
Abp King held him in great efteem; and the friendfhip of that
prelate was of great ufe to him in fcreening him from two
attempts made to profecute him, for daring to take upon him
the education of youth, without having qualified himfelf by
fubfcribing the ecclefiaftical canons, and obtaining a licenfe from
the bifhop. He had alfo a large fhare in the efteem of the primate Boulter, who, through his influence, made a donation to
the univerfity of Glafgow of a yearly fund for an exhibitioner,
to be bred to any of the learned profeffions. A few years after
his Enquiry into the Ideas of Beauty and Virtue, his " Treatife on the Paffions" was publifhed: thefe works have been often
reprinted, and always admired both for the fentiment and language; even by thofe, who have not affented to the philofophy
of them, nor allowed it to have any foundation in nature.
About this time he wrote fome philofophical papers, accounting
for laughter in a different way from Hobbes, and more honourable to human nature; which papers were publifhed in the collection called " Hibernicus's Letters." Some letters in the
" London Journal, 1728," fubfcribed Philaretus, containing
objections to fome parts of the doctrine in " The Enquiry, &c."
occafioned his giving anfwers to them in thofe public papers.
Both the letters and anfwers were afterwards publifhed in a feparate pamphlet.

After

After he had taught in a private academy at Dublin for seven or eight years with great reputation and success, he was called in 1729 to Scotland, to be a professor of philosophy at Glasgow. Several young gentlemen came along with him from the academy, and his high reputation drew many more thither both from England and Ireland. After his settlement in the college, he was not obliged, as when he kept the academy, to teach the languages and all the different parts of philosophy, but the profession of morals was the province assigned to him ; so that now he had full leisure to turn all his attention to his favourite study, human nature. Here he spent the remainder of his life in a manner highly honourable to himself, and ornamental to the university of which he was a member. His whole time was divided between his studies and the duties of his office ; except what he allotted to friendship and society. A firm constitution and a pretty uniform state of good health, except some few slight attacks of the gout, seemed to promise a longer life ; yet he did not exceed his 53d year. He was married soon after his settlement in Dublin, to Mrs. Mary Wilson, a gentleman's daughter in the county of Longford ; by whom he left behind him one son, Francis Hutcheson, M. D. By this gentleman was published, from the original MS. of his father, " A System of Moral Philosophy, in three books, Glasgow, 1755," 2 vols. 4to. To which is prefixed, " Some Account of the Life, Writings, and Character of the Author," by Dr. Leechman, professor of divinity in the same university. Dr. Hutcheson had high thoughts of human nature, of its original dignity ; and was persuaded, that even in this corrupt state it is capable of great improvements by proper instructions and assiduous culture. This is the foundation on which he has built his system : which will therefore pass for visionary with the followers of Montaigne, Hobbes, Mandeville, and others; who have set human nature as low as possible, by drawing it in the meanest and most odious colours.

HUTCHINS (John) [D], a native of Dorsetshire, and rector of the church of the Holy Trinity in Wareham, began in 1737, while curate of Milton-Abbas, to collect materials for the history of that county, which, after many difficulties, he lived to see put to press. He was rather a man of diligence than of extraordinary genius ; his collections were many years making, and a great part of them fell into his hands on the death of a prior collector. The book was most liberally conducted through the press, by a very handsome subscription of the gentlemen of the county, and the kind patronage of Dr. Cuming and Mr. Gough, for the benefit of the author's widow and daughter. Several articles were added, relative to the antiquities and natural history ; and

[D] Anecdotes of Bowyer, by Nichols p. 150.

such a number of beautiful plates were contributed by the gentlemen of the county, that (only 600 copies having been printed, a number not quite sufficient for the subscribers) the value of the book increased, immediately after publication, to twice the original price, which was only a guinea a volume. The title of it is, " The History and Antiquities of the County of Dorset, compiled from the best and most ancient Historians, *Inquisitiones post mortem*, and other valuable Records and MSS. in the public Offices, Libraries, and private Hands; with a Copy of Domesday-book and the Inquisitio Gheldi for the county: interspersed with some remarkable Particulars of Natural History, and adorned with a correct Map of the County, and Views of Antiquities, Seats of the Nobility and Gentry, Lond. 1774," 2 vols. folio. Mr. Hutchins was born in 1698 at Bradford-Peverell, where his father Richard Hutchins was curate, who died rector of All-Saints in Dorchester, 1734, having held it from 1693. He was educated at Baliol-college, where he cultivated an acquaintance with Mr. Godwin and Mr. Sandford; to the friendship of the former, who closed a long and worthy life about three years before him, he bears ample testimony in his preface. Upon being presented to Wareham, he married Anne, daughter of the Rev. Mr. Steevens, rector of Pimpern, whose grandfather had been steward to Mr. Pitt's family, who permitted Mrs. Steevens to present to the living for the next turn, in hopes of keeping it for her son; but the presentee, Mr. Andrews, dying within the year, she lost her turn [1]. Mr. Hutchins was presented to Swyre, 1729, to Melcomb-Horsey, 1733, and to Wareham, 1743; and, after a long combat with the infirmities of age and gout, and a severe loss by the fire at Wareham, in 1762, died June 21, 1773, and was buried in Mary's church at Wareham, in the ancient chapel under the south aile of the chancel.

HUTCHINSON (JOHN), an English author, whose writings have been much discussed, and who is considered as the founder of a sect, was born at Spennythorn in Yorkshire in 1674. His father was possessed of about 40l. per ann. and determined to qualify his son for a stewardship to some gentleman or nobleman. He had given him such school-learning as the place afforded; and the remaining part of his education was finished by a gentleman that boarded with his father. This friend is said to have instructed him, not only in such parts of the mathematics as were more immediately connected with his destined employment, but in every branch of that science, and at the same time to have furnished him with a competent knowledge of the writings of antiquity. At 19, he went to be steward to Mr. Bathurst of Skutterskelf in Yorkshire, and from thence to

the

the earl of Scarborough, who would gladly have engaged him in his fervice; but his ambition to ferve the duke of Somerfet would not fuffer him to continue there, and accordingly he removed foon after into this nobleman's fervice. About 1700, he was called to London, to manage a law-fuit of confequence between the duke and another nobleman; and during his attendance in town, contracted an acquaintance with Dr. Woodward, who was phyfician to the duke his mafter. Between 1702 and 1706, his bufinefs carried him into feveral parts of England and Wales, where he made many obfervations, which he publifhed in a little pamphlet, entitled, " Obfervations made by J. H. moftly in the Year 1706."

While he travelled from place to place, he employed himfelf in collecting foffils; and we are told, that the large and noble collection, which Woodward bequeathed to the univerfity of Cambridge, was actually formed by him. Whether Woodward had no notion of Hutchinfon's abilities in any other way than that of fteward and mineralogift, or whether he did not fufpect him at that time as likely to commence author, is not certain: Hutchinfon however complains in one of his books, that " he was bereft, in a manner not to be mentioned, of thofe obfervations, and thofe collections; nay, even of the credit of being the collector." He is faid to have put his collections into Woodward's hands, with obfervations on them, which Woodward was to digeft and publifh, with further obfervations of his own: but putting him off with excufes, when from time to time he folicited him about this work, he firft fuggefted to Hutchinfon unfavourable notions of his intention. On this Hutchinfon refolved to wait no longer, but to truft to his own pen; and that he might be more at leifure to profecute his ftudies, he begged leave of the duke of Somerfet to quit his fervice. The requeft at firft piqued the pride of that nobleman; but when he was made to underftand by Hutchinfon, that he did not intend to ferve any other mafter, and was told what were the real motives of his requeft, the duke not only granted his fuit, but made him his riding purveyor, being at that time mafter of the horfe to George I. As there is a good houfe in the Mews belonging to the office of purveyor, a fixed falary of 200l. per ann. and the place a kind of finecure, Hutchinfon's fituation and circumftances were quite agreeable to his mind; and he gave himfelf up to a ftudious and fedentary life [F]. The duke alfo gave him the next prefentation of the living of Sutton in Suffex, which Hutchinfon beftowed on the Rev. Julius Bate, a great favourite with him, and a zealous promoter of his doctrines.

[F] See art. BATE.

In 1724, he published the firſt part of his " Moſes's Principia;" in which he ridiculed Woodward's " Natural Hiſtory
of the Earth," and his account of the ſettlement of the ſeveral
ſtrata, ſhells, and nodules, by the laws of gravity; which, he
tells him, every dirty impertinent collier could contradiƈt and
diſprove by ocular demonſtration. " Moſes's Principia," wherein
gravitation is exploded, is evidently oppoſed to " Newton's
Principia," wherein ſhat doƈtrine is eſtabliſhed. Hutchinſon
alſo threw out ſome hints concerning what had paſſed between
Woodward and himſelf, and the doƈtor's deſign of robbing him
of his colleƈtion of foſſils. From this time to his death, he continued to publiſh a volume every year, or every other year;
which, with the MSS. he left behind him, were colleƈted in
1748, amounting to 12 vols. 8vo. An abſtraƈt of them was
alſo publiſhed in 1723, in 12mo. Hutchinſon's followers look-
upon the breach between Woodward and him, as a very happy
event; becauſe, ſay they, had the doƈtor fulfilled his engagements, Hutchinſon might have ſtopped there, and not have extended his reſearches ſo far as he has done; in which caſe the
world would have been deprived of writings deemed by them in-
valuable. Others are as violent oppoſers and cenſurers of his
writings and opinions; and the diſpute has been carried on with
no ſmall degree of warmth.

In 1727, Hutchinſon publiſhed the ſecond part of " Moſes's
Principia;" which contains the ſum and ſubſtance, or the principles, of the Scripture-philoſophy. As Sir Iſaac Newton made
a vacuum and gravity the principles of his philoſophy, this author on the contrary aſſerts, that a plenum and the air are the
principles of the Scripture-philoſophy. In the introduƈtion to
this ſecond part, he hinted, that the idea of the Trinity was to
be taken from the three grand agents in the ſyſtem of nature,
fire, light, and ſpirit; theſe three conditions of one and the
ſame ſubſtance, namely, air, anſwering wonderfully in a typical or
ſymbolical manner to the three perſons of one and the ſame eſ-
ſence. This, we are told, ſo forcibly ſtruck the celebrated Dr.
Samuel Clarke, that he ſent a gentleman to Mr. Hutchinſon
with compliments upon the performance, and deſired a conference with him on that propoſition in particular: which, however, it is added, after repeated ſolicitations Hutchinſon thought
fit to refuſe. This doƈtrine a certain admirer of Hutchinſon,
particularly in his opinions on natural philoſophy, has lately
attempted to revive and illuſtrate, in a pamphlet entitled, " A
ſhort Way to Truth, or the Chriſtian Doƈtrine of a Trinity in
Unity, illuſtrated and confirmed from an Analogy in the Natural Creation." It was publiſhed in 1793.

Some time in 1712, Hutchinſon is ſaid to have completed a
machine of the watch-kind, for the diſcovery of the longitude

at

at fea, which was approved by Sir Ifaac Newton; and Whifton, in his "Longitude and Latitude, &c." has given a teſtimony in favour of his mechanical abilities. "I have alſo," ſays he, "very lately been ſhewn by Mr. Hutchinſon, a very curious and inquiſitive perſon, a copy of a MS. map of the world, made about 80 years ago, taken by himſelf from the original; wherein the variation is reduced to a theory, much like that which Dr. Halley has ſince propoſed, and in general exactly agreeing to his obſervations.—But with this advantage, that therein the northern pole of the internal loadſtone is much better ſtated than it is by Dr. Halley—its place then being, according to this unknown very curious and ſagacious author, about the meridian, &c. which ancient and authentic determination of its place, I defire my reader particularly to obſerve."

Hutchinſon had been accuſtomed to make an excurſion for a month or ſo into the country for his health: but neglecting this in purſuit of his ſtudies, he is ſuppoſed to have brought himſelf into a bad habit of body, which prepared the way for his death. The immediate cauſe is ſaid to be an overflowing of the gall, occaſioned by the irregular ſallies of an high-kept unruly horſe, and the ſudden jerks given to his body by them. On the Monday before his death, Dr. Mead was with him, and urged him to be bled; ſaying at the ſame time in a pleaſant way, "I will ſoon ſend you to Moſes." Dr. Mead meant, to his ſtudies, two of his books being entitled, "Moſes's Principia:" but Hutchinſon, taking it in the other ſenſe, anſwered in a muttering tone, "I believe, doctor, you will;" and was ſo diſpleaſed with Mead, that he afterwards diſmiſſed him for another phyſician. He died Aug. 28, 1737, aged 63. He ſeems to have been in many reſpects a ſingular man. He certainly had eminent abilities, with much knowledge and learning; but many people have thought it very queſtionable, whether he did not want judgment to apply them properly. His temper ſeems to have been violent: ſince much ill language, and a ſtrong propenſity to perſecution, but too plainly appear in his writings. The leading feature of Hutchinſon's doctrine was, that all knowledge, natural as well as theological, is contained in the Hebrew Scriptures. To maintain this opinion, he had recourſe to the moſt fanciful and extravagant etymologies; and taught that every Hebrew root has ſome important meaning; or, as his diſciples expreſſed it "repreſents ſome obvious idea of action or condition, raiſed by the ſenſible object which it expreſſes, and further deſigned to ſignify ſpiritual or mental things." The air of myſtery and cabaliſm which appeared in theſe doctrines, added to the overbearing manner of the teacher, raiſed for a long time a vaſt contempt and abhorrence of Hutchinſon's ſyſtem; and the name of

Y 2   Hutchin-

Hutchinfonism has frequently operated as a bar to the preferment of perfons otherwife well worthy of it. It appears that thefe motions have been carried too far; or at leaft the danger, if there was any, is now nearly over. Few now adhere to the opinions of Hutchinfon; and fome who do, have given up his etymologies, and enmity to human learning [o].

HUTTEN (ULRIC DE), a gentleman of Franconia [R], of uncommon parts and learning, was born in 1488 at Sieckenburg, the feat of his family; was fent to the abbey of Fulde at 11 years of age; and took the degree of M. A. at 18, at Frankfort on the Oder, being the firft promotion made in that newly opened univerfity. In 1509, he was at the fiege of Padua, in the emperor Maximilian's army; and he owned that it was want of money, which forced him to make that campaign. His father, not having the leaft tafte or efteem for polite literature, thought it unworthy to be purfued by perfons of exalted birth; and therefore would not afford his fon the neceffary fupplies for a life of ftudy. He wifhed him to apply himfelf to the civil law, which might raife him in the world; but Hutten had no inclination for that kind of ftudy. Finding however that there was no other way of being upon good terms with his father, he went to Pavia in 1511, where he ftayed but a little time; that city being befieged and plundered by the Swifs, and himfelf taken prifoner. He returned afterwards to Germany, and there, contrary to his father's inclinations, began to apply himfelf again to literature. Having a genius for poetry, he began his career as an author in that line; and publifhed feveral compofitions, which were much admired, and gained him credit. He travelled to various places, among the reft to Bohemia and Moravia; and waiting on the bifhop of Olmutz in a very poor condition, that prelate, who was a great Mæcenas, received him gracioufly, prefented him with a horfe, and gave him money to purfue his journey. The correfpondence he held with Erafmus was of great advantage to him, and procured him refpect from all the literati in Italy, and efpecially at Venice.

At his return to Germany in 1516, he was recommended in fuch ftrong terms to the emperor, that he received from him the poetical crown; and from that time Hutten had himfelf drawn in armour, with a crown of laurel on his head, and took vaft delight in being fo reprefented. He was of a very military difpofition, and had given many proofs of courage, as well in the wars as in private rencounters. Being once at Viterbo, where an ambaffador of France ftopped, there happened a general quar-

[o] See Jones's Life of Bifhop Horne.   [R] Melchior Adam de vitis, &c. Bayle's Dict. Niceron, Hamerus Illuftres, Tom. XV.

[o]

5

rel to arife; in which Hutten, forfaken by his comrades, was
attacked by five Frenchmen at once, and put them all to flight,
after receiving fome fmall wounds. He wrote an epigram on
that occafion, " in quinque Gallos à fe profligatos," which may
be feen in Melchior Adam. He had a coufin John de Hutten,
who was court-martial to Ulric duke of Wirtemberg, and was
murdered by that duke in 1515, for the fake of his wife, whom
the duke enjoyed afterwards as a miftrefs. The military poet,
as foon as he heard of it, breathed nothing but refentment ; and
becaufe he had no opportunity of fhewing it with his fword,
took up his pen, and wrote feveral pieces in the form of Dialogues,
Orations, Poems, and Letters. A collection of thefe was printed
in the caftle of Steckelberg, 1519, 4to.

He was in France in 1518, whence he went to Mentz,
and engaged in the fervice of the elector Albert ; and attended
him a little after to the diet of Augfburg, where the elector
was honoured with a cardinal's hat. At this diet, articles were
exhibited againft the duke of Wirtemberg, on which occafion
the murder of John de Hutten, marfhal of his court, was not
forgotten: and a league was after formed againft him. Ulric Hutten ferved in this war with great pleafure ; yet was foon difgufted with a military life, and longed earneftly for his ftudies
and retirement. This we find by a letter of his to Frederic Pif-
cator, dated May 21, 1519: in which he difcovers an inclination for matrimony, and expreffes himfelf very fingularly on that
fubject. He informs his correfpondent, " that he wanted a
wife to take care of him ; that whatever fine things might be
faid of a fingle life, yet he was by no means fit for it, and did
not like even to lie alone ; that he wanted a female, in whofe
company he might unbend his mind, footh his cares, play, joke,
and tattle ; that fhe muft be beautiful, young, well-educated,
merry, modeft, and patient ; that he did not require much money
with her, nor infift much on her high birth, fince whoever married him would be fufficiently ennobled :—ad genus quod per-
tinent, fatis nobilem futuram puto, quæcunque Hutteno nup-
ferit."

Believing Luther's caufe a very good one, he joined in it with
great warmth ; and publifhed Leo the Xth's Bull againft Luther
in 1520, with interlineary and marginal gloffes, in which that
Pope was made an object of the ftrongeft ridicule. The freedom with which he wrote againft the irregularities and diforders
of the court of Rome, exafperated Leo in the higheft degree ;
and induced him to command the elector of Mentz to fend him
to Rome bound hand and foot, which however the elector did
not do, but fuffered him to depart in peace. Hutten then withdrew to Brabant, and was at the court of the emperor Charles V.

but

but did not ſtay long there, being told that his life would be in danger. He then retired to Ebernberg, where he was protected by Francis de Sickingen, Luther's great friend and guardian, to whom the caſtle of Ebernberg belonged. There he wrote in 1520 his complaint to the emperor, to the electors of Mentz and Saxony, and to all the ſtates of Germany, againſt the attempts which the Pope's emiſſaries made againſt him. From the ſame place alſo he wrote to Luther in May 1521, and publiſhed ſeveral pieces in favour of the Reformation. He did not declare openly for Luther, till after he had left the elector of Mentz's court; but he had written to him before from Mentz, and his firſt letter is dated June, 1520. While he was upon his journey to Ebernberg, he met with Hochſtratus; upon which he drew his ſword, and running up to him, ſwore he would kill him, for what he had done againſt Reuchlin and Luther: but Hochſtratus, throwing himſelf at his feet, conjured him ſo earneſtly to ſpare his life, that Hutten let him go, after ſtriking him ſeveral times with the flat ſword. This ſhews the heat of his zeal: it was indeed ſo hot, that Luther himſelf, warm as he was, blamed it. During his ſtay at Ebernberg, he performed a very generous action in regard to his family. Being the eldeſt ſon, and ſucceeding to the whole eſtate, he gave it all up to his brothers; and even, to prevent their being involved in the miffortunes and difgraces which he expected, by the ſuſpicions that might be entertained againſt them, he enjoined them not to remit him any money, nor to hold the leaſt correſpondence with him.

It was now that he devoted himſelf wholly to the Lutheran party, to advance which he laboured inceſſantly both by his writings and actions. We do not know the exact time when he quitted the caſtle of Ebernberg; but it is certain that, Jan. 1523, he left Baſil, where he had flattered himſelf with the hopes of finding an aſylum, but on the contrary had been expoſed to great dangers. Eraſmus, though his old acquaintance and friend, had here refuſed a viſit from him, for fear, as he pretended, of heightening the ſuſpicions which were entertained againſt him: but this was only a pretence; his true reaſon, as he afterwards declared it in a letter to Melancthon, being, " that he ſhould then have been under a neceſſity of taking into his houſe that proud boaſter, oppreſſed with poverty and diſeaſe, who only ſought for a neſt to lay himſelf in, and to borrow money of every one he met." Take his words: " quod Hutteni colloquium deprecatur, non invidiæ metus tantum in cauſa fuit; erat aliud quiddam. Ille egens & omnibus rebus deſtitutus quærebat nidum aliquem, ubi moraretur. Erat mihi glorioſus ille miles cum ſua ſcabie in ædes recipiendus, &c. This refuſal of Eraſmus provoked

voked Hutten to attack him feverely, and accordingly he publifhed an " Expoftulatio" in 1523, which chagrined Erafmus
extremely. He anfwered it however the fame year, in a very
lively piece, entitled, " Spongia Erafmi adverfus adfperginès
Hutteni." Hutten would certainly have made a reply, had he
not been fnatched away by death ; but he died in an ifland of the
lake Zurich, where he had hid himfelf for fecurity, Aug. 1523.
He is faid to have died a martyr to debauchery ; which, though
fome treat as a calumny, is generally and upon good grounds
believed to have been the cafe: for, not to infift on his having
declared that he could not live without women, although he was
never married, he publifhed a Latin work in 1519, " Of curing
the Lues by Guiacum Wood :" in the dedication of which to
the elector of Mentz, a fpiritual prince, he was not afhamed to
own, that having been grievoufly afflicted with the diftemper
which is the fubject of his book, he had recovered his health
wholly by the application of this medicine. What a ftrange
mixture of character !—Hutten, abjuring all connexions with
temporalities and the things of this world ; Hutten, wandering
from place to place on account of his religion ; Hutten, bearing
perfecution with the moft ardent zeal, carried a difgraceful difeafe with him wherever he went, and at laft died of it !
He was a man of little ftature ; of a weak and fickly conftitution ; extremely brave, but much too paffionate : for he was
not fatisfied with attacking the Roman Catholics with his pen,
he attacked them alfo with his fword. He acquainted Luther
with the double war, which he carried on againft the clergy.
" I received a letter from Hutten," fays Luther, " filled with
rage againft the Roman Pontiff, declaring he would attack the
tyranny of the clergy both with his pen and fword : he being
exafperated againft the Pope for threatning him with daggers
and poifon, and commanding the bifhop of Mentz to fend him
bound to Rome." Camerarius fays, that Hutten was vaftly impatient, that his air and difcourfe fhewed him to be of a cruel
difpofition ; and applied to him what was faid of Demofthenes,
namely, that " he would have turned the world upfide down,
had his power been equal to his will." Neverthelefs they all admired him for his genius and learning. His works are very numerous, though he died young ; which made Bayle fay, that
had he lived 35 years longer, (being that age when he died) he
would have overflowed Europe with a deluge of books and libels.
A collection of his " Latin Poems" was publifhed at Frankfort
in 1538, 12mo ; all which, except two poems, were reprinted
in the third part of the " Deliciæ Poetarum Germanorum."
He was the author of a great many works, chiefly fatirical, In
the way of dialogue ; and Thuanus has not fcrupled to compare

him

him to Lucian. Of this caſt were his Latin Dialogues on Lutheraniſm, publiſhed in 4to. in 1520, and now very ſcarce. He had alſo a conſiderable ſhare in the celebrated work, called, " Epiſtolæ virorum obſcurorum."

HUTTEN (JACOB), a Sileſian of the 16th century, the founder of the ſect called the Bohemian or Moravian Brethren, a ſect of Anabaptiſts. Hutten purchaſed a territory of ſome extent in Moravia, and there eſtabliſhed his ſociety. They are conſidered as deſcended from the better ſort of Huſſites, and were diſtinguiſhed by ſeveral religious inſtitutions of a ſingular nature, but well adapted to guard their community againſt the reigning vices of the times [i] When they heard of Luther's attempts to reform the church, they ſent a deputation to him, and he, examining their tenets, though he could not in every particular approve, looked upon them as worthy of toleration and indulgence. Hutten brought perſecution upon himſelf and his brethren by violent declamations againſt the magiſtrates, and the attempt to introduce a perfect equality among men. It has been ſaid, that he was burnt as a Heretic at Inſpruck, but this is by no means certain. By degrees theſe ſectaries, baniſhed from their own country, entered into communion with the Swiſs church; though, for ſome time, with ſeparate inſtitutions. But in the ſynods held at Aſtrog in 1620 and 1627, all diſſentions were removed, and the two congregations were formed into one under the title of *the Church of the United Brethren.* The ſect of Herrenhutters or Moravians, formed by count Zinzendorff in the beginning of the preſent century, pretend to be deſcended from theſe brethren, and take the ſame title of *Unitas Fratrum;* but Moſheim obſerves, that " they may with more propriety be ſaid to imitate the example of that famous community, than to deſcend from thoſe who compoſed it, ſince it is well known that there are very few Bohemians and Moravians in the fraternity of the Herrenhutters; and it is extremely doubtful, whether even this ſmall number are to be conſidered as the poſterity of the ancient Bohemian Brethren, who diſtinguiſhed themſelves ſo early by their zeal for the reformation [ĸ]."

HUTTER (ELIAS), a Proteſtant divine, born at Ulric in 1553, and died at Nuremberg after 1602. He was deeply verſed in languages, oriental and occidental; particularly Hebrew, which he ſeems to have taught at Laipſic. He publiſhed, 1. " A Hebrew Bible," remarkable for being printed with the radical letters in black, the ſervile in hollow types, and the quieſcent or deficient letters in ſmaller characters above the line. At the end is the 117th Pſalm in thirty different languages. 2. " Two Polyglotts;" one in four languages, printed at Hamburg in

[i] Moſheim iv. 102.   [ĸ] Ibid. Vol. V. p. 84.

1596; the other in fix languages, at Nuremberg, in 1599; both in folio.

HUTTER (LEONHARD), was alfo, a native of Ulm, and born in 1563. He ftudied at Strafbourg, and early applied himfelf with great diligence to theology: he was afterwards at Leipfic, Heidelberg, Jena, and Wirtemburg, and in the latter place, was appointed one of the public profeffors of theology. He married a lady of illuftrious birth in 1599; and died of a fever in 1616, being then for the fourth time rector of the univerfity. The opinion held of his principles, may be judged by five anagrams of his names, *Leonardus Hutterus*, four of them implying that he was another Luther. They are formed, fays the author who gives them [L], " per literarum haud vanam tranfpofitionem ;" thus, " Redonatus Lutherus ;" " Leonhartus Hutterus ;" " Ah tu nofter Lutherus ;" " Notus arte Lutherus ;" " Tantus ero Lutherus." His works are very numerous; a great part of them controverfial, directed againft the church of Rome. Befides thefe, 1. " Compendium Theologiæ, cum Notis D. Gotofredi Cundifii." 2. " Explicatio Libri Concordiæ Chriftianæ," 8vo. 3. " Loci Communes Theologici," folio. 4. " Formulæ concionandi," 8vo. 5. " Difputationes de verbo Dei fcripto, ac traditionibus non fcriptis," in 4to. 6. " Collegium Theologicum, five XI difputationes de articulis confeffionis Auguftanæ," 8vo. 7. " Libri Chriftianæ Concordiæ," 8vo, and feveral pieces in defence of the *Formulæ Concordiæ*, which in his time were highly efteemed. Befides many other tracts in Latin and in German, all of which are enumerated by Freher, but feem too uninterefting at the prefent day to be tranfcribed.

HUYGENS (CHRISTIAN), a very great mathematician and aftronomer, was born at the Hague in Holland, April 14, 1629 [M], and was fon of Conftantine Huygens, lord of Zuylichem, who had ferved three fucceffive princes of Orange in the quality of fecretary. He fpent his whole life in cultivating the mathematics; and not in the fpeculative way only, but in making them fubfervient to the ufes of life. From his infancy he applied himfelf to this ftudy, and made a confiderable progrefs in it, even at nine years of age, as he did alfo in mufic, arithmetic, and geography; in all which he was inftructed by his father, who, in the mean time, did not fuffer him to neglect the belles lettres. At thirteen, he was initiated in the ftudy of mechanics; having difcovered a wonderful curiofity in examining machines and other pieces of mechanifm: and two years after had the affiftance of a mafter in mathematics, under whom

[L] Freher, Theatrum Virorum Erud. claror. p. 366.
[M] Huygen. vita, præfixed to his Opera Varia.

he

be made a furprifing progrefs. In 1645, he went to ftudy law at Leyden under Vinnius; yet did not attach himfelf fo clofely to that fcience, but that he found time to continue his mathematics under the profeffor Schooten. He left this univerfity at the end of one year, and went to Breda, where an univerfity had juft been founded, and put under the direction of his father; and here, for two or three years, he made the law his chief ftudy. In 1651, he gave the world a fpecimen of his genius for mathematics, in a treatife entitled, "Theoremata de quadratura Hyperboles, Ellipfis, & Circuli, ex dato portionum gravitatis centro:" in which he fhewed very evidently what might be expected from him afterwards.

After his return to the Hague in 1649, he went to Holftein in Denmark, in the retinue of Henry count of Naffau; and was extremely defirous of going to Sweden, in order to fee Des Cartes; but the fhort ftay of the count in Denmark would not permit him. In 1655, he travelled into France, and took the degree of doctor of laws, at Angiers. In 1658, he publifhed his "Horologium" at the Hague. He had exhibited in a preceding work, entitled, "Brevis inftitutio de ufu Horologiorum ad inveniendas longitudines," a model of a new invented pendulum; but as fome perfons, envious of his reputation, were labouring to deprive him of the honour of the invention, he wrote this book to explain the conftruction of it; and to fhew, that it was very different from the pendulum of aftronomers invented by Galileo. In 1659, he publifhed his "Syftema Saturninum, five de caufis mirandorum Saturni phænomenôn, & comite ejus planeta novo." Galileo had endeavoured to explain fome of the furprifing appearances of the planet Saturn. He had at firft perceived two ftars, which attended it; and fome time after was amazed to find them difappear. Huygens, defirous to account for thefe changes, laboured with his brother Conftantine to bring the telefcopes to greater perfection; and made himfelf glaffes, by which he could view objects at a greater diftance, than any that had yet been contrived. With thefe he applied himfelf to obferve all the phafes and appearances of Saturn, and drew a journal of all the different afpects of that planet. He difcovered a fatellite attending it, for none of the five were then known any thing of; and, after a long courfe of obfervations, perceived that the planet is furrounded with a folid and permanent ring, which never changes its fituation. Thefe difcoveries gained him an high rank among the aftronomers of his time.

In 1660, he took a fecond journey into France, and the year after paffed over into England, where he communicated his art of polifhing glaffes for telefcopes, and was made a fellow of the Royal Society. About this time the air-pump was invented, which

which received confiderable improvements from him. This
year alfo he difcovered the laws of the collifion of elaftic bodies; as did afterwards our own countrymen, the celebrated
Wallis and Wren, with whom he had a difpute about the honour of this difcovery. After he had ftayed fome months in
England, he returned to France in 1663, where his merit became fo confpicuous, that Colbert refolved to fix him at Paris,
by fettling on him a confiderable penfion. Accordingly, in
1665, letters, written in the king's name, were fent to him
to the Hague, where he then was, to invite him to Paris, with
the promife of a large ftipend, and other confiderable advantages. Huygens confented to the propofal, and refided at Paris
from 1666 to 1681; where he was made a member of the Royal
Academy of Sciences. All this time he was engaged in mathematical purfuits, wrote feveral works, which were publifhed
from time to time, and invented and perfected feveral ufeful inftruments and machines. But continual application began then
to impair his health; and, though he had twice vifited his native
air, in 1670 and 1675, for the fake of recovering from illnefs, he
now found it permanently neceffary to his conftitution. He left
Paris in 1681, and paffed the remainder of his life in his own
country, occupied in his ufual purfuits and employments. He
died at the Hague June 8, 1695, in his fixty-feventh year, while
his "Cofmotheoros," a Latin treatife concerning the plurality
of worlds, was printing: he provided, however, in his will for
its publication, defiring his brother Conftantine, to whom it was
addreffed, to take that trouble upon him. But Conftantine was
fo occupied with bufinefs, as being fecretary in Holland to the
king of Great Britain, that he died alfo before it could be
printed; fo that the book did not appear in public till 1698. A
fimilar fate feemed to attend Kepler's "Somnium aftronomicum,"
a book on a fimilar fubject. While it was in the prefs, he
died. The perfon to whom the care of the impreffion fell, died
too, before it was finifhed; fo that, as we have related in his
life, a third perfon was unwilling to undertake it, left the fame
misfortune fhould attend him.

In 1703, were printed at Leyden, in one vol. 4to, Huygens's
" Opufcula Pofthuma, quæ continent Dioptricam, Commentarios
de vitris figurandis, Differtationem de Corona & Parheliis, Tractatum de motu & de vi centrifuga, defcriptionem Automati Planetarii." Huygens had left by will to the univerfity of Leyden
his mathematical writings, and requefted de Volder and Fullenius, the former profeffor of natural philofophy and mathematics at Leyden, and the other at Franeker, to examine thefe
works, and publifh what they fhould think proper. This was
performed in the volume here mentioned. Huygens had written
in Low Dutch the fecond of the tracts it contains, relating to
the

the art of forming and polishing telescope-glasses, to which he
had greatly applied himself; but Boerhaave, for this work, translated into Latin. In 1704, were published in 4to, his " Opera
Varia." This collection is generally bound in four volumes.
It contains the greatest part of the pieces which he had published separately, and is divided into four parts. The first part
contains the pieces relating to mechanics; the second, those relating to geometry; the third, those relating to astronomy; and the
fourth, those which could not be arranged under any of the former titles. Gravesande had the care of this edition, in which he
has inserted several additions to the pieces contained in it, extracted
from Huygens's manuscripts. In 1728, were printed in two
volumes, 4to, at Amsterdam, his " Opera Reliqua: which new
collection was published also by Gravesande. The first volume
contains his " Treatises on Light and Gravity;" the second his
" Opuscula Posthuma," which had been printed in 1703. His
whole time had been employed in curious and useful researches.
He loved a quiet and studious life; and, perhaps through fear of
interruption, never married. He was an amiable, chearful,
worthy man; and in all respects, as good as he was great.

HYDE (EDWARD), earl of Clarendon, and chancellor of
England, was descended from an ancient family in Cheshire,
and born at Dinton in Wiltshire, Feb. 16, 1608 [N]. In 1622,
he was entered of Magdalen-hall in Oxford, and in 1625, took
the degree of Bachelor in Arts; but failing of a fellowship
in Exeter-college, for which he stood, removed to the Middle-Temple, where he studied the law for several years, with application and success. When the lawyers resolved to give a public
testimony of their dissent from the new doctrine advanced in
Prynne's " Histriomastix," wherein was shewn an utter disregard of all manner of decency and respect to the crown, Hyde
and Whitelocke were appointed the managers of the masque,
presented on that occasion to their majesties at Whitehall on
Candlemas-day, 1633-4. At the same time he testified, upon
all occasions, his utter dislike to that excess of power, which
was then exercised by the court, and supported by the judges in
Westminster-hall. He condemned the oppressive proceedings of
the high-commission court, the star-chamber, the council-board,
the earl-marshal's-court, or court of honour, and the court of
York. This just way of thinking is said to have been formed
in him by a domestic accident, which Burnet has related in the
following manner. " When he first began," says that historian,
" to grow eminent in his profession of the law, he went down to
visit his father in Wiltshire; who one day, as they were walk-

[N] Athen. Oxon.　　[O] Life of the lord-chancellor Hyde, prefixed to several
of his pieces, &c. p. 2. Lond. 1727.

ing in the fields together, obferved to him, that ' men of his profeffion were apt to ftretch the prerogative too far, and injure liberty: but charged him, if ever he came to any eminence in his profeffion, never to facrifice the laws and liberty of his country to his own intereft, or the will of his prince.' He repeated this twice, and immediately fell into a fit of apoplexy, of which he died in a few hours; and this advice had fo lafting an influence upon the fon, that he ever after obferved and purfued it [P]."

In the parliament which began at Weftminfter, April 10, 1640, he ferved as burgefs for Wotton-Baffet in Wiltfhire; in which parliament he diftinguifhed himfelf upon the following occafion. His majefty having acquainted the houfe of commons, that he would releafe the fhip-money, if they would grant him twelve fubfidies, to be paid in three years, great debates arofe in the houfe that day and the next; when Hampden, feeing the matter ripe for the queftion, defired it might be put, " whether the houfe fhould comply with the propofition made by the king, as it was contained in the meffage?" Hereupon ferjeant Glanvile the fpeaker, for the houfe was then in a committee, endeavoured in a pathetic fpeech to perfuade them to comply with the king, and fo reconcile him to parliaments for ever. No fpeech ever united the inclination of a popular council more to the fpeaker than this did; and if the queftion had been prefently put, it was believed that few would have oppofed it. But, after a fhort filence, the other fide recovering new courage, called again with fome earneftnefs, that Hampden's queftion fhould be put; which being like to meet with a concurrence, Hyde, being very folicitous to keep things in fome tolerable calmnefs, then ftood up; and, giving his reafons for his diflike to that queftion, propofed, that " to the end every man might freely give his yea or no, the queftion might be put only upon giving the king a fupply; and if this was carried, another might be put upon the manner and proportion: if not, it would have the fame effect with the other propofed by Mr. Hampden." This, after it had been fome time oppofed and diverted by other propofitions, which were anfwered by Hyde, would, as it is generally believed, have been put and carried in the affirmative, though pofitively oppofed by Herbert the folicitor-general, if fir Henry Vane the fecretary had not ftood up, and affured them as from his majefty, that if they fhould pafs a vote for a fupply, and not in the proportion propofed in his majefty's meffage, it would not be accepted by him, and therefore defired that the queftion might be laid afide. This being again urged by the folicitorgeneral, and it being near five in the afternoon, it was readily confented to, that the houfe fhould adjourn till the next morn-

[P] Hiftory of his own Times, Vol. I. B. 2.

ing,

ing, at which time they were suddenly dissolved. And within an hour after Hyde met St. John, who was seldom known to smile, but then had a most chearful aspect; and observing Hyde melancholy, asked him, " what troubled him?" who answered " The same he believed that troubled most good men, that, in a time of so much confusion, so wise a parliament should be so imprudently dissolved." St. John replied somewhat warmly, " that all was well; that things must grow worse, before they would grow better; and that that parliament would never have done what was requisite [Q.]."

This parliament being dissolved, Hyde was chosen for Saltash in Cornwall in the long parliament, which commenced Nov. 3, the same year, where his abilities began to be noticed; and when the commons prepared a charge against lord chief baron Davenport, baron Weston, and baron Trevor, he was sent up with the impeachment to the lords, to whom he made a most excellent speech. It begins thus: " My lords, there cannot be a greater instance of a sick and languishing commonwealth, than the business of this day. Good God! how have the guilty these late years been punished, when the judges themselves have been such delinquents? It is no marvel, that an irregular, extravagant, arbitrary power, like a torrent, hath broken in upon us, when our banks and our bulwarks, the laws, were in the custody of such persons. Men, who had left their innocence, could not preserve their courage; nor could we look that they, who had so visibly undone us, themselves should have the virtue or credit to rescue us from the oppression of other men. It was said by one, who always spoke excellently, that ' the twelve judges were like the twelve lions under the throne of Solomon;' under the throne of obedience, but yet lions. Your lordships shall this day hear of six, who, be they what they will else, were no lions: who upon vulgar fear delivered up their precious forts they were trusted with, almost without assault; and in a tame easy trance of flattery and servitude, lost and forfeited, shamefully forfeited, that reputation, awe, and reverence, which the wisdom, courage, and gravity of their venerable predecessors had contracted and fastened to the places they now hold. They even rendered that study and profession, which in all ages hath been, and, I hope, now shall be of honourable estimation, so contemptible and vile, that had not this blessed day come, all men would have had that quarrel to the law itself which Marius had to the Greek tongue, who thought it a mockery to learn that language, the masters whereof lived in bondage under others. And I appeal to these unhappy gentlemen themselves, with what a strange negligence, scorn, and indignation, the faces of all

[Q] History of the Rebellion, &c. B. ii.

men,

men, even of the meaneſt, have been directed towards them, ſince, to call it no worſe, that fatal declenſion of their underſtanding in thoſe judgements, of which they ſtand here charged before your lordſhips." The concluſion runs thus: " If the excellent, envied conſtitution of this kingdom hath been of late diſtempered, your lordſhips ſee the cauſes. If the ſweet harmony between the king's protection and the ſubject's obedience hath unluckily ſuffered interruption; if the royal juſtice and honour of the beſt of kings have been miſtaken by his people; if the duty and affection of the moſt faithful and loyal nation have been ſuſpected by their gracious ſovereign; if, by theſe miſrepreſentations, and theſe miſunderſtandings, the king and people have been robbed of the delight and comfort of each other, and the bleſſed peace of this iſland been ſhaken and frightened into tumults and commotions, into the poverty, though not into the rage, of war, as a people prepared for deſtruction and deſolation; theſe are the men, actively or paſſively, by doing or not doing, who have brought this upon us: ' Miſera ſervitus falſo pax vocatur; ubi judicia deficiunt, incipit bellum [a]."

But though Hyde was very zealous for redreſſing the grievances of the nation, he was no leſs ſo for the ſecurity of the eſtabliſhed church, and the honour of the crown. When a bill was brought in to take away the biſhops vote in parliament, and to leave them out of all commiſſions of the peace, or any thing that had relation to temporal affairs, he was very earneſt for throwing it out, and ſaid, that, " from the time that parliaments begun, biſhops had always been a part of it; that if they were taken out, there was nobody left to repreſent the clergy; which would introduce another piece of injuſtice, that no other part of the kingdom could complain of, who, being all repreſented in parliament, were bound to ſubmit to whatever was enacted there, becauſe it was, upon the matter, with their own conſent: whereas if the bill was carried, there was nobody left to repreſent the clergy, and yet they muſt be bound by their determination [s]." He was one of the committee employed to prepare the charge againſt the earl of Strafford: but, as ſoon as he ſaw the unjuſtifiable violence with which the proſecution was puſhed, he left them, and oppoſed the bill of attainder warmly. He was afterwards appointed a manager at the conference with the houſe of lords, for aboliſhing the court of York, whereof that earl had been for ſeveral years preſident; and was chairman alſo of ſeveral other committees, appointed upon the moſt important occaſions, as long as he continued his preſence among them. But, when they began to put in execution their or-

[a] Ruſhworth's Hiſt. Collect. Vol. II.   [s] Hiſt. of the Rebel. p. iii.

dinance

dinance for raifing the militia againft his majefty, Hyde, being
perfuaded that this was an act of open rebellion, left them; and
they felt the blow given to their authority by his abfence fo fenfibly, that in their inftructions fhortly after to the earl of Effex
their general, he was excepted with a few others from any grace
or favour [τ].

Hyde withdrew to the king at York, having firft obtained the
great feal to be fent thither on May 20, 1642: and, upon his
arrival, was taken into the greateft confidence, though he was
not under any official character in the court for fome months.
But, towards the latter end of the year, upon the promotion of
fir John Colepepper to be mafter of the Rolls, he fucceeded him
in the chancellorfhip of the Exchequer, and the fame year was
knighted, and made a privy-counfellor. With thefe characters
he fat in the parliament affembled at Oxford, Jan. 1643; and,
in 1644, was one of the king's commiffioners at the treaty of
Uxbridge [υ]. Not long after, the king fending the prince of
Wales into the Weft, to have the fuperintendency of the affairs
there, fir Edward Hyde was appointed to attend his highnefs,
and to be of his council; where he entered, by his majefty's
command, into a correfpondence with the marquis of Ormond,
then lord-lieutenant of Ireland. Upon the declining of the
king's caufe, he with the lords Capel and Colepepper failed
from Pendennis caftle in Cornwall to Scilly, and thence to Jerfey, where he arrived in March, 1645; but being greatly difgufted at the prince's removal thence the following year to
France, he obtained leave to ftay in that ifland. His difguft at
the prince's removal into France, is ftrongly expreffed in the
following letter to duke of Ormond:

"My lord,

"Your lordfhip hath been long fince informed, whither my
lord Digby attended the prince; and from thence have pardoned
my not acknowledging your grace's favour to me, from the im-
poffibility of prefenting it to you. I confefs, in that conjunc-
ture of time, I thought the remove from Jerfey to Ireland to
be very fit to be deliberately weighed, before attempted; but I
would have chofen it much more chearfully than this that is embraced, which I hope will be a memorial to my weaknefs; for
it is my misfortune to differ from thofe with whom I have hitherto agreed, and efpecially with my beft friend, which I hope
will not render me the lefs fit for your charity, though I may
be for your confideration. Indeed, there is not light enough
for me to fee my way, and I cannot well walk in the dark;
and therefore I have defired leave of the prince to breathe in

[τ] Whitelocke's Memorials, &c. p. 62, and Hift. of the Rebellion, B. vi.
[υ] Lives of the Lord Chancellors, &c. Vol. I. p. 46. Lond. 1708.

this

this ifland a little for my refrefhment, till I may difcern fome
way in which I may ferve his majefty. I hope your lordfhip
will never meet with any interruption in the exercife of that
devotion, which hath rendered you the envied example of three
kingdoms, and that I fhall yet find an opportunity to attend
upon your lordfhip, and have the honour to be received by you
in the capacity of [x],

"My Lord, your Lordfhip's, &c.

"June 22, 1646.   "EDWARD HYDE."

We fee here not barely a difguft, but even a refentment
fhewn to the prince's going to Paris; the ground of which undoubtedly lay in the manifeft danger his religion was thereby
brought into from the reftlefs endeavours of his mother; fince it
is notorious, that the chancellor was never upon any tolerable
terms with the queen, on account of his watchfulgefs againft
every attempt of this kind.

During his retirement in Jerfey, he began to write his "Hiftory of the Rebellion," which had been particularly recommended to him, and in which he was affifted alfo by the king,
who fupplied him with feveral of the materials for it. We
learn from the hiftory itfelf, that upon lord Capel's waiting on
the king at Hampton-court in 1647, his majefty wrote to the
chancellor a letter, in which he "thanked him for undertaking
the work he was upon; and told him, he fhould expect fpeedily
to receive fome contribution from him towards it: and within a
very fhort time afterwards, he fent to him memorials of all that
had paffed from the time he had left his majefty at Oxford,
when he waited upon the prince into the Weft, to the very day
that the king left Oxford to go to the Scots; out of which memorials the moft important paffages, in the years 1644 and
1645, are faithfully collected." Agreeably to this, the ninth
book opens with declaring, that "the work was firft undertaken
with the king's approbation, and by his encouragement; and
particularly, that many important points were tranfmitted to
the author by the king's immediate direction and order, even
after he was in the hands and power of the enemy, out
of his own memorials and journals." Thus do we trace the
exact time when this hiftory was begun. The time when it
was finifhed may be afcertained with the fame degree of exactnefs, from the dedication of the author's "Survey of the
Leviathan," wherein he addreffes himfelf to Charles II. in thefe
terms: "As foon as I had finifhed a work, at leaft recommended, if not enjoined, to me by your bleffed father, and approved, and in fome degree perufed by your majefty, I could
not, &c." This dedication is dated Moulins, May 10, 1673;

[x] Collection of letters to and from the duke of Ormond, by Carte, No. 378.

whence it appears, that the hiftory was not completed till the beginning of that, or the latter end of the preceding year: and this may account for thofe paffages in it, where facts are related which happened long after the Reftoration; as for inftance, that " fir John Digby lived many years after the king's return ;" and that the " earl of Sandwich's expedition was never forgiven him by fome men:" which, we fee, might very confiftently be ob-ferved in this hiftory, though that nobleman did not lofe his life till 1672.

In May, 1648, fir Edward received a letter from the queen to call him to Paris; where, after the king's death, he was conti-nued both in his feat at the privy-council, and in his office of the exchequer, by Charles II. In Nov. 1649, he was fent by the king with lord Cottington ambaffador extraordinary into Spain, to apply for affiftance in the recovery of his crown; but returned without fuccefs, in July, 1651. Soon after his arrival, the king gave him an account of his efcape after the battle of Worcefter, in that unfortunate expedition to Scotland, which had been undertaken during fir Edward's abfence, and much againft his judgement. He now refided for fome time at Ant-werp, but left no means unattempted, by letters and meffages to England, for compaffing the Reftoration; wherein, however, he folely relied upon the epifcopal party. In 1653, he was accufed of holding a correfpondence with Cromwell; but being declared innocent by the king, was afterwards fecretary of ftate. More attempts were made to ruin him with the king; but in vain; for, in 1657, he was made chancellor of England. Upon the Reftoration, as he had been one of the greateft fharers in his mafter's fufferings, fo he had a proportionable fhare in his glory.

Befides the poft of lord chancellor, in which he was conti-nued, he was chofen chancellor of the univerfity of Oxford, in Oct. 1660; and, in November following, created a peer, by the title of baron Hyde of Hindon, in Wiltfhire; to which were added, in April, 1661, the titles of vifcount Cornbury in Oxfordfhire, and earl of Clarendon in Wiltfhire. Thefe ho-nours, great as they were, were however by no means beyond his merit. He had, upon the Reftoration, fhewn great prudence, juftice, and moderation, in fettling the juft boundaries between the prerogative of the crown and the liberties of the people. He had reduced much confufion into order, and adjufted many clafhing interefts, where property was concerned. He had en-deavoured to make things eafy to the Prefbyterians and mal-con-tents by the act of indemnity, and to fatisfy the Royalifts by the act of uniformity. But it is not poffible to ftand many years in a fituation fo much diftinguifhed, without becoming the object of envy; which created him fuch enemies, as both wifhed and attempted his ruin, and at laft effected it. Doubtlefs nothing

more

more contributed to inflame this paſſion againſt him, than the
circumſtance of his eldeſt daughter being married to the duke of
York, which became known in a few months after the king's
return. She had been one of the maids of honour to the prin-
ceſs-royal Henrietta, ſome time during the exile, when the duke
fell in love with her [Y]; and being diſappointed by the defeat
of ſir George Booth, in a deſign he had formed of coming with
ſome forces to England in 1659, he went to Breda, where his
ſiſter then reſided. Paſſing ſome weeks there, he took this opportunity, as Burnet tells us, of ſoliciting miſs Hyde to indulge
his deſires without marriage; but ſhe managed the matter with
ſuch addreſs, that in the concluſion he married her, Nov. 4,
that year, with all poſſible ſecrecy, and unknown to her father.
After their arrival in England, being pregnant, ſhe called upon
the duke to own his marriage; and though he endeavoured to
divert her from this object, both by great promiſes and great
threatenings, yet ſhe had the ſpirit and wiſdom to tell him,
" She would have it known that ſhe was his wife, let him uſe
her afterwards as he pleaſed." The king ordered ſome biſhops
and judges to peruſe the proofs of her marriage; and they re-
porting, that it had been ſolemnized according to the doctrine of
goſpel and the law of England, he told his brother, that he muſt
live with her whom he made his wife, and at the ſame time
generouſly preſerved the honour of an excellent ſervant, who
had not been privy to it; aſſuring him, that " this accident ſhould
not leſſen the eſteem and favour he had for him."

The firſt open attack upon lord Clarendon was made by the
earl of Briſtol; who, in 1663, exhibited againſt him a charge
of high-treaſon to the houſe of lords. There had been a long
courſe of friendſhip, both in proſperity and adverſity, between
the chancellor and this earl; but they had gradually fallen into
different meaſures in religion and politics. In this ſtate of
things, the chancellor refuſing what lord Briſtol conſidered as a
ſmall favour, (which was ſaid to be the paſſing a patent in favour of a court lady), the latter took ſo much offence, that he
let looſe his fiery temper, and reſolved upon nothing but revenge. The ſubſtance of the whole accuſation was as follows:
" That the chancellor, being in place of higheſt truſt and confidence with his majeſty, and having arrogated a ſupreme direction in all things, had, with a traiterous intent to draw contempt
npon his majeſty's perſon, and to alienate the affections of his
ſubjects, abuſed the ſaid truſt in manner following. 1. He had
endeavoured to alienate the hearts of his majeſty's ſubjects, by
artfully inſinuating to his creatures and dependents, that his
majeſty was inclined to popery, and deſigned to alter the eſta-

[Y] Carte's Hiſt. of the duke of Ormond, Vol. II. p. 188.

bliſhed

blished religion. 2. He had said to several persons of his majesty's privy-council, that his majesty was dangerously corrupted
in his religion, and inclined to popery: that persons of that religion had such access and such credit with him, that, unless
there were a careful eye had upon it, the protestant religion
would be overthrown in this kingdom. 3. Upon his majesty's
admitting sir Henry Bennet to be secretary of state in the place
of sir Edward Nicholas, he said, that his majesty had given
10,000l. to remove a most zealous Protestant, that he might
bring into that place a concealed Papist. 4. In pursuance of
the same traiterous design, several friends and dependents of his
have said aloud, that, ' were it not for my lord chancellor's
standing in the gap, Popery would be introduced into this kingdom.' 5. That he had persuaded the king, contrary to his
opinion, to allow his name to be used to the pope and several
cardinals, in the solicitation of a cardinal's cap for the lord Au-
bigny, great almoner to the queen: in order to effect which, he
had employed Mr. Richard Bealing, a known Papist, and had
likewise applied himself to several popish priests and Jesuits to
the same purpose, promising great favour to the Papists here,
in case it should be effected. 6. That he had likewise promised
to several Papists, that he would do his endeavour, and said, ' he
hoped to compass taking away all penal laws against them;' to
the end they might presume and grow vain upon his patronage ;
and, by their publishing their hopes of toleration, increase the
scandal designed by him to be raised against his majesty throughout the kingdom. 7. That, being intrusted with the treaty
between his majesty and his royal consort the queen, he concluded it upon articles scandalous and dangerous to the Protestant religion. Moreover, he brought the king and queen together without any settled agreement about the performance of
the marriage rites ; whereby, the queen refusing to be married
by a Protestant priest, in case of her being with child, either the
succession should be made uncertain for want of the due rites
of matrimony, or else his majesty be exposed to a suspicion of
having been married in his own dominions by a Romish priest.
8. That, having endeavoured to alienate the hearts of the king's
subjects upon the score of religion, he endeavoured to make use
of all his scandals and jealousies, to raise to himself a popular
applause of being the zealous upholder of the Protestant religion, &c. 9. That he further endeavoured to alienate the hearts
of the king's subjects, by venting in his own discourse, and
those of his emissaries, opprobrious scandals against his majesty's
person and course of life ; such as are not fit to be mentioned,
unless necessity shall require it. 10. That he endeavoured to
alienate the affections of the duke of York from his majesty, by
suggesting to him, that ' his majesty intended to legitimate the
duke

duke of Monmouth.' 11. That he had perſuaded the king, againſt the advice of the lord general, to withdraw the Engliſh garriſons out of Scotland, and demoliſh all the forts built there, at ſo vaſt a charge to this kingdom; and all without expecting the advice of the parliament of England. 12. That he endeavoured to alienate his majeſty's affections and eſteem from the preſent parliament, by telling him, ‘ that there never was ſo weak and inconſiderable a houſe of lords, nor never ſo weak and heady a houſe of commons;' and particularly, that ‘ it was better to ſell Dunkirk, than be at their mercy for want of money.' 13. That, contrary to a known law made laſt ſeſſion, by which money was given and applied for maintaining Dunkirk, he adviſed and effected the ſale of the ſame to the French king. 14. That he had, contrary to law, enriched himſelf and his treaſures by the ſale of offices. 15. That he had converted to his own uſe vaſt ſums of public money, raiſed in Ireland by way of ſubſidy, private and public benevolences, and otherwiſe given and intended to defray the charge of the government in that kingdom. 16. That, having arrogated to himſelf a ſupreme direction of all his majeſty's affairs, he had prevailed to have his majeſty's cuſtoms farmed at a lower rate than others offered; and that by perſons, with ſome of whom he went a ſhare, and other parts of money reſulting from his majeſty's revenue [2].”

A charge urged with ſo much anger and inconſiſtency as this was, it is eaſy to imagine, could not capitally affect him: on the contrary, we find, that the proſecution ended greatly to the honour of the chancellor; notwithſtanding which, his enemies advanced very conſiderably by it in their deſign, to make him leſs in favour with his maſter, leſs reſpected in parliament, and leſs beloved by the people. The building of a magnificent houſe, which was begun in the following year, 1664, furniſhed freſh matter for obloquy. “ The king,” ſays Burnet, “ had granted him a large piece of ground, near St. James's palace, to build upon. He intended a good ordinary houſe; but not underſtanding theſe matters himſelf, he put the management of it into the hands of others, who run him to a vaſt expence of above 50,000l. three times as much as he had deſigned to lay out upon it. During the war, and in the year of the plague, he had about 300 men at work; which he thought would have been an acceptable thing, when ſo many men were kept at work, and ſo much money was daily paid circulated about. But it had a contrary effect; it raiſed a great outcry againſt him. Some called it Dunkirk Houſe, intimating that it was built by his ſhare of the price of Dunkirk; others called it Holland Houſe, becauſe he was believed to be no friend to the war, ſo it was given out he

had the money from the Dutch. It was vifible that, in a time
of public calamity, he was building a very noble palace. Another accident was, that before the war there were fome defigns
on foot for the repairing of St. Paul's, and many ftones were
brought thither for the purpofe. That project was laid afide;
upon which he bought the ftones, and made ufe of them in
building his own houfe. This, how flight foever it may feem
to be, had a great effect by the management of his enemies
[A]." To this remark it may be added, that this ftately pile
was not finifhed till 1667; fo that it ftood a growing monument
for the popular odium to feed upon, almoft the whole interval
between his firft and his laft impeachment; and to aggravate
and fpread that odium, there was publifhed a moft virulent fatirical fong, entitled, "Clarendon's Houfe-warming," confifting
of many ftanzas, to which, by way of fling at the tail, was
added, the following clumfy but bitter epigram:

> **UPON THE HOUSE.**
> Here lie the facred bones
> Of Paul beguiled of his ftones.
> Here lie the golden briberies
> Of many ruined families.
> Here lies the cavaliers debenture wall,
>   Fixed on an eccentric bafis:
> Here's Dunkirk town and Tangier-hall,
> The queen's marriage and all,
>   The Dutchmen's Templum Pacis.

In Auguft, 1667, he was removed from his poft of chancellor,
and in November following was impeached by the houfe of commons of high-treafon, and other crimes and mifdemeanors: upon
which, in the beginning of December, he retired to France,
and on the 19th, an act of banifhment was paffed againft him
[B]. Echard obferves, how often "it has been admired, that
the king fhould not only confent to difcard, but foon after ba-
nifh a friend, who had been as honeft and faithful to him as the
beft, and perhaps more ufeful and ferviceable than any he had
ever employed; which furely could never have been brought to
bear without innumerable enviers and enemies." But to conceive how thefe were raifed, we need only remember, that during
the height of his grandeur, which continued two years after the
Reftoration without any rivalfhip, as well as the reft of his
miniftry, he manifefted an inflexible fteadinefs to the conftitution
of the church of England, in equal oppofition to the Papifts on
one fide, and the Diffenters on the other; fo that none of thefe
could ever be reconciled to him or his proceedings. Yet at firft

[A] Hift. of his own Times, Vol. I.   [B] Hift. of England, ad annum, 1667.

he feemed fo forward to make a coalition of all parties, that the
cavaliers and ftrict churchmen thought themfelves much neglected; and many of them upon that account, though unjuftly,
entertained infuperable prejudices againft him, and joined with
the greateft of his enemies. But the circumftances which were
fuppofed to weaken his intereft with, and at length make him
difagreeable to the king, were rather of a perfonal nature, and
fuch as concerned the king and him only. It is allowed on all
hands, that the chancellor was not without the pride of confcious
virtue; fo that his perfonal behaviour was accompanied with
a fort of gravity and haughtinefs, which ftruck a very unpleaf-
ing awe into a court filled with licentious perfons of both fexes.
He often took the liberty to give reproofs to thefe perfons of
mirth and gallantry; and fometimes thought it his duty to advife the king himfelf in fuch a manner that they took advantage
of him, and as he paffed in court, would often fay to his majefty, "There goes your fchoolmafter." The chief of thefe
was the duke of Buckingham, who had a furprifing talent of
ridicule and buffoonery; and that he might make way for his
ruin, by bringing him firft into contempt, he often acted and
mimicked him in the prefence of the king, walking in a ftately
manner with a pair of bellows before him for the purfe, and
colonel Titus carrying a fire-fhovel on his fhoulder for the mace:
with which fort of farce and banter the king, fays Echard, was
too much delighted and captivated. Thefe, with fome more
ferious of the Popifh party, affifted by the folicitations of the
ladies of pleafure, made fuch impreffions upon the king, that
he at laft gave way, and became willing, and even pleafed, to
part both from his perfon and fervices. It was alfo believed,
that the king had fome private refentments againft him, for
checking of thofe who were too forward in loading the crown
with prerogative and revenue; and particularly, we are told, that
he had counteracted the king in a grand defign which he had, to
be divorced from the queen, under pretence, "that fhe had been
pre-engaged to another perfon, or, that fhe was incapable of
bearing children." The perfon defigned to fupply her place was
Mrs. Stuart, a beautiful young lady, who was related to the
king, and had fome office under the queen. The chancellor, to
prevent this, fent for the duke of Richmond, who was of the
fame name; and feeming to be forry, that a perfon of his worth
and relation to his majefty fhould receive no marks of his favour,
advifed him to marry this lady, as the moft likely means to advance himfelf. The young nobleman, liking the perfon, followed his advice, made immediate application to the lady, who
was ignorant of the king's intentions, and in a few days married her. The king thus difappointed, and foon after informed
how the match was brought about, banifhed the duke and his

new

new dutchefs from court, referving his refentment againft the chancellor to a more convenient opportunity. Be this as it will, the private reafons that induced the king to abandon the chancellor were expreffed in a letter to the duke of Ormond; then in Ireland; which the king wrote to that nobleman for his fatisfaction, knowing him to be the chancellor's friend. Echard obferves, that this letter was never publifhed, nor would a copy of it be granted; but that he had been told the fubftance of it more than once by thofe who had read it; and the principal reafon there given by the king was, " The chancellor's intolerable temper."

Being now about to quit the kingdom in exile, before he departed he drew up an apology, in a petition to the houfe of lords, in which he vindicated himfelf from any way contributing to the late mifcarriages, in fuch a manner, as laid the blame at the fame time upon others. The lords received it Dec. 3, and fent two of the judges to acquaint the commons with it, defiring a conference. The duke of Buckingham, who was plainly aimed at in the petition, delivered it to the commons; and with his ufual way of infult and ridicule, faid, " The lords have commanded me to deliver to you this fcandalous and feditious paper fent from the earl of Clarendon. They bid me prefent it to you, and defire you in a convenient time to fend it to them again; for it has a ftyle which they are in love with, and therefore defire to keep it." Upon the reading of it in that houfe, it was voted to be " fcandalous, malicious, and a reproach to the juftice of the nation [c];" whereupon they moved the lords, that it might be burnt by the hands of the common hangman, which was ordered and executed accordingly. The chancellor retired to Rouen in Normandy; and, the year following, his life was attempted at Evreux near that city by a body of feamen, in fuch an outrageous manner, that he with great difficulty efcaped. In the Bodleian library at Oxford, there is an original letter from Mr. Oliver Long, dated from Evreux, April 26, 1668, to fir William Cromwell, fecretary of ftate, where the following account is given of this affault. " As I was travelling from Rouen towards Orleans, it was my fortune, April 23, to overtake the earl of Clarendon, then in his unhappy and unmerited exile, who was going towards Bourbon, but took up his lodgings at a private hotel in a fmall walled town called Evreux, fome leagues from Rouen. I, as moft Englifh gentlemen did to fo valuable a patriot, went to pay him a vifit near fuppertime; when he was, as ufual, very civil to me. Before fupper was done, twenty or thirty Englifh feamen and more came and demanded entrance at the great gate; which, being ftrongly barred, kept them out for fome time. But in a fhort fpace they

broke

broke it, and prefently drove all they found, by their advantage
of numbers, into the earl's chamber; whence, by the affiftance
of only three fwords and piftols, we kept them out for half an
hour, in which difpute many of us were wounded by their
fwords and piftols, whereof they had many. To conclude,
they broke the windows and the doors, and under the conduct
of one Howard an Irifhman, who has three brothers, as I am
told, in the king of England's fervice, and an enfign in the
company of canoneers, they quickly found the earl in his bed,
not able to ftand by the violence of the gout; whence, after
they had given him many blows with their fwords and ftaves,
mixed with horrible curfes and oaths, they dragged him on the
ground into the middle of the yard, where they encompaffed
him around with their fwords, and after they had told him in
their own language, how he had fold the kingdom, and robbed
them of their pay, Howard commanded them all, as one man,
to run their fwords through his body. But what difference arofe
among themfelves before they could agree, God above, who
alone fent this fpirit of diffenfion, only knows. In this interval their lieutenant, one Swaine, came and difarmed them.
Sixteen of the ringleaders were put into prifon; and many of
thofe things they had rifled from him, found again, which were
reftored, and of great value. Monf. la Fonde, a great man
belonging to the king of France's bed-chamber, fent to conduct
the earl on his way hither, was fo defperately wounded in the
head, that there were little hopes of his life. Many of thefe
affaffins were grievoufly wounded; and this action is fo much
refented by all here, that many of thefe criminals will meet
with an ufage equal to their merit. Had we been fufficiently
provided with fire-arms, we had infallibly done ourfelves juftice
on them; however, we fear not but the law will fupply our
defect."

Being greatly afflicted with the gout, and not finding himfelf
fecure in that part of France, he went in the fummer to Mont-
pelier; where, recovering his health to a good degree, he continued three or four years. In 1672, he refided at Moulins,
and removing thence to Rouen, died Dec. 9, 1673, in that
city; from whence his body was brought to England, and interred on the north fide of Henry VIIth's chapel in Weftminfter-abbey. He was twice married: firft to Anne, daughter
of fir Gregory Ayloffe, of Robfon in Wiltfhire, knt. and this
lady dying without iffue, to Frances, daughter, and at length
heirefs, to fir Thomas Aylefbury, bart. in 1634; by whom he
had four fons and two daughters. Anne his eldeft daughter was
married, as we have already obferved, to the duke of York, by
which match fhe became mother to two daughters, Mary and
Anne, who were fucceffively queens of England. Befides thefe,

fhe

she brought the duke four sons and three daughters, who all died in their infancy. The last was born Feb. 9, 1670-1, and her mother died on March 31 following; having a little before her death changed her religion, to the great grief of her father, who on that occasion wrote a most pathetic letter to her, and another to the duke her consort.

Besides the "History of the Rebellion" already mentioned, the chancellor wrote other pieces, theological as well as political. In 1672, while he resided at Moulins, he wrote his "Animadversions upon Mr. Cressy's Book, intituled, "Fanaticism fanatically imputed to the Catholic Church by Dr. Stillingfleet, and the Imputation refuted and retorted by J. C." He is supposed to have been led to this work from the knowledge he had of Cressey, by means of an acquaintance commenced at Oxford, where that gentleman was his contemporary; and a motive of a similar nature might probably induce him to draw up his "Survey of Mr. Hobbes's Leviathan," which he dedicated the year following to Charles II. from the same place. He wrote also some things of a smaller kind, which have been collected and published with his "Miscellaneous Tracts." And lastly, in 1759, was published "An Account of his own Life from his Birth to the Restoration in 1660; and a Continuation of the same, and of his History of the Grand Rebellion, from the Restoration to his Banishment in 1667." Written by himself; and printed in one volume, folio, and three in 8vo, from his original MS. given to the university of Oxford by his heirs.

HYDE (Dr. THOMAS), a most learned writer, was son of Mr. Ralph Hyde, minister of Billingsley near Bridgenorth in Shropshire, and born there June 29, 1636. Having a strong inclination for the Oriental languages from his youth, he studied them first under his father; and afterwards, in 1652, being admitted of King's-college in Cambridge, he became acquainted with Mr. Abraham Wheelock, an admirable linguist, who encouraged him to prosecute his study of them in that place. By him Hyde, when he had been at Cambridge little more than a year, was sent to London, and recommended to Walton, afterwards bishop of Chester, as a person very capable of assisting him in the Polyglott Bible, in which work he was then engaged. Hyde rendered him great services; for, besides his attendance in the correction of it, he set forth the Persian Pentateuch. He transcribed it out of the Hebrew characters, in which it was first printed at Constantinople, into the proper Persian characters; which by Usher was then judged impossible to have been done by a native Persian, because one Hebrew letter frequently answered to divers Persian letters, which were difficult to be known. He translated it likewise into Latin. What he did farther in the Polyglott, is specified by the editor in these words:
"Nec

" Nec prætereundus eſt D. Thomas Hyde, ſummæ ſpei juvenis, qui in linguis Orientalibus ſupra ætatem magnos progreſſus fecit, quorum ſpecimina dedit tum in Arabibus, Syriacis, Perſicis, &c. corrigendis, tum in Pentateucho Perſico characteribus Perſicis deſcribendo, quia antea ſolis Hebraicis extitit, ejuſque verſionem Latinam concinnando."

In 1658, he went to Oxford, and was admitted of Queen's-college, where he was ſoon after made Hebrew reader. The year after, Richard Cromwell, then chancellor of that univer-ſity, directed his letters to the delegates thereof, ſignifying, that " Mr. Hyde was of full ſtanding, ſince his admiſſion into the univerſity of Cambridge, for the degree of maſter of arts, and that he had given public teſtimony of his more than ordinary abi-lities and learning in the Oriental languages;" upon which they made an order, that he ſhould accumulate that degree, by read-ing only a lecture in one of the Oriental languages in the ſchools; and having accordingly read upon the Perſian tongue, he was created M. A. in April 1659, Soon after he was made under-keeper of the Bodleian library, upon the ejection of Mr. Henry Stubbe; and behaved himſelf ſo well in this employment, that, when the office of head-keeper became vacant, he was elected into it with the unanimous approbation of the univerſity. In 1665, he publiſhed a Latin tranſlation from the Perſian of Ulugh Beig's " Obſervations concerning the Longitude and Latitude of the fixed Stars," with notes. This Ulugh Beig was a great Tar-tar monarch, the ſon of Shâhrokh, and the grandſon of Timur Beig, or, as he is uſually called, Tamerlane. In the preface he informs us, " that the great occupations of government hin-dered him from performing in perſon, ſo much as he would have done towards the completing this uſeful work: but that he relied chiefly on his miniſter Salaheddin, and that he dying before the work was finiſhed, his colleague Gaiatheddin Giam-ſhed and his ſon Ali al Couſhi were afterwards employed, who put the laſt hand to it." It was written originally in the Arabic tongue, but afterwards tranſlated twice into the Perſian.

About this time Hyde became known to Mr. Boyle, to whom he was very uſeful in communicating from Oriental writers ſe-veral particulars relating to chemiſtry, phyſic, and natural hiſ-tory [D]. Oct. 1666, he was collated to a prebend in the church of Saliſbury. In 1674, he publiſhed " A Catalogue of the books in the Bodleian library." In 1678, he was made arch-deacon of Glouceſter; and, in 1682, took the degree of doctor in divinity. Dec. 1691, he was elected Arabic profeſſor, on the death of Dr. Edward Pocock; and the ſame year publiſhed the " Itinera Mundi" of Abraham Peritſol, the ſon of Mordecai

[D] Boyle's Works, Vol. V. p. 580, &c.

Peritſol,

Peritfol, a very learned Jew. This was done to fupply in fome meafure the Arabic geography of Abulfeda, which, at the requeft of Dr. Fell, he had undertaken to publifh with a Latin tranflation: but, the death of his patron putting an end to that work, he fent this fmaller performance abroad, and dedicated it to the earl of Nottingham, then fecretary of ftate, in hopes that it might excite a ftronger curiofity amongft the learned to fearch into this branch of literature. In 1693, he publifhed his " De Ludis Orientalibus libri duo ;" a work, which is ftill held in very high efteem. Dr. Altham, regius-profeffor of Hebrew, and canon of Chrift-church, being, on fome difpute about the oaths, removed from both preferments, Hyde became poffeffed of them, the one being annexed to the other, in July 1697.

Three years after he had ready for the prefs, as Wood tells us, an excellent work, on a fubject very little known even to the learned themfelves, " The Religion of the Ancient Perfians:" a work of profound and various erudition, abounding with many new lights on the moft curious and interefting fubjects, filled with authentic teftimonies, which none but himfelf could bring to public view, and adorned with many ingenious conjectures concerning the theology, hiftory, and learning of the Eaftern nations. This work was printed at Oxford in 1700, in 4to, containing 550 pages; and is now become fo exceedingly fcarce, that it fells from 1l. 16s. to 2l. 2s. according to the condition it happens to be in, or the humour of the bookfeller who may chance to be poffeffed of it. Of this curious work the title will give an idea fufficiently accurate for moft readers. " Hiftoria Religionis Veterum Perfarum, eorumque Magorum. Ubi etiam nova Abrahami, & Mithrae, & Veftae, & Manethis Hiftoria, &c. Atque Angelorum officia & praefecturae ex Veterum Perfarum fententiâ. Item Perfarum annus antiquiffimus tangitur, is tū Giemfhid detegitur, verus tō Yefdegherdi de novo proditur, is tō Melicfhah, is tā Selgjûk & tō Chorzemfhâd notatur, & is tōr Katâ & tēs Oighûr explicatur. Zoroaftris vita ejufque & aliorum vaticinia de Mefliah è Perfarum aliorumque monumentis eruuntur: Primitivae opiniones de Deo & de Hominum origine referantur: Originale Orientalis Sibyllae myfterium recluditur: atque Magorum liber Sad-dor, Zoroaftris praecepta feu religiònis Canones continens, è Perfico traductus exhibetur. Dantur veterum Perfarum fcripturae & linguae, ut hae jam primo Europae producantur & literato orbi poffliminio reddantur, fpecimina. De Perfiae ejufdemque linguae nominibus, deque hujus dialectus, & à moderna differentiis ftrictim agitur. Auctor eft Thomas Hyde, S. T. D. Linguae Hebraicae in univerfitate Oxon. profeffor Regius, & ling. Arabicae profeffor Laudianus. Praemiffo capitum Elencho accedunt Icones, & Appendix variarum differtationum." This work was dedicated to lord Somers. Foreign writers

writers, as well as those of our own country, have spoken of it
with high admiration and applause ; and, if Hyde had left us
no other monument of his studies, this alone had been sufficient
to establish and preserve his reputation, as long as any taste for
Oriental learning shall remain. He published however many
others, and had many more ready to be published, or at least in
some forwardness towards it: of which a catalogue is preserved
by Wood. But the study of Oriental literature was at that time
overlooked, or rather the worth of it was not sufficiently understood: the consequence of which was, that this learned man's
abilities, application, and strong inclination to enrich the republic
of letters, with numerous acquisitions of a most laborious research, at the same time new, curious, and useful, were neglected, till it was too late; and the loss has been ever since, in vain,
though deservedly, regretted.

In April 1701, he resigned the office of principal keeper of the
Bodleian library, on account of his age and infirmities; and
died Feb. 18. 1703, at his lodgings in Christ-church, in his
67th year. He had occupied the post of interpreter and secretary
in the Oriental languages, during the reigns of Charles, II.
James II. and William III. and, it is said, had, in the course
of this employment, made himself surprisingly acquainted with
whatever regarded the policy, ceremonies, and customs of the
Oriental nations. He was succeeded in his archdeaconry of Glou--
cester by Mr. Robert Parsons ; and, what was singular enough,
in the chair of Hebrew professor and in his canonry of Christ-
church by his predecessor Dr. Altham.

HYDE (HENRY), earl of Clarendon [E], son of the chancellor, was born in 1638. Having received the rudiments of
education, he early entered into business: for his father, apprehending of what fatal consequence it would be to the king's affairs, if his correspondence should be discovered by unfaithful
secretaries, engaged him, when very young, to write all his letters in cypher; so that he generally passed half the day in writing in cypher, or decyphering, and was so discreet, as well as
faithful, that nothing was ever discovered by him. After the
Restoration, he was created Master of Arts, at Oxford, in 1660;
and, upon settling the queen's houshold, appointed chamberlain
to her majesty. He was much in the queen's favour ; and, his
father being so violently prosecuted on account of her marriage,
she thought herself bound to protect him in a particular manner.
He so highly resented the usage his father met with, that he
united himself eagerly to the party which opposed the court, and
made no inconsiderable figure in the list of speakers. Mr. Grey
has preserved a great number of his speeches. On his father's

[E] Editor's preface, and Biog. Brit.

death in 1674, he took his feat in the houfe of lords ; ftill corr-
tinued his oppofition, and even figned a proteft againft an addrefs voted to the king on his fpeech. He ftill, however, held
his poft of chamberlain to the queen ; and afterwards, fhewing
himfelf no lefs zealous againft the bill of exclufion, was taken
into favour, and made a privy-counfellor, 1680. But he foon
fell under the difpleafure of the prevailing party in the houfe of
commons ; who, unable to carry the exclufion bill, fhewed their
refentment againft the principal oppofers of it, by voting an addrefs to the king, to remove from his prefence and councils, the
marquis of Worcefter, and the earls of Halifax, Feverfham, and
Clarendon.

On the acceffion of James II. he was firft made lord privy-
feal, and then lord-lieutenant of Ireland : but being too firmly
attached to the Proteftant religion for thofe times, he was recalled
from his government, to make room for lord Tyrconnel ; and
foon after removed from the privy-feal, that lord Arundel, another Papift, might fucceed him. About this time he was made
high-fteward of the univerfity of Oxford. After the landing of
the prince of Orange, he was one of the Proteftant lords, fummoned by the king, when it was too late, to repair the ill confequences of his Popifh councils, and had fpirit enough to take
the lead, and to fpeak his mind frankly and openly in that memorable affembly. Yet though he had fo great a regard to the
conftitution, as to oppofe king James's encroachments, he would
not transfer his allegiance to the new eftablifhment, nor take
the oaths to king William : on which account he was, with
fome others, fufpected of evil defigns againft the government ;
and, when the king was in England, and the French fleet appeared on the Englifh coaft, the regency thought proper to fecure him in the Tower. After fome months he was releafed,
and fpent the remainer of his days privately at his own houfe in
the country ; where he died 1709, aged 71.

His State Letters, during his government of Ireland, and his
Diary for the years 1687, 1688, 1689, and 1690, were publifhed, in 2 vols. 4to, 1763, from the Clarendon prefs in Oxford.

HYGINUS (CAIUS JULIUS), an ancient Latin writer, who
flourifhed in the time of Auguftus ; and of whom Suetonius, in
his book " De illuftribus Grammaticis," has given this account.
" He was a freedman of Auguftus, and by nation a Spaniard ;
though fome think that he was an Alexandrian, and brought by
Cæfar to Rome when Alexandria was taken. He was a diligent
follower and imitator of Cornelius Alexander, a celebrated
Greek grammarian ; and was alfo himfelf a teacher at Rome.
He was made keeper of the Palatine library ; was very intimate with the poet Ovid, and with Caius Licinius, a man
of confular dignity and an hiftorian, who has taken occafion to
                                                              inform

inform us, that he died very poor, and, while he lived, was supported chiefly by his generosity [F]." Vossius asks, who this consular historian Caius Licinius is? and thinks it should be Caius Asinius, who wrote a history of the civil war, and was consul with Cneius Domitius Calvinus, U. C. 723.

Hyginus wrote many books, which are mentioned by ancient writers. Gellius quotes a work " of the Lives and Actions of illustrious Men [G]." Servius, in his " Commentary upon the Æneid," tells us, that he wrote upon " the Origin and Situation of the Italian Cities:" which same work is also mentioned by Macrobius. Gellius again mentions his " Commentaries upon Virgil;" as does Macrobius a book " Concerning the Gods." He wrote also " about Bees and Agriculture;" and lastly, a book of " Genealogies," of which he himself has made mention in the only undoubted work of his remaining; that is, in his " Poëticon Astronomicon, de mundi & sphæræ ac utriusque partium declaratione, libris quatuor, ad M. Fabium conscriptum." The first book treats of the world and of the doctrine of the sphere; the second of the signs in the zodiac; the third gives a description and history of the constellations; and the fourth treats of several things relating to the planets. Here, while Hyginus describes the constellations in the heavens, and notes the stars which belong to each, he takes occasion to explain the fables of the poets from which the constellations were supposed originally to have taken their rise and name; and hence his work seems to have been called " Poëticon Astronomicon." It has come down to us, however, very imperfect; and all that part of it, which, as he tells us, treated of the month, the year and the reasons of intercalating the months, is entirely lost. To this is joined a book of fables, in which the heathen mythology is reduced into a compendium: but this is imperfect, and suspected to be spurious. The best edition of these books is that which Munker published, together with some other pieces of antiquity upon the same or a similar subject, under the title of " Mythographi Latini, Amst. 1681," 2 vols. 8vo. The third book of the Astronomics, is adorned with illustrated with several copper-plates of the constellations elegantly engraved, which Grotius had published from the Sulian MS. but which, Schetter tells us, he had omitted in his edition of 1674, because he knew those ancient delineations to be very erroneous, and very ill done.

HYPATIA, a most beautiful, virtuous, and learned lady of antiquity, was the daughter of Theon, who governed the Platonic school at Alexandria, the place of her birth and education, in the latter part of the fourth century. Theon was famous among

[F] De Hist. Lat. p. 103. L. B. 1651.　　[G] Lib. I. c. 13.

his

his contemporaries for his extensive knowledge and learning;
but what has chiefly rendered him so with posterity, is, that he
was the father of Hypatia, whom, encouraged by her prodigious
genius, he educated not only in all the qualifications belonging to
her sex, but likewise in the most abstruse sciences. She made
an amazing progress in every branch of learning, and the things
that are said of her almost surpass belief. Socrates, the ecclesiastical historian, is a witness whose veracity cannot be doubted,
at least when he speaks in favour of an heathen philosopher;
and he tells us [н], that Hypatia "arrived at such a pitch of
learning, as very far to exceed all the philosophers of her time:"
to which Nicephorus adds, "those of other times [i]." Phi-
lostorgius, a third historian of the same stamp, affirms, that
"she was much superior to her father and master Theon, in
what regards astronomy [к]:" and Suidas, who mentions two
books of her writing, one "on the Astronomical Canon of
Diophantus, and another on the Conics of Apollonius," avers,
that "she not only exceeded her father in astronomy, but also
that she understood all the other parts of philosophy [l]." But
our notions of Hypatia will be prodigiously heightened, when
we consider her succeeding her father, as she actually did, in
the government of the Alexandrian school: teaching out of that
chair, where Ammonius, Hierocles, and many great and celebrated philosophers had taught; and this also at a time, when
men of immense learning abounded both at Alexandria, and in
many other parts of the Roman empire. Her fame was so extensive, and her worth so universally acknowledged, that we
cannot wonder, if she had a crouded auditory. "She explained
to her hearers," says Socrates, "the several sciences, that go
under the general name of philosophy; for which reason there
was a confluence to her, from all parts, of those who made philosophy their delight and study." One cannot represent to himself without pleasure the flower of all the youth in Europe,
Asia, and Africa, sitting at the feet of a very beautiful lady, for
such we are assured Hypatia was, all greedily swallowing instruction from her mouth, and many of them doubtless love
from her eyes: though we are not sure that she ever listened to
any solicitations, since Suidas, who talks of her marriage with
Isidorus, yet relates at the same time, that she died a maid.

Her scholars were as eminent as they were numerous: one of
whom was the celebrated Synesius, who was afterwards bishop
of Ptolemais. This ancient Christian Platonist every where
bears the strongest, as well as the most grateful testimony to the
learning and virtue of his instructress; and never mentions her

[н] Lib. vii. c. 15.　　　[i] Lib. xiv. c. 14.　　　[к] Lib. viii. c. 9.
[l] In Theon.

without the profoundest respect, and sometimes in terms of affection coming little short of adoration. In a letter to his brother Euoptius, "Salute," says he, "the most honoured and
the most beloved of God, the PHILOSOPHER; and that happy
society, which enjoys the blessing " of her divine voice [M]."
In another, he mentions one Egyptus, who "sucked in the
seeds of wisdom from Hypatia [N]." In another, he expresses
himself thus: " I suppose these letters will be delivered by Peter,
which he will receive from that sacred hand [o]." In a letter
addressed to herself, he desires her to direct a hydroscope to be
made and bought for him, which he there describes. That famous silver Astrolabe, which he presented to Peonius, a man
equally excelling in philosophy and arms, he owns to have been
perfected by the directions of Hypatia [P]. In a long epistle,
he acquaints her with his reasons for writing two books, which
he sends her; and asks her judgement of one, resolving not to
publish it without her approbation [Q].

But it was not Synesius only, and the disciples of the Alexandrian school, who admired Hypatia for her great virtue and
learning: never woman was more caressed by the public, and
yet never woman had a more unspotted character. She was held
as an oracle for her wisdom, which made her consulted by the
magistrates in all important cases; and this frequently drew her
among the greatest concourse of men, without the least censure
of her manners. "On account of the confidence and authority," says Socrates, "which she had acquired by her learning,
she sometimes came to the judges with singular modesty. Nor
was she any thing abashed to appear thus among a crowd of men;
for all persons, by reason of her extraordinary discretion, did at
the same time both reverence and admire her." The same is
confirmed by Nicephorus, and the other authors; whom we have
already cited. Damascius and Suidas relate, that the governors
and magistrates of Alexandria regularly visited her, and paid their
court to her [R]; and, to say all in a word, when Nicephorus
intended to pass the highest compliment on the princess Eudocia,
he thought he could not do it better, than by calling her " another Hypatia [s]."

While Hypatia thus reigned the brightest ornament of Alexandria, Orestes was governor of the same place for the emperor
Theodosius, and Cyril bishop or patriarch. Orestes, having
had a liberal education, could not but admire Hypatia, and, as
a wise governor, frequently consulted her. This created an intimacy between them that was highly displeasing to Cyril, who

[M] Epist. iv.   [N] Ibid. cxxxv.   [o] Ibid. cxxxii.   [P] Ad Pæon.
[Q] Epist. cliv.   [R] Apud Pho.   [s] Lib. viii. c. 5.

VOL. VIII.   A a   had

had a great averfion to Oreftes: which intimacy, as it is fuppofed, had like to have proved fatal to Oreftes, as we may collect from the following account of Socrates. " Certain of the Monks," fays he, " living in the Nitrian mountains, leaving their monafteries to the number of about five hundred, flocked to the city, and fpied the governor going abroad in his chariot : whereupon approaching, they called him by the names of Sacrificer and Heathen, ufing many other fcandalous expreffions. The governor, fufpecting that this was a trick played him by Cyril, cried out that he was a Chriftian ; and that he had been baptized at Conftantinople by bifhop Atticus. But the Monks giving no heed to what he faid, one of them, called Ammonius, threw a ftone at Oreftes, which ftruck him on the head ; and being all covered with blood from his wounds, his guards, a few excepted, fled, fome one way and fome another, hiding themfelves in the crowd, left they fhould be ftoned to death. In the mean while, the people of Alexandria ran to defend their governor againft the Monks, and putting the reft to flight, brought Ammonius, whom they apprehended, to Oreftes ; who, as the laws prefcribed, put him publicly to the torture, and racked him till he expired [τ]."

But though Oreftes had the luck to efcape with his life, Hypatia afterwards fell a facrifice. This lady, as we have obferved, was profoundly refpected by Oreftes, who much frequented and confulted her : " for which reafon," fays Socrates, " fhe was not a little traduced among the Chriftian multitude, as if fhe obftructed a reconciliation between Cyril and Oreftes. This occafioned certain hot-brained men, headed by one Peter a lecturer, to enter into a confpiracy againft her ; who watching an opportunity, when fhe was returning home from fome place, firft dragged her out of her chair ; then hurried her to the church called Cæfar's ; and then, ftripping her naked, killed her with tiles. After this, they tore her to pieces ; and, carrying her limbs to a place called Cinaron, there burnt them to afhes." Cave endeavours to remove the imputation of this horrid murder from Cyril, thinking him too honeft a man to have had any hand in it ; and lays it upon the Alexandrian mob in general, whom he calls " leviffimum hominum genus," " a very trifling inconftant people." But though Cyril fhould be allowed to have been neither the perpetrator, nor even the contriver of it, yet it is much to be fufpected, that he did not difcountenance it in the manner he ought to have done : which fufpicion muft be greatly confirmed by reflecting, that he was fo far from blaming the outrage committed by the Nitrian Monks upon the

[τ] Lib. vii. c. 14.

governor

governor Oreftes, that " he afterwards received the dead body
of Ammonius, whom Oreftes had punifhed with the rack;
made a panegyric upon him, in the church where he was laid,
In which he extolled his courage and conftancy, as one that had
contended for the truth; and, changing his name to Thaumafius,
or the Admirable, ordered him to be confidered as a martyr.
However, continues Socrates, the wifer fort of Chriftians
did not approve the zeal, which Cyril fhewed on this man's
behalf; being convinced, that Ammonius had juftly fuffered for
his defperate attempt [υ]." We learn from the fame hiftorian,
that the death of Hypatia happened in March, in the 10th year
of Honorius's, and the 6th of Theodofius's, confulfhip; that
is, about A. D. 415.

HYPERIDES, an Athenian Orator, difciple of Plato and
Ifocrates, flourifhed about 335 years before the Chriftian Æra.
He was a fincere patriot, and fo ftrenuous a lover of juftice and
liberty, that he did not hefitate to accufe his friend Demofthenes
of receiving money from Harpalus, and actually drove him into
banifhment. They were afterwards reconciled, and perifhed
about the fame time. When the Athenians were beaten at
Cranon, he was dragged out of the temple of Ceres, and delivered
up to Antipater. He died about 322. He publifhed many
of his orations, of which one only is extant, and that in fome
degree dubious. It ftands the 17th among thofe of Demofthenes.
There are alfo fome fragments. His ftyle of eloquence
has been varioufly eftimated by the critics of his own country.

HYPSICLES, of Alexandria, a difciple of Ifidorus, flourifhed
under M. Aurelius, and Lucius Verus. He has been
fuppofed to be the author of a certain work called " Anaphoricus,"
or a book of afcenfions, which was written in oppofition
to the doctrines of fome aftronomer. It was publifhed in Greek,
with the Latin verfion of Mentelius, and in conjunction with
the Optics of Heliodorus, at Paris in 1680, 4to. Voffius, in
his book de Scientiis Mathematicis, has erroneoufly fuppofed
him to have lived at a much earlier period.

HYRCANUS (John), high prieft and fovereign of the Jews;
fucceeded his father Simon Maccabæus, who had been treacheroufly
killed by his fon-in-law Ptolemy. This traitor, having been
gained over by Antiochus Sidetes king of Syria, was defirous of
deftroying his brother-in-law Hyrcanus after he had murdered
his father-in-law, but John caufed the affaffins to be taken up
and put to death. Ptolemy then perfifting in his perfidy, invited
Antiochus into Judea, and Hyrcanus was fhut up in Jerufalem,
and befieged there by him. After a long and obftinate

[υ] Lib. vii. c. 14.
A a 2

fiege, during which Antiochus fhewed fome extraordinary marks
of generofity to the befieged, a peace was concluded. The
conditions were, that the Jews fhould give up to him their arms,
and the tribute they received from Joppa, and other towns not
properly within their territory.—After the death of Antiochus,
Hyrcanus took the opportunity of avenging his country. He
took feveral towns in Judea, fubdued the Idumæans, feized Samaria, and demolifhed the temple of Gerizim. He died 106
years before Chrift.

JAAPHAR

J.

JAAPHAR EBN TOPHAIL, an Arabian philofopher, was contemporary with Averroes, who died about the year 1198. He compofed a philofophical romance, entitled, "The Life or Hiftory of Hai Ebn Yokdhan:" in which he endeavours to demonſtrate, how a man may, by the mere light of nature, attain the knowledge of things natural and fupernatural; more particularly the knowledge of God, and the affairs of another life. He lived in Spain, as appears from one or two paſſages in this work. He wrote fome other pieces, which are not come to our hands; but, that this was well received in the Eaſt, appears from its having been tranſlated by R. Mofes Narbonenſis, into Hebrew, and illuſtrated with a large commentary. It was publiſhed in 1671, with an accurate Latin verſion, by Mr. Edward Pococke, fon of Dr. Pococke, profeſſor of the Oriental languages at Oxford; and, in 1708, an Engliſh tranſlation of it from the Arabic was given by Simon Ockley, foon after Arabic profeſſor at Cambridge. See article OCKLEY.

JABLONSKI (DANIEL-ERNEST), a learned Poliſh Proteſtant divine, was born Nov. 20, 1660, at Dantzick, and had the firſt part of his education in Germany; after which he travelled into Holland, and thence croſſed the water to England, for further improvement in his ſtudies. Thus accompliſhed, he became fucceſſively miniſter of Magdebourg, Liſſa, Koningſberg, and Berlin, and was at length ecclefiaſtical counfellor and prefident of the fociety of fciences in this laſt city. His zeal againſt infidelity, both in the Atheiſts and Deiſts, ſhewed itſelf on all occafions; and he tonk a deal of pains to effect an union betwixt the Lutherans and Calviniſts, but to no purpofe. The truth is, confidering the rooted prejudices on each fide, fuch a coalition like that between the church of England and the Diffenters, is rather to be wiſhed than expected. Mr. Jablonſki died in May, 1741.

There is a Latin tranſlation by him of "Bentley's Sermons at Boyle's Lectures [A];" there are alfo feveral Latin "Differtations upon the Land of Geffen;" "Meditationes de divinâ origine fcripturæ facræ;" alfo a piece entitled, "Thorn affligée," homilies, and fome other works in good efteem.

[A] Dictum. Portat.

JABLONSKI (THEODORE), counsellor of the court of Pruffia, and secretary of the Royal Society of Sciences at Berlin, was also a perfon of diftinguifhed merit. He was a man of the moft exact probity and a ftrict piety, united to a fweetnefs of temper, a polite urbanity, and an inclination to oblige all that applied to him. He loved the fciences, and did them honour, without that ambition which is generally feen in men of learning. It was owing to this modefty that he did not put his name to the greater part of his works; the chief of which are, " Dictionaire François-Allemand & Allemand-François," printed in 1711; " A Courfe of Morality in the German Tongue, 1713;" Dictionaire Univerfel des Arts & des Sciences, 1721;" a tranflation into High Dutch of " Tacitus de moribus Germanorum," with remarks, 1724.

JABLONSKI (PAUL-ERNEST), the fon of Daniel-Erneft, above-mentioned, was a native of Berlin, a Proteftant divine, and a profeffor of theology at Frankfort on the Oder, as well as paftor there. He was born in 1693, and in 1714 publifhed a learned differtation entitled, " Difquifitio de Lingua Lycaonica," ad Act. Apoft. xiv. 11. It appeared at Berlin in quarto. A great expectation of his talents was excited by this publication, which he fully juftified in his fubfequent life. He publifhed alfo, 2. " De Memnone Græcorum, 1753, Frankfort, 1753. 3. " Inftitutiones Hiftoriæ Ecclefiafticæ," in 2 vols. 8vo. But his moft learned and important work was, 4. " Pantheon Ægyptiorum: five de Diis eorum Commentarius, cum Prolegomenis de religione & theologia Egyptiorum," in three volumes, 8vo, publifhed at Frankfort in 1750, and 1752. It is a book of great and extenfive erudition. Jablonfki died in 1757.

JACETIUS (FRANCIS DE CATANEIS), an Italian writer, was born at Florence, in 1466, and was the difciple of Marfilius Ficinus, under whom he ftudied the Platonic philofophy, and became a great mafter of it. He was alfo a good orator, and fucceeding Ficinus in his profefforfhip, held it till his death, which happened in 1522. There is extant by him, " A Treatife of Beauty," and another of " Love," according to the doctrine of Plato, befides feveral others, which were all printed together at Bafil in 1563.

JACKSON (THOMAS), a learned Englifh divine, was born at Willowing, in the bifhopric of Durham, 1579 [n]. Many of his relations being merchants in Newcaftle, he was defigned to have been bred in that line; but his great inclination to learning being obferved, he was fent to Oxford, and admitted into Queen's-college in 1595, but removed to Corpus-Chrifti the

[n] Athen. Oxon.

year

year after. He took his degrees in arts at the stated times; and May 10, 1606, became probationer-fellow, being then well-grounded in arithmetic, grammar, philology, geometry, rhetoric, logic, philosophy, the Oriental languages, history, &c. with an insight into heraldry and hieroglyphics. But he made all his knowledge subservient to the study of divinity, to which he applied with great vigour, and became so distinguished in it, that he not only read a divinity-lecture in his college every Sunday morning, but another on the week-day at Pembroke-college (then newly founded) at the request of the master and fellows. He was also chosen vice-president of his college for many years successively, by virtue of which office he moderated at the divinity disputations, with remarkable learning, and no less candour and modesty. He commenced D. D. in 1622, and quitted the college two years afterwards, being preferred to a living in his native country, and soon after to the vicarage of Newcastle. In that large and laborious cure, he performed all the duties of an excellent parish-priest, and was particularly admired for his discourses from the pulpit. At this time he was a rigid Calvinist, and was first convinced of the errors of absolute predestination by Dr. Richard Neile, bishop of Durham, who took him for his chaplain, and joined with Dr. Laud in bringing him back to his college, where he was elected president by their interest, in 1630. Upon this promotion he resigned the vicarage of Newcastle; and, in 1635, was collated to a prebend of Winchester, having been made king's chaplain some time before. Dr. Towers being advanced to the bishopric of Peterborough, Dr. Jackson succeeded him in the deanery in 1638; but he did not enjoy this dignity quite two years, being taken from it by death, in 1640. He was interred in the inner chapel of Corpus-Christi-college. He was a man of a blameless life, studious, humble, courteous, and remarkably charitable, pious, exemplary in his private and public conversation; so that he was respected and beloved by the most considerable persons in the nation; and indeed the greatest esteem was no more than his due, on account of his learning, for he was well skilled in all the learned languages, arts, sciences, and physics. As an instance of his charitable disposition, we are told, that while he was vicar of Newcastle, whenever he went out, he usually gave what money he had about him to the poor, who at length so flocked about him, that his servant took care he should not have too much in his pocket. Dr. Jackson was profoundly read in the fathers, and endued with an uncommon depth of judgement, which however did not clear him from some of the received errors of the times. His works are very numerous [c],

[c] Life of Dr. Jackson, prefixed to his works in 1653.

A a 4 printed

printed at different times, but were all collected and published in 1672 and 1673, in three volumes, folio, consisting chiefly of sermons, besides his " Commentaries on the Apostles' Creed," which are his principal work. His writings were much admired and studied by the late bishop Horne, in the account of whose life his merits are thus displayed by the biographer. " Dr. Jackson is a magazine of theological knowledge, every where penned with great elegance and dignity, so that his style is a pattern of perfection. His writings, once thought inestimable by every body but the Calvinists, had been greatly neglected, and would probably have continued so, but for the praises bestowed upon them by the celebrated Mr. Merrick, of Trinity-college, Oxford, who brought them once more into repute with many learned readers. The early extracts of Mr. Horne, which are now remaining, shew how much information he derived from this excellent writer, who deserves to be numbered with the English fathers of the church [D]."

JACKSON (JOHN), an English divine [E], son of the Rev. John Jackson, first rector of Lensey, afterwards rector of Rossington, and vicar of Doncaster in Yorkshire; was born at Lensey, April 4, 1686. He was educated at Doncaster-school under the famous Dr. Bland; who was afterwards head master of Eton-school, dean of Durham, and from 1732 to 1746 provost of Eton-college. In 1702, he was admitted of Jesus-college, Cambridge; and, after taking the degree of B. A. at the usual period, left the university in 1707. During his residence there, he learned Hebrew under Simon Ockley, the celebrated Orientalist; but never made any great proficiency. In 1708, he entered into deacon's orders, and into priest's two years after; when he took possession of the rectory of Rossington, which had been reserved for him from the death of his father by the corporation of Doncaster [F]. That politic body, however, sold the next turn of this living for 800l. and with the money paved the long street of their town, which forms part of the great northern road. In 1712, he married Elizabeth, daughter of John Cowley, collector of excise at Doncaster; and, soon after, went to reside at Rossington.

In 1714, he commenced author, by publishing three anonymous letters, in defence of Dr. S. Clarke's " Scripture-Doctrine of the Trinity," with whom he soon after became personally acquainted; and nine treatises by Jackson on this controversy, from 1716 to 1738, are enumerated in the supplementary volume of the " Biographia Britannica." In 1718, he offered himself at Cambridge for the degree of M. A. but was refused on ac-

[D] Jones's Life of bishop Horne, p. 75.   [E] Life of Jackson, 1764, 8vo.
[F] Anecdotes of Bowyer, by Nichols, p. 226.

count of his heretical principles. Upon his return, he received
a confolatory letter from Dr. Clarke, who alfo procured for him
the confraterfhip of Wigfton's hofpital in Leicefter; a place which
is held by patent for life from the chancellor of the dutchy of
Lancafter, and was particularly acceptable to Jackfon, as it
requires no fubfcription to any articles of religion. To this he
was prefented, in 1719, by lord Lechmere, in whofe gift it
was then, as chancellor of the dutchy of Lancafter, and from
whom Dr. Clarke had the year before received the mafterfhip of
that hofpital. He now removed from Roffington to Leicefter;
where, between politics (Leicefter being a great party-town)
and religion, he was engaged in almoft continual war: and, to
fay the truth, his fpirit was not averfe from litigation. In May,
1720, he qualified himfelf for afternoon-preacher at St. Martin's church in Leicefter, as confrater; and, in the two following years, feveral prefentments were lodged againft him in the
bifhop's and alfo in the archdeacon's court, for preaching heretical doctrines; but he exerted all his fpirit, and vindicated himfelf fo ftrenuoufly, as to defeat the profecutions. Yet, after the
" Cafe of the Arian Subfcription" was publifhed by Dr. Waterland, he refolved, with Dr. Clarke, never to fubfcribe the
articles any more. By this he loft, about 1724, the hopes of a
prebend of Salifbury, which bifhop Hoadly refufed to give him
without fuch fubfcription. " The bifhop's denial," fays my
author, " was the more remarkable, as he had fo often intimated
his own diflike of all fuch fubfcriptions:" Jackfon, however,
had been prefented before by fir John Fryer to the private prebend of Wherwell in Hampfhire, where no fuch qualification
was required.

On the death of Dr. Clarke, in May, 1729, he fucceeded,
by the prefentation of the duke of Rutland, then chancellor of
the dutchy of Lancafter, to the mafterfhip of Wigfton's hofpital, which fituation he preferved to his death. The year before, 1728, he had publifhed, in 8vo, " Novatiani Opera, ad
antiquiores editiones caftigata, & à multis mendis expurgata:"
and now, intent upon books, and perhaps the more fo by being
incapable of rifing to preferment, he continued from time to time
to fend out various publications. In 1730, " A Defence of
Human Liberty, againft Cato's Letters;" and, in the fecond edition, " A Supplement againft Anthony Collins, efq; upon the fame
Subject." In 1730 and 1731, " Four Tracts in Defence of
Human Reafon, occafioned by bifhop Gibfon's fecond Paftoral
Letter." In 1731, a piece againft " Tindal's Chriftianity as
old as the Creation;" in 1733, another by way of anfwer to
Browne bifhop of Corke's book, entitled, " Things Divine
and Supernatural, conceived by Analogy with Things Natural
and Human;" in 1734, " The Exiftence and Unity of God,
&c."

&c." which led him into a controversy with Law, and other writers; and, in 1735, "A Differtation on Matter and Spirit," with remarks on Baxter's "Inquiry into the Nature of the human Soul." In 1736, he publifhed "A Narrative of his being refufed the Sacrament of the Lord's Supper at Bath:" this had been done in a very public manner by Dr. Coney, and was the fecond affront of that kind he had experienced; for, in 1730, he had been denied the ufe of the pulpit at St. Martin's in Leicefter, by the vicar, who fet the facriftan at the bottom of the ftairs to reftrain him from afcending. Thofe attacks, however, he repelled with vigour, and ufually came off victorious, at leaft unhurt.

In 1742, he had an epiftolary debate with his friend William Whifton, concerning the order and times of the high priefts. In 1744, he publifhed "An Addrefs to the Deifts, &c." in anfwer to Morgan's "Refurrection of Jefus confidered by a Moral Philofopher;" and, in 1745, entered the lift againft Warburton, in "The Belief of a future State proved to be a fundamental Article of the Religion of the Hebrews, and held by the Philofophers, &c." two or three polemic pieces with Warburton were the confequence of this. His next work was, "Remarks upon Middleton's Free Inquiry into the Miraculous Powers, &c." and, after this, he does not appear to have publifhed any thing till 1752, except that, in 1751, he communicated to Mr. John Gilbert Cooper, for the ufe of his "Life of Socrates," fome learned notes; in which he contrived to avenge himfelf upon his old antagonift Warburton. At the fame time he expofed the young and incautious writer to the refentment of that veteran, who did not fail to fhew it in one of his notes upon Pope. In 1752, came out his laft and capital work, "Chronological Antiquities," in 3 vols. 4to. He afterwards made many collections and preparations for an edition of the New Teftament in Greek, with Scholia in the fame language; and would have inferted all the various readings, had not the growing infirmities of age prevented him. An account of the materials of this intended edition, with notes containing alterations, corrections, additions to his "Chronology," are inferted in an appendix to "Memoirs" of him printed in 1764, by Dr. Sutton of Leicefter.

He died May 12, 1763. By his wife, who died before him, he had twelve children; but only four furvived him. He was a man of great application and learning, but not of parts or genius, and totally devoid of tafte. His knowledge too was confined to the precincts of Greek and Latin: for he knew nothing of Oriental languages, except a little Hebrew; and of the modern languages, even the French, was altogether ignorant. Though of a fpirit fomewhat litigious, and not a little opinionated,

aled, he was good-natured, hospitable, and chearful even to
mirth; and, upon the whole, easy, complacent, and agreeable
to all who were connected with or dependent upon him.

JACOB (Ben Naphtali), a famous rabbi in the fifth century, was one of the principal Maforets, and bred at the school
of Tiberias in Palestine, with Ben Afer, another leading man
of the fame fect. The invention of the points in Hebrew, to
ferve for vowels, and of the accents, to facilitate the reading of
that language, is ascribed to these two rabbies. This is said to
have been done in an assembly which the Jews held at Tiberias
in 476. This is the opinion of Gerebrand and several other
learned men, but it is not universally received [c].

JACOB (Ben Hajim), a rabbi of the sixteenth century,
who rendered himself famous by the collection of the Masora,
which was printed at Venice in 1525 with the text of the Bible,
the Chaldee paraphrase, and the commentaries of some rabbies
upon Scripture. This edition of the Hebrew Bible, and those
which follow it with the great and small Masora compiled by
this rabbi, are much esteemed by the Jews; there being nothing
before exact or accurate upon the Masora, which is properly a
critique upon the books of the Bible in order to settle the true
reading. In the preface to his great Masora, he shews the use-
fulness of his work, and explains the keri and ketib, or the different readings of the Hebrew text: he puts the various readings in the margin, because there are just doubts concerning the
true reading; he observes also, that the Talmudish Jews do not
always agree with the authors of the Masora. Besides the various readings collected by the Masorets, and put by this rabbi
in the margin of his Bible [H], he collected others himself from
the MS. copies, which must be carefully distinguished from the
Masora.

JACOBÆUS (Oliger), a professor of physic and philosophy at Copenhagen, was born in July, 1650-1, at Arhufen in
the peninsula of Jutland, where his father was bishop [ı], who
took all possible care of his son's education; but dying in 1671,
he was sent by his mother, the famous Jasper Bartholin's daughter, to the university of Copenhagen, where he took the usual
degrees, and then travelled to the principal courts of Europe.
In this tour he ran through France, Italy, Germany, Hungary,
England, and the Netherlands. His view was to improve himfelf in his profession, and he omitted no opportunity that offered.
Upon his return home in 1679, he received letters from his
prince, appointing him professor of physic and philosophy in the

[o] Dictlon. Perot.
[n] Simon's Crit. Dict.
[ı] His great-grandfather, Mr. Jaco-
laeus, was also bishop of Falster, and his
grandfather first physician to Christian IV.
king of Denmark.

capital of his kingdom. He entered upon the discharge of this post in 1680, and performed the functions of it with the highest reputation; so that besides the honour conferred on him by the university, Christian V. king of Denmark, committed to him the charge of augmenting and putting into order that celebrated cabinet of curiosities which his predecessors had begun; and Frederic IV. in 1698, made him a counsellor in his court of justice. Thus loaded with honours, as well as beloved and respected by his compatriots, he passed his days in tranquillity, till an unforeseen stroke deprived him for ever of his happiness. This was the loss of his wife, Anne Marguerete, daughter of Thomas Bartholin, who, after seventeen years of marriage, died in 1698, leaving him father of six boys. The loss threw him into a melancholy which at length proved fatal. In vain he sought for a remedy, by the advice of his friends, in a second marriage with Anne Tistorph: this proved ineffectual, his melancholy increased, and, after languishing under it near three years, he died at the age of 51 [κ].

His works are as follow: 1. "De Ranis dissertatio, Romæ, 1676." 2. "Bartholomei Scalæ equitis Florentini historia Florentinorum, &c. Romæ, 1677:" the famous Magliabecchi furnished him with this MS. from the Medicean library. 3. "Oratio in obitum Tho. Bartholini, 1681." 4. "Compendium institutionum medicarum, Hafniæ, 1684," 8vo. 5. "De Ranis & Lacertis dissertatio, 1686." 6. "Francisci Ariosti de oleo montis Zibinii, seu petroleo agri Mutinensis, &c. 1690." 7. "Panegyricus Christiano Vto dictus, 1691." 8. "Gaudia Arctoi orbis ob thalamos angustus Frederici & Ludovicæ, 1691." 9. "Museum regium, sive catalogus rerum, &c. quæ in basilica bibliotheca Christiani V. Hafniæ asservantur, 1696." He had a great talent for poetry, and composed several excellent poems upon various subjects, some of which have been published. He left the character of a good husband, a good master, a good neighbour, and a good friend.

JACOPONE (DA TODI), an ancient Italian poet, a contemporary and friend of Dante. His true name was *Jacopo de' Benedetti*, and he was born at Todi of a noble family. Late in life he became a widower, upon which he distributed his wealth to the poor, and entered into the order of Minors, where through humility, he remained always in the class of Servitors. (*converi*). He died, at a very advanced age, in 1306; and the reputation of sanctity he had acquired procured him the title of *The happy*. He composed sacred Canticles, full of fire, and zeal; which are still admired in Italy, notwithstanding their uncultivated style, which abounds with barbarous words, from the Calabrian

[κ] Moreri. L'Advocat.

Sicilian,

Sicilian, and Neapolitan dialects. He wrote also some poems of the same stamp in Latin, and was the author of the *Stabat Mater*. The completest edition of his Canticles is that of Venice, printed in 1617, in quarto, with notes.

JACQUELOT (ISAAC), son of a protestant minister of Vassy, was born in 1647, and became colleague to his father at the age of twenty-one. After the revocation of the edict of Nantz, he went to Heidelburg, and thence to the Hague, where the king of Prussia accidentally heard him preach, and immedially took him to Berlin as his chaplain. He also settled upon him a considerable pension, which he enjoyed till his death, in 1708. Jacquelot, a virtuous and learned minister, was author of several works abounding in strong argument, but defective in method and precision. 1. "Dissertations on the Existence of God," in quarto, 1697. He argues here against Epicurus and Spinosa. 2. Some controversial tracts against Bayle. 3. "Dissertations on the Messiah," 8vo. 1699. 4. "A treatise on the inspiration of the sacred books," 8vo. 1715. 5. "A Critique on Jurieu's Picture of Socinianism," which involved the author in persecution. 6. "Sermons," in two volumes, 12mo. which, like his other works, abound with genius, sagacity, and learning, but want method. 7. "Letters to the bishops of France," the intention of which was to dispose them to behave with gentleness and moderation towards the Protestants, as becomes men and christians, and particularly the servants of the God of peace.

JÆGER (JOHN WOLFGANG), a Lutheran divine, was born at Stutgard, 1647, of a father who was counsellor of the dispatches to the duke of Wirtemberg. After he had finished his studies, he was entrusted with the education of duke Eberhard III. with whom he travelled into Italy in 1676, as preceptor. This charge being completed, he taught philosophy and divinity; and in 1698 was nominated a counsellor to the duke of Wirtemberg. The following year he became consistorial counsellor and preacher to the cathedral of Stutgard, and superintendant-general and abbot of the monastery of Adelberg. At last he was promoted in 1702 to the places of first professor of divinity, chancellor of the university, and provost of the church of Tubingen. He died in 1720. We have a great number of works of his, the chief of which are [1]. 1. "Ecclesiastical History compared with Profane History." 2. "A System or Compendium of Divinity." 3. "Several Pieces upon Mystic Divinity, in which he refutes Poiret, Fenelon, &c." 4. "Observations upon Puffendorf and Grotius, de jure belli & pacis." 5. "A Treatise of Laws." 6. "An Examination of the Life and

[1] Diction. Portat.

Doctrine

Doctrine of Spinofa." 7. "A Moral Theology, &c." All his works are in Latin.

JAGO (Richard), an English minor poet, was born October 11, 1715. He was the third fon of Richard Jago, rector of Beaudefert near Henley, Warwickfhire, a gentleman of Cornifh extraction. He was educated at the fchool of a Mr. Crompton, at Solihul, in Warwickfhire, where he formed an intimacy with Shenftone, which continued throughout their lives. About 1732 he went, as a fervitor, to Univerfity College, Oxford, where Shenftone, then a commoner of Pembroke, continued his friendfhip to him, and introduced him to feveral of his friends. One of thefe, Mr. Graves, author of the Spiritual Quixote, &c. has animadverted with fome feverity, on the illiberal prejudice which obliged thefe friends to vifit Jago privately, becaufe he was only in the rank of a fervitor. This prejudice is now much foftened, and the fame circumfpection would hardly be thought neceffary, in the cafe of a young man of merit. Mr. Jago took orders in 1737, and the degree of Mafter of Arts in 1738. In 1744, he married Dorothea Sufanna Fancourt, daughter of a clergyman in Leicefterfhire. The two fmall livings of Harbury and Chefterton were given him by lord Willoughby de Broke, about 1746, and at the former he refided till 1751, when he was unfortunately left a widower with feveral fmall children. In 1754, lord Clare, afterwards earl Nugent, procured for him from the bifhop of Worcefter, the vicarage of Snitterfield in Warwickfhire, worth about 140l. a year, and here he refided for the remainder of his life. He took a fecond wife in the year 1759, who was a daughter of Mr. Underwood of Budgely in Staffordfhire. In all fituations he continued to indulge his early propenfity to poetry, and correfponded with Shenftone, on the fubject of their literary purfults.

His Elegy on the Blackbirds was publifhed in 1752, by Dr. Hawkefworth in the Adventurer, and at firft attributed to Gilbert Weft. When it afterwards appeared in Dodfley's collection with the name of the real author, it is faid that a manager of the Bath theatre claimed it as his own; and affured his friends that *Jago* was merely a fictitious name, which he had taken from the tragedy of Othello. Hawkefworth probably received the poem from Weft, and certainly thought it his, as Dr. Johnfon obferves, but abundant evidence has fince proved it to be the performance of Jago. In 1771, lord Willoughby de Broke prefented him to the living of Kilmcote in Leicefterfhire, worth near 300l. a year, which had been held by the father of his firft wife. He then refigned the vicarage of Harbury.

In the latter part of his life, as infirmities came upon him, he feldom went far from home; but amufed himfelf in improving his vicarage houfe, and ornamenting his grounds, which

we e

were agreeably fituated), and had many natural beauties. After
a fhort illnefs, he died on the 8th of May 1781, in the 66th year
of his age, and was buried in a vault which he had made for his
family at Snitterfield [M]. By his firft wife, he had three fons,
who died before him, and four daughters, three of whom were
living in 1784. His fecond wife brought him no children.

The other poems of Jago were " Edgehill," a defcriptive
poem in blank verfe, publifhed in 1767, by which his poetical
reputation was moft exalted: " Labour and Genius," a fable,
infcribed to Shenftone, who is the fubject of its panegyric:
Some " Elegies, Eclogues," &c. His character appears to have
been in all refpects amiable and refpectable; particularly as defcribed by his friend and biographer Mr. Hylton [N]. With
ftrangers he was rather referved, among his friends lively, eafy,
and entertaining. As a poet he cannot take a very high rank;
but has perhaps fufficient merit to fecure him from oblivion.

JAMBLICUS, the name of two celebrated Platonic philofophers, one of whom was a native of Chalcis, and the other of
Apamea, in Syria. The firft, who is equalled by Julian the
Apoftate to Plato himfelf, was a difciple of Anatolius and Porphyry; after which he became a teacher, and had a great number of difciples, who flocked to him, not fo much for his eloquence, as for his probity and the good cheer which he gave
them. He began to grow famous in the time of Dioclefian,
and died under the reign of Conftantine. The fecond Jamblicus flourifhed under Julian the Apoftate, who wrote feveral letters to him, and feems to be the fame man to whom Symmachus
wrote, defiring to cultivate a friendfhip with him; he is faid
to have been killed by poifon under the emperor Valens. It is
not certain to which of thefe two we are to afcribe the works
that we have in Greek, under the name of Jamblicus, namely,
1. " The Hiftory of the Life and Sect of Pythagoras." 2.
" An Exhortation to Philofophy." 3. A piece, under the name
of Abamon, againft Porphyry's " Letter upon the Egyptian
Myfteries."

There is alfo cited [O], a collection of the dogmata of Pythagoras by Jamblicus; and Julian quotes a piece of Jamblicus
of Chalcis upon the fun, from which he borrows a great part of
his treatife upon the fame fubject.

JAMES (THOMAS), a learned Englifh critic and divine, was
born about 1571, at Newport in the Ifle of Wight; and, being
put to Winchefter-fchool, became a fcholar upon the foundation,
and thence a fellow of New-college in Oxford, 1593. He commenced M. A. in 1599; and the fame year, having collated

[M] Dr. Anderfon's Life of Jago. Brit. Poets, Vol. XI.   [N] Life prefixed
to an Edition of his Poems.   [O] Moreri, L'advocat.

several MSS. of the Philobiblion of Richard of Durham, he published it in 4to at Oxford, with an appendix of the Oxford MSS. and dedicated it to Sir Thomas Bodley, apparently to recommend himself to the place of librarian to him, when he should have completed his design. Mean while James proceeded with the same spirit to publish a catalogue of all the MSS. in each college-library of both universities, and in the compiling of it having free access to the MSS. at Oxford, he perused them carefully; and, when he found any society careless of them, he borrowed and took away what he pleased, and put them into the public library. These instances of his taste and turn to books effectually procured him the designation of the founder to be the first keeper of the public library; in which office he was confirmed by the university in 1602. He filled this post with great applause; and commencing D. D. in 1614, was promoted to the subdeanery of Wells by the bishop of that see. About the same time, the Abp. of Canterbury also presented him to the rectory of Mongeham in Kent, together with other spiritual preferments. These favours were undeniably strong evidences of his distinguished merit, being conferred upon him without any application on his part. In 1620, he was made a justice of the peace; and the same year resigned the place of librarian, and applied himself more intensely to his studies. Of what kind these were, we learn thus from himself: " I have of late," says he in a letter, May 23, 1624, to a friend, " given myself to the reading only of manuscripts, and in them I find so many and so pregnant testimonies, either fully for our religion, or against the Papists, that it is to be wondered at." In another letter to archbishop Usher, the same year, he assures the primate he had restored 300 citations and rescued them from corruptions, in thirty quires of paper [P]. He had before written to Usher upon the same subject, Jan. 28, 1623, when having observed that in Sixtus Sinensis, Alphonsus de Castro, and Antoninus's Summæ, there were about 500 bastard brevities and about 1000 places in the true authors which are corrupted, that he had diligently noted, and would shortly vindicate them out of the MSS. being yet only conjectures of the learned, he proceeds to acquaint him, that he had gotten together the flower of the English divines, who would voluntarily join with him in the search. " Some fruits of their labours," continues he, " if your lordship desires, I will send up. . And might I be but so happy as to have other 12 thus bestowed, four in transcribing orthodox writers, whereof we have plenty that for the substantial points have maintained our religion (40l. or 50l. would serve); four

[P] These two letters are in the collection at the end of Parr's " Life of Usher," numb. 66 and 77.

to compare old prints with the new ; four other to compare the
Greek translations by the Papists, as Vedelius hath done with
Ignatius, wherein he hath been somewhat helped by my pains ;
I would not doubt but to drive the Papists out of all starring-
holes. But alas! my lord, I have not encouragement from our
bishops. Preferment I seek none at their hands ; only 40l. or
60l. per ann. for others is that I seek, which being gained, the
cause is gained, notwithstanding their brags in their late books."
In the convocation held with the parliament at Oxford in 1625,
of which he was a member, he moved to have proper commissioners appointed to collate the MSS. of the fathers in all the
libraries in England, with the Popish editions, in order to detect
the forgeries in the latter. This project not meeting with
the desired encouragement [q], he was so thoroughly persuaded
of the great advantage it would be both to the Protestant religion
and to learning, that, arduous as the task was, he set about executing it himself. He had made a good progress in it, as appears from his works, a catalogue of which may be seen below [r ;
                                                              and

[q] We may form a probable conjecture of his plan, from a passage in the
just cited letter to Usher, where he expresses himself thus : " Mr. Briggs will
satisfy you in this and sundry other projects of mine, if they miscarry not for
want of maintenance : it would deserve a
prince's purse. If I was in Germany, the
state would defray all charges. Cannot
our estates supply what is wanting ? If
every churchman that hath 100l. per
annum and upwards, will lay down but
1l. for every hundred towards these public
works, I will undertake the reprinting of
the fathers, and setting forth of five or six
orthodox writers, comparing of books
printed with printed or written ; collating
of Popish translations in Greek ; and generally whatsoever shall concern books or
the purity of them. I will take upon me
to be a magister of S. Patalii in England,
is I be thereunto lawfully required."

[r] A list of his publications, 1. "Philobiblion R. Dunelmensis, 1599," 4to. 2.
" Ecloga Oxonio-Cantabrigiensis, Lond.
1600," 4to. 3. " Cyprianus Redivivus,
&c." printed with the " Ecloga." 4.
" Spicilegium divi Augustini : hoc est,
libri de fide ad Pet. Diacon collatio &
castigatio," printed also with the " Ecloga."
5. " Bellum papale seu concordia discors
Sext. V. & Clementis VIII. circa Hiero-
nym. Edition. Lond. 1600," 4to, and
1678, 8vo. 6. " Catalogus librorum in
bibliotheca Bodleiana, Oxf. 1605, 4to,
printed with many additions in 4to, 1620,
Vol. VIII.

to which was added an appendix in 1636 :
in this catalogue is inserted that of all the
MSS. then in the Bodl. library. 7. " Con-
cordantiæ S. patrum, i. e. vera & pia libri
Canticorum per patres universos, &c. Daf.
1607," 4to. 8. " Apology for John Wickliffe, &c. Oxf. 1608," 4to, to this is
added the " Life of John Wickliffe." 9.
" A Treatise of the Corruption of Scriptures, Councils, and Fathers, &c." Lond.
1611," 4to, and 1688, 8vo ; this is reckoned his principal work. 10. " The Jesuits Downfall threatened—for their wicked Lives, accursed Manners, heretical Do-
trine, and more than Machiavilian Policy,
Oxf. 1612," 4to ; to this is added " The
Life of Father Parsons, an English Jesuit."
11. " Filius Papæ papallis" ch. 1. Lond.
1621 ; translated from Latin into English
by William Crashaw : the author's name
is not put to it. 12. " Index generalis
sanct. Patrum ad singulos versus cap. v.
secundum Marlharum, &c. Lond. 1624,"
8vo. 13. " Notæ ad Georg. Witzelium
de methodo concordiæ ecclesiasticæ, &c.
1695," 8vo. 14. Vindiciæ Gregorianæ,
seu restitutus Gregorius Magnus et MSS.
&c. de Geneva, 1625." 15. " Manu-
duction, or Introduction unto Divinity, &c.
Oxf 1625," 4to. 16. " Humble and
earnest Request to the Church of England,
for and in the behalf of Books touching
Religion," in one sheet 8vo, 1615. 17.
" Explanation or enlarging of the ten Articles in his Supplication lately exhibited
to the Clergy of the Church of England,

and no doubt would have proceeded much further towards completing his design, had not he been prevented by death. This happened in 1622. at Oxford. Wood informs us, that he left behind him the character of being the most industrious and indefatigable writer against the Papists, that had been educated in Oxford since the Reformation; and in reality his designs were so great, and so well known to be for the public benefit of learning and the church of England, that Camden, speaking of him in his life-time, calls him " a learned man and a true lover of books, wholly dedicated to learning; who is now laboriously searching the libraries of England, and proposeth that for the public good which will be for the great benefit of England."

JAMES (RICHARD) [s], nephew of the preceding, was born in the same place, and entered of Exeter-college, Oxford; but being chosen scholar of Corpus-Christi 1608, took his degrees in arts at the regular times, became probationer-fellow of his college in 1615, and entered into orders. About 1619, he travelled through Wales into Scotland; and thence to Shetland, Greenland, and into Russia: on which country he wrote observations the same year. He proceed B. D. in 1624, and not long after assisted Selden, in composing his " Marmora Arundeliana," published in 1628. He was also very serviceable to Sir Robert Cotton and his son Sir Thomas, in disposing and settling their noble library: and with the former of these (who was no friend to the prerogative) he was committed close prisoner, by order of the house of lords, in 1629. During his confinement he composed a copy of verses in English, which he prefixed afterwards to a copy of all the printed works of his own original composition, bound in one volume, and presented to the Bodleian library some time before his death, which happened in 1638. Wood tells us, that he was esteemed a person well versed in most parts of learning; and particularly was a very good Greek scholar, a poet, an excellent critic, antiquary, divine, and admirably well skilled in the Saxon and Gothic languages. That nothing was wanting but a sinecure or prebend, either of which, if conferred upon him, would have carried him through Herculean labours;

Oxf. 1625," 4to. 19. " Specimen Corruptelarum pontificiorum in Cypriano, Ambrosio, Greg. Magno, &c. Lond 1626." 19. " Index librorum prohibitorum i pontificii, Oxf. 1627," 8vo. 20. " Admonitio ad theologos protestantes de libris pontificiorum caute legendis," MS. 21. " Enchiridion theologicum," MS. 22. " Liber de suspicionibus & conjecturis," MS. These three Wood says he saw in the Lambeth library, under D. 42, 3; but whether printed, says he, I know not, perhaps the " Enchiridium" is. Dr. James

likewise translated, from French into English, " The Moral Philosophy of the Stoics, Lond. 1598," 8vo; and published two short treatises against the order of begging friars, written by Wickliffe; with a book entitled, " Fiscus papalis, sive catalogus indulgentiarum, &c. Lond. 1617," 4to: but some were of opinion this book was published by William Crashaw, already mentioned. Several letters of our author are in the appendix to Parr's " Life of Usher."

[s] Ath. Oxon.

finally,

finally, that he was of a far better judgement than his uncle ;
and, had he lived to his age, would have furpaffed him in publifhing books. His uncle himfelf, in a letter to Ufher, gives
the following charaéter of him : "A kinfinan of mine is at this
prefent, by my direélion, writing Becket's life, wherein it fhall
be plainly fhewed, both out of his own writings, and thofe of
his time, that he was not, as he is efteemed, an arch-faint, but
an arch-rebel ; and that the Papifts have been not a little deceived by him. This kinfinan of mine, as well as myfelf,
fhould be right glad to do any fervice to your lordfhip in this
kind. He is of ftrength, and well both able and learned to ef-
feétuate fomewhat in this kind, critically feen both in Hebrew,
Greek, and Latin, knowing well the languages both French,
Spanifh, and Italian, immenfe and beyond all other men in reading of the MSS. of an extraordinary ftyle in penning ; fuch a
one as I dare balance with any prieft or Jefuit in the world, of
his age, and fuch a one as I could with your lordfhip had about
you : but *paupertas inimica bonis eft moribus*, and both fatherlefs
and motherlefs, and almoft (but for myfelf) I may fay (the more
is pity) friendlefs."

JAMES (Dr. ROBERT), an Englifh phyfician of great eminence, and particularly diftinguifhed by the preparation of a
moft excellent fever-powder, was born at Kinverfton in Staffordfhire, A. D. 1703. His father was a major in the army, his
mother a fifter of fir Robert Clarke. He was educated at St.
John's-college in Oxford, where he took the degree of A. B.
and afterwards practifed phyfic fucceffively at Sheffield, Litchfield, and Birmingham. He then removed to London, and became a licentiate in the college of phyficians ; but, in what year,
we cannot fay. At London, he applied himfelf to writing as
well as practifing phyfic ; and, in 1743, publifhed a " Medicinal
Dictionary," 3 vols. folio. Soon after, he publifhed an Englifh
tranflation, with a fupplement by himfelf, of " Ramazzini de
morbis artificum ;" to which he alfo prefixed a piece of Frederic
Hoffman upon " Endemial Diftempers," 8vo. In 1746, " The
Practice of Phyfic," 2 vols. 8vo ; in 1760, " On Canine Madnefs," 8vo ; in 1764, " A Difpenfatory," 8vo. June 25, 1755,
when the king was at Cambridge, James was admitted by mandamus to the doctorfhip of phyfic. In 1778, were publifhed
" A Differtation upon Fevers," and " A Vindication of the
Fever-Powder," 8vo ; with " A fhort Treatife on the Diforders
of Children," and a very good print of Dr. James. This was
the 8th edition of the " Differtation," of which the firft was
printed in 1751 ; and the purpofe of it was, to fet forth the fuccefs of this powder, as well as to defcribe more particularly the
manner of adminiftering it, The " Vindication" was pofthumous and unfinifhed ; for he died March 23, 1776, while he
was employed upon it. The editor informs us, that " it is only

a part of a much larger tract, which included a defence of his
own character and conduct in his profession; and was occasioned," he fays, " by the violent and calumnious attacks of his
brethren of the faculty."

The affectionate remembrance of Dr. James, by Johnson in
his Life of Smith, deferves to be preferved among the honourable teftimonies to the character of the former. " At this man's
table," fays the biographer, fpeaking of Mr. Walmfley, " I enjoyed
many chearful and inftructive hours, with companions fuch as
are not often found; with one who has lengthened, and one who
has gladdened life; with Dr. James, whofe fkill in phyfic will
be long remembered: and with David Garrick, whom I hoped
to have gratified with this character of our common friend: but
what are the hopes of man!" &c. It appears from the life of
Johnfon, that he had gained fome knowledge of phyfic from
James, which he in return made ufeful to his friend, by affifting
him in his Medicinal Dictionary. " My knowledge of phyfic,"
faid he, " I learnt from Dr. James, whom I helped in writing
the propofals for his dictionary, and alfo a little in the dictionary
itfelf." Bofwell adds, " I have in vain endeavoured to find out
what parts Johnfon wrote for Dr. James. Perhaps medical
men may [T]." There can be very little doubt, from the ftyle
of the addrefs, that Mr. Bofwell is right in afcribing the dedication of that work entirely to the pen of Johnfon. The elegance
and originality of the compliments in it fufficiently mark the hand
of that great mafter. It may not be amifs to infert it here, as
a model of dedicatory addrefs, highly honourable to Dr. James
if his own, and creditable even to have deferved from Johnfon.

" Sir,

" That the *Medicinal Dictionary* is dedicated to you, is to
be imputed only to your reputation for fuperior fkill in thofe
fciences, which I have endeavoured to explain and facilitate:
and you are therefore, to confider this addrefs, if it be agreeable
to you, as one of the rewards of merit; and if otherwife, as
one of the inconveniences of eminence. However, you fhall
receive it, my defign cannot be difappointed; becaufe this public
appeal to your judgement will fhew, that I do not found my
hopes of approbation upon the ignorance of my readers, and
that I fear his cenfure leaft, whofe knowledge is moft extenfive.
I am, Sir, &c.

                                   R. JAMES [U]."

The dictionary is, in effect, confidered as a work highly
honourable to the author, and retains its credit, unimpaired
after the continued progrefs of medicine for feveral years.
Dr. Johnfon certainly held James in high efteem, and though
he did not burft out into any paffionate exclamation of grief,

on reading of his death, (as his biographer relates), he doubtlefs felt confiderable regret, as appeared not only by his manner of returning to the fubject [x]; 'but by his mention of
him above-cited from the life of Smith. The regret which remains upon the mind after reflection, is as fincere, if not as
violent, as that which fhews itfelf at firft in impatient lamenta-
tions. "No man," faid he, on fome occafion, "brings more
mind to his profeffion than James;" and undoubtedly no man
was better able to judge of mind, than the perfon who pronounced
that opinion.

Dr. James was rough in his manners, and, if not very generally mifreprefented, far from temperate in his habits; but ftrong
fenfe ufually appeared in his coarfe expreffions, and no man
had more fagacity, when his head was clear, which of a morning was always the cafe. Several whimfical ftories, perhaps of no
precife authority, are told of his evening prefcriptions: and he
is faid, in comparing his patient's pulfe with his own, fometimes to have confufed the two; and, finding that one was
quickened by intemperance, to have bluntly accufed the *patient*,
perhaps a delicate Lady, of being in liquor. But James,
whatever failings he might have, was without doubt an able
and acute phyfician, and his dictionary will remain a noble
monument of his Knowledge. His perfon had not more delicacy than his manners, being large and grofs.

His *fever powder* was for a long time violently oppofed by the
faculty, who, as the compofition was kept a fecret, confidered
it as a noftrum, and refufed to prefcribe or countenance it. The
admirable effects experienced from it, forced it into general ufe,
and it is now confidered as the moft efficacious medicine for fevers
that is known. Dr. Pearfon, who took great pains to analyze
it, concludes that "by calcining bone afhes, that is, phofphorated
lime, with antimony in a certain proportion, and afterwards
expofing the mixture to a white heat, a compound may be formed
containing the fame ingredients, in the fame proportion, and poffeffing the fame chemical properties" [y]; and the London Phar-
macopœia now contains a prefcription, under the title of *Pulvis
Antimonialis*, which is intended to anfwer the fame purpofes.
"It is well known," fays Dr. Pearfon, "that this powder cannot be prepared by following the directions of the fpecification in
the Court of Chancery." He therefore inftituted a laborious
chemical enquiry, firft analytical, and then fynthetical, in order
to afcertain the compofition.

Whether James was the real inventor of the powder, may admit of a doubt. "The calcination of antimony and bone-afhes
produces," fays Dr. Pearfon, "a powder called *Lile's* and
Schwanberg's fever powder; a preparation defcribed by Schroeder

[x] *Life*, Vol. II. p. 366.   [y] *Philof. Tranf.* for 1791, p. 367.

and

and other chemists 150 years ago."—" According to the receipt in the possession of Mr. Bromfield, by which this powder was prepared forty-five years ago, and before any medicine was known by the name of James's powder, two pounds of hartshorn shavings must be boiled, to dissolve all the mucilage, and then, being dried, be calcined with one pound of crude antimony, till the smell of sulphur ceases, and a light grey powder is produced. The same prescription was given to Mr. Willis above forty years ago, by Dr. John Eaton of the College of Physicians, with the material addition however, of ordering the calcined mixture to be exposed to a given heat in a close vessel, to render it white."—" Schroeder prescribes equal weights of antimony and calcined hartshorn ; and *Poterius* and *Michaelis*, as quoted by *Frederic Hoffman*, merely order the calcination of these two substances together (assigning no proportion) in a reverberatory fire for several days." It has been alledged, that Dr. James obtained the receipt for his powder, of a German Baron named Schwanberg, or one Baker, to whom Schwanberg had sold it. This account we have not been able to verify, but if it be true, Baron Schwanberg ; as he is called, was probably the descendant of the Schawanberg mentioned so long ago. Be it as it may, Dr. James was able to give that credit and currency to the medicine which otherwise it would not have had, and the public are therefore indebted to him for publishing, if not for inventing, a preparation of most admirable effect.

Dr. James was married, and left sons and daughters. His eldest son, Robert Harcourt James, was educated at Merchant-Taylor's-school, and afterwards at St. John's-college in Oxford, for the profession of physic. The powder has proved a noble fortune to the family.

JAMYN (AMADIS), a French poet, was, in his youth, a great traveller, and run over Greece, the isles of the Archipelago, and Asia Minor. Poetry being his delight, he applied himself to it from his infancy ; and his writings, both in verse and prose, shew that he had carefully studied the Greek and Latin authors, especially the poets. He is esteemed the rival of Ronsard, who was his contemporary and friend ; but he is not so bombastical, nor so rough in the use of Greek words, and his style is more natural, simple, and pleasing. Jamyn was secretary and chamber-reader in ordinary to Charles IX. and died about 1585. We have, 1. his " Poetical Works," in 2 vols. 2. " Discours de philosophie a Passicharis & à Pedanthe," with seven academical discourses, the whole in prose, Paris, 1584, 12mo. 3. " A Translation of Homer's Iliad," in French verse, begun by Hugh Salel, and finished by Jamyn from the 12th book inclusive, to which is added a translation of the three first books of the " Odyssey."

JANICON

JANICON (FRANCIS MICHAEL), was born at Paris in 1674, the son of a Protestant, and sent early into Holland for education. For a time he quitted his studies for the army, but at the peace of Ryswick, he resumed his literary labours, and became concerned in the gazettes of Amsterdam, Rotterdam, and Utrecht. A simple, and historical style, with a clear head, and much political sagacity, seemed to promise great success to these labours; but his press being silenced, on account of a political tract (in which, however, he had no concern), he retired to the Hague, and became agent to the landgrave of Hesse. He died of an apoplexy in 1730, at the age of fifty-six. Of his works there are, 1. His " Gazettes," written in a good style, and with sound political knowledge. 2. A translation of Steele's " Ladies Library," published in 1717 and 1719, in 2 vols. duodecimo. 3. A translation of an indifferent satire against monks and priests, written originally by Antony Gavin, and printed in 1724, in 4 vols. 12mo. 4. " The present State of the Republic of the United Provinces, and their Dependencies," published in 1729, in 2 vols. 12mo. This is the most correct work that is extant, though it has been considered by Niceron as not altogether devoid of faults.

JANSEN, or JANSENIUS (CORNELIUS), bishop of Ypres, principal of the sect called Jansenists, was born in a village called Akoy, near Leerdam in Holland, of Roman Catholic parents [?], and, having had his grammar-learning at Utrecht, went to Louvain in 1602. Afterwards he went to Paris, where he met with John du Verger de Hauranne, afterwards abbot of Saint-Cyran, with whom he had contracted a very strict friendship in Louvain. Some time after, du Verger removing to Bayonne, he followed him thither: where pursuing their studies with unabated ardour, they were noticed by the bishop of that province, who, conceiving a great esteem for them, procured du Verger a canonry in his cathedral, and set Jansen at the head of a college or school. He spent five or six years in Bayonne, applying himself with the same vigour to the study of the fathers, St. Austin in particular; and, as he did not appear to be of a strong constitution, du Verger's mother used sometimes to tell her son, that he would prove the death of that worthy young Fleming, by making him overstudy himself.

At length, the bishop being raised to the archiepiscopal see of Tours, prevailed with du Verger to go to Paris; so that Jansen being thus separated from his friend, and not sure of the protection of the new bishop, left Bayonne; and after twelve years residence in France returned to Louvain, where he was chosen

[a] His father's name was Jan Otie, by trade a carpenter, his mother was called Lyntse Gisberts.

principal of the college of St. Pulcheria. But this place was not altogether so agreeable, as it did not afford him leisure to pursue his studies so much as he wished, for which reason he resused to teach philosophy. He took his degree of D. D in 1617, with great reputation, was admitted a professor in ordinary, and grew into so much esteem, that the university sent him twice, in 1624, and the ensuing year, upon affairs of great consequence, into Spain; and the king of Spain, his sovereign, made him professor of the Holy Scriptures in Louvain, in 1630; notwithstanding the Spanish inquisition lodged some information against him in 1627 [A], with Basil de Leon, the principal doctor of the university of Salamanca, at whose house he lodged. But the complaint was chiefly that he was a Dutchman, and consequently an heretic; and Basil answered them so much to the advantage of Jansen, that his enemies were quite out of countenance. Mean while, the king of Spain observing, with a jealous eye, the intriguing politics, and growing power of the French, put his new professor upon writing a book, to expose them to the pope, as no good Catholics, since they made no scruple of forming alliances with Protestant states. Jansen performed the task, in his " Mars Gallicus [B]," which is replete with invidious exclamations against the services France continually rendered to the Protestants of Holland and Germany, to the great injury of the Romish religion; in which the Dutch are treated as rebels, who owe the Republican liberty they enjoy to an infamous usurpation. It was this service that procured him the mitre, in 1635, when he was promoted to the see of Ypres.

Some years before, he had maintained a controversy against the Protestants upon the subject of grace and predestination, which happened thus: the States-General published an edict in 1629, forbidding the public exercise of the Romish religion in Boissleduc; and having appropriated the ecclesiastical revenues of the mayoralty of that city to the service of the Protestant religion, appointed four ministers to preach there. These, hearing that many slanders concerning their doctrine were secretly spread, published a manifesto, declaring that they taught nothing but the pure gospel, and intreating their adversaries to propose whatever objections they might have to make in a public manner. This was answered only by Jansen, in a piece entitled, " Alexipharmacum," in 1630. Gilbert Voetius, one of the four ministers who preached in Boissleduc, wrote " Remarks[c]," which Jansen refuted in another piece, entitled, " Notarum Spongia,"

[A] See a letter of his, dated Dec. 31, that year.

[B] The title of it is, " Alexandri patricii armacani theolog. Mars Gallicus;

five, de justitia armorum & foederum regis Galliæ libri duo 1635."

[c] The remarks were entitled, " Philonius Romanus correctus,"

in

in 1631. The author of thefe " Remarks," replying in a large book, entitled, " Defperata caufa papatus," in 1635; this was anfwered by Fromond, a friend of Janfen, who ftiled his piece, " Caufæ defperatæ Gifberti Voetii, adverfus fpongiam Janfenii, crifis offenfa." This was printed at Antwerp in 1636, and refuted by Martin Schoockius, profeffor of hiftory and eloquence at Deventer, the title of whofe anfwer was, " Defperatiffima caufa papatus," this was publifhed in 1638 : and here the difpute ended [D].

But Janfen had another war to maintain, which may be called a Proteftant one ; for Theodore Simonis, a wavering Roman Catholic, who wanted a mafter, waited upon him at Louvain, defiring him to clear up fome doubts he had about the pope's infallibility, the worfhip of the eucharift, and fome other points. Janfen, being puzzled with this man's objections, told him one day, that he would not difpute with him by word of mouth, but in writing; and that he faw plainly he had to do with a Roman Proteftant Catholic, who would foon go to Holland, and there boaft he had overcome him. Simonis, with fome difficulty, complied with the propofal; but after both had written twice on the fubject in queftion, his lodgings were furrounded with foldiers, and himfelf threatened with the punifhment due to heretics. The duke d'Archot's fecretary exclaimed aloud againft him, and faid, that there was wood enough in his mafter's forefts to burn that heretic. But as the perfon who examined Simonis, in the name of the archbifhop of Malines, declared that he had found him a good Catholic, and fully refolved to perfevere in the Romifh communion, the prifoner was fet at liberty, and Janfen obliged to pay the expences of the foldiers [E].

Janfen was no fooner poffeffed of the bifhopric of Ypres, than he undertook to reform the diocefe ; but before he had completed this good work, he fell a facrifice to the plague, May 16, 1638. He was buried in his cathedral, where a monument was erected to his memory; but in 1665, his fucceffor, Francis de Robes, caufed it to be taken down privately in the night ; there being engraved on it an eulogium of his virtue and erudition, and particularly on his book entitled, " Auguftinus;" declaring, that this faithful interpreter of the moft fecret thoughts of St. Auftin, had employed in that work a divine genius, an indefa-

[D] Unlefs the piece belongs to it which was publifhed by Fromondus, in 1640, with the title of " Sycophanta: epiftola ad Gifbertum Voetium." See Valerius Andreas's Bibliotheque among Fromondus's works.

[E] Yet Simonis two years after turned Proteftant, and publifhed a book entitled, " De ftatu & religione propriâ papatus adverfus Janfenium." This man firft quitted the Lutheran communion to go over to that of Rome, then turned Lutheran again, and at laft Socinian : he was principal of the Socinian college of Kiffelin in Lithuania, was well verfed in the Greek tongue, and tranflated Comenius's " Janua linguarum" into that language. Bayle.

tigable labour, and his whole life-time; and that the church
would receive the benefit of it upon earth, as he did the reward
of it in heaven; words that were highly injurious to the bulls of
Urban VIII. and Innocent X. who then had censured that work.
The bishop destroyed this monument by the express orders of
pope Alexander VII. and with the consent of the archduke
Leopold, governor of the Netherlands, in spite of the resistance
of the chapter, which went such lengths, that one of the principal canons had the courage to say, " it was not in the pope's
nor the king's power to suppress that epitaph;" so dear was
Jansen to this canon and his colleagues. He wrote several other
books besides those already mentioned; 1. " Oratio de interioris
hominis reformatione." 2. " Tetrateuchus sive commentarius
in 4 evangelica." 3. " Pentateuchus sive commentarius in 5
libros Mosis." 4. The Answer of the Divines of Louvain,
" de vi obligandi conscientias quam habent edicta regia super re
monetaria." 5. Answer of the Divines and Civilians, " De
juramento quod publica auctoritate magistratui designato imponi
solet." But his " Augustinus" was his principal work, and he
was employed upon it above twenty years. He left it finished
at his death, and submitted it, by his last will, in the completest
manner to the judgement of the holy see. His executors, Fromond and Calen, printed it at Louvain, in 1640, but suppressed
his submission. The subject is divine grace, free-will, and predestination. " In this book, says Mosheim, " which even the
Jesuits acknowledge to be the production of a man of learning
and piety, the doctrine of Augustine, concerning man's natural
corruption, and the nature and efficacy of that divine grace
which alone can efface this unhappy stain, is unfolded at large,
and illustrated, for the most part, in Augustine's own words.
For the end which Jansenius proposed to himself in this work,
was not to give his own private sentiments concerning these important points; but to shew in what manner they had been understood and explained by that celebrated father of the church,
whose name and authority were universally revered in all
parts of the Roman Catholic world. No incident could be
more unfavourable to the Jesuits, and the progress of their religious system, than the publication of this book; for as the
doctrine of Augustine differed but very little from that of the
Dominicans; as it was held sacred, nay almost respected as
divine, in the church of Rome, on account of the extraordinary
merit and authority of that illustrious bishop; and at the same
time was almost diametrically opposed to the sentiments generally received among the Jesuits; these latter could scarcely consider the book of Jansenius in any other light, than as a tacit
but formidable refutation of their opinions concerning *human
liberty* and *divine grace*; and accordingly they not only drew
their

their pens againſt this famous book, but alſo uſed their moſt
ſtrenuous endeavours to obtain a public condemnation of it from
Rome [F]." In Louvain, where it was firſt publiſhed, it excited prodigious conteſts. It obtained ſeveral violent advocates,
and was by others oppoſed with no leſs violence, and ſeveral
theological theſes were written againſt it. At length, they who
wiſhed to obtain the ſuppreſſion of it by papal authority, were
ſucceſsful; the Roman inquiſitors began by prohibiting the pe-
ruſal of it, in the year 1641; and, in the following year, Urban
VIII. condemned it as infected with ſeveral errors that had been
long baniſhed from the church. This bull, which was publiſhed at Louvain, inſtead of pacifying, inflamed matters more;
and the diſputes ſoon paſſed into France, where they were carried on with equal warmth. At length the biſhops of France
drew up the doctrine, as they called it, of Janſen, in five propoſitions, and applied to the pope to condemn them. This was
done by Innocent X. by a bull publiſhed May 31, 1653; and he
drew up a formulary for that purpoſe, which was received by
the aſſembly of the French clergy. Theſe propoſitions contained the following doctrines:

1. That there are divine precepts, which good men, notwithſtanding their deſire to obſerve them, are nevertheleſs, abſolutely unable to obey; nor has God given them that meaſure
of grace which is eſſentially neceſſary to render them capable of
ſuch obedience.

2. That no perſon, in this corrupt ſtate of nature, can reſiſt
the influence of divine grace, when it operates upon the mind.

3. That in order to render human actions meritorious, it is
not requiſite that they be exempt from *neceſſity*, but only that they
be free from *conſtraint*.

4. That the Semipelagians err grievouſly in maintaining that
the human will is endowed with the power of either receiving
or reſiſting the aids and influences of preventing grace.

5. That whoever affirms that Jeſus Chriſt made expiation by
his ſufferings and death, for the ſins of all mankind, is a Semi-
pelagian.

Of theſe propoſitions the pontiff declared the firſt four only
heretical, but he pronounced the fifth, raſh, impious, and injurious
to the ſupreme Being. Janſenius, however, was not named in the
bull, nor was it declared that theſe five propoſitions were maintained in the book entitled, Auguſtinus, in the ſenſe in which
the pope had condemned them. Hence the ſubtile Antony Ar-
nauld, doctor of the Sorbonne, invented a diſtinction, which
the other Janſeniſts took up as a defence. He ſeparated the
matter of *doctrine*, or *right*, and of *fact* in the controverſy; and

[F] Moſheim, Eccleſ. Hiſt. Cent. XVII. Sect. 2. Part I.

acknow-

acknowledged that they were bound to believe the five propositions justly condemned by the Roman pontiff, but did not acknowledge that these propositions were to be found in the book
of Jansenius, in the sense in which they were condemned.
Hence arose the famous distinction between the *fact* and the
right. They did not, however, long enjoy the benefit of this
artful distinction. The restless and invincible hatred of their
enemies pursued them in every quarter, and at length engaged
Alexander VII. the successor of Innocent, to declare by a solemn bull, issued in 1656, that the five propositions were the
tenets of Jansenius, and were contained in his book. The
pontiff did not stop here; but to this flagrant instance of impru-
dence, added another still more shocking: for, in the year
1665, he sent into France the form of a declaration which was to
be subscribed by all who aspired to any preferment in the church;
and in which it was affirmed that the *five propositions* were to be
found in the book of Jansenius, in the same sense in which they
had been condemned by the church. This declaration, the un-
exampled temerity of which, as well as its contentious tendency,
appeared in the most odious light, not only to the Jansenists, but
also to the wiser part of the French nation, produced the most
deplorable divisions and tumults. It was immediately opposed
with vigour by the Jansenists, who, thus provoked, went so far
as to maintain that, in *matters of fact*, the pope was fallible,
especially when his decisions were merely personal, and not confirmed by a general council; and consequently that it was neither obligatory or necessary to subscribe this papal declaration,
which had, as they alledged, only a matter of fact for its object.
The assembly of the clergy, nevertheless, insisted upon subscription to the formulary; and all ecclesiastics, monks, nuns, and
others, in every diocese, were obliged to subscribe. Those who
refused, were interdicted and excommunicated; and they even
talked of entering a process against four bishops, who in their
public instruments had distinguished the fact from the right; and
declared, that they desired only a respectful and submissive silence
in regard to the fact. The affair was at length accommodated
in 1668, under the pontificate of Clement IX. who was satisfied that the bishops should subscribe themselves, and make others
subscribe purely and simply; though they declared expressly,
that they did not desire the same submission for the fact, but for
the right. This accommodation, stiled the peace of Clement,
was for a time complied with; yet the dispute about subscribing
was afterwards renewed both in Flanders and France; whereupon Innocent XII. by a brief, in 1694, directed to the bishops
in Flanders, declared that no addition should be made to the
formulary, but that it should be sufficient to subscribe sincerely,
without any distinction, restriction, or exposition, condemning
the

the propositions extracted from Janfen's book, in the plain and
obvious fenfe of the words. A refolution of a cafe of confcience, figned by forty doctors, in which the diftinction of the
fact from the right was tolerated, reinflamed the difpute in
France, about the beginning of the prefent century: when
pope Clement XIII. by a bull dated July 15, 1705, declared,
that a refpectful filence is not fufficient to teftify the obedience
due to the conftitutions; but that all the faithful ought to condemn as heretical, not only with their mouths, but in their
hearts, the fenfe of Janfen's book, which is condemned in the
five propofitions, as the fenfe which the words properly import;
and that it is unlawful to fubfcribe with any other thought,
mind, or fentiment. This conftitution was received by the general affembly of the French clergy in 1705, and publifhed by
the king's authority. Nevertheless, it did not put an end to the
difputes, efpecially in the Low Countries, where various inter-
pretations of it were made; it may even be faid that the conteft
grew hotter than ever, after the pope, by his conftitution of
Sept. 13, 1713, condemned 101 propofitions, extracted from
the "Paraphrafe on the New Teftament," by Pere Quefnel,
who was then at the head of the Janfenifts. There was another
Cornelius Janfen, bifhop of Gand, who died in 1576, and publifhed fome theological works.

JANSON (ABRAHAM), of Antwerp, an excellent painter in
the 16th century. He was born with a wonderful genius for
painting, and in his youth executed fome pieces, which fet him
above all the young painters of his time: but love took fuch
poffeffion of his heart, that he facrificed his profeffion to the
devotion he paid to a young woman at Antwerp; and as foon as
he obtained her in marriage, thought of nothing but diverfions
and feafting. This way of life foon drained his purfe; and,
inftead of imputing this to his idlenefs, he took offence at the
little regard which he thought was paid to his merit. He grew
jealous of Rubens; and fent a challenge to that painter, with a
lift of the names of fuch perfons as were to decide the matter,
fo foon as their refpective works fhould be finifhed; but Rubens, inftead of accepting the challenge, anfwered that he willingly yielded him the preference, leaving the public to do them
juftice. There are fome of Janfon's works in the churches at
Antwerp. He painted alfo a defcent from the crofs for the
great church of Buifleduc, which has been taken for a piece of
Rubens; and, in reality, it is no ways inferior to any of the
works of that great painter.

JAQUELOT. See JACQUELOT.

JARCHI (SOLOMON BEN ISAAC), otherwife RASCHI and
ISAAKI, a famous rabbi, was born in 1104, at Troyes in
Champagne in France. Having acquired a good ftock of Jewifh
learning

g

learning at home, he travelled at thirty years of age; vifiting Italy, Greece, Jerufalem, Palefline, and Egypt, where he met with Maimonides. From Egypt he paffed to Perfia, and thence to Tartary and Mufcovy; and laft of all, paffing through Germany, he arrived in his native country, after he had fpent fix years abroad. After his return to Europe, he vifited all the academies, and difputed againft the profeffors upon any queftions propofed by them. He took a wife, and had three daughters by her, who were all married to very learned rabbies. Jarchi was a perfect mafter of the Talmud and Gemara; and he filled the poftils of the Bible with fo many Talmudical reveries, as totally extinguifhed both the literal and moral fenfe of it. Many of his commentaries are printed in Hebrew, and fome have been tranflated into Latin by the Chriftians, among which is his " Commentary upon Joel, by Genebrard;" thofe upon Obadiah, Jonah, and Zephaniah, by Pontac; that upon Efther, by Philip Daquin. But the completeft of thefe tranflations is that of his Commentaries on the Pentateuch, and fome other books by Fred. Breithaupt, who has added learned notes. The ftyle of Jarchi is fo concife, that it is no eafy thing to underftand him in feveral places, without the help of other Jewifh interpreters. Befides, when he mentions the traditions of the Jews recorded in their writings, he never quotes the chapter nor the page; which gives no fmall trouble to a tranflator. He introduces alfo feveral French words, of that century, which have been very much corrupted, and cannot be eafily underftood. M. Breithaupt has overcome all thofe difficulties. The ftyle of his tranflation is not very elegant; but it is clear, and fully expreffes the fenfe of the author. It was printed at Gotha, in 1710, 4to. There are feveral things in this writer, that may be alledged againft the Jews with great advantage. If, for inftance, the modern Jews deny that the Meffias is to be underftood by the word Schilo, Gen. xlix. 10. they may be confuted by the authority of this interpreter, who agrees with the Chriftians in his explication of that word. M. Reland looks upon rabbi Jarchi as one of the beft interpreters we have; and tells us in his preface to the Analecta Rabbinica, that when he met with any difficulty in the Hebrew text of the Bible, the explications of that Jewifh doctor appeared to him more fatisfactory than thofe of the great critics, or any other commentator.

Jarchi wrote alfo commentaries upon the Talmud, and upon Pirke-Avon, and other works. It is faid that he was fkilled in phyfic and aftronomy, and was mafter of feveral languages befides the Hebrew. He died at Troyes, in 1180; and his body was carried into Bohemia, and buried at Prague. His decifions were fo much more efteemed, as he had gathered them from the mouths of

all

all the doctors of the Jewish academies in the several countries through which he had travelled. His "Commentary upon the Gemara," appeared so full of erudition, that it procured him the title of "Prince of Commentaries." His commentaries upon the Bibles of Venice are extant; his glosses or commentaries upon the Talmud are also printed with the text. They were published collectively in 1660, in 4 vols. 12mo. He was so highly esteemed among the Jews, as to be ranked among the most illustrious of their rabbies.

JARDINS (MARY CATHARINE DES), a French lady, famous for her writings; was born about 1640, a native of Alençon in Normandy, where her father was provost. Her passions as well as her genius came forward very early. Being obliged to quit Alençon, in consequence of an intrigue with one of her cousins, she went to Paris, where she undertook to support herself by her genius. She studied the drama, and published at the same time some little novels, by which she acquired a name. She had, by her own description, a lively and pleasing countenance, though not amounting to beauty, nor entirely spared by the small-pox. Her attractions, however, soon furnished her with lovers, and among them she distinguished M. Villedieu, a young captain of infantry, of an elegant person and lively genius. He had been already married about a year, but she persuaded him to endeavour to dissolve his marriage. This proved impracticable; nor was it likely from the first to be effected; but the attempt served her as a pretext for her attachment. She followed her lover to camp, and returned to Paris under the name of madame de Villedieu. This irregular union was not long happy; and their disagreements had arisen to a considerable height, when Villedieu was ordered to the army, where soon after he lost his life. The pretended widow comforted herself by living among professed wits, and dramatic writers, and leading such a life as is common in dissipated societies. A fit of devotion brought on by the sudden death of one of her female friends, sent her for a time to a convent, where she lived with much propriety, till her former adventures being known in the society, she could no longer remain in it. Restored to the world, in the house of madame de St. Romaine her sister, she soon exchanged devotion again for gallantry. She now a second time married a man who was only parted from his wife; this was the marquis de la Chasse, whom she met in this society. By this marriage she had a son, who died when only a year old, and the father not long after. The inconsolable widow was soon after united to one of her cousins, who allowed her to resume the name of Villedieu. After living a few years longer in society, she retired to a little village called Clinchemare in the province of Maine, where she died in 1683. Her works were printed in 1702, and form ten volumes, 12mo, to which

two

two more were added in 1721, confifting chiefly of pieces by other writers. Her compofitions are of various kinds: 1. Dramas; as Manlius, a tragi-comedy; Nitétio, a tragedy; the Favourites, a tragi-comedy. 2. Mifcellaneous poems, fables, &c. 3. Romances; among which are, " Les Difordres de l'Amour ;" " Portraits des foibleffes Humaines ;" " Les Exilés de la Cour d'Augufte ;" which are reckoned her beft productions in this ftyle; alfo, " Cleonice," " Carmente," " Les Galanteries Grenadines," " Les Amours des Grands Hommes," " Lyfandre," " Les Memoirs du Serail," &c. 4. Other works of an amufing kind, fuch as, " Les Annales Galantes, " Le Journal Amoreux," &c.

The ftyle of this lady is rapid and animated, but her pencil is not always correct, nor her incidents probable. Her fhort hiftories certainly had the merit of extinguifhing the tafte for the old tedious romances, and led the way to the novel, but were by no means of fuch excellence in that ftyle as thofe that have fince been written by Duclos, Marivaux, Marmontel, and others. She has alfo the fault of attributing her feigned adventures to great perfonages known in hiftory, and thus forming that confufion of fictitious and real narratives which is fo pernicious to young readers. Her verfe is inferior to her profe, being languid and feeble.

JARRY (LAURENCE JUILLARD DU), a French preacher and poet, was born in the village of Jarry, near Xantes, about 1658. He went young to Paris, where the duke of Montaufier, M. Boffuet, Bourdaloue, and Flechier, became his patrons, and encouraged him to write. He gained the poetical prize in the French academy in 1679 and in 1714, and it is remarkable that, on this latter occafion, Voltaire, then very young, was one of his competitors. The fuccefsful poem was, however, below mediocrity, and contained fome blunders, with which his young antagonift amufed himfelf and the public. One of his verfes began, " Poles, glacés, brûlans." " Thefe torrid Poles," could not eafily efcape ridicule. At the fame time he was celebrated as a preacher. He was prior of Notre Dame du Jarry of the order of Grammont, in the diocefe of Xantes, where he died in 1730. We have of his, a work entitled, " Le Miniftere Evangelique ;" of which the fecond edition was printed at Paris in 1726. 2. " A Collection of Sermons, Panegyrics, and Funeral Orations," 4 vols. 12mo. 3. " Un Recueil de divers ouvrages de pieté, 1688," 12mo. 4. " Des Poefes Chrétiennes Heroiques & Morales, 1715," 12mo.

JAUCOURT (LOUIS DE), a man of a noble family, with the title of chevalier, who preferred ftudy and literary labour, in which he was indefatigable, to the advantages of birth, which in his time were very highly eftimated. His difintereftednefs, and his virtues, were confpicuous, and his knowledge extended

to

to medicine, antiquities, manners, morals, and general literature; in all which branches he has furnished articles that are
reckoned to do honour to the French Encyclopedie. He conducted the " Bibliotheque Raifonnée," a journal greatly esteemed,
from its origin to the year 1740. In conjunction with the professors Gaubius, Muschenbroék, and Dr. Massuet, he published
the " Musæum Sebæanum," in 1734, a book greatly esteemed,
and of high price. He had also composed a " Lexicon Medicum universale," but his manuscript, which was just about to
be printed in Holland, in 6 vols. folio, was lost with the vessel
in which it was sent to that country. Some other works by him
are also extant, on subjects of medicine and natural philosophy.
He was a member of the Royal Society of London, and of the
academies of Berlin and Stockholm; and, having been a pupil
of the illustrious Boerhaave, was, by his interest, strongly invited
into the service of the stadtholder, on very advantageous terms.
But promises had no effect upon a man who was, as he paints
himself, " a man without necessities, and without desires, without ambition, without intrigues; bold enough to offer his compliments to the great, but sufficiently prudent not to force his
company upon them; and one who sought a studious obscurity, for the sake of preserving his tranquillity." He died in
February, 1780, but his age is not exactly known.

JAY (GUI MICHEL LE), an advocate in the parliament of
Paris, very remarkable for his profound knowledge of languages.
He printed a Polyglott at his own expence, and thus purchased
glory with the loss of his fortune. The whole edition was offered to sale in England, but too great a price being set upon it,
the Polyglott of Walton was undertaken in a more commodious
form. Le Jay might still have made great profit by his work if
he would have suffered it to appear under the name of cardinal
Richelieu, who was very desirous to emulate the fame of Ximenes in this respect. Being now poor, and a widower, Le
Jay became an ecclesiastic, was made dean of Vezelai, and
obtained a brevet as counsellor of state. He died in 1675. The
Polyglott of Le Jay is in ten volumes, large folio, a model of
beautiful typography, but too bulky to be used with convenience.
It has the Syriac and Arabic versions, which are not in the
Polyglott of Ximenes. The publication commenced in 1628,
and was concluded in 1645. We cannot suppose the editor to
have been less than two or three and thirty, when he had finished
a volume of this kind, in which case he must have been near
eighty at the time of his death. It is not improbable that he was
still older.

JANSONIUS. See JENSON.

IBAS, bishop of Edessa in the fifth century, from about 436,
was first a Nestorian, and afterwards an orthodox divine. While

he was under the former perfuafion, he wrote a letter to a Perfian, named Maris, which afterwards became the fubject of
much difpute. In this letter he blamed Rabulas, his predeceffor,
for having unjuftly condemned Theodore of Mopfueftia, whom
he extolled in the higheft manner. In the following century,
Theodore bifhop of Cefarea in Cappadocia, being a violent favourer of Origen, counfelled Juftinian to condemn, 1. The
writings of Theodore of Mopfueftia. 2. The counter-ana-
themas of Theodoret of Cyrus, in reply to the anathemas of
Cyril againft the Neftorians. 3. This very letter of Ibas. This,
which was done in the council of Conftantinople, in 553, under
pretence of giving peace to the church, produced a fchifm that
lafted above a century, and was called the difpute on *the Three
Chapters*, by which were meant the three writings above-mentioned [H]. Ibas was by birth a Syrian. He was harraffed with
accufations for herefy, but more than once acquitted honourably. In the council of Ephefus, in 449, (called the *Synod of
Robbers*), he was depofed, banifhed, and imprifoned; but in
the council of Chalcedon, in 451, he was reftored to his dignity. Many years after his death he was condemned for Nefto-
rianifm.

IBBOT (Dr. BENJAMIN), an ingenious and learned writer,
and a judicious and ufeful preacher, fon of the Rev. Mr. Thomas Ibbot vicar of Swaffham, and rector of Beachamwell, in
the county of Norfolk, was born at Beachamwell in 1680[1].
He was admitted of Clare-hall, Cambridge, July 25, 1695,
under the tuition of the Rev. Mr. Laughton, a gentleman juftly
celebrated for his eminent attainments in philofophy and mathematics, to whom the very learned Dr. Samuel Clarke generoufly
acknowledged himfelf to be much indebted for many of the
notes and illuftrations inferted in his Latin verfion of " Rohault's
Philofophy [K]." Mr. Ibbot having taken the degree of B. A.
1699, removed to Corpus-Chrifti, in 1700, and was made a
fcholar of that houfe. He commenced M. A. in 1703, and was
elected into a Norfolk fellowfhip, in 1706, but refigned it next
year, having then happily obtained the patronage of archbifhop
Tenifon. That excellent primate firft took him into his family
in the capacity of his librarian, and foon after appointed him his
chaplain.

In 1708, the archbifhop collated Ibbot to the treafurerfhip
of the cathedral church of Wells. He alfo prefented him to
the rectory of the united parifhes of St. Vedaft, alias Fofter's,
and St. Michael le Querne. George I. appointed him one of

[H] See the article FACUNDUS.
[I] Life prefixed to his fermons, 1776.
[K] " —permulta duchiffimo & in his

rebus exercitatiffimo Viro Ricardo Laugh-
tono,—debere me gratus futurus." PRAEF.L
Edit. quartae, 1718, p. 3.

4

his

his chaplains in ordinary, in 1716; and when his majesty made
a visit to Cambridge, Oct. 6, 1717, Dr. Ibbot was, by royal
mandate, created D. D. together with the very Rev. William
Gregg, the vice-chancellor, Mr. Daniel Waterland, and other
learned and worthy clergymen. In 1713 and 1714, by the appointment of the archbishop, then the sole surviving trustee of
the Hon. Robert Boyle, our author preached the course of sermons for the lecture founded by him. Dr. Ibbot expressed his
desire in his last will, that these sermons should be published.
They bear evident marks of the solidity of his judgement, and
are well adapted to his professed design of obviating, by perti-
nent observations and just reasonings, the insidious suggestions
and unjust censures of Collins, in his "Discourse of Free-
thinking." In these sermons the true notion of the exercise of
private judgement, or free-thinking in matters of religion, is
fairly and fully stated, the principal objections against it are answered, and the modern way of free-thinking, as treated by
Collins, is judiciously refuted. To this publication is annexed,
"A List of the several learned persons who had preached the
Boylean Lectures, from their Commencement in 1692 to the
year 1726, with a particular Account of their different subjects."
Some time after he was appointed preacher-assistant to Dr. Samuel Clarke, and rector of St. Paul's, Shadwell. But his
constitution could no longer endure the fatigue of constant preaching in places so distant from one another, especially in the summer seasons. His health was gradually impaired, and his
strength and spirits greatly exhausted; and having been installed
a prebendary in the collegiate church of St. Peter, Westminster, Nov. 16, 1724, he retired to Camberwell for the recovery
of his health; where he closed the scenes of a studious, laborious, and pious life, April 5, 1725, in the 45th year of his
age, and was buried in the abbey-church of Westminster.
Soon after his death, "Thirty Sermons on Practical Subjects,"
were selected from his MSS. by his worthy friend Dr.
Samuel Clarke, and published for the benefit of his widow, in
2 vols. 8vo, 1726, for which she obtained a very large subscription, and was honoured by the generous donations of some persons
of the first rank and character. Besides these sermons, he had published six others, on several public occasions. He also published,
without his name, a translation of Puffendorf's treatise, entitled, "De habitu Religionis Christianæ ad vitam civilem," of
the relation between the church and the state; or how far Christian and civil life affect each other; with a preface giving some
account of the book, and its use with regard to the present
controversies, 1719, 8vo.

JEANNIN (PIERRE), a native of Burgundy, and bred only
as an advocate in the parliament of Dijon, who rose by his ta-

lents and probity to the highest situations in his profession. The states of Burgundy employed him to administer the affairs of that province, and had every reason to felicitate themselves upon their choice. When the orders for the massacre of St. Bartholomew were received at Dijon, he opposed the execution of them with all his might, and a few days after arrived a courier to forbid the murders. The appointments of counsellor, president, and finally chief president, in the parliament of Dijon, were the rewards of his merit. Seduced by the pretences of the leaguers to zeal for religion and for the state, Jeannin for a time united himself with that faction; but he soon perceived their perfidy and wickedness, as well as the completely interested views of the Spaniards, and repented of the step. After the battle of *Fontaine Françoise*, in which the final blow was given to the league, Henry IV. called him to his council, and retained him in his court. From this time he became the adviser, and almost the friend of the king, who admired him equally for his frankness and his sagacity. Jeannin was employed in the negotiation between the Dutch and the court of Spain, the most difficult that could be undertaken. It was concluded in 1609. After the death of Henry IV. the queen-mother confided to him the greatest affairs of the state, and the administration of the finances, and he managed them with unparalleled fidelity; of which his poverty at his death afforded an undoubted proof. He died in 1622, at the age of eighty-two, having seen seven successive kings on the throne of France. He published a folio collection of negotiations and memoirs, in the year 1659, which were long held in the highest estimation. The regard which Henry IV. felt for him was very great. Complaining one day to his ministers that some among them had revealed a state secret of importance, he took the president by the hand, saying, " As for this good man, I will answer for him." Yet, though he entertained such sentiments of him, he did little for him. He felt conscious that he had been remiss in this respect, and said sometimes, " Many of my subjects I load with wealth, to prevent them from exerting their malice, but for the president Jeannin, I always say much, and do little."

JEBB (SAMUEL, M. D.), a native of Nottingham, and a member of Peter-house, Cambridge, became attached to the Nonjurors, and accepted the office of librarian to the celebrated Jeremy Collyer [L]. While he was at Peter-house he printed a translation of " Martin's Answers to Emlyn, 1718," 8vo; reprinted in 1719; in which latter year he inscribed to that society his " Studiorum Primitiæ ;" namely, " S. Justini Martyris cum Tryphone Dialogus, 1719," 8vo. On leaving the uni-

[L] Anecdotes of Bowyer, by Nichols, p. 32, 81, &c.

versity,

verfity, he married a relation of the celebrated apothecary Mr.
Dillingham, of Red-lion-fquare, from whom he took inftructions in pharmacy and chemiftry by the recommendation of Dr.
Mead, and afterwards practifed phyfic at Stratford by Bow. In
1722, he was editor of the "Bibliotheca Literaria," a learned
work, of which only ten numbers were printed, and in which
are interfperfed the obfervations of Maffon, Waffe, and other
eminent fcholars of the time. He alfo publifhed, 1. "De
Vita & Rebus geftis Mariæ Scotorum Reginæ, Franciæ Dota-
riæ." "The Hiftory of the Life and Reign of Mary Queen
of Scots and Dowager of France, extracted from original Records and Writers of Credit, 1725," 8vo. 2. An edition of
"Ariftides, with Notes, 1728," 2 vols. 4to. 3. A beautiful
and correct edition of "Joannis Caii Britanni de Canibus Britannicis liber unus; de variorum Animalium & Stirpium, &c.
liber unus; de Libris propriis liber unus; de Pronunciatione
Græcæ & Latinæ Linguæ, cum fcriptione novâ, libellus; ad
optimorum exemplarium fidem recogniti; à S. Jebb, M. D.
Lond. 1729," 8vo. 4. An edition of Bacon's "Opus Majus,"
folio, "neatly and accurately printed for W. Bowyer, 1733."
5. "Humphr. Hodii, lib. 2. de Græcis illuftribus Linguæ
Græcæ Literarumque humaniorum inftauratoribus, &c. Lond.
1742," 8vo. "Præmittitur de Vita & Scriptis ipfius Humphredi
Differtatio, auctore S. Jebb, M. D." He wrote alfo the epitaph infcribed on a fmall pyramid between Haut-Buiffon and
Marquife, in the road to Boulogne, about feven miles from Calais, in memory of Edward Seabright, efq; of Croxton in Norfolk, three other Englifh gentlemen, and two fervants, who
were all murdered Sept. 20, 1723 [M]. The pyramid, being
decayed, was taken down about 1751, and a fmall oratory or
chapel erected on the fide of the road [N]. In 1749, Dr. Jebb
poffeffed all Mr. Bridges's MSS. relative to the "Hiftory of
Northamptonfhire," which were afterwards bought by fir Thomas Cave, bart. and finally digefted, and publifhed in 2 vols.
folio, by the Rev. Peter Whalley, in 1791. Dr. Jebb practifed
at Stratford with great fuccefs till within a few years of his death,
when he retired with a moderate fortune into Derbyfhire, where
he died March 9, 1772, leaving feveral children, one of whom
was fir Richard Jebb, M. D. one of the phyficians extraordinary
to his majefty.

JEBB (JOHN), fon of Dr. John Jebb, dean of Cafhell, was
born in London, early in 1736. He was a man much cele-

[M] See "Political State," Vol. XXVI.
p. 333: 441; and, "A Narrative of the
Proceedings in France, for difcovering and
detecting the Murderers of the Englifh
Gentlemen," where there is a print of the
pyramid, with the infcription.

[N] From the Information of a gentleman who has been in the chapel, where
mafs, he was told, is occafionally performed for the fouls of the perfons who
were murdered.

brated

brated among the violent partizans for unbounded liberty, religious and political; and certainly a man of learning and talents, though they were both fo. much abforbed in controverfy as to leave little among his writings of general ufe. His education was begun in Ireland and finifhed in England. His degrees were taken at Cambridge, where he bore public offices, and obtained fome church preferment. His college was Peter-houfe. He early took up the plan of giving theological lectures, which were attended by feveral pupils, till his peculiar opinions became known in 1770, when a prohibition was publifhed in the univerfity. How foon he had begun to deviate from the opinions he held at the time of ordination is uncertain, but in a letter dated Oct. 21, 1775, he fays, " I have for feven years paft, in my lectures, maintained fteadily the proper unity of God, and that he alone fhould be the object of worfhip." He adds, that he warned his hearers that this was not the received opinion, but that his own was fettled, and exhorted them to enquire diligently [o]. This confeffion feems rather inconfiftent with the defence he addreffed to the archbifhop of Canterbury, in 1770. He was a ftrenuous advocate for the eftablifhment of annual examinations in the univerfity, but could not prevail. In 1775, he came to the refolution of refigning his ecclefiaftical preferments, which he did accordingly; and then, by the advice of his friends, took up the ftudy of phyfic. For this new object he ftudied indefatigably, and in 1777, obtained his degree by diploma from St. Andrew's, and was admitted a licentiate in London.

Amidft the cares of his new profeffion, he did not decline his attention to theological ftudy, nor to what he confidered as the caufe of true liberty. He was, as he had been for many years, zealous for the abolition of fubfcription, a warm friend to the caufe of America againft England, an inceffant advocate for annual parliaments, and univerfal fuffrage (thofe pernicious engines for deftroying the Britifh conftitution), a writer in newf-papers, and a fpeaker in public meetings. So many eager purfuits feem to have exhaufted his conftitution, and he died, apparently of a decline, in March, 1786.

Dr. John Jebb was a man of various and extenfive learning, mafter of many languages, among which were Hebrew and Arabic; and during his laft illnefs, he ftudied the Saxon, with the Anglo-Saxon laws and antiquities. He was twice a candidate for the profefforfhip of Arabic at Cambridge. Befides his theological and medical knowledge, he was not a little verfed in the fcience of law, which he once thought of making his profeffion, even after he had ftudied phyfic. He was alfo a mathematician and

[o] Difney's Life of Jebb, p. 106.

philo-

philofopher, and was concerned with two friends in publifhing at Cambridge a fmall quarto, entitled, " Excerpta quædam e Newtonii principiis Philofophiæ naturalis, cum notis variorum ;" which was received as a ftandard book of education in that univerfity. His other works have been collected into 3 vols. 8vo, publifhed in 1787 by Dr. Difney, and contain chiefly, (befides the plan of his lectures, and harmony of the gofpels, fix fermons, and a medical treatife on paralyfis,) controverfial tracts and letters, on his intended improvements at Cambridge, on fubfcription, on parliamentary reform, &c. He feems to have been an active, enterprifing, and rather turbulent, but a fincere man.

JEFFERY (JOHN), an Englifh divine, was born in 1647, at Ipfwich, where he had his grammar-learning; and thence removed in 1664 to Catharine-hall, Cambridge, under the tuition of Dr. John Eachard [P]. Here he took his firft degree, and as foon after as he could, he went into orders, and accepted of the curacy of Dennington in Suffolk. He applied very clofely to his ftudies, lived quite retired, and was not known or heard of in the world for fome years. At length, becoming known, he was, in 1678, elected minifter of a church in Norwich; where his good temper, exemplary life, judicious preaching, and great learning, foon recommended him to the efteem of the wifeft and beft men in his parifh. Sir Thomas Brown, fo well known to the learned world, refpected and valued him. Sir Edward Atkyns, lord chief baron of the Exchequer, took great notice of his fingular modefty of behaviour, and rational method of recommending religion in fermons; gave him an apartment in his houfe, took him up to town with him, carried him into company, and brought him acquainted with Dr. Tillotfon, then preacher at Lincoln's-inn, and with feveral other eminent men. In 1687, Dr. Sharp, then dean of Norwich, afterwards archbifhop of York, obtained for him, without follicitation, the two fmall livings of Kirton and Falkenham in Suffolk; and, in 1694, archbifhop Tillotfon made him archdeacon of Norwich. In 1710, he married a fecond wife; and after his marriage, difcontinued his attendance on the convocation: and when he was afked the reafon, would pleafantly excufe himfelf out of the old law, which faith, " that, when a man has taken a new wife, he fhall not be obliged to go out to war." He died in 1720, aged 72.

He publifhed, " Chriftian Morals, by Sir Thomas Browne." " Moral and religious Aphorifms, collected from Dr. Whichcote's Papers." Three volumes of fermons, by the fame author, 1702.

[P] Memoirs of his Life prefixed to his Works.

In 1701, he had printed a volume of his own discourses, and occasionally various sermons and tracts separately, for twenty years before. All these were collected, and published in 2 vols. 8vo, in 1751. Dr. Jeffery was an enemy of religious controversy, alledging, " that it produced more heat than light." He left behind him many manuscript volumes, entitled, TA EIΣ EATTON, affording an irrefragable proof of his great industry.

JEFFERY of Monmouth (ap ARTHUR), the famous British historian, flourished in the time of Henry I. [q], was born at Monmouth, and probably educated in the Benedictine monastery near that place; for Oxford and Cambridge had not yet risen to any great height, and had been lately depressed by the Danish invasion; so that monasteries were at this time the principal seminaries of learning. He was made archdeacon of Monmouth, and afterwards promoted to the bishopric of St. Asaph in 1152. He is said by some to have been raised to the dignity of a cardinal also, but on no apparent good grounds. Robert earl of Gloucester, natural son of Henry I. and Alexander bishop of Lincoln, were his particular patrons; the first a person of great eminence and authority in the kingdom, and celebrated for his learning; the latter, famous for being the greatest patron of learned men in that time, and himself a great scholar and statesman.

Leland, Bale, and Pits inform us, that Walter Mapæus, alias Calenius, who was at this time archdeacon of Oxford, and of whom Henry of Huntingdon, and other historians, as well as Jeffery himself, make honourable mention, as a man very curious in the study of antiquity, and a diligent searcher into ancient libraries, and especially after the works of ancient authors, happened while he was in Armorica to meet with a history of Britain, written in the British tongue, and carrying marks of great antiquity. Being overjoyed at this, as if he had found a vast treasure, he in a short time came over to England, where enquiring for a proper person to translate this curious but hitherto unknown book, he very opportunely met with Jeffery of Monmouth, a man profoundly versed in the history and antiquities of Britain, excellently skilled in the British tongue, and besides (considering the time) an elegant writer, both in verse and prose, and to him he recommended the task. Jeffery accordingly undertook to translate it into Latin; which he performed with great diligence, approving himself according to Matthew Paris, a faithful translator. At first he divided it into four books, written in a plain simple style, a copy whereof is said to be at Benet-college, Cambridge, which was never yet

[q] Tanner's Bibliotheca, sub voce, &c. Oxonofridus Marmoretensis.

published,

published; but afterwards made fome alterations, and divided it into eight books, to which he added the book of " Merlin's Prophecies," which he had alfo tranflated from Britifh verfe into Latin profe. A great many fabulous and trifling ftories are inferted in the hiftory, upon which account Jeffery's integrity has been called in queftion; and many authors, fuch as Polydore Virgil, Buchanan, and fome others, treat the whole as fiction and forgery. But, on the other hand, he is defended by very learned men, fuch as Ufher, Leland, Sheringham, fir John Rice, and many more. His advocates do not deny, that there are feveral abfurd and incredible ftories inferted in this book; but, as he tranflated or borrowed them from others, the truth of the hiftory ought not to be rejected in grofs, though the credulity of the hiftorian may deferve cenfure.

Camden alledges, that his relation of Brutus, and his fucceffors in thofe ancient times, ought to be entirely difregarded, and would have our hiftory commence with Cæfar's attempt upon the ifland: and this advice has fince been followed by the generality of our hiftorians. But Milton purfues the old beaten tract, and alledges that we cannot be eafily difcharged of Brutus and his line, with the whole progeny of kings to the entrance of Julius Cæfar; fince it is a ftory fupported by defcents of anceftry, and long continued laws and exploits, not plainly feeming to be borrowed or devifed. Camden, indeed, would infinuate, that the name of Brutus was unknown to the ancient Britons, and that Jeffery was the firft perfon who feigned him founder of their race. But this is certainly a miftake. For Henry of Huntingdon had publifhed, in the beginning of his hiftory, a fhort account of Brutus, and made the Britons the defcendants of the Trojans, before he knew any thing of Jeffery's Britifh hiftory; and he profeffes to have had this account from various authors. Sigibertus Gemblacenfis, a French author, fomewhat more early than Jeffery, or Henry of Huntington (for he died, according to Bellarmine, in 1112) gives an account of the paffage of Brutus, grandfon of Afcanius, from Greece to Albion, at the head of the exiled Trojans [R]; and tells us, that he called the people and country after his own name, and at laft left three fons to fucceed him, after he had reigned twenty-four years. Hence he paffes fummarily over the affairs of the Britons, agreeably to the Britifh hiftory, till they were driven into Wales by the Saxons.

Nennius abbot of Banchor, who flourifhed according to fome accounts, in the feventh century [s], or however, without dif-

[R] Chronographia, &c.   adjecit, Thomas Oslcus. Nennii procm.
[s] Hiftoria Britonum, five Eulogium ad Hift. Brit.
Britanniæ, Oxon. 1691, edidit notafque

pute, some hundreds of years before Jeffery's time, has written very copiously concerning Brutus; recounting his genealogy from the patriarch Noah, and relating the sum of his adventures in a manner that differs but in few circumstances from the British history. He tells us from whence he compiled his account in the following words: "Partim majorum traditionibus, partim scriptis, partim etiam monumentis veterum Britanniæ incolarum, partim & de annalibus Romanorum; insuper & de Chronicis sanctorum patrum, S. Jeronymi, Prosperi, Eusebii; nec non & de historiis Scotorum, Saxonumque licet inimicorum, non ut volui sed ut potui, meorum obtemperans jussionibus seniorum, unam hanc historiunculam undecunque collectam balbutiendo coacervavi." Giraldus Cambrensis, contemporary with Jeffery, says, that in his time the Welch bards and singers could repeat by heart, from their ancient and authentic books, the genealogy of their princes from Roderic the Great to Belim the Great; and from him to Sylvius, Ascanius, and Æneas; and from Æneas lineally carry up their pedigree to Adam. From these authorities it appears, that the story of Brutus is not the produce of Jeffery's invention, but, if it be a fiction, is of much older date.

There are two editions of Jeffery's history extant in Latin, one of which was published in 4to, by Ascensius, at Paris, A. D. 1517; the other in folio by Commeline, at Heidelberg, 1587, among the "Rerum Britannicarum Scriptores vetustiores & præcipui," which is much the fairer and more correct edition. A translation of it into English by Aaron Thompson, of Queen's-college, was published at London, 1718, in 8vo, with a large preface concerning the authority of the history.

JEFFREYS (lord GEORGE), baron Wem, commonly known by the name of judge Jeffreys [T], was the sixth son of John Jeffreys, esq; of Acton in Denbighshire. He was educated at Westminster-school, where he became a good proficient in the learned languages; and was thence removed to the Inner-Temple, where he applied himself very assiduously to the law. His father's family was large, and his temper parsimonious, consequently the young man's allowance was very scanty, and hardly sufficient to support him decently: but his own ingenuity supplied all deficiencies, till he came to the bar; to which, as is affirmed by some, he had no regular call. In 1666, he was at the assize at Kingston, where very few counsellors attended, on account of the plague then raging. Here necessity gave him permission to put on a gown, and to plead; and he continued the practice unrestrained, till he reached the highest employments in the law. Alderman Jeffreys, a namesake, and pro-

[T] Lives of the Lord Chancellors, &c. North's Life of the late Lord-keeper Guilford.

bably

bably a relation, introduced him among the citizens; and, being
a jovial bottle companion, he became very popular among them,
came into great bufinefs, and was chofen their recorder. His
influence in the city, and his readinefs to promote any meafures
without referve, introduced him at court; and he was appointed
the duke of York's folicitor.

He was very active in the duke's intereft, and carried through
a caufe which was of very great confequence to his revenue: it
was for the right of the Penny-poft-office. He was firft made
a judge in his native country; and, in 1680, was knighted, and
made chief juftice of Chefter. When the parliament began the
profecution of the abhorrers, he refigned the recorderfhip, and
obtained the place of chief juftice of the King's-bench; and,
foon after the acceffion of James II. the great feal. He was
one of the greateft advifers and promoters of all the oppreffive
and arbitrary meafures of that unhappy and tyrannical reign;
and his fanguinary and inhuman proceedings againft Monmouth's
miferable adherents in the Weft will ever render his name infamous. There is, however, a fingular ftory of him in this expedition, which tends to his credit; as it fhews, that when he
was not under ftate influence, he had a proper fenfe of the natural and civil rights of men, and an inclination to protect them.
The mayor, aldermen, and juftices of Briftol, had been ufed to
tranfport convicted criminals to the American plantations, and
fell them by way of trade; and finding the commodity turn to a
good account, they contrived a method to make it more plenti-
ful. Their legal convicts were but few, and the exportation
was inconfiderable. When, therefore, any petty rogues and
pilferers were brought before them in a judicial capacity, they
were fure to be terribly threatened with hanging; and they had
fome very diligent officers attending, who would advife the ignorant
intimidated creatures to pray for tranfportation, as the only way
to fave them; and, in general, by fome means or other, the advice was followed. Then, without any more form, each alderman in courfe took one and fold for his own benefit; and fometimes warm difputes arofe among them about the next turn.
This trade had been carried on unnoticed many years, when
it came to the knowledge of the lord chief juftice; who,
finding upon enquiry, that the mayor was equally involved in
the guilt of this outrageous practice with the reft of his brethren,
made him defcend from the bench where he was fitting, and
ftand at the bar in his fcarlet and furs, and plead as a common
criminal. He then took fecurity of them to anfwer inform-
ations; but the amnefty after the Revolution ftopt the proceedings, and fecured their iniquitous gains.

North, who informs us of this circumftance, tells us likewife, that, when he was in temper, and matters indifferent
came

came before him, no one better became a feat of Juſtice. He
talked fluently, and with ſpirit; but his weakneſs was, that he
could not reprehend without ſcolding, and in ſuch Billingſgate
language as ſhould not come from the mouth of any man. He
called it " giving a lick with the rough ſide of his tongue." It
was ordinary to hear him ſay, " Go, you are a filthy, louſy,
nitty raſcal;" with much more of like elegance. He took a
pleaſure in mortifying fraudulent attornies. His voice and viſage
made him a terror to real offenders, and formidable indeed to
all. A ſcrivener of Wapping having a cauſe before him, one
of the opponent's counſel ſaid, " that he was a ſtrange fellow,
and ſometimes went to church, ſometimes to conventicles; and
none could tell what to make of him, and it was thought that
he was a Trimmer." At that the chancellor fired. " A Trimmer!" ſaid he, " I have heard much of that monſter, but never
ſaw one; come forth, Mr. Trimmer, and let me ſee your ſhape:"
and he treated the poor fellow ſo roughly, that, when he came
out of the hall, he declared " he would not undergo the terrors
of that man's face again to ſave his life; and he ſhould certainly
retain the frightful impreſſions of it as long as he lived."

Afterwards, when the prince of Orange came, and all was
in confuſion, the lord chancellor, being very obnoxious to the
people, diſguiſed himſelf in order to go abroad. He was in a
ſeaman's dreſs, and drinking a pot in a cellar. The ſcrivener,
whom he had ſo ſeverely handled, happening to come into the
cellar after ſome of his clients, his eye caught that face which
made him ſtart; when the chancellor ſeeing himſelf obſerved,
feigned a cough, and turned to the wall with his pot in his hand.
But Mr. Trimmer went out, and gave notice that he was there;
and the mob immediately ruſhed in, ſeized him, and carried
him to the lord-mayor. Thence, under a ſtrong guard, he was
ſent to the lords of the council, who committed him to the
Tower; where he died April 18, 1689, and was buried privately the Sunday night following.

JEFFREYS (GEORGE), educated at Weſtminſter-ſchool
under Dr. Buſby, was the ſon of Chriſtopher Jeffreys, eſq; of
Weldron in Northamptonſhire, and nephew to James, the eighth
lord Chandos [U]. He was admitted of Trinity-college, Cambridge, in 1694, where he took the degrees in arts, was elected
fellow in 1701, and preſided in the philoſophy-ſchools as moderator in 1706. He was alſo ſub-orator for Dr. Ayloffe, and not
going into orders within eight years, as the ſtatutes of that college require, he quitted his fellowſhip in 1709. Though Mr.
Jeffreys was called to the bar, he never practiſed the law, but,
after acting as ſecretary to Dr. Hartſtronge biſhop of Derry, at

[U] Nichols's Select Collection of Poems, Vol. VI. p. 57.

the

the latter end of queen Anne's and the beginning of George the
Firſt's reign, ſpent moſt of the remainder of his life in the families of the two laſt dukes of Chandos, his relations. In
1754 he publiſhed, by ſubſcription, a 4to volume of " Miſ-
cellanies, in Verſe and Proſe," among which are two tragedies, " Edwin," and " Merope," both acted at the theatre-royal
in Lincoln's-inn-fields, and " The Triumph of Truth," an
oratorio. " This collection," as the author obſerves in his dedication to the preſent duke of Chandos, then marquis of Car-
narvon, " includes an uncommon length of time, from the
verſes on the duke of Glouceſter's death in 1700, to thoſe on his
lordſhip's marriage in 1753." Mr. Jeffreys died in 1755, aged
77. In ſir John Hawkins's " Hiſtory of Muſic [x]," his grandfather, George, is recorded as Charles the Firſt's organiſt at
Oxford, in 1643, and ſervant to lord Hatton in Northamptonſhire, where he had lands of his own; and alſo his father,
Chriſtopher, of Weldron in Northamptonſhire, as " a ſtudent
of Chriſt-church, who played well on the organ." The anonymous verſes prefixed to " Cato," were by this gentleman,
which Addiſon never knew. The alterations in the Odes in
the " Select Collection," are from the author's corrected
copy.

JENKIN (ROBERT), a learned Engliſh divine, ſon of Thomas Jenkin, gentleman, of Minſter in the Iſle of Thanet,
where he was born Jan. 1656; and bred at the King's ſchool at
Canterbury [y]. He entered as ſizar at St. John's-college,
Cambridge, March 12, 1674, under the tuition of Mr. Francis
Roper; became a fellow of that ſociety March 30, 1680; de-
ceſſit 1691; became maſter in April, 1710 [z.]; and held alſo
the office of lady Margaret's profeſſor of divinity. Dr. Lake,
being tranſlated from the ſee of Briſtol to that of Chicheſter, in
1685, made him his chaplain, and collated him to the precen-
torſhip of that church, 1688. Refuſing to take the oaths at the
Revolution, he quitted that preferment, and retired to his fellowſhip, which was not ſubject then to thoſe conditions, unleſs
the biſhop of Ely, the viſitor, inſiſted on it; and the biſhop
was, by the college ſtatutes, not to viſit unleſs called in by a
majority of the fellows. By theſe means he and many others
kept their fellowſhips. Retiring to the college, he proſecuted
his ſtudies without interruption, the fruits whereof he gave to

[x] Vol. IV. p. 64. Ib. 523.
[y] Anecdotes of Bowyer, by Nichols,
p. 15.
[z] On the death of Dr. Humfrey
Gower; who left him a country-ſeat at
Thriplow, worth 20l. per ann. on the death

of Mr. Weſt, his nephew and heir; and
500l. to buy a living for the college, to
which ſociety he alſo left two exhibitions
of 10l. each, and all his books to their
library.

the public in several treatises which were much esteemed [A].
Upon the accession of George I. an act was passed, obliging all
who held any post of 5l. a year to take the oaths, by which Dr.
Jenkin was obliged to eject those fellows who would not comply,
which gave him no small uneasiness [B]; and he sunk by degrees
into imbecillity. In this condition he removed to his elder brother's house at South Rungton in Norfolk, where he died April
7, 1707, in his 70th year; and was buried, with his wife (Su-
fannah, daughter of William Hatfield, esq; alderman and merchant of Lynne, who died 1713, aged 46), his son Henry, and
daughter Sarah, who both died young in 1727, in Holme chapel,
in that parish of which his brother was rector. Another daughter Sarah survived him. A small mural monument was erected
to his memory, inscribed as below [c].

Dr. Jenkin had an elder and a younger brother, Henry and
John. John was a judge in Ireland, under the duke of Ormond.
Henry, elder brother of the master, was vicar of Tilney in
Norfolk, and rector of South Rungton cum Wallington, where
he died in 1732, and had three sons, Thomas, William, and
Robert.

JENKINS (Sir LEOLINE), a learned civilian and able statesman, was descended from a family in Wales, being the son of
Leoline Jenkins, who was possessed of an estate of 40l. a year,
at Llantrisaint in Glamorganshire, where this son was born, about
1623. He discovered an excellent genius and disposition for
learning, by the great progress he made in Greek and Latin, at

[A] These are, 1. "An Historical
Examination of the Authority of General
Councils, 1688." 2. "A Defence of the
Profession which bishop Lake made upon
his Death-bed." 3. "Defensio S. Augus-
tini adversus Jo. Pherepomum, 1707." 4.
"An English translation of the Life of
Apollonius Tyaneus, from the French of
Tillemont." 5. "Remarks on Four
Books lately published; viz. Basnage's
History of the Jews; Whiston's Eight
Sermons; Locke's Paraphrase and Notes
on St. Paul's Epistles; and Le Clerc's
Bibliotheque Choisie;" and was also au-
thor of, 6. "The Reasonableness and
Certainty of the Christian Religion;" of
which a fifth edition, corrected, appeared
in 1721.

[B] The true account of the ejection
is this: The statutes of that college require
the fellows, as soon as they are of proper
standing, to take the degree of B. D. But
the oath of allegiance is required to be
taken with every degree: so that, after the
Revolution, twenty-four of the fellows
not coming in to the oath of allegiance,

and the statutes requiring them to commence B. D. they were constrained to part
with their fellowships. As to those who
had taken the degree before the Revolution, there was no cause for rejecting them,
till they refused the abjuration oath, which
was exacted upon the accession of Geo. 1.

[c]   S. M.
Reverendi admodum ROBERTI
JENKIN,
Sanctæ Theologiæ pro Domina
Margareta
In Academia Cantabrigiensi Professoris,
Omni laude dignissimi,
Et Collegii Divi Johannis Evangelistæ
Præfecti
Vigilantissimi, spectatissimi;
Qui doctrinæ, pietatis, religionis,
Ornamentum fuit illustre;
Exemplar venerabile,
Vindex fidelissimæ,
Et usque vixit
Monumentum perpetuum.
Ob. 7 die Aprilis,
Anno Domini 1727,
Æta. 70.

Cowbridge

Cowbridge school, near Llantrisaint; whence he was removed,
in 1641, to Jesus-college in Oxford, and, upon the breaking out
of the civil war soon after, took up arms, among other students,
on the side of the king. This, however, did not interrupt his
studies, which he continued with all possible vigour; not leaving Oxford till after the death of the king. He then retired to
his own country, near Llantrythyd, the seat of fir John Aubrey,
which, having been left void by sequestration, served as a refuge
to several eminent loyalists; among whom was Dr. Mansell,
the late principal of his college. This gentleman invited him
to fir John Aubrey's house, and introduced him to the friendship
of the rest of his fellow-sufferers there, as Frewen Abp. of York,
and Sheldon afterwards Abp. of Canterbury; a favour, which,
through his own merit and industry, laid the foundation of all
his future fortunes. The tuition of fir John Aubrey's eldest
son was the first design in this invitation; and he acquitted himself in it so well, that he was soon after recommended in the
like capacity to many other young gentlemen of the best rank
and quality in those parts, whom he bred up in the doctrine of
the Church of England, treating them like an intimate friend
rather than a master, and comforting them with hopes of better
times.

But this could not long continue unobserved by the parliament
party, who grew so jealous, that they were resolved to put a
stop to it: and, as the most effectual means of dispersing the
scholars, the master was seized by some soldiers quartered in
those parts; and, being sent to prison, was indicted at the quar-
ter-sessions, for keeping a seminary of rebellion and sedition.
He was however discharged by the interest of Dr. Wilkins, then
warden of Wadham-college in Oxford: to which place he removed with his pupils, in 1651, and settled in a house, thence
called Little Welch-hall, in the High-street. During his residence in Oxford, he was recommended to the warden of Wad-
ham by the famous judge David Jenkins; and employed on several messages and correspondences between the judge, Dr. Sheldon, Dr. Mansell, Dr. Fell, and others. But Dr. Wilkins,
his protector, being promoted to the mastership of Trinity-college Cambridge, in 1655, Jenkins was obliged to remove; and,
being talked of as a dangerous man, sought his safety by flight.
He withdrew with his pupils out of the kingdom, and resided
occasionally in the most famous of the foreign universities. He
thus kept a kind of moving academy; and by that method, the
best opportunities of improving the students in all sorts of academical learning were obtained; while they had the further advantage of travelling over a great part of France, Holland, and
Germany. They returned home in 1658; and Mr. Jenkins,
delivering up his pupils to their respective friends, gladly accepted

cepted an invitation to live with fir William Whitmore, at his feat at Appley in Shropshire.

He continued with that patron of distressed cavaliers, enjoying all the opportunities of a well-furnished library, till the Restoration; when he returned to Jesus-college, and was chosen one of the fellows. He was created LL. D. in Feb. 1661, and elected principal in March following, upon the resignation of his patron Dr. Mansell; and fir William Whitmore soon after gave him the commissaryship of the peculiar and exempt jurisdiction of the deanery of Bridgenorth in Shropshire. In 1662, he was made assessor to the chancellor's court at Oxford; and the same year Dr. Sweit appointed him his deputy professor of the civil law there. In 1663, he was made register of the consistory court of Westminster-abbey; and his friend Sheldon, newly translated to the fee of Canterbury, soon after appointed him commissary and official for that diocese, and judge of the peculiars. Jenkins was very serviceable to that prelate, in settling his Theatre at Oxford; of which, as soon as it was finished, he was made one of the curators. He was useful to the archbishop on other occasions also relating to church and state; and it was by his encouragement, that Dr. Jenkins removed to Doctor's-Commons, and was admitted an advocate in the court of arches in the latter end of 1663. Here he was immediately made deputy-assistant to Dr. Sweit, dean of this court, as he had been to him before in the office of professor; and this situation brought his merit nearer the eye of the court. Upon the breaking out of the first Dutch war in 1664, the lords commissioners of prizes appointed Dr. Jenkins, with other eminent civilians, to review the maritime laws, and compile a body of rules for the adjudication of prizes in the court of admiralty, which afterwards became the standard of those proceedings. Then, by the recommendation of Sheldon, he was made judge-assistant in that court, March 21, 1664-5; Dr. Exton, the judge, being then very aged and infirm: and upon his death soon after, became principal, and sustained the weight of that important office alone, with great reputation. He had advanced the honour and esteem of that court to a high degree, by a three years service; when finding the salary of 300l. per annum, allowed by the king, not a competent maintenance, he petitioned for an additional 200l. per annum, which was granted Jan. 29, 1668. He was now considered as so useful a man by the government, that the king became his patron; and having recommended him to the archbishop, as judge of his prerogative court of Canterbury, which appointment he obtained in 1668, employed him the following year in an affair of near concern to himself.

The queen-mother, Henrietta Maria, widow of Charles II. dying Aug. 1, 1669, in France, her whole estate, both real and

personal,

personal, was claimed by her nephew, Louis XIV [D]: upon which matter, Dr. Jenkins being commanded to give his opinion, it was approved in council; and a commission being made out for him, with three others [E], he attended it to Paris. He demanded and recovered the queen-mother's effects, discharged her debts, and provided for her interment; when, returning home, his majesty testified his high approbation of his services, by conferring on him the honour of knighthood, Jan. 7, 1669-70. Immediately after this honour, he received a greater; being nominated one of the commissioners of England, to treat with those authorized from Scotland, about an union between the two kingdoms. In 1671, he was chosen a representative in parliament for Hythe in Kent, one of the cinque ports.

He did not approve the rupture, which brought on the second war with the Dutch in 1672. Being appointed an ambassador and plenipotentiary, with others, for settling a treaty of peace, and resigning his place of principal of Jesus-college, he arrived in his new character at Cologne, in June 1673: but after several fruitless endeavours to effect it, he returned to England in 1674. On his arrival in May, he gave the privy-council an account of his negotiation, which was well received; and, in December, was appointed one of the mediators of the treaty at Nimeguen. He continued there throughout the whole course of that long and laborious negotiation; and the chief part of the business, at least the drudgery of it, lay upon him, as is acknowledged by sir William Temple, his brother mediator: who in his pleasant manner observes, that, "where there were any ladies in the ambassadors houses, the evenings were spent in dancing or play, or careless and easy suppers, or collations. In these entertainments," says he, "as I seldom failed of making a part, and my colleague never had any, so it gave occasion for a *bon mot*, a good word, that passed upon it: *Que la mediation estoit toujours en pied pour faire sa fonction:* that is, that the mediation was always on foot to go on with its business; for I used to go to bed and rise

[D] She had resided at Colombe in France ever since her departure from England in July 1644, being entertained there at the charge of Lewis XIV. Upon the Restoration, she came to London; and having settled her revenues here, went back to France, to bestow her daughter Henrietta in marriage to the duke of Anjou. July 1661, coming again into England, she settled her court at Somerset-house, where she resided till May 1665. But falling into a bad state of health, she returned to her native country, where she died. Under these circumstances it was pretended, that she was not only a native, but an inhabitant of France; consequently, that whatever estate she possessed there, ought to be subject to the laws and usages of that country, and that madame royale of France, the aforesaid dutchess of Anjou, was by those laws the only person capable of succeeding; Charles II. and the duke of York, as well as the princess of Orange, her other children, being expresly excluded and disabled by the Droit d'aubaine, because they were not born nor inhabitants within the allegiance of the French king. But our court's claim was at length admitted.

[E] Ralph Montague, Esq; ambassador at that court, the earl of St. Alban's, and lord Arundel.

late, while my colleague was a bed by eight and up by four; and to say the truth, two more different men were never joined in one commission, nor ever agreed better in it [F]."

The detail of this negotiation is well known, and may be seen in sir Leoline's letters, and his colleague's works, to which we must refer; it being sufficient to observe here, that all expedients proposed by the two mediators were rejected. Sir Leoline quitted the place on Feb. 16, 1679; and retiring to Neerbos, received a warrant from his royal master, dated Feb. 14, three days after the date of his letter of revocation, appointing him ambassador extraordinary at the Hague, in the room of sir William Temple, who had been then recalled. He accordingly arrived there, March 1; but continued in that station no longer than the 25th of the same month: for, by a new commission, dated Feb. 20, and which came to his hands six days after, he returned to Nimeguen March 26, authorised to resume his mediatorial function, at the desire of the prince of Orange and the States, and the earnest intreaty of the Northern princes. His instructions now left him in a great measure to himself, without other direction than to act as he should find most consistent with his majesty's honour, and the good of the general peace; which, as he was a modest man and very diffident of himself, put him under great anxiety. He happily succeeded, however, in accommodating all differences, and returned home, Aug. 1679, after having been employed about four years and a half in this tedious treaty.

Soon after his arrival in England, he was chosen one of the burgesses for the university of Oxford; and, in the parliament which met Oct. 17 following, opposed, to the utmost of his power, the bill brought in for the exclusion of the duke of York from the crown. He was sworn a privy-counsellor before the expiration of this year; and received the seals as secretary of state, April 1680, being first secretary for the northern province, and in 1681 for the southern. He entered upon this arduous office in critical and dangerous times, which continued so all the while he enjoyed it; yet he escaped the then common fate of being assailed by addresses against him, committed and impeached. Being chosen again for Oxford, in the parliament which met there, March 21, 1681, he earnestly again opposed the exclusion of the duke of York, as he did also the printing of the votes of the house of commons; a practice which had then been lately assumed [G], but was considered by him as inconsistent with the gravity of that assembly, and a sort of impro-

[F] " Temple's Memoirs," p. 185, first to be printed 22 Oct. 1680. See that edit. 1692, 8vo. collection.
[G] The votes of the commons begin

.per

per appeal to the people. With fimilar zeal he withflood the
command of the houfe, to carry their impeachment of Edward
Fitz-Harris up to the lords, regarding it as defigned to reflect
upon the king in the perfon of his fecretary ; nor did he comply, till he faw himfelf in danger of being expelled the houfe
for refufing [n]. But when the corporations began to be new
modelled by the court, and a quo warranto was brought againft
the city of London, the fecretary fhewed a diflike of fuch violent meafures ; and gave his opinion for punifhing only the moft
obnoxious members in their private capacities, without involving
the innocent, who would equally fuffer by proceeding to the for-
feiture of the city's privileges [1]. In many other inftances, fir
Leoline differed from the general difpofition of the court. He
was a determined foe to all ideal projects that came before the
privy-council ; and had refolution to diffent, and experience
enough to diftinguifh what was practicable and really ufeful,
from what was merely chimerical. He alfo conftantly declared
againft every irregular or illegal proceeding ; but, not having
ftrength to fuftain the bufinefs and conflicts of thofe turbulent
times, he begged leave to refign for a valuable confideration,
which was granted by his majefty on April 14, 1684. Having
obtained his wifh, he retired to a houfe in Hammerfmith, where
learning and learned men continued to be his care and delight.
Upon the acceffion of James II. he was fworn again of the
privy-council, and elected a third time for the univerfity of Oxford. He had gained fome little return of ftrength, and frefh
application was accordingly made to him to appear in bufinefs ;
but, indifpofition foon returning, he was never able to fit in that
parliament, and paid the laft debt to nature on Sept. 1, 1685.
His body was conveyed to Oxford, and interred in the area of
Jefus-college chapel. Being never married, his whole eftate
was bequeathed to charitable ufes ; and he was, particularly, a
great benefactor to his college. All his letters and papers were
collected and printed in two folio volumes, 1724, under the title
of his " Works," by W. Wynne, Efq; who prefixed an ac-

[n] The words which gave offence, befides thofe mentioned in the text, were,
" And do what you will with me, I will
not go." Whereupon many called, " To
the bar," and moved that his words fhould
be written down before he explained them.
The chief fpeakers againft him were the
famous J. Trenchard and fir William Jones.
At length the fecretary made a foftening
fpeech, alledging, he did apprehend the
fending of him to be a reflection upon his
mafter, and under that apprehenfion he
could not but refent it. " I am heartily

forry," continues he, " I have incurred
the difpleafure of the houfe, and I hope
they will pardon the freedom of the expreffion." To which he added a little
after, " I am ready to obey the order of
the houfe, and am forry my words gave
offence." Collection of Debates, p. 315.
336.

[1] Some of the city were fo much fatisfied with the part he acted in this affair,
that he was prefented with his freedom,
and afterwards chofe mafter of the Salters
company. Wynne, p. 37.

count

count of his life ; which has furnished the chief materials of this memoir.

JENNENS (CHARLES, Esq; [K]) a gentleman of considerable fortune at Gopsal in Leicestershire, and a diffenter, was descended from a family, which was one among the many who have acquired ample fortunes at Birmingham, where they were equally famous for industry and generosity [L]. In his youth he was so remarkable for the number of his servants, the splendor of his equipages, and the profusion of his table, that he acquired the title of "Solyman the Magnificent." He is said to have composed the words for some of Handel's oratorios, and particularly those for "the Messiah;" an easy task, as it is only a selection of verses from scripture. Not long before his death, he imprudently exposed himself to criticism by attempting an edition of Shakspeare, which he began by publishing "King Lear," in 8vo; and printed afterwards, on the same model, the tragedies of "Hamlet," 1772; "Othello" and "Macbeth," 1773. He would have proceeded further, but was prevented by death, Nov. 20, 1773. The tragedy of "Julius Cæsar," which in his life had been put to the press, was published in 1774. He had a numerous library, and a large collection of pictures, both in Great Ormond-street [M] and at Gopsal.

JENSON (NICOLAS), or Jansonius, a celebrated printer and letter-founder of Venice, but by birth a Frenchman, flourished in the fifteenth century. He is said to have been originally an engraver of coins and medals at Paris. About the year 1458, the report of the invention of printing at Mayence being circulated, he was sent by the king, Charles VII. to gain private information on the subject of that art. He fulfilled the object of his mission, but, on his return to France, finding that the king was dead, or perhaps having heard of his death, he removed to Venice. Such is the purport of an account in two old French manuscripts on the coinage, except that one places the mission of Jenson under Louis XI, which is less probable. Jenson excelled in all branches of the art, and more than are now united with it. He formed the punches, he cast the letters, and conducted the typography. He first determined the form and proportion of the present Roman character: and his editions are still sought on account of the neatness and beauty of his types. The first book that issued from his press is a scarce work in

[K] Anecdotes of Bowyer, by Nichols, p. 442.

[L] John Jennens gave, in 1651, 3l. 10s. for the use of the poor; and Mrs. Jennens 10l. to support a lecture. The land on which the neat and elegant church of St. Bartholomew was built in 1749 was the gift of John Jennens, Esq; of Gopsal,

then proffessor of a considerable estate in and near Birmingham; and Mrs. Jennens gave 100l. towards the building.

[M] Dispersed by public auction soon after his death. See a catalogue of them in "The Connoisseur," 8vo. and in "London and its Environs."

quarto,

quarto, entitled, "Decor Puellarum," the date of which is
1471; and in the same year he published in Italian "Gloria
Mulierum," a proper sequel to the former. After these are
found many editions of Latin Classics and other books, for ten
years subsequent; but, as no books from his press appear after
1481, it is conjectured that he died about that time.

JENYNS (SOAME), a modern English writer of some eminence, was born in London in 1704, the only son of sir Roger
Jenyns, knt. of Bottisham in Cambridgeshire [N]. He was
educated privately, till he went to St. John's college, Cambridge,
where he resided about three years, studying diligently; but took
no degree. He appeared as a poet so early as in 1728, when
he published his "Art of Dancing." Several other productions
followed at different periods, which he collected into a volume
in 1752. He was elected into parliament for Cambridge in
1741, and continued to sit there chiefly for that place, but once
or twice for others, till 1780. He assisted Moore in the periodical paper entitled *The World*, in 1753. In 1755, he was appointed one of the Lords of Trade, which place he held during
every change of administration, till it was abolished in 1780.
Though no speaker, he was an active and diligent member of
the house of commons. He was twice married. He died of a
fever, December 18, 1787, in his 83d year, leaving no issue;
and was buried at Bottisham.

The poems of this author were three times published collectively in his life, first, in a small 8vo, in 1752; the second time
in 2 vols. small 8vo, 1761; lastly, in one large 8vo, 1778. He
wrote also, 2. "A Free Enquiry into the Origin of Evil,"
8vo, 1757. 3. "A View of the internal Evidence of the Christian Religion," 12mo. 1776. 4. "Several political Tracts, and
short Philosophical Disquisitions." All these were published
together in four volumes, 8vo, by Nalson Cole, Esq; in 1790,
with a short sketch of his life. The character of S. Jenyns
seems to have been amiable and respectable. As an author he
attained no small degree of reputation, by powers which had
every aid that useful and polite learning could bestow. His poetry is characterized by elegance and correctness, rather than by
invention or enthusiasm. He is a pleasing and elegant, not a
very animated or first-rate writer. His expression is concise,
his wit lively, his humour delicate, his versification easy and
agreeable. He had a critical judgement, an elegant taste, and a
rich vein of wit and humour. He is entitled to great praise for
the excellence of his style and purity of his language. His view
of the internal evidence of the Christian religion contains many
just and important observations, but his method of reasoning is

[N] See Dr. Anderson's Life of Jenyns, in his *British Poets*.

liable

liable to confiderable objections: and it was accordingly anfwered by Dr. Maclaine and others, who were defirous to feparate the perfect parts from thofe which are lefs judicious. The courfe of his religious fentiments was rather fingular. From early impreffion or ftrong conviction, he had been originally a zealous believer of revelation, and had even been fufpected of a tendency to certain fanatical opinions. Gradually lofing ground in faith, he wandered into paths obfcured by doubt, and became a profeffed Deift; till, by a retrograde progrefs, he meafured back his fteps to the comforts of chriftianity. On his death-bed, it is faid, he revie ! !.- life, and with a vifible gleam of joy, he gloried in the belief, that his *View of the internal Evidences* had been ufeful. He fpoke of his death as one prepared to die. A very honourable teftimony to the goodnefs of his heart, was infcribed in the regifter of Bottifham, by the Rev. W. L. Manfell, then fequeftrator of that vicarage: and indeed the only blemifh upon this part of his character, is the revengeful attack upon Dr. Johnfon, ...er his death, in a fevere epitaph which ftands againft its author in his works. It was amply punifhed by a counter-epitaph upon him, written while he was alive. His pique againft Johnfon is fuppofed to have arifen from a fevere critique upon his book on the Origin of Evil, which appeared in the Literary Magazine for 1757. But this offence fhould have been punifhed earlier, if at all.

JEREMIAH, the fecond of the greater prophets, the fon of Hilkiah, of the prieftly race, and a native of Anathoth, in the tribe of Benjamin. He was born in the reign of Jofias, about 629 years before Chrift; and was fet apart for the prophetic office from his very birth Jeremiah inveighed againft the diforders of his country, and predicted the evils that were to fall upon it. He alfo prophefied againft feveral neighbouring nations, as the Egyptians, Philiftians, Tyrians, Phœnicians, &c. In the fourth year of Jehoiakim, he foretold the captivity of the Jews, and that it would endure feventy years. Thefe predictions were very offenfive to the great men of Jerufalem, and they threw him into prifon. When the city was taken by Nebuchadnezzar, Jeremiah was among the captives, but the general gave him leave to choofe, whether he would go to Babylon or ftay in Judea. He preferred the latter, and went to Gedaliah at Mifpah, where he was joined by feveral Jews, whom the war had difperfed into feveral quarters. Ifhmael having treacheroufly murdered Gedaliah, Johanan collected as many Jews as he could at Bethlehem, and there confulted Jeremiah whether they fhould ftay in Judea, or retire into Egypt. The prophet advifed that they fhould ftay in Judea, the contrary however was determined by the principal perfons, and Jeremiah, and his difciple Baruch, were compelled to go with the reft. Several of the ancients,

and

and among them St. Jerome, maintain, that Jeremiah was put
to death by the Jews at Tapahnes in Egypt, about 586 years before Chrill : while some rabbins assert, that he returned to Judea, and others, that he went to Babylon and there died.

The prophecies of Jeremiah, of which the circumstantial ac-
complishment is specified in the Old and New Testament, are
of a very distinguished and illustrious character [o]. He foretold the Babylonish Captivity, the precise time of its duration,
and the return of the Jews. He described the destruction of
Babylon, and the downfall of many nations. He foreshewed
the miraculous conception of Christ, the virtue of his atonement, the spiritual character of his covenant, and the inward
efficacy of his laws. His style, though neither deficient in elegance nor sublimity, has been considered, by bishop Lowth, as
inferior in both respects to that of Isaiah. His images are perhaps less lofty, and his expressions less dignified than those of
some others among the sacred writers ; but the character of his
work, which breathes a tenderness of sorrow calculated to interest the milder affections, led him probably to reject the ma-
jestic tone in which the prophetic censures were sometimes conveyed.

JEROM, St. (See HIERONYMUS).

JEROME of Prague, so called from the place of his birth,
where he is held to be a Protestant martyr. It does not appear
in what year he was born, but it is certain that he was neither a
monk nor an ecclesiastic : but that, being endowed with excellent natural parts, he had a learned education, and studied at
Paris, Heidelberg, Cologne, and perhaps at Oxford ; the degree of M. A. being conferred on him in the three first-menti-
oned universities, and he commenced D. D. in 1396. He began to publish the doctrine of the Hussites in 1408, and it is
said he had a greater share of learning and subtlety than John
Hufs himself. In the mean time, the council of Constance
kept a watchful eye over him ; and, looking upon him as a
dangerous person, cited him before them April 18, 1415, to
give an account of his faith. In pursuance of the citation, he
went to Constance, in order to defend the doctrine of Hufs, as
he had promised ; but, on his arrival, April 24, finding his
master Hufs in prison, he withdrew immediately to Uberlingen,
whence he sent to the emperor for a safe-conduct ; but that was
refused. The council, it seems, were willing to grant him a
safe-conduct to come to Constance, but not for his return to Bohemia. Upon this, he caused to be fixed upon all the churches
of Constance, and upon the gates of the cardinal's house, a paper, declaring that he was ready to come to Constance, to give

[o] Gray's Key to the Old Testament.

Dd 4   an an account of his faith, and to answer, not only in private and under the seal, but in full council, all the calumnies of his accusers, offering to suffer the punishment due to heretics, if he should be convinced of any errors; for which reason he had desired a safe-conduct both from the emperor and the council; but that if, notwithstanding such a pass, any violence should be done to him, by imprisonment or otherwise, all the world might be a witness of the injustice of the council. No notice being taken of this declaration, he resolved to return into his own country: but the council dispatched a safe-conduct to him, importing, that as they had the extirpation of heresy above all things at heart, they summoned him to appear in the space of fifteen days, to be heard in the first session that should be held after his arrival; that for this purpose they had sent him, by those presents, a safe-conduct so far as to secure him from any violence, but they did not mean to exempt him from justice, as far as it depended upon the council, and as the catholic faith required. This pass and summons came to his hands: nevertheless, he was arrested in his way homewards, on April 25, and put into the hands of the prince of Sultzbach; and, as he had not answered the citation of April 18, he was cited again May 2, and the prince of Sultzbach sending to Constance in pursuance of an order of the council, he arrived there on the 23d, bound in chains. Upon his examination, he denied the receiving of the citation, and protested his ignorance of it. He was afterwards carried to a tower of St. Paul's church, there fastened to a post, and his hands tied to his neck with the same chains. He continued in this posture two days, without receiving any kind of nourishment; upon which he fell dangerously ill, and desired a confessor might be allowed. This being granted, by that means he got a little more liberty. July 19, he was interrogated afresh, when he explained himself upon the subject of the Eucharist to the following effect: That, in the sacrament of the altar, the particular substance of that piece of bread which is there, is transubstantiated into the body of Christ, but that the universal substance of bread remains[P]. Thus, with John Huss, he maintained the " universalia ex parte rei." It is true, on a third examination, Sept. 11, he retracted this opinion, and approved the condemnation of Wickliff and John Huss; but, on May 26, 1416, he condemned that recantation in these terms; " I am not ashamed to confess here publicly my

[P] It is not easy for a person, unskilled in logic, to comprehend the meaning of this visionary distinction. It is enough to observe, that, according to the doctrine of the schools, universals have a proper and real existence of their own, independent of, and in the nature of things prior to the existence of the individuals, whose genera and species they constituted. But these universals are now well known to be nothing else but abstract ideas, existing only in the mind, which is their sole creator.

weakness,

weaknefs. Yes, with horror, I confefs my bafe cowardice. It was only the dread of the punifhment by fire, which drew me to confent, againft my confcience, to the condemnation of the doctrine of Wickliff and John Hufs." This was decifive, and accordingly, in the 21ft feffion, fentence was paffed on him; in purfuance of which, he was delivered to the fecular arm, May 30. As the executioner led him to the flake, Jerome, with gr. at fleadinefs, teftified his perfeverance in his faith, by repeating his creed with a loud voice, and finging litanies and a hymn to the bleffed Virgin; whence he was adjudged by his party, to have merited the martyr's crown, and to have his name, together with Wickliff and Hufs, inferted in the Proteftant martyrology.

JERVAS (CHARLES), a painter of this country, more known from the praifes of Pope, who took inftructions from him in the art of painting, and other wits, who were influenced probably by the friendfhip of Pope, than for any merits of his own. He was a native of Ireland, and ftudied for a year under fir Godfrey Kneller. Norris, framer and keeper of the pictures to king William and queen Anne, was the firft friend who effentially ferved him, by allowing him to ftudy from the pictures in the royal collection, and to copy them. At Hampton-court he made fmall copies of the cartoons, and thefe he fold to Dr. George Clark of Oxford, who then became his protector, and furnifhed him with money to vifit France and Italy. In the eighth number of the Tatler, (April 18, 1709), he is mentioned as " the laft great painter Italy has fent us." Pope fpeaks of him with more enthufiafm than felicity, and rather as if he was determined to praife, than as if he felt the fubject. Perhaps fome of the unhappieft lines in the works of that poet are in the fhort epiftle to Jervas. Speaking of the families of fome ladies, he fays,

" Oh, lafting as thy colours, may they fhine,
Free as thy ftroke, yet faultlefs as thy line;
New graces yearly, like thy works difplay,
Soft without weaknefs, without glaring gay,
Led by fome rule, that guides, but not conftrains,
And finifh'd more through happinefs than pains."

In this paffage the whole is obfcure, the connection with the preceding part particularly fo; and part is parodied from Denham. It is no wonder that Jervas did not better infpire his friend to praife him, if the judgement of lord Orford be accurate, on which we may furely rely. He fays, that " he was defective in drawing, colouring, and compofition, and even in that moft neceffary, and perhaps moft eafy talent of a portrait-painter, likenefs. In general, his pictures are a light, flimfy kind of fan-painting, as large as life." His vanity, inflamed

perhaps

perhaps by the undeferved praifes he received from wits and poets, was exceffive. He affected to be violently in love with lady Bridgewater; yet, after difpraifing the form of her ear, as the only faulty part about her face, he ventured to difplay his own as the complete model of perfection. Jervas appeared as an author in his tranflation of Don Quixote, which he produced, as Pope ufed to fay of him, without underftanding Spanifh. It is the fate of Cervantes to be fo reprefented in England, for the fame objection has been made to Smollet. Warburton added a fupplement to the preface of Jervas's tranflation, on the origin of romances of chivalry, which was praifed at the time, but has fince been totally extinguifhed by the acute criticifms of Mr. Tyrwhitt [q]. Jervas died about 1740.

JESUA (LEVITA), a learned Spanifh rabbi in the fifteenth century, is the author of a book entitled, " Halichot olam," " The Ways of Eternity;" a very ufeful piece for underftanding the Talmud. It was tranflated into Latin by Conftantin l'Empereur; and Bafhuyfen printed a good edition of it in Hebrew and Latin, at Hanover, in 1714, 4to.

JEUNE (JEAN LE), was born in the year 1592, at Poligni in Franche-Comté. His father was a counfeller in the parliament at Dole. The piety of Le Jeune was of the moft exemplary kind. He delighted in the moft arduous offices of his profeffion; and refufed a canonry of Arbois, to enter into the then rifing, but ftrict fociety of the Oratory. His patience and humility were no lefs remarkable than his piety. He loft his fight at the age of 35, yet did not fuffer that great misfortune to deprefs his fpirits. He was twice cut for the ftone, without uttering a fingle murmur of impatience. As a preacher he was highly celebrated, but totally free from all oftentation. As a converter of perfons eftranged from religion, or thofe efteemed heretical, he is faid to have poffeffed wonderful powers of perfuafion. Many dignitaries of the church were highly fenfible of his merits; particularly cardinal Berulle, who regarded him as a fon, and La Fayette bifhop of Limoges, who finally perfuaded him to fettle in his diocefe. Le Jeune died in 1672, at the age of 80. There are extant ten large volumes of his fermons, in 8vo, which were ftudied and admired by Maffillon. They have been alfo tranflated into Latin. His ftyle is fimple, infinuating, and affecting, though now a little antiquated. He publifhed alfo a tranflation of Grotius's tract, De Veritate Religionis Chriftianæ,

The JEW (WANDERING), is fo often mentioned by various authors, that fome account of the phantom may be expected

[q] Supplemental Obfervations on Love's Labour Loft.

here.

here [x]. The unapposite examples of Enoch and Elias, who
never tasted death: the firm persuasion of the Jews, who confi-
dently believe, that the prophet Elias is present, invisibly, at
the ceremony of circumcising their children: the words of Jesus
Christ, in the Gospel, where speaking of St. John the Evan-
gelist, he says, "If I will that he tarry till I come, what is
that to thee," which are understood by several of the ancients,
and some modern authors, to contain a promise to that apostle,
that he should not die till the day of judgement: these, and
other vague notions, added to the prevalent love of the marvellous, have contributed to raise a belief, that there is such a personage as the Wandering Jew. The partizans of this opinion
appeal likewise to the legend of the Mahometan authors; who
mention, in the sixteenth year of the Hegira, a captain named
Fadhila, that had the command of 300 horse; and being arrived with his troop, about the close of the day, between two
mountains, and bidding the evening prayer with a loud voice,
by these words, "God is great," heard a voice which repeated
the same words, and so continued to pronounce with him the
whole prayer to the end. Fadhila thought at first, that this was
nothing more than an echo; but observing, that the voice repeated distinctly and entirely every word of the prayer, he said,
"O thou who answerest me, if thou be'st of the order of angels, the virtue of God be with thee; if thou art of the kind
of any other spirits, well and good; but if thou art, as I am,
of the human species, shew thyself to my eyes." He had no
sooner ended this speech, than an ancient man, bald-headed,
holding a staff in his hand, and having the air of a dervis, stood
before him. Fadhila, after a civil salutation, asked the old man
who he was; to which he answered, that his name was Zerib,
the grandson of Elias; I am here, continues he, by the order
of the Lord Jesus, who hath left me in this world to live here,
till his second coming upon earth. I wait for this lord, who is
the fountain of all happiness; and, in pursuance to his orders,
I make this mountain my last residence. Fadhila asked him, in
what time the Lord Jesus was to appear? He answered, at the
end of the world, and at the last judgement. And what are the
signs of the approach of that day? replied Fadhila. Zerib,
then assuming the prophetic tone of voice, says, "When men
and women mingle together without distinction of sex; when
the abundant plenty of provisions shall not cause the price
thereof to fall; when innocent blood shall every where be shed;
when the poor shall beg an alms, and no one shall communicate
to them; when charity shall be extinguished; when men shall

[a] At some curious particulars are collected in this article, it has been suf- fered to retain its place; though there was surely very little reason originally, for in- serting so fabulous an account, in a col- lection of real biography.

make

make ballads of the holy Scriptures; and the temples dedicated to the true God shall be filled with idols: know then, that the day of judgement is at hand." Having finished these words, the figure immediately vanished. This wild story has been supposed to be a testimony to the existence of the Wandering Jew.

His story, who can wonder, is related somewhat differently by different authors. Matthew Paris, under the year 1229, tells us, that there came that year an Armenian prelate to England, who brought letters of recommendation from the pope, intreating the bishops there to shew him the principal relics of that country, and the manner of divine worship in their churches. Paris, who was then living, assures us, that several persons talked with this strange archbishop upon many subjects; and, among other things, enquired the news concerning the Wandering Jew, who was in the East, asking several questions about him; whether he was still alive, who he was, and what account he gave of himself? The archbishop assured them, that this Jew was an Armenian; and an officer of the prelate's train told them, that the Jew was Pontius Pilate's porter, whose name was Caraphilus, who seeing them drag Jesus Christ out of the judgement-hall, struck him with his fist upon the back, in order to push him faster out of doors, and that Jesus Christ said to him, "The son of man goes his way, but thou shalt wait his coming." Thereupon the porter was converted, and baptized by Ananias with the name of Joseph. He lives for ever; and as soon as he comes to be 100 years old, he falls sick and into a swoon, during which he grows young again, returning to 30, the age he was of when Christ died. This officer assured us, that Joseph was known by his master; that he had seen him eat at his table a little before his departure from Jerusalem; that he answered with sufficient gravity, and without the least smile, when he was interrogated upon ancient facts, such, for instance, as the resurrection of the dead, who came out of their graves at the crucifixion of Jesus Christ; the history of the apostles and holy personages of old. He stands, added he, continually afraid of Jesus Christ's coming to judge the world, since that day is to be the last of his life: the fault that he committed in striking Jesus makes him tremble; he is, however, not without hopes of being forgiven, as he did it through ignorance. Several such impostors as these have appeared from time to time, each of whom, abusing the credulity of the people, have given out themselves to be the Wandering Jew; and taking advantage of some knowledge in ancient history, and the Eastern languages, have persuaded the simple, that they were this pretended personage.

One of these impostors appeared at Hamburgh, in 1547. A Christian writer assures us, that he saw him and heard him

preach

preach in one of the churches of that city ; that he feemed to be about fifty years of age, of a tall ftature, with long hair fpreading over his fhoulders. He frequently was obferved to groan, which was attributed to the grief and pain that he felt for his fault. He faid, that, at the time of Jefus Chrift's paffion, he was a fhoemaker at Jerufalem, and lived near the gate through which our Saviour was to pafs in his way to Calvary: that he was then a Jew, and his name Affuerus: that Jefus being fatigued, and going to reft himfelf upon his ftall, Affuerus ftruck him: whereupon Jefus faid to him, " I fhall reft myfelf here, but thou fhalt run about till I come." From that moment, Affuerus began to run, followed Jefus Chrift, and hath continued wandering ever fince. Another of thefe pretenders ftarted up, many years ago, in England. Calmet has given us the copy of a letter written by the countefs of Mazarin to madam Bouillon, giving un account, that there was a man in that country, who pretended to have lived upwards of 1600 years; he fays he was one of the Sanhedrim at Jerufalem, at the time that Jefus Chrift was condemned by Pontius Pilate ; that he pufhed our Saviour out of the judgement-hall in a rude manner, faying, " Go along, get you out, what do you ftay here for?" That Jefus Chrift anfwered him, " I indeed will go, but you fhall' ftay till I come back." He remembers to have feen all the apoftles; can tell you the features and air of their faces, the colour and manner in which they wore their hair, and defcribe their drefs. He hath travelled through all parts of the world, and is to wander to the end of ages. He pretends to heal the fick with a touch; he fpeaks feveral languages, and gives fuch an exact and particular account of every thing that hath paffed in every country, that thofe who have heard him know not what to think of him. The two univerfities have fent their doctors to difcourfe him; but they have not been able, with all their knowledge, to catch him in a contradiction. A gentleman of great learning fpoke to him in Arabic, to whom he anfwered immediately in the fame language, telling him that there was hardly fo much as one true hiftory in the world. The gentleman afked him what he thought of Mahomet; " I knew his father," faid he, " very well, at Ormus in Perfia; and as for Mahomet, he was a perfon of great penetration and knowledge, but fubject, neverthelefs to error, as well as other mortals, and that one of his principal errors was his denying the crucifixion of Jefus Chrift ; for, " fays he, " I was prefent at it, and faw him nailed to the crofs with my own eyes." He told this gentleman further, That he was at Rome, when Nero fet the city on fire: that he faw Saladin after his return from the conquefts in the Levant. He related feveral particulars concerning Solyman the Magnificent. He likewife knew Tamerlane, Bajazet, Eterlan,

and

and gave a large recital of the wars of the Holy Land. He
talks of coming in a few days to London, where he will satisfy
the curiosity of all persons who shall please to address themselves
to him. This is the purport of the countess of Mazarin's letter.
Her ladyship moreover observes, that the common and simple
sort of people ascribe many miracles to this wonderful person,
but that the more knowing ones look upon him as an impostor [s].

JEWEL (JOHN), an English bishop, and one of the ablest
champions of that church against popery, was descended from
an ancient family at Buden in Devonshire, where he was born
in 1522. After learning the rudiments of grammar under his
maternal uncle Mr. Bellamy, rector of Hamton, and being put
to school at Barnstaple, he was sent to Oxford, and admitted a
postmaster of Merton-college at 13; but, being chosen scholar
of Corpus-Christi, in 1530, he removed thither. He pursued
his studies with indefatigable industry, usually rising at four in
the morning, and studying till ten at night; by which means he
acquired a masterly knowledge in most branches of learning:
but, taking too little care of his health, he contracted such a
cold as fixed a lameness in one of his legs, which accompanied
him to his grave. Oct. 1540, he proceeded B. A. became a
celebrated tutor, and was soon after chosen rhetoric lecturer in
his college. In Feb. 1544, he commenced M. A.

He had early imbibed Protestant principles, and inculcated
them among his pupils; but this was carried on privately till the
accession of Edward VI. in 1546, when he made a public declaration of his faith, and entered into a close friendship with
Peter Martyr, who was professor of divinity at Oxford. In
1550, he took the degree of B. D. and frequently preached
before the university with great applause. At the same time he
preached and catechised every other Sunday at Sunningwell in
Berkshire, of which church he was rector. Thus he zealously
promoted the Reformation during this reign, and, in a proper
sense, became a confessor for it in the succeeding [T]; so early,
as to be expelled the college by the fellows, upon their private
authority, before any law was made, or order given by queen
Mary. Unwilling, however, to leave the university, he took
chambers in Broadgate-hall, now Pembroke-college, where

[s] Moreri. Calmet Dict. de la Bible.
[T] In the primitive church, the title
of confessor was given not only to those
who actually suffered torture for the faith,
but to such as were imprisoned in order to
suffer torture or death. See Cyprian " de
unitate ecclef." And perhaps Jewel was
not inferior to any of the ancients in point
of piety, and much superior in regard to

learning. Prince, in his " Worthies of
Devonshire," tells us, that Mr. Jewel's life,
during his residence in college, was so exemplary, that Moren, the dean of it, used
to say to him, " I should love thee, Jewel,
if thou wert not a Zuinglian; in thy faith
I hold thee an heretic, but surely in thy
life thou art an angel; thou art very good
and honest, but a Lutheran."

many

many of his pupils followed him, besides other gentlemen, who were induced by the fame of his learning to attend his lectures. But the strongest testimony to his literary merit was given by the university, who made him their orator, and employed him to write their first congratulatory letter to her majesty. Wood indeed observes, that this task was evidently imposed upon him by those who meant him no kindness; it being taken for granted, that he must either provoke the Roman Catholics, or lose the good opinion of his party. If this be true, which is probable enough, he had the dexterity to escape the snare; for the address, being both respectful and guarded, passed the approbation of Tresham the commissary, and some other doctors, and was well received by the queen.

Burnet informs us, that her majesty declared, at her accession, that she would force no man's conscience, nor make any change in religion. These specious promises, joined to Jewel's fondness for the university, seem to have been the motives which disposed him to entertain a more favourable opinion of Popery than before. In this state of his mind, he went to Clive, to consult his old tutor Dr. Parkurst [u], who was rector of that parish; but Parkhurst, upon the re-establishment of Popery, having fled to London, Jewel returned to Oxford, where he lingered and waited, till, being called upon to subscribe some of the Popish doctrines under the several penalties, he submitted. Yet his compliance did not answer his purpose; for the dean of Christ-church, Dr. Martial, alledging his subscription to be insincere, laid a plot to deliver him into the hands of bishop Bonner; and would certainly have caught him in the snare, had he not set out the very night in which he was sent for, by a bye-way to London. He walked till he was forced to lay himself on the ground, quite spent and almost breathless: where being found by one Augustine Berner, a Swiss, first a servant of bishop Latimer, and afterwards a minister, this person provided him a horse, and conveyed him to lady Warcup's, by whom he was entertained for some time, and then sent safely to the metropolis. Here he lay concealed, changing his lodgings twice or thrice for that purpose, till a ship was provided for him to go abroad, together with money for the journey, by sir Nicolas Throgmorton, a person of great distinction, and at that time in considerable offices. His escape was managed by one Giles Lawrence, who had been his fellow-collegian, and was at this time tutor to sir Arthur Darcy's children, living near the Tower of London. Upon his arrival at Frankfort, in 1554, he made a public confession of his sorrow for his late subscrip-

[v] He had been his tutor at Merton-college, and was afterwards bishop of Norwich.

tion to Popery; and foon afterwards went to Strafburgh, at
the invitation of Peter Martyr, who kept a kind of college for
learned men in his own houfe, of which he made Jewel his
vice-mafter: he likewife attended this friend to Zurich, and
affifted him in his theological lectures. It was probably about
this time that he made an excurfion to Padua, where he contracted a friendfhip with Sig. Scipio, a Venetian gentleman, to
whom he afterwards addreffed his " Epiftle concerning the
Council of Trent."

Upon the death of Queen Mary, in 1558, he returned to
England; and we find his name, foon after, among the fixteen
divines appointed by queen Elizabeth, to hold a difputation in
Weftminfter-abbey againft the Papifts. July, 1559, he was in
the commiffion conftituted by her majefty to vifit the diocefes of
Sarum, Exeter, Briftol, Bath and Wells, and Gloucefter, in
order to exterminate Popery in the Weft of England; and he
was confecrated bifhop of Salifbury at the end of the fame year,
and had the reftitution of the temporalities April 6, 1560. This
promotion was prefented to him as a reward for his great merit and
learning; and another atteftation of thefe was given him by the
univerfity of Oxford, who, in 1565, conferred on him, in his
abfence, the degree of D. D. in which character he attended
the queen to Oxford the following year, and prefided at the
divinity difputations held before her majefty on that occafion.
He had, before, greatly diftinguifhed himfelf, by a fermon
preached at St. Paul's-crofs, foon after he had been made a
bifhop, wherein he gave a public challenge to all the Roman
Catholics in the world, to produce but one clear and evident
teftimony out of any father or famous writer who flourifhed
within 600 years after Chrift, for any one of the articles which
the Romanifts maintain againft the church of England; and two
years afterwards he publifhed his famous " Apology" for that
church. Meanwhile, he gave a particular attention to his diocefe, where he began, in his firft vifitation, and perfected in his
laft, a great reformation, not only in his cathedral and parochial
churches, but in all the courts of his jurifdiction. He watched
fo narrowly the proceedings of his chancellor and archdeacons,
and of his ftewards and receivers, that they had no opportunities
of being guilty of oppreffion, injuftice, or extortion, nor of
being a burden to the people, or a fcandal to himfelf. To prevent thefe, and the like abufes, for which the ecclefiaftical courts
are often cenfured, he fat in his confiftory court, and there faw
that all things were conducted rightly: he alfo fat often as an
affiftant on the bench of civil juftice, being himfelf a juftice of
the peace.

Amidft thefe glorious employments, the care of his health
was too much neglected. He rofe at four o'clock in the morning;

ing; and after prayers with his family at five, and in the cathedral about six, he was so fixed to his studies all the morning, that he could not, without great violence, be drawn from them. After dinner, his doors and ears were open to all suitors; and it was observed of him, as of Titus, that he never sent any sad from him. Suitors being thus dismissed, he heard, with great impartiality and patience, such causes debated·before him, as either devolved to him as a judge, or were referred to him as an arbitrator; and, if he could spare any time from these, he reckoned it as clear gain to his study. About nine at night, he called all his servants to an account how they had spent the day, and then went to prayers with them: from the chapel he withdrew again to his study, till near midnight, and from thence to his bed; in which, when he was laid, the gentleman of his bedchamber read to him till he fell asleep. Mr. Humfrey, who relates this, observes, that this watchful and laborious life, without any recreation at all, except what his necessary refreshment at meals, and a very few hours of rest, afforded him, wasted his life too fast, and undoubtedly hastened his end. In his 50th year, he fell into a disorder which carried him off in Sept. 1571. He died at Monkton Farley, in his diocese, and was buried in his cathedral, where there is an inscription over his grave, written by Dr. Laurence Humfrey, who also wrote an account of his life, to which are prefixed several copies of verses in honour of him. Dr. Jewel was of a thin habit of body, which he exhausted by intense application to his studies. In his temper he was pleasant and affable, modest, meek, temperate, and perfectly master of his passions. In his morals he was pious and charitable; and when bishop, became most remarkable for his apostolic doctrine, holy life, prudent government, incorrupt integrity, unspotted chastity, and bountiful liberality. He had naturally a very strong memory, which he greatly improved by art, so that he could exactly repeat whatever he wrote after once reading [x]. He professed to teach others this art, and actually taught it his tutor, Dr. Parkhurst, at Zurich. He was a great master of the ancient languages, and skilled in the German and Italian. His writings, a list of which is inserted below [y], have rendered his name famous over all Europe.

IGNATIUS

[x] See his Life by Humfrey and Featly. Wood's Ath. Oxon. Vol. I. and Hist. and Antiq. Oxon.

[y] These are, 1. "Exhortatio ad Oxonienses." The substance printed in Humfrey's Life of him, p. 35, 1573, 4to. 2. "Exhortatio in collegio CC. five concio in fundatorii Foxi commemorationem," p. 45, &c. 3. "Concio in templo B. M. Virginis, Oxon. 1550," preached for his degree of B. D. It is reprinted in Humfrey, p. 49. 4. "Oratio in aula collegii CC." His farewell speech on his expulsion in 1554, printed by Humfrey, p. 72, &c. 5. A short tract, "De Usura," ibid. p. 217, &c. 6. "Epistola ad Sciplonem Patritium Venetum, &c, 1559," and reprinted in the appendix to father

IGNATIUS (furnamed THEOPHRASTUS), one of the apoftolical fathers of the church, was born in Syria [z], educated
under the apoftle and evangelift St. John, intimately acquainted
with fome other of the apoftles, efpecially St. Peter and St.
Paul; and being fully inftructed in the doctrines of Chriftianity,
was, for his eminent parts and piety, ordained by St. John [A],
and confirmed, about the year 67, bifhop of Antioch [B] by
thefe two apoftles, who firft planted chriftianity in that city,
where the difciples alfo were firft called Chriftians. In this important feat he continued to fit fomewhat above 40 years, both
an honour and fafeguard to the Chriftian religion; in the midft
of very ftormy and tempeftuous times, undaunted himfelf, and
unmoved with the too fure a profpect of fuffering a cruel death.
So much feems to be certain in general, though we have no account of any particulars of his life till the year 107; when Trajan the emperor, flufhed with a victory he had obtained over the
Scythians and Daci, came to Antioch to prepare for a war againft
the Parthians and Armenians. He entered the city with the
pomp and folemnities of a triumph; and, as he had already commenced a perfecution againft the Chriftians in other parts of the

ather Paul's "Hiftory of the Council of
Trent," in Englifh, by Brent, 3d edition,
1619, folio. 7. "A Letter to Henry
Bullinger at Zurich, concerning the State
of Religion in England," dated May 22,
1559, printed in the appendix to Strype's
"Annals, No. 11." 8. Another letter
to the fame, dated Feb. 2, 1566, concerning his controverfy with Hardynge, ibid.
No. 16, 37. 9. "Letters between him
and Dr. Henry Cole, &c. 1560," 8vo.
10. "A Sermon preached at St. Paul's
Crofs, the fecond Sunday before Eafter,
anno 1560," 8vo. Dr. Cole wrote feveral
letters to him on this fubject. 11. "A
Reply to Mr. Hardynge's Anfwer, &c.
1566," folio, and again in Latin, by Will.
Whitaker, fellow of Trinity-college,
Cambridge, at Geneva, 1578, 4to; and
again in 1585, in folio, with our author's
"Apologia ecclefiæ Anglicanæ." 12.
"Apologia ecclefiæ Anglicanæ, 1562,"
8vo: it was feveral times printed in England and abroad, and a Greek tranflation
of it was printed at Oxford, in 1614, 8vo.
The Englifh tranflation by the lady Bacon,
wife to fir Nicolas Bacon, entitled, "An
Apology or Anfwer in Defence of the
Church of England, &c. 1562," 4to.
This "Apology" was approved by the
queen, and fet forth with the confent of
the bifhops. 13. "A Defence of the
Apology, &c. 1564," 1567, folio, again
in Latin, by Tho. Braddock, fellow of

Chrift's-college, Cambridge, at Geneva,
1600, folio. Th's was ordered by queen
Elizabeth, king James, king Charles, and
four fucceffive archbifhops, to be read
and chained up in all parifh churches
throughout England and Wales. 14.
"An Anfwer to a Book written by Mr.
Hardynge, intituled, 'A Detection of fun-
dry foul errors,' &c. 1568," and 1570,
folio. 15. "A View of a feditious Bull
fent into England from Pius V. &c. 1582,"
8vo. 16. "A Treatife of the Holy
Scriptures," 8vo. 17. "Expofition on the
two Epiftles to the Theffalonians, 1594,"
8vo. 18. "A Treatife of the Sacra-
ments, &c. 1583." 19. "Certain Sermons preached before the Queen's Majefty
at Paul's Crofs, and elfewhere." All
thefe books (except the firft eight) with
the "Sermons" and "Apology," were
were printed at London, 1609, in one vol.
folio, with an abftract of the author's life,
by Dan. Featly; but full of faults, as
Wood fays, 20. "An Anfwer to certain
frivolous Objections againft the Government of the Church of England, 1641,"
4to, a fingle fheet. 21. Many letters in
the collection of records in part iii. of Burnet's "Hiftory of the Reformation."

[z] Jortin's "Remarks on Ecclef.
Hiftory," Vol. I. p. 349.
[A] Wafterland's "Importance of the
Trinity," Chap. VI.
[B] Cave in the Life of this Martyr.

empire, he now refolved to carry it on here. However, as he was naturally mild and humane, though he ordered the laws to be put in force againſt them, if convicted, yet he forbad them to be fought for puniſhment.

In this ſtate of affairs, Ignatius, thinking it more prudent to go than ſtay to be ſent for, of his own accord prefented himfelf to the emperor; and, it is ſaid, there paſſed a large and particular diſcourſe between them, wherein the emperor expreſfing a ſurpriſe how he dared to tranſgreſs the laws, the biſhop took the opportunity to aſſert his own innocence, and the power which God had given Chriſtians over evil ſpirits; declaring, that "the gods of the Gentiles were no better than dæmons, there being but one ſupreme Deity, who made the world, and his only begotten ſon Jeſus Chriſt, who, though crucified under Pilate, had yet deſtroyed him that had the power of ſin, that is, the devil, and would ruin the whole power and empire of the dæmons, and tread it under the feet of thoſe who carried God in their hearts." The iſſue of this was, that he was caſt into priſon, and this ſentence paſſed upon him, that, being incurably overrun with ſuperſtition, he ſhould be carried bound by ſoldiers to Rome, and there thrown as a prey to wild beaſts. It may ſeem ſtrange that they ſhould ſend an old man by land, at a great expence, attended with ſoldiers, from Syria to Rome, inſtead of caſting him to the lions at Antioch: but it is ſaid, that Trajan did this on purpoſe to make an example of him, as of a ringleader of the ſect, and to deter the Chriſtians from preaching and ſpreading their religion: and, for the ſame reaſon, he ſent him to be executed at Rome, where there were many Chriſtians, and which, as it was the capital of the world, ſo was it the head quarters of all ſorts of religions. Ignatius was ſo far from being diſmayed, that he heartily rejoiced at the fatal decree. "I thank thee, O Lord," ſays he, "that thou haſt condeſcended to honour me with thy love, and haſt thought me worthy, with thy apoſtle St. Paul, to be found in iron chains." With theſe words he cheerfully embraced his chains; and, having frequently prayed for his church, and recommended it to the divine care and providence, he delivered up himſelf into the hands of his keepers. Theſe were 10 ſoldiers, by whom he was firſt conducted to Seleucia, a port of Syria, at about 16 miles diſtance, the place where Paul and Barnabas ſet ſail for Cyprus. Arriving at Smyrna in Ionia, Ignatius went to viſit Polycarp, biſhop of that place, and was himſelf viſited by the clergy of the Aſiatic churches round the country. In return for that kindneſs, he wrote letters to ſeveral churches, as the Epheſians, Magneſians, Trallians, beſides the Romans, for their inſtruction and eſtabliſhment in the faith; one of theſe was addreſſed to the Chriſtians at Rome, to acquaint them with his preſent ſtate and paſ

ſionate

sionate desire not to be hindered in that course of martyrdom which he was now hastening to accomplish.

His guard, a little impatient at their stay, set sail with him for Troas, a noted city of the lesser Phrygia, not far from the ruins of old Troy; where, at his arrival, he was much refreshed with the news he received of the persecution ceasing in the church of Antioch. Hither also several churches sent their messengers to pay their respects to him, and hence too he dispatched two epistles, one to the church of Philadelphia, and the other to that of Smyrna; and together with this last, as Eusebius relates, he wrote privately to Polycarp, recommending to him the care and inspection of the church of Antioch. All this while his keepers, the 10 soldiers, used him very cruelly and barbarously. He complains of it himself: " From Syria even to Rome" says he, " both by sea and land, I fight with beasts; night and day I am chained to the leopards, which is my military guard, who, the kinder I am to them, are the more cruel and fierce to me." From Troas they sailed to Neapolis, a maritime town in Macedonia, thence to Philippi, a Roman colony, where they were entertained with all imaginable kindness and courtesy, and conducted forwards on their journey, passing on foot through Macedonia and Epirus, till they came to Epidaurum, a city of Dalmatia, where again taking shipping, they sailed through the Adriatic, and arrived at Rhegium, a port town in Italy.

The Christians at Rome, daily expecting his arrival, had come out to meet and entertain him, and accordingly received him with an equal mixture of joy and sorrow: but when some of them intimated, that possibly the populace might be dissuaded from desiring his death, he expressed a pious indignation; intreating them to cast no obstacles in his way, nor do any thing that might hinder him, now he was hastening to his crown. The interval before his martyrdom was spent in prayers for the peace and prosperity of the church. That his punishment might be the more pompous and public, one of their solemn festivals, the Saturnalia, was chosen for his execution; when it was their custom to entertain the people with the conflicts of gladiators, and the hunting and fighting with wild beasts. Accordingly, Dec. 20, he was brought out into the amphitheatre; and the lions, being let loose upon him, quickly dispatched their meal, leaving nothing but a few of the hardest of his bones. These remains were gathered up by two deacons who had been the companions of his journey, and transported to Antioch.

His epistles are very interesting remains of ecclesiastical antiquity on many accounts. He stands at the head of those Antenicene fathers, who have occasionally delivered their opinions in defence of the true divinity of Christ, whom he calls the Son of God, and his eternal word. He is also reckoned the great champion

pion

pion of the episcopal order, as distinct and superior to that of priest and deacon. He is constantly produced as an instance of the continuation of supernatural gifts, after the time of the apostles, particularly that of divine revelation. But the most important use of his writings respects the authenticity of the holy scriptures, to which he frequently alludes, in the very expressions which are extant.

ILIVE (JACOB), was a printer, and the son of a printer; but he applied himself to letter-cutting in 1730, and carried on a foundery and a printing-house together [c]. He was an expeditious compositor, and was said to know the letters by the touch; but being not perfectly found in mind, produced some strange works. In 1751, he published a pretended translation of " The Book of Jasher;" said to have been made by one Alcuin of Britain. The account given of the translation is full of glaring absurdities; but the publication, in fact, was secretly written by him, and printed off by night. He published, in 1733, an Oration, intended to prove the plurality of worlds, and asserting that this earth is hell, that the souls of men are apostate angels, and that the fire to punish those confined to this world at the day of judgement will be immaterial. This was written in 1729, and spoken afterwards at Joiners-hall, pursuant to the will of his mother [D], who had held the same extraordinary opinions. A second pamphlet called " A Dialogue between a Doctor of the Church of England and Mr. Jacob Ilive, upon the Subject of the Oration," appeared in 1733. This strange Oration is highly praised in Holwell's third part of " Interesting Events relating to Bengal." For publishing " Modest Remarks on the late Bishop Sherlock's Sermons," Ilive was confined in Clerkenwell Bridewell from June 15, 1756, till June 10, 1758; during which period he published " Reasons offered for the Reformation of the House of Correction in Clerkenwell, &c. 1757," and projected several other reforming treatises, enumerated in Gough's " British Topography [E];" where is also a memorandum, communicated by Mr. Bowyer, of Ilive's attempt to restore the company of Stationers to their primitive constitution. He died in 1763.

ILLYRIUS (MATTHIAS FLACIUS, or FRANCOWITZ), a most learned divine of the Augsburgh confession, was born, 1520, at Albona in Istria, anciently called Illyria. He was instructed in grammar and the classics by one Ignatius at Venice, till he was seventeen years of age; and afterwards became a good master in Greek and Hebrew. In 1541, having for some time conceived a strong dislike to the old religion, and being

[c] Anecdotes of Bowyer by Nichols, p. 130.
[D] Elizabeth, daughter of Thomas James, a benefactor to Sion-college library, and defendant of Dr. Thomas James, librarian of the Bodleian. She was born 1689, and died 1733.
[E] Vol. I. p. 637.

inclined

inclined to the Reformation, he went to Wittenberg, to finish his studies under Luther and Melancthon. The latter gave him a thousand proofs of his good-nature and generosity; but Illyrius, growing fanatical, strongly opposed the Interim, with all the pacific measures Melancthon had suggested; and also wrote with so much virulence against this excellent person, as to call him *Echidna Illyrica*. He had the chief direction of the "Centuriæ Magdeburgenses," and was the author of several learned works. He was indeed a man of excellent parts, very great learning, and of a just and well-grounded zeal against Popery; but at the same time of so restless, passionate, and quarrelsome a temper, as to overbalance all his good qualities, and raise innumerable disturbances among the Protestants. He died in 1575, very little, if at all, lamented.

IMBERT (JOHN), a learned advocate in France, was born at Rochelle, and, after serving the office of *lieutenant-criminel* at Fontenay-le-comte, died towards the end of the 16th century. He was considered as one of the most able practical lawyers of his time, and has left the following works as monuments of his learning. 1. "Enchiridion juris scripti Galliæ;" or "a Manual of written Law of France," 4to, 1559. It was translated into French by Théveneau. 2. "Institutiones forenses," or "The Practice of the Bar," 8vo, 1541. These books were formerly much consulted, and have been illustrated by learned commentators.

IMBERT (JOSEPH-GABRIEL), a painter of Marseilles, who studied some time under Vander-Meulen and Le Brun. Being disgusted with the world, at the age of 34, he entered into the order of St. Bruno: but the superiors of the order, perceiving his great talents in his art, encouraged him to exert them, and furnished him with opportunities. By their interest he was employed to paint for many societies of Carthusians, but the pictures most esteemed, are those which he executed for that of Ville-neuve, at Avignon, where he made his vows, and where he died, at the age of 83, in the year 1740. His most perfect picture is (or was) at the high altar of the Chartreux, at Marseilles. It is a canvas of unusual size, representing a view of Calvary. The design is full of taste, the colouring and contrasts highly picturesque, the expression just, with fine touches of the pathetic, and the whole executed with much good sense and propriety.

IMHOFF (JAMES-WILLIAM), a very famous genealogist, born of a noble family at Nuremberg, in 1651, was a lawyer in that city, and one of its senators. He was considered as having a singular and profound knowledge of the interests of princes, the revolutions of states, and the history of the principal families in Europe. He died in 1728. His works were,

were, 1. " Genealogiæ excellentium in Gallia familiarum," folio, Norimb. 1687. 2. " Genealogiæ familiarum Dellomaneriæ, &c." Norimb. 1688, folio. 3. " Hiftoria Genealogica Regum Magnæ Britanniæ," Norimb. folio, 1690. 4. " Notitia procerum S. R. imperii," Tubingen, 1693, folio. 5. " Hiftorica Italiæ et Hifpaniæ genealogica," Norimb. folio, 1701. 6. " Corpus Hiftoriæ genealogicæ Italiæ et Hifpaniæ," Norimb. folio, 1702. 7. " Recherches Hiftoriques et Genealogiques des Grands d'Efpagne," Amfterd. folio, 1708. 8. " Stemma regium Lufitanicum," folio, Amfterd. 1708. 9. " Genealogiæ 20 illuftrium in Hifpaniâ familiarum," folio, Leipfic, 1720.

IMPERIALI (JOHN BAPTIST), a celebrated phyfician, was born at Vicenza in 1568, of the noble family of his name, which is one of the twenty-four nobles of Genoa. He ftudied at Verona, and afterwards at Bologna, under Jerome Mercurialis and Frederic Pendofius. He made a great progrefs in the languages and the fciences, and became one of the moft able men of his time. He excelled particularly in philofophy and phyfic, which he taught with fuccefs at Padua. Upon his return to Vicenza, he practifed his profeffion with extraordinary reputation till his death, which happened in May, 1623, at 54 years of age. He was a fkilful writer in Latin, both of profe and verfe; and particularly imitated Catullus. There is by him a quarto volume, " Exercitationum exoticarum," Venice, 1607.

IMPERIALI (JOHN), fon of the former, was equally celebrated as a phyfician and as a writer. He was born in 1602. His two principal works were printed at Venice, in 1640, in one volume, namely, 1. " Mufeum Hiftoricum," a collection of hiftorical eulogies. 2. " Mufeum Phyficum, five de humano ingenio." He died in 1653.

IMPERIALI (GIUSEPPE-RENATO), born at Genoa in 1651, was chiefly celebrated for the magnificent library which was formed by him, and continues one of the ornaments of the city of Rome. He was employed by the popes in many important negotiations, and always conducted them with fuccefs. Being raifed to the dignity of cardinal, he was propofed in the conclave of 1730, as pope, and loft that nomination only by a fingle vote. He died in 1737, at the age of 86. A defcriptive catalogue of his library was publifhed at Rome in 1711, in folio, by Juftus Fontanini.

INCHOFER (MELCHIOR), a German Jefuit, born in 1584 at Vienna. In the beginning of his ftudies, he particularly applied himfelf to the law; and, being endowed with excellent parts, quickly furpaffed his fellow ftudents in that faculty. He had acquired the character of a good lawyer at the age of

E e 4

twenty-three years, when he refolved to enter among the Jefuits; for which purpofe he went to Rome, and enrolled himfelf a member of that fociety in 1607. Here turning his thoughts upon philofophy, mathematics, and divinity, he became mafter of thefe fciences; and afterwards taught them a great while at Meffina, where he publifhed a piece in 1630, entitled, " Epiftolæ B. Mariæ Virginis ad Meffanenfes veritas vindicata," or " The Bleffed Virgin Mary's Letter to the People of Meffina proved to be genuine," folio. This gave fo much offence, that complaints were made of it to the congregation of the Index at at Rome, whereupon he was fummoned before them; but the reafons he pleaded in defence of what he had advanced, gave fo much fatisfaction to the judges, that they ordered him only to alter the title, and, far from fuppreffing it, gave him leave to reprint it, with fuch alterations or additions as he thought proper. With this requifition he readily complied, and the fecond edition came out at Viterbo in 1633, entitled, " Conjectatio ad epiftolam beatiffimæ Mariæ Virginis ad Meffanenfes," " A Conjecture concerning the bleffed Virgin Mary's Letter to the People of Meffina." Inchofer, however, was not pleafed with the Jefuits, among whom he fuffered many difcontents; and, in revenge, wrote a fatire upon them, which was publifhed in 1648, in Holland, foon after his death, which happened that year at Milan. The title of it is, 2. " Monarchia folipforum." The author calls himfelf " Lucius Cornelius Europæus." Some maintain that the real author was Julius Scotti. He publifhed feveral other works, which fhew him to have been a very learned man, though tinctured with credulity. Thefe works are, 3. " Annalium Ecclefiafticorum regni Hungariæ, Tomus primus," folio, 1644; a book full of refearch. 4. " Hiftoria trium Magorum," 4to, 1639. Here he manifefts as little judgement as in his treatife on the Virgin's epiftle. 5. " De facra Latinitate," 4to, 1635.

INGUIMBERTI (Dominic, Joseph, Marie d'), an exemplary and learned bifhop of Carpentras, at which place he was born in 1683. He was firft a Dominican, and in that order he fuccefsfully purfued his theological ftudies; but, thinking the rule of the Ciftertians more ftrict and perfect, he afterwards took the habit of that order. His merit quickly raifed him to the moft diftinguifhed offices among his brethren, and being difpatched on fome bufinefs to Rome, he completely gained the confidence and efteem of Clement XII. By that prelate he was named archbifhop of Theodofia in partibus, and bifhop of Carpentras in 1733. In this fituation he was diftinguifhed by all the virtues that can characterize a Chriftian bifhop; excellent difcernment, and knowledge, united with the completeft charity and humility. His life was that of a fimple monk, and his
wealth

wealth was all employed to relieve the poor, or ferve the public. He built a vaft and magnificent hofpital, and eftablifhed the moft extenfive library thofe provinces had ever feen, which he gave for public ufe. He died in 1757, of an apopleftic attack, in his 75th year. This excellent man was not unknown in the literary world, having publifhed fome original works, and fome editions of other authors. The principal of thefe productions are, 1. " Genuinus charaċter Reverendi admodùm in Chrifto Patris D. Armandi Johannis Butillierii Rancæi," 4to, 1718, at Rome. 2. An Italian tranflation of a book, entitled, " Theologie Religieufe," being a treatife on the duties of a monaftic life, 3 vols. folio, Rome, 1731. 3. An Italian tranflation of a French treatife, by father Didier, on the infallibility of the pope, folio, Rome, 1732. 4. An edition of the works of Bartholomew des Martyrs, with his life, 2 vols. folio. 5. " La Vie feparée," another treatife on monaftic life, in 2 vols. 4to, 1727.

INGULPHUS, was born at London in 1030[r], and educated at Weftminfter and Oxford, in which latter place he became particularly attached to the ftudy of Ariftotle and Cicero. His father, having fome employment at the court of Edward the Confeffor, introduced his fon Ingulphus to queen Editha, with whom he frequently converfed. In 1051 he went over to Normandy, where he was gracioufly received by William, duke of that country, who made him his fecretary. In 1064 he went in an expedition to the Holy Land, and after his return became a Benedictine in the monaftery of Fontanelle in Normandy, where he was foon after elected prior. In 1076, William, now king of England, fent for Ingulphus, and appointed him abbot of Croyland. In this fituation he continued many years, in high favour with the king, and archbifhop Lanfranc. He rebuilt the monaftery of Croyland, and obtained for it many privileges. Du Pin fays, that fome time before his death, he obtained leave to retire from the abbey, but his authority for this affertion is dubious. Ingulphus died in 1109. There is extant by him, a hiftory of the monaftery over which he prefided, entitled, " Hiftoria monafterii Croylandenfis, ab anno 664 ad 1091," publifhed among the " 5 Scriptores," by fir H. Saville, London, 1596, folio. It was alfo printed at Frankfort, in 1601, and at Oxford in 1684, and the laft is the moft complete of the three editions.

INNOCENT III. (properly LOTHARIO CONTI), one of the popes diftinguifhed for learning and talents. He was a native of Anagni, of the family of the counts of Segui, and born in 1161. The fame of his learning raifed him to the dignity of cardinal, and he was raifed to the papacy in 1198, as fucceffor to Celeftin III. The power and influence of this pope,

[r] Berkenhout's Biographia Literaria, p. 9.

who had abilities to take advantage of the difposition of the times, were very great. He encouraged the crufades to the Holy Land, he excited one againft the unfortunate Albigenfes in Languedoc, he put the kingdom of Philip Auguftus of France under interdict, and excommunicated king John of England, and Raimond count of Touloufe. He obtained the fovereignty of feveral places in Italy, which had not been fubject to his predeceffors; and greatly extended his authority even in the city of Rome itfelf. Innocent convened the fourth Lateran council, in which were paffed feveral important regulations. One of thefe was a canon forbidding to increafe the number of religious orders, left they fhould introduce confufion into the church: neverthelefs, the Dominicans, the Francifcans, and fome others, originated under his pontificate. Innocent died in 1216.

From his youth, Innocent had been diftinguifhed for his abilities, and fome proofs of them are ftill extant. 1. Two folio volumes of letters by him, were publifhed in 1680, by Baluze; but whatever merit they may have of a theological or moral kind, they are not diftinguifhed for their ftyle. 2. There is a work of his in three books, entitled, " De contemptu mundi, five de miferia humanæ conditionis," which has been feveral times publifhed. 3. Finally, his works were publifhed collectively at Cologn, in 1575. The profe hymn of the Romifh church, beginning " Veni fanctè fpiritus," was compofed by him; and other hymns have been afcribed to him of which he was not the author, among which is the " Stabat Mater," which was written by Todi.

INVEGES (Augustino), a Sicilian Jefuit, and a celebrated hiftorian and antiquary, was born in 1595. Little is known of him, except the works he produced; which were, 1. " Il Palermo antico facro et nobile, et Annali della felice città di Palermo," 3 vols. folio, publifhed in 1649. 2. " Hiftoria Paradifi terreftris," 4to, 1641. 3. " La Cartagine Siciliana," which was the hiftory of the city of Caccamo. This was printed at Palermo, in 1651, 4to. In this work he jocularly alludes to the horrid Sicilian Vefpers, giving the people of Caccamo and Palermo the honour of finging the firft ftrain in them, as he expreffes it. He died in 1677.

JOAN (Pope), called by Platina, John VIII. having obtained a place in the hiftory of the popes, deferves to fill an article in thefe memoirs, notwithftanding her very exiftence is at leaft uncertain. This fubject has been treated with as much animofity on both fides, between the Papifts and the Proteftants, as if the whole of religion depended on it. There are reckoned upwards of fixty of the Romifh communion, and among them feveral monks and canonized faints, by whom the ftory is related thus:

About

About the middle of the ninth century, viz. between the pontificates of Leo IV. and Benedict III. [G] a woman, call'd Joan, was promoted to the pontificate, by the name of John; whom Platina, and almost all other historians, have reckoned as the VIIIth of that name, and others as the VIIth: some call her only John. This female pope was born at Mentz, where she went by the name of English John [H]; whether because she was of English extraction, or for what other reason, is not known: some modern historians say she was called Agnes, that is, the chaste, by way of irony, perhaps, before her pontificate. She had from her infancy an extraordinary passion for learning and travelling, and in order to satisfy this inclination, put on men's clothes, and went to Athens, in company with one of her friends, whom the scandalous Chronicle calls her favourite Lover. From Athens she went to Rome, where she taught divinity; and, in the garb of a doctor, acquired so great reputation for understanding, learning, and probity, that she was unanimously elected pope in the room of Leo IV [I].

Hitherto there is nothing in this story but what does great honour to Joan, and the fair sex in general; but several modern historians add many particulars of a more delicate nature. They pretend, that Joan carried her gratitude too far towards this friend, to whose assistance she owed her advancement in learning; and that he, on his side, as much struck by the beauties of her person as by those of her mind, taught her somewhat more than mere Greek and philosophy. This commerce, however, might have remained a secret, had it not been for an unlucky accident: Joan, mistaken, without doubt, in her reckoning, ventured to go to a procession, where she had the misfortune to be brought to bed in the middle of the street, between the Colosseum and the church of St. Clement. History, or fable, says she died there: whether of her pains, or out of grief at having so badly concerted her measures, is what we are left to guess. To whatever it might be owing, Joan, it is said, died in labour, after having held the pontifical see about two years. It is pretended, that whenever the most holy father passes by this fatal spot, he never fails to turn his head aside, in token of his abhorrence of what happened there [K]: and an author, whose testimony ought not to be suspected in these matters, assures us, that the marble statue, which was to be seen

[G] See Moreri. N. B. Blondel, Desmarets, and Bayle, are the chief of those who absolutely denied it. Spanheim, L'Enfant des Vignolles, among those who have affirmed it.

[H] Her true name was Gilberta, and it is said she took the name of English, or Anglus, from Anglus, a monk of the abbey of Fulda, whom she loved, and who was her instructor, and travelled with her. Crespin's L'etat de l'English.

[I] Marianus Scotus, Chron. l. iii. Ætat 6, ad ann. 854.

[K] Id. & Sigebert's Chronogr. made the same year.

in his time in the very place, was originally set up there as a monument of the fact [L]. As an appendage to this story, we are told of a pierced chair in which the popes elect were afterwards obliged to sit, to preclude such another mistake by actual examination. This ceremony has, at all events, been long discontinued.

Such is the story, with its most curious circumstances, as related in the history of the popes. It was certainly received and avowed as a truth for some centuries. Since it became a matter of dispute, some writers of the Romish church have denied it; some have apologized for it absurdly enough; others in a way that might be admitted, did not that church claim to be infallible: for it was that claim which first brought the truth of this history under examination. The Protestants alledged it as a clear proof against the claim; since it could not be denied that, in this instance, the church was deceived by a woman in disguise. This put the Roman Catholics upon searching more narrowly than before into the affair; and the result of that enquiry was, first a doubt, and next an improbability, of Joan's real existence. This led to a further inquiry into the origin of the story; whence it appeared, that there were no footsteps of its being known in the church for 200 years after it was said to have happened [M]. Æneas Sylvius, who was pope in the 15th century, under the name of Pius II. was the first who called it in question, and he touched it but slightly, and as it were with fear; observing, that in the election of that woman there was no error in a matter of faith, but only an ignorance as to a matter of fact: and also, that the story was not certain. Yet this very Sylvius suffered Joan's name to be placed among those of the other popes in the register of Siena, and transcribed the story in his historical work printed at Nuremburg in 1493. The example of Sylvius emboldened others to search more freely into the matter, who, finding it to have no good foundation, thought proper to give it up.

But this did not silence the Protestants. On the contrary, they thought themselves the more obliged to labour in support of it, as an indelible blot and reproach upon their adversaries; and to aggravate the matter, several circumstances were mentioned with the view of exposing the credulity and weakness of that church, which, it was maintained, had authorized them. In this spirit it was observed, not only that Joan, being installed in her office, admitted others into orders, after the manner of other popes; made priests and deacons, ordained bishops and

---

[L] Theodoric à Niem in lib. de privil. & juribus imperf.

[M] Marianus is the first who mentions it, and he lived 200 years after,

Blondel's Eclaircissm. de la question : Si une femme à esté assise au siege papal, p. 17.

abbots, fung mafs, confecrated churches and altars, adminiftered the facraments, prefented her feet to be kiffed, and performed all other actions which the popes of Rome are wont to do: but, that whilft fhe was thus in poffeffion of that high dignity, fhe was got with child by a certain cardinal, a chaplain of hers, who knew very well of what fex fhe was; that fhe was delivered and died as before related; that on account of fuch fin, and becaufe fhe was thus delivered in public, fhe was deprived of all the honours which are ufed to be paid to the popes, and buried without any pontifical pomp; and that the fearching-chair, now no longer in ufe, had been laid afide, becaufe the popes, while they are cardinals, give fo many unqueftionable proufs of their virility, that there is no longer any occafion for fo holy a ceremony.

This ftory of pope Joan, in the church of Rome, is well matched by that of the Nag's-head confecration of archbifhop Parker, at the Reformation in England; and the difputes concerning them, between the two churches, are little worth maintaining with much eagernefs or animofity.

JOACHIM, abbot of Corazzo, and afterwards of Flora in Calabria, diftinguifhed for his pretended prophecies, and remarkable opinions, was born at Celico near Cofenza, in the year 1130. He was of the Ciftertian order, and had feveral monafteries fubject to his jurifdiction, which he directed with the utmoft wifdom and regularity. He was revered by the multitude as a perfon divinely infpired, and even equal to the moft illuftrious of the ancient prophets. Many of his predictions were formerly circulated, and indeed are ftill extant, having paffed through feveral editions, and received illuftration from feveral commentators. He taught erroneous notions refpecting the holy Trinity, which amounted fully to tritheifin; but what is more extraordinary, he taught that the morality of the Gofpel is imperfect, and that a better and more complete law is to be given by the Holy Ghoft, which is to be everlafting. Thefe reveries gave birth to a book attributed to Joachim, entitled, " The Everlafting Gofpel," or " The Gofpel of the Holy Ghoft." It is not to be doubted, fays Mofheim, " that Joachim was the author of various predictions, and that he, in a particular manner, foretold the reformation of the church, of which he might fee the abfolute neceffity. It is however certain, that the greater part of the predictions and writings, which were formerly attributed to him, were compofed by others. This we may affirm even of the *Everlafting Gofpel*, the work undoubtedly of fome obfcure, filly, and vifionary monk, who thought proper to adorn his reveries with the celebrated name of Joachim, in order to gain them credit, and render them more agreeable to the multitude. The title of this fenfelefs production is taken from Rev. xiv. 6. and it contained three books. The first was entitled, *Liber concordiæ veritatis*, or the book of the harmony of truth: the second, *Apocalypsis nova*, or new revelation ; and the third, *Psalterium decem Chordarum*. This account was taken from a MS. of that work in the library of the Sorbonne[N]." It is necessary, we should observe, to distinguish this book from the " Introduction to the Everlasting Gospel," written by a friar named Gerhard, and published in 1250. Joachim died in 1202, leaving a number of followers who were called Joachimites. His works have been published in folio, Venice, 1516, &c. and contain propositions which have been condemned by several councils. The part of his works most esteemed is his commentaries on *Isaiah*, *Jeremiah*, and *the Apocalypse*. His life was written by a Dominican named Gervaise, and published in 1745, in 2 vols. 12mo.

JOBERT (LOUIS), a pious and learned Jesuit, was a native of Paris, where he was born in 1647. He taught polite literature in his own order, and distinguished himself as a preacher. He died at Paris in 1719, at the age of 72. There are several tracts of piety of his writing, besides a piece entitled, " La Science des Medailles," in good esteem; of which the best edition is that of Paris, in 1739, 2 vols. 12mo.

JODELLE (STEPHEN), lord of Limodin, was born, in 1532, at Paris, and so much distinguished himself by his talents for poetry, as to be one of the Pleiades[o], so named by Ronsard. He was the first French poet who wrote comedies and tragedies in his own language. His tragedies had chorusses in the manner of the Greek stage; and though very imperfect, were then greatly admired. His Cleopatra having been acted before the king with vast applause, Ronsard and other poets, in a bacchanalian frolic, meeting with a goat, presented it, with a kind of humorous solemnity, to Jodelle; in imitation of the ancients, who sacrificed a goat to Bacchus, as the patron of tragedy. But this act of homage was deemed very profane and heathenish by the clergy of the time. Besides poetry, Jodelle had other accomplishments. He was an orator; well skilled in architecture, sculpture, and painting; and a good master of the sword, which he always wore, having a right to it as a gentleman. In his younger years he embraced the reformed religion, and lived at Geneva, where he wrote one night, extempore, (for he had a wonderful talent of that kind) 100 Latin verses, in which he described the mass, with strong sarcasms. But he returned ere long, to Paris, and to that mass which he he had so much cried down in his Latin verses. Hence the

[N] Mosheim, Vol. III. p. 83.
[O] That is, seven principal French poets, according to the number of the stars in that constellation.

Huguenots

Huguenots probably called him an impious man, and even
an atheist ; epithets that must unavoidably be fixed upon him by
the thirty sonnets, which he made immediately after the maffacre on St. Bartholomew's day, in order to charge their minifters with being the caufe of the executions, murders, and wars,
which had raged in France fince the beginning of the Reformation. He is faid to have received for thefe fonnets a large fum
of money [P]. He might have been fupported by royal patronage, but neglected his intereft at court, and died very poor
in 1573, aged 41. In 1574, his friends publifhed a volume of
his works, which contains two tragedies, " Cleopatra," and
" Dido ;" a comedy named " Eugene ;" befides fongs, fonnets,
odes, elegies, &c.

JOHN of Salifbury, an Englifhman, bifhop of Chartres,
and one of the moft learned men in the twelfth century. In
his youth he lived with Peter de Celles, abbot of St. Rheims,
as his clerk ; but leaving the abbot for fome time, he went to
finifh his ftudies at Paris, where he was fupported by the liberality of Theobald IV. furnamed the Great, count of Champagne in France. In this univerfity he took his doctor's degree,
and afterwards went to Rome to make his devoirs to pope Adrian
his countryman, who received him very gracioufly, and fhewed
him feveral marks of friendfhip. From Rome he returned to
Paris, where he eftablifhed a fchool ; and among other fcholars
had the honour of teaching the learned Peter de Blois. After
fome time, he took a voyage to England, where he was entertained by Theobald, archbifhop of Canterbury ; and, after the
death of that prelate, lived with Thomas à Becket, his fucceffor, whofe companion he was till the death of the latter. In
1177, he was chofen bifhop of Chartres by the clergy of that
diocefe. This promotion was obtained by the recommendation
of Louis the Young, king of France, and the folicitation of
his friend William of Champagne, fon of Theobald IV. who
had been tranflated from that fee to the metropolitan chair of
Sens. Thefe friends were probably procured by his patron
Thomas à Becket, to whofe merits he always afcribed his election [Q]. He governed this church with admirable prudence ;
and, having affifted at the council of Lateran in 1179, died two
years after. He wrote feveral books, which are loft. Thofe
which remain, are his " Life of St. Thomas of Canterbury ;"
" A Collection of Letters ;" and his " Polycraticon," or " De-
nugis Curialium, & veftigiis philofophorum, Libri octo, &c."

[P] Memoirs de l'eftat de France,
Tom. I.
[Q] This be expreffed by an infcrip-
tion upon the greateft part of his letters,

In thefe terms : " Joannes, divina miferra-
tione, & meritis S. Thomæ martyri., Car-
potenfis ecclefiæ minifter humilis, &c.

JOHNSON

JOHNSON (SAMUEL), an Englifh divine of remarkable learning and fleadinefs in fuffering for the principles of the Revolution in 1688. He was born in 1649, in Warwickfhire; and being put to St. Paul's fchool in London, fludied with fuch fuccefs and reputation, that as foon as he was fit for the univerfity, he was made keeper of the library to that fchool. In this ftation he applied himfelf to the Oriental languages, in which he made great progrefs. He was of Trinity-college, Cambridge, but left the univerfity without taking a degree. He entered into orders, and was prefented by a friend, in 1669-70, to the rectory of Corringham in Effex. This living, which was worth no more than 80l. a year, happened to be the only church preferment he ever had: and, as the air of the place did not agree with him, he placed a curate upon the fpot, and fettled himfelf at London: a fituation fo much the more agreeable to him, as he had a ftrong difpofition for politics, and had even made fome progrefs in that ftudy, before he was prefented to this living.

The times were turbulent: the duke of York declaring himfelf a Papift, his fucceffion to the crown began to be warmly oppofed; and this brought the doctrine of indefeafible hereditary right into difpute, which was ftrongly difrelifhed by Johnfon, who was naturally of no fubmiffive temper [a]. This inclination was early obferved by his patron, who warned him againft the danger of it to one of his profeffion; and advifed him, if he would turn his thoughts to that fubject, to read Bracton and Fortefcue " de laudibus legum Angliæ," &c. that fo he might be acquainted with the old Englifh conftitution; but by no means to make politics the fubject of his fermons, for that matters of faith and practice furmed more fuitable admonitions from the pulpit. Johnfon, it is faid, religioufly obferved this advice; and though, by applying himfelf to the ftudy of the books recommended to him, he became well verfed in the Englifh conftitution; yet he made a proper ufe of this knowledge, and never introduced it in his fermons.

[a] Of this truth we cannot have a ftronger evidence, than from himfelf. In a piece printed 1689, fpeaking of bifhop Burnet's Paftoral Letter, publifhed a little before, in order to place king William's right to the crown upon conqueft, he expreffes himfelf thus: " I will prefently join iffue with this conquering bifhop, for I have not been afraid of a conqueror thefe 18 years; for fo long fince I ufed to walk by the New-Exchange-gate, where ftood an overgrown porter with his gown and ftaff, giving him a refemblance of authority, whofe bufinefs it was to regulate the coachmen before the entrance; and would make nothing of lifting a coachman off his box, and beating him, and throwing him into his box again. I have feveral times looked up at this tall meddening fellow, and put the cafe: Suppofe this conqueror fhould take me up under his arm, like a giffard, and run away with me; am I his fubject? No, thought I, I am my own, and not his; and, having thus invaded me, if I could not otherwife refcue myfelf from him, I would fmite him under the fifth rib. The application is eafy." Tract concerning king James's abrogation. In our author's works, p. 207, 208.

But

But he employed his difcourfes with zeal to expofe the ab-
furdity and mifchief of the Popifh religion, which was then too
much encouraged, and would, he thought, unavoidably be eftablifhed, if the next heir to the crown was not fet afide. This
point he laboured inceffantly in his private converfation, and
became fo good a mafter of the arguments for it, that the oppofers of the court, gave him fuitable encouragement to proceed. The earl of Effex admitted him into his company; and
lord William Ruffel, refpecting his parts and probity, made him
his domeftic chaplain. This preferment fet him in a confpicuous point of view; and in 1679, he was appointed to preach
before the mayor and aldermen at Guildhall-chapel, on Palm-
Sunday. He took that opportunity of preaching againft Popery; and from this time, he tells us himfelf, " he threw away
his liberty with both hands, and with his eyes open, for his
country's fervice [s]." In fhort, he began to be regarded by his
party, as their immoveable bulwark; and to make good that
character, while the bill of exclufion was carried on by his patron, at the head of that party in the houfe of commons, his
chaplain, to promote the fame caufe, engaged the ecclefiaftical
champion of paffive obedience, Dr. Hickes [t], in a book entitled, " Julian the Apoflate, &c." publifhed in 1682. This
tract being written to expofe the doctrine, then generally received, of paffive obedience, was anfwered by Dr. Hickes, in a
piece entitled, " Jovian, &c." to which Johnfon drew up a
reply, under the title of " Julian's Arts to undermine and extirpate Chriftianity, &c." This was printed and entered at Stationers-hall, 1683, in order to be publifhed; but, feeing his
patron lord Ruffel feized and imprifoned, Johnfon thought proper
to check his zeal, and take the advice of his friends in fuppref-
ing it.

The court however, having information of it, he was fummoned, about two months after lord Ruffel was beheaded, to
appear before the king and council, where the lord keeper
North examined him upon thefe points: 1. " Whether he was
the author of a book called ' Julian's Arts and Methods to undermine and extirpate Chriftianity?" To which, having anfwered in the affirmative, he was afked, " Why, after the book
had been fo long entered at Stationers-hall, it was not publifhed?"
To which he replied, " That the nation was in too great a
ferment to have the matter further debated at that time." Upon
this he was commanded to produce one of thofe books to the
council, being told that it fhould be publifhed if they approved
it; but he anfwered, " he had fuppreffed them himfelf, fo that

[s] Abrogation of king James, &c.
p. 264.
[t] Dr. Hickes's production here attacked, was a fermon preached before the
lord-mayor in 1681, and publifhed in
1682.

VOL. VIII. F f they

they were now his own private thoughts, for which he was not accountable to any power upon earth." The council then dismissed him; but he was sent for twice afterwards, and the same things pressed upon him, to which he returned the same answers, and they sent him prisoner to the Gatehouse. His warrant of commitment was dated Aug. 3, 1683; and signed by sir Leoline Jenkins, one of the privy-council, and principal secretary of state. He was bailed out of prison by two friends, and the court used all possible means to discover the book; but, being disappointed in the search, recourse was had to promises, and a considerable sum, besides the favour of the court, was offered for one of the copies, to the person in whose hands they were supposed to be lodged. This was refused; and as neither threats nor promises prevailed, the court was obliged to drop the prosecution upon that book, and an information against Johnson was lodged in the King's-bench, for writing "Julian the Apostate, &c." The prosecution was begun and carried on by the interest of the duke of York. The following was one of the first of the passages on which the information was founded; " And therefore, I much wonder at those men who trouble the nation at this time of day, with the unseasonable prescription of prayers and tears, and the passive obedience of the Thebean legion, and such-like last remedies, which are proper only at such a time as the laws of our country are armed against our religion." The attack of this apparently innocent sentence gives a strong idea of the violence of the times.

When Mr. Johnson was brought to trial, he employed Mr. Wallop as his counsel, who urged for his client, that he had offended against no law of the land; that the book, taken together, was innocent; but that any treatise might be made criminal, if treated as those who drew up the information had treated this. The judges had orders to proceed in the cause, and the chief justice Jeffries upbraided Johnson for meddling with what did not belong to him; and scoffingly told him, that he would give him a text, which was, " Let every man study to be quiet, and mind his own business:" to which Johnson replied, that he did mind his business as an Englishman, when he wrote that book. He was condemned, however, in a fine of 500 marks, and committed prisoner to the King's-bench till he should pay it. Here he lay in very necessitous circumstances, it being reckoned criminal to visit or shew him any kindness; so that few had the courage to come near him, or give him any relief; by which means he was reduced very low. Notwithstanding which, when his mother, whom he had maintained for many years, sent to him for subsistence, such was his filial affection, that though he knew not how to supply his own wants, and those of his wife and children, and was told on this occasion, that " charity begins

al

at home," he fent her forty fhillings, though he had but fifty in the world, faying, he would do his duty, and truft providence for his own fupply. The event fhewed, that his hopes were not vain; for the next morning he received 10l. by an unknown hand, which he knew afterwards to have been fent by Dr. Fowler, afterwards bifhop of Gloucefter.

Having, by the bonds of himfelf and two friends, obtained the liberty of the rules, he was enabled to incur ftill further dangers, by printing fome pieces againft Popery in 1685, and difperfing feveral of them about the country at his own expence. Thefe being anfwered in three Obfervators by fir Roger L'Eftrange, who alfo, difcovering the printer, feized all the copies that were in his hands, Johnfon took care to have a paper pofted up everywhere, entitled, "A Parcel of wry Reafons and wrong Inferences, but right Obfervator." Upon the encampment of the army the following year, 1686, on Hounflow-heath, he drew up, "An humble and hearty Addrefs to all the Proteftants in the prefent Army, &c." He had difperfed about 1000 copies of this paper, when the reft of the impreffion was feized, and himfelf committed to clofe cuftody, to undergo a fecond trial at the King's-bench; where he was condemned to ftand in the pillory in Palace-yard, Weftminfter, Charingcrofs, and the Old Exchange, to pay a fine of 500 marks, and to be whipped from Newgate to Tyburn, after he had been degraded from the priefthood. This laft ought to have been done according to the canons, by his own diocefan, the bifhop of London, Dr. Compton; but that prelate being then under fufpenfion himfelf, (for not obeying the king's order to fufpend Dr. Sharp, afterwards archbifhop of York, for preaching againft Popery in his own parifh church of St. Giles's in the Fields) Dr. Crew, bifhop of Durham, Dr. Sprat, bifhop of Rochefter, and Dr. White, bifhop of Peterborough, who were then commiffioners for the diocefe of London, were appointed to degrade Mr. Johnfon. This they performed in the chapter-houfe of St. Paul's, where Dr. Sherlock, and other clergymen attended; but Dr. Stillingfleet, then dean of St. Paul's, refufed to be prefent. Johnfon's behaviour on this occafion was obferved to be fo becoming that character of which his enemies would have deprived him, that it melted fome of their hearts, and forced them to acknowledge, that there was fomething very valuable in him. Among other things which he faid to the divines then prefent, he told them, in the moft pathetic manner, "It could not but grieve him to think, that, fince all he had wrote was defigned to keep their gowns on their backs, they fhould be made the unhappy inftruments to pull off his: and he begged them to confider, whether they were not making rods for themfelves." When they came to the formality of putting a Bible in his hand and taking it from him again, he was much affected, and parted from it with difficulty, kissed it, and said, with tears, "That they could not, however, deprive him of the use and benefit of that sacred depositum." It happened, that they were guilty of an omission, in not stripping him of his cassock; which, as slight a circumstance as it may seem, rendered his degradation imperfect, and afterwards saved him his living [v].

A Popish priest made an offer for 200l. to get the whipping part of the sentence remitted: the money was lodged, by one of Johnson's friends, in a third hand, for the priest, if he performed what he undertook. The man used his endeavours, but to no purpose; the king was deaf to all intreaties: the answer was, "That since Mr. Johnson had the spirit of martyrdom, it was fit he should suffer." Accordingly, Dec. 1, 1686, the sentence was rigorously put in execution; which yet he bore with great firmness, and went through even with alacrity. He observed afterwards, to an intimate friend, that this text of Scripture, which came suddenly into his mind, "He endured the cross, despising the shame," so much animated and supported him in his bitter journey, that, had he not thought it would have looked like vain-glory, he could have sung a psalm, while the executioner was doing his office, with as much composure and chearfulness as ever he had done in the church; though at the same time he had a quick sense of every stripe which was given him, to the number of 317, with a whip of nine cords knotted. This was the more remarkable in him, because he had not the least tincture of enthusiasm [x]. The truth is, he was endued with a natural hardiness of temper to a great degree; and being inspirited by an eager desire to suffer for the cause he had espoused, he was enabled to support himself with the firmness of a martyr. After the execution of this sentence, the king gave away his living; and the clergyman who had the grant of it, made application to the three bishops above-mentioned for institution; but they, being sensible of his imperfect degradation, would not grant it without a bond of indemnity; after which, when he went to Corringham for induction, the parishioners opposed him, so that he could never obtain entrance, but was obliged to return re infecta. Mr. Johnson thus kept his living, and with it, his resolution also to oppose the measures of the court; insomuch, that, before he was out of the surgeon's hands, he reprinted 3000 copies of his "Comparison between Popery and Paganism." These, however, were not then published; but not long

---

[v] He came with it on to the pillory, where Mr. Rouse, the under-sheriff, tore it off, and put a slighter coat upon him. Report of the committee in 1689.

[x] Excepting this, he seems to have been cast in much such a mould as John Lilburn; to whom he bore a great resemblance, both in the hardiness of his temper, and in the quarrelsomeness of it.

after, about the time of the general toleration, he publifhed,
" The Trial and Examination of a late Libel, &c." which was
followed by others every year till the Revolution. The parliament afterwards, taking his cafe into confideration, refolved,
June 11, 1689, that the judgement againft him in the King's-
bench, upon an information for a mifdemeanor, was cruel and
illegal ; and a committee was at the fame time appointed to
bring in a bill for reverfing that judgement. Being alfo ordered
to enquire how Mr. Johnfon came to be degraded, and by what
authority it was done, Mr. Chrifty, the chairman, fome days
after reported his cafe, by which it appears, that a libel was then
exhibited againft him, charging him with great mifdemeanors,
though none were fpecified or proved ; that he demanded a copy
of the libel, and an advocate, both which were denied : that he
protefled againft the proceedings, as contrary to law and the
132d canon, not being done by his own diocefan, but his pro-
teflation was refufed, as was alfo his appeal to the king in chancery ; and that Mrs. Johnfon had alfo an information exhibited
againft her, for the like matter as that againft her hufband. The
committee came to the following refolutions, which were all
agreed to by the houfe, " That the judgement againft Mr. Johnfon was illegal and cruel : that the ecclefiaftical commiffion was
illegal, and confequently, the fufpenfion of the bifhop of London,
and the authority committed to three bifhops, null and illegal :
that Mr. Johnfon's not being degraded by his own diocefan, if
he had deferved it, was illegal : that a bill be brought in, to
reverfe the judgement, and to declare all the proceedings before
the three bifhops null and illegal : and that an addrefs be made
to his majefty, to recommend Mr. Johnfon to fome ecclefiaftical
preferment, fuitable to his fervices and fufferings." The houfe
prefented two addreffes to the king, in behalf of Mr. Johnfon ;
and, accordingly, the deanery of Durham was offered him,
which however he refufed, as an unequal reward for his fervices.

The truth is, he was his own chief enemy ; and his difap-
pointment, in his expectations of preferment, was the effect of
his own temper and conduct. For, with very good abilities,
confiderable learning, and great clearnefs, ftrength, and vivacity of
fentiment and expreffion, of which his writings are a fufficient
evidence ; and with a firmnefs of mind capable of fupporting the
fevereft trials, for any caufe which he confidered as important, he
was paffionate, impatient of contradiction, felf-opinionated, haughty, apt to overrate his own fervices, and undervalue thofe of others,
whofe advancement above himfelf was an infupportable mortifi-
cation to him. The roughnefs of his temper, and turbulency of
his genius, rendered him alfo unfit for the higher ftations of the
church, of which he was immoderately ambitious. Not being

able

able to obtain a bishopric, lady Ruffel made use of the influence she had with Dr. Tillotfon, to folicit a penfion for him [7]; whereupon king William granted him 300l. a year out of the poft-office, for his own and his fon's life, with 1000l. in money, and a place of 100l. a year for his fon.

Violence produces violence; and his enemies were fo much exafperated againft him, that his life was frequently endangered. After publifhing his famous tract, entitled, " An Argument proving that the Abrogation of King James, &c." which was levelled againft all thofe who complied with the Revolution upon any other principles than his own, in 1692, a remarkable attempt was actually made upon him. Seven affaffins broke into his houfe in Bond-ftreet, Nov. 27, very early in the morning; and five of them, with a lantern, got into his chamber, where he, with his wife and young fon, were in bed. Mr. Johnfon was faft afleep, but his wife, being awaked by their opening the door, cried out, Thieves; and endeavoured to awaken her hufband: the villains, in the mean time, threw open the curtains, three of them placed themfelves on that fide of the bed where he lay, with drawn fwords and clubs, and two ftood at the bed's feet, with piftols. Mr. Johnfon ftarted up; and, endeavouring to defend himfelf from their affaults, received a blow on the head, which knocked him backwards. His wife cried out with great earneftnefs, and begged them not to treat a fick man with fuch barbarity; upon which they paufed a little, and one of the mifcreants called to Mr. Johnfon to hold up his face, which his wife begged him to do, thinking they only defigned to gag him, and that they would rifle the houfe and be gone. Upon this he fat upright; when one of the rogues cried, " Piftol him for the book he wrote;" which difcovered their defign; for it was juft after the publifhing of the book laft mentioned. Whilft he fat upright in his bed, one of them cut him with a fword over the eye-brow, and the reft prefented their piftols at him; but, upon Mrs. Johnfon's paffionate intreaties, they went off without doing him further mifchief, or rifling the houfe. A furgeon was immediately fent for, who found two wounds in his head, and his body much bruifed. With due care, however, he recovered; and, though his health was much impaired and broken by this and other troubles, yet he handled his pen with the fame unbroken fpirit as before. He died in May, 1703.

In 1710, all his treatifes were collected, and publifhed in one folio volume; to which were prefixed, fome memorials of his life. The fecond edition came out in 1713, folio.

[7] Tillotfon laboured the matter very heartily, though Johnfon continued abufing him and reviling him all the time. While he was in prifon alfo, Tillotfon had sent him 50l. which, though his neceffities obliged him to accept, yet he did it with an air of the utmoft contempt. Birch's Life of Tillotfon, p. 201.

JOHNSON (JOHN), a learned divine among the Nonjurors, was born, 1662, at Frindsbury near Rochester, of which place his father was vicar. After acquiring his classical literature at Canterbury-school, he was sent to Magdalen-college, Cambridge, in 1677; and, in 1682, removed to Benet or Corpus-Christi, of which he became fellow in 1685. In 1686, he received priest's orders: and, the year after, was presented by archbishop Sancroft to the vicarages of Baston and Heron-hill near Canterbury. In this neighbourhood were two Popish families of good estates, which made him apprehensive about his parishioners: but his fears were dissipated by the Revolution, to which he was then a hearty well-wisher. In 1694, he published, but without his name, " An Answer to Mr. Henry Wharton's Defence of Pluralities;" with which queen Mary was said to be exceedingly pleased. In 1697, archbishop Tenison placed him at Margate; but, because that benefice was small, added the vicarage of Apuldre, on which he resided altogether, giving up Margate in 1703.

About 1705, was printed the first volume of, what may be deemed his capital work, " The Clergyman's Vade-Mecum;" large additions were made to it in 1707, and a second volume was printed in 1709; both in 12mo. As a continuation of his work, he published, in 1720, " A Collection of Ecclesiastical Laws, Canons, &c." 2 vols. 12mo.

The nation was now much heated in the business of Sacheverell; and Johnson in particular, was so over-heated, that he forsook not only his old principles, but all his old friends and acquaintance, to whom he would scarce pay even common civility. The clergy, however, had an high opinion of his learning and abilities; and he was twice, in 1710 and 1713, chosen proctor in convocation for the diocese of Canterbury. The latter year, he published, " The Unbloody Sacrifice and Altar unveiled and supported;" in which treatise he paid a singular deference to the judgement of Dr. Hickes. From an attachment to this divine, he soon grew, not only to have a mean opinion of the articles and liturgy of the Church of England, but to entertain also unfavourable thoughts of the Protestant succession, for which he had formerly been so zealous. He even denied the king's supremacy, and refused to read the customary prayers on the accession of George I. This refusal brought him into some difficulties; and he was at last forced to submit. Having once admitted the spirit of contumacy, he continued to the end of his life self-willed, restless, and unhappy. He died Dec. 15, 1725. Besides what we have mentioned, he published several tracts of a smaller kind, upon religious subjects.

In 1689, he married Margaret, the daughter of Thomas Jenkin, gent. of the ise of Thanet, and half-sister of Dr. Robert Jenkin, master of St. John's-college in Cambridge. He had some children; and among them a son, who died in 1723, after having been fellow of the above college, and rector of Standish in Lancashire.

JOHNSON, or JANSEN (CORNELIUS), an excellent painter, both in miniature and full size, but particularly admired in portraits. He was a native of Amsterdam, where he resided many years; but coming to England in the reign of James I. he drew several fine portraits of that monarch, and most of his court. He lived also in the time of Charles I; and was contemporary with Vandyck, whose greater fame soon eclipsed that of Jansen; though it must be owned his pictures had more of neat finishing, smooth painting, and labour in drapery throughout the whole [A]: but he wanted a true notion of English beauty, and that freedom of draught, of which the other was master. He died in London.

JOHNSON (MARTIN), bred as a seal-engraver, and famous in that art, was also an extraordinary landscape-painter after nature. He arrived at a great excellence in views, which he studied with application, making a good choice of the delightful prospects of England for his subjects; which he performed with much judgement, freedom, and warmth of colouring. Some of his pieces are now in the hands of the curious in England; though they are very scarce. He died in London about the beginning of James the Second's reign.

JOHNSON (CHARLES), originally bred to the law [B], and a member of the Middle-Temple, being a great admirer of the Muses, and finding in himself a strong propensity to dramatic writing, quitted the studious labour of the one, for the more spirited amusements of the other; and, by contracting an intimacy with Mr. Wilks, found means, through that gentleman's interest, to get his plays on the stage without much difficulty. Some of them met with very good success, and, being a constant frequenter of the meetings of the wits at Will's and Button's coffee-houses, he, by a polite and inoffensive behaviour, formed so extensive an acquaintance and intimacy, as constantly insured him great emoluments on his benefit-night; by which means, being a man of œconomy, he was enabled to subsist very genteelly. He at length married a young widow, with a tolerable fortune, on which he set up a tavern in Bow-street, Coventgarden, but quitted business at his wife's death, and lived privately on an easy competence which he had saved. At what time he was born we know not, but he flourished during the reigns of

[A] Essay towards an English School of Painting   [B] Biographia Dramatica,

queen

queen Anne, king George I. and part of George II. His firſt
play was acted in 1702, and his lateſt is dated in 1733; but
Cibber informs us that he did not die till about 1744. As a dramatic
writer, he is far from deſerving to be placed amongſt the loweſt
claſs: for though his plots are ſeldom original, yet he has given
them ſo many additions, and has clothed the deſigns of others
in ſo pleaſing a dreſs, that a great ſhare of the merit they poſſeſs ought to be attributed to him.

Though we have obſerved before that he was a man of a very
inoffenſive behaviour, yet he could not eſcape the ſatire of Pope,
who, too ready to reſent even any ſuppoſed offence, has, on
ſome trivial pique, immortalized him in the " Dunciad;" and
in one of the notes to that poem has quoted from another piece,
called, " The Characters of the Times," the following account
of him: " Charles Johnſon, famous for writing a play every year,
and for being at Button's every day. He had probably thriven
better in his vocation, had he been a ſmall matter leaner; he
may be juſtly called a martyr to obeſity, and be ſaid to have
fallen a victim to the rotundity of his parts." The friends of
Johnſon might triumph that Pope could find no better object
for his ſatire; and, though we may ſmile at the humour, we
cannot think very ill of a man of whom nothing more degrading
could be ſaid than that he was fat. The dramatic pieces this
author produced, nineteen in all, are enumerated in the Biographia Dramatica.

· JOHNSON (MAURICE), an excellent antiquary, and founder
of the Gentleman's Society at Spalding, was deſcended from a
family much diſtinguiſhed in the laſt century [c]. At Berk-
hamſtead, the ſeat of one of his relations, were half-length
portraits of his grandfather old Henry Johnſon and his lady,
and ſir Charles and lady Bickerſtaff, and their daughter, who
was mother to ſir Henry Johnſon, and to Benjamin Johnſon [D],
poet-laureat to James I. Sir Henry was painted half-length,
by Frederick Zuccharo; and the picture was eſteemed capital.
The family of Johnſon were alſo allied to many other families
of conſideration. Mr. Johnſon, born at Spalding, a member of
the Inner Temple, London, and ſteward of the ſoke or manor of
Spalding, married early in life a daughter of Joſhua Ambler, eſq;
of that place. She was the grand-daughter of ſir Anthony Oldfield,
and lineally deſcended from ſir Thomas Greſham, the founder
of Greſham-college, and of the Royal Exchange, London. By
this lady he had twenty-ſix children, of whom ſixteen ſat down
together to his table,

Mr. Johnſon in the latter part of his life was attacked with a
vertiginous diſorder in his head, which frequently interrupted

[c] Hiſtory of the Spalding Society.
[D] The poet ſpelt his name Jonſon, agreeably to the orthography of that age.

his

his studies, and at last put a period to his life, Feb. 6, 1755. He acquired a general esteem from the frankness and benevolence of his character, which displayed itself not less in social life than in the communication of his literary researches. Strangers who applied to him for information, though without any introduction except what arose from a genuine thirst for knowledge congenial with his own, failed not to experience the hospitality of his board. While their spirit of curiosity was feasted by the liberal conversation of the man of letters, their social powers were at the same time gratified by the hospitable frankness of the benevolent Englishman. The following eulogium on him by Dr. Stukeley, is transcribed from the original in the " Minutes of the Society of Antiquaries;"—" Maurice Johnson, esq; of Spalding in Lincolnshire, counsellor at law, a fluent orator, and of eminence in his profession; one of the last of the founders of the Society of Antiquaries, 1717, except Br. Willis and W. Stukeley; founder of the Literary Society at Spalding, Nov. 3. 1712, which, by his unwearied endeavours, interest, and application in every kind, infinite labours in writing, collecting, methodizing, has now [1755] subsisted forty years in great reputation, and excited a great spirit of learning and curiosity in South Holland [in Lincolnshire]. They have a public library; and all conveniences for their weekly meeting. Mr. Johnson was a great lover of gardening, and had a fine collection of plants, and an excellent cabinet of medals. He collected large memoirs for the " History of Carausius,' all which, with his coins of that prince, he sent to me, particularly a brass one which he supposed his son, resembling those of young Tetricus. A good radiated CAES SPFA. Rev. a woman holds a cornucopia, resting her right hand on a pillar or rudder LOCIS or CISLO. In general the antiquities of the great mitred priory of Spalding, and of this part of Lincolnshire, are for ever obliged to the care and diligence of Maurice Johnson, who has rescued them from oblivion."

An accurate account of his many learned communications to the Society of Antiquaries of London, as well as of those which he made to the Society he founded at Spalding, may be seen in the curious work which furnishes this article.

JOHNSON (SAMUEL), the greatest English writer within the memory of the present generation, was born at Litchfield, Sept. 7, 1709. After the many able details of his life which have been produced, such a sketch as can here be admitted, will serve rather to refresh memory than to satisfy curiosity. Michael Johnson, the father of Samuel, was a bookseller; and had no other child, except Nathaniel, about three years younger, who died in 1737. Strong marks of genius were displayed by Samuel Johnson, both at the free-school in Litchfield, where, with

Dr.

Dr. James, Dr. Taylor, and fome others, he received the chief
part of his education, and at the fchool of Mr. Wentworth, at
Stourbridge in Worceflerfhire, where he paffed a year. Some
of his exercifes have been accidentally preferved, and well juftify the expectations which determined a father, not opulent, to
continue him in the paths of literature. After paffing two years
at home, in voluntary and defultory ftudy, he was entered as a
commoner at Pembroke-college, Oxford, in October, 1728,
being then, by the teftimony of the learned Dr. Adams, the
beft qualified young man that he ever remembered to have feen
admitted. Of the compofitions produced by him at Oxford,
the moft remarkable is his Latin verfion of Pope's Meffiah,
which, if not faultlefs in point of Latinity, is written with
uncommon vigour. Pope is reported to have gone fo far in its
praife as to fay, "that the author would leave it a queftion for
pofterity, which poem had been the original." Oppreffed by
the difficulty of finding money for fubfiftence, Johnfon was
obliged to make an interrupted and a fhort refidence at Oxford,
and finally gave it up as impracticable, in the autumn of 1731;
after having ftruggled as long as poffible with fevere indigence,
completed by the infolvency of his father.

From the univerfity, he returned to Litchfield, with little
improvement of his profpects: his character, however, procured him fome valuable friends, whofe hofpitality at leaft fupported his fpirits, and alleviated his diftreffes. The firft of thefe
was Mr. G. Walmfley, whom he has immortalized by his ce-
lebration. It is true, that he has thrown fome dark fhades into
the picture; but it is no lefs evident, that he means them as
traits of the party character of his friend, not of his native difpofition as a man. Soon after his return to Litchfield, he loft
his father, and found on the divifion of his effects, that his own
fhare amounted to only twenty pounds. The place of ufher to
a fchool at Bofworth in Leicefterfhire, was offered to him, when
thus deftitute of fupport. It promifed well; and he went to it
on foot. But he was placed in the houfe of a tyrannical patron,
and found it intolerable. He removed, after fome months of
mifery, by the invitation of his friend Mr. Hector, to Birmingham, where his career as an author may be faid to have
commenced: for he was fupported partly by his efforts for Mr.
Warren, a bookfeller; and here his tranflation of "Lobo" was
publifhed. He returned in 1734 to Litchfield, and there iffued
propofals for the works of "Politian," with a life; but the
plan was not encouraged, and failed.

Johnfon was not infenfible to female attractions, and is faid
to have been once or twice in love; but his ferious attachment
was fixed in 1735, on Mrs. Porter, a widow, of Birmingham,
much older than himfelf, and, according to the report of friends,

not

not very engaging in perfon or manners. He appears, however, from the whole tenor of his memoirs, to have felt for her
a fincere and ftrong affection ; and though fhe was poffeffed of
800l. a vaft fum to him at that time, he cannot juftly be fufpected of having married her from interefted motives. They
were married in July, 1735, and he foon after fitted up a houfe
at Edial near Litchfield, where he undertook to keep a fchool.
This plan alfo failed for want of encouragement. He obtained
only three fcholars, David and George Garrick, and a Mr. Offely,
and did not very long perfevere in the attempt. About this
time he began his tragedy of Irene, in which he was encouraged
to proceed by Mr. Walmfley. In March, 1737, having relinquifhed his fchool, he formed his firft expedition to London;
the more memorable for being undertaken with his pupil David
Garrick, both intent to try their talents in that great field of
exertions, and both deftined to rife in it to the higheft celebrity.
In this preparatory vifit he was not accompanied by Mrs.
Johnfon; but he continued his tragedy, formed a literary connection with Cave, the editor of the Gentleman's Magazine,
and acquired fome other friends. He returned in the courfe of
the fummer to Litchfield, where he finifhed Irene; but returned in about three months to fix himfelf and wife in London.
His tragedy was now offered to Mr. Fleetwood, the manager of
Drury-lane, but, probably for want of fome recommendation,
was not accepted. His principal employment for feveral years
was that of writing for Cave in the magazine, where the firft
of his performances is a Latin ode in Alcaic ftanzas, of great
elegance and beauty, addreffed to the editor. It was inferted in
March, 1738. His account of the parliamentary debates forms
a very interefting part of his communications to this work. His
fole compofition of them, (for Guthrie affifted before) extends
from Nov. 19, 1740, to Feb. 23, 1743.

Johnfon now became intimate with Savage. Together they
fuffered the miferies of extreme poverty, and in their folitary
wanderings conceived a mutual regard, which produced, long
after, the partial, but eloquent and inftructive life of Savage.
It was in May, 1738, that the celebrity of Johnfon as an author
commenced, by the publication of his imitation of Juvenal's
third fatire, entitled, "London, a Poem." Like all authors
not yet famous, he found a difficulty in getting it publifhed.
But when it appeared, it was noticed by Pope, (whofe fatire entitled, 1738, appeared on the fame day) was admired by other
wits, and proceeded to a fecond edition in the courfe of a week.
Still, the profits of authorfhip were too fcanty to encourage him
to continue in that line. He attempted to be mafter of a free-
fchool in Leiceflerfhire, but failed, though recommended by
lord Gower, from not being a mafter of arts. He next made an
effort

effort to be admitted at Doctor's-Commons, but a degree in civil law was here indispensible. Forced in this manner to continue an author, he followed the direction of his apparent destiny. His " Marmor Norfolciense," an anonymous attack upon the ministry, and the house of Hanover, published in 1739, has been said to have exposed him to the danger of prosecution; but this account seems to be refuted by a later enquiry. For several years, his principal productions, consisting chiefly of the lives of eminent persons, appeared in the Gentleman's Magazine. His life of Savage was published separately, in 1744. He planned much more than he executed. A list of his literary projects, amounting to near forty articles, has been preserved by sir John Hawkins; all of which, from indolence, versatility, or want of encouragement, remained unexecuted. In 1747, at length, he proceeded to greater things; he was employed upon his edition of Shakspeare, and published the plan of his English Dictionary. The price stipulated in his agreement with the bookfellers for this great work was 1575l. The plan was addressed to lord Chesterfield, in an elegant strain of dignified compliment; and though this was done at the suggestion of Dodsley, it is evident from the plan itself, that the earl had favoured the design, and had been confulted on the subject. To enable him to complete this vast undertaking, Johnson hired a house in Gough-fquare, Fleet-street, fitted up one of the upper rooms in the manner of a counting-house, and employed fix amanuenfes. The words, partly taken from other dictionaries, and partly supplied by himself, were first written down with spaces left between them. He then delivered in writing, the etymologies, definitions, and various significations; and the authorities were copied from books, in which he had marked the passages with a pencil.

While he was employed upon his dictionary, he formed, in 1748, a club for literary diffussion, at a coffee-house in Ivy-lane, Paternoster-row. His pupil David Garrick had now raised himself, by his transcendent theatrical abilities, to the situation of joint-patentee, and manager of Drury-lane theatre. At the opening of the house, after this event, Johnson had furnished him with an admirable prologue, and in 1749, he shewed, in return, his kindness for his friend, by bringing forward the tragedy of Irene. The tragedy, however, did not please, and the author acquiefced in the decision of the public, by declining all further attempts in that species of composition. It does not indeed appear, that this style of writing was fuited to his genius. Irene had been written confefledly with labour, and flow progress, contrary to his usual method, which was rapid and fluent; and though the sentiments are frequently of great value and energy, the language is stiff and unpleasing. In the attack of Lauder upon

upon the fame of Milton, Johnfon co-operated this year, by writing the preface and poftfcript to his book; but he was deceived by the forgeries of the man, and approved no longer than while he believed the allegations to be juft. On the 20th of March, 1750, he publifhed the firft paper of the Rambler, which he continued without interruption, every Tuefday and Friday, till the 17th of March, 1752. In this very excellent work, he proceeded almoft without affiftance, only five papers in the whole having been fupplied by other writers.

Soon after the clofe of the Rambler, Johnfon fuffered a lofs which affected him in the deepeft manner. His wife died in March, 1752, after an union of feventeen years, and left him a childlefs and afflicted widower. Whether the greatly deferved his affection has been doubted; that he fincerely loved, and profoundly regretted her, there is abundant proof. Society, to which he had now abundant accefs, became his chief refource: he excelled in converfation, and he delighted in it. As the publication of his dictionary approached, lord Chefterfield, who had been firft addreffed as its patron, but during the whole interval had neglected the author, whofe manners were not fufficiently graceful to fuit his courtly tafte, grew anxious to repair his fault, and retain the glory of fuch patronage. He wrote two papers in its praife, to prepare the public for its appearance, in the periodical work, entitled, "The World;" but thefe unhappily produced from the dignified lexicographer no other return than that celebrated letter, which by its delicate farcafms, and fevere, though refpectful chaftifement, muft infallibly immortalize his difgrace. "With little affiftance of the learned, and without any patronage of the great," this national monument of labour, ta'ents, and judgement, was completed, and appeared in May, 1755; the author having been previoufly honoured, in February, with the degree of mafter of arts, by diploma, in teftimony of his abilities and merit. With whatever frigidity the great mind of Johnfon might perfuade itfelf to difmifs this noble work, while its reception was yet dubious, he muft undoubtedly have been gratified in no fmall degree, by the abundant praifes it extorted from domeftic and foreign literati. The attacks upon it were fuch as he had declared himfelf to expect; the commendations muft have furpaffed his hopes, though not his deferts. Garrick, in an epigram upon this fubject, well turned, though not very carefully written, has afferted from it, the fuperiority of our countrymen to the French; and, comparing the fingle labour of Johnfon, with the united efforts of the forty academicians of Paris, in producing their dictionary, fays,

And Johnfon, well-arm'd like a hero of yore,
Has beat forty French, and will beat forty more!

Never-

Nevertheless, he had not yet emerged from poverty. The sum stipulated for his dictionary had been expended during its progress, he had subsisted afterwards principally on his subscriptions for Shakspeare: but, in March, 1756, we find him under arrest for a debt of five guineas, and liberated by the aid of the celebrated Richardson. He now for some time produced only occasional compositions, in various works; but on the 15th of April, 1758, he began to publish "The Idler," which was continued in a weekly newspaper called the Universal Chronicle, till April 5, 1760. At the death of his mother, in January, 1759, his piety taxed his genius; and to pay the expences of her funeral, and a few debts she had left, he wrote his "Rasselas." The copy produced 100l. and abundantly answered his purpose.

At length, in 1762, he was placed, by royal munificence, above the necessity of subsisting by occasional and precarious efforts. The king granted him a pension of 300l. per annum, expressly as a reward for the merit and moral tendency of his writings; without any kind of stipulation relative to the future use of his pen. The person most active in obtaining for him this deserved and honourable reward, was Mr. Wedderburne, now lord chancellor Loughborough. Some have attempted to fix on the philosopher the charge of inconsistency for receiving this pension, after the indignant definition of a pensioner given in his dictionary. But Johnson was no hireling: it was long after the grant of his salary before he wrote at all for the court, and then it was in defence of his own well-known sentiments, no less than of ministerial measures. The love of Johnson for conversation induced him, in 1764, to form a club, since distinguished by the name of "The Literary Club," which after many losses, and many honourable accessions, still subsists, retaining two of its original members, Mr. Burke and Mr. Langton. The rest were, sir Joshua Reynolds, Dr. Nugent, Mr. Beauclerk, Mr. Chamier, sir John Hawkins, Goldsmith, and Johnson himself. In July, 1765, he was complimented by the university of Dublin with the degree of doctor of laws; "ob egregiam scriptorum elegantiam et utilitatem," as the diploma expresses it. In the same year appeared, after long delay, his edition of Shakspeare, of which the preface and the summary account of each play are the most valuable parts.

The king, who had rewarded the merit of Johnson by pecuniary independence, took an opportunity afterwards to prove that he was duly sensible of the merit of the writer he had thus favoured. In a conversation with him at the Queen's-house, in February, 1765, the king asked if he intended to publish any more works? Johnson modestly answered, that he thought he had written enough: "And so should I too," replied the king,

"if

" if you had not written so well." Johnson had now arrived
at that eminence which cultivated genius always seeks, but seldom obtains. His fortune, though not great, was adequate to
his wants, and of most honourable acquisition; for it was derived from the produce of his labours, and the rewards which
his country, in the person of the sovereign, had bestowed upon
his merit. He received during life that unqualified applause
from the world, which in general is paid only to departed excellence, and he beheld his fame firmly seated in the public
mind, without the danger of being shaken by obloquy or shared
by a rival. He could number among his friends, the greatest
and most improved talents of the country. His company was
courted by wealth, dignity, and beauty. His many peculiarities
were overlooked and forgotten in the admiration of his understanding; while his virtues were regarded with veneration, and
his opinions adopted with submission [s]. It has been said, that
in 1771, he was ambitious of adding to his other honours, that
of a seat in the house of commons. His fame was now high as
a politician, from the celebrity of his pamphlets, entitled, " The
false Alarm," and the " Thoughts on the late Transactions respecting Falkland's Islands;" but though an attempt was made
for this purpose, by Strahan, the King's printer, who was himself in parliament, no step was taken for him by the ministry,
and nothing was effected. It is possible, from his great facility
of expression, that he might have shone as a speaker, late as it
was in life to begin the attempt, for he was now sixty-two.

In March, 1775, his title of Doctor was confirmed to him
by the university of Oxford, which sent him this degree also by
diploma; an honour seldom granted, and never certainly to one
who would be more sensible of its value. His tour in Scotland
in the summer of 1773, produced his book, entitled, " A Journey to the Western Islands of Scotland," which was published
this year; and this incidentally brought on his altercation with
Macpherson respecting the poems of Ossian, and that famous
letter, in which he beats his antagonist more effectually with his
pen, than he could with the cudgel which he provided for
his defence, in case of the personal attack Macpherson had
been foolish enough to threaten. In 1777, he undertook his
last great work, " The Lives of the English Poets," which was
completed in 1781. Some time in March, says he in his meditations, " I finished the Lives of the Poets, which I wrote in
my usual way, dilatorily and hastily; unwilling to work, and
working with vigour and haste." In a previous memorandum,
he says of them, " Written, I hope, in such a manner as may
tend to the promotion of piety." Though this work was begun

[s] Anderson's Life of Johnson, p. 145.

in

in his fixty-eighth, and finifhed in his feventy-fecond year; it
betrays no fymptom of the flighteft declenfion of faculties.
His judgement, tafte, fpirit, and force of thought, appear as
ftrongly in this as in any of his former works, and his ftyle is
more level to the general tafte, than in the Rambler, and fome
other compofitions. From the clofe of this ufeful and pleafing
labour, his decline in health and happinefs was confiderable.
In May, 1781, he loft his friend Mr. Thrale, in whofe houfe
and fociety he had paffed, for fifteen years, the happieft of his
hours. The palfy in 1783, and the afthma, with a degree of
dropfy, in 1784, gave him warnings of the failure of his conftitution. He would at that time have tried to renovate his powers
by the milder air of Italy, but his penfion did not appear adequate
to the expence ; and the attempt to procure an augmentation,
for that exprefs purpofe, unfortunately was not fuccefsful. It
was probably too late for any effential benefit to be received, and
he relinquifhed his defign. He did not, however, view the approach of death with tranquillity. A melancholy, which in him
was conftitutional, and had harraffed him more or lefs through
every period of his life, joined to a very fcrupulous fenfe of
duty, filled him with apprehenfion of an event, which few men
can have fo good a right to meet with fortitude. That event
approached, as it dues to all, not the lefs for being apprehended ;
the dropfy and afthma became more and more oppreffive; yet,
in his fleeplefs nights, he retained fufficient vigour of intellect to
amufe himfelf by tranflating into Latin verfe feveral of the
Greek epigrams in the Anthologia. A truly claffical employment for a declining author! On the 13th of December, 1784,
the fatal period of his life arrived ; and the laft days of his exiftence having been lefs clouded by gloomy apprehenfions, he departed full of refignation, ftrong in faith, and joyful in hope,
dying the enviable death of the righteous.

Dr. Johnfon was buried in Weftminfter-abbey, at the foot of
Shakfpeare's monument, and clofe to the grave of his friend and
pupil Garrick. His monument was referved for St. Paul's
church ; and the expences having been defrayed by a liberal and
voluntary contribution, it ftands with that of Howard, one of the
firft tributes of national admiration and gratitude admitted into that
cathedral. The fculpture was defigned and finely executed by
Bacon. The epitaph is the compofition of Dr. Parr, and is concife, but ftrongly appropriated. The monument was completed
early in 1796. The principal works of Johnfon, and the time
of their publication have already been mentioned. The fmaller
pieces are fo numerous, that to enumerate them would occupy a
confiderable fpace. They were publifhed collectively, with his
life, by fir John Hawkins in 1787, forming eleven volumes in
octavo. In this edition feveral pieces are attributed to Johnfon

without foundation. A new edition, amounting to twelve volumes, 8vo, with an essay on his life and genius by Arthur Murphy, esq; was published in 1792. Besides these, his " Prayers and Meditations," were published from his manuscripts, by George Strahan, A. M. in 8vo, 1785. " Letters to and from Samuel Johnson, LL. D." were published by Mrs. Piozzi, in 2 vols. 8vo, 1788. The " Sermons left for Publication by Dr. Taylor," were unquestionably Johnson's; and besides the internal evidence of the style, and cast of thought, the fact is now ascertained on the authority of the editor, Mr. Hayes. They are in two volumes, 8vo, published in 1788, and 1789. His " Debates in Parliament," were collected in two volumes, 8vo, from the Gentleman's Magazine, by Mr. Stockdale, in 1787; the real names of the speakers being substituted throughout, for the fictitious or mangled names employed in the Magazine; they are arranged also in chronological order.

The figure of Johnson was large, robust, and latterly unwieldy from corpulency. His carriage was disfigured by sudden motions, which appeared to a common observer to be involuntary and convulsive. But, in the opinion of sir Joshua Reynolds, they were the consequence of a depraved habit of accompanying his thoughts with certain untoward actions. Of his limbs he is said never to have enjoyed the free and vigorous use. His strength, however, was great, and his personal courage not less so. Among other instances which exemplify his possession of both, it is related, that being once at the Litchfield theatre, he sat upon a chair placed for him behind the scenes. Having had occasion to quit his seat, he found it occupied upon his return, by an innkeeper of the town. He civilly demanded that it should be restored to him; but, meeting with a rude refusal, he laid hold of the chair, and with it, of the intruder, and flung them both, without further ceremony into the pit. In his dress he was singular and slovenly, and though he made some improvement under the advice of Mrs. Thrale, at Streatham, his progress was not great. In conversation he was violent, and impatient of contradiction. " There is no arguing with him," said Goldsmith, alluding to a speech in one of Cibber's plays, " for if his pistol misses fire, he knocks you down with the but-end of it." In the early part of his life he had been too much depressed, in his latter years he was too lavishly indulged; but in the wit and wisdom of his conversation, and his warm goodness of heart, his friends found an ample recompence for the submission he exacted. With all his defects of temper, there was scarcely a virtue which he did not in principle possess. He was humane, charitable, affectionate, and generous. His most intemperate sallies were the effect of an irritable habit; he offended only to repent. Another great feature of his mind was

the

the love of independence, which he in no degree gave up when
he accepted the bounty of his fovereign. The grand characte-
riftic of his genius was gigantic vigour. He had an indolence
which often reprefled his efforts, but what he ferioufly attempted
he never failed to execute, with a mafterly boldnefs which leaves
us to regret that he fhould ever have relapfed into literary idlenefs. He united in himfelf, what are feldom found in union,
a vigorous and excurfive imagination, with a ftrong and fleady
judgement. His memory was remarkably tenacious, and his
apprehenfion wonderfully quick and accurate; and to this he
was indebted for that pointed and judicious difcrimination which
elucidated every queftion, and aftonifhed every hearer. His
reading was cafual and defultory, but from this cafual reading
he rofe with a mind feldom fatigued, endowed with clear and
accurate perceptions. The variety of his ftudies relieved without perplexing him; the ideas arranged in order were ready for
ufe, adorned with all the energy of language and force of manner. But the labour of literature was a talk from which he always wifhed to efcape; and we fcarcely fee any attempt beyond
a periodical paper, which he did not profefledly continue with
unwillingnefs and laffitude. His piety was truly venerable and
edifying, yet, from his morbid melancholy, not always confolatory to himfelf. His prejudices in a few inftances were ftrong,
and occafionally biafled his judgement, which otherwife might
have had a perfection to which a parallel example would be fought
in vain. Thefe traits of his character, taken in part from Dr.
Anderfon's judicious account of his life, will be found, perhaps,
to give as correct an idea of his merits and abilities as can be
conveyed in fo many words. We cannot further expatiate, and
leave him to be finally appreciated by the inftructive ftudy of his
works.

JOHNSTON (ARTHUR), was born at Cafkieben, near
Aberdeen, the feat of his anceftors [τ], and probably was educated at Aberdeen, as he was afterwards advanced to the higheft
dignity in that univerfity. The ftudy to which he chiefly applied, was that of phyfic; and to improve himfelf in that fcience
he travelled into foreign countries. He was twice at Rome, but
the chief place of his refidence was Padua, in which univerfity the
degree of M. D. was conferred on him in 1610, as appears by
a MS. copy of verfes in the advocate's library in Edinburgh.
After leaving Padua, he travelled through the reft of Italy, and
over Germany, Denmark, England, Holland, and other countries, and at laft fettled in France; where he met with great
applaufe as a Latin poet. He lived there twenty years, and by
two wives had thirteen children. At laft, after twenty-four years

[τ] Anecdotes of Bowyer by Nichols, p. 151.

abfence,

abfence, he returned into Scotland, in 1632. It appears by the council-books at Edinburgh, that the doctor had a fuit at law before that court about the fame time. In the year following, it is very well known that Charles I. went into Scotland, and made bifhop Laud, then with him, a member of that council, and by this accident, it is probable, the acquaintance began between the doctor and that prelate, which produced his " Pfalmorum Davidis Paraphrafis Poëtica." We find that, in the fame year, the doctor printed a fpecimen of his Pfalms at London, and dedicated them to his lordfhip, which is almoft as plain a proof as can be defired that the bifhop prevailed upon Johnfton to remove to London from Scotland, and then fet him upon this work; neither can it be doubted but, after he had feen this fample, he alfo engaged him to perfect the whole, which took him up four years; for the firft edition of all the Pfalms was publifhed at Aberdeen in 1637, and at London in the fame year. In 1641, Dr. Johnfton, being at Oxford, on a vifit to one of his daughters, who was married to a divine of the church of England in that place, was feized with a violent diarrhœa, of which he died in a few days, in the 54th year of his age, not without having feen the beginning of thofe troubles which proved fo fatal to his patron. He was buried in the place where he died, which gave occafion to the following lines of his learned friend Wedderburn in his " Sufpiria," on the doctor's death:

" Scotia mœfta, dole, tanti viduata fepulchro
Vatis; is Angligenis contigit altus honos."

In what year Johnfton was made phyfician to the king, does not appear; it is moft likely that the archbifhop procured him that honour at his coming into England in 1633, at which time he tranflated Solomon's Song into Latin elegiac verfe, and dedicated it to his majefty. His Pfalms were reprinted at Middleburg, 1642; London, 1657; Cambridge, ...; Amfterdam, 1706; Edinburgh, by William Lauder, 1739; and at laft on the plan of the Delphin claffics, at London, 1741, 8vo, at the experce of auditor Benfon, who dedicated them to his late majefty, and prefixed to this edition memoirs of Dr. Johnfton, with the teftimonies of various learned perfons. A laboured, but partial and injudicious comparifon, between the two tranflations of Buchanan and Johnfton was printed the fame year in Englifh, in 8vo, entitled, " A Prefatory Difcourfe to Dr. Johnfton's Pfalms, &c." and " A Conclufion to it." His tranflations of the " Te Deum, Creed, Decalogue, &c." were fubjoined to the Pfalms. His other poetical works are his Epigrams, his Parerga, and his " Mufæ Aulicæ," or commendatory

datory Verſes upon perſons of rank in church and ſtate at that time, printed in 8vo. at London, 1635.

JOINVILLE (JOHN, Sire de), an eminent French ſtateſman, who flouriſhed about 1260, was deſcended from one of the nobleſt and moſt ancient families at Champagne. He was ſeneſchal, or high-ſteward, of Champagne, and one of the principal lords of the court of Louis IX. whom he attended in all his military expeditions; and was greatly beloved and eſteemed for his valour, his wit, and the frankneſs of his manners. That monarch placed ſo much confidence in him, that all matters of juſtice, in the palace, were referred to his deciſion; and his majeſty undertook nothing of importance without conſulting him. He died about 1318, at not much leſs than ninety years of age. Joinville is known as an author by his "Hiſtory of St. Louis," in French, which he compoſed in 1305. It is a very curious and intereſting work. The beſt edition is that of Du Cange, in 1668, folio, with learned remarks. On peruſing this edition, however, it is eaſily ſeen, that the language is not that of the Sire de Joinville, and has been altered. But an authentic MS. of the original was found in 1748, and was publiſhed without alteration, in 1761, by Mélot, keeper of the royal library at Paris. This edition is alſo in folio.

JOLY (CLAUDE), a French writer, was born at Paris in 1607; and obtained a canonry in the cathedral there in 1631. Diſcovering alſo a capacity for ſtate affairs, he was appointed to attend a plenipotentiary to Munſter; and, during the commotions at Paris, he took a journey to Rome. In 1671, he was made precentor of his church, and ſeveral times official. He lived to the great age of 93, without experiencing the uſual infirmities of it; when, going one morning to matins, he fell into a trench, which had been dug for the foundation of the high altar. He died of this fall in 1700, after bequeathing a very fine library to his church. He was the author of many works in both Latin and French, and as well upon civil as religious ſubjects. One of them in French, 1652, in 12mo, is entitled, "A Collection of true and important Maxims for the Education of a Prince, againſt the falſe and pernicious Politics of Cardinal Mazarine;" which, being reprinted in 1663, with two "Apologetical Letters," was burnt in 1665 by the hands of of the common hangman. The ſame year, however, 1665, he publiſhed a tract called "Codicil d'Or, or The Golden Codicil," which is relative to the former; being a further collection of maxims for the education of a prince, taken chiefly from Eraſmus, whoſe works he is ſaid to have read ſeven times over.

JOLY (GUY), known by his long and faithful attachment to the famous cardinal de Retz, whom he attended both in his prosperity and adversity. He wrote "Memoirs of his times," from 1641 to 1665, which, as Voltaire expresses it, "are to those of the cardinal, what the servant is to the master."

JONAS (ANAGRIMUS), a learned Icelander, who acquired a great reputation for astronomy and the sciences. He was co-adjutor to Gundebrand of Thorbac, bishop of Holum in Iceland, who was also of that nation, a man of great learning and probity, had been a disciple of Tycho Brahe, and understood astronomy very well. After his death, the see of Holum was offered by the king of Denmark to Anagrimus, who begged to be excused; desiring to avoid the envy that might attend him in that high office, and to be at leisure to prosecute his studies. He chose therefore to continue as he was, pastor of the church of Melstadt, and intendant of the neighbouring churches of the last-mentioned diocese. He died in 1640, at the age of 95, having entered into a second marriage with a young girl about nine years before.

He wrote several books in honour of his country, against the calumnies of Blefkenius and others, which are well esteemed; the titles whereof are, "Idea veri magistratus." Copenhagen, 1589, 8vo. "Brevis commentarius de Islandiâ, ibid. 1593," 8vo. "Anatome Blefkeniana [α]. Holi in Iceland, 1612, 8vo, and at Hamburgh, 1618, 4to. "Epistola pro patria defensoria," ibid. 1618. "Ἀποτρίβη calumniæ," ibid. 1622, 4to. "Crymogæa [Ν], seu rerum Islandicarum libri tres, ibid. 1630," 4to. "Specimen Islandiæ historicum et magnâ ex parte chorographicum," Amstelod. 1634, 4to [Ι]. "Vita Gundebrandi Thorlacii," Lugd. Bat. 1630, 4to.

[α] This book is a refutation of one printed at Leyden in 1607, entitled, "Islandia, seu descriptio populorum & memorabilium hujus insulæ."

[Ν] This was written in 1603, and printed at Hamburg in 1609, with a map of Denmark, and, in 1710, without the map.

[Ι] This piece is a vindication of the author's opinion against the arguments of John Isaac Pontanus. Anagrimus maintained that Iceland was not peopled till about the year 874, and therefore cannot be the ancient Thule.

:.

INDEX

EIGHTH VOLUME.

3

Hooke,

END OF THE EIGHTH VOLUME.

www.ingramcontent.com/pod-product-compliance
Lightning Source LLC
Chambersburg PA
CBHW031047110726
47900CB00003B/844